A PASSIONATE WOMAN

was Ginger McKinntock, her tempestuous life intertwined with that of America's greatest pleasure playground, Palm Springs.

Her lovers were Tonito, the handsome Native American who awakened her youthful sensuality . . . Jason, the fascinating outdoorsman who taught her new ways to love nature—and man . . . and ever-*simpatico* Avery, the tender doctor she tried desperately to forget, but couldn't stop loving.

Her enemies were her ruthless sister, Ella, a world-famous movie star . . . and all those who tried to exploit her beloved desert paradise for the sake of a quick buck.

Her passions were the desert itself . . . the elegant hotel she founded . . . and above all her family— whose adventures swept them in war and peace from the California desert to Paris and Rome, to modern Mexico, and finally back home to the most glamorous spa in the American sun . . .

PALM SPRINGS

PALM SPRINGS

by
Trina Mascott

AN ONYX BOOK

NEW AMERICAN LIBRARY

A DIVISION OF PENGUIN BOOKS USA INC.

For Holly, Cindy, and Owen

PUBLISHER'S NOTE

This book is a work of fiction. Names, characters, places, and incidents either are the product of the author's imagination or are used fictitiously, and any resemblance to actual persons, living or dead, events, or locales is entirely coincidental.

NAL BOOKS ARE AVAILABLE AT QUANTITY DISCOUNTS
WHEN USED TO PROMOTE PRODUCTS OR SERVICES.
FOR INFORMATION PLEASE WRITE TO PREMIUM MARKETING DIVISION,
NEW AMERICAN LIBRARY, 1633 BROADWAY,
NEW YORK, NEW YORK 10019.

ONYX TRADEMARK REG. U.S. PAT. OFF. AND FOREIGN COUNTRIES
REGISTERED TRADEMARK—MARCA REGISTRADA
HECHO EN DRESDEN, TN, U.S.A.

SIGNET, SIGNET CLASSIC, MENTOR, ONYX, PLUME, MERIDIAN
and NAL BOOKS are published by New American Library, a division of
Penguin Books USA Inc., 1633 Broadway, New York, New York 10019

First Printing, February, 1990

1   2   3   4   5   6   7   8   9

PRINTED IN THE UNITED STATES OF AMERICA

Prologue

1987

Lost in a bittersweet reverie, Ginger stood quietly on her bedroom balcony, high on a rocky hillside overlooking Palm Springs. In front of her was a panorama of rooftops, palm trees, swimming pools, and golf courses, with Mt. San Jacinto casting its broad shadow over the town. Behind her was her bedroom. There, for most of her life, she had laughed and wept and slept and made important decisions. But most of all . . . there she had loved.

She shivered, remembering the sounds of lovemaking that had reverberated against these walls. Yes, she had been blessed with a healthy body and a talent for loving that had given her more hours of sensual pleasure than anyone could expect of life. But she was greedy. She wanted more—more life, more pleasure, more passion, more youthful vigor. Granted, today was her eighty-seventh birthday. So what? *Screw the years!* she thought. She had never allowed age to be a big factor in her life. Not when she was young, and not now. And damn it all, *she wanted a future!*

This balmy desert winter twilight—Friday, February 13—marked the seventy-fifth anniversary of her arrival in Palm Springs, a memorable Tuesday in 1912, her twelfth birthday. Whenever possible during the intervening years, she had made it a birthday ritual to stand on this hillside balcony while watching night settle upon the California desert. Never had she forgotten one tiny detail of the view from her balcony as it had been in 1912, and over the years the loss of that original panorama had caused her great sorrow.

In those early days, clumps of cottonwood and palm trees had sheltered the village's handful of cottages, while rows of meandering palo verde and smoke trees had delineated the routes of water ditches. Randomly scattered rocks and rain-carved gullies had given the land a rugged texture which caught every nuance of the constantly changing light as the sun moved through the sky. And what a sky! She had stared at its intense deep blue until her eyes had ached from the dazzle of it.

But now, wherever she looked, she saw rooftops. Rooftops, rooftops, *rooftops* that had spread like lava to obliterate the landmarks of her childhood vista. Well, at least the sky was still incredibly blue. The mountains were as magnificent as ever. As for the city, changes and growth were inevitable. *Be glad you're still here to see it,* she gently chided herself. *Be grateful you were lucky enough to enjoy seventy-five years in this very special place.*

Tonight, to commemorate the anniversary of her arrival in Palm Springs, she would be honored at a blacktie banquet attended by two former presidents of the United States and some of the most influential men and women in the world. She knew that many of the people coming to her banquet sincerely admired and respected her, and some even loved her. So why didn't she feel happier about it? Was it because the dinner was a testimonial to her past, and what she really wanted was some assurance that she still had a future?

The people who would honor her tonight saw her as a symbol, as one of the oldest living survivors from Palm Springs' early days. But she preferred to be admired as the feisty woman who had screamed and hollered whenever the city's desert character had been threatened. She had helped keep out gambling and high-rises. "Damn it," she had scolded at meetings with developers who wanted to buy her land, "if you assholes want Las Vegas, then for God's sake leave *us* alone and *go* to Las Vegas."

Once, in the early days, she had gone into a gambling club with an ax and hacked to pieces two roulette tables. The hoodlums who owned that club never had dared press charges against her. And not once had she sold a piece of her precious acreage at *any* price unless the buyer gave her the right to approve the building plans.

Now she was the dignified *grande dame* of Palm Springs.

In recent years she had been grand marshal of the annual Circus Parade, she had addressed innumerable holiday banquets, had lent her name to more fund-raising drives than she could remember, and the Agua Caliente band of Cahuilla Indians had selected her as an honored guest at their last big powwow.

Still, she hated being venerated simply because she had reached a venerable age. It was unkind of people to put a symbolic plastic dome over her and turn her into a relic. It was like being stuffed alive. Didn't they realize that she never had lost her zest for living, that she still relished new ideas, that she was constantly growing in wisdom and knowledge, that she would welcome challenges until the day she died?

Of course, she was smart enough to realize that most people venerated her money far more than her age. If she were a darker-skinned welfare recipient in North Palm Springs, living in a slum shack, she could be a *hundred* and eighty-seven and nobody would think twice about her.

Ginger chuckled. She liked to think of herself as inadvertently wealthy. She hadn't started out with the desire to get rich. It had simply happened, and nobody had been more surprised than she was. That was the difference between her and some of the people who would be attending tonight's banquet. To her, being wealthy was a pleasant accident that allowed her to gratify her philanthropic nature and to lead a wonderfully indulgent life. To many of those others, being rich was their main reason for living, and they pursued the goal of getting even richer with a monomania that crushed any obstacles in their paths. For all their cultural and philanthropic pretensions, they were nothing but greedy money-grubbers. She knew the type well: she had been related by blood to men like them.

Some of the people sponsoring tonight's festivities in her honor were the very ones with whom she had battled bitterly over their schemes for irresponsible development. It would serve them right if she decided to play truant tonight. She could mount Se-San, named after her very first horse, and ride up Mt. San Jacinto to her favorite lookout point. There was a full moon tonight—how many more full moons did she have left, anyway? She could spend her eighty-seventh birthday and her seventy-fifth anniversary with her horse instead of with some of those overweight, overdressed, overrich horses' asses. At least her mare knew that Ginger still was a whole, viable person and not just an ancient memento of the past.

In 1912, when she had arrived in Palm Springs, its entire population had consisted of less than twenty hardy white families and fifty impoverished Indian families, all living in symbiotic harmony beneath the steep eastern flanks of eleven thousand-foot Mt. San Jacinto. Set in the mountain's protective embrace at the edge of the vast sandy desert, the village had been a secret paradise far removed from the rest of the world, not so much in miles as in spirit.

Now, millions of visitors inundated the city every year. Many fell in love with the fragrant dry air and health-giving sunshine and settled here permanently, but their overwhelming presence threatened to destroy the very qualities that had attracted them to the desert in the first place. Much as Ginger sympathized with their love of this climate, these newcomers were inadvertently damaging the fragile land far more than any natural disaster ever had.

Ginger knew all about natural disasters. She had been caught in floods that swept away people and bridges and tore up the land. She had survived earthquakes that toppled houses and started rock slides. She had watched fires burn irreplaceable groves of thousand-year-old palm trees. She had withstood harrowing sandstorms that pitted cars and ruined vegetation. But the never-ending invasion of humanity shook her equanimity almost as much as the calamities that nature had thrown at her.

She could feel the massive presence of Mt. San Jacinto rising behind her house. Its powerful energy wrapped itself around her like a comforting cloak. How many countless times had she climbed its Indian trails? Clambered over its sharp inhospitable rocks? Memorized its stands of creosote bush and manzanita? She knew where to find acres of pink sand verbena and purple heliotrope and red chuparosas and yellow daisies and white primrose. She could tell from a winter's rainfall which month each variety of wildflower would bloom and when the fluffy white seeds would waft down from the cottonwood trees to make the sun-baked ground look like ski slopes.

She knew from the color and clarity of a sunrise what kind of day to expect. She considered herself a human weather vane, able to predict from the sound and direction of the wind whether it would bring maddening heat or a cloudburst or shriek all night and strip bare the vegetation in its path.

She could walk down any street in Palm Springs and recite the year each structure had been built and what had previously occupied that piece of land. The public library named for Dr. Welwood Murray covered part of the orchard where the crusty old Scot once had grown the finest figs, oranges, dates, grapefruit, apricots, and lemons. Pearl McCallum McManus's lovely old adobe mansion was gone; in its place were the nondescript Tennis Club time-share condominiums. The cozy cottage made of railroad ties which years ago had belonged to the dignified White sisters—Dr. Franilla, Miss Isabel, and Miss Cornelia—had been moved a block to the Village Green on Palm Canyon Drive and was part of a Visitors' Center.

The simple hot-springs bathhouse of the Agua Caliente tribe had been replaced by the six-story Spa Hotel, but the Indians still owned the valuable land and collected a handsome rent for it. A swank shopping mall and a fancy new hotel stood on the sites of Nellie Coffman's world-famous Desert Inn and Zaddie and Ed Bunker's 1913 sheet-metal garage where that gutsy couple had learned how to fix cars from a handbook. And of course there were dozens and dozens of other examples of "progress," including all the parcels she herself once had owned and had sold or given away.

Ginger could describe in detail all the people who had lived here long, long ago. She knew their children, their grandchildren, and their great-grandchildren. She knew their achievements, if any, and their sorrows, often many, and the dates of their births and their marriages and their divorces and, inevitably, their deaths. She knew where they were buried and what their legacies may have been to the city, to the country, and even on occasion to mankind.

For a moment she felt faint, with the threat of a

gripping headache, as though all the people she had known during her seventy-five years of living in Palm Springs were a vast army tramping through her head. While she stood on the balcony reminiscing, dusk gradually softened the sky to a rich purple glow, just dark enough for the lights to come on all over the valley and for the first few stars to make their presence known, one by one.

From the moment she had arrived in this desert oasis she had felt protective of it. But now it no longer was a real desert and it no longer was an oasis. Thousands of swimming pools were constantly evaporating moisture into the air, along with all the sprinklers required for grass lawns and flowerbeds and for the seventy-odd emerald-green golf courses. As a result, her precious desert was not as arid as a desert ought to be. It was insane the way some people insisted upon making Palm Springs look like tropical Hawaii, and disgraceful that the local per-capita consumption of water was *ten times* that of San Francisco. She smugly prided herself on never having planted anything that couldn't thrive on the desert with a minimum of water.

Besides the higher humidity, sometimes smog crept out through the San Gorgonio Pass from Los Angeles, and frustrating traffic jams clogged the entire length of Palm Canyon Drive most winter weekends. Now there were the inevitable afflictions of "civilization": murders and kidnappings and muggings and burglaries and bank robberies. During the Easter holidays the city was plagued by hordes of insolent drunk and doped-up college students who came to Palm Springs to have "fun" and ended up attacking the police and throwing rocks at innocent people and fornicating in public.

Lately, no matter how much Ginger had tried to stop this mad despoliation of her beloved village—the overbuilding and the lack of respect for the fragile desert's needs—she felt she had been trying to stop an avalanche with a lace hankie.

She was shaken by nostalgia for the early days, when the local residents had taken delight in simple activities. She remembered when Easter meant going up the mountain to Inspiration Point for sunrise services, which were thrilling even if you weren't one bit religious. She remembered bathing in the Indians' hot springs in the days when you waited at the old wooden bath-shack for one of the four cubicles to be free. Then you stepped into the hot water and the sand sucked you down and lifted you up, and you giggled; it was like a massage, being pulled down and raised up, over and over, until you staggered out as though you were high on champagne.

She remembered the days when nobody had locks on their doors and the tiny public library was on the honor system, before the village could afford a librarian, and not one book ever was stolen. She remembered horseback rides under the full moon, and mad gallops across the desert floor in the rare lashing rains, she and her friends drenched and roaring with hilarity and the jubilation of living. She remembered impromptu square dances and watermelon parties and potluck picnics and stew suppers where if too many people showed up you threw more rice in the pot. And after all these years she suddenly thought of the long-gone elegant Anza Dining Room at the Desert Inn, where she had celebrated her twentieth birthday by dancing half the night with the beautiful young man who had given her so much happiness . . . and so much pain. Had it all been as wonderful as she remembered? Or was she a victim of faulty recollection, of the "good-old-days" syndrome that so often afflicts the elderly?

Oh, but it *had* been wonderful! She and her girlfriends had skipped arm in arm down the middle of Indian Avenue singing at the top of their voices. With umbrellas attached to their handlebars they had pumped their bicycles all the way up Palm Canyon Drive, in the days when it still was called Main Street, and then, with their feet off the pedals, they had let the wind carry them screeching downhill. They had ridden their horses all over the desert floor with a security that today's children couldn't match even when locked up in their own high-walled gardens.

But the memories made Ginger melancholy, made her feel out of sync with the world. She knew damn well that life in retrospect often seemed a lot more carefree than it actually had been. And she certainly didn't want to waste the precious present by living in the irretrievable past.

Despite all her complaints about today's Palm Springs

. . . yes, she *did* still love it. Although the city now contained a lot of god-awful jerry-built buildings, it also boasted some of the most imaginative houses and gardens and public buildings in the world. The place had its detractors, very often people who never even had been there, snobs from San Francisco and Santa Barbara and the East Coast who said Palm Springs was too fake-elegant, or too honky-tonk, or too lacking in culture, or too tame, or too boring, or too noisy, or too quiet, or too hot. Now, it was all very well for *her* to find fault with her city, but she bitterly resented the complaints of outside critics. Such people didn't begin to understand the desert. To them, inhaling the pungent dry air meant nothing more than another breath, and the dazzling cloud-free sunlight meant only a quick tan.

She considered the desert sun and air a cure for every physical and spiritual ailment known to mankind. All her life, whenever she had been defeated by tragedy, the desert had saved her sanity and restored her sense of exhilaration.

Yes, it was a crazy, unique, amazing community, this city spread out between the mountains and the desert, this city created for pleasure. It probably had more restaurants, hotels, swimming pools, tennis courts, and golf courses per square mile than any other place on earth. Its theaters and civic buildings and art galleries and churches were grander than those found in most cities its size, the result of generous endowments by its horde of wealthy citizens who had turned philanthropy into a fiercely competitive game. Civic buildings, hospitals, theaters, wide boulevards, and even mountains were named for altruistic inhabitants, many of them movie stars or former United States presidents. Most of all, though, she loved the streets that were named for the early Indian families—Alejo, Ramon, Vista Chino, Lugo . . . The list went on and on.

For those who loved parties, there were enough lavish festivities to keep one dining and dancing every night of the season, black-tie affairs to benefit all the diseases and charities in existence. There were endless holiday celebrations, costume parties, Art Museum openings, first-night galas for plays and concerts and ballets and operas. There were balloon races and turtle races and polo matches, and almost weekly there were world-famous tennis and golf tournaments. There were nature walks and birding tours and equestrian trails and bicycle paths and jogging tracks.

There was an annual Circus Parade and a Vintage Car Parade and an Easter Parade, and up the Tramway at the top of Mt. San Jacinto one could enjoy ice skating and skiing and sled-dog races. There were authentic Indian powwows and antique shows and a Mounted Police Rodeo and a Date Festival and a Corn Carnival and art fairs and chili cook-offs and curling contests and dog and cat shows. There were state and national and international conventions for every business and profession listed in the Yellow Pages. And for God's sake, there was even a Water Park where, a hundred and ten miles from the ocean, one could go surfing on four-foot waves!

And who was she to say it was good or bad? Just because she would rather enjoy a cookout under the desert moon than go to the fanciest nightclub didn't mean that one was intrinsically better than the other. Anyhow, she smiled to herself, when you're eighty-seven you're entitled to be a little old-fashioned. There had to be some compensation! Still, looking back, those early residents should have put a thick medieval wall around their village, complete with a moat, to keep this unique place forever safe from the invaders who brought wave after wave of change to it. From the vantage point of hindsight, she saw the last seventy-five years as a war between Us and Them, except that *They* kept becoming *Us.*

The sound of an approaching car put an abrupt end to her reflections. With a deep sigh of satisfaction she watched her grandson's red Toyota swoop up the long curved driveway and come to a squealing stop beneath her balcony. She waved at him in the dusk, loving his dark appealing face and his trusting brown eyes.

He has inherited the best of all of us, Ginger told herself, *all of us whose loves and hatreds, intelligence and stupidity, goodness and evil, wealth and poverty somehow combined to produce this one delightful twenty-three-year-old, this beloved companion of my old age.*

Dear God, how she loved this boy! He was her hope for the future of humanity at a time when she was growing progressively disenchanted with today's world and fearful of tomorrow's. But she sometimes worried that he might use his enormous inheritance not to better the world but for selfish purposes, as his father and his great-uncle had done before him. And she cringed at the thought of what might happen to him when "floozy gold diggers," as she still called them, discovered this good-looking young heir to a great fortune.

You're not God, she reminded herself, *and if there's one thing you should have learned all these years, it's that life is bound to kick you in the ass once in a while.* But that didn't mean you had to accept it without trying to kick back!

Ah, Ginger, Ginger, she chided herself, you should start getting dressed for the banquet. She knew that if she began thinking about all the people who had shared her life, she would be standing there all night, lost in a flood of heartbreaking memories.

Had it been wise, she wondered, to love as passionately as she had? But she could no more have stopped love from crashing down upon her than she could have stood beneath a waterfall and commanded the plunging cascade to halt in midair.

Nor would she ever have tried.

CHAPTER

1

1912

George McKinntock and his three children stared out the Pullman-car window and gasped in unison as the train reached the crest of the San Gorgonio Pass. Spread out below them was a vast shimmering desert so spectacular that the four McKinntocks could only exclaim in wonder. The train rushed out of a fogbank and plunged into a sea of warm air which quickly replaced the February chill that had accompanied the family all the way from San Francisco.

The dazzling sunlight awed ten-year-old Ella, an exceptionally beautiful child who had been pouting and predicting during the entire journey that she was going to *hate* the desert. This unexpected jolt of wonder made her sit very quietly. Since she had trouble absorbing new sensations, this entire journey had been painful for her. She was furious with her father for taking them from their fine Pacific Heights mansion and making them pack up all their belongings and move to this horrible place at the ends of the earth. Grudgingly she admitted to herself that the sunshine felt good, especially after all the dampness that had enveloped them during the trip, but that wasn't going to make up for leaving all her adoring friends, whom she probably never would see again. The idea of going to all the trouble of gathering a new set of admirers made her sigh with weariness.

The immensity of the valley impressed eight-year-old Neil, who usually was too ill and too cranky to take much notice of his surroundings. But hand in hand with his amazement at finding so enormous a space was his sense of bewilderment and his terrible fear of being lost, all alone, in that vast, empty land. With a tremor he grasped his father's hand and turned away from the window. He forced a coughing fit, which brought him instant worried attention from his father and his two older sisters. He kept coughing as long as he could without making his throat sore; then he lay back against his father's arm and closed his eyes, lulled by a sense of smug self-satisfaction.

For Virginia, whom everyone called Ginger, coming to the desert was the best gift she could have been given, particularly since that February day—the thirteenth—was her twelfth birthday. She had known all along that this land would be magnificent. Her mother and grandfather had told her so dozens of times. The arid air rushed through the train's open windows and ruffled her unruly auburn curls. Inhaling deeply, with utter delight, she felt euphoric and buoyant, as though she could float out of the train and soar above Mt. San Jacinto, whose steep rocky flanks guarded the pass.

The train picked up speed as it rushed downhill, clattering noisily over the uneven roadbed, shaking so alarmingly that its passengers rocked from side to side like metronomes. The engineer blew his whistle again and again, as though intent upon impressing the train's raucous presence upon the silent, empty land.

Sitting opposite the McKinntocks was a stylishly dressed blond who watched them with open curiosity. Polly Rutherford often was described by friends as regal, or stately, or dignified, or all three. She prized these traits, in herself and in others, but now, though she appeared sedately self-possessed, her inner turmoil was intense. She kept darting quick admiring glances across the aisle at George McKinntock's heavily lashed blue eyes, his narrow aristocratic nose, his finely defined lips, his thick, neatly combed fair hair, his impeccable, expensive clothes. What a splendid-looking couple he and she would make!

She guessed that he was in his mid-thirties, just the right age. Never again would she marry a man twice her age simply because he was wealthy. Never again would she deprive herself of the romantic love to which she felt entitled. She was quite certain that the handsome man across the aisle was a recent widower, for she sensed in him a great sadness. She tried to think of an acceptable way to speak to him, but she felt very strongly that it would be unseemly for her to initiate a conversation.

Covertly she watched the younger girl, the one they called Ella, blond and fair, with eyes to match the vivid desert sky. Polly ached to take Ella in hand, to embellish her fragile beauty with clothes of the finest silks and lace instead of the unbecoming starched white middy blouse and blue serge skirt she now wore. And that shimmering mass of pale hair, the color of a canary's underbelly! It should be curled and caught up in jeweled combs and not be permitted simply to fall haphazardly to her shoulders.

The sick little boy was a pale replica of his attractive father. The lad treated his two older sisters with an imperious air which Polly found quite charming. Yes, she would be happy to mother such a child, to cuddle him and have Cook make him the most enticing dishes to flesh out his puny body.

But Polly instinctively disliked the older sister, the one they called Ginger. The girl's exuberance was extremely unbecoming in a female. Her skirt was shockingly short— well above her ankles—her blouse was too tight across her budding breasts, and her straw hat was sitting upside-down in the aisle instead of on her head, where it belonged. Polly sensed the girl's wild spirit, and longed to contain it in some way.

Surely this Ginger was living proof that these were indeed motherless children, for no decent woman would allow a young girl to behave so badly, showing absolutely no deference to her father, asking far too many questions, displaying such unbridled curiosity, first jumping up to look out of one side of the train, then bouncing back to her seat and sticking her head out of the window so that her long wild hair tangled in the wind. Disgraceful!

Ginger was keenly aware of the woman's hostility, and utterly bewildered by it. Whatever had she done to deserve it? Gazing across the aisle, she couldn't help but admire the woman's fashionable clothes: the blue silk dress with dainty white flowers embroidered on the collar and cuffs, the matching narrow-brimmed hat, and the darker blue pocketbook and gloves lying neatly on the red plush seat beside the woman.

Ooh-la-la, French mama! Ginger felt like crooning: wasn't that what her mother would say about so fancy a lady? That is, if her mother were still alive to say anything at all. Not that her mother had been without attractive clothes. Helene McKinntock had owned an extravagant wardrobe. But she never had looked as chic as the woman across the aisle. Ginger remembered fondly, and sorrowfully, that her mother always had seemed storm-tossed, as though she had moved in the center of a private gale. Her auburn hair, moments after being expensively coiffed, had looked utterly windblown. Clothes wrinkled quickly on her active body, and she had been careless about what she wore, throwing together a rainbow of colors and textures that wildly clashed. She had adored fringed shawls and fur-trimmed velvet capes and anything made of lace.

Ginger had loved the way her mother looked, so unique, such a contrast to the other "ladies" in the McKinntocks' upper-class milieu. Only in her casket had Helene finally been well-groomed, with every hair sleekly in place and without a single crease in her gold satin ball gown.

Ginger sat quietly for the first time since they had begun this long slow journey from San Francisco. Traveling in easy stages because of Neil's fragile health, they had spent only a few hours on the train each day, so that the boy would never get overtired. Now, as always when she thought about her mother, Ginger felt a slow, grinding pain grip her body, making her breathing shallow and her stomach tight. She had to fight hard to keep from crying. There was nobody in the world Ginger had loved as much as her mother. Helene had been her teacher, her protector, her playmate. They had been so similar, looking alike and thinking alike, that they might have been identical twins born twenty years apart.

But now this exciting journey was helping Ginger to let go of her sorrow. She enjoyed the new sights and the elegant hotels where they had stopped each evening. The previous night at Riverside's Mission Inn, they had even had the Presidential Suite, the very rooms, the maid had told her, where Teddy Roosevelt once had slept! And when they reached Palm Springs there would be a whole new world to explore. Her father had promised them real Indians, and exotic palms trees like the pictures she had seen of the Holy Land in their illustrated children's Bible, and sweet oranges they could pick right off the trees, and their own horses, and a Spanish-style pink mansion that her mother's father had built back in 1890, ten years before Ginger was born.

It was going to be fun. Soon little Neil would be healthy again. She would teach him how to ride a horse, and together they would explore the desert. Ella, of course, would never in a million years get on a horse, little Miss-Ladylike-Prune, Ginger thought disdainfully. But surely Neil would want to? Sometimes her little brother baffled her. He was getting bossier and more selfish every day. Did being sick make him behave so unpleasantly? Or would he have been that way even if he had been healthy? She shook her head sadly.

Ginger wasn't the only McKinntock who noticed the elegant passenger across the aisle. George had been admiring the dainty face, the golden hair drawn back becomingly in a bun, the *haute couture*, the decorous manners, the air of gentility that clung to the woman like a veil. He was well aware of her frequent admiring glances in his direction and he was flattered, very flattered. He always had been attractive to women, but the disasters of the past year had made him all but forget about that side of life.

First there had been Helene's debilitating illness and death, followed by the collapse of his own family's business. Now, for the first time in his life, George had to worry about money. Helene's legacy was of little help: two thousand worthless acres of scrubby desert land which her father had foolishly bought for two dollars an acre in the 1880's, when he thought Palm Springs would become a fashionable resort. But it never had, and never would, and now it was just a sleepy village with several dozen Agua Caliente Indians working their miserable dirt farms and a handful of diehard whites who somehow managed to maintain a few shops and boardinghouses and a sanatorium or two.

But Helene's sun-baked land was all George had. Oh, there was still a few thousand dollars between him and starvation, but it was going fast. Too fast. He hadn't the faintest notion of how to economize. He could no more walk into a hotel and ask for the cheapest rooms than he could turn himself into a bird and fly away from his troubles. No, he had to have the best. He could function in no other fashion.

When it came to money, he and Helene had lived like two spoiled children "playing house." Both of them had had rich fathers who had provided them with generous allowances. Whoever would have thought it could all disappear so quickly? Even the mansion his father had given them for a wedding present had turned out to be too heavily mortgaged to keep.

George's stomach churned with frustration when he thought about his financial problems. There was no longer anyone he could turn to: no rich father, no wealthy relatives; all of them were either dead or had their own money woes. Now the only way he could possibly survive was for him and the children to live in Helene's father's old Palm Springs house—provided it wasn't too run-down after sitting empty in the desert heat for the two years since his father-in-law had died. And even before that, during the six years his father-in-law had been a widower, had the old man kept the house in good condition?

As for the land Helene—and now he—had inherited, maybe by some miracle there would be a boom in desert real estate. If not, he would have to seek work, but the very idea nauseated him. What could he do in Palm Springs? Sell pianos to the Indians so their daughters could play Mozart in their shabby shacks? Be a teacher, when he had forgotten everything he himself had ever learned in school? Dig ditches with his dainty white hands? It was laughable; he was so totally unfit for any job.

What's more, the knowledge that three children depended upon him sent him into panic. When they were cute little babies, he never had dreamed that someday they would become so great a responsibility. So great a burden!

He looked over at Ginger: she was such a wild tomboy, so unlike the ladylike Ella. Ginger's clothes didn't fit, her hair was a tangled mess, she was too gawky and too thin, and he had no idea how to make her behave more sedately. She jumped at life, full of enthusiasms that Helene had understood perfectly, but which left him limp with exasperation and a sense of failure as a parent. And yet there were rare moments of repose when Ginger looked positively beautiful, when she reminded him so much of Helene that he wanted to cry.

Helene! Beautiful, extravagant, passionate—his beloved playmate. But despite her air of frivolity, she *had* taken full responsibility for their lives. Only when he lost her had he realized how much she had protected him from day-to-day problems. Like paying bills. Even when money was plentiful, he never had given a moment's thought to paying creditors. Nor had he realized how much work was involved in procuring food, and hiring servants, and running a household. Helene had done it all for him.

He remembered how she had taken charge after the earthquake, that appalling April morning in 1906 when they had been awakened by the thunderous crash of houses collapsing all around them. The previous night, he and Helene had gone to the San Francisco Opera House to hear Caruso in *Carmen*, and for a moment, when the earthquake struck, George had confused the roar in his ears with the appreciative roar of the audience the night before.

Miraculously, their house had stood, damaged but intact, while the mansions on either side of them had collapsed into mountains of rubble. By another miracle, their little family had survived without injury. But it had been Helene who arranged for them to stay with relatives in Atherton during the first days, when the city was without water or food. And it had been Helene who later got them rooms at the Fairmont Hotel while waiting for their house to be repaired. Now there was no Helene to come to his rescue.

He shrugged. Something would turn up. Why worry now, when it would do no good? If he tried hard to be frugal, and if the house in Palm Springs were halfway livable, he had enough money for them to last at least another year. *Then* he'd worry.

Through his thick lashes he gazed once more at the woman across the aisle. Was she going to Palm Springs too? Only desert rats and people with bad lungs ever went there, and she hadn't coughed once during the entire train trip. Would she think him uncouth if he spoke to her without a proper introduction? He decided to take a chance. "Forgive me, madam," he began tentatively, "but . . . I say, are you at all familiar with Palm Springs?"

She turned toward him slowly and he thought he saw a

flash of relief cross her features. "Why, yes," she replied, "yes, I know it very well. What there is of it," she added disparagingly.

"Then perhaps you can recommend a doctor?" He nodded toward Neil. "For my son here?"

Her laugh was soft and throaty. "Well! It just so happens you asked the right person! My younger sister lives in Palm Springs, and even though her husband has only been a doctor for two years, he's had tremendous success with respiratory patients. Dr. Avery Rowland."

George raised his eyebrows. "The Pasadena Rowlands?" She nodded. "You know them?"

"Not personally. They were friends of my parents."

"Yes, well, you'd never know that Avery comes from such a wealthy family, the simple way he and my sister live. Poor Adele has respiratory problems herself. That's why they moved to the desert when Avery finished his training. Anyway, he's an excellent doctor and I'd be more than happy to introduce you to him."

"I'd be eternally grateful." As their eyes met across the aisle, George felt a long-unfamiliar wave of desire. Did the flush on the woman's cheeks mean that she was excited by the same impulse? He leaned toward her. "Listen . . . I hope you'll be kind enough to overlook our not having been properly introduced . . ."

She nodded. "Well, one can't always . . ."

"My name is George McKinntock. And these are my children. Virginia, Ella, Neil." He lowered his voice and added hesitantly, "My wife died eight months ago."

"Actually, we're in the same boat, Mr. McKinntock. I lost my Harry two years ago. By the way, I'm Polly Rutherford." She gestured at the seat opposite her own. "Won't you join me and tell me . . . um . . . uh . . . a little more about your son's illness?"

Ginger watched her father with a mixture of scorn and concern as he moved across the aisle and sat down near the woman. Her father was so transparent! Asking the woman about a doctor when he already had arranged for this Dr. Rowland to treat Neil. And Ginger didn't like the intimate way her father and this Mrs. Rutherford were looking at each other. What if he married her? She looked like a wicked, mean stepmother if ever there was one!

Ginger often wondered why her mother had married her father. Her mother had been intelligent and well-educated and lively, while her father was a stick-in-the-mud, so stiff and formal and proper, without a serious thought in his head. Of course Ginger loved him, but now her love for him no longer was the unconditional adoration of a child for a parent, but more like the exasperated love of an adult for a naughty boy.

Ella also was keenly aware of her father's flirtation with the woman across the aisle, but her reaction was the opposite of her sister's. Ella regarded their father as her personal property, since Ginger had preempted their mother to a degree that had quite shut out the two younger children. Every time she thought about her mother, Ella experienced a queasy feeling in her stomach. The truth of the matter was that Helene hadn't cared much for this second daughter of hers, had resented the unwanted pregnancy and the birth of an infant whose very existence intruded upon Helene's overwhelming love affair with her firstborn. The intense anger Ella had felt at her mother's outrageous rejection had had to be suppressed because Ella discovered soon enough that tears and temper tantrums brought her nothing but more rejection.

How hard she had tried to please her mother! But the sweeter Ella had behaved, the less Helene had seemed to like her, always turning to Ginger with the fierce mother love that Ella craved. It was as though Ginger had drained off Helene's entire supply of maternal adoration, leaving none for Ella or Neil.

Even though she was jealous of Ginger, Ella had nothing but scorn for her older sister. Silly Ginger, always reading books about history or people in other lands, or else talking about how fresh the rain smelled or how she liked to look at the sky when it was especially blue. What good were those things? You couldn't touch them or use them. God, wasting time learning the names of flowers and trees! And mooning over sunsets! How dumb could a person be?

As for Neil, Ella felt a kinship with him that she never would feel for Ginger. Neil was one of Ella's greatest admirers. And Ella divided the whole world into two categories: those who idolized her and those who didn't.

A true chameleon, she could play any part her admirers desired. No matter how she might actually feel, she always acted the loving daughter, and teacher's pet, and to each and every playmate she gave the impression of being that child's *very* best friend.

The pretty lady across the aisle already was a member of Ella's favored category because Ella was well aware of the woman's admiration for her; she could see it in the woman's eyes. Yes, this Polly Rutherford would be a good choice of stepmother. Ella knew exactly how to manipulate such people, using outrageous flattery and doing everything expected of a sweet little girl. And presto! The expensive presents would come cascading down upon her in no time at all.

As the train gained momentum, Ginger grew weary of sitting quietly. She pushed her way past Ella's and Neil's knees and proceeded to march down the aisle, looking for someone to talk to. A salesman in the next seat, sleeping with his head on his sample case, made her smile because his ear kept bouncing on the hard leather every time the train clickety-clacked over an uneven section of railbed. She hesitated before an elderly woman holding an ear trumpet in her lap, then gave up her search for company and returned to her family. But before she could sit down, the train lurched and threw her against Polly Rutherford, knocking that lady's hat off her head and onto the floor.

Polly screamed, Ginger cried out in alarm, George grabbed Ginger off Polly and retrieved the hat in one magnificent swooping movement, while Ella shouted, "Ginger! You clumsy *fool!*" and Neil chortled loudly at Ginger's discomfiture.

Blushing with dismay, Ginger stood hesitantly in the aisle. Her father's fingers still painfully circled her arm, and she could almost feel his disgust flow through his hand and into her skin. "I'm s-sorry, Mrs. Rutherford," she stuttered. But the woman stared straight ahead, angrily replacing her hat without acknowledging Ginger's apology.

Defiantly Ginger yanked her arm away from her father's hurtful grasp. She already disliked Mrs. Rutherford enormously. It wasn't as if Ginger had fallen onto her on purpose. *Well,* Ginger told herself as she returned to her seat, *at least now the horrid woman has a reason to hate me.*

Resolutely she stared out the window, trying to ignore the looks she was receiving from Ella and Neil. How do these things happen? she wondered forlornly. It had all been an accident anyhow, her falling on that woman. Why couldn't her family help her when something like that happened, instead of acting like she was in the wrong?

She realized with a jolt of fresh misery that no one had remembered her birthday, not her father, not her sister, not her brother. Her mother always had made a big party for her, with cake and ice cream and party favors and presents. But her father! She glared at him across the aisle. How could he have forgotten? The loss of her mother and the realization of how little she could count on anyone else made her want to cry: she suddenly felt so completely *alone.*

At that moment the train jolted to a jarring halt. There was a great commotion as the conductors carried luggage from the Pullman car and dragged steamer trunks out of the baggage car. A few minutes later the McKinntocks and Polly Rutherford were standing on the platform of the small Palm Springs station alongside the McKinntocks' four brown leather trunks and Polly's six French brocade valises.

"Hey, where's the town?" Neil wailed, looking in every direction at the surrounding desert. It was empty, except for the one-room station, a small grove of palm trees, and a water tank standing beside the tracks. Flat sandy soil stretched as far as they could see, interrupted only by occasional wind-sculptured low dunes. The sky was a rich royal blue, a deeper hue than any of the McKinntock children ever had seen it. But it was the mountains that captured their attention, pink and lavender in the afternoon sun.

"The village is six miles from here," Mrs. Rutherford explained to Neil. "A buggy meets the train and takes the passengers into Palm Springs."

As if on cue, a ramshackle open wagon came creaking toward them, pulled by a mule and driven by a dark-skinned Indian with a shaggy black mustache. Sitting on the worn buckboard seat next to the driver was an alert fifteen-year-old boy whose black hair glistened like a beacon in the sunlight. Man and boy were dressed in overalls, khaki shirts, red bandannas around their necks, and carrying straw hats.

"Johnny Pete," Mrs. Rutherford cried in exasperation at the driver, "why on earth didn't you bring the closed buggy?" She looked down with despair at her immaculate dress and shoes.

"The buggy, it is broke," the Indian replied, not at all regretfully.

"Oh! I knew I should have telegraphed Adele!" Polly turned a tragic face to George. "Usually Avery sends his Oldsmobile for me. But this time I came a few days early, and like a fool, I didn't bother to let them know." She sighed in exasperation.

The two Indians hoisted the trunks and valises into the front part of the wagon while George helped Polly and the children climb into the rear.

"This is Johnny Pete Alvarez and his son Antonio. But everyone calls the boy Tonito. They're from our local Indian tribe," Polly explained to the children, "but don't you worry, our Agua Caliente Indians are nice and friendly. Good hard workers too. Not savages, like other Indians you hear about." Polly lowered her voice. "Now, remember, children, even though Indians are allowed to attend the local school with the white children, Indians are *not* socially acceptable and you mustn't be too friendly with them."

Ginger took offense at Polly's remark, but she had caused enough trouble already, so she kept quiet. However, she thought the boy—Antonio, Tonito, whatever he was called—was the most beautiful human being she had ever seen. She stole a look at him as he lifted a trunk onto the wagon, and she caught him staring admiringly at Ella's pale, ethereal blond beauty.

Please, God, make him look at me too, Ginger prayed, but the boy gazed only at Ella. Hey, Ginger wanted to shout at him, *I'm* the nice one! *I'm* the smart one! *I'm* the adventuresome one! Even if I have these damn freckles and ordinary brown eyes and even if I'm plain compared to Ella, you can at least look at me! *Acknowledge that I exist!*

The wagon began its slow, jouncing journey toward

the village, swaying along a dusty road that was little more than the memory of ruts made by previous wheels. Ginger blinked away a few tears: Tonito hadn't once looked in her direction. Would it always be like this? Everyone ignoring her and making a fuss over silly-dumb-selfish Ella instead?

Ginger gave her sister a baleful sidelong look. She had to admit that Ella had been born gorgeous and would be a great beauty if she lived to a hundred. But Ginger had been furious—and hurt—when thoughtless visitors to their San Francisco home had gone into ecstasies over Ella's looks. "Ella's the beautiful one," they invariably had said, and then as an afterthought, "and of course Ginger's the smart one." As if any girl would rather be smart than beautiful!

And yet, mixed with the jealousy, Ginger felt a pang of pity for Ella. The younger girl would probably go through life without ever experiencing any of the joys so readily available to an inquisitive spirit. Never to ride a horse, or climb a mountain! Never to take chances, to really look at the world, to try to understand and enjoy people and not just use them. All her life, Ella would most likely just sit and smugly accept all the praise and admiration that came her way. But was that really living?

Ginger noticed that her father and Mrs. Rutherford, sitting side by side, still were involved in animated conversation. She hadn't seen her father look so handsome and debonair for a long time. She saw, too, that Mrs. Rutherford's eyes sparkled, and a becoming rosiness had risen to her cheeks. The woman continued to look well-groomed, despite the strong wind that swirled around the wagon and threw whorls of dust on everyone. Mrs. Rutherford held on to her hat, her dignity unimpaired, and any discomfort she may have felt was entirely submerged in the pleasure she seemed to be taking in George McKinntock's company.

Suddenly the wagon hit a deep rut. Passengers and baggage slammed toward the rear, knocking the tailgate open and spilling adults, children, trunks, and valises onto the dirt road. While cries and shouts filled the air, the terrified mule bolted free of his traces and tore off down the road. At the same moment, the wagon tilted onto its side, throwing the driver and his son onto the sand.

For a stunned minute, no one moved. Then slowly, carefully, they sat up and took inventory, feeling their arms and legs. No bones were broken, but everyone was bruised. Ginger's knees were scraped, and a deep gash on her arm was bleeding. Neil had a bloody nose. Ella whimpered and stared in horror at the scraped skin on her palms and knees. George groaned because of a bruised cheek and even more over the rips in his favorite cashmere jacket. Polly Rutherford had a tiny cut on her forehead, and her blue dress had turned a dusty beige. All of them had sand and dirt on their faces and hands and in their hair.

Silently the Indian assessed the damage to his wagon: a wheel had fallen off and lay in splinters beside the road. Like curious onlookers, a screeching flock of thrushes wheeled toward them, then swooped away from the wrecked wagon and its disgruntled passengers. Between gusts of wind, the silence was formidable.

"What happened to the mule?" Neil wailed. "Where'd he go?"

"He probably ran home," Tonito said. "He always does when he's scared."

"Now, Johnny Pete, and you too, Tonito," Polly ordered, "run into the village and tell Dr. Rowland to send his car."

The Indian shook his head. "I am too slow, missus. My boy will go alone." He touched his son's arm fondly, proudly. "Run, Tonito. Soon it will be dark."

Ginger walked away from the others and sat by herself on the sand, still nursing her feelings of estrangement from the rest of them. She didn't know what was wrong with her today, because she kept wanting to cry. That wasn't like her; she usually was so brave. She took a handkerchief from her pocket and wound it tightly around her bleeding arm.

They were a glum group. George rested Neil's head on his thigh and stanched the boy's nosebleed, while Mrs. Rutherford wiped Ella's palms. Ella was smiling adoringly up at Mrs. Rutherford, a look Ginger knew from experience that Ella pasted onto her face whenever she was about to flatter someone outrageously.

"You're the prettiest lady I ever saw," Ginger heard Ella tell the woman.

Oh, you silly little fool! Ginger wanted to shout at her sister. *How can you be such a bare-faced liar? And how can you be so disloyal to our mother's memory? Mama was much, much prettier!*

She turned away from the others and gazed at the desert surrounding her. She was amazed at the variety of wildflowers and prickly-looking shrubs she saw—big sharp-needled barrel-shaped cactus and skinny ones that looked like humorous stick figures. The plants stood far apart, as if each one owned a private territory. They were not as colorful as the mist-protected flowers in San Francisco, but they were beautiful, she thought, in their own special way.

"Hey, Ginger, a snake'll bite you out there," Neil taunted. He was standing up now, holding a handkerchief to his nose.

"Don't worry, Neil, I'll just bite him back!" All the same, she peered under the nearby shrubs to make sure no reptiles lurked there. Uneasy now, she joined the others.

She gazed up at the sky. The late-afternoon sun slanted obliquely across the desert, making the quartz particles in the sand glitter like slivers of diamonds. The distant mountains were a deepening purple, and rugged Mt. San Jacinto, rising steeply behind her, was in silvery shade as the sun moved behind it. The silence was searing, a presence, part of the landscape.

An hour passed and the travelers grew weary of waiting. They sat uncomfortably on the sand, leaning against the bottom of the overturned wagon. There, in the shade of the looming mountain, it was growing chilly, although farther out on the desert floor, away from the mountain's shadow, the sun still blazed hotly.

Gusts of cold wind began whipping across the flat land. As though a giant kept scooping up a handful of sand and throwing it at them, they were lashed again and again by the stinging sharp particles. They all put their arms over their eyes to protect them.

"That Tonito!" Polly Rutherford complained. "He must've stopped running the minute he was out of our sight."

"That's not so, missus," the Indian strongly objected. "My son, he runs like the wind. He is a good boy." He paused. "It may be, missus, that the doctor's driver, he is often someplace else and must be found."

While Polly shook her head in disgust, the Indian, whose name really was Juan Pedro, wondered why white people always called him Johnny Pete. And why did they call his sacred Mt. San Jacinto by the silly name of Saint Jack?

He found these things disrespectful, though not enough to make a fuss over. After all, the Agua Caliente Indians were lucky. The white men had let them keep some of their beautiful land, and except for an occasional fight over water rights, the tribal members got along reasonably well with their white neighbors. White children and Indian children attended the same grammar school in the village, and there was less of the racism here than other tribes experienced.

Yes, except for this stuck-up Mrs. Rutherford, Juan Pedro respected most white people—white Indians, his great-grandfather used to call them, because in the beginning all people were Indians and the white ones went off and did things differently, while the red ones stayed on the land and kept in touch with the Spirits. When the red Indians needed help, they fasted and prayed to the Spirits. But when the white people wanted help, they didn't pray or fast. Instead they invented machines to do things for them, machines that raced over the earth on wheels more swiftly than the fastest Indian runners, and some machines that even flew in the air! They made telegraphs and telephones that sent sound from one place to another like magic, and they made ice in summer, and lights that shone all through the night without fire or fuel.

Yes, he admired white people. His son Tonito was the smartest boy in the entire Agua Caliente tribe and was getting a white education. Someday he would use that education to teach the rest of the tribe how to obtain all the advantages the whites had. Still, Juan Pedro prayed that if his people ever did lift themselves out of their poverty and ignorance, they would do so without losing their reverence for the land.

Juan Pedro glanced over at this new family sitting on the sand with Mrs. Rutherford and he wondered what had brought them to the desert. He could tell, just by looking at them, that the father and the two younger children weren't going to like it here. It showed right away in people's eyes if they liked it—their eyes lighting up with pleasure the first time they looked around in amazement at the mountains and the sand dunes. Except for the older girl, this little family viewed the desert like it was some kind of terrible enemy.

As if to echo the Indian's thoughts, Neil whimpered, "I hate it here, Daddy. It's scary!"

"Oh, God, Neil, you're such a baby," Ginger groaned.

"I'm scared too," Ella whispered. "Daddy, it's awful!"

George sighed. He secretly agreed that the place was desolate; yes, "scary" was the right word. But he tried to sound cheerful. "Come on, now, you two. You'll like it better when we get to the village and—"

"Yes," Polly interrupted, eager to help George. "In the village there are actually some very nice houses and a few shops, and pretty trees and flowers. You'll see." If the truth be known, she also hated the desert and she only came here for a few weeks every winter out of sisterly duty to Adele, who was a semi-invalid. Polly had to admit that this fragrant, dry desert air did make her feel years younger. But still, it was a godforsaken place, so far from everything. There was no gas, no electricity, no telephones. She didn't know how Adele could stand it.

Polly saw that her little speech had failed to cheer the children. In a burst of courage born of the unusual circumstances in which they were trapped, she reached out and squeezed George's hand in commiseration.

George returned the pressure of Polly's hand. They smiled at each other and both felt a jolt of optimism . . . and desire. Polly was confident that with some judicious, very subtle aggression on her part, this coming month on the desert might well change both their lives.

The sky was purple with a stunning band of turquoise behind the darkened mountains when the flickering headlights of Dr. Rowland's Oldsmobile came probing up the road toward them. They all gave a shout of relief at their deliverance. Polly took charge, telling the children where to sit in the big black touring car, showing Henry, the chauffeur, where to stow the luggage, and ordering Juan Pedro to stay there and guard the four trunks that didn't fit into the automobile.

"Guard them from what?" Juan Pedro laconically inquired. "The coyotes?"

"Just stay here until Henry comes back for you," she insisted.

Juan Pedro shrugged his passive assent.

Once the automobile started back toward Palm Springs, Polly sighed with relief. "Actually, I didn't want that dirty Indian sitting here in the car with us," she whispered to George.

He turned toward her, startled. "Why not? He looked clean enough."

"One can't be sure—"

"And there really was room for him," George went on. "I should think the trunks'd be safe out there, too."

She shook her head. "I tell you this, George, it's one thing to *act* friendly toward the Indians. But it never would do to treat them like equals. They're no better than niggers."

George pondered her words for some time. Snob he might be, but a bigot he was not, so he had to count her prejudice as a point against the lady. And at this stage of their developing friendship he was loath to admit that she might be anything less than perfect.

Night had settled over Palm Springs by the time the Oldsmobile carried the weary travelers into the village. Light from candles and kerosene lanterns glowed in a few windows, but the most overwhelming illumination, as they stepped out of the automobile, came from the stars.

"How close they are!" Ginger exclaimed. She waited for the others to voice their wonder at the amazing sky, but they were all too busy smoothing their clothes and shaking off the dust.

George had arranged by mail to stay with the children at Nellie Coffman's boardinghouse—the sign on her porch called it "The Desert Inn Hotel and Sanatorium"—until he could determine whether or not his father-in-law's house was livable. Conveniently, the boardinghouse was just down the street from Adele and Avery Rowland's home. The Rowlands rushed out to greet them, full of concern about Polly's accident on the desert. They were joined by Nellie and her Chinese cook who had kept dinner warm for the McKinntocks.

Although the two sisters' faces were similar, with delicate, sculptured features, Ginger was surprised at how different Polly Rutherford was from Adele. Polly was elegantly dressed; small, frail Adele wore a simple plaid shirt, faded blue knickers, and boots. Her blond hair was carelessly caught back in a bun, while Polly's was perfectly coiffed, despite the windy ride on the desert. But the greatest difference was in their expressions: Polly looked forbiddingly haughty to Ginger, whereas Adele had a sweet, friendly, welcoming smile.

Adele's husband, Dr. Avery Rowland, also wore a plaid shirt, knickers, and boots, but on his tall, sturdy body they looked stylish. He had a strong, handsome face with a square chin and a high forehead framed by smooth light brown hair. His eyes were so bright a blue that they glowed even in the dim lantern light. His cheerful good humor enveloped the group like a caress, holding them together longer than anyone needed to stay. He shook George's hand and each child's hand and repeated their names as they were introduced. When he saw the gash on Ginger's arm, he insisted that she come with him to have it cleaned and properly bandaged. As for the rest of the McKinntocks, Avery could see that they had only superficial wounds that needed no treatment.

"Well, come on, Polly. You must be starved." Adele took her sister's arm while smiling shyly at the McKinntocks. "I'm so happy to meet all of you!"

Avery put a protective arm around Ginger and led her around the side of the house to his office. All at once his kindness unlocked the tears she had been suppressing all day. He took her hand and let her cry, all the while stroking her hair and making little comforting sounds.

"I'm s-sorry," she whispered when the tears abated. She gave him a shaky smile. "I was crying because I m-miss my mother," she said, "and because nobody remembered my birthday." *And because Tonito never once looked at me,* she added to herself.

"Never apologize for crying, Virginia. There's nothing wrong with it." He helped her onto a stool, cleaned and cauterized her wound—grimacing in sympathy when she winced at the sting of the disinfectant. Then he bandaged her arm neatly.

Only when he helped her down from her perch did she

notice eight bright paintings on his office's white walls. Half were bold, brilliantly colorful landscapes and the others were covered with strange multihued geometric shapes.

"D'you like them?" he asked with a wry smile.

"Well, yes, but they're so . . . different!" She pointed at a forest with scarlet leaves and twisted purple trunks. "I mean, I know they're trees, but they don't really *look* like trees." She cocked her head. "Oh, but they're really interesting!"

"Poor Adele dislikes them, I'm afraid. Her taste runs to classical art." He laughed ruefully. "That's why I keep them out here. Trouble is, my patients all hate them too."

Ginger walked closer to the wall and examined each painting: "Well, I guess they are pretty unusual. But *I* think they're beautiful."

"I'm glad you do, Virginia. I just wish more people appreciated them." He sighed. "I spent a year in Paris when I was eighteen, trying to be a painter. These paintings were farewell gifts from some of the artists who befriended me." He pointed at the signatures and read them off. "Matisse. Dufy. Vlaminck. Braque. Léger. My only souvenirs of that wonderful year. Besides my memories."

"Paris." Ginger smiled at him wistfully. "My parents went there for their honeymoon." She hesitated. "Why did you become a doctor? I mean, if you really wanted to be a painter?"

He shrugged. "I wasn't a bad painter. Just not good enough."

"Who said?"

"*I* said."

"Did you paint like that too?" She gestured at the pictures on the wall.

"No. I tried. But my work wasn't bold enough. Not free enough."

"Why didn't you keep on trying?"

"Because my father and I made an agreement that if I didn't have a gallery show by the end of the year, I'd come home and go to medical school."

"Don't you like being a doctor?"

"Oh, sure. Once I got started learning medicine, I

began to enjoy it. And after a while I married Adele and we moved here, and now Paris seems like . . . well, like a dream I had . . . almost as if it never really happened."

She heard the disappointment in his voice and thought she ought to say something comforting to him, but she didn't know what. "My mother loved Paris," Ginger told him. "She promised she'd take me there"—her voice quavered—"some day."

"Well, who knows?" he said heartily, trying to cheer her. "Maybe someday Adele'll be strong enough, and *we'll* take you to see Paris." He picked up his lantern and accompanied her across the dark road to Nellie's boardinghouse. The night air was cool and dry, permeated with the fragrance of desert plants and orange blossoms. At the door, he took her hand and leaned over to kiss her forehead. "Happy birthday, little girl," he said, "and many, *many* more!"

"Oh, thank you!" She was standing on the high doorstep, so that her face and the doctor's were the same height. They smiled at each other for a moment in the dim light. He was still holding her hand, and all at once she was aware of a strange tingling sensation that started in her fingers and swooped up her arm and through her whole body, leaving her breathless.

"Well, good night," she finally said, reluctantly sliding her hand out of his warm grasp. She opened the boardinghouse door and stepped inside. "And thank you again, Dr. Rowland, for . . . for *everything*."

CHAPTER
2

Ginger awoke at dawn. She crept quietly to the window of the tent-cabin she shared with Ella, who slept on a cot across the small room. Cautiously lifting the drapery, Ginger clapped her hand over her mouth to keep from crying out with pleasure and waking her sister. There before her glowed Mt. San Jacinto, gilded by the rising sun. The foothills were a cluster of bright gold clumps. Behind them, the deep, steep folds of the mountain were pale blue beside orange sunlit outcroppings. High above this pageant of color the snow on the mountain's peak was pink. The luminescent blue sky was all of a piece with the rest of the dramatic view and thus a continuation of it. The air was absolutely still, as if holding its breath in awe.

Close by, a small forest of palm trees lined a narrow water-filled ditch which cut through the boardinghouse grounds. Down the road was Dr. Rowland's house. Now, in daylight, Ginger could see that it was a low tree-smothered structure with a deep porch across the front. Two beige dogs frolicked in the yard while a white cat stretched itself on the porch steps.

Ginger smelled bread baking in the boardinghouse kitchen. Grinning at the wonder of it all, she dressed quickly and left the tent-cabin. She looked around at the boardinghouse grounds: a dozen or so tents with wooden floors, peaked canvas roofs, and white awnings—just like the one she and Ella occupied—stood behind the neat cottage that housed the kitchen and dining room. Rock-edged round flower gardens were interspersed among the tents, along with randomly placed rocking chairs and canvas chaises. Shade trees were everywhere. But over-whelming the near view was the rocky mountainside that rose steeply behind the boardinghouse grounds.

Ginger let herself out the gate and skipped along the dirt street while deeply inhaling the delicious air. She never had felt so alive. Under her breath, to the tune of "My Country 'Tis of Thee," she sang over and over, "Palm Springs I lu-uv you . . . and the sky abu-uve you : . ."

Everywhere she looked, she saw lines of tall palms and acres of pink and white and yellow wildflowers, and always, always, looming over the town, the bronze rock-strewn flanks of San Jacinto mountain. And everything, every stone and leaf and flower, looked crisply sharp in the clear early-morning air.

When she passed a two-story rustic hotel she waved at the elderly man with a full white beard who was standing on the long covered porch. "Hello," she called out hap-pily. "I'm Ginger McKinntock and I've come here to live!"

He nodded gravely at her. "Welcome, my dear. I'm Dr. Welwood Murray and I've lived here for twenty-five years!"

"Did you know my Grandpa John?"

"Sure did. He was my very best friend."

She pointed at a pond behind his property. "Is that your pond?"

He shook his head. "Nope. That's the Indians' hot springs. The one the village is named after."

She nodded and continued along Main Street, first passing a small brand-new wooden church and then a schoolhouse, which she eyed with great curiosity as the future seat of her education. At Blanchard's Feed and Grocery Store she stopped to read a small handwritten notice announcing a special sale of soap for a nickel and women's union suits for seventy-five cents. A second, more permanent sign said: "United States Post Office."

Ginger strolled up another dirt road, one which rose gently uphill toward Mt. San Jacinto. There, on a mesa abutting the mountainside, she found a big pink adobe house whose windows all were shuttered. She knew at once, from her mother's description of it, that this delightful mansion with arched windows, wrought-iron balconies, and a turret had been her grandparents' home. Here her mother had lived during her vacations from the Marlborough School in Los Angeles.

The red tile roof was nearly covered by overgrown drooping trees. Dried-up flowerbeds curved around dusty stretches of gravel. Behind the garden lay a stone-lined ditch full of rushing, sparkling water. The house was completely circled by a porch with deep overhangs to protect it from the sun. Ginger walked around the entire porch, trying to peer into the windows, but she found it impossible to pry open the peeling white wooden shutters.

She stood on the porch and looked out at the view. The house was on a sharp rise, so that she could see for miles, clear across the valley. There were tall dunes of beige sand, and clumps of pale green trees, and long expanses of gray-beige flatlands, and rocky alluvial fans at the base of a mountain range southeast of the village, and blue ponds that looked from a distance like lakes but that she knew from her grandfather's descriptions were actually salt-flats.

Next to her mother, Grandpa John had been the most important person in Ginger's life. A tall, dapper man, he always wore a dark blue suit, white shirt, and blue bow tie—his "city clothes"—when he visited with Helene and her little family in San Francisco. "But you should see me out on my desert," he would chortle to Ginger, his face alight with pleasure. "There I live in riding pants and boots! I tell you, my little darling, out in God's country people and their horses are always together, like Siamese twins."

Until he died two years earlier, Grandpa John had come to San Francisco every summer to escape the desert's searing heat. But home to him was his pink adobe mansion in the shadow of Mt. San Jacinto.

"I have land, Ginger, lots of land," Grandpa John had told her during his last, his final visit. "Someday my little oasis will be famous. And when that happens, whoever owns land out there is going to make a pile of money. But, child, it's not going to happen in my lifetime. So, by God, your generation better make darn sure our little Eden grows properly! You build a house out there with thick walls and plenty of shade, it'll always be comfortable, even in our hot summers. Same goes for the trees and gardens. It's all got to be native to the desert. If you don't preserve the qualities that make the desert so special, you'll end up with nothing but a hot, humid copy of Los Angeles out there." His eyes had misted. "Save my desert, sweetheart," he had whispered in a voice hoarse with emotion.

But this warm, clear morning, she could see nothing that was threatening the land. It was as quiet and peaceful as she imagined heaven to be.

As she was about to retrace her steps toward Main Street, she heard a hearty male voice behind her. "*Good* morning, young lady!" She turned and recognized Dr. Avery Rowland. "Oh, good morning, Dr. Rowland," she replied, delighted to see him. He made her feel so . . . alive! So *excited* to be alive! And a little breathless.

"Everyone calls me Dr. Avery," he corrected her. "How're you feeling this morning, Virginia?"

"Oh, fine. And everyone calls *me* Ginger."

"Yes, I like that better. Well, then, Ginger-girl, been making the grand tour of our little village?"

"Yes."

"Do you like it?"

"Oh, yes, I do!" she inhaled deeply. "I especially like your air."

"*My* air?" He laughed. "Well, I guess you might call it mine at that. This wonderful dry air helps my patients far more than any medicine." *Except it hasn't helped Adele,* he thought sadly. Then he brightened and gestured at the pink mansion behind him. "I love that house. I tried to buy it from your grandfather before he died, but he wouldn't sell it. He always hoped you'd live here someday."

"I can't wait to see the inside," Ginger said.

"It's a beauty. Well-built, too. It had to be, to keep from getting washed away in ninety-three. We get real killer storms every now and then."

"Did you see it?"

"No, sweetheart, that was before my time. But your Grandfather John said it was the ditches and culverts he'd put all around the land that saved it. He said the entire mountainside looked like Niagara Falls."

She looked up at the peaceful scene. "It's hard to imagine such a storm."

"Well, if you stay here long enough, you'll surely see one," he said. "So! What brings you out so early?"

"It's too nice to stay indoors."

"A girl after my own heart! Best time of day, dawn." He pointed at the mountain behind them. "There are paths up there made by the Indians, God knows how many centuries ago. I climb them all, when it's barely light out. That way, I get to see the sunrise in all its glory."

"Oh! That must be beautiful!"

"It is. Tell you what, Ginger. If you'd like to hike up my favorite trail with me tomorrow morning, be out in front of Nellie's place just before dawn."

Ginger gave the mountain behind them a skeptical look. "My brother says it's crawling with rattlesnakes up there."

"Oh?" Avery was amused. "Just when did Neil climb San Jacinto and see all these snakes?"

"He didn't. He only heard about it."

"I see. Well, you tell Neil that in the two years I've been going up and down that mountain, I've never once been bitten."

"But did you ever *see* a snake?"

"Yeah, a few times. But y'see, Ginger-girl, snakes are like people *ought* to be: if you don't bother them, they won't bother you."

"Well, in that case . . . sure, I'd love to hike with you tomorrow." As she looked back at the mountain, a graceful beige animal with huge curved horns appeared on an outcropping of rock far above her head. "Oh," she breathed in awe, "what's *that*?"

He followed her line of vision. "Ah!" He smiled with pride. "That's a bighorn sheep. I call him 'Curly.' Sometimes he follows me, leaping from crag to crag. He keeps his distance, though." He turned and gestured down at the village. "It's a big change from San Francisco, isn't it?"

"I like them both."

"Well said, Ginger-girl. Some people think if you love one place, you've got to hate everywhere else. This'll take getting used to, though. No streetlights like you have up north. Now, there's no sense in lighting up all that air, is there, when it only takes one small lantern for a person to go wherever it is he's going? No telephones here either. No, thanks! How can you have your privacy when any jerk can ring you up anytime he wants and interrupt whatever it is you're doing?"

They passed a strange, shaggy edifice whose walls and roof were made of palm fronds. Dogs, goats, sheep, horses, mules, and a cow lay indolently on the ground, soaking up the early-morning sun. "That's an Indian brush house," Avery explained. "G'morning, Dolores!" He nodded and waved at an Indian woman weaving a basket under a canopy of fronds. "Now, then, that open area with a thatched roof where Dolores is sitting, that's called a ramada. Nice and cool in the hottest weather. Nellie's got one, out back of the boardinghouse. Nowadays, though, most of the Indians are copying us newcomers and building wood or stucco houses. I'm not so sure it's an improvement."

"Do you know all the Indians here, Dr. Avery?"

"Sure. There aren't that many—maybe fifty families. But don't let their poverty give you the wrong impression, Ginger-girl. They're fine, fine people. They've got a good sense of humor, most of them. They're honest and intelligent—hard workers, too—so don't pay any attention if you hear prejudiced white people making them out to be an inferior breed."

Like your sister-in-law, Mrs. Rutherford, Ginger wanted to say.

They turned onto Indian Avenue, a broad dirt thoroughfare paralleling Main Street. Huge cottonwood trees framed the mountain, still pink under the rising sun. "You see, Ginger," he said, "this little village is special. There's a magic to it. But it's not for everyone. Most of us here want to keep this little oasis as our own very special secret."

"Don't worry," Ginger laughed, "I won't tell a soul."

"Is that a promise?" He smiled. "Now, I happen to know that your father has a couple thousand acres he's he's just dying to get rid of at a big fat profit. Me, I'm just the opposite. I bought three thousand acres when I first got here and I'll *never* sell them. That way they'll remain open desert forever."

He stopped in the middle of the dirt road between his house and Nellie's boardinghouse. Solemnly he enfolded Ginger's small smooth hands in his large firm ones. "I can tell you're a real desert rat, honey, just like the rest of us here."

As had happened the previous night, she felt a jolt of excitement run through her body when he touched her hands. "Grandpa J-John always called himself a d-desert rat too," she stuttered, confused and embarrassed by the way she reacted to the doctor's touch.

Avery beamed. "Wonderful man, John. Just about my very best friend in the world, even though he was old enough to be my father."

"I guess he was everybody's best friend," Ginger said wistfully, remembering the white-haired man she had met earlier that morning, and missing her grandfather with a fresh gust of grief.

Avery, who was as adept at diagnosing people's sorrows as he was at determining their physical ailments, could see that this girl was too sensitive for her own good, though it was balanced by a lot of spunk. He felt that she was on the brink of an abyss, at a vulnerable age when she could fall into a sea of lifelong disappointments, or else she could soar, away from the brink, away from the abyss, into a life of achievement and joy.

I'll help her all I can, he promised himself. *She's special, this one. She has spirit and soul.*

His thoughts were interrupted when Nellie Coffman sailed out of the boardinghouse and put a protective arm around Ginger. "Where've you been, child? Your papa was afraid you'd been kidnapped." Nellie was a large handsome woman whose cheerful rosy face was framed in a pink bonnet.

"Who'd kidnap *me*?" Ginger scoffed, liking the feel of this motherly woman's arm around her.

"*Voilà, madame*," Avery said airily. "I saved her from the child-snatchers, *n'est-ce pas*?"

"Oh, you and your French," Nellie laughed. "Let me warn you, Ginger, this man is a complete fraud. Just because he spent a year in Paris trying to be a painter, he puts on airs in front of us plain folk."

"Believe me," Avery sighed, "my French was a lot better than my painting." He pointed at Nellie's simple white Mother Hubbard. "And, Ginger-girl, don't let the way Nellie dresses fool you for one minute. She isn't 'plain folk' any more than I'm the King of France. She's one smart, high-class lady!" He gave Ginger and Nellie a mock salute and crossed the street to his house.

Bursting with the wonders of her new hometown, and delighted by her growing friendship with the kind young doctor, Ginger impulsively hugged Nellie. "I'm going to live here forever!" she vowed. "Forever and ever, Mrs. Coffman. Till I'm an old, old lady!"

Later that afternoon, George took the children with him to investigate the pink house. While he unlocked doors, released shutters, and flung open the casement windows, the children ran from room to room and up the stairs to claim their own territories.

Ginger was the first to find the corner upstairs bedroom in the turret, facing Mt. San Jacinto on one side and the entire valley on the other. Surely this round room had been her mother's: the description fitted perfectly. It was large, with a varnished wood floor, a stone fireplace, and a semicircle of arched windows. A glass door opened onto a small balcony. When Ginger pulled the protective sheets off the furniture, she discovered a high bed with a floral-embroidered counterpane. Against one wall an enormous chest of drawers stood next to a marble-topped dressing table.

She rushed down the steps to find her father. In the living room she stopped in awe before the stone fireplace: each rock was a perfect oval, created not by a mason's tools but by centuries of wind and rain. The high mantel held a truncated grandfather clock whose brass pendulum was motionless. The room's leather-and-rosewood couches and chairs had been uncovered—a pile of yellowed sheets sat in the middle of the braided carpet.

She found her father in the blue-and-white-tile kitchen staring with perplexity at the cast-iron stove whose doors and sides were covered with intricate wrought-iron designs.

"Does it work, Papa?" Ginger asked.

"I haven't the faintest idea."

"Papa, I found the bedroom I want. I think it was Mama's. Can I have it? Please? Please?"

"Sure, that's fine," he readily agreed. So vast was George's relief at finding the house in a livable condition that he would have promised anything she asked. The furniture was like new. The linens and curtains would need laundering, and a general housecleaning and some painting and polishing were necessary, but Polly had assured him that the village Indians were more than eager for such work, at reasonable rates.

Together Ginger and George went out to the porch. "Everything will have to be replanted," he said, gesturing at the garden, "and the trees need trimming."

"Oh, Papa, I love it!"

Looking at Ginger, George was reminded of Helene. They had met, nearly fourteen years earlier, on this very porch, when he came to Palm Springs with his father to buy a commercial building that Helene's father had owned in Oakland. Helene had smiled up at George and offered to show him the gardens. The flowers had been beautiful then, pink oleanders and red hibiscus, he remembered, and coral-throated water lilies in the pond.

He sighed deeply. The house was in good shape and he was glad that Ginger was happy here. But he knew that Neil and Ella were not so easy to please. As for himself, he would shrivel up and die if he had to stay here too long. There was nothing to do! No restaurants, no theaters, no society, no sports, nothing but this godforsaken vast desert to stare at and wish he were hundreds of miles away. What kind of a life was that?

Maybe Polly would be his salvation. Pretty, rich Polly. She had made sure yesterday that he knew all about her splendid mansion in Pasadena and her yearly shopping trips to Paris and New York. Very obviously she was eager to replace the late Mr. Rutherford in her heart and hearth. And in her bed.

George liked her well enough, was even attracted to her physically. If he married her it would mean good schools and fashionable clothes for his children, and above all, the kind of luxurious life to which he was accustomed: servants, travel, the best of everything. And why not? He and Polly both would be getting what they wanted out of such a marriage. They could have a good life together . . . if he didn't mind being a "kept man."

But he did mind. He had his pride. No, he couldn't propose to Polly while he was penniless. He had to approach her with something in his pocket. *Oh, God,* he silently prayed, *let me sell that damn worthless land!*

When the McKinntocks finished inspecting the pink mansion and returned to Nellie's boardinghouse, they found Tonito waiting for them with two horses. He approached Ella with a grin. "Want to ride?"

Ella drew back, offended. "Are you *crazy?*"

"All the girls here ride," he insisted.

Ginger approached a light brown colt and gazed with rapture into its eyes. "What's his name?"

"He's called Se-San," Tonito told her, "after one of our bravest warriors. From the old days."

"He's beautiful, Tonito." She stroked the animal's neck. "I'd love to ride him."

"You know how?"

"Of course I know how!"

He glanced back regretfully at Ella. "Sure you won't come, Ella?"

"I'm sure!"

Tonito shrugged. "All right, Ginger," he said ungraciously, frowning with disappointment, "come on, then."

He took off at a gallop and Ginger strained to keep up with him. They flew across miles of flat desert floor, racing over sun-baked ground as hard as pavement. Then they climbed a dune, where the horses sank ankle-deep in soft sand. At the crest, Tonito stopped and peered at a line of jagged peaks to the southeast of them.

"Do those have a name?" Ginger asked shyly, intimidated by his silence. She couldn't stop looking at him—he was so beautiful. His skin glowed like polished copper. He was so graceful, he made her feel awkward in comparison.

"Santa Rosa," he replied tersely.

"And those lacy trees?" she ventured, emboldened.

"Mesquites." He hesitated, as though every word he spoke were a torture. "There's water hidden in the sand under them. Good to know if you're ever out here dying of thirst."

They rode in silence until Tonito stopped his horse, slid off the animal, and motioned for Ginger to do the same. He led her to a strange cleft in the earth with stairs dug out of its side. "C'mon!" he ordered.

She followed him down twenty curving steps to an opening in the wall.

"It's an Indian well," he whispered.

"Why are you whispering?"

"I don't know, it's spooky down here."

She caught his fright and dashed up the steps with Tonito close behind her. "Whew!" she cried with relief at the top, then burst out laughing. "I wasn't the least bit scared until you said *you* were."

"I wasn't," he scoffed as he jumped up on his horse. "I was only trying to scare you."

They entered a narrow shady canyon, a tree-filled oasis where a creek lapped and trickled along a series of pools and cascades. Ginger looked up at the forest of palms whose stiff fan-shaped fronds made a harsh swishing clatter above their heads.

"I love palm trees," Ginger said.

"Those're called fan palms. Some are a thousand years old!" Tonito said proudly. "My tribe owns this entire canyon—Palm Canyon, we call it. But wait till you see Tahquitz Canyon! There's a waterfall there."

"That's a funny name."

"Tahquitz?" He thought about it. "There's an old tribal legend that an ugly magician named Tahquitz lived far up the canyon. He'd lure innocent people to his cave and make slaves of them. Especially beautiful young maidens. Anyhow, my people used to believe it was Tahquitz throwing a tantrum when there was rumbling and landslides in the canyon."

Tonito stopped his horse beside a glassy pool rimmed with rocks and boulders and surrounded by tall fan palms and thick low ferns. A meadow of wild fiddlehead and chuparosa, vivid pink primrose, and sand verbena separated the pool from the canyon's steep bare walls. Robins and meadowlarks chattered and swooped with excitement as they feasted on mistletoe berries.

Beyond the clearing, where the canyon narrowed, Ginger saw a blue haze. Was it smoke? She worried for a moment, until her eyes focused more clearly. "Blue trees!" she cried out, astonished. "How can there be blue trees?"

Tonito smiled for the first time that afternoon. Straight white teeth, upturned mouth, shining eyes, cheeks dimpled with humor—the sight of his unexpected mirth took Ginger's breath away. "They're called smoke trees," he explained to her, "because they get those blue blossoms that look like smoke. We had lots of rain this year, so they bloomed early." He pointed at a stand of trees whose smooth trunk and branches were light green and whose leaves were hidden by a profusion of yellow flowers. "And those're palo verdes. My favorites."

"What a place!" Ginger gushed. "It's like . . . like a fairyland!"

He shook his head, his smile gone.

She was puzzled. "Well, don't you think it's beautiful, Tonito?"

"Yes," he replied so softly she barely could hear him. "We call our land *La Palm del Dios*. The Palm of the God's Hand. But its beauty makes me sad."

"Why?"

"Because in a few days I have to leave it. I'm going to the high school in San Bernardino and I'll be living there with some cousins."

Their eyes met, then wavered, and as each looked away, Ginger felt a hollow lurch in her stomach. "You're going away?" she whispered.

"I don't want to, but it's my duty," he said bitterly. "For years now the government's been promising to officially divide our land among us Indians. But the men in Washington don't have time for our problems." He gestured in the direction of the village. "We're farmers. We work hard. When our men have time, they do odd jobs for the white people, working in their gardens or painting their houses, anything for a little extra money."

"And your women? What do they do?"

"They clean the white people's houses and take care of the white people's children. And they make beautiful baskets in their spare time."

He stopped and stared up at the stark canyon walls. His bare arms and feet, his graceful neck and meditative face, were a warm amber color, his cheeks tinged with red. Youthful health radiated from every pore as he slouched on his horse.

"You know," he mused, "since the beginning of time, long before the first whites came, my tribe farmed part of the year down here in the desert, and during the hot summers they went up to the cool mountains. Down here we had our magic hot spring and plenty of pure water from the mountain. My ancestors had a good life, even if it was simple. Then the white men came, first the Spanish, and they gave us their Catholic Church and their Spanish names. But you whites have made us dissatisfied with the way we live. Now we all want stucco houses with real windows, and fancy clothes like you people wear, and money to hire other people to do our work like white people do." He sighed deeply.

"You hate us, don't you?" Ginger felt torn between sympathy and guilt. He made her feel as though she personally were responsible for his tribe's plight.

"Hate you?" He thought about it. "No. I only hate those men in Washington who don't give a damn about us. Someday they'll listen to us! I'll *make* them!"

"You? How?"

"Why do you think everyone in the tribe is contributing to my education? When I finish high school, they're sending me to college and then to law school. After I graduate, I'll come back here and fight for the tribe's rights."

"I'm sorry you're going away, Tonito. I was hoping you'd show me that waterfall in Tahquitz Canyon sometime."

He shrugged. "Sure, I'll show you all the other canyons too . . . when I'm home for vacation. But only if you get Ella to come too."

Ginger stared at him, stunned by his cruelty. Anger and disappointment swept through her, knotting her throat and stinging her eyes. Abruptly she turned her horse and raced out of the canyon. She hated him. *Hated him!* She heard his horse behind her and she urged the colt to go faster.

"Wait!" Tonito called. "Hey, Ginger, wait! Hey, I didn't mean anything . . ."

She pressed her knees against Se-San and together girl and horse sped across the desert. Slowly a delicious sense of power crept through her. She felt sorry for people who always went about in buggies or automobiles and never felt this symbiotic union between human and horse, the horse guided by the human's intelligence, the human absorbing the animal's physical strength.

She rode for an hour, trying to forget Tonito, who at some point had given up chasing her and had gone back toward the village. But no matter how fast she went, she couldn't shake her anger at Tonito . . . and at Ella.

Two weeks later, George and his children moved into the freshly painted pink house along with an Indian couple, Rosa and Marcus, who would cook and take care of the place. Once they were settled and he had someone to look after the children, George missed the excitement of San Francisco more than ever. He and Helene had been popular young socialites, accustomed to dining and dancing at friends' homes or at the city's fashionable hotels and restaurants two or three times a week. Now, for companionship, he had only Polly and Adele and Avery and the few permanent residents who took pity on a widower with three children.

But the Palm Springs social whirl consisted mainly of sunset horseback rides across the desert or picnics in the palm-choked canyons. Sometimes a party of adults went swimming at night in the pond beside the hot springs belonging to the Indians. Since George neither rode nor swam, his socializing consisted of a few informal suppers with an hour of small talk on the front porch afterward. He was going out of his mind with boredom.

After several days of nagging, Ginger talked George into buying Se-San for her from Tonito's father, Juan Pedro. George hated to spend the money, but he had too much pride to say that to Ginger. Ella still refused to get on a horse, even though she was the only girl at the little Palm Springs school who didn't ride.

Neil's health was improving under Dr. Avery's care, which consisted of mild medication, a healthy diet, and daily baths in the hot springs. By September, Avery predicted, Neil would be healthy enough to attend school with the other children.

Mid-March approached and Polly's visit was drawing to a close. George still hadn't mentioned marriage, although each day the handsome young widow hinted that his proposal would be joyfully accepted. He hesitated and procrastinated, one day thinking he would like to get married and the next day feeling trapped. Besides, he had his pride. So long as he was penniless, he could not ask her to marry him.

Desperate, Polly decided to take matters into her own hands. She spent hours making lavish dinners for the McKinntock family. She taught Ella how to sew, and together they made two new dresses for the girl. Polly fussed over Neil, making sure that the little invalid ate properly. Even Polly's aversion to Ginger seemed to have receded a little.

Since settling down in their pink house, Ginger either was at school, which she loved, or was off with her new girlfriends, including Tonito's younger sister, Maria. The girls rode their horses so far, so fast, for so long, that Dr. Avery dryly remarked he half-expected the poor animals to wear their hooves down to their ankles. Tanned and bareheaded, eyes dancing and hair flying, the girls rode without saddles, fearlessly, usually at a dead run, all of them uproariously happy.

When Ginger and her friends weren't out riding, they gathered in Ginger's room or in the garden next to the newly filled lily pond, sometimes romping like rowdy children and other times chatting with exaggerated lady-like decorum.

The first weekend that Tonito returned home from San Bernardino he came over to the pink mansion and apologized to Ginger for having spoken so thoughtlessly the day he took her to Palm Canyon. He invited her to have a picnic with him in Tahquitz Canyon and see the waterfall.

They tethered their horses and settled themselves on a flat rock near the plunging water. Happily munching chicken sandwiches, they watched hummingbirds and finches flit and flutter around an old palo-verde tree rooted beside the creekbed. Tonito gestured at a lizard sunning on a nearby rock. "Watch," he said. He picked up a small pebble and lobbed it so that it gently bounced a few inches from the lizard's head. Startled, the lizard slid into a crevice and disappeared.

"Is that some kind of fat little snake?" Ginger asked worriedly.

"No, silly, it's a lizard. A chuckwalla."

"Do they bite?"

He shook his head. "But if you tried to pull him out of his hiding place, he'd blow up his body, you know, like blowing up a balloon? You'd never be able to budge him."

"How about if I stuck a pin in him and let the air out?" Ginger asked playfully, and when Tonito shot her a look of horror at the idea, she laughed and touched his arm reassuringly. "Don't worry. I'm only kidding."

"It's fun, being with you," Tonito said with one of his tooth-flashing grins.

"With you too, Tonito."

"I never met a girl like you." He ducked his head shyly. "What I'm trying to say is, well, usually it's hard, talking to white girls."

"You mean, because you're an Indian?"

"Because I'm a *boy*, silly." He gestured helplessly. "If Ella ever stopped acting like I was invisible and actually looked at me, I'd be tongue-tied for a week. But it's really easy, talking to you."

Ginger glared at him. "If you want to be my friend, Tonito, don't mention my stupid sister."

He grinned. "Oh, but it's so much fun to tease you about her!"

Ginger knew how much Ella hated Palm Springs. She hated their little one-room school and she hated the other girls her age. She scorned her vivacious sister and her sister's friends and refused their invitations to join them. Instead, after school Ella held court sitting on the front porch. Wearing her new full-skirted white dotted-swiss dress with a pink satin sash, her pale-blond hair a mass of curls—thanks to Polly—Ella looked far older than a ten-year-old. Somehow, with an air of complete innocence, she managed to look demure and haughty and mysterious all at the same time.

Before long, every village boy between the ages of ten and eighteen meandered past the pink mansion. The bold ones came right up to Ella with a grin and draped themselves on the front steps or the low railing. The shy ones sauntered back and forth on the dirt street, then slowly came up the driveway blushing with embarrassment as they joined the others, until the porch looked ready to collapse with adolescent yearning.

Ella seldom spoke, and none of the boys addressed her directly. Their words to each other, full of taunts and bravado, were meant to impress her, though most of what they said was pitifully foolish. But every now and then Ella favored one of them with a slight seductive smile. When that happened, the chosen boy nearly fell off the railing with ecstasy.

Meanwhile, the days passed swiftly and Polly grew desperate. She was in love, deliriously, in her mid-thirties, as she never had been in love before. And the more standoffish George behaved, the more frantic became her desire to marry him. She daydreamed of trips to Europe together, in the *Mauretania*'s bridal stateroom. She grew damp with physical longing for the man, for his touch, for their first lingering kiss.

Harry, her late husband, had been an energetic lover, demanding his marital rights every night without fail. At first she had resented his painful intrusions into her body. He had been a big man with a red face and a hairless pink body. Slow to climax, he would lie on top of her, crushing her slender torso into the soft mattress as he grunted and groaned and shrieked and sobbed himself to an enormous ejaculation. Then one night, two years into their twelve-year marriage, all his pushing and pounding suddenly brought her to an astonishing, unexpected climax. After that it had happened almost every time.

Now she was eager to resume "that side" of life. Too ladylike to give it a name, nevertheless she longed for a man to bestow upon her the same secret pleasure. Maybe with George "it" would be even better. Certainly George was the first man she had met in two years of widowhood who aroused her interest. She was gripped by desire whenever she saw him or thought about him. Why on earth was he waiting to propose to her?

She had thrown all her wiles at him, to no avail. How many times had she stretched her long, smooth neck for him to admire? She had shown off all her French frocks, sometimes changing her attire two or three times a day for his benefit. She had even sat with her skirt slightly lifted so that George could admire her trim ankles. She studied her face for hours in the mirror, looking for flaws, though she found none. What was the matter with the man?

But Polly was, above all, practical. If she couldn't win him with love and physical charms, she would buy him. Harry had left her more money than she could ever need. And George obviously was nearly bankrupt. But he was proud too. She sensed that only if he had some money of his own would he consider marrying her.

Two days before she was to leave Palm Springs, she had a sudden inspiration. George had inherited his father-in-law's two thousand acres of worthless sand when his wife died. Polly's lawyer could play the role of a buyer, and she would secretly provide the money to purchase George's acreage.

She approached George at once, using the pretext of walking Neil home from his daily visit to Avery. "George," she began lightly, "would you do me a favor?"

"Of course, my dear Polly. Anything you want."

"I've had a letter from a friend in Pasadena asking me to find him a bit of property while I'm here. He actually has some crazy idea he'd like to build a rather fancy hotel." She smiled with pity for her mythical friend. "I think the poor man has more faith in the future of this desolate place than sensible people like you and me."

George was alert at once. "I say, Polly! You know, don't you, that I own some land I'd really like to sell? I'd even throw in the house."

"Yes, well, he doesn't want a house, just the acreage. So I thought perhaps I should get the two of you together."

"Wonderful! That's simply bully, Polly, bully! When's he coming out?"

"Well, that's the trouble, George. You see, he's a bit too lame to make the trip, especially now, with the hot weather coming and all."

"Hmmm. Then how . . . ?"

"I was wondering . . . would it be worth your while to come back with me to Pasadena for a week or two? Rosa could look after the children, and of course Adele and Avery would keep an eye on them too. You're welcome to stay at my place if you like. It's simply enormous and actually much more comfortable than a hotel."

"Polly! You're too good to me."

"So? Will you come?"

"*Will I*? Of course I will!"

Polly suppressed a grin of triumph. The negotiations

over the purchase could take weeks. She'd see to that! And once she had George ensconced in her magnificent estate, with her silk sheets and marble bathrooms, her staff of well-trained chefs and servants, her formal four-acre walled garden, her swimming pool and her tennis court, her box seats for concerts and ballet, and a few choice dinner parties with her most entertaining friends . . . after she'd spoiled George absolutely and completely rotten, he'd *never* want to come back and live in boring, hot, uncivilized Palm Springs!

CHAPTER
3

1913–1916

Ginger's first year in Pasadena was outright war. She fought Polly's domination the way a drowning swimmer struggles for life. Ginger thrashed and screamed, but to no avail.

Ginger waylaid George in the mansion's entry hall one afternoon. She wasn't supposed to be in that part of the house without her stepmother's permission, but she was desperate to see her father. "Please, Papa, you've got to help me," she begged.

"What with?" he asked absently.

"Oh . . . everything! Papa, I'm so unhappy here . . ."

"Unhappy?" He was mystified. He gestured at the grand hall where they were standing. Double stairways curved gracefully up both sides of the high-ceilinged room to meet beneath a beveled-glass dome which splashed rainbow colors on the white walls. "But, Ginger," George exclaimed in honest perplexity, "how can you be unhappy in such a beautiful house?"

"Oh, sure, the house *is* beautiful. But, Papa, I hardly ever see you! Polly only lets us come into your part of the house for a half-hour in the afternoon, *if* we've been good. Polly's definition of 'good' means that I hardly ever get to. Haven't you even missed me?"

"Sure, sweetheart. But . . ." He fidgeted, eyeing the door in his eagerness to escape. "Look, I'm late for an appointment. Talk to Polly—"

"Papa, what good would it do for *me* to talk to Polly? She's so mean to me . . ."

"It's only for your own good, sweetie." He touched her arm—half in affection, half in apology—and left her standing there.

"Papa!" she screamed. She ran after him, out to the porte cochere, and watched in frustration as he jumped into his plum-colored Mercedes limousine and was driven away. She went down the driveway as far as the iron gates and peered out. "Please open the gate," she asked Jack, the good-natured Negro gateman, who wore a fancy gold uniform with epaulets and sat in a little brick guard-house all day.

He shook his head. "Orders have to come from Miz McKinntock, little lady."

"It's like being in jail," she told him sadly.

He looked up across the terraced lawn at the stately mansion. "Pretty fancy jail, missy."

She nodded, gazing critically at her gilded prison. Like all Gaul, Polly's mansion was divided into three distinct parts: the lavishly furnished drawing rooms and salons and master bedroom suite were in one wing; the second wing consisted of the children's bedrooms, bathrooms, classrooms, library, and a cheerful white-and-yellow dining room where Ginger and Ella and Neil ate with their tutors; the third wing held the servants' quarters. The formal gardens surrounding the estate were tended by four full-time gardeners, who kept the rolling lawn looking as smooth as green felt. The well-tended flowerbeds were so perfect they hardly looked real.

Ginger walked slowly back to the sprawling house, which had been patterned after a Normandy château. Ivy climbed up its gray stone walls, each leaf in shiny good health. Oh, how she hated it! She hated every inch of this beautiful house and perfect garden and fashionable neighborhood and rich man's city. She even hated the stirring view of Mt. Wilson and the surrounding orange groves whose blossoms wafted sweet smells all over the area. She hated her father for abandoning her to Polly's cruelty.

And most of all, she hated Polly.

Polly-the-tyrant. Polly, who made Ginger wear fancy boots and beige jodhpurs and a fitted red jacket and white shirt and red tie and black derby hat when she went horseback riding. Sitting astride an English saddle, Ginger was forced to go daintily around a fenced riding ring at the Altadena Stables once a week. She, who rode like the wind on the desert, had to go round and round a silly ring that would bore a toddler!

Polly-the-tyrant chose Ginger's clothes, and the books she was permitted to read, and the friends she could have, and she forced Ginger to attend boring tea parties where all the girls stood around stiffly in expensive dresses and hats and gloves and girdles. Girdles! Ginger was outraged. But it was good training for their "coming-out" parties when they were eighteen, Polly-the-tyrant explained. Polly-the-tyrant found fault with everything Ginger said and did, and punished her by locking her in her bedroom without books or paper or pen.

Unlike Ginger, Ella and Neil lapped it all up. They adored Polly and rejoiced the day their father married her and moved them into her grand estate. *"Slaves!"* Ginger hissed at them under her breath. *"Serfs! Lackeys! Fools!"*

Ginger finally had surrendered after a long talk with Avery on the first of what became the McKinntock family's annual two-week visit to Palm Springs during Easter vacation. Sitting side by side on a ledge high up Mt. San Jacinto's eastern slope while trying to reestablish the easy companionship they had enjoyed before the McKinntocks moved to Pasadena, Ginger and Avery had silently stared out at the desert valley and watched the fast-moving shadows that the clouds cast as they scampered across the sky. Avery's heart constricted with worry at the misery he saw in the girl's face. She was too thin and pale. The sparkle and enthusiasm which he had so admired the previous year had disappeared entirely.

Avery listened patiently to Ginger's outpouring of anguish. "Look, little friend," he said, "I know exactly how you feel. But you've got to stop fighting with Polly. It's making you sick. You're thirteen, and in a few years you'll be old enough to live your own life. Until then, concentrate on learning all you can. At least Polly is providing you with some excellent tutors. Take advantage of them. And, honey, if Polly orders you to wear a green dress, go ahead and wear the damn green dress. What's the difference? If she wants you to ride a horse around a silly ring, go ahead and ride it. Ginger-girl, I want you to be a fighter, but only when you have a chance of winning."

"You don't know how awful she is, Dr. Avery."

"Oh, yes I do! I've known Polly a long time."

"I feel like I'm in prison," Ginger said glumly.

"Well, someday when you get out of your prison, you'll appreciate your freedom that much more."

Ginger smiled wanly. "As for Polly's choosing my clothes, it so happens that I look awfully ugly in green."

Avery smiled gently. "Ginger, you couldn't look ugly no matter what color you wore."

"I think Polly wants me to look terrible. It makes Ella look even more beautiful in comparison."

"Ginger, you have a beauty of spirit that Ella will never have. So concentrate on your blessings . . . and please, please stop making yourself sick."

"All right, I'll try it your way, Dr. Avery," Ginger finally conceded. "But someday I'm coming back here to live, and I'll wear whatever I please, and ride however I please, and do whatever I please, and I'll never, *ever* leave!" The tears she had been suppressing engulfed her and she leaned against Avery's comforting chest while he quietly held her and let her cry.

When Ginger ran out of tears, she remained leaning against Avery, relishing the feel of his arms around her. Her ear was against his chest, where she could hear the steady beat of his heart. Oh, how she wished she could stay like this forever! She felt so happy when she was with this dear, kind man. Her mind and body came alive in his presence as at no other time.

That night, with Adele's consent, Avery asked Polly and George if he and Adele could keep Ginger with them in Palm Springs for a few months, "to get back the roses in her cheeks," but Polly vigorously shook her head. "She's got to learn how to behave! She's nothing but a little barbarian."

"Polly, you're much too hard on her," Avery objected. "You're making her ill."

"She has a lot to learn, Avery, so stay out of it! She's *my* problem, not yours!"

New Year's Day of 1916, Polly and George were invited to ride in a very special horse-drawn open carriage in the Rose Parade. The ornate gilded carriage dated back to 1860 and had belonged to Empress Eugenie of France. Polly was dressed in a gold velvet fitted gown copied from a portrait of the empress, while George wore a blue velvet suit with lace jabot and cuffs, a replica of Napoleon III's.

The excitement in the mansion that morning mounted in intensity as the time approached for the family's departure to the event. The three children were being accompanied to the parade by two of their tutors. They were to sit in special seats and watch their parents and the rest of the parade go past. Their clothes had been bought for the occasion weeks earlier, and all was in readiness.

As they waited under the porte cochere for the chauffeur to bring around their Packard touring car, Polly cast a critical eye over Ginger's attire.

She's looking for something to criticize, Ginger thought angrily—and fearfully. But knowing Polly would do this, Ginger had been extra-careful to dress properly.

Polly pinched Ginger's hip. "You're not wearing your girdle."

"Oh, Polly, I'm so thin, it won't stay up."

"March upstairs, young lady, and put it on!"

"Polly, it hurts me. The stays poke into me—"

"Did you hear me or didn't you?" Polly demanded.

"I heard you," Ginger replied sullenly, but she didn't move.

"That's it!" Polly turned to George. "Take her up to her bedroom and lock the door. She can miss the parade."

"Ah, come on, Polly . . ." George objected.

With an impatient grunt, Polly grabbed Ginger's arm and pulled her back into the house. "Get upstairs!" she commanded.

Ginger remembered Dr. Avery's advice: only fight when you're sure of winning. With a sigh, she surrendered. "Okay, I'll go put on my girdle."

"Ladies don't say 'okay.' It's crude."

"I'm sorry."

"Now, hurry! Or we'll go without you."

Later, sitting in the rose-covered gilt carriage with George, Polly still seethed with anger at Ginger. As they rode slowly up Orange Grove Avenue past one elaborate mansion after the other, Polly's ire was fueled by envy. The Wrigley mansion was even bigger than hers. And look at those incredible roses along the driveway to the Waltons' Greek Revival house. Why couldn't her stupid gardeners do as well? She hated the strange-looking Gamble house designed by those crazy Greene brothers, and at least her estate was much more luxurious than the Simpsons' brick English Tudor they were passing. But then they rolled past the Chandlers' magnificent new Colonial that overshadowed everything in sight. . . .

Finally Polly burst out to George, "I tell you, Ginger is simply impossible!"

"Ginger?" George hated being involved in the day-to-day problems with the children, but he hid his annoyance behind a wide-eyed attempt at looking concerned. "Yes, she can be . . . Wave to the people, darling."

Polly waved with her left hand and took his arm with her right hand. They smiled fondly at each other. Their four-year-old marriage was even more successful than either of them had expected. They both were strikingly attractive, always dressed in the latest fashions, and one of the most popular couples in Pasadena society. Daily, a waterfall of party invitations flowed through their mail slot. They had box seats reserved on opening nights for every concert, play, and opera that came to the Los Angeles area. Septembers, they traveled to New York and Europe, always in grand style, indulging their every whim.

"It's that mocking air of docility Ginger puts on," Polly said as she continued to wave and smile at the crowd on her side of the carriage. People were lined up three deep along the curb. Others watched from balconies and even rooftops.

"Be fair, Polly. I know she was a lot of trouble that first year. But for the last three years she's tried awfully hard to please you."

"You can't see through her like I can, George. She's nothing but a damn little hypocrite!"

"C'mon, Polly, she's still a child . . ."

"She's not a child anymore, she's almost sixteen. And you should see the way she looks at me, George, like I'm just a big . . . I don't know what—a big fool, I guess." She squeezed his arm. "Sweetheart, let's send her away to boarding school."

George frowned. "Polly, for pity's sake! How many times do I have to tell you? It's out of the question!" He forced a smile and waved at the bystanders.

"Oh, George. Just because you promised that silly Helene that you'd never—"

"Don't you dare call Helene silly!"

"I'm sorry, darling. But it *was* terribly unfair of her to make you promise—"

"It wasn't at all unfair. Helene hated boarding school herself. So it's perfectly understandable that she didn't want her own children subjected—"

"Yes, yes, you're right," Polly sighed, quickly giving in. George seldom crossed her, but she knew from painful experience that it was unwise to push him too far when he did disagree with her, because then he would sulk for days, refusing to go out and thus ruining all of her carefully structured social plans.

George, savoring his victory, at once felt magnanimously conciliatory. "Tell you what, Polly," he conceded. "In April, when we visit Palm Springs, I'll get Avery to have another talk with Ginger. He'll straighten her out if she's being impertinent to you. He's the only one in the whole world she ever really listens to."

The marching band from Whittier High School, in formation behind Polly and George's carriage, struck up a rousing Sousa number and drowned out all further conversation. George looked up at the blue sky with a sigh of contentment. If the band continued to play for the rest of the parade, maybe Polly would forget about Ginger and give him a little peace.

In 1916 the McKinntocks' annual two-week Easter visit to Palm Springs still was made by train. Automobile travel to the desert remained slow and hazardous. The road from Banning into Palm Springs had finally been paved, only to wash out two weeks after its completion in a devastating rainstorm that had sent flash floods over miles of desert and had turned the village's mild little creeks into wild rivers.

Sitting docilely on the red Pullman seat, neatly dressed in a dark blue travel suit, a gray felt hat with matching purse, shoes, and gloves, and underneath her clothes a damn tight girdle, Ginger could not help but compare this trip with her very first one to the desert, four years earlier. How excited she had been then! What freedom she had enjoyed! She sighed. A flame of resentment burned right up through the middle of her body, and it took all of her energy to keep it from exploding into her stepmother's face.

Ginger glanced over at Ella, sitting beside her. As usual, Ella was basking in the admiring glances of the other passengers. Everywhere Ella went, people stared with awe at her beauty, and Ella accepted the adulation with a smugness that made Ginger want to pinch her.

But Ginger had to admit that even at fourteen Ella was spectacular to look at. Polly took special pains with Ella's hair, which tended to be straight and stringy. The two of them would look enviously at Ginger's thick, shiny auburn waves, which fell into place naturally, without any coaxing. Ella was taller than Ginger and even more curvaceous. Her blue eyes were the biggest Ginger ever had seen; in certain lights they looked violet. The younger girl's skin was pale, flawless and luminous, as though a candle burned within. Ginger wasn't so much jealous of Ella as scornful of her. *Ella has so much beauty on the outside*, Ginger grumbled to herself, *that none was left for the inside*.

Neil sat across from them, restlessly shuffling a deck of cards. No longer an emaciated invalid, under Polly's care he had recovered his health and was growing plump. His self-satisfied face disturbed Ginger: she detected a slyness there, maybe even a cruelty, that seemed inappropriate in a twelve-year-old.

"Neil," she ventured, trying to establish some rapport, "will you come riding with me this year?"

He gave her a dubious look. "You mean, out on the desert?"

"Sure. I'll show you the Indian canyons—"

"Who'd want to see *them*!"

Ginger was taken aback. She remembered the Easter vacations from the previous three years, when she and Tonito spent hours each afternoon on horseback, exploring the desert and its surrounding mountains. "Well, I thought you might like them. I mean, they're so beautiful . . ."

He shook his head. "You can keep your silly old canyons."

"How about you?" Ginger nudged Ella.

"Are you *crazy*? I don't like to ride anywhere but the Altadena Stables. The desert's too dangerous." Ella glanced glumly out the train window at hulking Mt. San Jacinto, whose foothills were just coming into closer view. "God only knows what I'll do for two whole weeks in this awful place," she added with a sigh.

Ginger settled back in her seat with a pleased smile. Last year she had promised Tonito she would try to get Ella to ride with them, and now she could tell him, in all honesty, that she *had* tried and Ella had absolutely refused. Tonito would be disappointed—he was determined to make Ella accept him as an equal—but at least Ginger would have him all to herself for the whole ten days of his Easter vacation. Anyway, it really was time he gave up trying to make friends with Ella, who treated him like a flunky.

Ginger hugged herself happily, knowing she would see Tonito in two days. During last year's Easter vacation, just before they parted, he had given her a quick, almost frightened kiss on the lips. "I can't *imagine* spending my vacations with anyone but you," he had said. "I think of you all the time."

Ginger knew that Tonito still had long years of college and law school ahead of him. But the knowledge that he loved her—and she him—had made it easier for her to put up with Polly's persecutions these past fifty weeks.

The sight of her grandfather's pink adobe hacienda sitting on its low hill always gave Ginger a jolt of intense pleasure. She loved this house far more than she ever could care for Polly's fancy Pasadena mansion. It pained Ginger to think that the Palm Springs house sat empty fifty weeks of the year, except for Rosa, now a widow, who took care of it.

"I think we should paint the house white," Polly told George as Avery's chauffeur drove the family up the driveway.

"But Grandpa told me he wanted it to always be pink," Ginger objected.

Polly ignored her. "You have to admit, pink is so *déclassé*, George."

"Whatever you say, darling," George agreed morosely.

The desert's heat made him irascible. The seemingly endless space with its strong sun and gusting wind made him feel uncontrollably at the mercy of the elements.

Ginger gave him a disgusted look, but she remained quiet. She was too excited to be angry with Polly or George or anyone else. For three years—ever since she had decided to follow Avery's advice and submissively accept Polly's tyranny—these two weeks in Palm Springs were all Ginger lived for during the rest of the year. Here she felt free again. The dry air made her whole body come to life, as if it had been in hibernation during the long dull months since her last visit. And most important of all, in two days she'd see Tonito.

As soon as the Oldsmobile stopped, Ginger flew out of the car and ran to see Se-San in his stable. The horse neighed and rose on his hind legs in joyful greeting. When he calmed down, Ginger threw her arms around his neck and sobbed with happiness. She could feel his warm breath against her neck, waking her from the somnolence of her Pasadena life.

She ran up to her room, where she threw off her travel clothes and hid her girdle behind the dresser. In the closet she found her desert riding clothes from the previous year: a loose blue shirt and knee-length pants—they still fit her perfectly! Had she stopped growing? Barefoot, she raced down the steps and was about to rush out to the stable when Polly stopped her at the front door.

"And just where d'you think you're going, young lady?"

Ginger stared at Polly: wasn't it obvious where she was going? "To ride my horse," she replied politely.

"Like *that*? Go put on your proper riding clothes."

"I didn't bring them."

"You didn't *bring* them!" Polly echoed in a shocked voice.

"They're too hot for the desert," Ginger explained.

"Well then, Ginger, I guess that means you can't go riding!"

Without a word, Ginger whirled around and hurried through the kitchen and out the back door, blowing a kiss to Rosa on the way. Quickly she led Se-San out of the stable, jumped up on his bare back, and they galloped down the hill, away from the house. Away from Polly.

First Ginger explored the village, eager to see what changes had been made since her last visit. Seven new shops were altering the character of Main Street, and Ginger was sorry to see that a row of giant fig trees had been cut down to make room for them. Nellie Coffman's boardinghouse boasted a new, bigger sign: "The Desert Inn." It was awash with red oleanders, palms, and cottonwood trees—an oasis within an oasis. Nellie had acquired several more tent-houses for guests and had added a new dining room and a wide concrete front porch with tables and chairs set up for outdoor meals.

Across the street, Avery's orchard now spread over two more acres and his vegetable garden had a healthy crop of winter squash. Ginger felt a jolt of excitement at the thought of seeing Avery, but she didn't stop, knowing that at this hour of the afternoon the doctor would be busy with patients. The McKinntocks were all invited for dinner that night with Avery and poor, sweet, ailing Adele.

The village still enchanted Ginger, whichever way she looked. The palm trees seemed taller, the ferny desert plants thicker, and snow-topped Mt. San Jacinto more majestic than ever. She rode up and down the few short dirt streets, feeling a strong sense of belonging there. She paused in front of the schoolhouse she had briefly attended four years earlier, before her father's horrid marriage. She missed her old friends and felt shut out of their carefree lives, though undoubtedly they envied *her* life, erroneously believing that living in a grand mansion in a beautiful city like Pasadena must be far more exciting than their own lives on the desert.

Ginger stayed out until dusk. If the moon had been full, she would have been tempted to ride all night. She visited all her favorite places: the sand dunes, the three Indian canyons, the path behind her house that led up to the ledge where she and Avery liked to sit and talk. Then she stopped at Juan Pedro's farm, where Tonito's sister Maria confirmed that Tonito was coming home the next day.

Happily tired, glowing in anticipation of seeing Avery later at dinner, and eager for her reunion with Tonito the next day, Ginger led Se-San to the stable before she trudged back into the house and started up the steps toward her room.

"Stop . . . right . . . there!" Polly ordered when Ginger was halfway up the staircase.

Ginger looked down over the banister at her stepmother and father standing side by side on the red-tile floor of the entry hall. They both seemed so angry that Ginger, in her euphoric mood, assumed that something terrible had happened while she was out riding. "What's wrong?" she asked.

"*You*, young lady!" George snapped. "Get in your room this minute, and you will stay there until we go home. Rosa will bring you your meals."

"You mean . . . *the whole two weeks*?" Ginger's voice squeaked with disbelief.

"This time you'll learn to obey me!" Polly raged.

On the fourth day of her solitary confinement, Ginger developed a high fever. When Avery came into her room and stood beside her bed, she grasped his hands and tingled all over with the joy of seeing him. "Hey, Doctor, can being really angry give you a fever?"

"It sure can." He put a thermometer into her mouth and then reached for her wrist to take her pulse. As he looked down at her flushed face he was shocked: the young girl he so dearly admired had become a beautiful young woman. *What did you expect, you fool?* he asked himself. *She's sixteen now. Not much younger than Adele was when you married her.* He couldn't take his eyes from Ginger. Her hair was a thick mass of auburn waves, her eyes a warm brown shot through with amber lights. Her lips were smooth and lustrous, and he longed to lean down and kiss them. His sudden desire made his fingers tremble against her wrist.

"Is my temperature very high?" she asked when he examined the thermometer.

"It's high." He sat down on the bed and put his hand on her hot forehead. "Ginger, Ginger," he breathed, "why did you disobey her?"

Ginger made a helpless gesture. "Oh, Dr. Avery, I can't go on like this."

"Then don't go back to Pasadena. Stay here with me . . . with us."

"You know Polly would never let me." Ginger turned tragic eyes on him. "She won't let me see Tonito either. I heard him at the door a dozen times the last three days. She won't even let him in the house."

"Well, she wouldn't let me see you either. Not until you began running a fever."

"But Tonito's only going to be here a week," she wailed, then burst into tears.

What have I done to her? Avery asked himself with dismay. Until now, he had believed in the soundness of his advice to her three years earlier, but instead of helping her . . . had he made her life pure hell?

"It's not your fault," Ginger said, wiping her damp eyes with her sheet.

He smiled. "How on earth could you tell what I was thinking?"

"Because you looked so stricken." She reached up and lightly caressed his cheek. Guiltily, she quickly withdrew her hand, trembling with shame. Why did she always feel this strange thrill when she touched him? It was a silly schoolgirl crush and it was so inappropriate! So ridiculous! So utterly foolish! He was a dignified married man. She was just a child to him. He'd be too disgusted to ever talk to her again if he knew how she felt.

Avery saw the embarrassment on her face and quickly turned away. She was good at reading his face—had he let slip some sign of his feelings for her? Dear God, he had to be careful not to let it show! Still, it was all he could do not to lift her up and take her away—far, far away from Polly and George and her miserable siblings. He envisioned himself with Ginger in some exotic place among a sea of strangers, where he could be her protector and her teacher and her friend. *And her lover.*

Avery rose abruptly from the bed and went to the window, where he stared unseeingly at the steep rocky flank of San Jacinto. He had to compose himself. How could he even *think* of making love to her? He was fifteen years older than she was. He might feel like a love-struck youth, but to her he was an old man. As her trusted friend, it was his responsibility to help her, not woo her. He had to face reality and not get carried away with impossible fantasies.

Above all, he had to think of Adele—poor, sweet Adele, who still loved him fervently, even though these days his feelings for her had more to do with compassion than desire. He had to be very careful to keep his face from betraying his most inappropriate feelings for Ginger. Avery would never, never do anything to hurt Adele. She was so frail, yet so kind and loving and patient. The shock of his being in love with someone else would kill her.

Despite everything, being near Ginger filled him with an exultation he hadn't felt in years. He turned from the window and smiled at her. "Listen, Ginger-girl. I'll talk to Polly . . . and George—"

"What good will that do?" She sat up and tried to push her pillows against the bed's headrest so that she could lean back on them, but she was too weak. He rushed over to help her.

"I'll think of something to say to them," he promised. "After all, I'm sure that deep down they really do care about your welfare. . . ."

She shook her head. "I've tried so hard to please Polly. I can't understand why she's so mean to me. She's nice as can be to other people. I mean, she's wonderful to Ella and Neil, and you should see her with her friends. She's even pretty nice to the servants. She just has it in for *me*."

"You have to get away from her," he insisted. "She's become totally irrational where you're concerned. Look, if she won't let you stay with Adele and me . . . how about going to a boarding school?"

"Polly wanted to send me last month. But Papa refused."

"Do you want to go?"

"I guess. Anything's better than living with her."

"Well, that's easy, then. We'll just get George to change his mind."

It was *not* easy. Avery went downstairs and told them that Ginger wanted to go to boarding school. At this point George was willing to forget his promise to Helene, but now Polly had changed *her* mind. She felt she was locked in a desperate struggle with Ginger. And Polly was not going to back down until she had decisively won that struggle. "Sending Ginger to boarding school would simply be begging the issue," she stormed. "Her wild spirit has *got* to be broken, once and for all! My God, Avery, that girl's got a stubborn streak a mile wide!"

"And you don't?" Avery blurted angrily. "Polly, let her go. This present situation is unhealthy for all of you."

"Why don't you just mind your own business, Avery Rowland? Ginger's nothing to you. And being a doctor doesn't give you the right to butt in!"

"Polly, tell me something," Avery persisted. "I've known you a long time and I've always had high regard for you." He swallowed, hating to lie, but he was trying to win her trust. "So it's hard for me to understand why you're so strict with Ginger. What d'you have against her? Right from the start—"

Polly shook her head. "You don't understand, Avery. I have nothing against her personally but . . . God, she's . . . she's so uncivilized! I want George's children to have the best of everything, to be accepted by the best society—"

"Yes, but your kind of 'society' might not be right for Ginger."

"Then I'll *make* her right for it!"

"Yes," George spoke up. "She's got to learn to conform."

Avery threw his hands up in exasperation. "Polly, you can't change people—"

"Oh, yes I can!" Polly's voice turned venomous. "Ginger's upbringing was abominable when she was little!"

Avery threw a quick glance at George and was surprised to see no reaction to this slur on his first wife's ability as a mother. All at once Avery understood Polly's hatred of Ginger: the girl looked like her dead mother and had many of her mother's traits. Was Polly so wildly jealous of Helene, he wondered, that she would stoop to making life miserable for Helene's favorite daughter?

Their argument was interrupted by Ginger, who came downstairs in her nightgown and bathrobe.

"Get back to bed!" Polly barked.

Ginger resolutely shook her head. "Don't order me around, Polly, ever again." She turned to George. "Papa, you never once tried to stick up for me these past four years. You act like I'm a stranger, like I don't exist. Anyhow, I've decided not to go back to Pasadena with you."

"What'll you do, you silly child?" Polly demanded. "Camp out on the desert?"

"I'll stay here in Grandpa's house. With Rosa."

"It's no longer your grandfather's house. It belongs to your father now. He can turn you out."

"He wouldn't." Ginger looked squarely at her father.

"Well . . . maybe it would be best all around if she did stay here," George said hesitantly. All he cared about was ending this uncomfortable situation.

"Tell me, Ginger, just who do you think will pay for your food and clothes?" Polly continued. "You'll get no money from us."

"I'll get a job. Nellie Coffman's always looking for help."

"Doing what? Scrubbing floors? You know darn well we can't allow a child of George's to do menial work." Polly sighed in exasperation. "All right, Ginger, you win. You can go to boarding school."

"No. Now I don't want to. I was lying in bed thinking: Why go away to boarding school? Why go anywhere? *This* is where I'm happiest. *This* is the place I love more than anywhere else. Why shouldn't I stay here if I want to? I can keep studying. Maria told me there's a wonderful new teacher here. I could take lessons from him and do a lot of reading on my own. . . ." Suddenly feeling faint, Ginger sat down and wearily closed her eyes. "Anyway," she whispered, "there's no way you can stop me. I'm old enough to do what I want."

"We can disown you," Polly threatened.

"I don't care. I don't want your money."

Avery's head buzzed with excitement at the thought of Ginger living here, where he could see her every day. He would watch over her, give her all the help she needed. But he would also give her plenty of room to be independent. He had no doubt that this splendid girl had the gumption and ability to take care of herself. Her solution was so right and so wise that he wondered why he hadn't thought of it himself.

Ginger saw Tonito only once that April. He came and sat with her on the porch later in the week, while she was still recuperating from her fever. Her father and Polly had cut their visit short and returned to Pasadena with Ella and Neil the morning after their big confrontation with Ginger. Now, without their presence to bother her, and with Rosa and Avery taking care of her, Ginger's health speedily improved.

Strangely, she and Tonito were ill-at-ease with each other. Their conversation was stilted, and he didn't stay long. He was returning to college the next morning. "I guess we can only communicate when we're sitting on horses," she said wryly as he was leaving. She took his hand. "Are we . . . you know . . . still engaged?"

"Sure." He bent down and quickly kissed her cheek.

"Well, I'll see you this summer. After my graduation."

Watching him walk jauntily down the driveway, she realized that he had grown very tall. Always lithe, always as handsome as the Greek gods she loved to read about, at nineteen Tonito seemed to Ginger like a throwback to the strong Indian braves who had lived here in the days when his people owned this entire country, before they were reduced to the poverty-damaged lives of dirt farmers.

She felt sad that her visit with Tonito had been so unsatisfying. They had always had so much fun together, giggling and teasing and being fiercely competitive. She wondered whether in growing up they were growing apart. Or did they have to find a new way to be together? Not as children, but as grown-ups? As lovers?

Nellie Coffman, wearing a starched white gingham dress and a broad friendly smile, welcomed Ginger like an unexpected gift from heaven. "It's so difficult to get good help here," she confessed. "I tell you this, Ginger, if you work hard and pay attention, I'll teach you everything I know about the hotel business. You wait and see: this town is going places, and someday there won't be enough hotel rooms for all the people wanting to come here. My place already is full up most of the time."

Nellie and Ginger sat in Nellie's living room, which doubled as the hotel's lobby. It was a homey room furnished with wicker sofas and chairs whose cushions were covered with brightly printed cretonne. "Come on, I'll show you the rest of the place," Nellie said. She took Ginger around the grounds to inspect the new guesthouses. Some were made of wood and some were canvas tents stretched across posts over raised floors. Most of them had porches shaded by roofs of palm fronds. Nellie had managed to make these temporary buildings attractive, using colorful print curtains and bedspreads and cotton-rag rugs to brighten the dark interiors. And the rooms were surprisingly comfortable, considering that as yet Palm Springs had no electricity or gas and there was only one telephone in the entire village, in Carl Lykken's general store, with an extension in Nellie's lobby.

"Someday I'll build permanent rooms, when I have the money," Nellie continued. "In my mind's eye I can see plain as day the way it's going to look—everything Spanish-Mediterranean with turrets and arches and every luxury. You know, Ginger, my father thought I was crazy to open a boardinghouse in a village without a paved road into it—he owned a hotel in Santa Monica, so he figured he knew what he was talking about. But I told him, if you give your guests what they want—good food, clean lodgings, and warm hospitality—the roads and autos will come. I'm going to make Palm Springs attractive to attractive people. I'm going to make it southern California's play yard!"

The next day Ginger started working in the kitchen, helping Quon Woon, the Chinese cook. Together they prepared all the meals for the thirteen guests the boardinghouse could accommodate. Ginger learned how to follow Quon's recipes and cook on the wood-burning stove, until she could run the kitchen by herself on the days Quon was sick or needed a rest.

After helping to prepare the meals, Ginger took off her apron, put on a blue waitress uniform, and served the guests. She enjoyed bringing platters of delicious-smelling food to the buff-colored dining room with its granite fireplace warming the guests on cool nights. Each of the four round tables was covered with an immaculate white cloth, a bud vase, and a red candle. Mornings, at breakfast, the sun streamed into the room through mullioned windowpanes and was reflected on the gleaming wood floor.

Ginger watched Nellie carefully and tried to emulate her. Ginger never had met anyone as hardworking and cheerful as Mrs. Nellie Coffman. When Ginger had time, she helped Nellie tend the garden that provided fresh produce for the kitchen. Together they fed the chickens and milked the cows. Ginger learned how to keep accounts and pay bills, to greet guests and soothe capricious patrons, and, above all, to make the visitors want to return again and again.

At night, after the last dish had been washed and put away and the tables set for breakfast, Ginger would ride her bicycle home, greet Rosa, and read until she fell asleep. In the morning she would wake up before dawn entirely refreshed, meet Avery for a hike up the trail to watch the sunrise, ride Se-San for a half-hour, bathe and dress, and get to work in time to serve the guests their ample breakfast at eight o'clock.

She loved her life, despite the long hours and hard work, and she cherished her freedom. She was fascinated by the hotel business. Most of the guests stayed long enough to become friendly with the staff, giving Ginger insights into people with diverse backgrounds, personalities, and professions. When she told this to her employer, Nellie replied, "I think people are friendlier out here in the West. Maybe it's the vast open spaces, I don't know. There's less snobbery, too. I tell you this, Ginger, I've never had a monotonous day here. There's always something to laugh or cry over in this kind of work. Mostly laugh."

Nellie spoke little about her personal life. Ginger knew only that Nellie had been born in Illinois, that she and her husband, Harry, had separated, and that Nellie had two sons, George and Earl, who were away at school.

Determined that Ginger should continue her education, Nellie insisted that between meals the girl find a quiet place in the garden where she could sit under a tree or a shady ramada and study. Edmund Jaeger, the new teacher and an ardent desert naturalist, picked up Ginger's education where her tutors had left off. "You're fairly well-prepared," he said after testing her in various subjects. "A little weak in Latin, excellent in French and literature, a crackerjack in arithmetic. But you're woefully lacking in science, dear girl." He gestured at the open land surrounding the village. "First off, I'm going to make a naturalist out of you. You're going to learn about every last thing that lives and grows out there in the desert—plants, critters, rocks, soil."

Ginger smiled inwardly. This was, she felt, the beginning of her desert education.

*   *   *

One day in mid-May Ginger received a letter from Polly's and George's lawyers informing her that George McKinntock had sold the pink adobe mansion and all its furnishings to a Mrs. Leland Offenbach of Pasadena, who would take possession on June 1. "He *can't*! He *can't*!" Ginger screamed so hysterically that Rosa came running in alarm. Weak with grief, Ginger cried in Rosa's arms until she ran out of tears. How could her father be so cruel? He didn't need the money. This house was more than a place to live: it had been her grandfather's home, his dream, the start of a tradition, a family homestead to be passed from generation to generation. She hated her father. She hated this Mrs. Offenbach. Most of all she hated Polly, who undoubtedly had been the author of this vindictive scheme to sell the house.

She wanted to rush right over to Avery's and see if he could somehow stop the sale. But he had gone to Banning for the day and wasn't coming home until late that night. So she had to wait until the next day, during their morning hike, to tell Avery what had happened.

He stopped walking and stared at her in perplexity, as though he hadn't understood her words. Then he exploded. "Those goddamn fools! They had no *right* to sell that house!"

"I guess they did have the right, Dr. Avery. Legally, anyway."

Too angry to walk, he sat down on a rock beside the trail. "I'd have bought it," he said, weak with frustration. "If I'd known they were going to sell it." He hit his fist against the rock. "*Damn* them! That was John's house. Morally, it belongs to you." He was quiet for a few moments, trying to think of some way to stop the sale. "This woman they sold it to . . . this Mrs. Offenbach . . . I'll offer her twice what she paid." He nodded, pleased with the idea. "Yes, Ginger-girl, that's what I'll do, and I'll put the house in your name."

"Oh, Dr. Avery, would you? I promise I'll pay you back someday—"

"We'll worry about that later."

That afternoon he came to see her at Nellie's and found her alone in the kitchen, rolling pie dough.

She grinned when she saw him, until she noted the dejection in his face. "What happened?" she asked fearfully.

"Mrs. Offenbach wasn't interested."

"But . . . didn't you say you'd give her *twice* what she paid?"

He sighed deeply. "She's a very rich old lady. I could've offered her *ten* times as much, and she'd have turned me down. She just doesn't want to be bothered."

Once more Ginger's world collapsed around her. Weeping, she threw herself at Avery, wetting the front of his shirt with her tears.

He embraced her awkwardly, keeping his body from contact with hers, afraid that if he held her any closer he would be unable to restrain his desire to crush her to him and kiss her trembling mouth. And then he would lose her trust and friendship forever.

"Ah, come on, Ginger-girl, it's not the end of the world," he said soothingly.

"I know." She leaned back against the kitchen table and wiped her eyes on her apron. "Nellie said if you didn't buy the house back, I could stay in one of the old tent-cabins. I'll be okay." She sniffed. "But what about Rosa? She'll be out of work."

"Maybe Nellie can use her. She's always looking for help." He touched her arm lightly, in commiseration. "And, Ginger, don't worry. If it's the last thing I do, someday I'll buy back your Grandpa John's house for you!"

On the first day of June, Ginger had no alternative but to turn over the keys to Mrs. Leland Offenbach, a widow whose respiratory problems had prompted her move to the desert. Mrs. Offenbach arrived in a maroon Cadillac limousine accompanied by a Polish chauffeur whose uniform matched the car, two Negro maids, and three pampered Pomeranians. "Where will you be going now, dearie?" Mrs. Offenbach asked. "Back to your parents in Pasadena?"

"No, I work at the inn, Mrs. Offenbach," Ginger said, already hating the woman. "Mrs. Coffman gave me a tent-room there to live in."

"A *tent*, poor girl, and you with parents who own one of the finest mansions in Pasadena!" She looked at Ginger as though the girl had lost her mind. "Well, come and visit here anytime you like, my dear."

"Thank you," Ginger replied coldly. But as she lifted her meager belongings onto Se-San's back and started off toward the inn, Ginger was determined never again to set foot in her grandfather's house. Never!

Not until the day she could buy it back.

Ginger had little time to mourn the loss of her beloved house, which Mrs. Offenbach painted a bilious green with brown shutters. Not only did Ginger spend many hours working and studying, but every Monday, her day off, she and Edmund Jaeger and sometimes Avery scoured the desert to collect the plant specimens Edmund needed for the book he was writing.

Busy though she was, Ginger kept making new friends. The village was filling up with exciting newcomers, a special breed of people, rich and poor, who found the arid land a glorious place to live. Some camped out in lean-to shacks, some built modest stucco or wood houses, a few had enough money to create handsome adobe-brick villas, and a very few even constructed elaborate mansions.

These new arrivals had more in common than a love for the desert. Many of them, Ginger discovered, were delightfully eccentric or highly talented. Lois Kellog, an heiress, was building a castle that she called Fools Folly; a painter named Carl Eytel became known as "the Artist of the Palms"; and Jimmy Swinnerton, another fine painter, often invited Avery to join his sketching forays into the desert. They and others were quickly absorbed into the community whose small size and isolation made its established inhabitants eager to welcome new faces.

The favorite place for socializing was the post office in Carl Lykken's two-story clapboard general store. A stack of wooden crates doubled as mailboxes, and it was here that Ginger met friends old and new when she ran over to pick up the hotel's mail every afternoon.

For the first time in her young life, Ginger was surrounded by strong women who were doing "men's work." Besides Nellie, Ginger admired Zaddie Bunker, the first woman in California to get a chauffeur's license, and Zaddie's sister, Henrietta Parker, who always lifted Ginger's spirits with her friendly, humorous banter. Zaddie and her husband Ed had learned to repair automobiles from a handbook and the plucky couple now owned a thriving garage on Main Street. It seemed as though every automobile that managed to limp into Palm Springs had developed some malady on the atrocious unpaved road leading into the village.

Ginger also admired Pearl McCallum McManus, whose father had settled in Palm Springs in 1885. It was Judge McCallum who had cleared the land of cactus and creosote bushes, had constructed irrigation canals, and had created a village. After Pearl's father died, she continued to shrewdly manage the family's extensive acreage. Pearl also loved to ride on the desert early in the morning, and many a time she and Ginger galloped across the sandy soil in easy companionship.

Sometimes Ginger rode with Cornelia White, who always wore pants, a stylish jacket, and a pith helmet to protect her head from the sun. Cornelia and her two sisters—Isabel and Dr. Franilla—lived in a house made of old railway ties taken from a long-abandoned desert railroad. The three elegant sisters, born in New York, were inseparable until Isabel married an Englishman named J. Smeaton Chase, who wrote books glowingly describing the desert, which he called his "Araby."

There was very little talk in the village about the terrible war being fought in Europe. The conflict seemed far, far away from the isolated desert community. Yet the war did bring more visitors to Palm Springs, wealthy Americans who formerly had traveled to the Riviera every winter and now were forced to find domestic destinations for their vacations. Many of them found Nellie's Desert Inn.

With new business coming her way, Nellie expanded her hotel. She took Ginger away from cooking and waitressing and made her assistant manager. When summer came and the temperature rose above a hundred and ten degrees day after day, Nellie temporarily closed down the inn and escaped to the cool mountaintop above Palm Springs.

All at once Ginger found herself with an abundance of free time. In the early mornings, she walked with Avery, and in the cool evenings she rode on the desert with Tonito, who had graduated from college and was home for the summer before starting law school in the fall. During the heat of midday Ginger stayed in the shade and read while Tonito helped his father with farm chores.

She used some of her leisure hours to improve her little tent-house. Two large wooden crates from Carl Lykken's general store served as her dressing table and a bedside commode. A few dollars of her savings went for cheerful pink-and-white floral cretonne, from which she fashioned flounced skirts for the new "furniture" and a ruffled bedspread and pillows for her cot. She made matching curtains for her windows and splurged on an oval pink-and-blue braided rag rug for the wood floor. She used "sky-blue" paint on the battered kitchen chair and table Nellie had given her to use as a desk. Two of Avery's desert watercolors and one of Carl Eytel's pen-and-ink drawings pinned to the canvas walls completed the transformation. Then Ginger stood back and surveyed her eight-by-ten-foot tent, feeling blissfully creative.

Now she had enough idle hours to see her girlfriends, to attend impromptu cookouts in the canyons, take moonlight rides on the desert, and to catch up on her studies. She seldom thought about her family, and when she did, she felt as detached from them as though they lived on another planet.

Most of all, for Ginger the summer meant Tonito. They reverted to childhood behavior whenever they were together, as though fearful of the demands adulthood might make upon them. They were two silly playmates, refusing to take life seriously.

"Where's your gorgeous sister?" he teased as they rested on the sand from one of their wild competitive rides across the desert floor. "She's the only reason I pay any attention to you."

"You haven't got a chance with her," Ginger retorted. "You'd have to be a big cheese or have a fancy title for Ella to notice you."

"My great-grandfather was chief of our tribe. Doesn't that make me some kind of royalty?"

"Ha! It still makes you a low-class good-for-nothing redskin in Ella's eyes. Unfortunately for you, I'm the only McKinntock who likes Indians."

Only when Tonito was returning to school at the end of summer did they become serious. The night before he left, they packed a picnic of ham sandwiches and thick slices of watermelon, then rode into Tahquitz Canyon at dusk. They tethered their horses and spread a blanket beside the pool at the bottom of the waterfall . . . and then found they were too sad to eat.

"I'll miss you," Ginger said, putting down her sandwich after the first bite.

Tonito wanted to make a joke and found that he could not. The thought of life without seeing Ginger every day made his throat constrict with misery. "I have something to tell you." His voice was low and hoarse with pain. "I won't be back again for three years, Ginger."

"Three years! But—"

He spoke very fast. "I've been afraid to tell you . . . my professors in Los Angeles got me a scholarship at Harvard Law School, near Boston—"

"Harvard!" Ginger interrupted, impressed. "It's the best in the country."

"So they say. But the money I get from the tribe will pay only part of my expenses. I'll have to work weekends and holidays and summers to earn money for my room and board. I won't have time to come home at all. Besides, the train fare's too expensive." He gestured helplessly. "I don't know how I'm going to stand it, Ginger. I hate cities. I belong *here*! On my ancestors' land. I belong with you! But . . . I won't be able to come home till I've graduated."

She stared at him, silently shaking her head in protest.

He leaned back against the trunk of a fan palm and stared back at her in the dimming light, as though trying to memorize her features. Tonito loved the way she looked: her wavy auburn hair, her dark eyes and full lips, her lithe body. He found her more beautiful every day. Impulsively he reached for her and pulled her against him, his heart thumping with excitement and fear in equal measure. It was the first time in their four-and-a-half-year friendship that they had touched each other this way.

She was very quiet, trembling against him. He caressed her throat and felt her pulse beating wildly. "Oh, Lord!" he whispered as his lips touched hers. The inside of his head roared like a waterfall while desire welled up in him. He had never felt so wonderful.

With her eyes closed, Ginger clung to Tonito in the most mindless state she had ever experienced. She was aware only of her body's sudden flash of heat, as if it were a kerosene-soaked rag that someone had ignited. With a start, she realized that she was imagining it was Avery who was kissing her, not Tonito. . . .

Suddenly Tonito was frightened. *What was he doing?* He moved away from her with agonizing reluctance. He stood up and helped her to her feet. Embracing her lightly, he planted soft kisses on the top of her head while his heart crazily jumped around in his chest.

"Tonito, let's get married! I could go east with you . . . I'm sure I could get a job at a hotel in Boston. . . ."

He shook his head regretfully. "What if you got pregnant? I'd have to quit school and go to work . . . and you *know* that I have to finish law school. I owe it to the tribe after all they've invested in me. And, we're still so young . . ."

She knew he was right. Only . . . how was she going to stand three more years of hiding her schoolgirl crush from Avery, whose presence stirred her more and more every day? She was certain that once she was safely married to Tonito, her foolish attraction to Avery would disappear entirely.

Tonito rubbed his cheek against her hair. "Ah, Ginger, be patient. Someday we'll be together all the time." He gestured out toward the desert. "We'll ride at dawn and watch the sunrise. We'll walk in the rain with the wonderful smell of desert lavender all around us . . . and at night when the coyotes sing . . ." He stopped abruptly and took a deep breath to quell his misery. *Say something silly,* he warned himself, *or you'll surely start crying*.

He walked her over to Se-San and lifted her onto the horse. "Of course you know, don't you, that I'd always hoped to marry Ella. But she's too highfalutin a society girl for me now."

Ginger gasped. "You mean . . . I'm your *second* choice?" Her voice rose with indignation and horror.

"No, no, no, I was only trying to make a joke." Contritely he grabbed her hand. "I guess it wasn't a very good one."

"Don't *ever* joke about liking Ella."

"I'm sorry." He sighed. "It's only that . . . I was trying

to be funny because it's so hard to leave you. And if I don't find something to laugh about . . . dammit, Ginger, I'm going to cry."

"I'll cry too. Every day until you come home, Tonito."

"No you won't. You'll get busy when the hotel reopens and never even think about me."

She touched his cheek and let her hand slide down his strong neck to his bare chest. His skin glowed warmly in the fading light, smooth firm flesh that looked as if it would ooze honey instead of blood if it were cut. She stared into his dark, expressive eyes. Oh, he was so beautiful! Of course she loved him. And three years was such a long time to wait. Suppose he met a girl at college who would be there with him every day and every night? What if he decided he was in love with such a girl? What if he didn't want to wait three years to make love?

"Of course I'll forget you when the hotel reopens," she agreed mockingly, fighting tears. "I'll be too busy looking for some rich, handsome Prince Charming to come and steal me from you!"

He knew she was joking, but her words touched upon his greatest fear: that she *would* be swept off her feet by someone else while he was gone. The hotel guests often were glamorous, wealthy men from exciting places. Why should Ginger wait three years for a poor Indian who had no chance of ever making much money? The best he could hope to do was use his law degree to get the Indian land equitably divided, and even then his share probably wouldn't amount to much.

Their embrace had left his body aching with desire. Would the ache go away? Or would this painful need stay with him like a chronic disease? What if he couldn't stand it? What if he got to Boston and his sexual craving forced him to find some woman . . . any woman? No, he wanted to wait for Ginger so that making love would be their own private enchantment. He didn't want either of them to be saddled with memories of ever having shared that experience with anyone else.

Avery was shocked, numbed with jealousy, when Ginger told him that she and Tonito were engaged. Oh, he had known that she was spending practically every free moment that summer with the handsome young Indian, but Avery had thought it was just a matter of kids riding around the desert together.

Much to Avery's relief, Adele hadn't caught on yet that he was hopelessly, feverishly in love with Ginger. Poor Adele. She still was confident that someday she might recover her health. She would desperately cling to him at night as he gently made love to her, and afterward she would whisper about her desire for a child. "Someday I'll be strong enough," she would murmur, making it sound more like a prayer than a promise.

Ah, what could he do now? Nothing. *Nothing*! He could only wish Ginger well. Tonito was a fine human being, worthy of the girl in every way. In many ways they were right for each other. What would she want with a man fifteen years older than she was, anyway? Even if he were free, he wouldn't be so foolish as to try to win her away from Tonito. No, Ginger couldn't possibly give up that strapping, fine-looking young fellow for a man past thirty with prematurely graying hair.

Ginger continued to walk with Avery every morning, even though the hotel had reopened for the new season and she was as busy as a centipede with only fifty legs. Daily, Avery found something new about her to cherish, adding drop by drop to his love for her until he thought that his heart, mind, soul, and body would burst with anguished yearning.

He finally understood what people meant when they talked about "carrying a torch." He wasn't just carrying a torch, he was completely *scorched* by the damn thing. But, being a practical man—albeit with the soul of an artist, he liked to assure himself—he tried to let his unrequited love enhance his days instead of poisoning them, knowing that Ginger's affection and friendship were the finest part of his life.

CHAPTER
4

1919–1921

Ginger first realized that the village had become a town in 1919, when some of the people she passed on Main Street were strangers. Until now, except for the few tourists staying at other hotels or boardinghouses, she had known everyone. New homes and shops were going up on every street. A cacophony of hammers and saws and the grinding squeal of hand-cranked cement mixers overwhelmed the whistling of the wind and the dry rustling of the palm fronds. Now, to hear insects and birds and tall trees dancing in the desert breeze, she had to ride outside of town.

In the past three years Ginger had become much more than assistant manager at the Desert Inn. Nellie didn't bother much with titles, but if Ginger had a formal one it would be second-in-command. There was nothing about the hotel's operation that she didn't know. As the inn grew, so did its staff—an international mix of Indians, Filipinos, Chinese, Mexicans, anyone Nellie could find to train. Nellie believed in having almost as many employees as guests, so that every request for service could be quickly granted. The inn had become more and more luxurious, no mean feat in a town that still lacked electricity and gas and had only one paved road—Main Street.

The inn had been very busy that winter. Moviemakers from Hollywood had discovered that Palm Springs' setting and climate and clear dry air were perfect for filming westerns and any movie whose background was the Sahara Desert or Arabia. Even South Seas movies were shot there, with the ferny palm-filled Indian canyons doubling as exotic Pacific islands. Now, wherever Ginger walked in the village, she was sure to see Tom Mix being filmed as he galloped down Indian Avenue, or Rin Tin Tin jumping over a hedge, or Will Rogers sitting on a fence and chewing a strand of wild grass, or Fatty Arbuckle munching a sandwich. When Rudolf Valentino stayed at the inn, every female within fifty miles stormed the lobby for a look at him.

The inn also had become the unofficial social center for the entire village. Nellie threw fund-raising parties whenever some worthy cause needed money. Even without a cause, informal dances were held time and again on the big front porch or out back under the ramada. All it took were a few lively couples and Nellie's hand-cranked Victrola for a party to come alive. The screech of "There's Yes, Yes in Her Eyes" and "The Sheik of Araby" pierced the quiet desert night.

For three years Ginger and Tonito had been writing long letters to each other, sharing the details of their lives. Tonito wrote: "I live like a white man here, with my white education and my white friends and loving my white fiancée. But even though I may think like a white man now, my feet still are firmly planted on my tribe's sacred soil."

They both had matured greatly in three years. Sometimes Ginger compared Tonito's early letters with the ones he wrote now, and she would smile at his firmer grasp of language, his expression of ideas, and his ability to communicate his love for her. She was happy that he'd had this opportunity to attend Harvard's law school. As he explained to her, he now realized that all over the country there were many other groups with problems and petitions to be addressed by Congress, and that the needs of his small Agua Caliente band of Cahuilla Indians were of little interest to the politicians in far-off Washington. Instead of discouraging him, these insights gave him a more realistic approach to the task before him, and an even greater dedication.

Had he remained at a Los Angeles law school, he would not have made the valuable contacts he would need to bring about an equitable division of his tribe's land. Many of his fellow students, sons of the establishment, were headed for careers in Washington or on Wall Street, either in banks or courts or working closely with legislators; these young men had promised to help him when he needed them.

His letters to Ginger were filled with love for her. He wanted to marry her the day after he returned in June, and he begged her to make the arrangements.

But the more Ginger threw herself into the role of Tonito's loving fiancée, the more she longed to have Avery take her in his arms and never let go. She was so tired of fighting her desire for him. She tried staying away from him for a month, telling him that her new duties at the inn didn't leave time for her to walk with him at dawn, but she resumed the walks when she realized that the separation only increased her infatuation with him. She was convinced it was only that—a silly school-girl infatuation. She was reacting to his kindness, she told herself. He was a substitute father, and she was behaving most inappropriately. She was sure he would be utterly appalled if he knew how her body ached for him.

And even if Avery weren't appalled, Ginger had to consider dear sweet Adele, whose health finally seemed to be improving. Her pale cheeks were becomingly tinged with pink. Her delicate, fine features looked less pinched. She had gained a few pounds and even had the strength to attend some of the village potlucks and picnics. Ginger couldn't help responding to Adele's generous nature. Now that Adele had more energy, she began to mother Ginger, trying to compensate for Polly's—and George's—cruel neglect of the girl. Adele bought Ginger little gifts of cosmetics and lingerie at Lykken's store, and she had Nellie bring home a fashionable new dress or sweater for Ginger whenever Nellie went to Los Angeles on business. Adele constantly apologized to Ginger for Polly—as though it were Adele's fault that her sister was such a bitch!

Ginger found that the best antidote to her silly crush on Avery was to make plans for her future life with Tonito. Someday she wanted to open her own hotel, smaller and more intimate than the Desert Inn. Nellie's guests were mostly wealthy business magnates or movie people. For herself, Ginger envisioned a hideaway for writers and artists and creative people of all kinds. She was not as interested in luxury as Nellie was. Hers would be a simpler, more private place, with lush gardens, fountains, and deeply shaded vine-covered arbors.

One lazy afternoon when Ginger had a few hours free from her duties at the inn and Avery had no patients to see, she couldn't resist his invitation to ride their horses up into Chino Canyon. They heard guitar music and stopped to listen. "How lovely," Ginger said. "Where's it coming from?"

"Up there. See?" Avery pointed out a thatched hut farther up the canyon.

"Is that a naked man sitting there?" Ginger asked uneasily.

Avery laughed. "Yeah, Peter hates clothes." He raised his voice. "Hey, Peter! Peter Pester! Get some clothes on! You've got company!"

By the time Ginger and Avery reached the hut, the heavily bearded long-haired young man greeted them wearing a monk's robe and a broad smile. His cabin was constructed of thick upright logs for walls and neatly combed thatch on the roof. Inside were shelves of books and musical instruments.

"Oh, I've seen you," Ginger said when Avery introduced them. "You sell those canes you make to tourists on Main Street." She gestured at his robe. "Are you really a monk?"

Peter grimaced and shook his head. "I've seen you too—out riding with Tonito before he went east. Aren't you the girl he's going to marry?"

"Yes." Ginger smiled.

Peter frowned, looking from Avery to Ginger and back again. When Ginger turned away to admire his guitar, Peter gave Avery a long, pitying look. Obviously his sharp eyes had caught a glimpse of Avery's feelings for Ginger, making Avery realize that he had to be more careful.

Riding back toward Palm Springs from Chino Canyon, Ginger caught sight of a buckhorn cholla in bloom. "Oooh, look!" she cried, quickly slipping off her horse and running toward the colorful flowers.

Avery dismounted and joined her beside the flamboyant yellow blooms growing out of the spine-covered cholla. He turned when he heard the horses neigh in fright.

There on the trail, ten feet away, was the longest, fattest rattlesnake he had ever seen. Ginger saw it at the same moment, and with a squeal of terror she threw herself into Avery's arms.

The world stopped for both of them. Never before had their bodies been like this, groin pressed against groin, her soft breasts against his chest, their trembling lips hovering only inches from each other, their eyes locked in shock. Neither of them saw the snake slither away under the rocks. Neither of them heard anything but their own hearts banging with fear . . . and desire.

Every part of him wanted to lower his lips onto hers, to crush her closer against him, to make love to her then and there on the dusty trail—and to hell with the consequences. *But I can't, I can't,* he groaned to himself. *She'll hate me forever.* He grasped her arms and quickly separated their bodies. "There, there, it's nothing to be afraid of, the snake's gone now." He deliberately spoke in his most avuncular manner, maintaining the fiction that theirs was an innocent relationship—he being the older, wiser protector and she the child still needing protection.

She stood there in a daze, still terrified, not of the snake but of their brief embrace. How wonderful it had felt! Even better than all her erotic daydreams and tormented night thrashings when she imagined him holding her and making love to her. How many times had her pillow been his mouth and her hard mattress and crumpled blankets his virile body? Oh, she was ashamed! So ashamed! He was so good and kind to her, and all she could do was repay him with this disgusting, *totally* inappropriate lust!

She was certain that once she married Tonito, her cravings for Avery would be transferred to Tonito. But until then, she warned herself, she had to be careful not to show Avery how she felt or he'd lose all respect for her. And without his friendship, her life would be so empty.

They mounted their horses and turned toward home in silence, both filled with self-loathing for the feelings each secretly harbored for the other. Avery's love for her had become a chronic malaise to him, interspersed with waves of joy. He always felt slightly giddy in her company. When they were apart, their age difference seemed an impossible barrier to him. He was certain that her feelings for him remained those of a child for an adored uncle. But when they shared a spectacular sunrise or sat on rocks at their favorite lookout and exchanged thoughts about the books they both had read and about people they knew and about life in general—at such times he was convinced that the difference in their ages was the least important part of their relationship.

Then he would tell himself that Ginger was only infatuated with Tonito or that she was trying to get even with Polly by threatening to marry an Indian. Avery prayed that Tonito would fall in love with some girl in Boston so that Ginger finally would realize that she really had loved *him*, Avery, all along. And then what? Even if Ginger did love him, he couldn't desert Adele, who adored him, who lay in his arms night after night still convinced that she would become pregnant, when all along Avery knew that her frail body was incapable of conceiving. But he couldn't tell her that, couldn't bear to destroy her illusions, any more than he could leave her for Ginger.

But you only have one life to live, an inner voice cried out in grinding, frustrated pain. *The way you feel about Ginger is too beautiful to sacrifice. You can't just walk away from it! If nothing else, you and Ginger could be secret lovers. . . .*

He looked over at her, riding beside him. Her face was closed, almost sullen. Forgetting that she had thrown herself into his arms in the first place, he berated himself for their intimate embrace. Now she was afraid of him. Now she would withdraw her friendship from him. Without it, his life would be drab. Worthless. All the joy would go out of it.

At that moment she turned and gave him a brilliant smile. "Golly, wasn't that snake something, Avery? I'm glad I finally saw one. I can't wait to write and tell Tonito about it."

He smiled back with overwhelming relief. Thank God, she wasn't angry with him after all. *Paradise regained!*

When Ginger told Nellie she planned to marry Tonito in mid-June, Nellie threw her arms around the younger woman. "I'm so happy for you, Ginger! Why not have the wedding here? Out in the garden, under the ramada?

I'll have Quon make a fantastic banquet. Oh, it's so romantic! Tonito's such a gorgeous fellow! And he's kind and sweet to boot. I hope you'll have a dozen beautiful children—" Abruptly Nellie stopped speaking and bent over to pick up a cigarette butt someone had thrown onto the inn's gravel path. "Now, what kind of a rotten human being would do a thing like that?" She straightened up, shaking her head with disgust.

Ginger smiled fondly, long accustomed to Nellie's tirades against litterers.

Suddenly Nellie frowned. "Oh! But, Ginger . . . if you get married, how on earth will I ever manage without you?"

"Don't worry, I'll still work for you after I'm married," Ginger assured her. "The tribe can't pay Tonito much salary. Besides, I love working here."

"What a relief! Even with my boys helping now, I can't imagine running this place without your help. Oh, the dreams I have for the future! A few more profitable years and I'll be able to start on our permanent buildings."

"With a swimming pool?"

"Absolutely! Soon Palm Springs'll have electricity and telephones and a paved road all the way from Banning. *Then* watch us grow!"

A pale, inwardly suffering Avery gave the bride away. Gone were all his fantasies that someday Ginger would realize she loved him or that Tonito would fall in love with some girl back east. Because now the two handsome young people were actually getting married—to each other. All hope of ever being completely happy again drained out of Avery.

George and Polly failed to respond to the invitation Ginger sent them, but Tonito's family, and his tribe, and most of the village's original settlers, plus Nellie's entire staff, attended the noon ceremony in the Desert Inn gardens. All hundred and fifty guests wore their Sunday best, despite the warm June weather.

Gazing into her mirror before the ceremony, Ginger had giggled at how ethereal she looked in her white chiffon wedding gown and short veil, a surprise gift from Adele that Nellie had bought on a trip to Los Angeles. A wreath of white roses on her hair and her mother's gold locket were her only adornments.

During the ceremony Ginger gazed admiringly at Tonito, who was perspiring in the dark blue suit his buddies at law school had bought him as a wedding present. Ginger realized that during their three-year separation the beautiful boy had become a strikingly handsome man. His even white teeth contrasted with his dark skin whenever he smiled, which was often. His hair was thick and full. But when she looked into his lively brown eyes, all she felt was a warm affection toward him. *Oh, but I do love him!* she reassured herself in a sudden panic. *Of course I love him!*

She glanced over at Avery and saw that he was staring at her. Suddenly she felt faint, clammy cold in the hot June air, and she realized that everyone was staring at her, not just Avery, staring and smiling and waiting expectantly. As if from a great distance, like an echo, she realized that the clergyman had asked her a question: "Do you, Virginia McKinntock, take this man to be your lawful wedded husband?"

She was surprised when her lips moved without her willing them to do so and she said, "I do."

There were more words and then Tonito firmly said, "I do," and she heard the words "man and wife" and a roar of approval from the guests when Tonito took her in his arms and kissed her, hard. If he hadn't been holding her, she would have fallen down, and she clung to him, trying to get her bearings, eliciting another roar of delight from the audience, who mistook her embrace for passion. Then everyone was grabbing her and kissing her. She forced a smile as she was passed from one guest to another while their words of felicitation reverberated all around her.

Ginger began to feel faint again, but Avery quickly put an arm around her and led her away from the crowd of well-wishers. "Sit down," he ordered tersely, pushing her into a chair on the inn's deserted front porch.

"Oh, Avery!" she whimpered, leaning her head against his arm. She cried softly while he gently patted her back. She remembered how he had comforted her the night she arrived in Palm Springs. If only . . .

Tonito rushed onto the porch and knelt in front of her. "What happened?" he cried, taking her hands.

"Too much excitement," Avery said.

"I . . . I . . ." She wiped her tears on a corner of her short veil and groped wildly for an explanation. "I suddenly realized how . . . how much I missed my mother . . . at a time like this." She gave both men a wan smile, looking from one to the other, from the man who now was her husband to the man who . . . should have been. "I'm fine now." She stood up, holding Tonito's arm. "*Really* I am."

Avery looked at the two of them, so young, so beautiful, and he had a vision of them lustily making love and sharing exquisite orgasms. He forced a smile. "Well, then! Shall we join the party?"

Quon had prepared the entire wedding buffet by himself. His assistants had arranged long tables with platters of roast beef, lamb, turkey, chicken, scalloped potatoes, vegetable casseroles, fresh fruit salads, hot biscuits, cornbread, whipped honey-butter, and finally a six-tiered white-and-silver wedding cake complete with a toy bride and groom.

Nellie had been hard pressed to provide dishes, cutlery, chairs, and tables for so large a party. She ended up borrowing crockery and furniture from everyone she knew. She harmonized all the different styles and designs by putting white tablecloths and napkins and silver candles on every table. She had her gardener beg or steal every flower blooming in Palm Springs that morning, for centerpiece bouquets. When she was finished, there was room for all the guests to sit down and enjoy the meal.

As a wedding present, Avery handed Ginger and Tonito the deed to a ten-acre mesa in the foothills, adjacent to the pink mansion that Ginger's grandfather had built. It was a beautiful piece of land overlooking the village, the entire valley, and the mountain ranges beyond. "I stole that property right out from under your grandfather's nose," Avery told Ginger. "John really wanted that land, because it's a continuation of the mesa that his house was built on. Now I'm doubly glad *I* got it instead of him, or your father would've sold it with the rest of John's land. It's finally back where it belongs: with John's favorite grandchild."

After the banquet, Ginger and Tonito slipped off to her tent-cabin. He kissed her—their first private married kiss, a heady mixture of eroticism and trepidation. Swept along by the force of Tonito's passion, Ginger was stirred by the kiss, and heartened by it. Yes, if she could transfer all of her erotic feelings for Avery to Tonito, then she'd have nothing more to worry about.

Eager to inspect their newly acquired land, they removed their wedding finery and put on Levi's and shirts and walking shoes. They ran the half-mile to *their* property. Catching their breath, still a little shy with each other after their long separation, they stood hand in hand, looking out at their spectacular view. It was a bright day, dry and fragrant. They could see every ripple in the sand on the valley floor, every crevice in the mountains, and the long shadows cast by dark clumps of creosote bush and mesquite.

They exclaimed happily over the forest of ironwood and cottonwood trees on their land, and the row of windbreaking tamarisks that Avery had put in, an experimental tree only recently imported from Libya. They cooled their feet in the fast-flowing creek that ran alongside their mesa, then put down rows of rocks to delineate where they wanted the walls of their cabin to stand. They laughed as they outlined their future outhouse. They found the ideal sunny areas for their vegetable and flower gardens, and amiably disagreed over which crops to put in first. They paced off their orchard.

"I'll start building the cabin tomorrow," Tonito promised. "The men of my tribe will help me."

"There's no rush, Tonito. Nellie said we could live in my tent as long as we want."

"I know. But, Ginger, this will be our *home*! I can't wait to live here!" Hesitantly he drew her close. "It's very private up here," he murmured. "Better than a hot tent. Especially over there, behind the tamarisks."

Holding hands, they walked slowly toward the thick screen of trees, gradually discarding their clothes until they faced each other naked for the first time. Ginger's modesty evaporated when she saw in his eyes how much he admired her, *all* of her. She, too, marveled at his body: strong, copper-colored, bursting with youthful energy. He reached out and put his hands on her shoulders.

Then, with a sense of wonder, he slid his hands down over her firm flesh while she caressed his face and chest.

They kissed timidly. They put their arms around each other's waists and walked deeper into the grove, looking for a soft spot to lie in. With their feet they kicked some fallen leaves into a pile and threw themselves onto the leafy bed they had created. They kissed again, deeply this time, fumbling awkwardly in their eagerness to caress each other's bodies.

They were both such novices! But Tonito had paid keen attention when his more worldly friends at school had boasted about their sexual exploits. He remembered random phrases like "I sucked her tits till she was panting like a steam engine" and "I kissed every inch of her from her neck down to her cute little pussy" and "Hey, they really like it if you feel them up *all over* before you put it in."

Now, fighting his own impatience to quickly plunge ahead, he kept his mouth on hers and slowly trailed his hand down between her breasts, detouring to fondle each one. Then he tentatively kissed her nipples, not knowing whether to lick or suck them, and ending up doing both, letting his fingers slide down her abdomen slowly, slowly, and come to rest on her mound of red-gold hair, and all the while he vibrated with desire.

She was caught up in his voracious excitement, like being carried down a raging rapid. When he slid into her, she instinctively pushed against him, easing his way into her tight passage. Both of them were groaning with newly discovered pleasure, though neither was aware of their groans, or of time passing, or of the world around them, or of their bed of prickly crushed leaves, or of the sun or the sky or the hot breeze caressing them.

He was still on top of her, drained and sweaty. And ecstatic. "Was it like you thought it would be?" he asked, kissing her quivering eyelids.

She shook her head. "I never imagined . . . It's so amazing. I didn't know *what* to expect. . . ."

"I didn't either." He kissed her lips. "Just think! We can do this anytime we want!"

He rolled off her and they rested on their sides, facing each other. Ginger closed her eyes and snuggled closer against him. Oh, she *liked* this lovemaking! She thought it was delicious, even better than she had expected.

Guiltily she felt a sting of regret that this was Tonito holding her and not Avery. It had always been Avery with whom she had imagined making love. *But you're married now to Tonito, not to Avery,* she admonished herself. *You're in love with Tonito, not with Avery. Will you stop this Avery nonsense once and for all?*

For the next three months Ginger and Tonito lived in her tent at the Desert Inn while he built their cabin. They could not have been happier living in a palace. Though they both enjoyed their work, they couldn't wait for their nightly reunion on Ginger's narrow cot.

Ginger was enchanted with sex, and with Tonito's lusty young body. Wholly swamped by her own body's newfound sensuality, and by the alternating surges of desire and voluptuous satisfaction that swept over her day and night, she was able to entirely repress what she considered her "inappropriate" attraction to Avery. Now she could walk with him each morning without the yearnings that for years had filled her with so much guilt.

Nellie offered the newlyweds a larger bed, but Ginger blushed and shook her head. "We like sleeping close." She giggled. And sleep close they did, all tangled up in each other's limbs. Tonito always fell asleep with a hand on her breast, while she held his testicles. He had a small bump, perhaps a mole, embedded at the base of the soft loose skin—he laughingly called it his "magic button." If she stroked it, he would be aroused at once, even in a deep sleep, and then she would slide her hand up to feel him growing hard. It always amazed her, no matter how often it happened.

They muffled their laughter and giggles and shrieks, afraid of disturbing the hotel guests whose tents and cabins were nearby. Repeatedly they reminded each other how wonderful it would be when they moved onto their private mesa, where they could shout and bellow all night long. They were never tired, despite their long days of hard work. They spent half the night making love and talking, and then they slept so soundly that dawn found them bouncing out of bed totally refreshed.

Tonito took two days off from building their cabin to play the part of an Indian chief in a Tom Mix movie being filmed on the flatlands south of town. The makeup people slathered Tonito with oil to make his amber skin shine. He wore a long black wig and a colorful feather war bonnet that framed his face and hung down his back almost to his feet.

"They didn't give me any lines," he told Ginger ruefully, "even though it's a silent film. The director said I had a Harvard accent and people who lip-read might be able to tell. So all I get to do is grunt." He gave her a demonstration.

She laughed. "It's a good thing you have a law degree to fall back on!" But she was proud of his striking good looks and asked the cameraman for a still photograph of Tonito in his "Indian" costume.

I love him, I love him, I love him! she told herself a dozen times a day, especially when Tonito made love to her. She reveled in their shared sensuality. She was gratified that her body was so responsive. She took pride in his boundless love for her and in his amazing male beauty. Most important of all, she no longer suffered over her foolishly romantic "schoolgirl" crush on Avery. She considered him her good friend, really her *best* friend, but nothing more. She realized that she had always seen Adele as Avery's burdensome appendage, but now she saw the two of them as a couple and she felt more comfortable with Adele.

As for Avery, each morning during their hike, when he looked into Ginger's radiant face, he had to sigh. *Damn it! I should've scooped her up on my white horse four years ago and ridden off into the sunset, never letting Tonito nor anyone else ever get near her.* But he resigned himself to her marriage. What else could he do? He threw himself with renewed vigor into his work, building a four-bed clinic for the growing number of patients who needed hospitalization as the village population increased and as more visitors came to Palm Springs for their health. He began sketching and painting again. He was more attentive to Adele and more affectionate to her than he actually felt.

Still, he suffered from a great sense of loss. His enthusiasm and his *joie de vivre* diminished, as though a per-

manent dark cloud now stood between him and his inner
sun. He went through his days mechanically, subdued, a
man without hope.

Johnny Alvarez was born the following spring, in April
1920, two months after Ginger's twentieth birthday. Ginger was certain that the baby had been born smiling,
because he was so good-natured and lively. She couldn't
believe the pangs of fierce mother love she felt for him.
And Tonito behaved like a grinning idiot. "You have to
be the proudest daddy in the whole world," she told him
fondly.

Ginger's old housekeeper, Rosa, came to work for
them so that Ginger could return to her job at the Desert
Inn. Rosa arrived on weekdays after the little family had
had their breakfast. At midday Ginger would rush home
for a half-hour to nurse the baby; then Rosa would stay
on until the late afternoon, when Ginger finished work.
Weekends, Ginger and Tonito and Johnny managed without Rosa. They reveled in their privacy up on their mesa
in their cozy three-room cabin.

The days they were alone, Tonito enjoyed participating when Ginger nursed the baby. He would lie back
against the pillows on their bed and have Ginger rest
against him, with his arms enfolding her and the greedily
suckling infant. Beside himself with joyous beatitude,
Tonito would rest his cheek against Ginger's fragrant hair
and help her hold the baby's small, sturdy body. He
couldn't imagine being any happier than he was at such
moments. Nothing else mattered except being in this
cozy room holding *his* beautiful wife and *his* adorable
son.

As soon as Ginger sensed that the feeding was nearly
finished, she would playfully slide her free hand down
Tonito's groin and stroke his mole—his "magic button"
—instantly making him tense with desire. With a sated,
sleeping Johnny back in his crib, Ginger and Tonito
would tenderly make slow, voluptuous love. She was
amazed at how different his lips felt on her nipples than
Johnny's little mouth did—Tonito's so arousing, and Johnny's so fulfilling.

She gave a trembly sigh of happiness many times a
day. When she was at work, she enjoyed the excitement

of the busy, prosperous hotel that was constantly filled with people from all over the country. And when she was home, she was swamped with love for her two "men," one so big and loving, the other so tiny and lovable.

Mornings, she still got up just before dawn and hiked up the mountain with Avery to watch the sunrise. She hardly noticed that his hair was turning prematurely white or that he had become quiet and withdrawn. She was too wrapped up in her own happiness to sense his loss of vivacity. But as in the past, he remained her dearest, kindest friend.

Every once in a while, though, when she was with him, her mind would suddenly flash on the day they had seen the rattlesnake and she had thrown herself into his arms. But before the memory of that magic moment could proceed too far, she would chop it off—*bam!*—like Quon's hatchet hacking off the head of a chicken.

Avery, too, often remembered that brief, astonishingly wonderful feeling of her body pressed against his. But unlike Ginger, he cherished the memory and let it linger in his thoughts.

Every morning, Ginger looked over the list of guests arriving that day to see if any special services would be required. As she did so one day in April 1921, she was startled to see: "Mr. Neil McKinntock and Miss Ella McKinntock." They had reserved the two best rooms at the inn for seven nights.

Ginger was torn between curiosity and uneasiness. She hadn't seen them for five years. Days, even weeks went by without her thinking about them. But they *were* her sister and brother and there was no reason she couldn't have a civil relationship with them. Her argument had been with Polly and George, not with Neil and Ella. It seemed strange to her that they were coming to Palm Springs without Polly and George. It wasn't like Polly to allow them to travel alone. Of course Ella was nineteen now, and Neil seventeen, but Ginger knew that Polly had always been overprotective of them.

Ginger went about her work with one eye on the driveway. Were they coming on the afternoon train? In that case the hotel jitney would bring them to the inn about five o'clock. Or was Polly's chauffeur driving them here?

This month more than half of the inn's rooms were occupied by a film company's actors, actresses, and crew members. Frank Ricardo, one of Hollywood's most successful directors, was shooting a film set in ancient Egypt. The movie people were a demanding bunch, refusing to dress in the required suits and ties for dinner and always wanting to eat at odd hours. "We're too exhausted by dinnertime to bother changing our duds," Frank Ricardo protested. "Come on, Nellie, be a sport. Bend your rules a little." Nellie did so with great misgivings, and granted all their other requests too. She wanted their business. But it put a burden on the employees when their routine was upset.

"When I can afford to expand the hotel," Nellie confided to Ginger, "I'll put in two dining rooms—one with a dress code, and one for actors and others too busy or lazy to look spiffy for dinner."

"A keen idea," Ginger agreed.

Late in the afternoon, Ginger went to the kitchen to settle a dispute between Quon and his new assistant. She was hurrying from the kitchen to the lobby when she saw Ella and Neil at the registration desk. Suddenly Ginger was at a loss. Should she kiss them? Shake their hands? Since they hadn't yet seen her, she stood quietly in the doorway and observed them.

Ella was even more beautiful than she had been five years earlier. At nineteen she was tall and willowy. Her face could not have been lovelier had it been sculptured: each feature was absolute perfection. Her hair, so blond it was almost white, was marcelled in a cascade of waves that ended at her shoulders. She wore a clinging black travel suit that blatantly revealed her voluptuous curves. Everything about her was provocative, inviting men to desire her.

Seventeen-year-old Neil was well over six feet tall and strikingly handsome, though a bit overweight. His height and his Savile Row suit gave him an air of authority, despite his youth. Or was it his arrogance? He was the one who signed the register, while Ella stood nearby with the demeanor of a woman who was certain that some man would always take care of her.

"Wow!" Neil chortled when he looked up and caught sight of his older sister. "You're the cat's meow, Ginger. When did you get so pretty?"

"Why . . . thank you, Neil." Ginger went to him and kissed his cheek. She turned to Ella with an uncertain smile. "How about a sisterly kiss?"

Ella impatiently presented her cheek. "We have loads to tell you."

Ginger beckoned two porters waiting nearby. "Bill, Andy, take care of their luggage, please." She led her brother and sister to a quiet alcove furnished with comfortable wicker chairs and a round oak table covered with magazines. "Let's sit here and talk."

"First of all . . ." Ella drew a deep, shaky breath. "Polly and Papa are dead," she quavered.

Ginger gasped. "But they were so young!" she protested. Her head buzzed with shock. Despite all that had happened, George was her father, and when she was very young she had believed he was the most perfect man in the world. Despite the way he had treated her, a vestige of that love must have remained . . . or why would she feel such a sense of loss? Was it because now there was no chance of ever reconciling with him?

"They'd just bought a new Pierce-Arrow open touring car and they . . . they were on their way up to Lake Arrowhead. Anyway, their chauffeur . . . the police said he was driving too fast around a curve and . . . and the car ran right off the road and went over a cliff—" Ella's voice broke.

"Polly and Papa were both thrown from the car and killed instantly," Neil continued for her. "That son-of-a-bitch chauffeur didn't even get a scratch. I'd like to bash him in the kisser!"

"My God!" Ginger stood up and walked agitatedly about the room. "When did it happen?"

"Last week."

"The funeral . . . ?"

"Polly's lawyer arranged everything," Ella said. "We didn't think you'd want to come."

"Oh, but I would have!"

"They left everything to Ella and me," Neil blurted, a touch of spite in his voice. "We got Polly's money, and her mansion in Pasadena, and our grandfather's land here in Palm Springs."

"But, Neil," Ginger protested, "Papa sold that land ages ago."

"Yeah, but try to guess *who* he sold it to."

Ginger shrugged. "Wasn't it some old friend of Polly's?"

"You're all wet, kiddo. We just found out from the lawyer: Polly herself bought it secretly. I guess she didn't want Papa to look like a gigolo, marrying her when he was flat broke."

"Did Papa ever find out?"

"Nope. Polly was a humdinger at keeping secrets. Anyhow, now *we* own it—Ella 'n me." He looked at Ginger triumphantly. "I guess you're just a dumb Dora, Ginger. After the way you acted, they didn't leave *you* one red cent!"

"I didn't expect them to, Neil," she said sadly. "Anyway, it was all Polly's money, not Papa's."

"But doesn't it make you feel lousy to be disinherited?" Neil persisted.

"I guess so. A little. I'd love to have grandfather's land." Ginger was thoughtful. "It's a great location, so close to the village."

"Yeah. Pretty soon we're going to start putting a whole bunch of houses on it," Neil boasted. "Polly's lawyer told us that land values are about to go sky-high here in Palm Springs. Lots on the main drag already've shot up in price. He said movie people are building vacation homes here, they like this place so much. God knows why—it gives me the creeps. Anyway, the lawyer said anything we build now will make us a bundle."

"But . . . Polly was loaded. She must've left you both an enormous fortune!" Ginger shook her head. "So why bother making *more* money?"

Ella gave Ginger a pitying look. "You can never be rich enough. That's what Polly always said."

"And what'll you do with all this money?" Ginger asked. "How much can the two of you spend?"

"It's not so much having it to spend," Neil said seriously. "When you have gobs of money you can invest it and make even *more* money." He gestured at the lobby. "D'you still work here?"

Ginger nodded. "I'm Nellie's assistant."

"You'll never get rich working for her."

"Getting rich isn't my aim in life, Neil. It's amazing how little you need to be happy."

"Ah, that's a lot of hokum, Sis!"

"And I think you're all wet, Neil." Ginger paused. "For one thing, I'm married now . . ."

Ella gave her a curious look. "Who'd you find to marry in this godforsaken place?"

"Remember Tonito?"

"You married an *Indian*?" Ella shrieked. "Polly would've had a fit if she'd known."

"She did know, Ella. I sent all of you an invitation, almost two years ago—but none of you came to the wedding."

Ella shook her head. "Polly never told us."

"We have a little boy—Johnny. He's a year old now" —Ginger patted her still-flat abdomen—"and we're expecting another baby in December."

"God, it's hard to picture you as a mother," Neil said. "You still look like a kid yourself."

"I'm twenty-one, Neil."

"What's the brat look like? A little dark papoose?"

Ginger scowled at her brother, and chose to answer him without a shred of sarcasm. "Johnny's a cross between both of us, I guess. Not as dark as Tonito, not as light as I am. And twice as cute as any other living creature!" She stood up. "C'mon, I'll take you to your rooms. Then you'd better freshen up for dinner. I reserved a table for the four of us at seven o'clock."

Ella didn't know why, but she felt very cross after seeing Ginger and hearing about her marriage and her baby. Was it possible that she, Ella, was *jealous* of dumb old Ginger? Ah, but Ginger wasn't so dumb, and she'd gotten very pretty—not a great beauty, like Ella was, but still . . . Ginger had a certain bloom to her, probably from being in love, an emotion Ella never had experienced.

Ella despised men because they were such pushovers. It was so easy to trap them! She really found them ridiculous, they way they fell in love with her and carried on like idiots. Though she was addicted to the attention her beauty brought her, deep down she had nothing but contempt for men who were attracted only by a beautiful

face and voluptuous body. It was like falling in love with
a store dummy and not caring that it was filled with
straw. These men knew nothing about *her*, what kind of
person she was. And she was smart enough to know that
love should be more than simply being attracted by someone's appearance. That was a bunch of horsefeathers.
She'd met plenty of great-looking guys and they had
impressed her no more than plain men. If anything did
get her attention, it was when a man was peppy and
made her laugh a lot. She liked a man to be fun and
know how to have a good belly laugh and not just moon
around after her.

Now, here was Ginger, radiant with happiness, with an
adoring husband and a darling baby and a fun job . . .
and suddenly Ella felt that her own great beauty and
huge fortune were lacking in comparison. What good was
it all, Ella wondered, if *she* never felt radiantly happy?

That evening, when Ginger and Tonito escorted Ella
and Neil into the Desert Inn's elegant Anza Dining Room,
all the other guests stared at Ella. Their eyes followed
her from the door to the table, and they continued to
watch her avidly all evening.

Ella was accustomed to such attention, indeed would
have felt bereft without it. She was wearing a sparkling
green sequined gown with a plunging neckline that revealed the tops of her full creamy breasts. But it was her
face and cascade of pale blond waves that made people
stare at her.

"Green's a good color for you," Ginger told her. "But
aren't you in mourning?"

"Only during the day."

"Polly always used to make me wear green," Ginger
said with a residue of resentment. "She did it out of spite
because she knew darn well that green makes me look
sallow."

"Don't you dare say one word against her," Ella warned
coldly.

"I don't intend to, Ella. It's ancient history." Seeing
that Tonito was surreptitiously watching Ella, Ginger
playfully kicked his shin under the table and he grinned
at her.

"Who takes care of your baby while you work?" Ella asked.

"Remember Rosa, who worked for us when we first moved here? She's our nurse and housekeeper—" Ginger was interrupted by a stocky, dark-skinned, casually dressed man whose black hair was parted in the middle and slicked down with brilliantine. He had a neat mustache, big teeth, and an aura of authority. "Oh, hello, Frank," she said.

"Ginger, honey, how about an introduction?" He stared eagerly at Ella as he spoke.

"Sure," Ginger agreed. "Ella, this is Frank Ricardo. He's a movie director. Ella's my sister, Frank. And this is my brother, Neil. You've already met my husband."

Without taking his eyes from Ella's face, Frank shook hands with Neil and Tonito.

"Oooh, Mr. Ricardo, I've heard such wonderful things about you," Ella lied breathlessly, giving Frank a dazzling smile. "Everyone says you're Hollywood's *greatest* director."

"Thank you, my dear. May I join you for a moment?" Without waiting for a reply, he pulled over an unoccupied chair from the adjacent table and sat down next to Ella while giving Ginger an arch smile. "You never told me you had such a gorgeous sister!"

"It never occurred to me."

"But you know I'm always looking for new faces to put into my pictures." His brown eyes were shiny with excitement.

"C'mon, Frank, I'm a hotel manager, not a talent scout."

Frank turned back to Ella. "How would you like to be in my next movie, young lady?"

Ella gazed at him with the well-practiced look she reserved for men she wanted to impress. "Well . . . aren't you just the sweetest thing!" She tilted her head back, her moist mouth slightly open and her eyes partly closed. A provocative smile flickered on her lips. *You are the most wonderful creature who ever lived*, her look said. *I am expiring with admiration and desire for you*.

Frank asked the others to excuse him while he took Ella over to meet his producer and the stars of his film.

With much commotion the people at his table moved their chairs to make room for Ella.

"This always happens," Neil said, shoveling the last bite of food from his plate into his mouth and then taking over Ella's unfinished dinner. "Whenever we go anywhere, men fall all over her."

"Well, she is absolutely gorgeous," Ginger conceded.

"Gorgeous!" Tonito echoed.

"Yeah. Well, Ginger, I guess Ella got the looks and you got the brains," Neil chortled. "But you have a big advantage over her, Sis. You've become a real great looker yourself, but there's no way Ella's ever going to grow any brains!"

Frank Ricardo decided to put Ella into the movie he was shooting. He had a part written in for her, that of a Nordic princess visiting ancient Egypt. Frank realized at once that her pale blond beauty would stand out like a beacon in contrast to all the swarthy actors playing Egyptians. He immediately recognized that Ella couldn't act, but it was of no importance; there was no dialogue in silent movies. Even if she only stood quietly, a voluptuous blond Viking, she'd steal the film. He soon learned that people simply loved to stare at her. Her astonishing beauty gave men erections and woman spasms of jealousy. Her body was provocative in the tight, slinky, low-cut gowns that Frank's costume people designed for her and which became her hallmark. Even as Frank worked on his present movie, he began planning his next one, with Ella in the starring role.

Five days after meeting Ella, alone with her in the hotel cabin he used as an office, Frank proposed to her. From her repertoire of smiles she gave him her smoldering one, while her eyes told him he was the most marvelous, desirable man she'd ever met. When it came to manipulating men, Ella was a far better actress than Frank realized. "Oooh, you darling," she crooned. "I'm so flattered that a big, smart, important man like you wants to marry me! But, Frank, I'm only nineteen and I want a career first."

"For God's sake, Ella, I don't expect you to stay home and darn my socks. I want to make a *star* out of you, a Hollywood sex queen! You're oozing sex appeal. You've got great gams." He put his lips against hers and let his hand rest on her breast.

She let him savor the rippling pleasure of her wet kiss. When she swayed against him, his loins ached from the touch. Then, as though frightened by her own uncontrollable passion, she quickly tore herself away from him. "Oooh," she whispered, "what you *do* to me! But, Frank honey, I'm saving myself for marriage. A minute more in your arms and I wouldn't have been able to stop!"

"Then marry me now!"

"Shhhh." She put a finger to his mouth. "Dear man, please be patient. Don't you think I'm worth waiting for?"

"I'm sure of it, Ella. But patience isn't one of my virtues. Just how long do I have to wait?"

"Until I'm ready," she whispered provocatively.

Ella had absolutely no intention of marrying Frank Ricardo, not now, not ever. Her brief encounter with the glamorous movie world suddenly had given her an ambition and a purpose in life far beyond being anybody's wife. She'd just string Frank along until she'd gotten what she wanted out of him.

Stardom.

"What a bore this place is," Neil said after dinner. "Where can I get some hooch?"

Ginger shook her head. "Didn't you ever hear of prohibition? You've got to bring your own in a flask."

"No gin mills? No roadhouses?"

"Where do you think you are, Neil? People don't come out here to make whoopee."

"Nuts! How can you stand it here?" He excused himself, leaving Ginger and Tonito alone at the table.

Ginger gave her husband a wry smile. "You always had a crush on Ella, didn't you?"

"She's amazing. I remember the first time I saw her . . . what was she, ten years old? She was a real Sheba even then."

Ginger nodded. "I was furious! You didn't once look at me."

"Yeah. It took me a while to realize that Ella's all surface beauty. Not much underneath." He took Ginger's hand. *"You're* beautiful through and through!"

"Thanks. But tell me, what is it about Ella that makes men so gaga? Not all beautiful woman do that."

He pondered a moment. "It's the way she looks at a man. Like he's God's gift to women. Even when you *know* it's fake, all an act, it still makes you feel . . . terrific."

Ginger nodded, sighing. "It's really goofy."

"Yeah." He squeezed her hand. "You have nothing to worry about, sweetheart. Her old blond magic doesn't work on me anymore."

Ella was swallowed up by the movie people. Even when they weren't filming her scenes, she remained on the set. She ate all of her meals with Frank and the actors. Ginger and Neil seldom saw her, except at a distance.

Neil was busy conferring with Polly's lawyer and a building contractor from Los Angeles. They were going to put up eight small "villas" on part of their grandfather's land that Neil and Ella had inherited from Polly. If those sold well, they would build more. As soon as the preliminary plans were completed, Neil gave the contractor all the responsibility for the construction and prepared to return to Pasadena.

"I'm taking off," Neil told Ginger when he found her in the hotel kitchen. "This town gives me the creeps. Always has. How can you stand living here? I mean, there's a whole exciting world out there . . . places like New York and London and Paris. I've been to New York four times!"

"Someday I'll visit them. But right now, this is all I want." She touched his arm. "Tell me, what are you going to do now? Go to college?"

"Hell, no! I fired all my tutors the day Papa and Polly died." He took a chocolate éclair from a nearby tray and devoured it in two bites.

"But you're only seventeen, Neil. An education is important."

"Look, Polly kept us on a leash for nine long years. Now I'm going to enjoy my freedom."

"You'd be just as free at college as anywhere else, Neil."

"You're all wet if you think I'm going to sit still for

four years while a bunch of professors try to fill my head with a lot of bunk." He took another éclair and bit into it. "Besides, I already know everything I'll ever need to know."

"About what?"

"About making money."

"But you have so much!"

"Yeah, and I'm going to make it grow and grow. Wait and see. Someday I'm going to be the richest man in the world!"

"But why? What's so wonderful about that?"

"Power, kiddo, power. Honest to God, Ginger, I can't believe you're four years older than me. You're so naive! Look, when you're super-rich, everybody bows down to you! Believe me, nobody gets in your way."

"But aren't you interested in anything besides money?" she protested.

"Sure. Fast cars and faster floozies."

"What would you do if you were poor and *had* to work?"

"Like you?" He snorted in contempt. "I'd slit my throat!"

"I'll never understand you," she sighed. "And I'd like to, Neil. I'd like us to be friends. When you were little, I loved you a lot."

He gave her an amused smile. "Sure, we can be friends. Just don't try to borrow any money from me!" Abruptly he leaned down and kissed her cheek. "I'm only kidding. If you need a little dough, you can always count on me. Ta-ta, Sis."

She watched him walk cockily out of the kitchen and she suddenly had a vision of him as an enormous giant, squashing people who got in his way, like normal-size people stepping on cockroaches.

Ella was fed up with being an actress. Standing in front of the big clunky lens while all the cameramen and electricians and grips and gaffers fussed around with the equipment, and the makeup people and hairdressers and dressmakers fooled around with her appearance, and the director and producer and the moguls argued about how to proceed with the shooting—it was no fun, no fun at all. But she desperately wanted to be a star. Deep down she knew it was a silly aspiration—after all, she didn't need the money, and what difference did it really make if some creep in Kokomo knew who she was? But she couldn't help it: that was what she wanted. Fame.

She seldom saw Ginger except across the hotel dining room or passing through the gardens, but Ginger always looked so happy. And the happier Ginger looked, the angrier Ella became. It was so unfair!

Ella couldn't get over the idea that Ginger had found true happiness, while she, Ella, was floundering, often feeling downright miserable. It should be the other way around, it seemed to her. After all, *she* was the great beauty, *she* was the one who had dozens of men in love with her, *she* was the rich one, *she* would soon be the famous one. She should be the happiest person in the world. There was nothing she couldn't buy, no place in the world she couldn't go. She and Neil owned Polly's fabulous mansion in Pasadena. And all Ginger had was a low-class Indian husband and a half-breed kid and a dumb little three-room cabin to live in.

But Ginger was in love, Ella realized, something Ella never could hope to experience herself because she just didn't give a damn about other people. And Tonito loved Ginger for her kindness, her sympathy, her intelligence, her dignity, her verve, her joyful spirit—all traits that Ella never had possessed and doubted she ever would. And there was that whole business from early childhood when their mother had doted on Ginger and hadn't given a hoot about Ella.

God, Ella fumed to herself, Ginger was so insufferably good, so naively wholesome, so sweetly in love, and so unfairly blessed with friends who truly cared about her, that Ella felt an acute need to "get even" with her sister for the unfairness of it all. Ginger just had to have her comeuppance. And it was up to Ella to do something about it!

Gradually she worked out a plan. She secretly rented a bizarre mansion on the outskirts of town. Hidden behind a thick overgrown grove of fig trees and oleander bushes, the villa was a copy of an Arabian seraglio and had been built at tremendous cost by an elderly Canadian lumber magnate in imitation of a photograph he had seen in the *National Geographic*. On the hot sands of the California desert, with unlimited wealth and unlimited lust, the aging bachelor had hoped to create for himself the life-style of a sheik—complete with harem—the way he imagined that Valentino lived.

Unfortunately for him, by the time his exotic pleasure palace was completed and furnished and before even a single occupant of the harem could be installed, the Canadian had lost most of his money and all of his potency. Without spending one night there, he had put his dream house up for sale or lease. Ella never lived there either. She remained at the Desert Inn with the rest of the movie crowd—but she had a plan that finally would give Ginger what she deserved.

Ella knew that Tonito worked alone in the tribal office, a tiny shack near the Indians' hot-springs bathhouse. Many of the movie cast and crew had become addicted to the hot baths and took them daily. Ella hated the effervescent water that smelled of sulfur, but she went there one morning when she wasn't needed on the set, aware that she could walk behind a row of tall oleanders from the bathhouse to Tonito's office quite easily without being seen.

He was startled when she entered wearing a low-cut green sundress that clung to her body like adhesive tape. He was immersed in his work, making an inventory of the Indian reservation, looking up old government land Franks, reviewing every congressional law pertaining to the Indians, and searching for precedents in state and federal courts.

"Well, hel-*lo*, brother-in-law," she drawled.

"Hello, sister-in-law," he replied dryly.

"I was near here in the bathhouse and it occurred to me that I've never really welcomed you into the family." She gave him one of her searing looks.

Tonito was amused. Did she really think he was such a pushover? He'd known her too long and was onto her tricks.

"My goodness, Tonito, we hardly know each other," she cooed, sitting on the edge of his desk, close to him.

"Hmmmm." He found her huge blue-lilac eyes disturbing. Knowing that everything she did was an act, why was he so stirred? How could he be such a dope?

She lightly touched his arm. "I've always thought you

were just the handsomest thing around, Tonito, even when we were children. But you, you silly old thing" —she pouted—"you always preferred Ginger."

"I . . . I always thought you were very b-beautiful," he stammered, "but you weren't very friendly, Ella."

"Well, I want to make up for that. . . ." She slid into his lap and put her arms around his neck. "Kiss me!" she commanded in a hoarse whisper.

She's a witch, he thought helplessly. *She's put a spell on me. I hate her—but I can't help myself. . . .*

They met every day in the secrecy of her rented seraglio. He was a wild man with her. Their lovemaking was frenzied, frantic, greedy. They flung themselves at each other like growling animals on the oversize canopied bed in the master bedroom, and it wasn't anything remotely like love. It was more like they were using their bodies to punish each other for the madness they felt when they were together.

Ella had never had sex before. But he was a good teacher and she was a fast learner and she quickly became addicted to her savage orgasms. For a half-hour afterwards she would stagger about the Arabian castle, desperately pleading with her body to calm down so she could return to the hotel and resume the life of a self-possessed young movie star.

Tonito hated her. Even more, he despised himself. Copulating with Ella was lewd, like exquisite torture, in no way resembling the wonderfully voluptuous satisfaction he enjoyed with Ginger. Every time he withdrew from Ella he vowed to himself that he would never return to the canopied bed and her bewitching body. He tore himself away from her the moment he ejaculated. He didn't even say good-bye, but hastily dressed and flung out of the house, slinking behind the trees that edged the water ditches, feeling like a criminal all the way back to his office.

He kept reminding himself that Ella was shallow, that her beauty truly was only skin-deep, that she was entirely selfish and cruel, that she was incapable of loving anyone but herself.

Ah, he remembered, but wasn't he, too, thinking only about himself? *And, God, God, God, wasn't she beautiful? That soft, soft, pale skin? That golden hair? Those lips, those breasts, those smooth thighs*. And he knew he would go back to her again. And again.

Later, when he went home to his beloved Ginger and their adorable Johnny and their heavenly mesa, he couldn't believe that he had ever touched Ella. He became a skilled actor; for every minute he spent with Ella, he gave Ginger hours of tender, extra-loving attention. Going to sleep with Ginger in his arms, he was certain he would never again—*never-never-never again*—see Ella. He awoke with the same vow, and yet the day would drag and his mind would refuse to comprehend his books and charts and all the careful notes he had taken, because he was waiting for the appointed time so that he could *prove* to himself that he would not go to Ella. But in the end he went. Always.

When Ella realized she was pregnant, she was terrified. God, an illegitimate baby! And a half-breed! The scandal would ruin her career. She was afraid to tell anyone. She was certain that Tonito would be furious . . . she knew how guilty he already felt. What if he stopped seeing her? She couldn't bear that. But what should she do about the baby? She was so confused.

Yet if she were to tell Ginger, Ella decided, she'd finally get her revenge. With one sentence, she could kill Ginger's happiness forever. She practiced it in front of a mirror: "Well, Mrs. High-and-Mighty, your husband fucked me silly, again and again, and now *I'm* carrying his child too!" Twice she stopped Ginger at the inn, ready to blurt out her news. But there was something about Ginger's affectionate eyes, her innocent joy in life, her sweet smile, and her genuine pleasure that Ella's movie career was progressing so well, that made Ella lose her nerve.

Then, suddenly, the movie was almost finished. Everyone was planning to return to Hollywood before summer's scorching heat seared the desert. Nellie, too, was about to close the inn for the two hottest months and retreat to the cooler mountains. Only Ginger and Tonito and Avery and Adele and the Indians and a few other diehards in their thick-walled tree-shaded houses could tolerate the high temperatures of July and August.

Ella grew desperate. *She had to do something!*

On a Friday afternoon the final scene was filmed and

Frank Ricardo happily hollered, "It's a wrap!" Later the production threw a party for cast and crew in the inn's dining room. It was their last night in the desert and most of them were eager to return home. They celebrated with gusto, downing bottle after bottle of the bootleg "hooch" the company had sent in from Los Angeles. The phonograph blared out one hit song after another: "Ain't We Got Fun," "Running Wild," "Betty Coed." A starlet who'd had a small role in the film got up on a table and did a wild shimmy amid much clapping and hooting.

"Hey, let's enter her in that new beauty contest in Atlantic City!" the head electrician yelled.

"Yeah, our own Miss America!"

"Shit, more like Miss Floozy of 1921, if y'ask me!"

"Hell, any way you slice it, she's a hot number!"

Refusing to allow anyone to cut in, Frank tangoed and slow-fox-trotted all evening with a surprisingly affectionate Ella. Toward midnight he danced her out to the terrace, and there, under the stars, once more he pleaded with her to marry him. He had lost count of his proposals and had no expectation that her response this time would be any different from the others.

"Yes, dear boy," she whispered in his ear. "Oh, yes!"

He looked at her closely. Was she making fun of him?

"Let's get married right away," she murmured. "I've made you wait long enough, you poor old thing." She snuggled close against him. "Oh, Frank, I've loved you from the first minute I met you. But I had to be sure."

He held her close, at first too stunned to speak. His mind raced with plans. He would buy her the biggest estate he could find. Of course, he'd let her choose it . . . the Hollywood Hills, or out in Beverly Hills . . . or Hancock Park . . . whatever she wanted.

Ella's mind was racing too. Frank was a swarthy Italian, so if the baby turned out dark like Tonito, nobody would give it a second thought.

Meanwhile, she'd have her lawyers buy the Arabian mansion. In the fall, as soon as it was cool enough, she'd come back to the desert and live there until the baby was born. By then she'd have gathered the courage to tell Ginger exactly what had happened. Ginger had too much pride to stay with Tonito once she knew the truth. And when Ginger threw him out, Tonito could spend every night with her, Ella, in that crazy Arabian castle. As for Frank . . . well, she'd worry about him when the time came. There was always divorce, but at least her baby would be legitimate and have a name.

Ella decided her acting career could wait, though she'd be acting every minute she spent with Frank, making him think she loved him and that the baby was his. The thought of going to bed with him gave her pause: he attracted her about as much as the tree trunk they were leaning against. But all she had to do was close her eyes and make believe he was Tonito. Frank would never know that he wasn't the cause of her ardor.

As plans whirled through Ella's head, one now stood out loud and clear above all others: whatever she herself did, whatever Ginger did, whatever Frank did—nothing was going to make her give up Tonito!

CHAPTER
5

Ginger loved that summer. Mornings, she hiked with Avery for an hour at dawn, while the air was still cool. Avery encouraged her to walk as much as she wanted during her pregnancy, but he had forbidden her to ride. "Not the way you go galloping across the desert," he admonished.

"How about if I ride in a more ladylike fashion?" she coaxed.

"You wouldn't know how."

Most days, the two of them climbed to their favorite lookout on the side of San Jacinto and, breathing deeply, stood there in awe, both of them trembling with the very joy of existence. In that early hour the desert lay below them in a trance, vast and silent, suffused with the pale pink and golden rays of the rising sun.

At such moments Avery desperately wanted to put his arms around her and hold her close. But he didn't dare. Sometimes he held her hand to help her across a narrow ledge or up a very steep path, and then he would secretly scoff at himself for purposely choosing a trail where he *knew* he would have a chance to hold her hand.

His envy of Tonito bordered on hatred, not only because Ginger loved Tonito, not only because the young Indian could make love to her whenever he wished, but also because Tonito was the father of Johnny and the unborn child. Ah, Avery thought, to have a child with this precious young woman would be the ultimate joy.

Ginger had no inkling of the misery she caused Avery. She took him for granted as her friend and benefactor. He was as solid as the mountain they enjoyed climbing together. That he mooned over her like a lovesick school-boy never entered her mind.

With the inn closed for the two hottest months, Ginger could be lazy and spend her days playing with Johnny and lolling about in the evenings with Tonito. Their mesa caught a constant light breeze that kept the daytime heat from becoming unbearable. At sunset the temperature fell rapidly, making the nights delightfully balmy.

Sometimes she missed the excitement of her job and felt as though she had been banished from a beloved homeland. She enjoyed meeting new guests, and solving problems, and learning more and more from Nellie about the hotel business . . . and about life. Calm amidst strife, humor instead of anger, serenity replacing agitation; these were Nellie's—and now Ginger's—prescriptions for success and happiness. Whenever the summer's indolence threatened to make her restless, Ginger would anticipate September and the challenge of a new season at the inn. Knowing her exile from work was only temporary, she could relax and continue to savor her summer of laziness.

Johnny was a constant source of pleasure to Ginger and Tonito. The baby had a genial personality and unlimited curiosity. His parents doted upon his waddling walk and his amusing gibberish. Tonito built a picket fence around a small area directly behind the cabin—with a ramada for shade at one end—so that Johnny could play outside without danger of wandering off their land or falling into the creek. He galloped madly around his enclosed area on a stick-horse that Tonito's father had made from an old broom. Johnny also had a sandbox, and a stuffed animal Ginger had made from a cast-off brown caracal muff of Nellie's, and a roly-poly—a gift from Avery and Adele—which Johnny tried to imitate with a great deal of falling down amidst whooping gusts of glee.

Rosa, their housekeeper, was spending the two summer months with her married daughter in Hemet, on the other side of the mountain. More and more young Indians were marrying whites they met at the local school or at the high school in Banning. The Agua Calientes were handsome, cheerful people who were easily assimilated into the life of the fast-growing population of whites, though most of them still maintained a strong loyalty to their tribe.

Ginger thoroughly enjoyed Tonito's family. She had been best friends with his sister, Maria, since her first days in Palm Springs, and she had grown very fond of old Juan Pedro, her father-in-law. Tonito's mother had died before Ginger came to the desert, but Tonito had numerous aunts and female cousins who made Ginger feel welcome.

Though only fifteen months old that July, Johnny was almost as big and strong as a two-year-old. He loved following his father around, mimicking everything Tonito did. During the hot weather, Tonito worked at home, poring over his papers for an hour or two, then going out and inspecting the irrigation channels in his orchard or tending the gardens before returning to his desk. There was no keeping Johnny in his fenced enclosure when Tonito was working on the land. The boy would howl and try to tear down the fence if Tonito failed to take him along. One day in August Johnny suceeded in pulling off a loose picket, squeezing out through the opening, and toddling into the orchard to startle his father.

"I hope this one's a girl." Ginger patted her stomach when Tonito carried Johnny back to the house. She stood beside Tonito and watched him hammer the broken picket back onto the fence's wooden crossbars.

He grinned up at her, illuminating his dark face with a flash of even white teeth. "I'll bet you were as much trouble as Johnny," he teased. "You told me yourself you were a tomboy."

"Well, I didn't go around tearing down fences!" She caressed Tonito's thick dark hair.

Tonito grabbed her hand and kissed it. God, how he loved her! Her face was angelic, with a serenity he envied. He was certain that she suspected nothing of his ghastly behavior with Ella. His sister-in-law's departure had been an enormous relief to him. For weeks before she left, he had worried that Ella might spitefully tell Ginger about their affair. His lust for her had dissipated, but his self-loathing and his hatred for her remained.

Ella wrote them a letter announcing her marriage to Frank Ricardo and bragging about the huge Spanish-style estate they now owned in the hills above Hollywood. She described their indoor swimming pool—"But she hates to swim!" Ginger interjected as she read the letter to Tonito— and their grotto and acres of manicured gardens and their magnificent mountain and city views. She boasted about the parties they had attended, where she had met Chaplin and Valentino and Gloria Swanson and "everybody else who's anybody in this town." To Tonito's horror, Ella added that she also had bought the Arabian castle in Palm Springs and hoped to spend a lot of time in their "darling little village," which she found "so cute and healthy."

"She's such a phony!" Tonito fumed, taking the letter from Ginger and throwing it into the trash barrel. "She's as fake as that stupid Arabian monstrosity she's gone and bought."

"Ah, come on, darling," Ginger said, "what difference does it make what she does?"

He sank to his knees in front of her and took her hands. "I don't want her in Palm Springs, that's all. She's a bad person, Ginger. She's selfish and mean. I'm afraid she'll make you unhappy."

"Make *me* unhappy?" Ginger echoed in surprise. "Why should I care whether Ella's in Hollywood or Palm Springs or the North Pole? After all, *we* don't have anything to do with her, wherever she is."

Speak for yourself, he thought in despair.

Ella did not return to Palm Springs in the fall, after all. Frank wanted her to do another film before the baby was born. It was a story about the French Revolution and her costumes consisted of tight, low-cut bodices and voluminous skirts, so that her expanding girth was not visible. Most of her scenes were close-ups of her face and bosom anyway.

Frank was ecstatic about the baby. At forty he had been married twice before, both times to actresses, neither of whom had produced a child. He loved to reach up under Ella's costume and stroke her swollen abdomen. He was always feeling the baby, much to Ella's annoyance, though she seldom dared to show her irritation.

Right now, she needed Frank. A genius at creating female stars, he was renowned for his masterly development and handling of Hollywood's leading actresses. And the studio press agents now trumpeted that Ella was Frank's greatest achievement. Even with only one picture in release, Ella already had fan clubs in all the major American cities. Her classic features were reproduced weekly in the rotogravure sections of Sunday newspapers throughout the country. Always, she was shown in the most glamorous settings wearing exquisite gowns. The studio knew that with millions of women wanting to identify with her, and millions of men lusting after her, millions of dollars would deluge the studio's box offices.

Ella's pregnancy was never publicized, and as her belly swelled, she made no public appearances. She changed her mind about going to Palm Springs to wait out her pregnancy. For one thing, she didn't want Tonito to see her huge with child. And she was afraid she would blurt the truth to him, or even to Ginger in a fit of jealousy, and ruin everything, because if either of them knew about it, what would keep them from telling Frank? She was worried that Frank would do something violent if he ever found out that the baby wasn't his. He loved collecting guns and he kept them all over the house. He would kill himself, or kill Tonito, or maybe even kill her and the baby.

Her pregnancy excited Frank sexually, as if by entering her he felt some kind of ecstatic communion with the baby. She didn't really mind. An orgasm is an orgasm, she told herself, and she simply loved having them. All she had to do was close her eyes and imagine that Frank was Tonito. Frank was short and stocky, compared to Tonito's tall, sleek, muscular body, but once Frank was inside of her and she began vibrating with excitement, he didn't feel that different.

Still, Ella was confused about the future. She wasn't sure she wanted to stay with Frank after the baby was born and safely had Frank's name, and when her stardom was secure enough for her to continue without Frank's help. She no longer wanted to have anything to do with Tonito either. After all, he was nothing but a dirt-poor Indian, despite his great looks and his law degree. No, she wanted someone not only handsome but also famous, maybe a prince or a duke—oh, she just didn't know *what* she wanted! Maybe she should just throw respectability out the window and have lots of lovers, one after the other, or even all at once. It would be easy, now that her doctor had told her about birth control. At every Hollywood party she attended with Frank, the men swarmed all over her.

She sighed. God, she ought to be the happiest person in the world. She had everything! There was hardly a woman in the whole country who wasn't wildly jealous of her, except maybe Ginger. But despite all she had, Ella was lonely. She always felt so mixed up and sad, because when she came right down to it, there was no one that she really and truly cared about. Or wanted.

Not even this baby growing inside of her.

"You look like Johnny's roly-poly," Tonito teased Ginger early on the morning of December 7.

She gestured wryly at her bulging stomach. "At least a roly-poly can't fall down. If I fell now, I'd never be able to get up!"

"I'd give you a hug. If I could get close to you."

"You could hug my back," she laughed.

He stood behind her and nuzzled her neck, then covered it with butterfly kisses.

They were startled by a sudden gust of wind that slammed against the cabin's door and threw it open. As Tonito rushed to close it, the noise woke Johnny, and Ginger went to lift him out of his crib.

"Let me." Tonito was at her side. "He's too heavy for you now."

The three of them were having breakfast when Avery knocked. "I was out for my morning walk . . . there's a hell of a storm coming." He joined them at the table while Tonito poured a cup of coffee for him.

"Don't mention your morning walk, Avery. It's so frustrating that I'm too clumsy to go with you anymore."

"Patience, Ginger-girl. From the looks of things, you'll be relieved of your burden any minute now. So, with a bad storm coming, I'd feel a whole lot better if the three of you came on down to the village. I can send Jim up with the car as soon as I get home. Because once it starts raining, your road will be a sea of mud." He grimaced. "I don't want Tonito here delivering your baby."

Ginger went to the door and examined the sky. "It doesn't look all that bad. And I've got a million things to do before the baby is born." She paused. "Hey, come over here, you two."

When they joined her at the door, with Johnny close behind them, Ginger pointed at their forest of cotton-wood trees. "Look!"

All of them stared in wonder: overnight, the cotton-wood leaves had turned a glittery gold. Now, against the steel-gray clouds, it was a sight to make them marvel.

Avery gestured toward the mountaintop. "Now, you see that dirty-looking bank of clouds? Believe me, it's going to turn old San Jacinto into one great big waterfall."

"Oh, pooh!" She smiled at him fondly. "Tell you what. As soon as it starts to rain, send Jim over. Okay?"

"I'd feel better if you came now," Avery worried.

"Avery, I can't just drop everything—"

"Oh, all right," he conceded with a sigh, "we'll do it your way."

The rain came suddenly, like an explosion. With it, raging winds howled down the mountainside and slammed into the mesa, uprooting trees and ripping a corner of the roof off the cabin. Ginger screamed and picked up Johnny, who had been playing on the floor. As she did so, a searing pain sliced across the bottom of her abdomen.

Tonito was at the window, peering out. "Those god-damn trees!" he sputtered, pointing. "They're forming a dam! When it bursts, it'll wash away the cabin!"

She joined him at the window and looked out. A pile of downed cottonwoods lay across the creek, backing up the water behind it. As she watched, sheets of rain turned part of the mesa into a pond. The picket fence around Johnny's play area had already washed away. Their dirt road disappeared beneath a plummeting waterfall.

Tonito yanked open the cabin door. "I have to move those trees!" he shouted above the roaring storm.

"No!" she shrieked in terror. "Tonito! Don't go!"

He didn't hear her. He slammed the door shut and plunged into the torrent roaring off the cabin's roof. He fell, knocked down by the force of the water. Scrambling to his feet, he sloshed his way toward the creek.

"*Tonito!*" Ginger shouted, her voice drowned out by the screeching fury of the storm. Helplessly she peered out at him through the rain-stained window as he wrestled with the tree trunks blocking the creek. She watched while he slid one tree out of the way, then another. She cried out in alarm when he slipped and fell, but he got up at once, covered with mud.

The pain tore through her again, taking her breath away. Johnny was crying now, screaming for his daddy, kicking and trying to get out of Ginger's arms. As she put him down and bent over in pain, he ran to the door and tried to reach the knob, which fortunately was too high for him to turn.

Standing at the window again, Ginger saw that Tonito had managed to pull all but two of the trees away from the creek. He was struggling with those two now. She was relieved to see that water had begun to surge down the creek, past the downed trees, thus ending the danger of a dam bursting all at once and washing away the cabin.

While Ginger watched, Tonito slipped and fell into the rampaging creek. A scream louder than the storm tore out of her throat, and without thinking, she flung open the cabin door and ran outside. *She had to save him!*

She slid in the mud, fell hard onto her hands and knees, tried to get up, but couldn't. She scrabbled around on the slippery ground, her tears of panic almost blinding her. The sound of the rain was deafening as it whipped against her face. She saw Johnny start to run past her, still calling for his daddy. Whimpering, she lunged for him and fell onto her bulging stomach while grabbing his muddy diaper. She tried desperately to slide closer to him as the slippery cloth in her hand inched slowly down his legs toward his feet. Her pain returned, battering her with the force of a cannonball.

She was unconscious, clutching an empty diaper, when Avery and Jim slogged through the mud and found her. She opened her eyes for a moment as Avery knelt on the wet ground and lifted her bulging body in his arms.

When she next awoke she was in a bed, snug and dry in Avery's clinic. Avery was holding a crying baby in a blanket. Ginger felt her abdomen: it was flat again. Confused, she closed her eyes and sank once more into the comforting dark world of unawareness.

Searchers found Tonito's mangled body the next day, two miles downcreek from the mesa. Little Johnny, battered almost beyond recognition, was discovered wedged in a pile of debris nearby.

Avery attended the double funeral at the Indians' little Catholic church. He followed the mourners to the barren Indian cemetery, where he watched in stunned misery as father and son, sharing a wooden coffin, were lowered into the ground. Along with the other mourners, Avery threw a handful of dirt into the grave, as was the Indians' custom, before the pallbearers filled the grave and erected a cross.

He didn't tell Ginger about the funeral—he couldn't— because she was barely conscious, with a high fever, in a stupor edging on madness.

CHAPTER
6

1922

Ginger's new son was two months old before she recovered her health enough to name the baby. "Of course he must be named after Tonito," she said when Avery brought up the subject. "Antonio Alvarez. But let's call him Tony." She was sitting up in bed, still at Avery's house, holding the baby for the first time since his birth. "He looks a lot like Tonito, don't you think?" She looked tremulously up at Avery. Adele stood next to him, staring at the baby with admiration—and envy.

Avery examined the baby's face with a critical eye. "Hmmm. I suppose so." He sighed. He knew Ginger was physically recovered enough to go home, and even resume her work at the inn. But she still had sudden frantic fits of weeping and long dark hours of melancholy. "Are you sure you want to live up there on that isolated mesa again?" he asked hesitantly. "Why not move closer in—"

"No!" She was fierce about it. "That's my home!"

"But you aren't strong enough—"

"I'll be all right, Avery. Rosa doesn't mind working full-time and sleeping over. She'll take good care of us."

He nodded, wishing for the thousandth time that Ginger could stay with him forever. Not here, but in Paris, his beloved Paris. Or was that an impossible dream? Could a man approaching forty ever recapture the Paris of his youth? Somehow, in all his daydreams about running off with Ginger, Adele conveniently disappeared. But in reality she was very much present. Her illness had reached a plateau. She had enough strength to do a few housewifely chores, which made her feel that she was no longer a complete burden to Avery. At night she offered her frail, unresponsive body to him with so much love that he didn't have the heart to refuse it. She still tired easily, and some days she had to stay in bed, but she was cheerful and tried to be helpful, especially with little Tony. She was captivated by the infant and dreaded the day Ginger would take him home.

Meanwhile, Avery did what he could for Ginger. While she was recuperating, he hired a carpenter to repair the roof of her cabin. With Rosa's help Avery removed the rain-damaged rugs and bought new ones, put up fresh curtains, painted the walls. He had her road regraded and culverts installed and the creek widened to prevent future flood damage.

When he finally accompanied her back home in his new Packard, with Jim at the wheel, Avery held her hand tightly, afraid she would break down at the sight of her cabin. As the car climbed up the mesa and stopped, he kept a careful eye on her drawn face.

"If only we had listened to you that day," she said mournfully.

"Jim and I started out the minute it began to rain. By the time we got here, your road was like Niagara Falls, so we had to use the driveway to your grandfather's house and come around that way—slipping and sliding through the mud. But *I* should have insisted that you leave that morning."

"Don't blame yourself, Avery. It wasn't your fault." She got out of the car, handed the baby to Avery, fell into Rosa's arms, and wept anew. "Don't worry," she sobbed to Avery after a while, "someday I'll run out of tears."

She didn't run out of them soon enough, as far as Avery was concerned. He understood the need for grief, and the danger of trying to suppress it, but ever since Ginger had returned to the mesa, she had been unable—or unwilling—to recover from her sorrow in the slightest degree.

Avery came to see her every afternoon when he finished with his patients. Invariably he found her sitting on the porch, staring blankly out at the desert, tears flowing down her cheeks. To his repeated suggestions that she resume walking with him at dawn, her only reply was a despondent shaking of their head.

Nellie also visited Ginger daily, and each time Nellie urged her to come back to work, Ginger simply shook her head and made no other reply. Like Avery, Nellie found Ginger totally withdrawn.

Avery and Nellie both realized that Ginger, who had always been such an enthusiastic, devoted mother to Johnny, seemed to give little Tony only the most perfunctory attention, leaving his care almost entirely to Rosa.

Tony, too, was strangely quiet, as though he had been infected by his mother's sorrow. Avery couldn't help but compare him to Johnny at that age. Johnny had been bright and bouncy, with curious eyes and strong fingers ready to grasp everything in sight. Avery vowed to himself that he would do everything in his power to be a substitute father to Tony, but remembering Tonito's youthful, joyful enthusiasm for fatherhood, Avery knew he could never make up for Tony's loss.

Ginger knew that she was neglecting Tony, that her unrelenting sorrow was unhealthy for her, that she ought to start riding Se-San and go hiking with Avery again, and that it was time she returned to work. But she was paralyzed, trapped in a web of utter lassitude.

One day when Avery's visit and Nellie's coincided, they left the cabin together. "Heavens!" Nellie exclaimed, looking out at the view. "Wouldn't this be a heavenly spot for a small hotel!"

Avery gazed around the mesa. "Is there enough room up here?"

"Oh, sure. Ginger's often talked about having a small, intimate place." They started down the driveway at a rapid clip.

"Hmmm." Nellie's words had planted a seed in Avery's head. "Tell me, how is the hotel business, Nellie? Your place seems busy as a beehive."

"It couldn't be better, Avery. Palm Springs is getting so popular, I have to turn people away all the time."

Avery nodded. "So a small hotel up here might be a good investment?"

"Yup."

"I'll bet Ginger could run a crackerjack little hotel," he mused.

"She knows the business inside out," Nellie said. "Anybody who invested in it could make a bundle."

"And it might take her mind off her grief," Avery added cautiously.

Nellie jabbed his side with her elbow. "Come on, Avery, why don't you give her the money?"

He smiled wryly. "What makes you think I have that kind of money?"

"Don't try to kid me, kiddo. Everyone knows your family was loaded."

He was thoughtful. "Well, it's not such a bad idea. Maybe I'll bring it up with her . . . when the time seems right."

Tonito's sister, Maria, also visited Ginger daily. The young Indian woman felt triple sorrow: for her dearly loved brother, for her adorable nephew, and for her bereaved sister-in-law, who was her favorite friend. Maria's round face showed the ravages of days of weeping.

Maria was married now, to an Italian immigrant who a year earlier had taken the train from Los Angeles to Indio, planning to visit relatives working at a date farm there. By mistake, Vittorio had gotten off the train too soon and had ended up in Palm Springs instead. His talent as a master carpenter quickly was appreciated by Nellie, who was constantly on the lookout for competent workmen. So Vittorio had stayed on, had met Maria, and had been captivated by her merry dark eyes, rosy cheeks, and cheerful disposition.

Trying to distract Ginger from her lethargy, Maria began an amusing story about her efforts to teach English to Vittorio and how he mangled the language, but Ginger didn't even give her a wan smile. "Don't you see, Ginger? When Mrs. Coffman said she wanted the *whole* cabin remodeled, Vittorio thought she wanted him to dig a *hole* and he got mad and told her he was a master carpenter, not a common laborer who dug holes. Only he was so upset he told it to her in Italian, and she didn't know what on earth he was talking about . . ." Maria's voice trailed off. It was no use.

She took Ginger's hand and leaned forward, staring

intently into Ginger's face. "Listen, there's something important I have to tell you, Ginger, please pay attention. Look at me!"

Responding to the urgency in Maria's voice, Ginger slowly turned and stared at her. "What?"

"The tribe is going to have a Ceremony for the Dead tomorrow night—for Tonito and Johnny."

Abruptly Ginger pulled her hand out of Maria's grasp. "No! I won't go."

"Ginger, you *have* to. The tribe will never understand if you don't."

"I don't care."

"You have to care! Think of little Tony . . . he's half Indian, Ginger. You want him to care about the tribe, don't you? And for the tribe to care about him?"

Ginger shrugged.

"Look, if you don't go, you'll break Pa's heart—he's so broken up about Tonito and Johnny as it is . . ." Maria grabbed her hand again. "Ginger, Tonito would want you to go!"

"Oh?" Ginger asked forlornly. "Would he?"

"Of course he would! He loved all our old customs and ceremonies and beliefs."

"But he told me they were just old legends."

"Sure, we all say that. The priests don't like our old ways, and we want to be good Catholics too. So we say our old beliefs are just legends. But they still mean a lot to us."

Ginger blinked, looked down at Maria's hand holding hers, then up at Maria's face as though seeing her for the first time. Ginger nodded. "Okay. For Tonito . . . I'll go."

The next night, Avery drove Ginger to the Tribal Big House, the Agua Calientes' sacred round building where important ceremonies were held. There, on a wooden bench, Ginger sat between Avery and Juan Pedro; Maria was on the other side of the old man, now wizened and close to death himself. His face had collapsed into a web of tiny wrinkles and his eyes were nearly hidden by his loose-skinned lids. He took Ginger's hand as they sobbed together quietly.

Avery held her other hand and hoped fervently that

the ceremony wouldn't be too painful for her. He had no idea what to expect, nor did she. He gazed up at the room's high-pitched palm-frond roof and its steeply sloped arrow-weed walls. The only illumination came from a few torches and a coal fire burning in the center of the dirt floor. Circles of benches surrounded the fire and were filled with all the tribal members except Rosa, who was taking care of Tony.

Ginger gasped in horror when two women entered carrying life-size effigies of Tonito and Johnny. The figures were made of cotton and stuffed with grass. Noses and ears were stitched on, and the facial features were embroidered with surprising likeness. The large effigy wore Tonito's dark blue suit, the one he had been married in. The child's figure was dressed in Ginger's favorite of all Johnny's clothes, a pair of light blue rompers with red trim around the neck and arms—"Like Skeezix wears, in the funny papers," Tonito had said when he bought the rompers at Lykken's store the previous summer.

"How did they get those clothes?" Ginger asked indignantly.

"I got them out of your closet when you were still recovering at Avery's," Maria replied defiantly. "We had to have them."

Quickly Ginger hid her face against Avery's broad chest. He put his arms around her protectively, fervently wishing they hadn't come. God only knew what this would do to her, weak as she was. He watched disapprovingly as the two women carrying the effigies slowly danced around the fire while the women in the audience began a monotonous chant, their voices rising and falling, rising and falling.

Still leaning against Avery, Ginger turned her head and peeked at the dancers. She felt dizzy and the smoke from the fire was giving her a headache. She was glad Avery was there to hold her in his comforting arms. Ruefully she remembered how thrilled she would have been to have him hold her like this all the years she had fought her attraction to him, but now she felt nothing, nothing at all. They both might also have been stuffed effigies for all she cared.

For the next three hours she stared hypnotically at the dancers as they gradually increased their tempo, going faster and faster around the circle. A few times she dozed, then awoke, startled. She still held on to her father-in-law's hand, gathering strength from his frail presence.

Avery was disgusted with himself. In the midst of all the smoke and heat, the bizarre dancing and the wailing, he was happy because he was holding Ginger in his arms. Her head was against his cheek, he could smell the fragrance of her hair. He was sexually stirred, and felt ashamed, but he couldn't help it. There it was.

They sat that way for three hours, Avery savoring the feel of her body against him, Ginger in a trancelike state, Juan Pedro grasping her hand as though hanging on to life itself. The stuffy dark room harbored a cacophony of sounds: wailing, chanting, sobbing, wheezing, coughing, and the rhythmic stamping of the dancers' feet.

All at once the two women carrying the effigies stopped whirling and stood still. The audience fell silent, watching the two dancers carrying the effigies as they walked solemnly out of the Tribal Big House. The spectators rose and lit torches and followed in a mournful procession to the Indian burial ground. There the effigies were placed upon Tonito's and Johnny's joint grave while the tribal members seated themselves on the ground in a circle around the grave.

"Everyone's going to stay here till dawn, singing our traditional songs," Maria whispered to Ginger and Avery. "Then they'll set fire to the effigies. They'll all scream and cry . . ." She touched Ginger's cheek affectionately. "You'd better go now. It's enough that you came for the ceremony. You're not well enough to stay all night."

"Thanks," Avery murmured gratefully. He led Ginger to his waiting car and drove her back to her cabin. "Are you all right?" he asked when they reached her door.

She nodded.

It was a beautiful night, star-filled and moonlit. "Ginger, why don't you build your own hotel? Up here." He gestured at the mesa. "I'll lend you the money, and Nellie said she'd help you get started. . . ."

She turned her head and looked at the land, first at the view and then at the forest of dark trees and the shiny rocks of the foothills beyond. "What an idea," she said flatly.

He couldn't tell what she meant. That it was a silly

idea? Or a good one? When she eased her arm from his grasp and went inside, he was reluctant to let go of her. He hated himself for wanting her still, after all this time. *You crazy old fool*! he kept berating himself as he returned to his car and headed home.

In the room where Tony and Rosa slept, Ginger stopped at Tony's crib and touched the baby's face. He was beautiful, Tonito in miniature. She wondered if someday he'd have his father's verve and intelligence and capacity for joy. She certainly wasn't doing much to give him a happy infancy.

Without undressing, she dropped onto her bed and fell asleep at once. She woke up suddenly, just before dawn. Throwing a shawl over her shoulders, she ran outside and stood at the edge of the mesa. She could see several torches still burning down at the Indian burial ground. As she watched, a blaze like a bonfire shot up. It must be the effigies burning, she realized.

Ginger felt a lightening of her spirit, as though she had been encased in a suffocating shell and it was beginning to fall away. She went inside, where Rosa and Tony were stirring. As she took the baby from his crib, she was painfully aware of how much the little creature was being cheated. *Poor baby*, she silently mourned, *you have no father and a terrible mother.*

With choking pain she remembered the intimacy she had shared with Johnny while nursing him. But Tony had been on a bottle from birth. There had been no way she could have breast-fed him those first two months of his life, when she had barely been conscious most of the time.

Rosa started to get out of bed, but Ginger shook her head. "Sleep awhile longer, Rosa," she urged. "I'll give Tony his bottle." She held him while fixing his formula and warming it on the kerosene stove. But when she sat down and put the bottle to his mouth, he gazed at her face, startled. His little features bunched up and he wailed, looking over at Rosa.

"Shhh," Ginger crooned, stroking his head and smiling down at him. After a moment he reluctantly accepted the rubber nipple and sucked on it while staring up at her with perplexed eyes and making little whimpering sounds.

My God, she thought in panic, *he doesn't even know me*!

Ella's son was born two months after Tony. She had no trouble convincing Frank that "their" son was born prematurely, so certain was Frank of his paternity. Ella gave birth in a fashionable private maternity hospital, where she was attended by three obstetricians. At home in the Ricardos' hillside estate an elaborate nursery awaited the infant. Ella had ordered the custom-made nursery furniture from New York, and the little hand-sewn garments from France. Shelves of stuffed animals and toys filled the room's walls. Ella had hired a cheerful young Mexican woman named Juanita, from Palm Springs, to be his nursemaid.

In the delivery room, Ella had been given an anesthetic, but the moment she woke up she demanded to see the baby. A nurse brought him in and Ella quickly examined him. His skin was darker than hers, but no darker than Frank's, certainly not dark enough to give away his paternity. Expelling a sigh of great relief, Ella handed the infant back to the nurse.

"Aren't you nursing him?" the woman asked.

"Are you *crazy*?"

Far more thrilled about the baby than Ella, Frank pranced around the hospital like a drunk puppy. "My little Calvin, my adorable Cal," he cooed in glee, again and again rushing to the nursery window to see the baby. "He's gorgeous! Gorgeous! He looks just like his beautiful little mama!"

And so Tonito's son was legally named Calvin Ricardo. Ella had let Frank decide what the baby's name would be, to make up for the fact that it wasn't his. Frank had chosen "Calvin" because the nation's vice-president happened to be his personal friend and Frank greatly admired Mr. Coolidge.

Of course, Ella was the only person in the world who knew that Cal was Tonito's son and not Frank's. She was a little regretful that Tonito was dead and would never know that their passion had produced a child. She thought it was sort of romantic.

Yet she knew she was not as sorry about Tonito's death as she ought to be. Months before he died, her desire for him had cooled. After all, she had realized, when you came right down to it, he was just an unsophisticated, penniless Indian, despite his fancy education. There were plenty of other men around who were bound to be as thrilling as Tonito had been in bed. As soon as she was up and around and completely recovered, she was eager to do some fancy research on the subject.

Someday, Ella promised herself—if she could be sure it wouldn't get back to Frank—she was going to tell Ginger that Tonito was Calvin's father. Ella was no longer sure why she needed to "get even" with her sister. But get even she would.

One day in early March, Ginger was surprised to see Avery's car, driven by Jim, climb up to her cabin. The chauffeur helped Adele out of the back seat as Ginger came out to greet her visitor.

While hugging her and kissing her cheek, Ginger saw that Adele had dressed with obvious care for the visit and even wore a pale lipstick. Ginger took the older woman by the arm and led her out to the porch overlooking the view of the desert.

"May I hold Tony?" Adele asked as soon as she sat down.

"He's napping."

"Oh!" Adele leaned back in her chair, her pale, fine-featured face sagging with disappointment.

Ginger smiled. "Oh, well, he's slept long enough. I'll go get him." She brought the drowsy baby out and put him into Adele's eager arms.

Adele gazed dreamily at the infant, then smiled over at Ginger. "I haven't been much of an aunt to you, have I?"

"Aunt?" Ginger was surprised. She had always considered Adele a friend, despite the difference in their ages.

"Of course I'm your aunt. My sister was your stepmother, after all."

"I never thought of it that way." She touched Adele's arm fondly. "But you *have* been wonderful to me."

Adele shook her head. "I don't have the energy most days to be wonderful to anyone. But, Ginger, I do want to be a real aunt to Tony." She sighed wistfully. "Look, I'm thirty-six years old. I have to be realistic. I've finally accepted the fact that I'll never have a child of my own."

She gazed down at the sleepy baby in her arms. "But if you'll let me, I want to be close to Tony."

"*Let* you," Ginger echoed. "Of course I'll let you! How can you doubt it? Tony needs all the love he can get."

Adele nodded happily. "I know Avery adores him. More like a grandfather than an uncle, I'd say." She hesitated, then asked shyly, "Could you bring Tony over and let him stay with me an hour or two, like . . . maybe twice a week or so? So he'll get to know me?"

"Of course, Adele," Ginger assured her, "you can see him as often as you want."

Ginger leaned back and watched Adele caress the baby. She had always admired her, but for a long time she had resented Adele. After all, if Avery hadn't been married—and married to a helpless invalid at that—then she might not have felt so guilty about being attracted to him.

Ah, but what did it matter now? Ginger thought despondently. All that churning emotion she had endured, all that extraordinary desire—God, it seemed like a million years ago, in another life.

It turned out that Adele and Tony were a godsend for each other. Every time she spent a few hours with Tony, Adele felt refreshed and rejuvenated. As for Tony, he gurgled with pleasure whenever he saw his "Auntie." Adele fixed up a spare bedroom as a nursery, furnishing it and stocking it with toys far more elaborately than Tony's room at home.

Ginger added gratitude to her affection for Adele. Ginger was only too well aware that she was shortchanging her baby. But try as she might, she couldn't muster much maternal feeling for him. Not that she didn't love him—she did! she did!—but it wasn't enough. She just felt so empty inside, so dead, so incapable of feeling anything but grief, still weeping pitifully whenever she thought of Tonito and Johnny and the beautiful idyll they had shared before it was all swept away in the flood.

By late March the desert was awash with a phenomenal crop of wildflowers of every hue, the only happy result of the disastrous December storm. The sandy flatlands were covered with a thick carpet of purple verbena for miles and miles. On the slopes, clumps of other flowers thrust up amid the rocks. As Ginger climbed a trail, she reeled off the names: fiddlehead, chuparosa, heliotrope, daisy, wild primrose, marguerite—her floral knowledge the legacy of her year of study with naturalist Ed Jaeger. She listened to the shrill jabbering of robins, meadowlarks, bluebirds, hummingbirds, orioles, wild doves, and herons while she inhaled the heady fragrance of orange blossoms. Carrying her three-month-old son in a cloth "papoose" pouch with shoulder straps that Maria had made for her, Ginger was on her way to meet Avery and talk about building a hotel together.

But hard as she tried to enjoy the flowers and the birds and her infant son, she knew she was only *acting* the part of a young woman doing those things. Inside, she felt like a robot, removed from all human feeling. Worse, she didn't even care. Still, she didn't want to worry Avery, so as she climbed the trail she rehearsed what she would say to him. She would smile, and even joke a little, and act enthusiastic about the plans for the hotel. She didn't give a damn about the hotel or anything else, but life had to go on, didn't it?

On their favorite mountainside ledge she found Avery waiting for her. He was wearing baggy khaki pants stuffed into ancient hiking boots, a red plaid shirt with the sleeves rolled up, and a battered straw hat, and despite the casual attire, he managed to look handsome and distinguished. He hadn't heard her coming, so she stopped and watched him for a moment. She remembered how once the sight of him had thrilled her. Now she felt nothing. Nothing. For him or for anyone else.

"Someday I'd like to see you in white tie and tails," she said lightly, forcing a smile.

"When Nellie finishes her fancy new buildings, I'll need a tux just to go have coffee with her." He gestured at a flat-topped rock and they sat down together. "Now, about your hotel. Have you finished the preliminary plans?"

She nodded. "I'm working with Bob Jellico—the architect my brother Neil fired. Bob's wild about my mesa, thinks it's the most spectacular setting he's ever seen."

"Why did Neil fire him?"

"Well, you know Neil. First my dear brother tried to bargain down Bob's fee. Bob was intrigued by the challenge of building on the desert—he has some really good ideas, like having thick walls and deep overhangs to keep the houses cool. So he let Neil talk him into taking a much smaller fee than he usually gets. Then, when Bob finished the plans and wanted to be paid, Neil insisted that Bob settle for half of what they'd originally agreed on. Well, Bob refused, Neil fired him, and Bob tore up the plans and threw them in Neil's face." Ginger grimaced. "My brother's only eighteen—awfully young to be such a monster."

"Yeah, it usually takes years of practice." He hesitated. "That land is rightfully yours, Ginger."

"Sure. Go tell that to Ella and Neil. Maybe they'll be kind enough to hand it right over!" Ginger sighed. "I'm glad Grandpa can't see the junky houses Neil's building on his beloved land. In a few years it'll be a shantytown."

Avery gestured at the expanding village spread out below them. "My land is scattered up and down Main Street and Indian Avenue . . . and I have acreage farther out too. At least we'll always have some open space."

"I can't believe how fast the town's changing, Avery. By next year we'll have a paved highway all the way to Los Angeles. Y'know what that means?"

"It means the world will be coming to us. *Invading* us." Avery shook his head sadly.

"And," Ginger continued, "the power lines are coming in soon. We'll have electric lights, and Frigidaires . . ."

"And radios with trashy music blaring out of every house!" Avery exploded. "It's mental rape! Who wants to know what's going on in the rest of the country the minute it happens? Do I really have to hear if some guy gets gunned down in Chicago? Or if there's a subway accident in New York? Or a riot in Germany?"

"Still, it *will* be helpful to have electricity for running a hotel . . ." She gazed out at the view. "But I hate the thought of those ugly poles and wires scarring up our desert."

"Progress, dear girl, progress. The day I dread is when they bring in telephone lines. Then our privacy will be gone forever." He gestured helplessly. "Now, what about your hotel?"

"*Our* hotel," she corrected him.

"It's yours, Ginger. I'm just lending you the money."

"You don't want to be partners?"

He shook his head. "It's all yours." He took Tony out of Ginger's arms and held him against his chest. "D'you mind if I sing to him?"

"I don't mind, but *he* might."

Avery laughed. He hummed a few bars and then sang a simple tune off-key in his deep baritone.

Impatiently she took a folded paper from her pocket. "Do you want to see the plans?"

He stopped singing. "Sure."

Ginger unfolded the paper. "Well, this is just a sketch, but as you can see, the dining room and glassed-in breakfast veranda and lobby go here, where the view is best. The first twelve guest bungalows will be scattered around the mesa—I guess we'll have to chop down a few trees, but not too many. And here in the center, we'll have a round swimming pool . . . I want it to look like a natural pond. See?" She showed him a sketch on another piece of paper. "Bob wants to divert some of the creek for a little waterfall. We'll use mostly native rock and white-washed adobe bricks for the buildings. And over here, behind the ironwood trees, later on I'll put in two or three tennis courts. Of course, if I'm successful with twelve bungalows, I'll gradually add more, but not too many. I think maybe thirty is the most I'll ever want."

"What about your cabin?"

"Oh, it's not in the way. I'll plant oleanders around it for privacy, but Tony and Rosa and I will still live there."

"Have you decided on a name for the hotel yet?"

She was thoughtful. "How d'you like 'The Springs'? That's what the Hollywood people call our town. They say, 'I'm going down to the Springs this weekend.' They think it sounds more chichi than plain old 'Palm Springs.' "

"Swell. It has a nice lilt."

"I'm glad you like it. Now, here, along the driveway, I'm going to plant a line of royal palms, and we'll put in loads of purple bougainvillea and red hibiscus, and pink and white oleanders all over the place . . ."

Avery let her ramble on, about the garden, the built-in furniture, the fabrics and wallpaper, the bay windows, the plumbing. He was impressed by the plans. They promised a small hotel of great beauty, comfort, and privacy. And the project did seem to be taking her mind off her grief. That alone would be worth every cent this project was going to cost him.

He was encouraged to see that she was no longer ignoring Tony. He fervently hoped she could make up for the months when she had been too ill to give the infant any attention at all. Avery knew that with Tony she still lacked the overwhelming bond of mother love she'd had with Johnny. Was she afraid to love the boy, he wondered, afraid that if she lost him too, the pain would be beyond endurance?

But despite her apparent enthusiasm for the hotel, something about her still seemed off-key to him. Sure, she was efficient and pleasant, but he had the impression that she was going through the motions of living without letting herself *feel* anything. Or was he just imagining it? If only he could take her in his arms and make her forget all the misery she had suffered!

Affectionately he looked down into the baby's face; it had a solemnity that was almost comical. He worried that the little fellow sometimes looked melancholy. Again, was he imagining it? Could anyone tell so early? But then, when Tony smiled, it was a wonder to behold, for it lit up every feature in his tiny face. His hair was dark like Tonito's, his eyes were amber-brown like Ginger's, his rose-bud mouth and cunning little tongue were pink and healthy.

Be happy, little Tony, Avery willed him. *Be happy and healthy . . . and someday when you fall in love*—Avery sighed as he looked over at Ginger—*be sure she loves you back!*

Avery was unaware that Ginger still cried at night, but her tears had turned from grief to anger. Actually, grief and anger were the only emotions she could feel anymore. She was furious with Tonito. Furious! *Why* had he insisted on going out and moving those stupid trees? *Why* had he been so stubborn and ignored her when she had *begged* him not to go out? *Why* hadn't he stayed in the cabin and protected her and Johnny, as he should have done? *Why? Why? Why?* By running out, Tonito had committed suicide and murdered Johnny. *"Oh, Tonito, you bastard! You goddamn bastard! You killed my baby!"* she sobbed into her pillow.

Most nights, she would steal out to the porch and sit there wrapped in a blanket until dawn, fighting the rage that was consuming her. It was so frustrating to be furious with a dead man. If only she could hit him! Slap him silly and punch him with all her might! *Fool-fool-fool!* she wanted to bellow.

She got over it after a while. She knew he hadn't wanted to die any more than she had wanted him to, that he'd only been trying to save her and Johnny and their home. When her anger left, it took some of her grief with it. She was calmer now, more accepting of the tragedy that had almost destroyed her. She had to get on with her life, raise her child, build her hotel.

Of one thing she was adamantly certain: she would never love anyone else. Tonito's dazzling face and virile body were all tangled up in her own being, as though she now embodied both of them. She had never met a man as handsome as Tonito, or as perfect. Yes, he had been absolutely *perfect*! She vowed never to forget that he had loved her passionately, that he had died trying to save her, and that she owed it to him to be faithful to his memory—for the rest of her life.

CHAPTER
7

1931–1934

"Hey, Ginger-baby, you're in luck! Tits're back in fashion!"

Ginger had been resting on a chaise beside her hotel's pool while listening to the hissing lisp of the nearby waterfall. She opened her eyes and smiled up at Gracie Hudson, a gravel-voiced two-hundred-pound comedienne who was almost as popular with American movie audiences as Mary Pickford and Janet Gaynor and Ginger's sister, Ella.

"It's true, kiddo," Gracie insisted. "I just got back from New York and I tell you, the flat-chested straight-up-and-down look is *out*. Everything's feminine now. Not that it matters to me." She gestured comically at her own body. "I look my best in a tent!"

Ginger stood up and hugged her guest. "Welcome back, Gracie. I missed you." They sat together on a padded stone bench.

"I missed you too, tootsie!" Gracie boomed. "But here I am. I wouldn't miss February here for anything."

"So . . . how *are* you, Gracie?"

"Dead on my feet."

"And New York?"

"Dismal. It's been that way for two years now—ever since the market crashed."

"Did you lose much?"

"Yeah, a bundle," Gracie admitted. "Mostly on paper. I jumped out the window, but lucky me, I was on the ground floor. How about you? The Depression hurting you yet?"

"Just the opposite. People who can't afford Europe anymore are coming here instead. I have a long waiting list. Same thing at Nellie's."

"Wonderful. I hear El Mirador's having trouble."

"Yeah, that's the rumor."

"I can't imagine why. Everybody I know is staying there. Marlene, Paulette and Charlie, Gary, Claudette, Alice and Phil, Dolores and John, Mary and Buddy—I swear, half of Hollywood's there every weekend." Gracie grimaced. "That's why I like to stay here. Not that I don't like those people—I do—but I see enough of 'em in town."

"Who'd ever have thought the great Gracie Hudson was a recluse?"

"Seriously, Ginger, I'm 'on' all the time. I need a place where I can unwind without hordes of fans bothering me."

"That's what all my famous guests say, Gracie. But none of you would *be* famous if you didn't have fans."

"Yeah, don't I know it! Sometimes I wonder if it's worth it." Gracie shook her head. "I wish Palm Springs would stay just the way it is. No crowds, no fans."

Ginger laughed. "People used to say you could shoot a cannon down Main Street in August and not hit anything. But that's not true anymore."

Gracie suddenly sat up straight and stared across the pool at a young woman whose sleeveless shirt stopped just below her breasts and whose shorts began below her waist, leaving an eight-inch strip of tanned skin exposed. "Now, what the hell is *that*?"

"A bare midriff. It's the latest rage here."

"Christ, Ginger, I swear, every year the shorts get shorter and the tops get skimpier. Pretty soon you're going to be running a nudist colony. But without me. I got too much to show."

"I hear you just did a picture with Ella," Ginger said.

Gracie peered at her quizzically. "I hope this doesn't offend you, Ginger, but your sister is one nasty bitch."

"What's she done now?"

"What hasn't she done! Miss Prima Donna! She terrified everyone on the set. God, if her fans only knew what a hard-boiled cookie she really is. The studio flacks make her sound like Miss Angelic. Did you know that ever since she divorced Frank Ricardo she's been testing every cock in sight? I guess she did it before the divorce too, but at least she was more discreet then. How old is she, anyway?"

"Um . . . twenty-nine."

"Christ! She looks nineteen. The way she drinks and screws around, you'd think she'd look fifty! What's her secret?"

"Same as Dorian Gray's."

"Dorian whose?"

"Never mind. Talking about age, today's my birthday, Gracie."

"Let me guess . . . you're twenty-six."

"Thirty-one. It's easy to remember because I'm the same age as the century."

"Well, happy birthday, toots. What *is* it with your family? Don't any of you ever age?"

"Ah, you're sweet. Anyway, Avery and Adele and Nellie are having a little dinner for me tonight—at Nellie's house, not in the Desert Inn dining room. Can you make it?"

Gracie hooted. "You bet I can! With bells on!"

Smiling and humming to herself, Ginger walked slowly back to her office next to the lobby. She loved her beautiful little hotel. The Springs. It was absolutely perfect. There were "regulars," guests who drove out from Los Angeles every weekend, and others from the East or up North who came and stayed all winter. She seldom had a vacancy and was making more money than she could spend. The previous month she had repaid Avery's loan in full. She kept plowing money back into the hotel. She now had thirty bungalows, each one decorated in a different style. All of her rooms were furnished with expensive antiques and increasingly valuable desert paintings by Jimmy Swinnterton, who had become famous, and by Carl Eytel, the gifted "old-timer" who had died a few years earlier. But no matter how much money she spent on the hotel, her savings account at the new Bank of America kept growing and growing.

She stood at the bay window in her office and looked down at Palm Springs. It was a far different vista from the one she first had seen nineteen years earlier. In fact, the town seemed to grow bigger every time she looked out of her window. A sea of roofs now blotted out much of the land where wild grass, rattlesnakes, and lizards had lived undisturbed since the beginning of time. Now there were seven hundred permanent residents who had begun talking cityhood, and every weekend a steady stream of automobiles invaded the town, bringing visitors who wanted to stay anywhere from one night to the rest of their lives.

She looked over at the pink tower of the new El Mirador Hotel, the favorite of most movie people these days. Nellie's Desert Inn appealed more to business tycoons and captains of industry from the Midwest and Canada. Pearl and Austin McManus had built an attractive hotel south of Nellie's, the Oasis. In contrast, Ginger's much smaller place was a retreat for those wanting peace and quiet—a few movie stars, but mostly writers and composers. Inexpensive eight- or ten-room establishments were springing up east of Indian Avenue and a lot of townspeople rented out a room or two in their homes during the winter season. In the midst of the Great Depression, Palm Springs was holding its own.

The town had a new schoolhouse, and about time—the one-room school Ginger had briefly attended dated back to 1895. She was delighted with the education nine-year-old Tony was getting from his dedicated teacher, Miss Katherine Finchy. The town now had a newspaper, the *Desert Sun*. There was a library, out behind the Community Church, but no librarian—people were on the honor system. And new shops opened every month as more and more people decided to live there. Electricity and telephones now were commonplace, making the old-timers nostalgic for candles and kerosene lanterns, even as they happily took their ice-cold bottles of beer from their Frigidaires.

But Palm Springs remained a small town in many ways, with few of the attractions—or problems—of civilization. Most of the streets remained unpaved. There were few sidewalks. And no crime. People seldom locked their doors. Surprisingly, this town, a mecca for the Hollywood crowd, still had no real motion-picture theater. If you wanted to see a movie, you went over to the schoolhouse one or two nights a week and watched whatever was being shown.

A gentle knock on the door interrupted Ginger's musings. It was Avery, holding a slim, gaily-wrapped package. "Happy birthday!" he said, grinning. His hair was silver now, which gave him a distinguished air. Ginger took the package from him and shook it. "Hmmm. What *can* it be?"

"Don't try to guess, because you won't in a million years." He gestured impatiently. "Just open it, will you?"

She tore off the ribbon and wrapping paper and lifted the cover from the box. Puzzled, she picked up a blue envelope and withdrew two round-trip train tickets to New York in a Pullman stateroom . . . and two round-trip first-class tickets on the *Ile de France* from New York to Le Havre. She looked up at him. "I don't understand . . ."

"Simple! Adele and I are taking you and Tony to Paris for the summer. After you close this place down for July and August. We have reservations at the Plaza in New York and the Ritz in Paris."

"Avery! I don't know *what* to say!"

"Say, 'Thank you, Avery dear,' for God's sake."

"Thank you, Avery dear," she parroted obediently. She was stunned, overwhelmed, for a moment too thrilled to move. Then she kissed him warmly on the cheek. "You angel! Am I glad now that Polly made me study French. How I suffered with that language! But tell me, can you get away for two whole months?"

He nodded. "I just hired a second assistant."

Ginger hesitated. "And Adele? Is she really up to traveling so far?"

"She says she is. She'll have to take it easy, and rest a lot." He beamed at Ginger. "I have more good news. Old Mrs. Offenbach's heirs want to sell your grandfather's house. Wanna buy it back?"

She fell into her chair. "Oh, Avery, it's been my *dream*, ever since the day Papa sold it. I was after her for years, begging her to sell it to me, but she said her sons wanted it after she died."

"Well, the sons live in Seattle now, so I guess they changed their minds. Anyway, they phoned me because I took care of their mother and they didn't know who else to call."

"How much do they want for it?" she asked eagerly.

"The bargain of the century. Not much more than your father sold it for fifteen years ago."

"How *much*, Avery?"

"Ten thousand."

"I'll buy it!" She pointed at the phone on her desk. "Hurry! Call them and tell them I'll buy it!"

"Oh, there's plenty of time," he drawled.

"Avery, please! Someone else could grab it!"

"There's no hurry," he said slowly, pausing teasingly. "I already told them you'd buy it!"

"Oh, Avery!" She looked into his face with glowing eyes. "I haven't been inside the house since I was sixteen."

"Didn't Mrs. Offenbach ever invite you?"

"Oh, sure, every time I saw her on the street. But I wouldn't! I just couldn't! Especially after she painted it green!" She whirled around the room with joy. "Avery, I can't wait to move back in! *After* I have it painted pink, like it's supposed to be!" She stopped suddenly and looked stricken. "Oh! But it means leaving the cabin that Tonito built . . . that he *died* to save . . ." He voice trailed off sadly. She had made the cabin very comfortable, adding an indoor bathroom and two extra rooms.

"Look at it this way, Ginger-girl. You and Tony and Rosa are pretty crowded in the cabin, even with your addition. Besides, Tonito knew how much you loved your grandpa's house. He'd be very, very happy for you."

"You're right. But that cabin was mine and Tonito's . . . I can't bear to have anyone else live in it. I know! I'll have it torn down. I could use the land for another tennis court, anyway."

The birthday-dinner guests included Tony, Avery, and of course Nellie, as well as the comic Gracie Hudson in a bright red-and-white-striped dress that really did look like a tent. Maria was there with her Vittorio, who finally had learned English and spoke it with a charming accent. Pearl and Austin McManus brought Ginger an album with photographs of her mother and grandparents that Pearl's father had taken in the early days of the village. The final guest was Talbot Honeycutt, a successful screenwriter and heir to an eastern department-store fortune, who was spending his second winter in one of Ginger's bungalows.

"Your sister's back in town," Nellie whispered to Ginger before they sat down, "but I didn't think you'd want me to invite her."

"I'm glad you didn't, Nellie."

"I feel sorry for her son. Ella leaves the poor boy here all alone in that dreadful Arabian mansion of hers, month after month, with nobody to look after him but his Mexican nursemaid and a bunch of servants." Nellie shook her head in disapproval. "I did try to reach your brother," Nellie went on, "but his butler said Neil's in London."

"That was kind of you, Nellie. I know he's not your favorite person."

"He's not anybody's. Except maybe those floozies he's always got hanging around that garish monstrosity he built for himself."

Ginger nodded in agreement. Neil's mansion *was* a monstrosity. He had wanted the biggest, most imposing house in Palm Springs. But he had hired and fired so many architects and had insisted upon using such cheap contractors that his place was a hodgepodge of styles. Ginger duitifully invited him for dinner when he was in town, even though they constantly disagreed about the cracker-box developments he continued to build on their grandfather's land.

The guests formed an unusually convivial group. Tony, now nine, was accustomed to adult company, having lived most of his life at his mother's hotel surrounded by the adoring staff and guests. He resembled his father in many ways, not only physically—he had also inherited Tonito's scholastic and athletic abilities.

Avery had come without Adele—she'd had one of her poor days and had gone to bed early. He watched "his birthday girl" with pride. His secret yearning for her had been going on for so long now—*My God,* he thought, *fifteen years!*—that it had become like a chronic ailment he had learned in self-defense to tolerate without too much pain.

Talbot Honeycutt sat directly across the table from Ginger, and it was obvious to everyone there, even Tony, that Talbot was madly in love with her. He hardly spoke, but kept staring at her with a dazed expression. Often described in gossip columns as "dashing," "sophisticated," and "handsome as the movie stars whose roles he creates," Talbot was nearly forty and had been married and divorced twice, both times to socialites.

Ginger was well aware of Talbot's infatuation with her, but she didn't consider it "love." He led such a glamorous life—hopping from Cannes to Deauville to Bar Harbor to his Nob Hill mansion in San Francisco, forever place-dropping and name-dropping—that she believed he was too shallow to be capable of love. He did amuse her, and she was even fond of him. But *love*? She decided to put him in his place. She rose and held up her glass of bootleg Dom Perignon, which Avery had brought. "I want to make a toast to all you delightful people," she said loudly and clearly, "and to the one who is always in my thoughts . . . my beloved Tonito!"

Tony stood at once and enthusiastically lifted his glass of milk to toast his dead father. The others rose to their feet and held up their glasses, though Nellie and Avery showed some reluctance. Nellie was impatient with Ginger: to be young and beautiful and to pine for nine years after a dead man—even one as remarkable as Tonito— seemed a terrible waste to Nellie. Avery was equally annoyed with Ginger: why couldn't she put her dead husband to rest? She needed to fall in love again—God, if only he were free—but she never would love anyone, not until she let go of Tonito's ghost.

Talbot took her toast like a slap in the face. Still, he found her irresistible. If someone had asked him to portray a perfect woman in one of his scripts, he would simply have described Ginger. He loved the way she looked, the way she walked and talked, her intelligence, and her goodness of heart. Talbot always judged people by how they treated their servants—he'd divorced his last wife partly because of her imperious attitude toward their help—and here was Ginger, with a staff of thirty, always considerate and kind to the people who worked for her.

He, too, realized that she would never love him nor anyone else as long as she hung on to Tonito's memory with such fervor. He hoped that with patience and persistence he might someday make that memory fade.

* * *

Ella was having trouble with Cal. When she arrived in Palm Springs from Hollywood one afternoon, she found him dead drunk. She wasn't the most conscientious mother—far from it—but this really frightened her. Cal was only nine! She had the servants put him to bed and the next morning she slapped his face, hard. "If I ever catch you drinking again," she screamed, "I'll stop your allowance."

"I don't care! Daddy gives me all the money I want." He stared back at her belligerently. He was tall for his age, almost her height. His face was a male version of hers, with the same perfectly formed features. The only difference between them was that he had darker skin and brown hair and eyes instead of her blond, blue-eyed coloring.

"All right! I'm firing Juanita."

"No! Mummy, no! I promise! I'll be good!" Ella's threat threw Cal into a panic. Juanita Valenzuela was the only stability in his life. He loved her. She was his whole family! All his life, she had been there for him when no one else was. She played with him and took care of him when he was ill and saw to it that he was properly fed and that he studied. She had spoken Spanish to him since his infancy, so that now he spoke it as flawlessly as English.

Often she took him to her parents' house, an adobe shack with a palm-thatched roof that the Valenzuelas rented from an Indian family. Cal loved Juanita's parents, who treated him like the rest of their eleven children. Oh, the fun he had with all of them! He developed a lifelong craving for corn tortillas and tamales and beans and the Mexican ballads they all sang. He helped the Valenzuela children make candy from barrel cactus by carefully peeling off the sharp thorns and boiling the insides. They all played a noisy game of whacking date beetles with boards. He waded barefoot with them down the flooded dirt streets after the rain, squishing the mud through his toes. He went swimming with them in the irrigation ditches when the weather turned hot—much more fun than playing alone in his mother's fancy tile swimming pool. And always there were picnics, picnics, picnics. . . .

"Please, Mummy," he begged. "Please don't fire her."

Ella was unmoved. "Dammit, she let you drink, didn't she? Can you deny it?"

"No, no, Mummy, it was her day off, she didn't even know!" He was sobbing, hanging on to Ella's arm. "Someone else left the liquor cabinet unlocked! I didn't know I'd get sick from it. Mummy, Mummy . . . *pleeeease!*"

Ella was adamant. She called in the nursemaid and coldly told her to pack her things.

Cal threw himself at the stunned young Mexican woman. He clutched her around the waist and screamed hysterically. When Ella tried to pry him off, he kicked at her so furiously she was forced to retreat a few feet.

"Let *go* of her!" Ella raged. She took the fireplace poker and hit him across the buttocks. "Let *go*! Let *go*!" Cal's refusal enraged her further. She hit him harder, on his legs and arms, until he finally lost his grip and fell backward onto the floor, screaming in pain.

Juanita went to him at once, to comfort him and help him up, cooing soft soothing words in Spanish.

"Get *out* of here!" Ella shrieked hysterically. She raised the poker as though to hit the woman, then thought better of it. "Just get the hell *out*!"

Cal jumped up and started to run after Juanita, but Ella grabbed his arm. "It's time you grew up," she raged, breathing hard. "I'm sending you to military school!"

Frank Ricardo had tried several times to get custody of Cal. Ella knew that Frank was a far better parent than she was—he adored Cal—but Ella had fought Frank fiercely and even perjured herself in court, though nobody could prove it. She was enough of an actress to fool the judge into believing that she was motherhood personified, despite witnesses to the contrary. There was no way she'd let Frank have custody of a boy who wasn't really his.

She had the housekeeper buy a new lock for the liquor cabinet and a few days later she went up to The Springs to see Ginger.

"What a surprise," Ginger said dryly. "Let's go sit outside." She led the way. As always, she felt a quick lift of pleasure at the sight of her hotel's garden. She had planned it all: the border of majestic royal palms and the pink oleanders Tony had helped her plant when he was three years old, the masses of purple bougainvillea and pink hibiscus, the sparkling round blue pool surrounded by smooth slabs of slate, the gaily striped pink-and-white umbrellas and chaises. The only part for which she couldn't take full credit was San Jacinto's dramatic rocky flank rising up behind it all.

"I need your advice," Ella said quickly as they sat down at a table. "It's Cal. I don't know how to handle him."

"You haven't had much practice," Ginger said, not unkindly. She gazed at her younger sister: Ella wore a clinging blue sundress that hugged her lovely round breasts and tiny waist, then fell in graceful folds around her slim hips, stopping above her knees to reveal her shapely tanned legs. Her sandals looked like Cinderella's glass slippers with four-inch heels. Ella's long pale blond hair was beautifully curled and her skin was as smooth as a teenager's. Gracie was right: Ella did look a luscious nineteen.

"Well . . . what would you do, Ginger, if you found Tony drunk?"

"Tony? Drunk?" Ginger couldn't imagine it. "Why, I . . . I guess I'd talk to him . . ."

"That's just it! Cal won't *listen* to me! He laughs in my face." Ella frowned. "D'you think I should send him to a military academy?"

"Ella, how can I advise you? I hardly know Cal. A strict school might help, but then again, it might make him rebel even worse." Ginger saw that Talbot had emerged from his bungalow and was coming toward the pool.

Ella saw him too and her face underwent a swift change, from concerned mother to sexually aroused woman. "What a dreamboat," she cooed softly. "Who *is* he, Ginger?"

"I'm surprised you don't know him. He's doing a script for Gloria Swanson."

Talbot stopped at their table. "May I?" He put a hand on a vacant chair.

"Sure," Ginger said politely. "Talbot Honeycutt, my sister, Ella Ricardo."

"Of course. I recognized you at once," he said to Ella. "I didn't realize you were Ginger's sister."

Ella gave him a seductive smile. "Oooh, Talbot

Honeycutt, I've heard such wonderful things about you!"
She pouted. "How come you've never written a screen-
play for me?"

"Well, we happen to work for different studios, Mrs.
Ricardo—"

"Oh, please! Do call me Ella." She grinned impishly.
"And be sure you *do* call me." She took a card from her
purse. "Here's my number."

Talbot was taken aback, but he slipped the card into a
book he was carrying, then turned his attention to Ginger. "Where's Tony? I thought I'd ask him to go riding
with me after I swim."

"He's over at Avery's—helping 'Auntie' Adele in the
garden." Ginger smiled archly. "Aren't you working today? Or did your typewriter break down?"

He grinned. "Who could work on a gorgeous afternoon like this?"

Ella was utterly astonished. The man was *ignoring* her.
Was he some kind of pervert? Well, she wasn't going to
put up with such treatment. She'd just say something
scathing to him and then leave. She stood up. "Well, so
long, Ginger. As for *you*, Mr. Talbot Honeycutt"—
quickly Ella decided to give him a second chance—"I'll
be sitting by my little old telephone waiting for your call,
honey."

Talbot watched her leave. "What gall! Does she really
expect me to phone her?"

"Most men do."

"Christ, I can't believe she's your sister! The gossip is
that she's a hopeless nympho."

"A what?"

"A nymphomaniac. Crazy for sex." He laughed. "Good
God, Ginger, you're so innocent."

She blushed. "Is that a crime?"

"Come on, I didn't mean to offend you." He touched
her cheek. "Oh, dammit all, Ginger, I wish you'd give
me a chance!"

She looked away, hiding her annoyance. "Talbot, I'm
flattered that you want me, but I've told you a dozen
times, I'll never marry again."

"Hell, Ginger, you're too young to spend the rest of
your life in mourning. I *know* I could make you happy—"

"I'm quite happy as I am."

"Tony isn't. He needs a father."

"Avery's like a father to him."

"That old goat! I think he's in love with you himself."

Ginger gave him a shocked look. "Don't be ridiculous!"

"Oh, Christ, I give up!" Talbot rose angrily and dived into the pool. He swam underwater the length of the pool, and when he came up for air, Ginger had left.

The summer abroad was a magnificent adventure for all four of them. Tony's dark eyes absorbed every sight they beheld. Ginger, easily impressed and seldom one to disparage, constantly was "oohing" and "aahing" over the art, the architecture, the views, and the historical significance of everything they saw in New York and Paris. Adele had to limit her sightseeing to an hour or two a day, but her enthusiasm matched Ginger's and Tony's. For Avery much of the trip was *déjà vu*, but nevertheless seeing his favorite art treasures and buildings through the enthusiastic eyes of his companions heightened the pleasure he took in them.

It started in New York as they gawked up at the newly completed Empire State Building. "Hey," Tony cried, "it's almost as tall as good old San Jacinto!" Their adjoining suites at the Plaza, overlooking Central Park, were the most luxurious any of them ever had occupied, but the grandeur was quickly eclipsed by their first-class shipboard staterooms on the *Ile de France*, which contained more lace, satin, and gilt than any of them had seen at one time.

In Paris they thrilled to all the great sights—the Louvre, the Arc de Triomphe, the Opéra, the Seine, the Eiffel Tower, Montmartre, the Avenue des Champs Elysées. But what delighted Tony the most were the bathrooms at the Ritz, especially the gold-plated faucets in the shape of swans.

"Hey, Mom, compare this to our old cabin back home," Tony giggled their first day there. He gestured at the thronelike toilet, huge tub, and double marble sinks. "It's funny to think . . . until a few years ago, we still used a privy!" He scowled at the bidet. "What do you suppose this is? A bathtub for cats?"

"They're called bidets," Ginger said. "It's for . . . well, rinsing off, if you don't want to take a whole bath."

She smoothed his hair with a mixture of pride and worry. He was such a dear child. He did everything well, he was even-tempered, and he never gave her a moment's trouble. And that was exactly why she was worried about him.

"Shouldn't he be naughty sometimes?" she asked Avery later when Tony went downstairs to explore the lobby and Adele took a nap.

Avery nodded. "It sounds funny, a mother complaining that her kid is *too* good. But I know what you mean. I myself wonder: is Tony holding something in? Or is it possible that he actually *is* perfectly well-adjusted? I don't know the answer, Ginger."

"I wish I felt closer to him," she said softly. "I mean, we *are* close, very close. We can talk freely to each other, we do a lot together, I love him, he loves me. But . . ." Her eyes filled with tears. "Oh, Avery, I've never felt quite the same about Tony as I did about"—she swallowed hard—"as I did about Johnny. That incredible *surge* of maternal love—even after all these years, I still feel it every time I think of my poor dead baby."

Avery took her hand. "Ginger-girl, just enjoy Tony and stop analyzing the situation. Wait till he's a teenager. I'll bet anything he won't be so well-behaved by then."

Tony burst back into the suite's living room. "Guess what? They've got two big rooms downstairs where they serve *whiskey*! Can you believe that people just buy the stuff and drink it, right out in the open, without worrying about getting arrested?"

Ginger and Avery laughed. "*Vive la France*," Avery chortled. "Well, if the Democrats get elected next year, we'll all be drinking in public again, like we used to."

"Will we have bidets too?" Tony wanted to know.

"I don't think they'll dare go that far." Avery stood up. "Come on, it's time we tried some of their legal bubbly."

"Can I have some?" Tony asked eagerly.

"I'll give you a sip of mine," Ginger promised.

"Gosh," Tony sighed, "I wish I'd had a French nursemaid instead of Rosa. What good is Spanish going to do me here?"

Hand in hand, like three high-spirited school chums, they walked through the lobby toward the bar. "Hey, look!" Tony cried, pointing at a French newspaper lying on a coffee table. "There's a picture of Aunt Ella and Cal!"

Ginger snatched up the paper and quickly read the article. "It's Frank. Oh, Avery! Poor Frank Ricardo died of a cerebral hemorrhage."

Frank died a week before his fifty-first birthday. As part of the divorce agreement, Frank had been permitted to have Cal stay with him for two weeks at Christmas and for part of the summer. Frank also was permitted to visit Cal at Ella's homes in Hollywood and Palm Springs anytime he wished. A devoted father, he seldom missed a chance to see the boy.

One Saturday in late July, Frank drove out to Palm Springs to pick up Cal and bring him back to his home in Beverly Hills. Despite the suffocating summer heat on the desert, Cal was there alone with the servants, since Ella and her new lover were enjoying a nonstop sexual marathon in her Hollywood mansion and she didn't want Cal hanging around and distracting her.

Frank had just bought a new Stutz-Bearcat roadster. Eager to put it through its paces out on the flat desert highway, he got it up to one hundred and ten miles an hour. He was frightened of driving so fast, but at the same time he found it exhilarating. "Hey, I'm flying!" he yelled out exuberantly. Never enthralled by desert scenery, he discovered that speeding was the only way to relieve the tedium of the trip. East of Banning he was up to one hundred and twenty miles an hour. His heart was beating hard and fast, pounding in his ears. But he loved it. Loved it! He hadn't had so much fun in ages.

When he reached Ella's crazy Arabian villa, Frank burst through the front door, intent on telling Cal about his wild ride. As always, Frank and Cal were happy to see each other. They embraced, hugging hard and laughing. Then Frank staggered and fell to the floor.

"Daddy, get up. Hey, stop clowning around!" Cal stood above his father's prone body and scowled. "C'mon, Dad, it isn't funny." When Frank failed to move, Cal bent down and tugged at his arm. "Daddy, come *on*!"

The cook and gardener rushed in when they heard Cal scream. They found the boy with an ear pressed against

Frank's chest. "His heart isn't beating." Cal raised a terrified face to the two startled men. "Is . . . is Daddy dead?"

Ella seemed inconsolable at the funeral. Stunning in black, clutching her son to her bosom, she sat weeping all during the service. Photographs of her sorrowful poses on the church steps appeared in newspapers all over the world. For weeks the press marveled and fan magazines gossiped: was it possible, the writers speculated, that despite their divorce Ella really had loved Frank all along? Ella's fans sent condolence letters that filled eighty postal carts.

The public would never know that Ella had wept so bitterly because, first, she feared death—any death, even Frank's—and second, she knew that now the full burden of raising Cal fell on her lovely white shoulders. It had been bad enough having even half the responsibility. Oh, she could always send Cal off to military school, as she had threatened, but actually she didn't want to. She really and truly loved him, in her way. She simply didn't have enough time for him. And someone *had* to give him some love and attention, more than he'd get at a boarding school. These days, Cal was spending far too much time with his Uncle Neil, and Neil was a bad, bad influence with the "fast cars and faster women" that he loved to brag about. Even Ella recognized that.

Suddenly the solution flashed through her mind. It was so simple! She remembered a man—a very tasty one at that—sitting beside Ginger's pool and wanting to go horseback riding with Tony. All she had to do was marry a man like that, someone who obviously liked children, someone who would help her raise Cal!

Her tears dried up at once. Now, what was that fellow's name? A screenwriter, wasn't he? She remembered Ginger saying he was working on a Gloria Swanson script. Ella had put him completely out of her mind when he failed to call her. She figured he had lost her card. She couldn't *imagine* that he hadn't wanted to call her.

She phoned her agent. "I want the name of the man who wrote the movie Gloria Swanson's doing," she ordered. "Find out where he is and get me his phone number! Right away!"

* * *

Talbot Honeycutt was flattered to get Ella's phone call while he was taking a bath in Stockholm's Grand Hotel. Talbot still was in love with Ginger, but he had a pathological fear of celibacy; he was certain it was extremely unhealthy for a man. So while he waited for Ginger to change her mind about marrying him—he was sure that she would come around someday—he sought out sex wherever he could find it. He had been enjoying a string of strapping, jolly Swedish girls while researching a story about Alfred Nobel.

"How'd you find me?" he shouted to Ella. They had a poor connection.

"Well, I heard someone talking about you at Louella's, about your being in Sweden, and it just so happens I'm coming there on vacation next week. I'd like to see a friendly American face when I get there."

"Sure. I'll give you the deluxe tour."

Ella arrived in Stockholm but she never got the deluxe tour. Traveling incognito because for once she didn't want the press hounding her, she checked into her Grand Hotel suite wearing a black wig and dark glasses, and she met Talbot for dinner in the hotel dinning room. Immediately after the soup course, they went directly to her suite. They didn't leave it for almost two weeks.

"You really enjoy it, don't you?" he said one evening, sitting up in bed while smoking and waiting for room service to bring their dinner.

"Only with you," she lied, reaching over and taking a long drag on his cigarette.

"I can't always tell if the woman is pretending to have an orgasm. With you, I think it's probably the real McCoy." He looked her straight in the eye. "Why'd you come here?" he demanded.

"I told you—for a vacation."

"Come on, Ella. You're about as interested in seeing Stockholm as I am in seeing the South Pole."

She lay back and put her arm over her eyes. "All right," she said huskily, "I'll tell you the truth. When I met you at Ginger's pool . . . I really went gaga for you! And you never called me. I waited and waited. I didn't know what to do." Her voice trembled. "Finally, I couldn't stand it anymore. I was desperate!" She sat up and leaned over him so that her lovely pink nipples grazed his chest. "I want to marry you."

He got out of bed and bent double with laughter. "Oh, my God, Ella, you deserve a special Academy Award for that performance!"

She gave him a hurt look. "Why don't you believe me?"

"Because if you'd really gone gaga for me the day we met, you wouldn't have waited for me to call. You'd have called me first." He shook his head. "Come on, you don't love me any more than I love you. Give me the whole story. From the top."

"Okay, but you're only partly right. I didn't go for you then, not completely, back at Ginger's pool. But . . . I do want to get married again. I'm tired of . . . of . . ."

"Of fucking every man in sight?"

She wanted to slap him, but she decided it would be imprudent. "When I decided I wanted to get married again," she continued softly, "I tried to think who might make a good husband. That's when I thought of you. You can accuse me of sleeping around, but I bet you do it even more than I do."

She went to him and embraced him. "Honey, I admit I came here on purpose to snare you. But these past two weeks . . . honest to God, I *did* fall in love with you. I'm telling you the truth," she lied solemnly. "I've never felt this way about anyone. Ever."

He sighed and pushed her away. "That's your tough luck, baby. I happen to be very much in love with someone else."

"After making love to *me*," she asked, pouting, "how could you possibly love anyone else?"

"Listen, Ella, making love isn't the same as being in love. It's possible to be in love with someone you've never even been to bed with."

"Who is she?"

"None of your damn business." He started dressing. "I've finished my work here. I'm taking the night boat to London, and then I'm going straight back to the States."

"I see." She put on a gold satin dressing gown and began brushing her shining hair. "*Please* tell me who she is."

"C'mon, Ella, what's it to you?"

"It's Ginger, isn't it?" She frowned. "Sure. That's why you tried to butter her up that day, offering to take Tony riding. Of course! That's why you ignored *me* and talked to her the whole time. You asshole!"

He laughed. "You're not as dumb as you look."

"She'll never marry you," Ella jeered. "She's too much in love with the memory of that damn Indian."

"I'm going to change all that."

"Better men than you have tried." She lit a cigarette and exhaled loudly. "Talbot, I know what you think of me. I mean, it's obvious, and maybe I deserve it. But I'm telling you the truth. I do love you. I want to marry you. If you ever stop pining for Ginger, will you give me a chance?"

He was silent. She sounded sincere, but how could he believe an actress, even a lousy one? And what difference did it make, anyway? She was a good lay and she had a fantastic body, but he couldn't love Ella, no matter what happened between him and Ginger.

"Don't hold your breath," he told her.

As their European vacation entered its last week, Ginger was torn between wanting to stay in Paris and her eagerness to return to the desert.

"Look," Avery said, "we can come back here every summer."

It was dusk and the two of them were waiting for the sun to set while standing on the Pont de la Concorde, the bridge over the Seine where the river turned, giving them a view of the city's most famous architectural landmarks, from Notre Dame to the Eiffel Tower. Adele was resting before dinner and Tony had gone to see the puppets in the Bois de Boulogne with the family of a British boy he had met at the hotel.

"Oh, Avery, wouldn't that be heavenly? Palm Springs nine or ten months of the year and Paris the rest of the time. The best of both worlds."

"I could buy an apartment here—"

"And not stay at the Ritz? Tony would never forgive you."

"Even if I installed gold-plated swan faucets in the bathrooms?"

They leaned companionably on the railing and watched

a slow barge slide under the bridge. A couple were playing cards at a small table on the rear deck while two black dogs chased each other around the table. A line of wash flapped in the breeze along one side of the vessel.

"Look." Avery pointed toward the Place de la Concorde on their left. The first bronze rays of sunset had turned the chestnut trees surrounding the Petit Palais a mellow golden-green.

"Ooh, and look at that!" Ginger nodded toward their right, where the Invalides dome glistened against the deep blue sky.

They looked up, down, and sideways as the setting sun kept changing the colors and shadows of the panorama spread before them. Avery was so happy to be there alone with her that he thought his heart would burst. For a moment he was certain that if he took her in his arms and kissed her deeply, his own ardor might be contagious and ignite a rush of desire in her. It had never occurred to him that they could be secret lovers, that Adele would never have to know. . . .

But before he could reach out for her, Ginger gestured at the view. "If only Tonito could have seen all this!"

Her remark broke Avery's spell. Was he crazy? Did he want to make an utter fool of himself? Was he going to spoil the ease of their relationship with a kiss and a few words that would forever make her uncomfortable in his presence? There was no way she would agree to a clandestine affair with him. *Let go of this silly obsession*, he urged himself. *Cherish her friendship, and if you really care about her, hope for her sake that she finds a young, virile man to love, someone who will finally break Tonito's hold on her.*

As he had done several times that summer, Avery hired a car and driver to take them on an outing. Fontainebleau, sixty kilometers south of Paris, was the destination of this final trip, two days before they were to take the boat train to Le Havre and board the *Ile de France* for their return trip to New York. They stopped for lunch in the art-colony village of Barbizon, where, their driver assured them, a small brasserie boasted one of the finest young chefs in all of France. He proved to be right.

"Go ahead and lick your plate," Avery teased as Tony scraped up the last of his *mousse au chocolat.* "I won't tell anyone."

Tony said, "Can I?" and before Ginger could say no, he proceeded to do so. "Can I have seconds?" he asked eagerly, looking sideways at Adele's untouched dessert and grinning as she passed it over to him.

The chef, a dark young man with an enormous silky black mustache, came beaming to their table. "Is good?" he asked them.

"Is heavenly," Ginger told him. "Every course." They'd each had six.

"American or English?"

"American."

"I say to myself, *oui,* zey must be American. Zee English, zey never laugh so much."

"We've been in France all summer," Avery said in French, "and this is the best meal we've had."

The young man was delighted. "I come to America and cook for you, no?"

Avery, Ginger, and Adele exchanged amused looks. Then Ginger had an idea. "You mean, you really want to come to America? To live?"

"Is my dream. And that of my wife. She is my *sous-chef.*"

Ginger's eyes glowed. "Avery . . . Adele . . . can you imagine what a coup it would be to have him at The Springs? We'd serve the best French food west of New York City."

The young man, whose name was Jean-Paul LeFebvre, was in a state of shock when he realized that these Americans were serious about hiring him and his wife. "Palm Springs?" he kept murmuring. "California? *Mon Dieu! Mon Dieu!*"

Back at the Ritz, Avery made a few phone calls and, *voilà!* everything was arranged. Jean-Paul and Danielle would sail in two weeks and reach Palm Springs in time for Ginger's gala reopening dinner on October 1.

Ginger was ecstatic. "A real French chef! Menus keep floating through my head. *Croissants* for breakfast. *Omelettes* and *potage du Barry* for lunch. *Veau au beurre blanc avec les pommes dauphine* for dinner. *Ooh-la-la!* Tell me, should I print the menus in French? Or is that just too pretentious for our little desert town?"

Tony was unimpressed. "*Ooh-la-la* all you want, Mom. I mean, sure, the guy makes an okay chocolate pudding. But I can't wait to get home and have an honest-to-God hot dog!"

Ginger came home to find that Neil was planning to build an eyesore of a cheap hotel on part of their grandfather's land. "I've never seen such an ugly design," she chided her brother when he brought over the plans. "It's like an overgrown outhouse."

"So what? It's just a place for tourists to spend the night. And couples who need a private place for some hot sex. You think screwers are going to care about fancy architecture or a pretty lobby?"

"But, Neil, it doesn't cost any more to build attractively. You use the same materials. It's the design that stinks!"

"Aah, who cares?"

"Didn't you hire an architect?"

"They cost money."

"Then who's responsible for this? *You*?"

Neil grinned. "Well, between me and the contractor, it just sort of grew." He shook his head. "You're a real pain in the ass, Ginger. But I admire your spirit."

"I wish I could find something to admire in *you*!" she grumbled. She took a good look at this brother of hers. He now was twenty-seven years old and about fifty pounds overweight. There was no trace of the puny, sickly boy. His face had grown even more handsome, with their father's blue, heavily lashed eyes, a lot of dark blond hair, a shapely nose, sensual lips . . . and a double chin.

"Neil, come out on my balcony and see what you're doing to this town," she begged. "You're ruining the view with that sea of ugly flat roofs!"

"Look, Sis, if you don't like the view from up here, there's a very easy solution. Go buy a house down on the flats. That way, you won't have to look at my ugly roofs anymore!"

The door to Ginger's office was always open, to guests, to visitors, to staff, to friends, even to strangers. So

Ginger was not surprised when she looked up and saw a slender man of medium height whose well-worn clothes, though clean, looked ready for the trash barrel.

Before she could ask his business, he leaned over her desk and looked directly into her eyes with his expressive gray ones. "You need me!" he said slowly and firmly.

Though somewhat taken aback, she didn't say anything, waiting for him to continue.

He straightened up without breaking their eye contact. "Aren't you going to ask me why?"

"I figure you'll tell me soon enough."

"Well, I've been looking your place over. It's a perfect hotel. Perfect! Right size, great kitchen, everything. But it needs one thing more."

"Yeah? What are you selling?"

"Me!" He gestured at a chair. "May I?"

She nodded, a bit warily. Was the man crazy?

"Listen, let me start over," he said with a little laugh. "I think I got off on the wrong foot. Do you remember Ed Jaeger?"

"Of course! My old teacher."

"He's a professor now. A very distinguished naturalist and a desert authority. I worked under him for my doctorate."

"I'm happy to hear he's doing well."

"Ed suggested I come and see you." He leaned forward eagerly in his chair. "I'm what Ed calls a true desert rat. I'm not happy anywhere else. It's cost me a wife and a daughter—Mary hates the desert and she's turned little Vivien against it too. Well, anyway, I'm doing research for a couple of books, and if I don't get a job, I'll be sleeping with the kit foxes and eating rattlesnake meat." He smiled. "Not for the first time, either."

"What do you have in mind?" Ginger felt sympathetic toward the young man, whom she judged to be in his early twenties. She liked his spontaneous grin and happy air. He kept pushing a lock of his sandy-colored hair off his forehead, but each time it fell right back.

"Here's what I thought. Your guests come here because they like the desert. Right?" When she nodded, he continued. "But I'll bet most of them are too timid to poke very far out onto the desert, or into the canyons."

"Well, some of them go a few miles out on horses, but I can't get many of them to hike with me. I keep trying because I think they'd love it."

"That's where I come in," he said eagerly. "I'd organize groups, and also take individuals and small parties. Whatever. We'd start out on horses, or in a surrey if they don't like to ride, and then we'd get out and walk. I'd teach them desert lore, and after dinner I'd give informal slide lectures on the flora and fauna of the area. One or two evenings a week we'd go into the canyons for steak cookouts around a bonfire. When there's a full moon we can even have midnight rides. And breakfast rides are fun too. While they're eating, I can even entertain them. I earned my way through college playing the guitar and singing. Really, there's no end to the ways I can instruct and amuse your guest."

And maybe even me, Ginger thought with a smile. "I'm intrigued," she admitted. "What salary do you have in mind?"

He frowned. "I'm not very good about money. I need just enough to pay my daughter's support—"

"How old is she?"

"Seven, and pretty as can be." Proudly he took a worn photograph from his wallet and handed it to Ginger. "That's Vivien."

Ginger studied the young face: it was pretty enough, with a sweet smile. For a moment she regretted never having had a daughter . . . but of course now it was too late. "She's adorable." She handed back the picture.

"My ex-wife's remarried, so I don't have to send anything for her. But I like to pay for Vivien's dance lessons and clothes, things like that. I guess maybe ten dollars a week, plus board and a place for my horse, would see me through. You don't have to put me up—I'll pitch my tent somewhere. But I better warn you, I eat like an elephant."

"I haven't fed any elephants lately, so I'm not sure what I'm getting into. And really, you don't have to sleep in your tent. There's a bungalow behind the pool that's too small for guests. You might as well use it." Ginger took fifty dollars from her cash box. "Look, I provide uniforms for all my employees. Go on over to Carl Lykken's store and get yourself some new jeans and boots. And some shirts while you're at it."

He looked down ruefully at his neat but threadbare clothes and his boots, whose scuff marks he had vainly tried to hide with polish. He came over and took her hand in both of his. "You won't be sorry, ma'am . . ."

"Call me Ginger. Everyone does."

"Ginger." He seemed to taste the word and find it delicious. He gave her a face-splitting grin. "I promise, you'll get your money's worth."

Ginger realized he was still holding her hand. Gently she pulled it free. "You didn't tell me your name."

"I didn't? It's Jason. Jason Sisley." He started out the door, and then turned back for a moment. "Say, Ginger, what should my title be?"

She thought. "Recreation director? Resident naturalist?"

He grinned again. "They both sound good to me!"

Ginger started going along on some of Jason's outings. "I want to see firsthand what you're doing," she told him. "Just make believe I'm not here."

"Why? I'm glad you're here." He put an arm around Tony, who often joined Jason after school.

For Ginger, the outings were bittersweet reminders of the early days when she and Tonito had roamed all over the desert during his school vacations, furiously racing their horses, idling up washes, climbing old Indian trails.

She was surprised to find herself feeling a twinge of anxiety when she saw Jason in intimate conversation with one of her attractive young female guests. Jealous? she asked herself. Aren't you being a bit ridiculous? He's a hired hand. . . .

Jason's trips were imaginative and well-planned. His lectures were more serious. "Men haven't wrecked too much of this valley . . . yet," was one of his favorite themes, "but it's happening all over this great country of ours. For centuries the Indians lived in harmony with the land. They took care of it, and it took care of them. But there's a growing number of Americans who see the land as their own personal cookie jar. And I tell you this: they can't plunder the land, strip off the trees, rip out the minerals, gouge out the gold and silver, plow up the grasslands, and expect the land to keep on providing for them."

The guests adored Jason, and word spread to the towns-people, who began having dinner at The Springs and staying afterward to hear him speak. After Jason's first two weeks, tickets for his Wednesday- and Saturday-night steak cookouts were all sold by midmorning. Guests had to make their reservations several days in advance.

"You're a success, Jason," Ginger said appreciatively. "I'm giving you a raise."

"Aw, come on, Ginger, you don't have to do that. I'm eating a hundred dollars' worth of food a week as it is."

"Well, you need fattening up. Anyway, whether you like it or not, your salary is now twenty-five a week."

"Thanks, boss-lady."

Ginger smiled happily. "Jason, you're exactly what this place needed." *And maybe what I needed too,* she thought. *I always feel so cheerful when he's around.*

"And, Ginger, seeing as how you're in such a good mood, can I ask a favor?"

"Sure. What is it?"

"I'd like an extra day off next week. It's Vivien's birthday . . ."

"Of course. Anytime you want a few days off, just juggle your schedule around and . . . it's fine with me."

"Coming to the cookout tonight?" he asked.

"How can I? It's a sellout."

"Hey! The boss ought to get some special privileges around here. All we have to do is ask Jean-Paul to throw in an extra steak."

"Better get two extra. Tony'll want to come too."

Ginger and Tony had moved back into her grandfather's house the previous spring, before leaving for Europe. Rosa came with them and Ginger hired two young Mexican girls to help the aging Indian woman. The big old adobe mansion once more was a soft pink with gray shutters, the way Grandpa John had wanted it to be. Though old Mrs. Offenbach had neglected the place in recent years, two months of refurbishing had made it better than new. Ginger had had the entire interior re-painted too, the furniture restored, new mattresses and bathroom fixtures installed, chipped tiles replaced, and the gardens replanted.

Tony enjoyed living in the pink adobe. "Of course, it's not the Paris Ritz," he teased Ginger, "but I do love it."

"Didn't you like our old cabin that your father built?" she asked wistfully.

"Sure I liked it," he assured her. "Only . . . I like this better."

Tony had taken to following Jason around. He hung on every word Jason uttered. "He's the greatest teacher," Tony told Ginger. "I mean, everything he says is so interesting. And he's even funnier than Jack Benny."

Several times Ginger found Tony staring at the portrait of Tonito that she had hung over the living-room mantel. A local artist had made the large portrait, copying the likeness from the photograph taken when Tonito had played an Indian chief in a Tom Mix movie. Tonito was bare to the waist, with his strong muscular arms crossed over his broad chest. A bonnet of colorful feathers cascaded down his back. He looked far more like an Indian in the portrait than he ever had in life.

Ginger put her arms around her son. "He looks so young," she said as they both stared at the portrait. "He'll always be young," she added pensively, "while I grow old."

"How come you don't have a picture of my brother?" Tony asked cautiously.

Ginger was startled. How could she tell him that she couldn't bear to see Johnny's picture . . . that she had barely been able to deal with her grief for Tonito, that she never dared to let herself *think* about Johnny. "I . . . I don't have a good picture of J-Johnny," she said lamely. "Just of your father."

"What's it like to be in love?" Tony asked.

She gestured helplessly. "It's hard to describe. It's when . . . when someone makes you feel wonderful, and glad to be alive."

"You mean, you can't feel glad to be alive if you're not in love?"

"Well, of course you can, silly. I mean *extra* glad."

Tony looked at her curiously. "I think Uncle Avery loves you the way you said."

Ginger shook her head. "Tony! You're talking nonsense. You know he loves Adele. . . ."

"Well, sure, he loves Auntie Adele, but not the same way. Really, Mom, don't you ever see the way he looks at you? I noticed it a lot in Paris. He looked so *happy*. . . ."

Ginger hugged him. "Darling, Avery was just happy to be in Paris. He's been wanting to go back there for years, and he finally did. He's in love with Paris, not with me. So stop imagining things. Honestly!"

Still in Ginger's arms, Tony looked up once more at his father's portrait. "I guess you loved *him* a lot."

"I still do. He was perfect, Tony. Just *perfect*. He never did a bad thing in his life. I'll never meet anyone that wonderful again."

Talbot Honeycutt returned to his suite at The Springs and resumed his pursuit of Ginger. "This is the year you'll give in," he predicted as he checked in.

"I hope it's the year you give *up*," she laughed. "Y'know, Talbot, you ought to buy a house here. Why pay my exorbitant rates year after year?"

"I'd buy the best house in town if you'd move into it with me." He sighed with exasperation. "Christ, Ginger, if you only knew what you're missing!"

To Talbot's dismay, Ella was spending the winter at her Arabian villa. She needed a rest, she told her studio, and though they threatened her with suspension, she refused to work. Cal needed her, she rationalized, but Cal was away at military school most of the time, and even when he was home for vacation, Ella managed to spend most of her days at The Springs' pool instead of her own.

"D'you mind?" she asked Ginger. "It's too lonely at my pool. Besides, it's good for your business to have celebrities around."

"My clientele doesn't give a damn about celebrities. But of course you can come here anytime you like."

Talbot was annoyed. He couldn't go to the pool without Ella throwing herself at him, literally. He'd come up out of a dive and there she'd be, posing seductively in a daringly low-cut bathing suit. He refused to go to bed with her.

She pouted. "Don't you remember Stockholm?"

"Only too well. How many times do I have to tell you—"

"I know. I know. You're in love with my sister." Ella sighed. The more Talbot rejected her, the more Ella wanted him. Nobody ever had spurned her before. The nerve of the man! The pressure grew and grew until Ella felt she'd simply burst if something didn't give.

These days Avery worked only as a consultant on difficult cases; he spent most of his time sketching and painting desert scenery. He had turned his home office into a studio. His practice having grown with the town's population, he now had three younger doctors associated with him, and his clinic occupied its own modern building on Palm Canyon Drive, the new name for the town's major thoroughfare. But Avery, along with the other original settlers, still insisted on calling it Main Street.

Walking to his clinic late one afternoon in October, he saw Tony and Jason practicing with a baseball in the schoolyard. He stopped to watch. He couldn't help but admire Jason's lithe movements, his quick smile, and the relaxed manner in which he taught Tony a better way to hold the bat and catch the ball.

That evening, as was their custom twice a week, Avery and Adele went up to The Springs to have dinner with Ginger and Tony. "I'd eat Jean-Paul's cooking three times a day if I wasn't afraid of gaining weight," Avery told Ginger.

"Oh, pooh, Avery, you never gain an ounce, no matter how much you eat."

"Neither do you," he said.

"Yes, but I don't eat as much as you."

"Ah, you two," Adele said softly, fondly. "Be glad you have such healthy appetites." She grimaced at the food on her plate, still largely untouched, and put down her fork.

Ginger squeezed Adele's hand lovingly, and with commiseration. For years now, Adele had been so kind to her, buying Ginger thoughtful gifts in the days when she had been struggling financially, playing the loving aunt to Tony since he was an infant. Ginger worried whenever Adele's health declined alarmingly and she rejoiced when Adele had periods of partial recovery. Ginger was in awe of Adele's ethereal beauty, whose source was not only

the older woman's patrician features but also an inner
glow fueled by her serenity. Her quiet refinement sometimes made Ginger feel like a rowdy child in comparison.

Later, strolling around the hotel gardens, Avery, Adele,
and Ginger found Tony and Jason sitting near the pool.
Jason was teaching Tony how to play the guitar. Jason
had a clear voice, sweet and forthright. He was singing
"When It's Springtime in the Rockies" and then he
launched into "Yes, Sir, That's My Baby," the kind of
peppy song that made Avery want to tap his feet and clap
and hum along with the singer.

Avery looked over at Ginger to see if she shared his
pleasure in the music. Yes, she was smiling with delight,
making Avery wonder whether the cause of her pleasure
was Tony, or the music, or . . . Jason?

Jason. Jason and Ginger? Avery took a sharper look at
the young man and he couldn't help but like everything
he saw. Jason was intelligent, good-humored, and honorable. He was undoubtedly the world's greatest salesman
for the earth, deftly couching his information lectures in
such fun and showmanship that in the guise of entertain-
ment he could make frivolous audiences eager to defend
the desert's natural resources.

Above all, Jason was wonderful with Tony. Avery
tried to imagine himself loping under fly balls the way
Jason had that afternoon. No, Avery admitted to himself, he might be young *for his age*, but he'd lumber in
the outfield without grace and with more than a groan or
two. Nor could he induct Tony into the magic of music
the way Jason did with a melodious voice and quick, sure
fingers on the guitar.

While Avery was comparing, he had a sudden vision of
Jason and Ginger making love with a vigor and a passion
that he himself could never again muster. Come to think
of it, had he ever? His mild unions with Adele, his
occasional forays into clumsy adultery with lonely wives
and widows visiting Palm Springs, his obligatory visits to
prostitutes when he was a timid eighteen-year-old in
Paris . . . even his daydreams of making love to Ginger
were of sweet sex, languorous sex, not the kind of youthful ardor she deserved.

In that moment, standing under the stars next to the
pool, Avery realized just how foolish he had been been

all these years, hoping for a miracle that would make him and Ginger lovers instead of best, best friends. If she ever did shake off the paralysis of Tonito's memory, she would want to love a Jason—if not this particular young man, then someone very much like him. Someone still bursting with virility and vitality.

You've been as bad as she has, Avery scolded himself. *She stubbornly clings to her memory of Tonito, and you, you old goat, all these years you've kept hoping for the impossible.* But try as he would, he could not shake his forlorn hope that someday she would love him the way he loved her.

Looking crestfallen, Tony came into Ginger's office late one November afternoon. He threw himself into her lap and burst into tears.

She held him, letting him cry, and when the sobs subsided, he got up and walked to the window. "Come on," she coaxed softly, "spit it out."

"I did something really bad, Mom."

"Well, tell me."

"Promise you won't get mad?"

"Tony, you know I try to be fair. If it's something worth getting angry about, I'll get angry. Okay?"

He sighed. "You know how I've been saving my money in a piggy bank for two years? Part of my allowance and presents and stuff?"

She nodded.

"Well, it's all gone."

"Don't tell me someone stole your piggy bank!"

"*I* did. I mean, *I* took out all the money. There was seventy-four dollars and eighteen cents. I've still got the eighteen cents." He looked at her with stricken eyes. "After school today, some of us kids went over to that café on Indian Avenue . . . you know, the one that opened in September?"

"You couldn't have spent that much eating there, Tony. It's a cheap greasy spoon."

"No. We didn't eat anything." He hesitated. "We went into a room in back where they have these two wheels that spin around, with a little silver ball and a bunch of numbers. You try to guess which number the ball will land on . . . and you put down maybe a dollar. Then, if you guess right, you win a whole bunch of money."

"And if you guess wrong?"

"They get your dollar."

Ginger felt her anger rising. "They let kids play?"

He nodded. "And, Mom, I chose the wrong number every single time!" He looked up into her face. "Are you mad at me?"

She shook her head. "It was your money, Tony. You could have bought something nice with it."

He nodded, abashed. "I was saving for a new bicycle."

"Well, I hope you learned a good lesson." She kissed his forehead. "Now, run on home."

After he left, Ginger went down the hall to Jason's office. "Want to help me break the law?" she asked, her voice low with fury.

He didn't know her well enough to recognize her mood. "Who do you want murdered?" he asked flippantly.

She told him what had happened to Tony.

"Well, shouldn't you call the sheriff? Gambling's illegal."

"I called him several times, two months ago. When the place first opened. So did Nellie. So did Avery and a lot of other people. Everybody in town knew about it." She gestured angrily. "Nothing happened, and we all figured, oh, what the hell, it wasn't hurting anyone. And the tourists love it. Some of the locals too. But when they let ten-year-olds play . . . not in my village, they don't!"

"So? What are you going to do?"

"I want you to come with me, Jason. I need your moral support."

Jason was mystified as they walked down the hill from The Springs and headed toward the village. Ginger was carrying a laundry bag, but he couldn't tell what was in it. Something heavy. "Want me to carry that for you?" he asked.

She shook her head, looking grim.

"Come on, Ginger, are you going to talk to them or what? And what's in that stupid bag?"

"You'll see."

When they reached the café, they stopped and looked at each other. "What now!" he asked nervously.

"Wait here. I'll go in alone."

"No you won't. I'm coming in with you."

"No, Jason. *Please!* I don't want you to."

"Ginger, if you're going to do something dangerous, forget it. I won't let you—whatever you're planning to do."

She shook her head firmly. "Look, they won't *dare* hurt me. But they might attack you. I just want to know you're out here. If I don't come out in five minutes, then you can come in and get me."

He grabbed her arm to stop her from going inside. They stared at each other—he fearful, she determined.

"Let *go* of me, Jason!" she ordered. "I'm not crazy enough to do anything foolish. You've got to trust me!"

Reluctantly he relinquished her arm.

Ginger went into the café, a dingy room with green walls, spotted wooden tables, paper napkins in metal dispensers, rickety chairs, sugary doughnuts in a glass case, the smell of stale grease. She didn't think many people came here to eat. One man was hunched over a cup of coffee at the counter. The waitress looked up from her newspaper when Ginger entered, then shrugged when Ginger ignored her and stalked to the drape-covered doorway at the rear of the café.

She found herself in a small room with two roulette tables. There were no customers, and the two croupiers—heavy middle-aged men—were sitting on stools drinking beer. She didn't recognize either of them.

One of them stood up and lumbered over to his table. "Y'can play over here, lady."

"I'm Ginger Alvarez, owner of The Springs Hotel," she said coldly. "Is your boss here?"

"No, ma'am. He lives in L.A. Just comes out weekends."

Before either man could stop her, she reached into the laundry bag she was carrying, took out a heavy long-handled ax, raised it over her head, and brought it smashing down on the first table. The table sagged where she had hit it, and she brought the ax down again, this time collapsing the table.

When the two stunned croupiers both started toward her, she held the ax threateningly above her head. "You come any closer, you fat assholes, and one of you'll get the blunt end of this thing!" They retreated and watched as she destroyed the second table in three whacks. They stared, still in shock, as she calmly put the ax back in the laundry bag and left the room.

Out on the sidewalk, she gave Jason a quavery grin. "Okay, now you can carry the bag," she said. She was shaking so hard her teeth chattered.

Jason grabbed the bag with one hand and her arm with the other. He propelled her half-running back up the hill. "My God, Ginger, are you crazy? Why didn't you let the sheriff take care of it?"

"I told you! He wouldn't."

"Jeez! You're dealing with hoodlums, Ginger. Real gangsters!"

"Exactly. And they have to know that there's no place for them in this town!" She stopped walking and touched his arm in gratitude. "Thanks for coming with me."

He wanted to take her in his arms and assure her that there was nothing in this world he wouldn't do for her. But her eyes still signaled for him—for every man—to keep his distance. "Ginger," he blurted, knowing he was skirting danger, "Tony needs a father—"

Her voice was icy. "He has Avery."

"Ginger, he needs a *real* father. Living with him, in the same house. And, Ginger, you need—"

"Jason!" she warned. She turned away from him and walked quickly toward The Springs. She was furious with him. How dare he!

He caught up with her and grabbed her arm, forcing her to stop. "How can you be angry with a fellow for . . . caring about you? Is it a crime?"

She looked into his eyes a long moment. "You should know better," she said softly. "Everybody knows . . . I'll never marry again."

"Was your husband such a paragon that—"

"He was perfect!" she insisted fiercely.

When they returned to The Springs, Jason waited in fear for some retaliation against Ginger or her property. He stayed close to her the rest of the evening and had the entire hotel staff watching for signs of trouble. Ginger didn't know that she was guarded all night by Jason, Jean-Paul, and Avery, armed with a rifle he had once bought to kill stray dogs when there was an outbreak of rabies. The three men hid behind a tamarisk tree across from the pink mansion.

The next morning the café was boarded up and neither of the two croupiers—nor their boss—was ever again seen in Palm Springs.

In December, in honor of Tony's tenth birthday, Ginger invited Jason and Avery and Adele and Talbot and a few of Tony's school friends to a dinner at the pink adobe mansion. Out of pity, she invited Ella too. Cal was away at his military academy.

On the day of the party, Tony pulled Ginger over to a window. "Hey, Mom, did you see the cottonwoods? They've all turned bright gold."

She peered out. "Yes. It happens every December. I remember noticing them the day you were born." *And the day your father and brother died*, she thought with a fresh surge of grief.

Jason was the first to arrive. He was far more presentable than he had been when he had come to her seeking a job. His clothes were still casual, but no longer threadbare. He wore a blue plaid flannel shirt, snug Levi's, a beige suede vest, tooled-leather boots, and a broad-brimmed snappy cowboy hat.

"Heigh-ho, silver!" Ginger teased when she answered the door.

"What a lovely house you have, Ginger. And my, don't you look sensational this evening." He took off his hat and stared admiringly at her French frock, a lacy gold concoction with a flounce below her knees. He caught sight of Tonito's portrait and strode over for a closer look. "Your husband?" he asked, and when she nodded, he said, "Mighty handsome, wasn't he?"

"Mmmm," she agreed proudly. They stood together in front of the fireplace, looking at Tonito's likeness, until the other guests began to arrive.

Ella had arrived feeling downcast. Talbot's presence at the birthday dinner and his constant rejection of her still rankled. She no longer expected him to marry her, but his refusal to have sex with her was going too far. As she sat morosely through dinner, she noticed that Ginger was the focal point for all eyes. What a turn of affairs! Ever since Ella could remember, *she* had been the center of attention. Was she slipping? she wondered with sudden fright. Losing her looks? Finally showing her age? Even worse, everyone there seemed to *love* Ginger. You could see it in their eyes and in their smiles. She already knew that Talbot was crazy about her sister. She had a feeling that dumb old Dr. Avery also was gaga about Ginger. And this young nobody sitting next to her, this Jason, was he too? *Was everybody in the whole goddamn world in love with her stupid sister?* By God, it was time she did something about it, Ella told herself, seething with fury. It was time!

Seeing Ginger go into the kitchen as the other guests wandered into the living room after dinner, Ella darted after her sister and grabbed her arm. "I've got to talk to you."

"Now?" Ginger objected. "Ella, I'm busy. Can't it wait?"

"No." Ella dragged a reluctant Ginger out onto the empty back porch. "There's something I should've told you ages ago." She took a deep breath, hesitated a moment, then plunged ahead. "That spring, when I first came down here after Papa and Polly died, and Frank put me into that Egyptian movie . . . do you remember? You'd just gotten pregnant with Tony."

"Of course I remember. But why are you—"

"Shut up and listen! All that spring, I had an affair with Tonito. We used to meet every day at my house."

Ginger drew herself away from Ella as though she were a venomous snake. "What a dirty *lie!*"

"I'm not lying, Ginger. It really happened. I know you think Tonito was so perfect, but he fucked me silly! Every day for two whole months we fucked and fucked, like wild animals! And . . ." She paused dramatically. "Cal is Tonito's son. So you see, Cal and Tony are more than just cousins, they're actually half-brothers. But I don't ever want Cal to know, because he was so crazy about Frank."

Ginger stared at Ella a moment, then shrugged. "I don't know why you're doing this to me, Ella. You've always been a mean, hateful person. But I know you're lying. Tonito loved me until the day he died. And *only* me!"

"I didn't say he *loved* me, Ginger: I said he *fucked* me. *Fucked* me! You know what that means? Are you too pure to know such words?"

"Stop lying! Stop it, Ella!"

"I can prove it!" Ella crowed triumphantly. "You know that little mole he had on his balls? He called it his magic button. When I'd lick it he'd go stark raving out of his mind, and . . ."

Ginger was looking up at the moon when it suddenly exploded into a million pieces.

"We were standing out on the porch talking, and she suddenly just keeled over. She'd said earlier that she felt dizzy, I mean that's why we went on the porch in the first place." Ella spoke as Jason carried Ginger into the house and put her down on a couch.

Avery gently slapped Ginger's cheeks while Tony knelt beside his mother and begged her to wake up. They were both relieved when Ginger opened her eyes.

"I told them you were dizzy and fainted," Ella said quickly.

Ginger looked up at Ella, then closed her eyes again. "Yes, I still feel dizzy. I think I'd better go to bed."

Avery took her pulse. "People don't get dizzy just like that," he said worriedly. "Do you have other symptoms? Let me take your temperature."

"No, Avery. Please. *Please!* I just want to lie down . . . in my bed."

When Jason helped her up the stairs, she hastily said good night and closed her bedroom door in his face. She sat on her bed in the dark for a long time. She was beyond tears. Her world was in shambles.

For the past ten years her entire life had been based upon her love for Tonito and the memory of his love for her. *But he fucked Ella silly all that spring . . . he and Ella fucking like wild animals . . . and all that time I was so happy, like a fool, never knowing the truth!* Now all her beautiful memories of her own lovemaking with Tonito were a mockery.

Tony stuck his head into her room. "You okay, Mom?

Everybody's gone, except Avery. He took Adele home and then came back. He wants to know . . . He thinks he ought to take a look at you."

"No, darling, I'm fine. Tell him to go home. Then you go to bed."

After Tony left the room, Ginger undressed mechanically, washed her face, and stared at herself in the mirror. "Fool!" she whispered. "You've wasted ten years being faithful to the memory of a faithless man!"

All night, as she tried to sleep, she kept thinking that she might have been able to forgive Tonito had he been unfaithful with anyone else. But with Ella! Oh, my God, why Ella? Her sister's words kept shrieking through her head. *Tonito fucked me silly . . . we fucked and fucked like wild animals . . . he fucked me silly . . . fucked me silly . . . fucked me silly . . .*

Everybody who loved Ginger realized that something traumatic had happened between her and Ella out on the porch that night. But Ginger refused to talk about it, and they all pussyfooted around her, like people do around terminally ill patients. Ella left town the next morning, and that afternoon a For Sale sign went up on the front lawn of the Arabian mansion. Later they learned that Ella had sailed for an indefinite stay in London, leaving Cal behind in a military academy outside of Los Angeles.

Ginger was strangely quiet when she hiked with Avery. After a week of her silence, he lost patience. "Ginger-girl, what's the matter? Can't you tell me what's wrong?"

She shook her head. "Stop nagging me or I won't walk with you any more."

Avery was astonished. He had never heard her speak so crossly before, not to him, not to anyone. He changed his tack. "Shall I make reservations for next summer? Paris again?"

She waved him off impatiently. "Avery, please. My brain is tired."

He was hurt. What on earth had that little bitch done to Ginger? Whatever it was, he could cheerfully wring Ella's pretty little neck.

When Ginger returned home from her walk with Avery, she was shaking. She had experienced a violent flare-up of her old attraction to him. After all this time! She had thought when she married Tonito and threw herself into their erotic life together that her silly schoolgirl crush on Avery had been killed once and for all. Now she no longer was a silly young schoolgirl and here it was again, stronger than ever.

During the past ten years her prolonged mourning for Tonito and Johnny had frozen her sexual feelings. And now, suddenly released from her sorrow by Ella's confession, she had needed all her strength to keep from throwing herself into Avery's arms that morning.

Nothing could be worse! It was more inappropriate than ever. *Oh, God,* she moaned to herself in the privacy of her bedroom, *the dear man surely would hate me if he knew. It would ruin the wonderful friendship we've shared for so many years.* And Adele! After all she's done for Tony since he was a baby—she'd never talk to me again.

Ginger fell onto her bed and cried rare tears of self-pity. Life seemed so difficult, so full of unexpected pitfalls. After a few minutes she dried her eyes and went out onto the bedroom balcony. It was a beautiful December day—serene and warm, with a crisp blue sky. She took a deep breath and was filled with determination. She had managed to get over this foolish Avery business once before. And, by God, she promised herself, somehow, some way, she'd do it again!

Later that morning Jason asked Ginger to go riding with him up into the Santa Rosa Mountains. "There's an area I've never explored before. We could leave after lunch and poke around for a few hours and have a picnic up there at sunset . . . if you don't mind riding back to town after dark. There's a full moon tonight." He spoke quickly, certain of a curt refusal when he finished.

"Sure. Why not?" she agreed without enthusiasm, although she was eager for a distraction. She gestured southeast at the Santa Rosas. "I know every inch of them."

Her assent surprised him. But she sounded so devoid of enthusiasm that he wished he could take her in his arms and console her. But he didn't dare. Every since Tony's birthday party, Ginger's step had lost its bounce and her eyes no longer sparkled. Maybe she's really sick with something like a low-grade infection, he worried. He would rather believe that than think there was some deeper cause for her misery.

"What should we take for supper?" he asked, trying to cheer her. "How about some of Jean-Paul's pâté? And cheese? With bread and fruit and wine?"

"Sure. Anything."

"Would Tony like to come?" he asked.

She shook her head. "He's spending the night with his cousins. My former sister-in-law Maria's kids."

"The little Italian Indians?" He chuckled.

"C'mon, Jason, why is that any funnier that Tony being a little Scotch Indian?"

"Sorry, sorry, I was only trying to make you smile."

She turned away listlessly.

"I'll come by for you at one o'clock," he called after her.

Jason found it impossible to make conversation with her. They rode silently from the valley floor up through Cathedral Canyon, climbing across fields of burroweed and creosote bush, past beavertail cactus and hoffmannseggia and brittle bush. They wandered through dry washes among cat's-claw acacia and palo verde and smoke trees. But Ginger was so wrapped in gloom that nothing seemed to grab her attention, not even the doe who crossed their path or the bighorn ewe watching them from a nearby hillock or the comical plump chuckwalla that scuttled out of their way.

They climbed higher and higher until the entire Coachella Valley was visible far beneath them. As they ascended, the terrain changed. Huge beige boulders lay strewn about. The low desert plants were replaced with thick stands of junipers and, in sunny spots, manzanita. The late-afternoon sun made clumps of golden cholla shimmer with a startling electric brilliance.

A few feet downhill from the trail Jason found a cozy shelf protected from the winds that often came up as evening approached. He spread out their saddle blankets for Ginger to sit on. Then he gathered fallen tree branches and made a big crackling fire. He unpacked Jean-Paul's smooth pâté and cheese and crusty bread along with a bottle of French wine, but Ginger ate and drank very little.

The setting was spectacular, with a view of the valley and its surrounding mountains to the north and the far-off blue smear of the Salton Sea to the south. In the distance, Mt. San Jacinto was darkly, starkly outlined against the vermilion-and-gold-streaked western sky. The entire valley floor glowed pink and the eastern mountains were orange. It was the most dramatic sunset Jason had witnessed in all his years of desert sunset-watching.

Ginger was staring unseeingly at her hands, deep in thought.

"Hey," Jason urged softly, "take a look at the sunset! You might never see one like it again."

She glanced up and her eyes did widen with wonder. "Oh, Jason!" She smiled for the first time since Tony's birthday.

They sat in silence by the fire, watching the mountains and the sky until all the colors faded and the stars came out. Hypnotized by the flames, neither of them was impelled to move. They were seated side by side on the soft sand, breathing in the pungency of the high-desert plants.

He could sense that she was coming out of the trance-like state that had paralyzed her since the night she had fainted. He heard her soft breathing, and by the firelight he could see that her eyes had softened. He didn't want to break the spell by speaking, though his heart and mind were full of words. He wanted to tell her how wonderful she was to look at, and how exciting she was to be with. How much he admired her. How desperately he desired her. How she had turned his life around and given it direction.

He took her hand and was surprised that she let him hold it. With his other hand he lightly stroked her cheek. She turned her head and gave him a strange look. He didn't know what to make of it.

Actually, she was startled. All day, ever since the shock that morning of finding herself still so violently attracted to Avery, great leaping surges of desire had been roaring through her body. And here was Jason—youthful, attractive Jason—who so obviously worshiped her. Impulsively she reached for him and the next minute they were lying on the saddle blankets in each other's arms and his mouth was consuming hers.

Later, she couldn't help comparing his lovemaking with Tonito's. Jason's was more forceful, less soulful, more passionate, less gentle, more rollicking, more ecstatic, more stirring, more *fun*, more, more, more!

He fell asleep in her arms, the two of them wrapped in the saddle blankets. But Ginger felt too alert to sleep, too eager to savor every moment of this remarkable night: the stars, the full moon, the royal-blue sky, Jason's warm breath upon her cheek, the slow steady bump of his heartbeat against her breast. She was jubilant that she had so quickly found a solution to her terrifying feelings for Avery. Jason had saved her, and his strong, virile body would continue to save her, just as Tonito's lovemaking once had rescued her. She felt emancipated, as though she had emerged from a prison or been awakened from a long sleep. Yes, she was Sleeping Beauty and the Prince had kissed her awake. Ginger smiled: rugged Jason wasn't very princely. He was a desert creature, as fresh as the air, as warm as the sun, as breezy as the wind.

She touched his face and woke him up. She guessed it was past midnight. "Excuse me," she said, bubbling with playfulness, "but I think I'd like to do it again."

"Happy to oblige, ma'am," he said as his mouth eagerly sought hers.

In the morning, the fire was out, the food was gone, and they were starving. "What a disaster," he moaned cheerfully. "Shall I find a rattlesnake for breakfast?"

"I think you ought to marry me."

He gave her a sharp look. "Are you sure you want to marry *me*?"

"Don't you want to?"

"Want to." He sighed as he echoed her words. "Sure I want to. More than anything in the world."

"Then?"

"Well, I'll be accused of marrying you for your money."

"By whom?"

"By everyone!"

She laughed. "I tell you what. I'll sell my house and

the hotel and put all my money in trust for Tony. Then we can go live in your tent."

"We can't! I already threw it away." He hugged her to him. "As long as *you* don't think I'm a fortune-hunter . . ."

"How can I, Jason? I'm the one who proposed. Besides, I'm not that rich." She paused, frowning. "You don't think I'm too old for you, do you?"

"Too old? Ginger, I'm much older than you are. I'm twenty-nine."

"I'll be thirty-two in February."

"Oh, my, such an old lady! You sure don't look it." He grinned his face-splitting grin. "God, I can't believe this is happening. It's like a Christmas present from heaven. Ten days early."

"Yes. For me too."

"I want you to know"—he was very serious now—"I'll be the best father to Tony that I know how to be. I do love him, you know."

"I know. And I'll be as good a mother to Vivien as she'll let me be."

Nobody saw them for almost a week. They rode their horses as far as the date groves in Indio at the eastern end of the valley. There Ginger phoned Maria and asked her to keep Tony for a few more days. Then she called The Springs and instructed her assistant to take over until he heard from her.

They went shopping and loaded their horses with blankets and camping gear and dried food and then rode back into the mountains for a pre-wedding honeymoon. As they wandered away from civilization, they saw marvelous sights—jagged purple mountains, wind-sculptured hills, distant lakes, multicolored rocks, a shy mountain lion, galloping wild horses, nimble bighorn sheep, mischievous kit foxes, timid snakes, deep ravines, abandoned mines, shifting sand dunes. Whenever their aimless ramblings took them to a creek, they watered their horses and took sponge baths and replenished their canteens.

He taught her facts about the desert that she had never learned before, and she took him to fern-filled hidden canyons he had never seen before, and they stopped often to discover bodily sensations they had never felt before. By the end of the week their lips were swollen from fervent kisses and their bodies were bewildered by the constant seesawing between ardent arousal and the afterglow of fulfillment.

Sitting by a campfire each night, they shared thoughts and feelings and secrets, their words erupting like unstoppable geysers. He told her about the two books he wanted to write, one a serious study of the desert's biological features that he hoped would become the naturalists' bible, the other aimed for a popular audience to acquaint readers with the importance of respecting the fragile land—an expansion of his evening lectures.

She told him about her early days in San Francisco, her virtual imprisonment in Polly's Pasadena mansion, her fight for freedom, her pride in having taken care of herself since she was sixteen, her endless love affair with Palm Springs.

He told her about his childhood. "My father was a mining engineer. Ha, listen to me! That's what he used to call himself, the old phony—it was a euphemism for 'prospector.' Come to think of it, what I do isn't much different. He wandered over the desert looking for gold, and I do the same thing looking for knowledge.

"My parents never had any more kids after me. I guess it was hard enough having one, the way we lived. For months at a time he'd park my mother and me in towns like Reno or Boise while he went off into the hills digging glory holes. He never found much of value—I mean, by the time he came on the scene it had all been pretty much picked over. I had to change schools and make new friends at least twice a year, sometimes more. I didn't mind too much—I liked the adventure of new places.

"My mother would just vegetate, sitting around waiting for him to return. She had no other interest in life. It used to disgust me, even when I was a child. They had one thing going for them, though. I didn't understand it then, but there was tremendous sexual electricity between them. I realized it was pretty special, but at the same time it shut me out." He turned and gave her a solemn look. "We have to be careful not to do that to Tony. He's so accustomed to having you all to himself."

She nodded in agreement. "Where are your parents now?"

He sighed, saddened by the memory. "My father died

nine years ago in a mining accident, and my mother a year later. The only relatives I've got left are a few cousins up in Oregon."

One night he told her about his marriage. "It was nothing like this with Mary," he confided. "I'd just gotten my master's degree and my first job, teaching biology at Santa Monica High. We had a big church wedding—you know the kind: six bridesmaids in matching fancy dresses and six ushers in tails and Mary in white satin with a long train and the church decorated with a million dollars' worth of flowers. We were just doing what Mary's family expected of us. It never occurred to me to question whether I really wanted it.

"Mary was scared to death of sex, and I was much too eager. It's strange, too, because before the wedding she would kiss and pet like crazy. I really thought she was hot stuff. But on our wedding night she acted like a frigid nun. She wouldn't let me touch her for a week. I was baffled. I mean, I'd had a little experience by then, I thought I knew my way around a woman's body, but . . ." His voice trailed off.

"She got pregnant right away. First she was afraid intercourse would hurt the embryo, and then after Vivien was born Mary never had time for lovemaking. She never gave sex a chance, and I was too young and stupid to have any idea how to help her. I don't know . . . we grew apart. I met Ed Jaeger when he invited a bunch of us high-school biology teachers on a desert field trip. When he offered to get me a teaching fellowship so I could go for a doctorate, I grabbed it.

"I had to spend a lot of time on the desert for my research. Well, Mary hated it. She just hated it! She went with me only once. After that, she refused to go again. Then, while I was away, she met a nice steady man at church, a civil engineer who had a good job with the Santa Monica street department . . ." He inhaled deeply. "I suppose it sounds cruel, Ginger, but I've never been so relieved in my life! Except for Vivien. I was—I always will be—mad for that kid. But maybe it's best for her this way. We have a lot of fun when we're together, there's great love between us. Now she has stability in her life, a nice home, good schools, dancing lessons, she's a Brownie

Girl Scout, she's got all the advantages." He looked up at the stars. "All the same, I sometimes wonder if she wouldn't be better off with me, wandering free . . ."

Ginger rested her head on his shoulder. "Wouldn't it be fun if Vivien and Tony fell in love someday and got married?"

"They couldn't do better, either of them."

"Maybe she can spend her vacations with us, now that you'll have a real home."

"That would be great. I love your grandfather's house, Ginger. You know that it's the only reason I'm marrying you, don't you?"

"I thought so, you son-of-a-gold-digger, you!" She was quiet a moment. "My life with Tonito was . . . well, it was pretty wonderful. I can't deny that. We were so young. So in love. It seemed too good to be true. As it turns out, though, I guess it wasn't quite so true after all. Only . . . well . . . at the time, I didn't know it." She swallowed the painful lump in her throat and told him about Ella and Tonito.

Jason was shocked. "Is that what she told you out on the porch?"

Ginger could only nod.

He held her tight, as though to protect her from further pain. "Maybe it was for the best, though," he said softly. "If Ella hadn't told you . . . you might still be closing yourself off from me."

"I know," she whispered.

He felt the hurt still coursing through her. He could tell from the sudden stiffness of her body and the catch in her voice. Slowly and soothingly he stroked her arms and neck to relax her.

"Ella doesn't want Cal to know," Ginger said when she recovered her composure, "and I think she's right. The poor kid's a mess as it is. He'd go to pieces if he learned that Frank hadn't been his father."

"Really? Were Cal and Frank that close after the divorce?"

"Frank gave Cal the only real love the boy has ever known. Frank and Cal's old nursemaid, Juanita."

"And Tony? Does he know . . . ?"

"No. And there's no *point* in his knowing." She sat up straight and shook her head. "So far as the rest of the world is concerned, nothing happened between Tonito and Ella. All that really matters is that I've finally accepted the fact that Tonito is dead and gone and I'm ready to love *you!*"

At the end of the week they went back to Indio and found a justice of the peace. They were married just as they were, trail-dusty in their rumpled camping clothes.

They returned home two days before Christmas with the news of their marriage. Tony was thrilled. Nellie was delighted. Talbot Honeycutt was so shocked that Ginger had chosen to marry a "nobody" when she could have had him that he checked out and spent the rest of the winter in Florida. Neil thought Ginger was a fool to waste herself on a "penniless drifter."

Adele was happy for Ginger, who was like a favorite niece to her. But she also was relieved that Ginger was safely married. It hadn't escaped Adele's notice, the previous summer in Paris, that Avery's interest in Ginger might be something more than avuncular.

Avery had to steel himself against a sharp jolt of jealousy whenever he saw Ginger and Jason together. Wrapped in a cocoon of blatant eroticism, the newlyweds kept grinning at each other as though they shared a delicious secret. They couldn't leave each other alone. Ginger was forever smoothing Jason's arched brows or straightening his collar or pushing back the lock of sandy-colored hair that fell down over his forehead. Jason constantly held her hand or had a proprietary arm around her shoulders.

Avery was glad that Ginger had recovered from her ten years of unhealthy grief, and he toasted the newlyweds along with everyone else. But later, after Adele had gone to bed, he sat alone in his living room feeling sorry for himself. He finally had to accept the fact that Ginger wasn't ever going to fall in love with him. Ever!

By God, Avery fumed, he'd had his fill of unrequited love! Until now, he had been able to hope that one day Ginger would realize she loved him romantically and that they would at least become secret lovers. And as long as he had had hope, his love for her had been pleasantly bittersweet. Now it was only bitter.

What's more, Ginger's new bond with Jason couldn't help but exclude Avery to some extent. Sure, she would continue to hike with him mornings. Sure, she would include him and Adele in most of the family activities. Sure, he would always be Tony's proxy grandpa. But Ginger no longer would turn to him for comfort, for advice, for affection.

She had Jason to turn to now.

Two years later, in January 1934, Adele caught pneumonia and died within a week. As Avery sat beside her corpse, holding her lifeless hand, a grief so profound gripped him that he was beyond tears. At first he thought he was mourning for Adele, and it jolted him when he suddenly realized he was grieving for himself. He felt so old and tired—dear God, he was nearly fifty!

At that moment, he considered his life utterly wasted. Oh, sure, he was a successful doctor. But he hadn't *wanted* to be a doctor, successful or otherwise, he had wanted to be a great painter. Sure, he'd had a fairly pleasant marriage with Adele. But he hadn't *wanted* to be pleasantly married, he had wanted to be *ecstatically* married . . . to Ginger.

He thought back over his years with Adele. She had been so sweet and understanding when he came home from Paris crushed by disappointment at his failure as a painter. She had cheered him, made him feel better about going to medical school, propped up his sagging ego. Even after her health failed she had always tried to be a good wife to him. When she had been too weak to look after him herself, she had hired people who ably took care of his needs under her supervision. She seldom had allowed her illness to keep him from making love to her, and what she lacked in passion she made up for with tenderness. He felt tremendous guilt that he hadn't loved her more. Even though he had never actually been unfaithful to her with Ginger, Avery's many years of wanting Ginger certainly had eroded his desire for Adele.

After her death, Avery found it more difficult than ever to keep his avuncular facade intact in the presence of Ginger and Jason's happiness. He was wildly jealous of Jason, and spent many hours each day trudging through the desert, trying to overcome his unreasonable envy, but he was like a mountain climber sliding down a sheer cliff without a toehold in sight.

Finally he decided to go live in Paris and try once more to be a painter. After all, there was nothing to keep him in Palm Springs. He had largely retired from his medical practice. Ginger, after two years of marriage, still seemed happy with Jason. Even Tony didn't need Avery so much anymore, with Jason around.

As Avery packed, he kept trying to convince himself that he would find a wonderful new life in the City of Lights. But when he left Palm Springs he still was wallowing in the quicksand of sorrow. *Ginger, Ginger, Ginger,* was all he could think. *My girl! My darling! My love!*

CHAPTER
8

1940

"What's bothering you?" Gracie gave Ginger an amused look. "Your fortieth birthday next week?"

They were sitting beside The Springs' pool one warm February afternoon in 1940. The garden's masses of pink hibiscus and oleanders and purple bougainvillea were overshadowed by the wild yellow honeysuckle running rampant over San Jacinto's rocky slopes and casting an invisible cloud of heady fragrance over the hotel.

"Oh, my birthday." Ginger dismissed it with a wave. "No, it's everything that's happening in the world. Hitler threatening to overrun Europe, the Japanese invading Manchuria, our own country in a stew over whether or not we should get involved in Europe . . ."

"Ah, Ginger, try not to worry about things that're beyond your control." Gracie lit a cigarette. "You know what they say: if you're gonna be raped, lie back and enjoy it."

"I can't help worrying, Gracie. Roosevelt's been talking about a military draft, and Tony's eighteen now . . ." Ginger sighed. It wasn't only Tony's welfare that troubled her. There was Avery, still in Paris even though the Germans had declared war on France the previous summer; Avery, whom she hadn't seen in six years but who still managed to creep into her thoughts constantly, no matter how hard she tried to forget his existence.

They were interrupted by Ginger's secretary. "Mail time," the white-haired Indian woman called out, waving the envelopes in her hand.

"Thanks, Romalda." In the bright sunshine, Ginger squinted at the return addresses, then held on to one and gave the rest back to the woman. "I'll look at these later." As her secretary headed back toward the office, Ginger ripped open the envelope she had kept. "Oh, my God!" she shrieked, "Neil's getting married! In two weeks!"

"Your brother? Why're you so surprised?"

"You know Neil. He's never stayed with the same woman for more than a month or two!" Ginger passed the parchment invitation to Gracie.

Gracie glanced at it. "Who's this Jennie Warren?" She handed the invitation back to Ginger.

"She's a beautiful little creature, maybe sixteen or seventeen years old. Wants to be an actress. We met her at Neil's Christmas party and I liked her . . . but I never thought Neil was going to *marry* her."

"Is that why he built the biggest damn house in Palm Springs?" Gracie asked. "As a gift for his bride?"

"I guess so. You should see it, Gracie!"

"What's it like?"

"Well, he copied a sixteenth-century Florentine villa down to the last little piece of mosaic. It's got groined ceilings and frescoes all over the place, and a master bedroom as big as a ballroom, and a three-acre garden full of fountains and lagoons and waterfalls and grottoes."

"It sounds fantastic."

Ginger shook her head. "I don't know, it just doesn't work. Somehow it seems grotesque, all that ornate decor and lush greenery out here in the desert." Ginger gestured at Palm Springs, spread out below them. "The desert cries out for simplicity. But have you noticed what's happening to my sweet little village? I swear, every time I look out, I see a new golf course and a couple more tennis courts and a *dozen* new swimming pools. Is there a movie star or producer or director who doesn't have a fancy house here?"

"Listen, kiddo, with the publicity this town gets, you're lucky the place has stayed as small as it is. Kee-rist! Each time a famous star farts out here, his press agent has it in every paper in the country."

"Well, I think we ought to put a wall around Palm Springs and not let anyone else in." Ginger sighed in exasperation. "Dammit, we're even a *city* now with a real honest-to-God mayor and an official city council. Can you believe there are more than *five thousand* permanent year-round residents? And thousands more living here every winter? And all the congestion from God only knows how many visitors and their damn smelly cars?"

"What do you expect, Ginger? People love to come here. It's beautiful. The weather's gorgeous. You can't keep people out."

"I know. Whenever I complain to Nellie, she reminds me that our city exists for tourists and visitors." Ginger sighed. "Nellie says this is nothing, that some day *millions* of people will be coming here every year. And let me tell you, Nellie's always right about things like that."

Gracie dragged deeply on her cigarette. "Well, why worry? You're as pleasantly isolated up here on your mesa as you ever were."

Ginger looked around at her hotel's luxuriant grounds. "This'll change too," she said glumly. "Now that air-conditioning's becoming so popular in theaters and shops, people will start expecting every damn hotel room in the desert to be ice-cold too."

"You're sure full of complaints today." Gracie smiled.

"Oh, I've got more. Yesterday I kicked out a pushy salesman who wanted to put a jukebox in the bar and dime pinball machines in the lobby! Can you imagine the nerve?"

"Boy, you're in some mood, my friend. Expecting your period or something?"

Ginger shrugged. "Well, yes, but mostly I guess it's an attack of old-fashioned nostalgia. I don't know, Gracie, I liked the world better the way it used to be."

"Sure," Gracie said acidly, "the Depression was lots of fun."

"It didn't affect us that much out here."

"Lucky you! Did you know I was an Okie? That my family's farm blew away in the dust bowl? The Depression started for us long before it did for the rest of the country." Gracie jabbed out her cigarette in an ashtray. "We came to California in the twenties, three adults including my sick old grandma and five scared kids in one little sedan, with everything we owned in the world tied down on the roof. Sure, those days were a barrel of laughs. We thought it was hilarious to drive on dirt roads that busted your axles and your backs. We laughed ourselves silly when our old bald tires went flat every few miles and my father had to stop and patch them. Yeah, those sure were the good old days!"

"Gracie, I didn't know—"

"Why'd you think I used to be so fat? It was from eating nothing but potatoes and stale bread all that time." Gracie gestured at her slim, trim body, now a hundred pounds lighter than it had been a few years earlier. "But hell, that's ancient history. Tell me, did you ever think I'd be so skinny? Or turn into the contented middle-class wife of a middle-class furniture-store manager with an adorable little middle-class daughter? And live in a middle-class cracker box of a house?"

Fondly Ginger touched her friend's arm. "Don't you ever miss being a big Hollywood star?"

"Big was right! Nope. I've never regretted losing all that blubber and snagging myself a husband. When I saw how happy you were with Jason, I realized I was missing something. There I was, two years younger'n you, and looking old enough to be your mother. I kept getting fatter, and lonelier—"

"And richer!"

"Sure, but what good was it? I know Bert Elliott's no Cary Grant, but believe me, he's sexy as hell. He's the best thing that ever happened to me. Bert and little Amy both." She looked down at her flat stomach and shapely legs. Even after seven years, she couldn't believe it actually was her body. She still felt like a fat person, as if the rest of her existed but was simply invisible.

She had lied to Ginger. Sure, she missed the excitement of being a star. Nowadays, nobody even recognized her, especially with all her famous flab gone. As for giving up her career in the hopes of having a marriage like Ginger's, Gracie had to admit that her relationship with Bert lacked the magic that Ginger and Jason seemed to share. Just watching them together gave Gracie goosebumps—the way those two *looked* at each other was more erotic than a dozen stag shows. Abruptly Gracie stood up. "I'm going swimming," she announced.

As Ginger watched Gracie make a neat dive into the pool and do a fast crawl for six laps, she felt concern for her friend. At the Racquet Club the previous Saturday night, when Gracie was home nursing Amy's sore throat, Ginger had seen Gracie's Bert dancing with Ella. Ginger had recognized all the danger signs: Ella's big violet-blue eyes worshipfully gazing up at Bert with her "aren't-you-the-most-wonderful-creature" look that Ginger knew so well, and Bert staring hungrily at Ella as though he wanted to throw her down on the dance floor and ravish her right in front of Lucy and Dinah and Spence and Katie and Clark and Tyrone and Greer and Charlie and all the other regulars at the club.

For eight years, after confessing to Ginger about her affair with Tonito, Ella had stayed away from Palm Springs, afraid of Ginger's wrath. Ginger had heard that Ella had bought a mansion in Beverly Hills and had kept Cal in a military academy all that time. But suddenly, the previous November, Ella had returned to Palm Springs with Cal. She had bought the eighteen-room "Villa Moderne," a white-brick estate with a sixty-foot swimming pool and two tennis courts, all enclosed by a ten-foot-high stone wall.

Ginger and Ella never spoke to each other, not even when they passed on the street or met in a shop. "I'll never forgive her," Ginger had told Jason the first time she ran into Ella, "and I'll never forgive Tonito either! He's lucky he's dead or I'd kill him!"

"You wouldn't have to," Jason said. "I'd kill him for you."

Ginger had looked searchingly at Jason. "Do *you* think Ella is . . . well . . . ? Tell me the truth. Does she attract you? Even a little?"

For a reply, Jason had taken Ginger into his arms. "I think she's pathetic," he had said, and meant it.

Gracie got out of the pool and wrapped herself in her pink terry robe. "I saw your sister this morning, shopping at the Plaza," she said, as though reading Ginger's mind.

"Lucky you."

"She asked about you . . . you know, did I think you'd like to make up with her." Gracie stretched out on a chaise and lit another cigarette.

Ginger groaned in exasperation. "What did you tell her?"

"Well, I have no idea what your beef is against her,

but I dislike Ella on general principle. I wanted to tell her that if she was my sister, I'd pull out her bleached-blond hair and run her out of town. But I didn't have the nerve. I just told her I didn't know if you wanted to make up with her or not."

Ginger shook her head. "No, I don't want to. Not now. Not ever."

"But I have to tell you, Ginger, your sister still looks great. It just knocks me out. Did you hear, she was desperate to play Scarlett O'Hara? The studio said she was too old, so she broke her contract and quit cold. Just like that. She said she'd never make another picture."

Ginger felt a flash of hatred for her sister. Even after almost nineteen years, even though she was happy with Jason now, Ginger still couldn't bear the thought of Ella and Tonito making love. *Fucking themselves silly*, Ella had smugly boasted. And all that time Ginger had gone around deliriously happy, thinking that Tonito was madly in love with her. What a fool she'd been!

Ginger also resented the fact that Ella's son, Cal, was Tony's half-brother. Sometimes she yearned to tell Tony the truth about his father, but then thought better of it. Tony idolized his father's memory, and he'd be hurt to learn that his father had been unfaithful.

Despite her anger toward Ella, Ginger was morbidly curious to hear all the gossip about her sister. She remembered when they were children how she'd been driven crazy by Ella's ability to attract people just by looking beautiful and by outrageously flattering them. Yes, she admitted to herself, she had always been jealous of Ella's exceptional beauty. But then, Ella had always been jealous of Ginger's scholastic ability and, above all, of her happy disposition.

"Gracie," Ginger asked, trying to sound offhand, "since you know all the latest scoop . . . um . . . what's Ella doing? Now that she's retired from films."

"Husband-stealing."

"Nothing new about that," Ginger said bitterly.

"Yeah?" Gracie gave Ginger a penetrating look and wondered at the hurt in her voice. Had Ella been foolish enough to try her wiles on Jason? "It's a funny thing about her," Gracie continued. "She always passes up the rich-and-famous guys and goes after the most ordinary men."

"Yeah, I know. Years ago she told me that successful men expect *her* to worship *them*. But with ordinary men, *she's* the one who's worshiped."

"Well, she's busted up at least a half-dozen marriages that I know of," Gracie said.

And one you don't know about, Ginger thought, remembering Bert dancing with Ella. She frowned, waving Neil's invitation. "Y'know, Neil's wedding poses a real problem. If he invites Ella, I won't go. He'll have to choose between her and me."

Gracie stood up and began gathering together her belongings. "Don't be crushed, sweetie, if he chooses Ella. After all, they're business partners. . . ."

"Sure! Developing my grandfather's land that by rights should be mine!" Ginger tore the invitation in little pieces and threw it in the ashtray. "They can both go to hell!"

Gracie took hold of Ginger's arm. "Take it easy, hon."

"I'll walk you to your car," Ginger said, taking deep breaths to calm herself. She led the way through her cheerful red-carpeted cocktail lounge, formerly the hotel's glass-enclosed veranda, which she had converted into a bar when prohibition ended in 1933. The room reverberated with the Andrews Sisters' bouncy voices singing "Beat me, Daddy, Eight to the Bar," and Ginger impatiently gestured for the bartender to turn down the radio's volume.

"Someday, after Neil's wedding," Gracie said soothingly, "will you take me to see his Italian *palazzo*?"

"Sure. *If* he and I are still talking to each other." Ginger sighed sadly. "Can you imagine the good he could've done with the money he wasted on that monstrosity?"

"Like what?"

"Oh, he could've built a hospital, or a new library . . . we need more schools . . . and an art museum, things like that. Since Palm Springs is a city now, we might as well give it a little culture."

Gracie laughed. "Yeah, we're big on tennis and low on Tennyson." She turned serious. "Y'know, maybe I should start doing things like that. I've got dough stashed away from my films and radio shows like you wouldn't believe. How d'you think I feel, having to come begging to use your pool when I could afford to buy a *hundred* swimming pools? But no, Bert won't let me spend a dime of my own money, not even on a little pool for Amy. We have to live on *his* lousy income." Glumly she opened the door of her six-year-old black Chevrolet coupe. Then she forced a smile. "Oh, well, what's the difference? Say, how about you and Jason coming with us to the Chi Chi tonight? Artie Shaw's playing. Or we could rumba at the El Mirador. . . ."

"Thanks, Gracie, but John Steinbeck's here and we invited him for dinner tonight. Why don't you two join *us*?"

"Is he the guy who wrote that book about the Okies? The one they've made into a movie with Hank Fonda?"

Ginger nodded. "Right. *The Grapes of Wrath*."

"I'd love to meet him." Gracie shook her head regretfully. "But Bert only likes hobnobbing with your run-of-the-mill famous movie stars. Cerebral celebrities make him nervous. Thanks anyway."

Watching Gracie drive away, Ginger wondered when her friend was going to realize how much she resented being pushed around by her precious Bert, all in the name of "love."

Ella stretched out languorously on her chaise. She watched Cal dive off the high board and swim underwater the entire length of their oversize pool. She felt a mixture of pride and exasperation when she looked at her son. He was absolutely beautiful—except for his brown hair and eyes and darker skin, a male version of herself. He had Tonito's remarkable smile, but only she and Ginger would ever make the connection. Or had Ginger told anyone that Tonito was Cal's father? Maybe Jason.

The trouble was, Cal was eighteen now, and with a little simple arithmetic anyone could figure out that Ella no longer was twenty-seven, as she always told people she was. When Cal had been younger, Ella had kept him out of sight, at the military academy and summer camps, so it was easy to fib about his age—and hers. Now he was too old to be hidden away. He had already graduated from the academy, didn't want to go to college, and, being as money-mad as his uncle, was planning to work for Neil.

Just looking at Cal made Ella feel old, and she feared aging even more than she feared death. Sometimes, when she discovered a new wrinkle, she thought it might be less painful to just take a handful of sleeping pills and end it all than to go on constantly finding signs that her youth and beauty were fading. She kept a woman on her permanent staff named Daisy, who did nothing but give Ella massages and facials and take care of her hair and makeup. Ella wouldn't even go to L.A. for the night unless Daisy went too.

Ella knew damn well what Ginger would say: "For God's sake, Ella, relax and enjoy life. Nobody but you gives a damn how old you are." But there was no way Ella was going to lie back and accept the inevitable. She'd fight it every inch of the way!

She still seethed with anger at the very thought of Ginger. Ella was bright enough to realize that her attitude was unreasonable, but nevertheless, she couldn't help it: she had been jealous of her sister ever since she could remember. Hadn't Ginger robbed her of their mother's love, right from the start? What's more, Ella couldn't stand the way her sister was so happy all the time, while she herself was always fretting about something. Take Ginger's marriage to Jason. At first everybody had thought Jason was a dud, a penniless desert rat, and that Ginger had been out of her mind to marry him. But then he fooled them all by becoming a world-famous author and desert authority. And whenever Ella bumped into Ginger's friend Gracie, Gracie always made it a point to tell Ella that Ginger and Jason were crazy in love, in a wonderfully exciting way that Ella herself never had experienced.

When Ella had returned to Palm Springs three months earlier, she had decided to seduce Jason, as she'd done with Tonito, just to get even once more with Ginger. Ella had read in the L.A. *Times* that Jason was going to be signing his new book at a bookstore in Pasadena, and Ella made a special trip there, hoping to see him alone, without Ginger.

"Well, hel-*lo*," she had drawled seductively, "remember me?"

His face had hardened. "Ella."

She had pouted charmingly. "Is that the way to greet your sister-in-law?" And she had given him the wide-eyed look that always made men melt, the look that told him how wonderful he was and how much she desired him.

He had gestured at the copy of his book in her hand, *Anatomy of a Desert.* "Do you want me to sign it?" he had asked coldly, and when she held it out to him, he had autographed it silently and handed it back without a word.

Ella was still smarting over the only two other men who had ever rejected her advances. Years ago there'd been that vile Talbot Honeycutt, who had been in love with Ginger. And then there was Dr. Avery. Ella had bumped into him in Paris a couple of years earlier, when she had gone for lunch with some friends to Tour d'Argent.

"Why, Dr. Avery Rowland!" she had squealed in surprise, passing his table. She had suddenly realized that Avery was a very attractive man, with his strong tanned face and silver hair and tall robust body.

He had stood up and introduced her to the white-haired woman seated beside him. Then, politely, he had asked Ella if she cared to join them.

"Just for a minute," she had said. While the people she had arrived with were shown to their own table, Ella sat down with Avery and started to come onto him with her usual seductive wiles. She had been bored with Paris, bored with the people she knew there, and a fling with Avery had suddenly seemed like a lark to her.

Completely ignoring his companion, Ella had looked into Avery's eyes with her widest-eyed smoldering look. He had merely watched her with an amused smile while she plied him with compliments.

"My dear girl," he had finally said, "if you are finished, I'd like to return to my lunch."

Ella had stood up in shock and without another word had fled to her own companions' table. She hadn't seen Avery since, and was furious with him whenever she thought about that humiliating scene.

Now, lost in thought beside her pool, Ella was startled when Cal clambered onto the flagstone deck and purposely splashed her as he reached for a towel.

"Watch it!" she said sharply. "You almost got my hair wet!"

"Sorry, Mother *dear*," he said sarcastically. He went

into the house, dripping chlorinated water all over the expensive carpeting.

Cal's feelings for his mother were as ambivalent as hers were for him. He was entranced by her beauty, narcissistically so, since they looked so much alike. But he bitterly resented his mother for the very traits they shared—a selfish nature and an ability to attract the opposite sex. He wanted an unselfish mother who was *motherly*, one who doted on him, one who never would have sent away his beloved Juanita or put him in a military academy. He wanted a mother who would have given him a stepfather after his own father died, the way his Aunt Ginger had for Tony. Cal still felt like crying when he thought of Frank Ricardo and the fun they always had had together before Frank died in his arms eight years earlier.

Cal was jealous of his cousin Tony, jealous of all the love Tony had gotten, and still got, while he was growing up. But Cal also had contempt for Tony. Who'd want a dirt-poor Indian for a father? Tony was such a square, too, always hitting the books and apple-polishing for A's and listening to classical music. Cal would bet his last dollar that Tony never touched broads or booze.

Cal showered his strong bronze body, then dressed in snappy white shorts and polo shirt, grabbed his tennis racket, and went out to his car, a white Duesenberg convertible with flashy red leather seats. He ran a hand lovingly over the long, arrogant hood. To him the car was like a sculpture, with its swooping fenders and shiny nickel-plated trim, a perfect complement to his own good looks. The only car he considered more beautiful was his mother's silver-and-blue Bugatti Royal, but she never let him drive it.

Cal sped out Indian Avenue toward the Racquet Club, where he had a date with the most desirable girl he had ever met. For the first time in his life, he was in love. Every day for the last two months he and his date had played tennis for an hour. Then they spent two more hours making love in the club bungalow he had rented for his secret assignations with her.

Driving north toward the club that afternoon, he suddenly noticed how the afternoon sun gilded the side of Mt. San Jacinto. He felt as though the mountain were signaling to him. Mesmerized, he pulled over to the side of the road and stared up at the rocky slopes. Something expanded within him, almost taking his breath away. He felt strange, dizzy, and puzzled, because he never had cared about scenery or vistas or anything like that. He had hardly ever even looked at San Jacinto before. He shook his head to clear it, shifted the car into first, and laid rubber on the asphalt in his hurry to escape from his odd experience.

With a flourish, he parked in the Racquet Club lot, grabbed his racket, and leapt over the car door. He used his racket to salute the guard at the club entrance. Realizing he was late, he ran swiftly through the building and found his date waiting for him at the swimming pool, where she was watching a fashion show while seated at one of the umbrella tables set around the decking. By the time they walked over to the tennis court and started their practice volley, Cal had completely shaken the curious—and strangely mystical—experience he had encountered en route to the club. All he cared about now was beating the frilly pants off his lovely partner.

His date—the girl he was so crazy about—was seventeen-year-old Jennie Warren. She also happened to be his Uncle Neil's fiancée.

Whenever Cal and Jennie played tennis with each other, it was like an exhibition game. Everyone in the club came over to watch. Cal's game was good enough for international competition, though he laughed and shook his head when anyone suggested it. He had been playing tennis since he was big enough to hold a racket, and he had been coached by all the greats: Big Bill Tilden, Fred Perry, Don Budge. And Jennie on the tennis court was a joy to behold. With the grace of a ballet dancer, the speed of an Olympic sprinter, and an almost humming-bird lightness, she dazzled the audience with her breath-taking leaps and twirls, her luminous beauty, her glorious youth.

Their games were like exercises in perpetual motion, so evenly matched were they. Rarely did either miss a shot. Only when the ball went outside the line—and even then, just by an inch or two—did one or the other score a point.

Although Cal was extremely competitive and hated

losing to anyone, even Jennie, halfway through the game on this sunny February day he realized how impatient he was to be alone with her. As always, he tingled with desire for her, but he also had something important to discuss with her. Therefore, despite his initial intention of winning the set, he began to deliberately throw the game by skillfully hitting the ball slightly harder than he ordinarily would have, letting her win and thus quickly ending the match.

As usual after their game, they made a great show of saying good-bye. "Give Uncle Neil my love," Cal said loudly as he headed for the Bamboo Bar.

"See you tomorrow," Jennie said, going into the dining room, ostensibly to watch Rudy Vallee rehearse the songs for his evening radio broadcast from the club.

But Cal meandered out the bar's back door, and a few minutes later Jennie slipped out of the dining room. Taking paths that veered off in divergent directions, they circled through the grounds and met in Cal's bungalow, making sure that no one saw them entering.

Later, Cal gathered the courage to say what was on his mind. "Jennie, you simply *can't* marry Uncle Neil. He's old and fat . . . besides, you love *me*, not him."

"Just because I've given you two terrific orgasms this afternoon," she chided playfully, "doesn't give you the right to tell me what to do!" She rolled her sleek body on top of his and put her hands on either side of his face. She liked the way the tilted-up slats of the venetian blinds threw diagonal stripes of sunlight across them, as though they were a couple of rutting zebras. She kissed his eyelids, then slid her tongue into his mouth and let it playfully duel with his tongue.

He rolled both of them over so that he was on top of her. "Answer me!"

She caught his penis between her legs and squeezed it with the strong muscles of her upper thighs. "D'you like that?" she murmured.

"Mmmmm." He wove his fingers through her long blue-black hair, which came to a point in the middle of her forehead. God, she was beautiful! She could look like an aristocrat one minute and a tramp the next, or a svelte lady or a frisky gamine. She had the heady combination of very dark hair and vivid blue eyes, translucent pale skin highlighted by naturally rosy cheeks, a slightly upturned nose with flaring nostrils, a generous mouth, perfect little teeth, a long smooth throat, breasts that were firm mounds of voluptuous flesh, legs even classier than Marlene's . . . even Jennie's little pink toes were delightful.

When she kissed him she threw her whole body into it, undulating beneath him, pushing her breasts against his chest, breathing in frantic little spurts through her nose. She ran out of breath and tore her mouth away from his to gasp more air into her lungs. "Hurry!" she begged. "Oh, Cal, *now! Now! Now!*"

"Don't you have to shoot up more goop on your diaphragm?"

"God, no, not now! *Cal!*"

He let the tip of his hard penis rest against the outside of her vagina but he didn't push it in. "First answer me about marrying Uncle Neil!" he insisted.

"*Cal!*" she shrieked. She wiggled against him, trying to force him into her, but he pulled himself up too high for her to make contact. She was panting hard, almost in tears. "Oh, darling, darling, *please* . . . let's talk when we're finished."

"You promise?"

"Y-e-e-s. . . ."

He entered her very slowly, making her even more frantic. He was excited by her desperation, by the way she cried out and eagerly thrust herself against him. He was lost in the moment, in the sweet sensations radiating through his body from the epicenter where he melted into her. He realized that she was throbbing like an engine without a turn-off switch.

"Now," he said, still on top of her after they both came, imprisoning her with his strong body and capturing her arms above her head, "you promised. Answer me!"

She sighed contentedly. "What was the question?"

"Do you love me or my Uncle Neil?"

"You. You, you, *you!*" She paused to raise her head and kiss his chin. "I love him too, but in a different way. Not like I love you."

"Then why are you marrying him instead of me?"

"I'll marry you later on."

He stared down at her in astonishment. "Later on *when*?"

"Why . . . after I divorce Neil, dummy."

He rolled off her and lay on his back next to her. "Jennie," he said sadly. "Jennie."

She turned on her side, holding her head up with one hand. With her other hand she traced the shape of his brows, his nose, his lips, his chin. "You're too young now, Cal. I know your mother's rich, but you're not. What would we live on? Your allowance isn't nearly enough—"

Angrily he threw her hand off his face. "I see. Just because I can't afford to build you a stupid Italian palace on a goddamn three-acre knoll—"

"Shhhh. You don't understand at all." She leaned over and kissed his mouth lightly. "Look, Neil knows everybody in Hollywood. And, Cal, I want to be a big star. It's been my dream ever since I can remember. My mama's and Daddy-Joe's too. I've worked so hard all my life— taking dancing lessons every day, practicing with singing coaches, and going to drama classes. I've memorized everything from Shakespeare to Clifford Odets, and all of Noël Coward's plays—"

"Dammit, Jennie, being an actress isn't so wonderful. Look at my mother. It hasn't made her all that happy."

"Even if it makes me miserable, I've got to do it. I just *have* to! Cal, try to understand. I'm so *good* at it! I am! I can act. I *know* I can win an Oscar with the right role. I can dance, even better than Ginger Rogers and Eleanor Powell put together. And you heard me sing here at the club last Friday night, when I did that impromptu duet with Bing. Did you know that afterward Tommy and Artie both asked me to be their lead girl singer? But I don't want to be just a singer. I want to do everything!" She paused. "Don't you see, Cal? If you're born with wings, you just have to fly!"

He sighed in frustration. "Why can't you marry me and still be a star? My mother would help you. She knows even more film people than Neil does."

Jennie shook her head. "Forgive me, Cal, but your mother's been away from Hollywood too long. Besides, she might not want you to get married so young."

"*She* married young."

"It's different for girls." Jennie sat up and gestured excitedly. "Neil knows everyone. Not just actors and actresses. He knows directors and producers and the people who run the studios. He's going to finance a movie for me so I can be a star in my very first picture. You have to admit, Cal, neither of us could even walk into this place"—she waved her hand out at the exclusive club—"if it wasn't for Neil's being a member."

"That's not true. My mother's a member too." Cal, still lying down, put an arm over his eyes. "When you screw my uncle, do you think of me?" he asked bitterly.

"Oh, Cal, I've never been to bed with Neil!"

Cal took his arm from his eyes and stared at her in astonishment. "What? How come?"

"Well, Neil and I decided to wait until our wedding night. Two weeks from today."

"God, Jennie, are you saying that exactly two weeks from tonight you'll just stop loving me and start loving him?"

"No, silly, I'll still love you too."

"How will you stand having sex with Uncle Neil? He's so fat and old."

"Come on, Cal, he's only thirty-six. That's not so bad. You've got to be patient. After a couple of years I'll get a divorce and marry you."

"You mean, after all Uncle Neil's going to do for you, you'll just up and leave him?"

"No, I'd never do that. But Neil will *force* me to leave him."

Cal sat up. "How will he do that?"

She shrugged sadly. "He loves me now, but men never are satisfied very long with one woman, no matter how marvelous she is. So when Neil starts being unfaithful, I'll divorce him."

"What am I supposed to do until then?"

"I don't know, Cal. I guess find someone else in the meantime, because I plan to be absolutely faithful to Neil."

"You mean you won't even see me once in a while, all the time you're married to Uncle Neil?"

"Not like this." She gestured at their nude bodies on the bed. She giggled. "After all, I'll be your aunt!"

"You really mean it? You're actually going to be *faithful* to Uncle Neil?" His voice rose with incredulity.

"Of course. That's what I've been telling you."

"Jennie, I don't understand you!"

"It's just that I believe in being faithful when you're married."

"Jeez!" He flung out of bed and angrily stormed around the room.

"Cal, please," she begged softly, "don't spoil our last two weeks together. Don't you see? You'll want me to be faithful to you when *we're* married, won't you?"

"Sure, but . . ."

"Of course, after a while you'll also be unfaithful to me, the same as Neil. Men always are. So then I'll have to divorce you too."

He came back to bed, shoved her down onto the mattress, and got on top of her. He entered her savagely but it was no good, not for either of them. "Jennie, I can't believe you're doing this to me." He was close to tears. "To us."

"I'm sorry, Cal. But that's the way it has to be."

"In that case, the hell with you! I don't ever want to see you again!"

Jennie knew what she was talking about when she said men never were faithful to their wives. Her own parents had been a singing-and-dancing vaudeville team, and when Jennie was six her father ran off with a female ventriloquist. It sounded like a bad joke when she told people about it, but Jennie had vivid memories of how hurt she had been. Her mother had been devasted too. Young though Jennie had been at the time, she had vowed *never* to love a man so much that it would be painful to lose him.

She remembered her father very clearly, even though she hadn't seen him for eleven years. Tears still came to her eyes when she thought of him. He had been as handsome as her mother was beautiful, both of them with Jennie's coloring—dark, dark hair and bright blue eyes. She was sure that if she passed him on the street she would know him at once. She had a fantasy that someday, when she was famous, he would recognize her on the screen and come find her so that he could apologize and they'd be friends.

Two years after her father's desertion, when Jennie

was eight, her mother had teamed up with Daddy-Joe, who was a dancer too. The two of them had married, quit the stage, and become dance teachers and coaches on Hollywood musicals. They had worked with Fred and Ginger and helped them "dance down to Rio," up walls, and over furniture. And knowing that millions of girls wanted to step into Ginger's shoes, Jennie's mama and Daddy-Joe had made their main occupation the training of Jennie for stardom. When she outgrew their teaching, they sent her to the best coaches in Hollywood. The three of them were a team—after a while, in more ways than were obvious.

On Jennie's fifteenth birthday, Mama and Daddy-Joe decided that if she was going to be a "sex symbol," then she ought to know everything she could about sex. "It's not enough to just *look* voluptuous, you've got to *be* voluptuous," Daddy-Joe explained patiently. "But, honey, a lot of people wouldn't understand what we're about to do, so it has to be a big secret between just the three of us."

That afternoon Mama took Jennie to her gynecologist to be fitted with a diaphragm, and that night Jennie and Mama and Daddy-Joe got into bed together. First Daddy-Joe had sex with Mama, while Jennie carefully watched. They explained each step of what they were doing until they got too excited to talk. Then Daddy-Joe had sex with Jennie while Mama coached her as much as possible.

Afterward Daddy-Joe said, "Now, Jennie-doll, just like you practice your dancing, it's important to practice sex. There are millions of girls out there who will do anything to get into the movies. You have to be good at everything they do, and then some."

After that, they "practiced" almost every night. But what Mama didn't know was that on the three mornings a week she left the house early for a nine-o'clock tap-dance class, Daddy-Joe gave Jennie *extra* practice with a passionate frenzy he never dared display in front of Mama.

Daddy-Joe taught her all about oral sex too. "You see, honey, not many people do this. It's considered very . . . well, sort of perverted. But I've seen ambitious girls go from one producer's office to the next, all over the big studios, unzipping the men's flies and sucking them off. There's one producer who's famous for taking starlets to

the best restaurants in town and having the girls crawl
under the table and give him a blow-job while he's eating. So if anyone really important in films ever asks you
to 'go down on him'—that's what it's sometimes called
too—I want you to do it *better* than anyone else." He was
thoughtful a moment. "I'm hoping, sweetheart, that you'll
wow them with your talent alone and won't have to do
things like that. But it's best to be prepared."

Jennie was very fond of her mama and Daddy-Joe, and
grateful too. They had taught her so much, preparing her
for stardom! When Jennie met Cal, she especially appreciated the sex training Mama and Daddy-Joe had given
her.

Tony, a freshman at Stanford, came home from Palo
Alto for his mother's fortieth birthday party. He was
taking flying lessons and he flew down to Palm Springs
with his instructor. When Ginger drove to the little Palm
Springs airport to pick him up, Tony pointed excitedly at
his instructor's blue-and-white Navion two-seater. "Hey,
Mom! Isn't she a beaut?"

Ginger kissed him, then cast a critical eye at the small
plane. She wasn't thrilled about her son's love of flying.

"Want to go up and see Palm Springs from the air,
Mom?" He appealed to his instructor. "What d'you say,
Herb, can you take my mother up? Oh, Mom, this is
Herb Tannenbaum."

"I'll fly with you some other time," Ginger said hastily as
she shook hands with the flight instructor. "How about
me giving *you* a ride, Mr. Tannenbaum . . . here on the
ground?"

"Thanks a million, Mrs. Sisley, but some friends are
coming by for me any minute. I buzzed their house."

While Ginger drove home, Tony told her about his
classes and his friends. "Who's coming to your birthday
party tomorrow night?" he asked.

"All the usual. Grace and Bert and their Amy, and
Nellie, and your Aunt Maria and Uncle Vittorio and
their five kids, and a few other old friends."

"I'm really sorry Avery won't be here," Tony said.

"He shouldn't have stayed in Paris this winter," Ginger said worriedly. "It was just plain stupid of him not to

come home last September after the Germans declared war on France."

"Yeah, Mom, but nothing much has happened since then, and in his last letter Avery said that the French have a lot of faith in their Maginot Line."

"Sure, but who knows what'll happen when the Germans finally do invade? They could come around through Holland and Belgium, like they did in the First World War. I just wish he was here where he belongs!"

"Anyone else coming to your party?"

"Oh, yes, Neil's bringing his fiancée. Imagine, Tony, she's younger than you are! And Vivien's coming in tomorrow, on the afternoon train."

"Good old Viv. It's fun having a little stepsister."

"She's not so little anymore. She's nearly sixteen."

He hesitated. "I hope you won't take this the wrong way, Mom, but . . . well . . . I can't help wishing that Jason really was my father. I mean, it's not that I'm not proud of my own father, but I never knew him and . . . and Jason's been so good to me."

Ginger was silent as she drove. How could she admit to him that she wished so too? Her anger at Tonito was less intense than it once had been, but she doubted that she would ever get over his betrayal. Besides, Jason was such fun to live with. Her only regret was their failure to have a child together. They had tried. Oh, how they had tried! Sam Miller, one of the doctors who had taken over Avery's practice, had said their problem might stem from the trauma of Tony's birth. He had sent them to three different fertility specialists in Los Angeles, all in vain. Now Ginger nursed a fond hope that Tony and Vivien might fall in love someday and at least give her and Jason a grandchild in common.

"Gosh, I miss Auntie Adele," Tony said sadly. "It just doesn't seem like the same place without her."

"I know," Ginger said gently, trying not to feel jealous. When Tony had been small, there were times he actually seemed to prefer Adele to her.

"I miss Avery too, Mom. Every letter I get from him, all he talks about is how we've got to start preparing to fight the Germans."

"He's probably right. But . . ." She gestured out at the peaceful desert. "It all just seems so far away."

"Soon as we get into the war, Mom, I'm joining the Air Corps."

Ginger shuddered. Her vivid imagination pictured Tony looking handsome in his sharp khaki uniform, Tony gracefully jumping into the cockpit of his fighter plane, Tony being riddled by machine-gun fire while parachuting down from the sky—

But he interrupted her fearful reverie, making her jump and almost lose control of the car. "Are Aunt Ella and Cousin Cal still in Palm Springs?"

She threw him a curious look. "Why? You don't expect me to invite *them* to my birthday dinner, do you?"

"Cal's not so bad," Tony said cautiously. "I saw him at the Racquet Club a few times over Christmas. He was playing tennis with the most beautiful girl."

"Well, you can see him all you want at the club, but don't you *ever* invite him home!"

"That sure doesn't sound like you, Mom. You always sat that the sins of the parents shouldn't be visited on their kids."

"Well," she said, "it doesn't apply to Ella and Cal."

He gave her a speculative look. "What did Aunt Ella ever *do* to make you hate her so much?"

She shook her head. Tears unexpectedly blurred her vision and she blinked them away.

"Never mind," Tony said softly. "I don't think I *want* to know."

Tony borrowed his mother's car the next morning and went over to the Racquet Club to see if Cal and his lovely tennis partner were there. Cal fascinated Tony. Sure, Tony was jealous of the way girls flocked around his handsome cousin, but there was something else, something Tony couldn't quite put his finger on, a bond he felt with Cal, which he chalked up to their being cousins.

Cal wasn't there, but the girl who had been Cal's tennis partner during Christmas vacation was sitting beside the pool with Tony's Uncle Neil.

"Tony!" Neil lumbered up from his lounge chair and embraced his nephew. "Jennie, meet my other nephew, my favorite half-breed. Tony, this is my fiancée."

Jennie smiled up at Tony. "Half-breed?"

"Yeah." Tony grinned to hide the shock he felt when

he heard the word "fiancée." He sat down on a chair next to Jennie's chaise. "My father was an Agua Caliente Indian."

"Oh, you must be Ginger's son." Jennie gazed at Tony with interest. "I guess I've met all my future in-laws now."

"When's the w-wedding?" Tony stammered.

"Two weeks from yesterday," Neil boomed, sitting back down and anointing his heavy body with cocoa butter. He sniffed his arm. "Smells good enough to eat. You're invited, of course. To the wedding. Not to eat my arm."

"Thanks, Uncle Neil, but I have to be back in Palo Alto day after tomorrow." Tony stole a look at Jennie. He had never seen such a beautiful, sweet face. "I guess I'll see you at my mother's party tonight," he said. When Jennie smiled up at him again and nodded, he felt as though all the blood had rushed to his head and left the rest of him limp. He struggled to his feet, waved good-bye, and walked unsteadily away from them.

Neil watched Tony's wobbly gait with a sardonic smile. *Another young man bites the dust at Jennie's feet.* The girl was a man-killer, and Neil was going to see that every youth in America—and lots of older guys too—fell madly in love with her. He had a great script for her first picture and a fantastic publicity campaign all mapped out, and it wouldn't be long before his Jennie would knock 'em all dead. But he wasn't doing it just for love. The return on his financial investment would knock the established movie moguls dead with envy.

He didn't kid himself for a minute that Jennie was in love with him. But she was fond of him and very, very affectionate, and that was good enough. He was pretty much wiped out as far as sex was concerned, anyway. He had had too much, too often, and it had become old hat. Oh, he still liked a good fuck once or twice a week, but not the way Jennie was carrying on with Cal.

Neil chortled to himself: the two silly kids thought they were keeping their torrid affair a big dark secret from him, when he had half the club's employees on his pay-roll, spying on them. Well, there was no way Neil could keep up with her in the sack. He had hoped she'd go right on secretly seeing Cal after the wedding, but evidently they'd had a falling-out. Now it looked as though Jennie's healthy sexual appetite was going to be Neil's problem exclusively.

He wasn't too worried. Maybe the little doll would reawaken some of his old ardor. And once she started working with calls at six in the morning and late-night shooting, she might be too tired to go at it two, three, four times a day, the way she had with Cal.

He looked forward to being a married man. He was sick of women throwing themselves at him for his money. He was sick of being promiscuous. It took too much time and effort. And making money was more fun. Above all, he loved the idea that once he made Jennie Warren famous, she'd turn out to be the best financial investment he'd ever made.

"This girl, this Jennie," Tony said to Ginger as soon as he got home. "How come she's marrying Uncle Neil?"

"Who knows?" Ginger shook her head. "Love is strange."

"Jeez, Mom, she can't really love him."

"Well, I know it looks that way. At first I thought she must be marrying him for his money. And I suppose that can't help but be a factor, especially after he took her to Beverly Hills and bought her half a dozen fur coats and all kinds of fabulous clothes and precious jewels for an engagement present. And I guess the house itself is a wedding present. But actually, she seems genuinely fond of him." Ginger pondered for a moment. "Of course, she *is* an actress. Maybe it's all an act. But let's give her the benefit of the doubt."

"Why?"

"Well, there's just something so open about her. I don't think I've ever met a more delightful creature." She caressed Tony's cheek. "Female variety, that is. I understand she's terrifically talented."

"I think I'm in love with her!" Tony blurted.

Ginger gave him a sharp look. "You just met her!"

"So? Didn't you ever hear of love at first sight?"

Ginger waved her hand dismissively.

"Come on, Mom. You told me yourself that you fell in love with my father the very minute you first saw him."

"Oh, heavens, Tony, I was only twelve years old when

I met Tonito! What did I know? Besides, I didn't fall in love with him, I just thought he was very handsome." She sighed. "Listen, darling, don't be foolish. If you talk yourself into loving Jennie, you'll just be asking for a lot of heartache."

"It's easy to be sensible when you're old," he said.

"Old? Who's old?"

"I guess forty's as old as *I'd* ever want to get," he said with unintended cruelty.

She pulled his head down to her level and kissed his forehead just as Jason came in and put his arms around both of them. "We look like a football huddle," he laughed. "Listen, I'm going to pick Vivien up at the depot. Anyone want to come with me?"

"What's wrong with her coming in the hotel limousine?" Ginger asked.

"It's too impersonal. I'd rather drive the nine miles."

"Okay," Ginger conceded. "I'd go with you, love, but two busboys just quit and I need to find replacements pronto."

"I'll come, Jason," Tony said eagerly, always happy to spend time with his stepfather. "You can tell me all about the birds and the bees."

"It won't help you one tiny bit, Tony. I'm afraid the birds and the bees both do it a lot differently than we do!"

Vivien loved to visit her father and Ginger. They always made a fuss over her, made her feel she really belonged there. Her own mother didn't treat her half as well. It was wonderful to have her own room in a real mansion and eat at Ginger's exclusive hotel. Oh, Vivien was glad her father had married a rich woman!

Vivien was fond of Tony too. He was lots of fun. He often took her horseback riding on the desert, and the previous summer he had taught her how to drive a car. He took her to dances and introduced her to his friends, and even helped her with her homework when she brought it along. He was just like a real big brother to her.

But her visits to Palm Springs also made her self-conscious and tense. Her big problem was shyness. She blushed easily and then wanted to hide before people noticed. She knew she was pretty enough, with her father's dark blond hair and big gray eyes. But something was definitely missing from her life.

Vivien was struck dumb when she met Uncle Neil's fiancée at Ginger's birthday party. Here was Jennie, only a year older than Vivien, wearing a fabulous green satin strapless gown that must have cost hundreds of dollars, and a necklace set with huge emeralds, and the biggest diamond ring Vivien had ever seen. Vivien felt like a great big awkward infant in her pink shirtwaist dress with a Peter Pan collar.

Jason noticed. He put an arm around Vivien and took her out onto the front porch. "Honey," he said gently, "it's silly to go around comparing yourself to other people. Jennie's worked hard her whole life to make herself glamorous. Don't be jealous."

"I can't help it!" She burst into tears and cried softly while he held her head against his chest.

Jason waited until the sobbing abated. "Think of it this way," he said. "How much you enjoy each day is what counts. Did you ever see an animal or an insect worrying about how it looks? Or comparing itself to its neighbor? It just lives the best life it can. You'll save yourself a lot of grief if you do the same."

"Sure," Vivien sniffed. "That's great advice for a gopher or a spider."

"Why not for a very pretty, very sweet, nearly-sixteen-year-old girl?"

"Because life's only good for a girl if lots of boys like her."

"Hmmm. That's a pretty narrow view of life. Well, don't any boys like you?"

She shook her head.

"Tony does."

"He doesn't count. He's like a brother."

"I see. So the fact that we all love you and admire you just doesn't cut any ice with you."

"Come on, Daddy, you know what I mean!"

The next morning, when Tony invited Vivien to go with him to the Racquet Club, she hesitated, suddenly shy. "Well, I don't play tennis very well," she protested lamely.

"Neither do I, Viv. Let's just go and fool around." He didn't add that he was desperately hoping to see Jennie again.

He let Vivien drive there, for the practice, and his praise pleased her. She carefully parked next to a white Duesenberg. "Wow! Will you look at that car!" she groaned with hushed admiration.

"It's my cousin Cal's." Tony gave the car a critical look. "What a show-off."

"Then how come you just turned green?"

Tony shrugged. "Can I help it if my mom and dad still prefer horses to cars? And end up buying cheap cars to show their contempt?"

"Well, they do have that Cadillac limousine . . ."

"Yeah, but it's just for the hotel guests. Mom and Jason wouldn't be caught dead riding in it."

Vivien reverently touched the shiny grille of the white luxury car as they walked past it. "How come I've never met this Cal if he's your cousin?"

"He and his mother, my Aunt Ella—"

"The one who's a movie star? Ella Ricardo?"

"Right. Well, actually, Cal and Aunt Ella have been away from Palm Springs all the time my mom and Jason have been married. They just moved back here a few months ago."

Tony and Vivien meandered around the club swimming pool and then watched the tennis players for a while. After that they wandered through the grounds. Tony was crushed because Jennie was nowhere in sight.

"How come Ginger and my dad are members here?" Vivien inquired. "I thought only movie stars belonged."

"No, some locals do too. Charlie Farrell sometimes stayed at The Springs, back in the days before he and Ralph Bellamy built this place. Anyway, Charlie and my mom and your dad became good friends, so Charlie gave them an honorary membership."

They were walking back toward the tennis courts when they bumped into Cal. "My cousin, Cal Ricardo," Tony introduced them, "my stepsister, Vivien Sisley."

Cal took both of Vivien's hands in his. "Tony! Aren't you the lucky one! I didn't even know you had a stepsister." Cal gazed admiringly into Vivien's eyes, dazzling her.

She hoped she wasn't blushing too furiously. "How-do-you-do," she said in a small voice, looking away from his captivating dark eyes. She hated herself for not being able to keep eye contact with him. If only she could give him a smoldering look, like she'd seen in movies. If only she could act alluring and mature at a time like this, instead of like a silly child!

"How long are you both going to be in town?" Cal asked.

"I'm flying back up north tomorrow morning," Tony said.

"I'll be here until the day *after* tomorrow," Vivien added.

"Well!" Cal put his arms around their shoulders. "Since we're all family, what say we cut out of here and go on out to my place?"

"Will your mother mind?" Tony asked.

"She's in Los Angeles for a couple of days, but I'll get our cook to fix lunch for us. We can sit by the pool and get to know each other better."

Vivien looked eagerly at Tony, who, to her vast relief, nodded his agreement.

"Okay, Vivien," Cal ordered in his take-charge manner, "you come with me. Tony, follow us in your car."

Getting into the Duesenberg, Vivien felt like she was audibly buzzing with excitement. Her frenetic heartbeats were reverberating in her ears. She didn't know what was more exciting: riding in a car like this or sitting next to Cal. Both were utterly beautiful . . . and utterly fascinating. Speeding down Indian Avenue, she fervently wished they were driving across the entire United States together, instead of just two miles down the road.

Sitting beside Cal's glistening swimming pool, eating a plate of *fettuccine con vongole*, Tony was frightened. Anyone could see that Vivien was starry-eyed over Cal. God, she was young and foolish! Cal could have all the glamorous beauties he wanted. Showgirls, starlets, fashion models, society debutantes—they all just *crawled* to him. What if Cal seduced Vivien as a momentary diversion and then threw her away? Tony knew how shy Vivien was. She'd be brokenhearted for life. My God, he thought to himself, she'd go straight to hell in a basket!

When Cal walked them out to their car, he turned to Vivien and again took both of her hands in his, playfully swinging them back and forth. "How about lunch at El Mirador tomorrow?"

"She can't," Tony said hastily. "My mom's having some kind of ladies' get-together for Vivien tomorrow afternoon."

"Well, then, dinner at the Chi Chi, Viv? We can rumba—"

"Really, Cal," Tony again intervened, "she's only visiting for a couple of days. I'm sure Jason will want to spend her last evening with her."

Cal smiled at Vivien. "Does big brother here always talk for you?"

Vivien shook her head, momentarily too overwhelmed to speak. "I don't know how to rumba," she finally said lamely. "And it's true, Dad would be really upset if I went out tomorrow night."

"All right. Next time you come down, I'll teach you how to rumba." Cal put an arm around her shoulders and walked her to the passenger side of the Dodge. "I'll phone you in the morning," he whispered as he opened the door.

Driving home, Tony was furious. "You can't go out with him!" he said flatly. "Ever!"

Vivien stared at him sullenly. "Why not?"

"I don't trust him."

"Tony, he's family. He's only trying to be kind."

"Ha! Believe me, Vivien, he's only interested in one thing. Getting you into bed!"

"Tony! What a dirty mind you have!" She turned away from him and stared out the side window. "I think you're just plain jealous because Cal's so handsome and charming," she said after a while.

He didn't reply at once. "Well, maybe I am jealous, Viv. But I tell you, you're not safe with a guy like that. He's looking for a hot time, and you're just a kid. . . ."

Vivien was kind of pleased that Tony was trying to protect her, so she decided to assuage his fears. She knew that Ginger had nothing planned for the next afternoon, that Tony had made it up to keep her from having lunch with Cal. But Tony would be back in Palo Alto by lunchtime and would never know what she did. She turned back to him. "Yeah, maybe you're right, Tony. Maybe I shouldn't go out with Cal. And I didn't mean that about you needing to be jealous of Cal. Really, you're just as handsome and charming as he is." She hesitated. "In fact, you guys resemble each other."

"You think so?" He didn't know whether or not to be pleased. "Well, maybe we do. His mom and my mom are sisters, after all, so there's bound to be some resemblance."

All the time Tony was telling Ginger about their visit to Cal's house, Vivien noticed how displeased Ginger looked.

"You were at Ella's house?" Ginger shook her head disapprovingly. "Why did you go there, Tony? You know how I feel about her."

"She wasn't there, Mom. Just Cal and the servants."

"I don't care! I don't want you going there, and I don't want them coming here!" Ginger took a deep breath. "I'm sorry, Tony. I'm acting like you were five years old."

"It's okay, Mom. I didn't realize you felt that way."

When Cal phoned Vivien the next morning—a half-hour after Tony's plane took off—and again asked Vivien to have lunch with him, she decided she had better not let Ginger know she was going to see him. "I'll meet you at noon at El Mirador," she said softly into the phone.

"I'll be glad to pick you up, Viv . . ."

"No, no, I have some shopping to do first, down near there," Vivien insisted. Then, bursting with suppressed excitement, she told Ginger that she had run into a girlfriend from Santa Monica at the Racquet Club and was meeting her for lunch.

Seeing the heightened color in Vivien's cheeks and the starry look in her eyes, Ginger knew that no girlfriend could cause such animation. She had to be meeting Cal. What other young man did Vivien know in Palm Springs? Ginger hated to challenge Vivien's truthfulness, but she was even more afraid to have Vivien go out with Cal. "Where are you and your girlfriend going for lunch?" Ginger asked lightly.

"We're meeting at the Plaza arcade. We'll decide then where to eat."

"Why not bring her up to The Springs? I'll have Jean-Paul fix you something special."

"Oh, no! I mean, I want to do some shopping, you know, at Bullock's and Magnin's, and . . . and besides, my f-friend's on a diet. We'll just stop somewhere for a bite."

Ginger was in a quandary. She knew that if she accused Vivien of lying, she'd lose the girl's trust. Yet, if she let her go, Vivien might be seduced. *Oh, but Cal wouldn't dare, would he?* Still, Cal *was* Ella's son. Like mother, like son? If only Jason were home, Ginger inwardly fumed, but he had taken a geology professor from Cal Tech to see some unusual rock formations in San Andreas Canyon and would be gone most of the day.

In the end, Ginger decided she had to show her trust in Vivien. What else could she do? Lock the girl up in her room? Call her a liar? Ginger groaned to herself. Here was Tony madly and ever so foolishly in love with Jennie, and Vivien dangerously starry-eyed over Cal. *Damn it*, Ginger wanted to cry out, *why the hell couldn't Tony and Vivien feel that way about each other instead?*

Vivien changed her dress three times, then finally wore white slacks with a pink angora sweater. She caught a ride downtown in The Springs' limousine with two other guests and had the driver drop her at the Plaza, just in case he reported back to Ginger. She walked from there to the pink-towered El Mirador and was happy to see the white Duesenberg in the parking lot, because she didn't want to get there first.

Cal had reserved a poolside umbrella table and he helped her order, since he ate there often. Vivien was flustered at first, this being her first date with a man, but Cal quickly told her some droll stories that made her laugh and put her at ease. Cal knew all the famous movie stars staying there. He introduced her to Clara Bow and Dorothy Lamour and Paulette Goddard and Bing Crosby and—gee, her very favorite—Clark Gable!

"Have you ever been to Europe?" Cal asked.

"Not yet. How about you?"

"Yeah, my mother sent me on a couple of tours. You know, ten boys traveling with two prissy teachers. We were too busy being brats to see much."

"Tony got to go every summer, to visit Dr. Avery. But now, with the dumb war over there, I guess he won't be going this summer."

"I suppose you know that there's some big family secret," Cal said with a trace of bitterness. "That's why my mother and Aunt Ginger don't speak to each other."

He gave her a sharp look. "You don't happen to know what it is, by any chance, do you?"

Vivien shook her head, mystified. "I don't know anything about it. I once met your Uncle Neil, but I've never met your mother. I saw all her pictures, though."

Cal slowly sipped his Coke. At the mention of Neil, Cal had a sudden vision of Jennie making love to his uncle and it evoked a violent pain that made him shudder inwardly from head to toe. He didn't ever want to cause another person so much pain. Until now, he had never thought about how his behavior might affect others.

In the past, he might very well have thoughtlessly dallied with this little Vivien, out of boredom, or just to pass an afternoon. Now, knowing how painful it was to want someone you couldn't have, he had no intention of making time with her, as Tony so obviously had feared he might. Vivien was too young and too shy to be trifled with, and he truly had no desire to hurt her.

He reached across the table and took her hand. "Vivien, honey, I feel like we're family. I've never had much feeling of kinship . . . my mother's always been busy with her career and my dad died when I was only nine. And then there's the bad feelings between my mother and Aunt Ginger . . . ." He shook his head sadly. "Viv, I want to give you some advice. You're safe with me, but please, honey, don't go out with guys like me. Not yet. Spend the next couple years preparing yourself for the future. Take school seriously. Build up your self-confidence. Learn the latest dances and how to play tennis so you'll be good at them later on when you start going out. Forget about dating and love and sex for a while."

She made a face. "It sounds so boring!"

"No, it's not. Believe me, there isn't much happiness in being a playboy like me. It looks glamorous, but it . . . it doesn't have any substance." He squeezed her hand. "The kind of marriage Aunt Ginger and your dad have is what I'd like someday . . ." His voice trailed off. "Anyhow, that's what you should prepare yourself for."

When they finished eating their lunch of shrimp cocktail, chicken croquettes with mashed potatoes and peas, and chocolate cake à la mode, he said he would drive her home.

"But I told Ginger I was having lunch with a girlfriend,"

Vivien protested. "If she sees your car, she'll know I lied."

"I want you to *tell* her that you lied, and that you're sorry," he insisted. "Or you'll always feel guilty about seeing me."

He stopped the car briefly on a vacant side street, where he leaned over and kissed her. It was a chaste kiss, without body contact, though he let his lips linger on hers somewhat longer than he should have. He could see that she was stirred. "That's a promise for the future," he told her, smiling. "Someday when you're old enough, I'll kiss you good and proper. Maybe I'll even make love to you. *If* you're a good girl and do all the things I told you to do."

He drove her up to the pink mansion and went into the house with her. They found Ginger in the living room, looking concerned. She greeted him politely but coolly.

Vivien looked contritely at Ginger. "I lied to you," she confessed. "I'm so sorry! I promise, Ginger, I'll never do it again!" Vivien gestured at Cal. "Cal insisted that I tell you. I was afraid to."

"I'm glad you did, Vivien," Ginger said. She turned to Cal and took his hand. Her attitude toward him cautiously flip-flopped from hostility to respect. "I admire your honesty," she told him.

After Cal left, Vivien clung to Ginger's arm. "Cal was ever so nice to me, sort of like Tony is, like a big brother. He wants to be friends with you and Daddy, but he thinks you all hate him." She paused. "He's really sorry that you and his mother can't stand each other. He likes you a lot. He says you and Daddy have the kind of marriage he'd like to have someday."

When Vivien went upstairs to change her clothes, she tingled with excitement, as though she'd stepped into a whole new phase of her life. *She was in love . . . and he was so rich!* Cal filled her thoughts, and when she whispered his name, little tremors fluttered through her body. She closed her eyes and relived his kiss again and again. Each time, the unfamiliar jolt of pleasure she had experienced came back with renewed vigor. Until yesterday she hadn't even heard of Cal, and in these few short hours he had become her whole life. Her lips still burned, as though Cal's kiss had been his brand on her, the way cattle are branded to show which rancher owns them.

Now she had a purpose in life. She vowed to do exactly as Cal had suggested. She would study hard at school so she wouldn't ever sound stupid when he took her out with important people. She would learn how to do all the latest dances and how to play tennis expertly, and how to wear snazzy clothes with grace and pizzazz. By the time she was eighteen, she would be ready for him. *Maybe someday I'll make love to you,* he had promised. But would he actually marry her? She wanted to be part of the life he led. Driving Duesenbergs. Meeting famous movie stars. Living on gorgeous estates. *Oh, God, make it happen,* she prayed.

Downstairs, Ginger phoned Neil. "Look, little brother," she said, "I'll come to your wedding. Yes, yes, even if Ella's there too. I promise not to make a scene, but I won't talk to her, either." When Ginger hung up the phone, she turned and found Jason grinning at her.

"I heard that," he said. "Congratulations."

"For what?"

"For letting go of your hatred for Ella." He held her close and kissed the tip of her nose.

"I haven't let go. I'm only doing it for Cal's sake. He's really rather nice."

"You know, my sweet," Jason said thoughtfully, "sometimes I feel kind of sorry for Tonito, because I'm sure he loved you, and his guilt must have been excruciatingly painful. I know that's how I'd feel if I were ever foolish enough to do what he did."

"So you think I should stop being angry at him?" Ginger stiffened and moved out of Jason's embrace.

"He's been dead for eighteen *years,* Ginger. Don't you think it's time you forgave him?"

"No! It'll *never* be time. If I live to a hundred, Jason, I'll still never forgive him! *Or* Ella!"

Ella got back from Los Angeles to find her son moping around the house. "What's wrong, Cal?" she asked.

"Oh, nothing."

"I thought there was some girl you were crazy about."

"That's over." He tried to smile, but it looked more like a grimace.

"Tough. Come see what I bought." She led him through her all-white bedroom into the vast dressing room she had added onto the house. It contained over a hundred lineal feet of closet space, dozens of built-in drawers, and cabinets with tilted shelves for two hundred pairs of shoes. She took out a hanger from which was suspended an exquisite pale green sequined gown. "Like it? It's for Neil's wedding." Ella smiled. "Nobody'll look at the bride, with me in this dress."

"I guess you haven't met Jennie," Cal told her glumly, "or you wouldn't say that."

Ella gave him a hostile stare. "Just what do you mean by that?"

"Well, Mother dear, you're a very gorgeous lady, but this Jennie, she's something else. And she's twenty years younger."

"Don't you *dare* talk to me like that!"

"Like what?" he asked with mock innocence. "I just stated a fact."

She hung up the dress. "So tell me, are you just going to hang around the house all the time?"

"I'm supposed to start working for Uncle Neil as soon as he gets back from his honeymoon."

"Honeymoon," she repeated softly. "That's what I need, a honeymoon."

"Don't tell me you're getting married again, Mother dear."

"Stop sounding so snotty. No, not married. I have a new lover, a real sweetheart."

"Who is he?" Cal asked without much interest.

"Oh, nobody you know." Ella twirled gaily out onto the patio.

Cal followed her outside. "Mom . . ."

"Why don't you call me Ella?"

"Why?" he asked suspiciously.

She shrugged. "Oh, it just sounds more . . . ummm . . . more dignified."

"I see," he said bitterly. "You were a lousy mother for eighteen years . . . and now you don't want to be a mother at all. Tell me, *Ella*, have you ever been *really* in love?"

"What a question!"

"Well, answer it," he barked.

"You'd have to define 'love,' " she said after a long pause. "I mean, there's love and there's *love*. It all depends."

"I guess you haven't been in love, or you'd know." He sounded disappointed. "Didn't you even love my father?"

"Your *father*?" She was startled. "Oh, you mean Frank. Yes, dear, I was terribly fond of him, for a while."

He went over to her and put his hands on her shoulders. Looking down into her upturned face, he had to admit that she was simply stunning. Her skin was as flawless as a young girl's, despite her constant complaints about wrinkles. Her eyes were as beautiful as ever, huge and clear and framed by thick dark lashes. He had to force his hand to remain on her shoulders, when he so desperately wanted to move them up onto her graceful long neck and strangle her.

"Just how many lovers have you had?" he asked nastily.

"You really want to know?"

He nodded.

"Well, I'm sorry, I've lost count."

He started to walk away, hating her.

"Listen, Cal, this new man . . . I've asked him to move in here with me."

He turned around and faced her. "Are you telling me to move out?"

"Well, we might all be happier if you had your own place." She gestured toward the north. "I saw a darling house about a mile from here. In Las Palmas. I'll buy it for you, if you like it."

He shrugged. "Sure. When can I see it?"

She went into her bedroom and returned with a key and a card. "Here's the address. It's all furnished, so you can move right in."

He stood before her, deep in thought. "You know, Moth . . . Ella, I hate the idea of being Uncle Neil's flunky. I've been thinking. How about giving me your half of the real estate you own jointly with him?"

She was outraged. "Why should I do that?"

"Then I'd be Uncle Neil's partner instead of his employee." He gave her his most winsome smile. "Come on. You're so rich you'll never miss it."

She shook her head. "Look here, Cal, I've been very

generous to you. If it wasn't for me, you'd be nothing but a soda jerk."

"What do you mean, you've been generous? My allowance comes from Dad's trust fund."

"That's right, Cal. But I'm the executor. Frank set it up for you to get his estate when you're twenty-one. Why can't you wait three years?"

"Three years is a long time. I want to get going now! So why make me wait?"

"I see no reason—"

His smile faded. "There's one good reason. You owe it to me, lady."

"Owe you what, you greedy boy?"

"You owe me for all the mother love I needed from you and never got when I was growing up. You owe me for firing Juanita, who was the only person who loved me and was always *there* for me. You owe me for shipping me off to that goddamn academy while you traipsed all over the world with your lovers. You owe me for turning me into a selfish son-of-a-bitch in your image."

They stared at each other in the bright desert sunlight. She was the first to look away. "I'll think about it," she promised.

Cal liked the house well enough. It had three bedrooms and baths, a palatial gold-and-white living room with a marble fireplace, a built-in bar and stone fireplace in the oak-paneled rumpus room, a den whose bookcases were already filled with books—he'd heard how decorators bought books by the lineal yard, color-keyed to the decor. The gold-and-white tile kitchen had stainless-steel appliances which he assumed would please his future cook. Behind the house, a large oval swimming pool was surrounded by palms and jazzy plants and a long outdoor bar. A great party house. It would do until he made enough money to build a truly fabulous estate, one even fancier than his mother's or Uncle Neil's. He'd show Jennie!

Driving back to his mother's place to pack his things, Cal passed a neighborhood of nondescript stucco houses that his Uncle Neil had built. Each one was painted a sickening pale blue or pink or yellow and was surrounded by a low picket fence. Kids were screeching while playing kick-the-can in the street, housewives were standing around gossiping, husbands were mowing lawns or sitting on their steps drinking beer right out of quart-size bottles.

At that moment Cal would have traded all the lavish estates in the world for one of these cottages. One with him and Jennie and maybe a couple of snot-nosed kids living in it.

The day after Cal moved into his new house, Bert Elliott brought an overnight bag to Ella's mansion and unpacked a few items of clothing and toiletries in one small drawer of a bank of built-ins which Ella had set aside for him.

"Is that all you own?" Ella shrieked with laughter.

"Of course not. Gracie wouldn't let me take the rest." He embraced Ella and nodded toward her bed, an oversize four-poster that she called her "playpen."

"What's your hurry?" she asked coyly. "I thought we'd celebrate with some champagne and caviar first."

"Later," he murmured, nuzzling her neck. He was of medium height and stocky, forty years old with thinning blond hair and slightly bulging sexy green eyes. He had been handsome in his youth and he still retained the cocky air of a man who knows that women desire him. Boldly rubbing his genitals against hers, he two-stepped her back toward the bed, fumbling with her blouse as they moved.

"What did Gracie say?" she asked breathlessly as she slid her hands down his back and under his pants and lasciviously massaged his buttocks.

"Mmmm, that's nice. Well, first she screamed a lot. Then she cried a lot. Then she got abusive and started throwing things. That's when I left."

Chalk up one more victory for me, Ella congratulated herself triumphantly as he roughly pushed her back onto the bed and threw himself on top of her.

Ginger rushed down to Gracie's house the minute her friend telephoned. It was a modest pseudo-Spanish house, a carbon copy of its neighbors on both sides of the street: two bedrooms and den, bath-and-a-half, a single-car garage in the backyard. Not exactly the kind of house one would expect the famous Gracie Hudson to be occupying.

The expression "fit to be tied" sprang to Ginger's mind the minute she saw her friend. Ginger had hoped that Ella would tire of Bert before Gracie heard about their affair. Now Gracie was gulping brandy and doing everything but foaming at the mouth. "I sent Amy next door," she said, " 'cause I'm afraid I'll scare the shit ouf of her. Ginger, I want to *scream!*"

"Okay, let's drive out to the middle of the desert and you can scream your head off," Ginger suggested.

Gracie shook her head. "Ahh, it wouldn't do any good. Oh, that son-of-a-bitch Bert! And that shitty, shitty, *shitty* sister of yours! Ginger, I'm going *crazy!* I have half a mind to take one of Bert's stupid guns and go shoot them both."

Ginger put her arms around her distraught friend. "Believe me, Gracie, I know how you feel."

"How could you? You've had two perfect husbands. There's no way you could know what it's like to be hurt this way."

If only that were true! Ginger thought ruefully. But there was no point telling Gracie about Tonito and Ella. It wouldn't make Gracie feel any better. "Gracie, don't just sit around and stew over what's happened. The best way to get past your pain is to make plans for the future."

"Plans? Like what?"

Ginger gestured at the garish living-room furniture. "You've never really liked this house. It's strictly Bert's taste. You deserve better."

"You think buying a new house will cure my heartache?" Gracie scoffed.

"It'll help. A gorgeous place with a pool. You've always wanted your own pool. And don't deny that you miss acting. Your fans still love you. You could pick up your career right where you left off. Everyone at the club says so."

"You mean, put on a hundred pounds so I can be a funny lady again?" Gracie ran her hands down over her slender body. "Uh-uh! I don't ever want to be fat again."

"Gracie, skinny people can be funny too."

"Nah, Ginger, everyone'll expect me to be fat." She gestured comically. "It's like the audience is expecting Kate Smith and out walks Lily Pons."

"Darling, on the radio it doesn't matter if you're fat or

thin. Give it a try. You can broadcast from right here in Palm Springs. Amos and Andy do it, Walter Winchell, Jack Benny . . ."

Gracie sat down on an overstuffed couch and let the tears gush. "I still love Bert."

"I know."

"I could kill him."

"I know."

"I could cut his fucking *balls* off—"

"I know."

"—and everything attached to them too." Gracie hiccuped. "He's awfully well-hung," she added wistfully.

"So's King Kong," Ginger said dryly.

Gracie tittered.

Ginger took Gracie's hand and pulled her up from the ugly floral couch. "Come on, Gracie."

"Where to?"

"We're going to find you a new house."

Gracie hung back. "But what if . . . what if Bert changes his mind?" Gracie gestured at the living room. "He'll still want us to live *here*."

"Screw him!"

Gracie stared at Ginger in amazement. "I've never heard you talk like that!"

"No? Well, my friend, I say *screw* him, *fuck* him—"

"I'd like to."

"Stop it, Gracie! I tell you, it's good riddance."

"But I love him!"

"Don't you realize how much that rotten son-of-a-bitch was holding you back? You had to live *his* way. Do everything *his* way. *He* made all the decisions, big and small. You're too smart to let anyone do that to you, love or no love."

Gracie was thoughtful. "But if I admit that Bert was a mistake, it's like I threw away my career and seven years of my life for *nothing*."

"Look, you got Amy out of your marriage. Doesn't she makes it all worthwhile? Now, dammit, Gracie, it's time you returned to the kind of life you deserve!"

At the last minute, Cal realized he couldn't face watching his Uncle Neil marry Jennie. Instead, he got into his car and drove to the Santa Barbara home of his former roommate from the military academy, Chuck Williston. Cal phoned Ella with the lie that he was visiting Chuck in the hospital after Chuck had been in an auto accident, and for her to give Uncle Neil his regrets.

Ella said she'd tell Neil at once so he could get a substitute best man, probably Jason. Then she added, "You know what you asked me last week? About giving you my share of the real estate I own jointly with Neil?"

"Yeah?"

"Well, Cal, I admit I haven't been such a great mother . . . and I'd like to make it up to you. So I decided to give you all the Palm Springs property except for my house. My lawyers are drawing up the documents."

"Thanks," Cal said huskily, overcome with amazement and gratitude. After he hung up the phone he turned to a perfectly healthy Chuck. "Y'know, life's funny. You're always winning some things and losing others. I just lost the most wonderful girl in the world, but I gained a fortune."

"Which would you rather have?" Chuck asked. "The girl or the money?"

"Before long, Chuckie-boy, I expect to have both!"

On her wedding night, Jennie discovered that sex with Neil was a little bizarre.

First, he took her on a tour of the master-bedroom suite, which he had forbidden her to see before, wanting it to be a surprise. The bedroom itself was so large that Neil had to raise his voice when he spoke to her from across the room. The high groined ceiling was decorated with erotic frescoes of naked men and women gamboling in tropical gardens. Standing between two tall arched windows, the mammoth bed was draped with yards and yards of scalloped blue velvet.

Jennie explored twin oval alcoves and found a kitchen complete with refrigerator, cupboards, sink, and stove in one and a fully stocked bar in the other. "It's fabulous," she said, impressed. "It's really a whole separate apartment, isn't it?"

"Come see the bathroom," Neil urged. "It's designed like a miniature Baths of Caracalla."

"Like what, darling?"

"An ancient monument I saw in Rome."

"I've never been there," she said pensively. "I've never been anywhere."

"Soon as they stop fighting over there, baby doll, we'll take off and see the world."

She followed him into an immense pink marble fairyland full of arches and dominated by an oval sunken tub the size of a small swimming pool. Although the tub was made of pink marble, it was covered with hand-painted multicolored flowers, as were all the fixtures in the room. A fountain, highlighted by pink bulbs in the ceiling, splashed at one end of the room, creating foamy bubbles that cascaded over a foot-wide moat surrounding the tub. One wall of the room held two oval sinks standing side by side. Facing them, on the opposite wall, were two curved dressing tables. Two round alcoves with etched glass doors each held a toilet and a small sink. Jennie looked into a third round alcove, which proved to be a shower with eight heads embedded in the pink marble walls. Mirrors and soft indirect lights were everywhere.

"How come there's two of everything but only one shower and one tub?" Jennie asked dryly.

"So we can bathe and shower together," Neil replied coyly.

Jennie stopped to examine two matching pink fixtures that looked like toilets without seats, also side by side, on one wall. "What are these?" she asked.

"Bidets. From France. All the fixtures are from France."

"Bidets," she repeated. "What are they *for?*"

"I'll show you." He took off his formal wedding clothes and squatted on one of the bidets. When he turned a faucet, a miniature geyser sprayed up onto his genitals. He soaped himself, rinsed off, and took a small fluffy pink towel from a nearby rack and dried himself. "Now you do it," he said.

She removed her elaborate white satin gown and threw it over a brass chair with a pink velvet seat. Then she gracefully but gingerly sat down on the bidet and turned on the faucet. She shrieked with delight. "Hey, that feels good!" She increased the water pressure and rocked back and forth so that the spray tickled her entire pubic area. Then she washed and dried herself.

Mystified, she watched him spread a big pink bath

towel over the blue satin sheets on the bed. He lumbered into the kitchen and brought back a small pitcher and put it on the night table next to the bed.

He didn't kiss her or fondle her. Instead, while he stood naked next to the bed, he told her to lie down flat on her back. She lay there quietly, warily waiting to see what he would do next.

He clambered onto the bed and shoved her legs apart, squatting between them so that his face was close to her vulva. He gently parted her labia, grasped the pitcher, and poured a dark lukewarm substance all over her exposed parts.

"What's that?" she squealed in surprise.

"Chocolate fudge syrup, little darling."

She squirmed with delight as his tongue flicked back and forth, licking up the syrup. He'd lap at her in quick little darts, alternating with slow hard sucks on her clitoris. He was even better at it than Daddy-Joe had been. She moaned with pleasure. When the chocolate had been licked out of every crevice, he pulled himself up and slid inside of her. They both climaxed in a couple of minutes. He remained heavily on top of her while they felt each other's hearts jumping inside their chests.

"Do you always do it like that?" she giggled breathlessly.

"No. Sometimes I use honey or jam," he said very seriously.

She thought a minute. "How about that new stuff? Reddi-whip?"

"Good idea! Yeah! It might tickle you nicely when I spray it on."

"Does maple syrup work?"

"Sure! I love it mixed with ground cashews."

"How about trying the maple syrup now, Neil?"

"*Now?*" He was aghast. "Have a heart, Jennie! Maybe in three or four days." He rolled off her and wiped himself with the pink towel, then cleaned the remnants of chocolate syrup and semen off her. "Let's use the bidets again, Jen." He pulled the towel off the bed, threw it on the floor, and led the way into the bathroom, where they sat side by side, washing themselves.

He grinned at her. "Pretty neat, huh?"

"Yes," she agreed, grinning back at him. "But you're the only person I know who'll gain weight having sex!"

CHAPTER
9

1940–1941

Avery came home from France by way of Portugal and returned to Palm Springs in April 1940, shortly before the Germans invaded the Low Countries. For the past six years Avery had leased a spacious Quai Anatole France apartment overlooking the Seine and the Tuileries Gardens. Summers, Tony had visited him and they traveled together all over Europe. Avery's only contact with Ginger during those years had been by mail, cheerful letters in which they both wrote about everyday happenings and never mentioned how they felt, about each other or anything else.

Avery had taken up residence in Paris during the bitter winter of 1934, six weeks after Adele's death. The wind screeching off the river had made every breath an agony of endurance whenever he ventured outside his apartment. He had waddled like a polar bear in a fur-lined coat, heavy woolen hat and gloves, and fur-lined boots. Though he wore a scarf over the bottom half of his face, the frigid air still had managed to get into his lungs and sear them. The skies had remained slate-gray day after day, exactly matching his spirits.

With the arrival of warmer days he had become obsessed with walking in every *arrondissement* and visiting the churches he passed. Somehow, somewhere, in the broad fashionable boulevards radiating from L'Etoile, in the narrow cobbled streets of the Marais, in the parks named Luxembourg and Monceau and Boulogne, in the dark nave of St. Eustache or the glowing radiance of

Sainte Chapelle, he had found a solace that gradually overcame his sorrow.

In Paris he was exposed to the latest trends in art. He had given up painting stiff little desert scenes and he began doing big bold canvases in brilliant colors. He was taken on by one of the smaller galleries in the Rue de Seine, where his paintings enjoyed modest sales. Feeling guilty about accepting money when he already had so much, he secretly donated every franc he earned from his work to the French Red Cross. The thrill of knowing that a few people thought enough of his canvases to buy them and hang them on their walls was payment enough for him.

His exquisitely furnished apartment was on the top floor of a six-story fashionable building. His rooms were spacious, with high ceilings and tall French windows leading out onto small balconies from which he could see not only the Seine and the Tuileries Gardens but also the Right Bank all the way up to the gleaming white dome of Sacré Coeur atop Montmartre.

His apartment was full of handsome mahogany furniture and handmade needlepoint cushions. The walls were covered with mauve damask, the draperies were made of heavy burgundy velvet, the dishes were Limoges, the glassware Baccarat. His living and dining rooms faced the river; his bedroom and the two guest rooms overlooked a quiet courtyard choked with greenery. He had hired a couple to cook and clean for him, cousins of Ginger's chef, Jean-Paul.

Madame Odette Cassin lived in the apartment directly below Avery's. The widow of a doctor—she had an independent spirit and independent means—she drew Avery into her circle of friends. Avery didn't know quite how to define his relationship with Odette. They were good friends, certainly. And yes, they were lovers, in a mild way. Every Saturday night it was their custom to eat a magnificient meal and share an expensive bottle of wine at one of the finer Paris restaurants. Then, weather permitting, they sauntered along the Seine or up the Champs or the Rue Montaigne or out along Avenue Victor Hugo. They taxied back to their apartment building and had the elevator man drop them at their respective floors. After all, Odette was a respectable widow with a reputation to uphold.

It was Avery's responsibility to make his way down the service steps to Odette's apartment without being seen. Theirs was a gentle, passionless lovemaking, without rapturous sounds or frantic thrashing about. They both found it pleasant, and it greatly endeared them to each other.

When he finally decided it was prudent to leave Europe, he begged Odette to come with him to the safety of the United States.

"Mon Dieu!" she had protested. "I should die of cultural starvation in your hot desert."

"Then live in New York. It's an exciting city."

"You expect me to abandon my country to the Germans?"

"But my *dear* Odette, the Germans will come whether you're here or not. I'm afraid your presence won't stop them for a moment."

"Yes, my *dear* Avery," she had mimicked his slightly patronizing tone, "but if everyone felt that way, there would be no one left here to fight for France."

"No, seriously, *ma chérie*, no one expects a widow of a certain age to actually fight."

"Perhaps not. But I shall stay here all the same and do what I can!"

Once Avery returned to Palm Springs, he fretted, knowing that any day now the Germans would march into Paris, goose-stepping down the streets he loved, eating at his favorite cafés, probably sleeping in his bed. He was impatient with people in Palm Springs, who were more concerned about whether skirts should be longer or shorter this year, or how long Joe Louis would retain his heavyweight title, than they were about Europe's entering a new Dark Age. What would any of it matter if the Germans invaded all of Europe?

"Of *course* we'll have to help England, and eventually get into the war!" he would growl at anyone who would listen. "When are we going to wake up in this country? The Nazis are killing civilization! Don't you *care?*"

His feelings for Ginger were ambivalent. He no longer suffered quite so much when he saw Jason embrace her, but at the same time, he felt elated whenever he was alone with her, as though some hidden part of him came alive only for her. A feeling of joy simply pervaded him in her presence. All the years he had been in Paris she had been in his thoughts constantly. Whenever he had seen an exceptional painting or a remarkable building, he had wished she were there to enjoy it with him. Not a night had gone by that he hadn't longed for her, longed to talk to her and make love to her.

Ginger, too, had mixed feelings about his return. For eight years she had carefully cultivated her love for Jason and made their marriage a fun-filled, joyous union. She had planned special outings and trips up and down the West Coast to places that she knew she and Jason would both enjoy. All their meals—except for breakfast, which they made themselves—had been prepared by Jean-Paul with exquisite care. And in bed she had thrown herself into lovemaking with zestful ardor. She had stopped going up the trail that she and Avery had hiked every dawn for so many years because it reminded her too much of Avery and she wanted to concentrate all her energies on loving Jason. She had been *determined* to create a deeply satisfying marriage that finally would destroy her old attraction to Avery.

Still, she was utterly unnerved the day Avery returned to Palm Springs. He came into her office unexpectedly—she hadn't expected him until the following afternoon—and when she looked up from her desk and saw him standing there, she felt faint. Paralyzed. She stared up at him wordlessly, at his beloved face and silver hair, and her entire eight-year effort to kill her feelings for him simply vanished.

She forced herself to smile, to get up, to hug him and kiss his cheek, to play the part of a happily married woman greeting an old family friend. "Of course you'll have dinner with us," she said. "Jason's dying to see you."

She couldn't resist resuming their morning walks and sharing a big breakfast at his house afterward, since Jason never got up that early and Avery's housekeeper didn't come to work until lunchtime. "When we come up here," he told her one Monday morning in late April as they climbed the trail while watching a pink-and-gold dawn sky, "I feel like I'm still twenty-seven and you're twelve."

"I wouldn't want to be twelve again," she said.

"Well, I can tell you, I wouldn't mind being twenty-seven!"

"What was it like, living in Paris?" Ginger asked. "You haven't told me much about your life there."

"It was a strange experience, Ginger. When I decided to return there to live, I didn't realize how much it had changed. Even as a tourist, you don't see what's really going on. That summer you and I and Adele and Tony went, we stayed at the Ritz and spent our time going to museums and tourist attractions. We never visited the less affluent neighborhoods. And when I was there the first time, back in 1903, I was a starry-eyed eighteen and Paris was at the height of the *Belle Epoque*. Then, it truly was the City of Lights. It was full of artists from all over the world and I was sure that someday I'd be a famous painter. Truly, it was just the most exciting place you can imagine! But when I arrived in 1934, the City of Lights had turned dark and mean.

"Most of the American colony had gone home. The drunkards staggered back to the States as soon as booze became legal here again. The Depression made a big difference to the Americans who'd arrived there in the twenties, most of them young, with rich daddies to support them. But once the Depression started, the fathers stopped sending checks. The only ones who managed to stay on were the children of the very rich, like Gertrude Stein, or those Americans who were very successful, like Cole Porter.

"Suddenly, too, all Gaul was divided into three *thousand* parts, as if the French passion for individuality had exploded, each fragmented part full of hatred for all the others, and all of them unwilling to compromise or make concessions. Hordes of homeless slept in the Métros and under bridges. The middle class became miserly to the extreme, even cutting back on their wine consumption to a very un-French degree. People on the street looked pinched and cold and hungry, and very, very shabby.

"Almost every day there was some new financial scandal, or stories of government corruption. People rioted in front of the Bourse and the Chamber of Deputies. I tell you, Ginger, everybody hated somebody. Some hated Jews. Some hated Catholics. Some hated Stalin. Some hated Hitler. But unfortunately, there were those who saw Hitler and Mussolini and Franco as saviors.

"The arts suffered drastically. Many painters became

so interested in politics that they spent their time painting slogans on walls for one cause or another, mostly Marxist. I was fortunate enough to be part of a small group of painters who somehow persevered in their art. But after a while I began to feel guilty about dabbing paint on canvas when the world I cherished was in danger of being exterminated. I felt then and I *still* feel that I ought to be telling the free world that fascists are coming and that art and freedom are in jeopardy, and we've got to fight it, before it's too late!"

When he stopped speaking, he looked so woebegone that Ginger stopped walking and took his hand in commiseration. "Why did you stay there if it was so painful?" she asked softly.

"I was fascinated. With all its troubles, Paris made me feel alive! I was actually watching history unfold, distasteful though that history might be to me." They began trudging up the trail again.

"You've certainly changed, Avery," Ginger said.

"In what way?"

"Oh, you're much more wordly."

He wagged a finger at her. "You're the one who's changed."

"Me? Come on, I'm still your same old Ginger-girl."

He shook his head. "You're a grown woman now."

"Well, for God's sake, Avery, I'm forty years old! I've been a grown woman for at least twenty years!"

"Yes, but it's finally *dawned* on me. I can't think of you as my little 'Ginger-girl' anymore."

"Well," she said lightly, "I no longer think of you as 'good *old* Avery' either. The fifteen years' difference in our ages doesn't seem all that important anymore." She was thoughtful. "Maybe we can be even better friends, seeing each other as two equal adults."

"Two equal adults," he echoed musingly. They walked on without speaking, pondering their words. The trail widened and formed a flat shelf, their favorite lookout. They could see almost the entire Coachella Valley from there. Machines resembling wind-up toys were moving tons of earth near the small airport far below them: the Army's Ferry Command was installing modern concrete runways for military planes.

"Are you in a hurry?" he asked. "Or do you have time to sit here awhile?"

"Oh, I've got plenty of time," she said as they sat down side by side on a large flat rock. "Jason's gone to an all-day seminar in Riverside and it's a quiet morning at the hotel." She gestured at their surrounding. "I love this lookout. It always reminds me of you." She touched his arm fondly. "When you first went away, I used to come up here and send telepathic messages to you. I don't suppose you ever got them."

He took both her hands and looked into her eyes. He felt overwhelmed with love for her. "You're always with me, Ginger. Always. Wherever I am." He paused. "Why didn't you ever visit me in Paris? Every summer, I hoped you'd come with Tony."

She smiled, tingling with pleasure at his touch. "So many times, I longed to join you over there. But there was always something here that Jason had to do. Lectures. Deadlines on his books. As you probably guessed, Jason isn't terribly in love with Europe. . . ." Her hands still were in his, and as had happened so often in the past, desire for him flooded her.

There was a long silence between them. He saw that she was looking at him strangely, but he couldn't tell what she was thinking. He only knew that he found her beautiful, more beautiful than ever. He loved everything about her, her warm amber-brown eyes, her auburn hair, her fair skin and full red lips, even the sprinkle of freckles on her nose. He said impulsively, "I've been in love with you since you were sixteen."

Stunned, she looked into his eyes to see if he were serious. "*In* love, Avery? Man-woman love?"

He nodded. "I never told you. I was afraid . . . well, afraid it would frighten you . . . or make us self-conscious with each other."

She couldn't speak. It had never once occurred to her that he might be in love with her too. And all this time . . . Oh, God! The effort she had made to hide her own attraction to him, thinking he would hate her if he knew, trying to convince herself that it was only a silly school-girl crush, feeling guilty and berating herself for the overwhelming desire she had felt for him, desire she had frantically directed toward Tonito and then Jason, as a way of suppressing her erotic longing for Avery.

She saw that he was staring at her, perplexed, waiting for her reaction to his declaration of love. At fifty-five he still was slim and youthful, still handsome, his eyes as bright a blue as ever. His brief time back in the desert sun had tanned his skin again, replacing his Parisian pallor. Looking at him, she wondered if it were possible for all of one's internal organs to simply melt together and become a whirling mass of the most delicious desire, because that's what was happening to her right now.

"I've loved you longer," she finally said. "Since that night when I first arrived here. My twelfth birthday. I told myself it was puppy love. A schoolgirl crush. An infatuation. Oh, Avery, how I've fought it all these years!"

It was his turn to be astonished. "You've l-loved *me?*" he stuttered. "All this time?"

She nodded.

"Then why . . . Tonito? Why Jason?"

"Because there was always Adele." She caught her breath. "And, oh, Avery, now . . . now there's Jason."

Avery frowned and shook his head, as if by so doing he could deny Jason's existence. He stood and pulled her up, drew her close against him. Their kiss—their first real kiss beyond careful friendly pecks on foreheads or cheeks—was like falling through space. It made their ears roar and left them weak.

"Remember that time," he said huskily, "when we saw the snake . . . ?"

"And I threw myself into your arms? Oh, Avery, I think of it all the time. You felt so . . . *wonderful.*"

They stood there unsteadily, clinging to each other. "I can't believe it," he murmured into her hair. "When you desperately wish and hope and pray for something year after year . . . and finally it happens . . . it's hard to believe it's real."

Her lips were against his cheek. "Oh, darling, but it *is,*" she replied, holding on to him with all her strength.

Ginger was shocked at how incredibly voluptuous their sweet and tender lovemaking was. To have a powerful rolling orgasm quickly erupt from a few gentle movements was so startling that it seemed even more erotic than when it happened after riotously carnal gyrations. Clinging to each other in Avery's bed, they were stunned by their shared rapture.

Neither of them felt like talking. There were no words that could express what they were feeling. They kept smiling rather shyly at each other and touching each other's faces to reassure themselves it really was happening. After a while Ginger got up and put her hiking clothes back on. He didn't want her to leave, ever, but he didn't feel he should stop her. She stood at the door for a moment, reluctant to go, then smiled and took a deep breath, as though shaking herself out of a trance.

"Well," she said, "I guess it's back to reality," and she went home.

She was in a quandary all day long. She felt as though what had happened with Avery was entirely outside of her "real" existence, as though there were two of her, one who always had and always would belong entirely to Avery, and one still married to Jason. She loved Jason, but she knew that her morning of lovemaking with Avery had nothing whatsoever to *do* with Jason.

Still, she was tense and confused when Jason returned from Riverside in the late afternoon. He was so adorable, so *youthful*, and so utterly lovable. He hugged her as though he had been away for a month instead of a day. Then he swept her up the stairs to their bedroom.

Ginger's mind churned with misgivings. Not that she regretted her morning with Avery. Oh, God, no! But it irrevocably changed her relationship with Jason. How could it not? Ironically, that morning in Avery's arms she had felt no guilt whatsoever. But now, while Jason undressed her and interspersed the sensual process with a dozen long, dizzying kisses, she felt utterly unfaithful to Avery.

Nevertheless, she couldn't help responding to Jason. He was a dynamo in bed, taking charge, rolling her onto her stomach so he could titillate the backs of her knees and lovingly lick his way up her spine, then flipping her onto her back and kissing her all over until she trembled with desire.

She always felt as though he were enclosing her with his entire body when he entered her. She felt suffused by him and filled with him. His mouth held hers while he vigorously, joyously, lustily made love to her. Oh, it was fun!—a romp, a jolly sport that left them throbbing and giggling with orgasmic delight.

And afterward, while they lay resting in each other's arms, she couldn't help comparing him with Avery. How strange it was that the carnal act could be so different · with the two men. After all, with both it was basically a matter of kiss-caress-coitus-come. But sex with Jason was earthy; with Avery it was . . . heavenly. Jason's lovemaking was like a wild jitterbug; Avery's was like a voluptuous ballet. An orgasm with Jason delightfully convulsed her sexual organs, but an orgasm with Avery suffused her entire body and her very soul with staggering bliss, the ultimate manifestation of their long-standing, all-encompassing love for each other.

She suddenly shuddered with fear, and Jason hugged her tighter, thinking it was a lingering quiver of pleasure. Her fear was not for herself, but for him, for the unhappiness she might eventually cause him. He was so vulnerable where she was concerned. The thought of hurting him was unbearable. He was so dear to her! No, she couldn't do it—not even if it meant that for the rest of their lives she and Avery would have to be secret lovers during their morning hour or two together.

She stifled a sigh. She knew that Avery was fond of Jason, but he was bitterly jealous of him too, for the eight and a half years of happiness she and Jason had shared. To Avery, Jason was the interloper. "Ginger, I've loved you for twenty-four *years*," Avery had insisted that morning. "Jason only *borrowed* you from me. He should be grateful he had you as long as he did."

"But I can't leave him," she had protested, "any more than you could've left Adele."

"Jason's young and strong, darling. Adele was a helpless invalid."

"It has nothing to do with strength or weakness," she had insisted. "It has everything to do with being incapable of hurting the people you love."

For the next few weeks Ginger and Avery skipped their customary early-morning hike up the mountain and their habit of sharing breakfast at his house and instead went right to his bedroom. Their hours apart became more and more painful to bear. Avery felt as though his staid exterior hid a veritable volcano of desire. He was behaving like a seventeen-year-old sex maniac, making up for fifty-five years of deprivation.

They were so perfectly attuned to each other that they needed few preliminaries. After a deep kiss or two and the touch of their naked bodies pressed together, they were ready to explode again and again with the most intoxicating pleasure. They gently caressed each other afterward to calm themselves. Avery liked to hold his lips against the carotid pulse in her neck, to feel the tumultuous rush of her blood while his hands soothed her smooth body.

One June morning when he entered her a second time, his head buzzing with exhilaration, he felt even more urgent and sensual than usual. His love for her flowed over him in waves, like a balm, even as his body thrust and quivered and finally shuddered with lustful joy. He remained on top of her, his cheek against hers while he fought to catch his breath. He wanted to lie there until they died, and then have someone wrap them together for eternity, like double mummies.

It was getting late, time for her to go, but still she clung to him. He raised his head and looked down at her. They smiled at each other a little uncertainly. "Don't go," he whispered. She shook her head and forced herself to get out of bed. When she had put on her hiking clothes and he had also dressed, he waited for that moment when she always changed into the "other" Ginger, the self-sufficient one who was married to Jason and who ran a hotel and who had a complete life outside of his bedroom. She had always made that change, quite visibly, like switching gears, every time they had been together. But this day she didn't.

Frowning, she walked unsteadily to the front door. She stopped and mumbled good-bye, but as she put her hand on the doorknob, she hesitated, then rushed back to him and embraced him fiercely. Her breath was ragged as he held her close.

"Ginger," he murmured again and again.

Almost angrily she pulled away from him and stood with her hands on his shoulders. She tried, unsuccessfully, to smile. "I don't want to leave you," she whispered. "I *can't!*"

He grasped both her hands and held them tightly. "Then stay."

When she shook her head and ran from the house, he went into the kitchen and made some coffee. He took the cup out onto his back porch and slowly drank the hot liquid while staring unseeingly at San Jacinto. His head and heart were in a turmoil. Suppose he had told her he loved her when he first knew it, when she was sixteen? And in Paris nine years ago, standing on the Pont de la Concorde, he had been on the verge of declaring his love to her. Should he have told her then? Would it have done any good? But Adele had still been alive then. Could he and Ginger have been secret lovers all those years? Or hadn't the time been right for it until now?

What were they going to *do*? The day certainly would come when she wouldn't be able to leave him, or he would refuse to let her go. These two hours each morning weren't enough for him, nor for her. Their bodies were hogging that precious time, greedily making up for all the lost years. But he wanted time to talk to her, to walk with her again, to share their meals, to enjoy every aspect of life with her. But could they be happy together if she were guilt-ridden, knowing that their joy was causing Jason to suffer? For suffer Jason would. Despite his easygoing demeanor, he was deeply, ardently, fiercely in love with Ginger.

Though Avery's eyes reflected these troubled thoughts, a smile kept playing around his lips. He couldn't help it. He was certain that it was just a matter of time until she got up the courage to leave Jason and marry him. He wanted to sing every love song he had ever heard. He wanted to yodel, exult, dance a triumphant jig. He wanted to run through the streets with a megaphone and announce his incredible news to the whole world:

Ginger loves me!

Ginger staggered along the path through the foothills that led from Avery's house to her own pink mansion. She was a little dizzy. She had never been so euphorically in love. Not with Tonito, not with Jason. Theirs now seemed like puppy love in comparison. Neither of them ever had made her feel this jubilant, this outrageously physically intoxicated. Only Avery had.

She melted at Avery's touch, at the very *thought* of his touch. Her internal organs fluttered at the sight of him. When she was alone, she whispered his name to herself like a magic mantra. This past week, while she had been busy closing down her hotel for the summer, she had been distracted and forgetful, wanting only to see Avery, to touch him, to be with him. How cruel life was! If only she had told him she loved him when she was sixteen and he first fell in love with her. They could have belonged to each other for the last twenty-four years, even if they'd had to be secret lovers while Adele was alive.

Yet she still adored Jason, enjoyed their life together, their laughter, even their fun in bed. But when she combined the physical bliss she and Avery shared with all her years of loving him as her kindest, dearest friend, how could Jason compete with that?

She still didn't have the courage to tell Jason that she was in love with Avery. It would have to wait until . . . she didn't know when. All she knew was that she couldn't hurt him. Not now. Not yet. She'd have to keep acting as though nothing had changed, at least for a little while.

She found him having his breakfast in their cheerful kitchen.

"G'morning," he sang out, greeting her with a wave of his coffee cup. "What took so long?"

"Oh, we went for a longer hike than usual." How she despised lying! "And then we had a big breakfast."

He stared at her. "You look different."

"I do?" She glanced anxiously into the colorful Mexican mirror above the sink: her hair was mussed, her face radiantly rosy. She looked fantastic! "I'm windblown and a little sunburned, I guess." She tried not to sound flustered. She sat down across the kitchen table from him and poured herself a cup of coffee. She was starving, but now she couldn't possibly eat after just having said she'd had a big breakfast at Avery's. She forced herself to smile at Jason while she sipped her coffee. He was adorable. His light hair was thick and tousled—no amount of brilliantine could keep it in place. His gray eyes twinkled with wit and humor and kindness. She looked down at his youthful hand: tanned, capable, strong, and smooth, without the enlarged veins of a fifty-five-year-old hand.

But inwardly she shivered with erotic delight at the thought of the older, veined hand touching her.

"God, Jason, I completely forget that Tony's coming home tomorrow."

"Tomorrow? You sure?" He got up and looked at the calendar on the kitchen wall. "Right. Saturday." He turned back to her. "How long is he staying?"

"A week. He's getting a ride down with a fellow from Indio. Then they're driving back up to Palo Alto for summer school. *And* I'm sorry to say, Tony's going to take more flying lessons." *A whole week without being alone with Avery,* she thought with a sinking heart. Tony liked to walk with them in the morning.

"Why do you pay for his flying lessons if they make you so unhappy?" Jason asked.

"I don't. He works part-time for his flight instructor in return for the lessons."

"Doing what?"

She shrugged. "I don't know. Sweeping the hangar, maybe some office work. For all I know, he shines his shoes and cleans his house."

"Then I guess there's nothing you can do about it." He grinned at her. "You look marvelous! Let's go back to bed."

She didn't know how to refuse. She never had. "All right. I need a bath." She started toward the steps.

"Gimme a kiss first."

"I'm all dusty and sweaty," she said. "I'll owe you one." She was afraid to get too close to him until she had bathed and douched and washed her hair and brushed her teeth. She was pumped full of Avery's semen and her skin reeked of his shaving lotion. Her mouth still tingled from his kisses and their mingled saliva.

She would take a leisurely bath and soak Avery out of her body and out of her mind—at least temporarily. Then she would make love to Jason—sweet, adorable Jason. Afterward she would spend the entire day with Jason so that she could give him her undivided attention every single minute of it. But she knew that no matter how lovingly she treated him, it wouldn't get rid of the awful guilt she felt toward him, knowing that someday soon she would have to leave him.

Try as she would, she couldn't get aroused when Jason

made love to her. First she made excuses to herself, that she already had had three orgasms that morning, that she was all played out. But she knew that if Avery were in bed with her instead of Jason, she would climax like a howling hurricane without half-trying.

Then, just *thinking* about Avery made her respond to Jason's caresses. She did something that caused her great distress: she closed her eyes and made believe that Jason *was* Avery. She came at once and burst into tears.

Jason stared at her with perplexed eyes. "What's wrong, sweetheart?" He stroked her hair.

She shook her head and clung to him. "Nothing," she assured him in a muffled voice.

"You've been acting very strange lately."

She gave him a wry smile. "Early menopause."

"Not you." He let go of her and lay back on his pillow. He didn't know what to make of her. He felt that they had lost their connection, that she was drifting away, and when he tried to hold on to her, he found himself clutching thin air. They had always been so close, so able to talk to each other freely, but now she was evasive, unresponsive, moody, completely lost in thought much of the time.

He decided to talk to Avery about her as soon as Tony's visit was over. Avery had been her friend and confidant, as well as her doctor, for years and years. Maybe he had some inkling of what was ailing her.

Ginger pulled herself together. She smiled at Jason, feeling more like her old self. "Let's play hooky today," she said with animation. "Just the two of us. We can go somewhere different for lunch . . ."

"Can't," he said regretfully. "Remember? Today's the day I give a slide-show talk to five hundred ladies in Riverside. The National Garden Club luncheon."

"Damn! I completely forgot."

"They invited me months ago, for a nice fat fee. Boy, do I dread that long hot drive!"

"Want me to come with you?" she offered.

He shook his head. "No point your riding in a stifling car all that way. It's bad enough that I have to suffer."

After he left, she wandered aimlessly around the house. She didn't have to go to work—she had already finished the chore of closing down the hotel for the summer.

Then she called Avery. "Jason's gone to Riverside for the day," she said, trying to control the tremor in her voice. "Avery, I want to see you. Can I come over? Or can you come here if Hilda's there cleaning?"

He was quiet for a moment. "Hilda's sick today. So yes, come on over."

"Oh, Avery, what are we going to *do*?"

"Let's talk about it."

"Shall I come over right now?" she asked breathlessly.

"I'll be devastated if you don't!"

"It's a disease, isn't it?" she asked, turning in his arms to face him while the sweat on their glistening bodies dried in the hot air being circulated by his ceiling fan. Their lovemaking was growing wilder and wilder. "Is there a name for it?"

"Sure. It's called ecstasy."

She sighed happily. "I can't think straight when you hold me like this. Let's get dressed and talk."

He tightened his arms around her and gave her a long kiss that started out languorous, then became more and more passionate, and ended in another whirlwind of rapture.

She sat up. "I can't *believe* us! I've read books about people who act this way, you know, staying awake day and night and having one orgasm after another. And you know what? I always thought the writers were terrible liars. Or at least wildly exaggerating."

"Now you know."

"Did *you* know?"

He shook his head. "I wish I had. Sometimes patients used to ask me about sex. I must've given out a hell of a lot of bad advice."

Reluctantly she got out of bed and stepped into her light sundress. "We have to talk."

"I know." He put on his tennis shorts. "God, it's hot!"

They went into his living room and sat under the ceiling fan, facing each other across a coffee table. Avery had set out two chilled glasses and a pitcher of cold lemonade tinkling with ice cubes. They sipped the tart drink slowly, waiting for the other to say something brilliant that would solve their dilemma.

"What I'd like to do," he finally said, "is marry you, of course, so we could be together all the time."

"Oh, sure," she drawled sarcastically. "Shall we kill Jason and bury his body in a lonely canyon? Or push him off a ledge up on San Jacinto?"

"You could divorce him."

She made a wry face. "I'm certainly giving him grounds." She sighed. "I guess what it really boils down to is this: do I want to stay married to Jason, or do I want to divorce him and marry you?"

"And?"

"I desperately want to marry you, but I don't want to divorce Jason. I can't bear to hurt him."

"So what's left? Bigamy?" He paused. "Remember, Ginger, when you worry about leaving Jason—*I saw you first!* I've invested years and years into loving you."

"I don't think Jason'll buy that."

"Well, there's one other thing we might consider. We could simply tell Jason the truth about us."

"I couldn't bear to," she objected, "even if you did see me first."

"You can tell him you still love him and don't want to divorce him. But tell him we absolutely must spend some time together or we'll go crazy. We could go away for a while, maybe up north somewhere. It would give us a chance to see if being together is what we really want."

"I can tell you right now, Avery Rowland, it's what I really want!"

"Me too. I can't imagine that it would work out any other way."

She was thoughtful. "There's one advantage to going away like that. It would give Jason time to get used to the idea . . . you know, used to living without me." She shook her head and her eyes filled with tears. "But, Avery, I just don't know . . ." She suddenly smiled wickedly. "Wouldn't it be wonderful if Jason were secretly in love with someone else?"

"Sic Ella on him."

"Ella!" she cried indignantly. Then she told Avery about Ella's affair with Tonito. "I've never told another soul, except Jason," she concluded. "Until now, it hurt too much."

Avery was stunned. "Well! That explains everything! The night you fainted . . . at Tony's tenth birthday party. But it freed you from grieving over Tonito. After that, you were able to love Jason. . . ."

"Yes. And now you've freed me from my anger against Tonito because I realize that I'm as bad an adulterer as he was."

Quickly Avery came over and knelt in front of her while taking her hands. "Don't say that! *We* love each other. Ella and Tonito just *fucked*. That's what you said Ella called it. It was lust based on hatred."

She stroked his silver hair, then grasped his head and held it against her breasts. "What we have is so wonderful, Avery. But why should Jason have to suffer in order for us to be happy?" She sighed. "God, how I wish all of this had happened before I ever met Jason!"

"I wish so too, with all my heart." Avery sat down next to her and put his arm around her.

She rested her head on his shoulder. "Let's go away, then. As soon as Tony leaves. I won't tell him yet. He worships Jason."

"Don't forget, he worships me too," Avery reminded her.

"Yes, like a grandfather. But Jason's been a real father to him."

"I can't deny that." He kissed her lightly. "So where shall we go?"

"How about the Ahwahnee in Yosemite for a while? Then maybe up to Lake Tahoe? I love the Fallen Leaf Lodge, and there's wonderful hiking all around there. After that we could go to Carmel . . . and San Francisco . . . and on up the coast. . . ."

"It sounds great." He stood up and pulled her to her feet. He realized how fortunate he was—how fortunate they both were—to share such an extraordinary love. How ironic it was, too, that they were so deliriously happy at the very time that the world was plunged into the worst misery of its known existence.

He was a little abashed to think that he had lived fifty-five years, had always considered himself an intelligent, well-educated, well-traveled man, and yet he had been so ignorant about something as basic to humanity as love. He had let his love lie fallow for over two decades, mooning over this woman and letting her marry two other men in the process. Why hadn't he simply followed his instincts and told her how he felt about her? Right from the start. Despite Adele. They'd have worked it out somehow. *Hey, no more mourning over the past,* he chided himself. *Think only of the glorious months ahead!*

"How soon can you leave?" he asked.

"Tony stays till the morning of June 10. I'll tell Jason about us as soon as Tony's gone, and you and I can leave that afternoon."

He nodded. "Poor Jason. But lucky us! We'll be together day and night. Imagine, Ginger! All summer long!"

Tony's visit was a great strain on Ginger. The boy was so perceptive—she remembered that when he was only ten he had *told* her that Avery was in love with her—and now she was afraid he would notice a lot more. She also dreaded the moment she would have to tell Jason she was leaving him. He seemed especially dear to her the week Tony was home, so thoughtful and kind and loving.

She had such mixed feelings about her son! She had to keep reminding herself that his strong resemblance to Tonito did *not* mean that Tony was in any way responsible for his father's behavior. Physically, Tony was a watered-down version of Tonito, with the contribution of her fair skin making the boy less strikingly handsome than his darker-skinned father had been. Often, looking at Tony, she couldn't help passionately wishing she knew what Johnny would have been like, all grown, and it was unfair to Tony for her to long for her dead child while her very-much-alive son was needing her maternal love.

His first morning home, he was awake before Ginger and waiting for her downstairs, wearing his hiking clothes. "G'morning, Mom." He hugged her and kissed her cheek.

"Tony! Why'd you get up so early? You're on vacation." Her heart was pounding with fear: if he hiked with her and Avery, then there would be no chance that day for lovemaking.

"Oh, I slept enough," Tony assured her. "I wouldn't miss your morning hike with Avery for anything."

"But . . . you need your sleep . . ." she protested lamely.

"I hate sleeping late. I never do. So c'mon, let's go!" He opened the door for her and she had no choice but to go with him to meet Avery.

Tony hiked with Ginger and Avery every morning of his vacation. And each day, as was their custom, they went to Avery's for breakfast. Ginger could barely force down a mouthful of food. She would sip her coffee and feel guilty because she resented her son's being there. She could only think of Avery's bed and how much she wanted to be in it with him. *The lovesick matron*, she derided herself.

She was alone with Avery only once during the entire week, when Jason and Tony spent a day collecting rocks in Palm Canyon for a project Tony was doing at school. The rest of the time Jason and Tony had activities planned for every moment, and they expected her to join them.

When she had a few minutes to herself she made a list of what she would take with her when she and Avery left. She didn't dare start packing until she had talked with Jason. And after that, she'd have only a short time to get her things together.

"Is Viv coming to visit this summer?" Tony asked his first day home.

Jason shook his head. "She's got a job—counselor at a summer camp up near Sequoia."

"How is she?"

"Great. I saw her two weeks ago, when I lectured at USC. She's slimmed down, plays tennis every day. I took her dancing at the Coconut Grove and she taught me how to rumba. She's really good!" Gaily Jason executed a few fancy steps. "The tango too." He suddenly sighed. "She's growing up. Too damn fast."

"Yeah, we kids have a bad habit of doing that," Tony said dryly. "How's good old Uncle Neil?" he asked casually, really wanting to know about Jennie but not daring to ask outright.

"He and Jennie are in Hollywood, making Jennie's first movie," Ginger replied. "If I remember right, Neil said he's financing it himself, and he's building his own studio. That's all I know. Anyway, it's all Greek to me."

"Oh?" Tony waited for more news of Jennie, but none was forthcoming. "And Cal?" he asked.

"Cal?" He's been over for dinner a few times. I try to invite him once in a while, when there's someone especially interesting staying at The Springs. Now he's gone east for the summer, sailing with friends in Maine."

"And Aunt Ella?"

Ginger grimaced. "In Newport, living it up with Gracie's husband."

"And Gracie?"

Ginger laughed. "Do you want a rundown on *everyone* we know? Anyhow, Gracie's just fine. She has her own half-hour radio show on CBS, starting next fall, so she and little Amy moved to New York. She bought herself a smashing penthouse apartment and she's marrying her show's producer—a really fine fellow—as soon as her divorce from Bert is final."

"One more, and I'll quit," Tony promised. "How's Nellie?"

"She's fine too. Her sons pretty much run the Desert Inn now. Nellie and Pearl McManus sort of take turns being the *grande dame* of Palm Springs."

"Maybe someday you'll have that honor, Mom."

"Me?" She hooted. "Not for years and years."

One night they had dinner at the home of Maria and Vittorio and all of Tony's cousins. The talk turned to the status of the Indian land and the tribe's inability to get the federal government to allow them to legally divide it.

"It *still* hasn't been solved, after all these years!" Maria complained. "Tonito tried, Lee Arenas is trying. Meanwhile, all around us, white landowners are making a bloody fortune. All *we* can do with our land is farm it." Fondly she patted Vittorio's round face. "If I didn't have a nice fat Italian husband who makes a good living, we'd all be starving to death."

"Ah, Maria-baby, knock it off." Vittorio grinned. "Listen to me, sweetheart, the longer the government forces you to hang on to that land of yours, the richer you'll be. Land values are going to keep going up and up and up." He made escalating slashes with his hand, ending up by gesturing high above his head.

"Great! So we'll have rich great-great-grandchildren!" Maria said wryly. "*I* want to enjoy the money!"

Later, walking home, Tony linked arms with Ginger and Jason. "Y'know, try as I might, I just don't feel one bit Indian."

"That's too bad, because the Agua Calientes have a beautiful heritage," Ginger said. "Tonito always talked about their history and legends with great pride."

"Yeah. Well, maybe someday I'll get more interested. Right now, I only care about being an ordinary American and about getting my pilot's license this summer."

"I'm thrilled," Ginger said flatly.

The evening before Tony left, he asked Ginger to go for a walk with him after dinner.

Jason waved them off. "It was stupid of me," he berated himself. "It didn't occur to me that you two should have some time alone together."

They walked downhill toward the center of town, past the locked gates of The Springs. During the season, the gates remained open with a uniformed gateman stopping all cars but those of the guests. It went against Ginger's nature to keep people out, but she had to protect the privacy of her famous guests. Seclusion was The Spring's greatest asset. If her guests wanted to see and be seen, they would go to the Desert Inn or El Mirador or the Racquet Club.

"Is the hotel all closed up now?" Tony asked.

"Yes, thank goodness! Until mid-October."

When they came to a low stone wall, Tony gestured at it. "Let's sit a minute."

"Sure." They sat down and shared a brief silence, each waiting for the other to speak, but meanwhile they watched the dark blue sky turn to purple as dusk edged into night. Downhill from them, the lights on Palm Canyon Drive competed with the emerging stars.

Resolutely Tony turned and faced her. "Mom, what's going *on*?"

"With what?"

"With you, with Jason, with Avery. You're all so . . . I don't know, just *strange*."

"Are we?" She had tried so hard to behave normally while he was home. "In what way?"

He took a deep breath. "Well, like mornings, when we go hiking with Avery, and then have breakfast at his place . . . I don't know, the air seems full of something, like electricity. And you hardly ever eat anything, you just sit there sipping your coffee with a funny look on your face. And good old Avery . . . I've never seen him so *happy*. He's like a little boy who got a whole bunch of extra toys for Christmas that he didn't expect. And Jason seems sort of jumpy . . . like he's worried about something."

"You're very observant, Tony." She took his hand. How was she going to tell him the truth? Would he hate her? And hate Avery? But Tony had to know what was happening. It was better for him to hear it from her than to be shocked by phoning home and finding she was gone. "I might as well tell you . . ." She stopped, her voice hoarse with tension. "I'm going away with Avery for the summer."

"You mean like we went to Paris with him that year?"

"No." Her voice was so low he could barely hear her. "I mean . . . . as lovers."

He stared at her. "Come on, Mom! You and old Avery?"

"Yes."

"Well, wha . . . what about Jason?"

"I'm going to tell him tomorrow. Right after you leave. So please, Tony, don't say anything to him. I want to tell him myself."

"I just can't believe it!" He got up and walked in agitated circles. "I mean, sure, I love them both . . ."

"So do I, Tony. But I love Avery more."

"Isn't he awful old?"

"He's a little old, darling, but not *awful* old." She stood up and put her arms around him. "Someday I hope you and a wonderful girl will love each other the way Avery and I love each other. I'll probably divorce Jason and marry Avery before too long. I can't help it, Tony. I just have to be with him. All the time."

Tony was amazed that people his mother's age, let alone Avery's, could fall in love this way. But love or no love, how could she do this to Jason? It was too cruel. She was Jason's *wife*, for God's sake! How could she be so goddam selfish?

"Tony," she begged, seeing the dismay on his face, "please . . ."

"What do you want me to say?" he asked bitterly.

"I was hoping you'd understand."

"What's there to understand, Mom? You're going off with Avery and leaving Jason out in the cold."

"It's not that simple, darling. Jason and I have had a wonderful life together. But I can't begin to explain how

Avery and I feel about each other. It's as if all the years we've been such wonderful friends has erupted into an incredibly romantic love between us." She paused while sudden tears flooded her eyes, and she couldn't tell if they were tears of joy because of her love for Avery or tears of sorrow over her need to hurt Jason.

"I think you're *awful*!" Tony blurted. He ran up the hill, back toward their house, not waiting for her. When she reached home, Jason told her that Tony had gone upstairs to bed.

In the morning, Tony was sullen. He didn't want breakfast, and when his friend arrived to pick him up, Tony hugged Jason, then turned to Ginger. He hesitated, then threw his arms around her in a ferocious hug and rushed out of the house.

"What's bugging him?" Jason asked.

"I don't know," she replied vaguely. "Listen, there's something I have to tell you."

"Yeah?" He cleared his throat and looked at her questioningly.

She nodded, close to tears. "Let's go sit on the back porch." She led the way and they sat stiffly on canvas chairs facing each other across a small wooden table. She stared at the rocky slopes behind the house, as if to gain courage from the mountain.

"Well?" he prompted. "Is something wrong?"

"Yes. I'm sure you noticed . . . I haven't been myself lately."

"Of course I noticed." He looked concerned. "Are you ill, darling? Something you've been afraid to tell me?" He reached across the table and took her hand.

"Ill?" She gave a hollow laugh. "I guess you could call it that. Jason, this is so difficult." She paused, then blurted, "I'm in love with Avery!"

He stared at her, thinking it might be some kind of joke. "Avery?" he repeated blankly.

"Yes. I'm madly, *insanely* in love with Avery."

He shook his head in confusion. "I don't get it."

"I'm trying to tell you . . . I'm going away with him for a while."

He let go of her hand, almost flinging it from him. He got up and paced back and forth on the porch. "Maybe

I'm dense, Ginger," he finally sputtered, "but I just don't understand. You're going away with Avery—*good old Avery*—as what? As friends? Or are you trying to tell me . . . as *lovers*?"

She nodded. "As lovers."

"But you're married to *me*!" he cried out in anguish, finally understanding what she was telling him.

"Yes. It's . . . it's just . . . just a trial . . . an experiment. We want to see if it's what we really want. Maybe we'll find we can't stand being together all the time."

"How long'll you be gone?" he asked dully, coming back and sitting down again.

"I don't know. Two months. Maybe three."

"In other words, all summer."

"Probably."

He jumped up and pulled her roughly out of her chair. He shoved her against the wall with his body and strained against her while kissing her. Hard. Punishing her while tears slid down his cheeks.

With a groan, he backed off and looked at her, shaking his head. "Is it the sex? Are you tired of me? Is that it? It's better with him?"

"No, no, if it were only the sex . . . I'd never leave you over that."

"Then *what* . . . ?"

"Oh, Jason, it's everything. I've loved him almost all my life, but I never *realized* . . ."

"And if you and Avery find you want to be together permanently . . . ?" He looked at her fearfully while his voice dropped to a whisper. "Does that mean you'll . . . divorce me?"

"Let's not worry about that now," she begged, sitting down again.

"Easy for you to say," he rasped, crumpling into his chair. "First you kick me in the teeth, the butt, and the balls, and then you say not to worry!"

"I'm sorry," she whimpered.

"Oh, you're sorry!" he mimicked sarcastically. "Goody, goody, she's sorry! That excuses everything. What the hell do you expect me to *do*, Ginger? Congratulate the two of you? Tell you I want you to live happily ever after and to forget about *my* feelings?"

She shook her head, wanting to die. "I know you

won't believe me, Jason, but I can't stand hurting you. I still love you. I love you as much as I ever did."

"Sure! I can see that!" His voice vibrated with scorn.

"It's only that I . . . I love Avery more. I can't help it." She started to cry from the strain of watching Jason's misery. "Can't you see? If I stayed with you out of a sense of duty, I'd be so miserable! I'd only end up making you miserable too!"

He watched her in silence, watched as she jumped up and ran upstairs. He heard the sound of closet doors and dresser drawers opening and shutting. He knew that she was packing, that in a little while she would walk out of his life and he would be left here all alone. Pain gripped his skull, a full-blown headache whose intensity made his eyes squint. *How was he going to live without her?*

He sat there slumped in a daze until he heard a car in the driveway, and he went upstairs and carried down her two suitcases for her. He left them on the porch—he didn't want to talk to the man who was stealing his wife—and retreated into the house, but not before Ginger rushed out to greet Avery. Jason didn't want to watch them together, but he couldn't help seeing the elation in their eyes as Avery took her hand and led her to his shiny blue Packard.

They drove as far as a small motor court outside of Bakersfield that first day. Both of them were exhausted from the strain of leaving Jason so bereft. It was as if he were in the backseat berating them every mile of the way. They felt his hovering presence all during dinner at a mediocre roadside café, the only place they could find in that semirural area. Only when they threw off their sweaty travel clothes and showered and got into bed did they fully realize how extraordinary a moment this was for them.

They embraced and looked into each other's eyes, and the rest of the world faded away. Jason, the war, mankind's endless misery, all disappeared into a mist.

When Ginger awoke in the morning she was lying on her right side with Avery's chest and groin pressed against her back and his arms encircling her. His regular breath ruffled the hair behind her ear. She moved tighter against him, happily aware that her body was beginning to flood with desire. They had the whole summer to be like this, every day and every night. And after that . . . well, if Avery lived to a hundred and she to eighty-five, they'd have forty-five more years together!

She heard him take a deep breath, and when she turned her head she saw that his eyes were slowly opening. She watched, amused, as he came awake with a start, looked around the unfamiliar room, then stared into her laughing eyes. "G'morning," she said, bubbling with joy.

"Mmmmmm," he replied sleepily.

She turned in his arms so that they were face-to-face. They stared at each other in wonderment before slowly bringing their mouths together and losing all sense of time and place.

It was late July and Jason wondered if a person could die of a broken heart. Because that was what he had. He had heard all his life that men didn't cry, but this man sure did. The days weren't so bad. He kept busy, felt good about the new book he was writing, liked living in Ginger's pink mansion, was relaxed and peaceful while riding his horse every evening after the summer air cooled off. But at night the big empty house spooked him and the big empty bed he had shared with Ginger utterly defeated him. Soon after Ginger left, he moved into one of the guest rooms, but many nights he still cried into his pillow.

If only it hadn't been Avery. How could he possibly hate Avery? He always had adored the man, admired everything about him. Jason could understand Avery's attraction for Ginger. He could even understand how all the years of deep affection between Ginger and Avery could suddenly boil over into physical passion.

Nor could Jason entirely hate Ginger. His wonderful, beautiful Ginger. He went over and over the eight and a half years of their marriage, trying to see if he had failed her in some way. Had he ever been less than attentive to her needs? He didn't think so. Had his success somehow changed him? Well, of course it had, but surely for the better? It had given him more self-confidence, more pride in himself, made him more worthy of her love. He sighed, totally confused.

He had often felt that her falling in love with him had been too good too be true. The first couple of years they were married, he kept waiting for her to realize that she had made a mistake. But time had passed, and her love for him had seemed genuine, and he had gotten over worrying about her leaving him.

He reread her last card. A picture of Oregon's Columbia River Gorge. It was gorge-ous, *ha-ha*. She had warned him that she wouldn't write, would only send picture postcards to let him know she was all right, that they hadn't fallen off any mountains.

He looked at the other cards she had sent—he kept them propped up on his desk. There was Yosemite Falls, an aerial photo of Lake Tahoe's Emerald Bay, Carmel's oceanfront Seventeen-Mile Drive, San Francisco's Fairmont Hotel with a scribbled note about her having stayed there after the big earthquake when she was six years old, a grove of redwood trees south of Crescent City, the ocean view from Coos Bay, Oregon. He could visualize Ginger and Avery hiking the magnificent trails in the Sierras with their arms around each other. He could see them driving along the dramatic northern coast in Avery's immaculate blue Packard. He could imagine them making love passionately, endlessly, in every hotel room they shared. . . .

And he was ravaged by jealousy. He felt like a moth repeatedly flinging itself against a windowpane, ignoring the pain while trying to get inside at the light. And his light was Ginger.

His wife. *His* love. *His whole world!* And he knew he didn't have a chance in hell of winning her back from Avery. The breathless way those two had looked at each other when Avery came to take her away! Like they wanted to fly into each other's arms and never let go. Jason couldn't remember her ever looking at *him* like that.

She might as well divorce me now and get it over with, he though dismally. Why prolong the agony? Oh, sure, she had told him that this summer with Avery was just an experiment, to see if they wanted to make it permanent. But Jason couldn't forget the dazzling euphoria in her eyes when she spoke about spending the entire summer with Avery. After that, how could Jason possibly have any hope whatsoever that she would come back to him at the end of the summer? Or ever?

Knowing that she telephoned Tony at his dormitory every week, Jason called his stepson and asked him to have Ginger phone home. It was urgent, he said.

The call came two days later, in the evening.

"Is anything wrong?" Ginger asked the moment Jason picked up the phone.

"No, no," he replied, wanting to say that *everything* was wrong. "I thought I'd tell you"—he stopped to clear his throat: he was having trouble controlling the tremor in his voice—"I've given it a lot of thought, Ginger, so let's not kid ourselves. It's over for us." He spoke in a great rush, afraid that if he'd didn't get the words out quickly they might stick in his throat and he'd never be able to say them. "Look, why don't you and Avery go to Reno for the usual six weeks and get it over with? Accuse me of anything the lawyer suggests."

"But, Jason! Are you really sure it's—"

He could hear the lilt of relief in her voice. "Listen, Ginger," he interrupted, "just do it. Okay? Then we both can get on with our lives."

"But . . . will *you* be all right?"

He ignored her question: the selfish bitch didn't deserve an answer. *Oh, but he loved her!* He cleared his throat again. "We don't need any sort of financial agreement. I mean, you have your money and I have more than enough for my needs. So let's let it go at that. I don't want any of the things we bought together. Only thing is, do you mind if I stay here in your house a few more weeks? It'll take me time to get all my papers and things together."

"You can stay there indefinitely, Jason. Avery and I can live at his place when we get back."

"Thanks, but I don't want to stay here." *It will remind me too much of my misery and humiliation . . . and of what I've lost,* he wanted to say, but didn't. He had his pride.

"Oh, but really . . ." she insisted. "Really, Jason, I *want* you to stay there."

Madam Bountiful, he thought wearily. She could afford to be generous to him: she had gotten what she wanted. "Thanks, but I can't," he finally mumbled. "I may leave Palm Springs altogether."

"Don't do anything hasty," she warned. "And, Jason, I . . . I . . ."

"Ginger, please. Spare me the apologies." He hung up quickly, blindly, before the tears came again.

It was mid-September by the time Ginger completed the six-week residency required for a Nevada divorce. The day before her court date, she and Avery shared a picnic on the black sand beach of Pyramid Lake, thirty miles north of Reno. They leaned against one of the porous volcanic tufa rocks on the western shore, eating cold chicken salad and sipping champagne while watching flocks of white pelicans cavort in the water.

Except for her recurring guilt over Jason, the entire summer had been one long honeymoon, and tomorrow they finally would get married, right after she received her divorce papers. Everywhere they had gone, Avery had reserved the bridal suite. Of course they had had to register as Dr. and Mrs. Avery Rowland, and Ginger had had to continue wearing her wedding ring so they wouldn't be turned away by haughty hotel personnel.

She watched Avery as he sat beside her, relaxed and happy. How splendid he looked! They both felt wonderfully fit after their summer of wandering and their six weeks of enforced stay in Nevada.

With Reno as their base, they had spent many days hiking up Mount Rose in the High Sierras and swimming in frigid Lake Tahoe. They had explored Virginia City's steep streets and faded grandeur, and the pleasant State Capitol at Carson City, and the little historic cemetery in Genoa. They had hiked in the desert terrain of the Washoe Mountains east of Reno. They had sauntered through the noisy casinos lining downtown Reno's Virginia Street, stopping to put a few nickels into the slot machines at Harold's Club and enjoying the tinkle of coins being spit out of the machines when someone—never them!—got a jackpot.

Early in their Reno sojourn they had discovered Pyramid Lake, named after the triangular rock in the middle of the lake on the Paiute Indian reservation, and they went there often to picnic. After lunch on this final day of their waiting period, while Avery stretched out on the sand for a nap, Ginger took a pen and a pad of stationery out of the picnic basket and wrote a letter:

Dearest Jason,

Tomorrow we will no longer be husband and wife. Embedded in my present joy is great sorrow that our life together is over. I know you will have trouble believing this, but I still love you, and always shall.

I want you to understand one thing: I know you feel that Avery stole me from you, but actually, the reverse is true. *You* stole me from Avery! He and I have loved each other from the day we met, when I was twelve and he was twenty-seven. At first it was the love of a child for a very dear adult, but by the time I was sixteen, Avery realized it was much more than that. Both of us let our age difference keep us apart for a quarter of a century! All that time we were spiritual lovers, even though it took us so long to become physical lovers as well. But don't you see? If you hadn't come along and utterly charmed me, Avery and I undoubtedly would have realized what we really mean to each other much sooner. We belong to each other, heart and soul.

Dearest Jason, don't be bitter. Our years together were marvelous and my only regret is hurting you now. As I told you the day I left, I don't love you one bit less than I ever did. It is only that I love Avery more.

Jason, I know I've been cruel to you. Grabbing my happiness at your expense has been utterly selfish. But it's better than living a life of deceit with you. I hope in time you will be able to forgive me.

Oh, darling, try to be happy!

Ginger

She sighed as she addressed an envelope and inserted the letter. *Ah, Jason, Jason, Jason,* she thought regretfully, *if only you could accept our wonderful eight and a half years together as a beautiful time in both our lives and get on with your own life—without me.*

The next morning, walking out of the Washoe County

Courthouse into the dazzling sunshine of the mile-high city, Ginger stopped on the steps and took off the simple silver wedding band that Jason had bought for her nearly nine years earlier. Every year, on their anniversary, he had offered to get her a more expensive ring, but she had always declined, perfectly satisfied with the plain band. In a few minutes, Avery would replace it with an elegant gold wedding ring, while she would slip a matching one onto his finger. She carefully put Jason's ring in her purse and smiled up at Avery.

"Aren't you going to throw it in the Truckee?" he asked.

She shook her head.

"What's the point in keeping it? It's the custom here for divorcees to throw their wedding rings in the river."

"Only if they *hate* their former husbands." She took his arm and they walked toward the small gray stone church where the minister was waiting to marry them. They had chosen this church not because either of them had any allegiance to it, but because they liked its architecture and its location alongside the river, close to Idlewild Park, where they often went to commiserate with the buffalo kept penned up there.

During the wedding ceremony, Ginger only half-heard the minister's voice. She was entranced by the way the stained-glass windows splashed rainbow colors over the nave's white walls. She knew she never would forget this high point in her life and she wanted to memorize every detail, including Avery's very admirable profile. *He was her husband now!*

Dear God, keep him hearty and healthy for years and years and years, and in return I'll be as virtuous as I know how, she silently and fervently prayed. *I'll try to be kind and helpful every day of my life.* She knew better than to make deals with the Almighty, but she would do anything to keep Avery with her for as long as possible. She didn't want to think too far ahead, preferring to live each day as it came, but the thought of life without him was too threatening to contemplate.

To Avery, this moment was the culmination of his dreams. Never in all the years of longing for Ginger had he expected to marry her, or for her to love him so ardently. There *is* a God, he thought, because the events of the past few months were nothing short of miraculous. When the minister said, "Dr. Rowland, you may kiss your bride now," Avery did so carefully, mindful that he and Ginger were instantly inflamed by their passionate kisses. What would the little man do, Avery wondered with an inward smile, if this very respectable-looking couple suddenly fell to the floor and consummated the marriage right there in front of him?

After the ceremony, wrapped in an aura of exultation, Ginger and Avery strolled slowly back toward the Mapes Hotel, where they were occupying the bridal suite. Ginger stopped in front of a dress shop's display window whose back wall was mirrored. "Look," she said, "aren't we a handsome couple?" They both stared happily at their images. Her face was radiant and the sun made a golden halo of her auburn hair. She was wearing a rustling blue silk dress with a sweetheart neckline and tiny pearls down the front. She still carried the bouquet of tea roses that the minister's wife had given her. Avery was beaming, his eyes glowing with sheer happiness. He was dressed in a midnight-blue suit, white shirt, and a silver tie that matched his hair. He had been given a pink carnation for his buttonhole. They both looked very festive and youthful.

The loudspeaker in the Mapes lobby was blaring Dinah Shore's voice singing "The Nearness of You." The elevator man was humming "I Married an Angel." And when Avery and Ginger reached their suite, the radio was tuned to Bing Crosby crooning "Always." It seemed to Avery that the whole world was singing love songs to them—until the news came on abruptly with the grim report of a brutal German aerial attack on London.

With a flash of guilt over his own happiness when the world seemed to be dying, Avery impatiently snapped off the radio and drew Ginger to him. He felt as though they both were wired, so that when their mouths touched, electric shocks of desire flowed through every part of their bodies. It was this thoroughly carnal and thoroughly holy meshing of their physical and spiritual selves that bonded them, he thought, far more than the minister's words and the state of Nevada's marriage certificate.

When they finally let go of each other, Avery realized that it was exactly five months since the April morning he had declared his love for her and they had become lovers. She had rejuvenated him, had turned him from a dispirited old man into a veritable flaming youth. And in return, he was certain that he had brought her more joy than she had ever known.

He took her hand and kissed it. " 'Grow old along with me . . .' " he started to quote softly.

"You and Mr. Browning have it all wrong," Ginger interrupted with a smile. "It should be 'Stay *young* along with me. The best is yet to be.' "

A week before Christmas, Ginger realized that she might be pregnant. "It just occurred to me that I haven't had a period since October," she told Avery, "and come to think of it, I've been a little queasy some mornings."

Avery examined her and shook his head in amazement. "Your uterus is definitely enlarged," he said with a tremor of wonder in his voice.

"But . . . I tried so hard with Jason to get pregnant! And you and Adele never had a child. Darling, I simply assumed that you and I were both incapable of it."

"Before we get our hopes up too high, give me a urine specimen and I'll send it off to the lab."

A few days later, when Avery received the positive lab results, his euphoria knew no bounds. But then he became thoughtful. "I may not live to see our child as an adult," he said sadly. "I'm not just old enough to be its grandfather, but its *great*-grandfather!"

"Why are you always so concerned about your age? Look how long it kept us apart!" Ginger gestured angrily. "Dammit, Avery, you're strong, you're never sick, you never even get colds. So stop saying things like that!" But her anger at him masked her own fears about his longevity. How could she live in a world without him? For the first time in her life she understood the old Hindu practice of suttee—not that she could ever do such a thing herself. *Now* you *stop it!* she scolded herself. *People can die at any age. Look at Tonito. Look at your mother. Look at your father and Polly. So stop this nonsense!*

When Tony came home for the Christmas holidays, Ginger and Avery jubilantly shared their astonishing news with him. He hugged them both and acted pleased and joked about the fact that he would be almost twenty years older than his little sibling, actually old enough to be its father, he said. But underneath it all, he was riddled with dismay. He was certain that his mother would love this new baby far more than she ever had loved him. He could sense the rapture that she and Avery shared, a closeness that shut him out, no matter how hard they tried to include him in their love.

Above all, Tony missed Jason. Much as he loved Avery, the older man couldn't offer him the father-son bond that Tony had developed with Jason. Avery had no way of competing with all the years that Jason and Tony had played baseball and football together, or the hours that Jason had spent teaching Tony desert lore, or their camping trips, their shared love of jazz, or their simply having lived in the same house and having loved each other day after day, for eight years. True, Tony had spent all his summers in Europe with Avery, but even then their relationship had been more like a mature mentor imparting his knowledge to a young pupil.

Tony slipped into a depression that was all the more painful for his having to hide it from his mother and Avery. His dejection became almost unbearable when he attended a Christmas Day party at his Uncle Neil's gaudy estate and saw his adored Jennie looking radiant and more beautiful than ever in a clinging gold lamé gown.

"Tony!" she greeted him, lifting her face to his. "Give Auntie a great big kiss!"

He forced a smile and pecked at her cheek, feeling faint with desire for her. He watched her kiss other guests, and it seemed to him that she was genuinely happy. Whenever she was near Neil she caressed his cheek like a loving wife. Was it sincere? Tony wondered. Did she really love fat old Uncle Neil? After all, she *was* an actress, and a superb one at that. Her first picture had opened all over the country the previous week and critics couldn't stop raving about her.

Tony noticed, from across the huge living room, that his cousin Cal also was watching Jennie's every move. Tony made his way over to Cal. He clapped him on the back and said, "Our auntie's quite a dish."

Cal nodded, a little drunkenly. "Didja know, Tony, that Jennie and I were lovers 'fore she married dear old

Uncle Neil? Boy, 's she hot stuff!" Cal took a long swallow from the tumbler of bourbon he was holding.

Tony flinched with shock. "L-lovers?" he repeated inanely.

"She's fantastic, and someday, wait 'n see, I'm gonna get her back!" Cal gestured at the room full of people. "Jeez, I hate Christmas. Always have. What say we ditch this shindig?"

"Where d'you wanna go?"

Cal shrugged. "I dunno. Got any ideas?"

"Jason's having a party tonight, over in Santa Monica. Wanna go?"

Cal looked at his watch. It was only five o'clock, and the way he drove, they could make it in less than two hours. "Why not?" He gave Tony a curious look. "How come you're still friendly with Jason?"

"He's like a father to me. He calls me all the time at school."

"I used to think he 'n your mother had the perfect marriage." Cal sighed deeply. "Tell me, does he hate her for throwing him over for old Doc Avery?"

Tony caught sight of his mother smiling elatedly up at Avery, who stood beside her with his arm possessively around her shoulders. Tony was flooded with the most corroding jealousy he had ever experienced. "Jason's furious at her," he replied, "and I can't say I blame him."

"D'you?"

"Do I what?"

"Hate your mother," Cal sniggered, draining his glass. "I hate mine. 'S usual, the bitch left me all alone at Christmas. Been doing that every year 's long 's I can remember. Went to New York with her stupid boyfriend."

Tony felt a surge of pity for Cal, and for the first time he felt close to him. He took his cousin's arm. "C'mon, Cal, screw 'em all. Let's get the hell out of here!"

Jason was no more in the mood to throw a Christmas party than he was to jump into the cold Pacific Ocean near his rented bungalow. But Vivien had talked him into it and together they had bought the food and cooked it and she was trying very hard to cheer him up. She was worried about him, about his persistent dejection and bitterness. It was so unlike the cheerful, ebullient father she had known all her life, and it frightened her.

He had accepted no invitations during the four months he had lived in Santa Monica, even though he knew many people in the area. Some were colleagues he had met during the years he had come to Los Angeles for speaking engagements, and others were old, old friends from his college days. In the past he had been friendly and gregarious, but now he was a recluse.

Vivien had invited five couples who had known Jason for years. Jason had phoned Tony at his dormitory in Palo Alto a week earlier and had asked him to come, but at the time Tony had been certain he wouldn't be able to leave his mother and Avery on Christmas Day. Therefore, when Tony and Cal rang the doorbell, Jason was overjoyed to see his stepson, and Vivien was overwhelmed by Cal's unexpected presence.

Tony was amazed at the change in Vivien since he had seen her the previous February, during her brief visit to Palm Springs for his mother's fortieth birthday party. Vivien was slimmer and she seemed more sophisticated. More grown-up. More self-confident. And much, much prettier. Her clothes were chic and her hair was shorter, blonder, and curlier than he remembered it.

"Little sisters grow up," she laughed when he complimented her. She gave him a dubious look. "Or . . . are you still my big brother?"

"Sure I am. I'll always be."

When Tony went to get a drink, Vivien turned to Cal. "I took your advice," she said softly.

"What advice?"

"Remember last February? When you took me to lunch at El Mirador?"

He searched his mind. Since last February there had been so many girls, so many lunches at El Mirador. He laughed. "Well, whatever you've done, you look swell."

"Thanks," she said with a smile, but her eyes were serious and full of longing for him.

Cal was tired of having women look at him like that. He had been unable to respond with much enthusiasm to anyone since his loss of Jennie. But then, when he noticed the depth of Vivien's admiration for him, he did recall their talk and how he had advised her to forget about dating— she was still only sixteen, as he remembered —and to concentrate on making herself more attractive, more desirable. Well, she had succeeded admirably. He remembered, too, that he had promised to kiss her properly, even make love to her, if she followed his advice, and now it seemed like a damn good idea to him.

"I learned how to rumba," she laughed, "*and* play tennis. And I hardly ever blush anymore." Boldly she let her eyes hold his to prove her point. "Want to take me dancing?" she asked provocatively. "You can find out how well I . . . um . . . rumba."

"Well, sure. How about later tonight?"

"I'd love to. As soon as I can slip away." She squeezed his hand and went to the kitchen to get more dip and chips.

From across the room, with great misgivings, Tony had watched them talk. He still felt a brotherly protectiveness of Vivien, and she was no match for a womanizer like Cal. What could the little fool be thinking of? He followed her to the kitchen. "Viv," he demanded, "were you making a date with Cal?"

She turned hostile eyes on him. "C'mon, Tony. I'm a big girl now."

"No you're not! Listen, Viv, every female from fifteen to fifty runs after Cal. He doesn't give a damn about any of them. If you go out with him, you'll just be looking for trouble!"

She turned on him angrily. "What do you know about anything? You never even go out with girls."

"Viv, please. I don't want to see you hurt. . . ."

"Well, *big* brother, just mind your own business!"

Earlier, during the exhilarating drive into the city—Cal drove his Duesenberg like a demon—Tony's gloom had lifted a little. But now it descended upon him in full force. He went into the living room and sat next to Jason. He remembered what a comfort Jason always had been, like when Tony failed to make the high-school baseball team, or when the girl he asked to the junior prom turned him down, or after he flunked algebra. Now Tony wished he could just put his head on Jason's shoulder and tell him how he felt. But Jason looked like *he* was the one who needed comforting even more.

"How's your mother?" Jason asked with a coldness

that Tony knew was directed at Ginger, not at him personally.

"She's going to have a baby," Tony replied flatly.

Jason turned scarlet and jumped out of his seat with shock.

"I'm s-sorry," Tony stammered. "I guess I shouldn't have told you."

Jason fled to his bedroom, with Tony at his heels. Jason turned a ravaged face on Tony. "Why is life so cruel?" he cried out in agony.

Tony put his arms around Jason and they both fought tears.

Jason sat down heavily on his bed. "Do you have *any* idea how much I wanted a child with her?"

Tony shook his head. "What happened? Didn't she want one?"

"Oh, she did! As much as I did! But somehow she just didn't conceive. Now, how could that old man . . . ?" He choked back a sob. "It's so unfair! Oh, God, how I hate the bitch!"

Tony sat down next to him, torn between loyalty toward his mother and love for Jason. He could see that Jason was drunk, that he was saying things he probably would regret when he sobered up. "Jason, I know I'm still a kid in your eyes, but listen, hating her is destroying you. Nothing you say or do is going to bring her back to you."

Jason shook his head. "I can't help it. I can't forgive her."

"You used to be such a happy guy," Tony mourned. "Why ruin your life over something you can't change?"

Jason looked at him carefully. "Tell me the truth, Tony. Do you love Avery?"

"Well, yeah. I mean, he's been like a grandfather to me since the day I was born. But I don't love him as much as I love you."

"Yeah, just the reverse of what your mother said. She told me she still loves me, but she loves Avery more. Some consolation." Jason took Tony's hand. "Believe me, kid, I appreciate your love. God knows, you and Viv are all that keep me going. And listen, I'm sorry I talked about your mother like that. It isn't fair to you." He brightened. "You'll stay over won't you? I've got plenty of room. We can walk on the beach tomorrow . . ."

"Sure. I'd love that." Tony rose. "We better get back to your party."

By the time they returned to the living room, Cal and Vivien had left.

Cal and Vivien drove all the way down Willshire Boulevard to the Ambassador Hotel, only to find that the Coconut Grove was closed Christmas Day. They returned to his car, disappointed. "Let's go to my mother's house," he suggested. "She's out of town."

"But . . . I thought you wanted to go dancing."

"I do. My mom's got some great records. We can dance there."

Vivien hesitated. She looked a lot more sophisticated than she actually was. Sure, she wanted Cal to kiss her, but was she ready to be all alone with him in a big mansion like that? Was she really ready to be seduced? What if Tony was right?

Cal understood. "Listen, honey, maybe I just better take you back to your Dad's—"

"No!" she quickly protested, wanting to be with him. "Let's go to your mom's."

Ella's estate was north of Sunset Boulevard, up in the hills behind the Bel Air Hotel. The curving street narrowed and climbed through a jungle of greenery and dead-ended in front of a wrought-iron gate. Cal had a key that unlocked the gate and they drove up a long driveway to a Colonial mansion with eight white columns across the portico.

"It's beautiful," Vivien said with hushed awe. "Even bigger than her place in the desert."

"Yeah. She didn't get to play Scarlett, so she built her own Tara."

"Is it exciting to have a mother who's a big movie star?"

He nodded absently, wondering what he was getting into. He was drunk enough to feel horny, but sober enough to care about Vivien's welfare. After all, she was family, sort of. He unlocked the massive front door and turned on lights as they went from room to room.

"No servants?" she asked.

"Everybody's gone for the holidays." When they reached the rumpus room he switched on the bar light and put a small towel over one arm. "Can I get *mam'selle* a drink?" He rummaged in a small refrigerator. "Champagne?"

"Sure." She suppressed a giggle. She sat on a bar stool and watched him pop the bottle and pour the bubbly liquid into two tulip-shaped glasses. God, how she loved all this luxury! Oh, to have enough money to live in a mansion and go into Saks and Magnin's and buy everything in sight! Sure, Jason and her stepfather gave her a pretty good allowance, but this was *real* money. Class! And she wanted to be part of it.

She knew she never would be able to earn any money to speak of. She had no talent, no ability. Right now all she had was a pretty face and a nice body. Her only hope of ever being rich—*stinking* rich—was to marry someone like Cal.

He flipped a switch that turned on the pool light, sending a blue glow through the softly lit wood-paneled room. Then he found a Xaviar Cougat record and the strains of a rippling rumba filled the air. He came back to the bar and they sat side by side sipping the champagne.

"Well, this is very pleasant," he said, suddenly feeling amazingly contented. Vivien was soothing. A real nice kid. He was sick of worldly women who always wanted something from him. They wanted his prick, or his money, or to share his privileged place in the exotic movie-star world. They were attracted by his good looks, but they had no interest in what he was like beyond that.

He was certain now that Jennie was never going to marry him. Maybe he ought to settle down with someone like Vivien, he mused to himself. It might be fun. They could have lots of babies, a *real* life, instead of all the sham and pretense and loneliness that were making him utterly bored with his existence before he was even out of his teens.

He took her hand and led her onto the white marble floor. He held her close and let his body lead her in the rumba. She followed him expertly, rhythmically, pressing her vulva against him. He lost himself in the undulating motions as he hummed along with the music, suffused with euphoria. *This* was what he wanted. Someone sweet, yet sexy. Someone who adored him for himself.

He stopped dancing and kissed her, softly at first, letting his lips brush hers in little teasing touches, then with more pressure, and more, until their lips were making love.

He broke it off and caught his breath. She was staring up at him starry-eyed. God, what a pushover she was! But he was sure he saw love in her eyes. Her lips trembled with desire for him. "Let's get married," he said impulsively.

She smiled.

He put his arm around her and took her to his mother's gold-and-white bedroom with its oversize fur-covered bed. "Let's make believe it's our wedding night," he whispered as they entered the room.

She let him unbutton and unzip and turn her around and pull clothes off her until she stood mutely nude in front of him. She watched him remove his clothes. She gasped at the feel of their naked bodies against each other.

"My sweet little virgin," he said soothingly. "My own darling little Vivien." He guided her across the room and carefully lay down with her on the soft white bearskin covering the bed. He could feel her shivering. "Don't worry, my darling," he murmured, "I won't hurt you."

He was gentle, enjoying the dual role of tender husband and passionate seducer. He was a good teacher, doing nothing that would alarm her, none of the oral tricks he knew, nothing she might consider bizarre. He kissed her and fondled her and stroked her in all the right places, waiting until she began moaning and undulating before he entered her.

She cried out in fright and pain, but he didn't let that stop his slow but insistent passage until he was deep into her, past all resistance. He was patient, murmuring encouragement, until her ardor returned, but even though she was aroused, she couldn't reach an orgasm. He came twice before he gave up. Then he held her affectionately while she cried. "Don't worry, honey. It'll be better next time," he promised.

"Did you mean it?" she asked.

"Mean what?"

"You know. About getting married."

"Sure." He kissed her forehead. "We'll elope."

She sat up abruptly. "But . . . I've always dreamed of having a big church wedding."

He pulled her down again. "I hate big church weddings, sweetheart. And if we tell everyone, our parents will say we're too young. So let's just do what I say."

"Mmmmm." She snuggled against him and fell asleep.

They drove to Las Vegas in the morning, under a clear blue sky, and were married by a justice of the peace. By the time they returned to Santa Monica in the late afternoon, they found Jason's bungalow in an uproar, with Jason and Tony and Vivien's mother and stepfather all sick with worry about Vivien's running off with Cal.

"Where were you two all night?" Vivien's mother screamed.

"We got married!" Vivien announced proudly, and waited for their blessings. But her mother slapped her face and burst into tears, Jason collapsed on the couch, hiding his face in his hands, and Tony simply stared at Cal with disbelief.

"You're both so young," Jason mourned. "What's your hurry?"

"How could you do this to me?" Vivien's mother moaned.

"I didn't do anything to you," Vivien said coldly. "And if you can't share my happiness, then the hell with all of you!"

"You stupid fool!" Ella shouted at Cal when she stormed back into town a week later. "You've ruined your life! Getting married when you're not even nineteen yet!"

"You were married at nineteen," he jeered.

"That's different! I was pregnant!"

"You *were?*" He paused, shocked. "You always said I was premature."

"Sure, that's what I told everybody. I had to protect my reputation." She glared at him. "Who the hell is this Vivien, anyway? Some creepy little tramp who's after your money?"

He shook his head. "You've got it all wrong. She's Jason's daughter."

"Oh." Ella's anger deflated somewhat, then rose again. "But it's in all the papers! Now everyone knows I have a son who's almost nineteen!"

"Tough titty, Ma."

"Don't get snotty with me!" She wanted to hit him, but she was afraid he would hit her back. Oh, but she had to punish him! And she knew exactly how to do it. "There's something you ought to know," she said in a low, threatening voice. "Sit down!"

They were alone in the living room of Ella's Bel Air mansion. Cal had left Vivien in their bungalow at the Beverly Hills Hotel when Ella summoned him, thinking this might not be the most propitious time for Vivien and Ella to meet. He slumped on a couch while his mother carefully sat down opposite him, utterly gorgeous—he had to admit—in a lilac chiffon negligee. "Okay," he said jovially, "what d'you want to tell me that's so earth-shaking that I have to sit down to hear it?"

"Frank Ricardo wasn't your father."

He stared at her without moving, though her words slammed into his brain as jarringly as a bullet. He moved his lips, but no sound came out.

"Ginger's first husband was your father. Tonito, the Indian. Tonito Alvarez." She could see that he was devastated and she smiled exultantly, enjoying her revenge. "As a matter of fact, your cousin Tony is really your half-brother."

"Who knows?" he whispered.

"Well, Ginger for one. *I've* never told another soul, but I imagine she might've told Jason, and probably Avery too."

"And Tony?"

"I doubt if he knows. And don't you go telling him, Cal. It's up to Ginger, if she wants him to know that his sainted father was unfaithful to her."

They both were silent. Cal remembered seeing a portrait of Tony's father, in Indian regalia, above the fireplace in the pink mansion, but that had been years ago. Ginger had moved it from the living room to Tony's bedroom when she married Jason. Cal remembered a strikingly handsome dark face with very white teeth and deep brown eyes and a bonnet of Indian feathers. A goddamn Indian. "So I'm really Calvin Alvarez," he finally said. "Not Calvin Ricardo."

"Well, there's no point changing your name. You might louse up your inheritance from Frank when you're twenty-one."

"Did Frank know?"

"Of course not! I was pregnant and just starting my career. I'd have been ruined if I hadn't married him and let him think you were his son."

"Poor Frank. Did you love him at all?"

She shrugged. "Anyway, I'm annulling your marriage. I already talked to Art Braverman—"

"Keep your lawyer out of it!" He stood up and walked unsteadily to the door. He still was too shocked by what she had told him about his paternity to know exactly how he felt about it. He remembered all the times he had looked down on Tony for being the son of a dirt-poor Indian. What a bitch his mother was! She hurt everyone she came in contact with. Now he knew why Aunt Ginger refused to talk to her. "By the way," he said nastily, "where's that dumb furniture salesman you hang out with?"

"Bert? I dumped him just before Christmas. I met someone else."

"Who this time? The local ditchdigger?"

She threw him a murderous look. "For your information, I'm through with low-life types." She smiled smugly. "I'm seeing a UCLA student now."

"Yeah? How old is he?" Cal sneered. "Seventeen? Eighteen?"

"No, dear, he's in law school. He's twenty-six," she lied—he really was only twenty-three. "So I'd appreciate it if you'd stay away when he's around."

Cal grinned as the perfect revenge occurred to him. "Well, Mother, I have to admit, you're one up on me with that news about my father. But let me tell you, if Vivien isn't pregnant yet, I'm going to knock myself out trying to knock her up!"

Ella was puzzled. "Why? What's one thing got to do with the other?"

"Revenge, Mummy, sweet-sweet revenge! I can't wait till all the gossip columnists hear that the famous Ella Ricardo, who claims to be only twenty-seven, is going to be a goddamn grandmother!"

Ginger had an easy pregnancy and gave birth to a daughter in August 1941. The baby was named Virginia

Junior. When she was a few days old her parents began calling her Jiminy because she chirped like a cricket.

Ginger couldn't get her fill of looking at her daughter. The rosy little face, the perfect miniature mouth, the pale arched eyebrows, the surprising amount of reddish hair—she was absolutely beautiful. For Ginger, the baby was the living symbol of her love for Avery, and his for her. But more than that, little Jiminy was a complete person in her own right, one whose unique needs and traits Ginger hoped she would always remember to respect.

Avery felt like yodeling with glee every time he picked up his daughter. *My daughter!* How many years he had wanted the pleasure of saying those words. He had had to wait an inordinately long time for life's greatest blessings, but how lucky he was to have finally found them, and in such abundance!

It seemed to him that his link with this tiny infant was almost palpable, like an invisible umbilical cord. There had been times during Ginger's pregnancy when Avery actually had been jealous of her because she was in such close proximity to the growing infant. But once Jiminy was born and the actual umbilical cord had been cut, Avery was sure he felt as close to the baby as Ginger possibly could.

When he held Jiminy close and crooned to her, he could feel something inside of him expand. He refused to use his medical knowledge to explain away the phenomenon: it was magic, pure and simple.

His happiness no longer was marred by worries about the war in Europe or the suicidal follies of mankind. He did what he could. He was available as a consultant to the local doctors for difficult respiratory cases, he raised money for Bundles for Britain and the Red Cross, he wrote to his congressmen urging more Lend-Lease to Britain. But *his* life was here, in this marvelous old pink mansion, in this unique little city, in this awesome desert. He no longer even missed Paris.

He felt suffused with love. Sometimes he awoke in the middle of the night and quietly got up to look at the little creature in the white bassinet across the room, just barely visible in the dim night-light. He would get down on his knees so that his face was close to hers, and although it might have appeared to a casual observer that he was praying, he actually was lost in a reverie of delight. He no longer worried about living long enough to deliver his daughter into adulthood. He simply reveled in the present, in his love for Ginger and *their* baby.

Then, overwhelmed by his good fortune, he would return to bed and embrace Ginger. This sleeping woman in his arms was so passionately devoted to him—and he to her—that he felt they epitomized the ideal love between a man and a woman. When their bodies merged, they gave each other explosive orgasms that shook them from head to toe, not only because they were completely attuned erotically but also because it was the ultimate physical affirmation of their spiritual bond.

At such moments Avery would drift toward sleep filled with such euphoria that, despite his medical knowledge to the contrary, he was afraid his body would literally burst apart with joy.

Vivien gave birth to a son in late September after a miserable pregnancy. She had been nauseous not only mornings but also afternoons and evenings, quickly boring Cal with her complaints. He moved her out to his Palm Springs house, where he proceeded to spend most of his time at the Racquet Club or at his Uncle Neil's plush offices on Palm Canyon Drive. Once again he rented a club bungalow for discreet afternoon sex, this time with random partners.

Vivien and Cal named the baby Todd, but neither of them found him very interesting. Certainly neither of them knew anything about taking care of him. With Ginger's help, Cal hired a "nanny" named Clara, the younger sister of Lupe, little Jiminy's nursemaid.

Cal and Vivien were having trouble trying to decide whether they wanted to stay married to each other. Their lovemaking was perfunctory, and almost nonexistent. Vivien made no effort to enjoy sex—she just plain didn't like it. They had nothing to say to each other. And they had lost any delusions they once had shared about being "in love."

I was drunk and lonely, Cal berated himself. *Why did I ever think I was ready for family life?* But oh, how he hated to admit he had made a mistake and have his mother smugly say: I told you so!

Damn it, I'm only seventeen and I don't want to waste my best years stuck with a dumb baby, Vivien grumbled to herself. But still, she had gotten what she really wanted out of the marriage: money. Lots of it.

Shortly after the baby was born, Jason moved back to Palm Springs and rented a modest cottage close to Cal's house. Daily, Jason gave Todd his noon bottle, then cuddled him and sang to him until it was time to put him down for his afternoon nap.

Jason still couldn't bear the thought of seeing Ginger and Avery. He seldom went anyplace where he was likely to bump into them, preferring to go for late-night walks, when he wouldn't see anyone. He hired an elderly Mexican woman to cook and clean and shop for him—a far cry from the days when all his food had been prepared in The Springs' gourmet kitchen by Jean-Paul and his *sous-chefs.*

One afternoon Jason found Todd crying in his crib. He picked him up and put his lips to the baby's forehead: it was hot. He carried Todd through the house to the kitchen, where Clara was preparing his bottle. "He has a high fever," Jason said urgently.

Clara looked alarmed. "Oh, is it worse? He woke up very warm this morning."

"Where are his parents?"

She shrugged. "Every day, they go out."

"They went out *knowing* the baby had a fever?" Jason felt his wrath rise, but there was no point in taking it out on the nursemaid. He phoned their family doctor's office and arranged to bring Todd right over.

Jason returned from the doctor's an hour later and put the baby in his crib, then stormed out of the house and got into his car. Much as he hated to chance bumping into Ginger and Avery, he had to find his daughter and son-in-law. He tried El Mirador first and looked everywhere, in vain. At the Racquet Club he saw them sitting under an umbrella by the pool. They were sipping tall drinks and laughing it up with another young couple.

"I'd like a word with you," he said quietly when they looked up in astonishment at seeing him there.

"Okay." Vivien was subdued by the stern look on her father's face. She rose, followed by Cal, and the three of them went into the bar and sat in a quiet corner.

"Todd's sick," he said, trying to suppress his fury. "For God's sake, don't you *care?*"

"Well, sure we care," Cal said lamely. "What's wrong with him?"

"I took him to Dr. Appel. Todd's temperature is a hundred and four. The doctor gave him some medication and Clara's giving him an alcohol sponge bath."

"So what's the problem?" Cal asked calmly. "Sounds like everything's under control."

"What's the *problem?*" Jason exploded. "What if I hadn't come by?" He forced himself to calm down. "Listen, why don't you let me adopt Todd? Seriously. I mean it."

"Don't be silly, Dad," Vivien said sheepishly.

"Look, you two don't have the least bit of interest in him."

Cal smiled at his father-in-law. "Little Todd will just have to put up with Viv and me, I guess. I mean, people can't give their babies away, not even to a grandparent."

"But don't you see what you're doing, Cal?" Jason persisted. "You're giving him the same kind of neglected childhood that you yourself always complain about."

"So? What difference does it make?" Cal laughed. "*I* didn't turn out so badly, did I?"

Jason didn't answer that. He was disgusted with these two selfish and totally irresponsible young people. Did their extreme youth excuse them? he asked himself. They were still teenagers, much too young to be parents. He looked disapprovingly at his daughter and she returned his look defiantly. He wondered sadly how his adorable baby, his cute little girl, his pretty high-schooler, had turned into this quite unlikable young woman.

Jason realized that to Vivien motherhood meant buying the most expensive baby furniture and infant clothing she could find. It meant filling his nursery with countless stuffed animals and more toys than Todd could use in the next ten years. But she never picked up the baby, or cuddled him, or paid attention to what sort of care Clara gave him.

Todd was the baby Jason had longed for, the baby he should have had with Ginger, he told himself in frustration. Would Ginger have run off with Avery so quickly if she and Jason had had a child together? Well, he'd never know. At any rate, all that was part of the past, and now he had to think about his future. And Todd's.

He was determined to give Todd everything—the love, the attention, the concern—that Todd's own silly parents were unwilling, perhaps even unable, to give themselves.

Ella finally returned to her Palm Springs estate, having grown bored with her young law student, and by the time she reluctantly came to see her grandson, he was nearly two months old. For the first few days, Ella just looked at the little fellow but showed no interest in touching him. Then one day, when no one was around, she impulsively took him out of his crib and cradled him in her arms. She felt a thrill that made her gasp in surprise. She had never, ever felt this way about Cal.

Jason came into the nursery at that moment and smiled at the sight of the glamourous movie star looking so maternal. It seemed to him that she had never been so radiantly lovely. She wore a vivid lilac dress that matched her enormous eyes; with her flawless iridescent skin and long blond hair, she looked about eighteen. "Isn't our little Todd just wonderful?" he asked in awe.

Ella nodded, close to tears. Holding the baby had made her so *tired* of her aimless life!

Jason came closer and together they stared down at the infant in Ella's arms. "He's beautiful," he said, his voice hoarse with emotion. He looked over at her. "He looks just like you."

"Well, thanks . . . but he definitely has your eyes, Jason. They're so . . . so wonderfully expressive."

"You think so?" He was flattered.

They watched, fascinated, as the baby responded to all this attention by making soft little sounds and giving them a big openmouthed smile. He waved his arms and kicked his feet while his grandparents grinned back at him.

"I feel more like his father than his grandfather," Jason confessed. "Hell, I'm only thirty-nine."

"So am I." Astounding herself, Ella had uttered her true age for the first time in twenty years. She put the infant back in his crib, then turned her full charm on Jason. "Jason, let's be friends," she pleaded. "After all, we do share a grandson."

Jason grinned. "It sure would tick Ginger off if we were friends, wouldn't it?"

"Yes!" Ella laughed. "It most certainly would!" She put a hand on his arm and gave him her well-practiced Aren't-you-the-most-wonderful-man-in-the-world look.

Jason knew all about that look. She had tried it on him once, unsuccessfully, years earlier in a Pasadena book-store, and he had seen her use it very effectively on countless men at the Racquet Club. Still, he had to admit, it *was* beguiling. He took her in his arms and held her close. For the first time since the calamitous morning almost a year and a half earlier when Ginger had told him she was leaving him, he felt like a nearly whole human being. A sexual thrill grabbed his groin and spread throughout his body, but he didn't kiss her right away. They just needed to comfort each other for a while.

Her body was magical—soft, voluptuous, clinging, melting into him and making him feel strong and virile. And desirable. He stoked the back of her head.

"Nobody's ever held me like this. Ever." Her tears came so softly that at first Jason wasn't even aware that she was crying. Then her sobs intensified as she reacted to his compassionate caresses of her back and shoulders. All her life, men had given her adulation and gifts and praise, but never before had anyone given her sympathy.

When she ran out of tears she leaned her wet cheek against his and spoke so softly that he had to strain to hear her. "I don't remember either of my parents ever holding me. My mother was always hugging Ginger, but never me or Neil. My father kept telling me how beauti-ful I was, but he never kissed me. Men embrace me because they want sex, not affection."

She pulled her head back so that she could look into his eyes. "Oh, Jason, I'm so tired of my life! I'm so tired of the effort it takes to look young and beautiful. The tyranny of it! I'm so tired of men wanting to possess my body, but not really caring about *me*. Sometimes I won-der if there really *is* a me anymore. Or if there ever was anything inside this attractive shell."

She nodded toward the crib and fresh tears formed in her eyes. "That poor baby! What a rotten heritage he has! *My* mother didn't love me. *I* never loved Cal. And now *Cal* doesn't give a damn about his own kid. Tell me,

Jason, how many generations can it go on?" She stamped her foot. "I won't let it!"

He kissed her then, lightly, reassuringly. He reminded himself that she was an actress through and through, that nothing she said was necessarily to be taken at face value. But he didn't care. What difference did it really make? All that mattered to him now was that she was making him feel *alive*.

"Help me, Jason," she moaned. "Help me learn how to live."

For a week Jason patiently let Ella talk about her dissatisfaction with her life. He listened to her with caring and understanding. He held her hand and hugged her, but he didn't make love to her. Never before had she had a sympathetic friend who was willing to take her seriously and who cared about her thoughts and feelings.

Finally, after she had gotten rid of a lifetime's repressed laments, they became lovers and he moved into her mansion. They both frankly admitted that they weren't in love with each other, but they wanted to be together because they were lost and lonely and needy. Even more pressing was the love they shared for their grandson and their determination to get custody of him.

When Ginger heard about their liaison, she shook her head in horror. "Oh, my God! She'll eat him alive!" she wailed. "What have I done to him?"

"It's not your fault," Avery reminded her.

"He's absolutely out of his mind! And it *is* all my fault!" she insisted, her voice rising with distress.

"Now, stop it!" Avery reprimanded her gently. "Listen, my darling, I'm a great believer in miracles these days. Maybe they'll actually be happy together."

"Sure. Making little voodoo dolls marked 'Ginger' and sticking pins into them!"

They were standing at one of their bedroom windows, facing out toward the open desert. Jiminy was sleeping in her bassinet on the other side of the room. It was a clear, sparkling Saturday afternoon in early December, with a light breeze fanning the palm fronds surrounding the house.

"Y'know," Ginger said softly, "when I look at the desert framed through a window, it seems so tame. But when I'm out in the middle of it . . . I feel like a giant."

"Really? I feel dwarfed."

Ginger leaned her head against his shoulder. "Tomorrow's December 7. Tony's twentieth birthday." She sighed. "He's been so unhappy lately."

"I think he feels left out."

"But he doesn't *let* us get close to him anymore," Ginger complained. "He refuses to believe me when I tell him I love him. He doesn't even want to come home for Christmas, or to see Jiminy."

Avery remembered Tony's first two months of life, when Ginger had been too ill to touch him, when Avery and Adele had given the boy the only "mothering" he got. And even later, when Ginger had recovered physically but was still deranged with grief over her loss of Tonito and Johnny, it had taken her a long time to pay any real attention to the baby. Avery wondered if that deprivation had damaged Tony in ways that only now were becoming apparent.

He brushed away the thought. Everyone was somewhat deprived in infancy, one way or another. It was an inevitable part of living. Even the best parents made mistakes without realizing it.

Lovingly he squeezed Ginger's arm. "C'mon, my darling, it's such a beautiful day. Let's get Lupe to keep an eye on Jiminy for an hour while we get on our horses and go riding in Palm Canyon."

It was his favorite cure for getting rid of unhappy thoughts.

The next day, Ginger phoned Tony and wished him a happy birthday. "Please come home for Christmas," she begged. "We both love you so."

He cleared his throat. "Well, last year was such a disappointment . . ."

"Tony, I'm sorry about last year. I know I was all wrapped up in my new life with Avery, and thrilled over getting pregnant so unexpectedly. But this year . . . darling, *please* give me another chance. And don't you want to see your little sister? I know you'll love her."

"I . . . Hey, wait a minute, Mom, hold on—"

She heard a great commotion and the hubbub of shouting male voices in Tony's dormitory. He came back on the phone yelling. "Hey, Mom! Mom! The Japs! Oh my *God*! It's a disaster! Quick! Turn on your radio!"

"What? Tony . . . what's happening?"

"It's the Japs, Mom. The goddamn Japs!" He made a sound that was a cross between a sob and a whoop. *"They just bombed Pearl Harbor!"*

Tony came home at Christmas wearing a dashing blue uniform with the Royal Canadian Air Force wings over his left breast pocket and a round gold American eagle badge on his left sleeve. He was intoxicated with the excitement of going off to war to save the world, to slay the dragons, and to bring Hitler to his knees, all by flying one little Spitfire.

"The day after Pearl Harbor," he explained to his mother and Avery, "I flew up to Canada with Herb—remember him? My old instructor? We both joined the Eagle Squadron."

Ginger shook her head in confusion. "What's that?"

"It's a group of American pilots who've been flying with the RAF for over a year now."

Ginger still was bewildered. "What's wrong with our own Air Corps?"

"Nothing. Once our Army gets its air operations set up in England, the Eagle Squadron will transfer over to it. But it'll take months. This way, I'll get into action a lot faster."

"What's your rush?" Avery asked almost inaudibly.

Tony grinned. "Me heap brave Indian, Avery. Gotta show Hitler we redskin Americans aren't afraid of him!"

Ginger smiled to herself as she brushed some lint off Tony's shoulder: it was the first time she'd ever heard Tony speak proudly of his Indian heritage. "Well, it's a very spiffy uniform, darling," she said lightly to hide her dismay at what the uniform really meant—*his imminent exposure to danger.* "You'll knock 'em all dead at Neil's party."

Tony nodded. "Right after New Year's, they're sending me over to England—to a training unit up near the Scottish border."

"A training unit?" Ginger echoed. "But you already know how to fly."

He gave her the pitying look the young save for those who are both slow-witted and elderly. "Sure, but military flying is different. You have to know how to fly in formation, and when to attack, and how to shoot down the enemy—" He was stopped by the look of horror on her face.

"Shoot?" she cried out in alarm.

"Well, what d'you think war is all about, Mom?" he asked impatiently. "Did you think we'd just be flying around for the fun of it?"

"No, I thought you just dropped bombs and flew back." She sighed.

Tony seemed happier than Ginger had seen him in a long time. He couldn't sit still. He was overstimulated, too thrilled. But she also detected lingering signs of his bitterness toward her and Avery. She caught him giving them both angry looks when he thought she wasn't looking at him, particularly if she and Avery showed each other any affection.

Tony was intrigued by Jiminy. He even got down on the floor and played with his four-month-old sister. "She's a perfect combination of both of you," he told them. "You know, Mom's face and auburn hair, and Avery's blue eyes. . . ."

Ginger's first elation at seeing Tony happy was replaced by a state of painful anxiety. *To shoot and be shot.* Why would any sane young man be happy about going to war? she kept wondering. Oh, sure, there were the attractive uniforms and the marching bands and the adulation of silly girls to mask the truth of the situation. There were stirring speeches and the sight of the flag to bring tears of ardent patriotism to one's eyes. But the hard, basic truth was that one killed and *got* killed.

Tony wanted to reminisce. He talked a lot about the time when he and Ginger had lived in the cabin that his father had built, and he thought it was hilarious that they'd had to use a privy. He remembered being pampered by the hotel guests in the early days of The Springs. He recalled every trip through Europe he had made with Avery. But he also kept mentioning activities he had shared with Jason, and every time he did so, he looked at his mother defiantly . . . and reproachfully.

He asked a lot of questions about Tonito. He kept talking about his Indian blood. "I'm proud to be half Indian. It makes me feel even more American." He wanted to hear again the story of Tonito's struggle to become educated and his years at Harvard Law School so that he could come home and help his tribe seek justice. "He was really perfect, wasn't he?" he asked Ginger.

She didn't want to say anything to temper Tony's adulation of his father. Tony needed his hero. "Yes," she lied, "he really was quite perfect. And," she added truthfully, "you have all his *best* qualities, darling."

He was eager to go to Neil's Christmas party, "to show off my uniform," he said with a grin. "I expect all the girls to grovel at my feet. And wait till Cal sees it. He'll die of jealousy." Then he paused and looked worriedly from Ginger to Avery. "Will it bother you . . . you know, if Jason's there with Aunt Ella?"

Ginger sighed. "It's a big house. I guess we can keep out of each other's way."

"Maybe you shouldn't," Avery said.

Ginger's eyebrows shot up in surprise. "Shouldn't what?"

"Avoid Ella. I'm not suggesting that you become bosom buddies, but hatred is so unhealthy."

Ginger turned away, annoyed with Avery. They seldom disagreed, and when they did, he often turned out to be right. But he was dead wrong about her reconciling with her sister. She couldn't. *Wouldn't!*

When they arrived at Neil's party, at least two hundred people were swarming through the vast rooms and out onto the multilevel terraces. Jennie kissed Ginger and Avery effusively, but her eyes were on Tony all the while. She touched his uniform with awe, then raised her eyes to his. "That deserves a very special kiss, my darling nephew." She put her hands on the back of his neck and brought her mouth up to his. Her lips were smooth, her taste fruity, her shining eyes full of promise.

"I'm keeping you to myself," she whispered as she took his hand and led him outside, across a flagstone patio, and down a flight of brick steps to a small waterfall. They sat on a curved stone bench and stared at each other. "I'm leaving Neil," she told him. "Right after the holidays."

He was astounded. "B-but why?" he finally found the breath to ask.

"He's been unfaithful. Again and again."

"Where'll you go?" he asked worriedly.

"He's letting me keep this estate. After all, it was my

wedding present." She shrugged. "I really liked being
married to him. He can be so sweet. And he did so much
for me . . . for my career—"

"I saw your picture three times," Tony interrupted.
"You were wonderful!"

"Thanks." She touched his hand in gratitude and let
her fingers stay on his. "The movie made a pile of money
for Neil." She laughed delightedly. "And it made a star
out of me. You should see the fan letters I get! Everybody wants a picture of me."

He turned his hand around so that their palms were
clasped. "How could Uncle Neil be unfaithful?" he asked
in wonderment. "I mean, with a wife like you . . . he's
out of his mind!"

"All men are unfaithful. Eventually."

"I wouldn't be, Jennie. I've been in love with you since
the very first minute we met."

"Oh, you're sweet." She looked with a flash of anger
at the house above them; they could hear Neil up there,
telling a joke and then laughing boisterously. Her affection for him was just about gone. He got fatter and more
uncouth every day. He had lost all interest in having sex
with her, and when she tearfully had asked him why, he
had told her right out that he couldn't be faithful to one
woman. Not that he was even so crazy about sex, but
when he did have it, he wanted variety. Anyway, he
pointed out, her career was zooming, she had a lucrative
five-year contract with his studio, and he was giving her
both the Palm Springs estate and the Beverly Hills mansion. So he just couldn't see what the hell she was pissed
about.

Jennie saw no reason to be faithful to Neil any longer.
But she had to be true to someone, she had to feel "in
love," and as long as Cal was married there was no way
she would go to bed with him. Ever since Jennie's mother
and Daddy-Joe had introduced her to sex as something
she had to know for her work, Jennie had considered it
on a par with dancing—a physical act that she was very
good at performing. Oh, she liked the quivering pleasure
of the orgasm well enough. But what she really loved was
being *in* love.

Tony's arrival at the party in his darling uniform was
an absolute godsend to Jennie. He was exactly what she

needed: someone sweet, and innocent, and ready to be loyal to her forever. She leaned against him and kissed him lingeringly. Then she stood abruptly and took his hand again. "Come on."

She led the way down a path that curved through a jungle of palm fronds to a small Gothic-style stone building. Rummaging behind a rock, she found a key and unlocked the carved wooden door. Tony entered a room with stained-glass windows that cast an eerie dim light over a low couch and a few easy chairs arranged around a long marble coffee table.

"This is my retreat. I come here when I can't stand Neil and his obnoxious cigar-chewing cronies who're always hanging around the house." Jennie slid her arms around Tony's neck and pushed her slender body eagerly against his. "If you'll take off that absolutely adorable uniform," she whispered urgently, "I have a *very* special Christmas present for you!"

Ginger went to the powder room, and when she came out she walked straight into Jason. They both gasped in consternation and shrank back a little. It was the first time they had seen each other since the morning she had left him, a year and a half earlier.

Jason was appalled. He hadn't wanted to come to this god-awful party, had actually been terrified of seeing Ginger, but Ella had insisted, assuring him that they would keep their distance from her sister. "You've got to start getting out," Ella had told him. "I don't want to live with a hermit."

Now his heart was pounding at the nearness of Ginger. All at once, through the crust of hatred for her that had become second nature to him, he realized that beneath it all . . . he still loved her. And the knowledge made him miserable. Never mind that she was married to Avery and he was living with Ella, his heart still couldn't accept the fact that Ginger no longer was his wife. His *life*. Did he have to go through the pain of losing her all over again every time he saw her?

Oh, but he'd been hungry for the sight of her! His eyes devoured every detail of her appearance. Her auburn hair was longer, falling in soft waves around her face. She was as slim and lovely as ever. Her blue velvet dress was scooped low to reveal the tops of the smooth pale breasts that he had loved to kiss. He still was so achingly familiar with every inch of her body. He knew he was staring at her, knew it was rude, but he couldn't help it: he wanted to gorge himself on the sight of her.

"So you're living with Ella," she said with a strained smile.

He nodded. "Did you know that she and I share a grandson?"

"Yes, I heard." Even as they made polite conversation, she was profoundly aware of how much they once had meant to each other. Eight and a half years of shared intimacy, of uproarious laughter, of zestful sex, of sleeping entwined, of fun trips and chef Jean-Paul's candlelit dinners and jointly enjoyed books and jointly loved pets and blustery evenings spent holding hands in front of a campfire—God, how he must resent her for robbing him of their deeply satisfying life together.

For the first time, she wondered how she would feel if the situation had been reversed, if he had been the one who had walked out on her for someone else. Wouldn't she be as bitter as he was now? Of course she would. Probably even more so.

He knew he should congratulate her on the birth of her daughter, but he was afraid he would burst into tears if he mentioned it. He couldn't help remembering all the times he had held her in his arms as they climbed together toward orgasm, hoping that a child would result. He was reminded of the first time he made love to her, in front of a dancing campfire high in the Santa Rosa Mountains. They had melted together and had achieved such mutual bliss that he had thought it was going to last forever. It seemed unbelievably tragic to him that now he didn't even have the right to reach out and touch her.

"Do you ever remember . . . what it was like between us?" he whispered.

He looked so wretched that it was all she could do to keep from throwing her arms around him and comforting him. "I know you won't believe me, Jason," she said in a strangled voice, "but I still care about you. Deeply."

"Don't say that," he objected. "It's easier for me to hate you."

She winced. "Oh, Jason, I couldn't ever hate you. Not after all we once meant to each other."

"Well, why the hell should you hate me? I've never given you reason to." He stared at her with longing for a moment. "Ah, dammit, Ginger, why am I talking about hating you . . . when I still love you?" He turned and quickly strode away from her.

When Avery saw Ginger return from the powder room, he knew at once from her pale, stricken face that she had talked to Jason. His heart went out to the younger man—what terrible torture they had put him through. But it couldn't be helped. If Ginger had stayed with Jason from a sense of duty, they would all three have wound up utterly miserable. Now the poor guy was living with Ella. Talk about looking for trouble! But Avery had seen Ella across the room and he had to admit that she looked different—less alluring, perhaps, but more mature and much more human.

He put a protective arm around Ginger and lightly kissed the side of her head, to let her know he understood what she had been through. They had so much empathy for each other, it was a form of mind-reading.

Ginger smiled intimately into Avery's eyes as she drank in his solace. Then she realized that Avery was in the middle of a conversation with Cal, and she touched her lips to her nephew's cheek in greeting.

Cal returned her kiss, but his eyes were on Avery. "Come *on,* Uncle Avery," Cal beseeched him, "be a sport. We're desperate for those ten acres."

Avery shook his head good-humoredly. "Sorry, Cal. They're not for sale."

"But I *told* you . . . we've already bought the surrounding acreage. Hell, your property sticks right up through the middle of it like a sore thumb! We've got the plans all drawn up for an eighteen-hole golf course and a classy hotel and a bunch of fancy houses—"

"I don't care if you're building the Taj Mahal, Cal. The answer still is no."

Cal turned to Ginger. "Can't you talk some sense into him?" He jerked his thumb at Avery. "We've offered him five times what those lousy ten acres're worth."

"Cal," Avery said patiently, "with a war on, I doubt

you'll be able to get enough material to build a one-hole outhouse. Anyway, get it through your head—that land isn't for sale. At *any* price."

"Give me one good reason—"

"Because I've earmarked it for a park."

"A park?" Cal looked at Avery as though he were made. "A lousy *park*? Way out there in the empty desert?"

"It won't be empty desert for long. Not the way you and Neil and others like you are building up this town. We'll need all the pockets of open space we can get." Avery turned to Ginger. "Ready to go home?"

She nodded and gave Cal a sympathetic smile. "You've been a good influence on Neil," she said. "At least you finally convinced him to use architects."

Cal followed them to the door and tried one last desperate appeal. "Avery, sell us that land and we'll hire the goddamn architects who designed the Taj Mahal, for Chrissakes!"

Avery shook his head. "You're a few centuries too late, my young friend."

Cal had seen Tony arrive in his jazzy uniform, had seen Jennie kiss him, had seen the two of them go outside and down the stairs. Cal had followed them at a distance, had watched them go into the little stone house.

He went back to the bar and had three quick double bourbons. He saw Vivien across the sixty-foot living room. Even though she was putting on weight, she was looking very glamorous in a silver satin gown that set off her curly hair beautifully. She had taken to having her hair dyed gold with streaks of silver and he found it very becoming. How that girl loved to spend his money! He smiled to himself. It was funny, he thought, but people who were born wealthy didn't get nearly the kick out of being extravagant as those who were born with less. Vivien lived to shop. Trips to Beverly Hills. Trips to New York's Fifth Avenue. He supposed she did it to compete with Jennie. She couldn't wait until the war was over so she could shop in Paris. But he didn't care. He was making more money as his Uncle Neil's partner than he had ever dreamed possible.

Every now and then he and Vivien talked about separating, but they both found the marriage convenient.

Being a married man made it possible for Cal to have sex without the fear that one or another of his partners might become a nuisance and demand a wedding ring. He told them all right away that he had a wife and son. As for Vivien, she liked the status of being Cal's wife. It wasn't only the money, but the whole way of life. Even if he gave her a generous settlement, rich divorcees were a glut in their social circle and certainly didn't have the social position she now enjoyed as his wife.

Later, Cal saw Jennie and Tony come back into the house, holding hands and looking starry-eyed. He went over to them and put a possessive arm around Jennie. "I saw her first," he told Tony.

"Yeah," Tony retorted, "but didn't you know, cuz, 'He laughs last who laughs best'?"

Cal smiled to show he wasn't angry. Or was he? He didn't know; he was all mixed up and much too drunk to think straight. If it had been anyone else with Jennie, he certainly would have been furious, but after all, Tony was his brother, even if the poor sap didn't know it. Let him have his fling with Jennie before he went off to war.

Cal put his other arm around Tony's shoulders. "You make me feel like a goddamn coward, Tony."

Tony gave him a surprised look. "Hell, Cal, you can enlist too."

Cal shook his head. "No way. They'll have to come and drag me off screaming."

Tony was aghast. "But . . . don't you care about your country? Don't you want to stop Hitler? And the Japs?"

"Little old me?" Cal gave a self-deprecating laugh. "Tony, baby, I don't have a patriotic bone in my body. Soon as they try to draft me, I'll get dear old Uncle Neil to pull some strings and find me a cushy officer's job. You know, like sitting around a Hollywood studio making venereal-disease films for the Army."

"Cal, you're disgusting," Jennie said.

Cal suddenly felt forlorn. He wondered why he was making such an ass of himself. He wondered why he didn't hug Tony and *tell* him they were brothers. He wanted to ask Tony about Tonito, the mysterious, handsome Indian who had fathered them both. But Ella had warned him not to do that, and although he usually didn't obey Ella, this was no time to upset Tony; the guy was probably nervous as hell underneath all that patriotic horseshit. After all, he wasn't going off to some country club. He was going to go kill Germans, and probably get killed himself in the process.

"Listen, pal, write to me, huh? I promise to answer." Cal shook Tony's hand and then quickly headed for the door.

Tony was glad to see Cal leave. It bothered him that his cousin had once been Jennie's lover. But he wasn't going to worry about anything today. Oh, he felt cocky! What a Christmas present Jennie had given him! He had had a few sexual experiences with girls at school, but they all were as inept at it as he was. But Jennie! What talented muscles she had hidden inside that beautiful silky body of hers. She had been all over him, using her hands and mouth and her sweet luscious breasts in ways he never would have dreamed possible.

He could just imagine what a hero he would be if he boasted to his fellow officers that he had made love to Jennie Warren, the famous movie star. *Wah-hoo!* They'd never believe him, though. Anyway, he wasn't about to kiss and tell.

Jennie made him stay until all the other guests had gone and just she and he and Neil were left. "I'm going to marry Tony when the war's over," she told Neil defiantly.

Neil gave Tony an amused look. "Keep the little doll in the family, huh?"

Tony nodded numbly, his head giddy with shock.

Neil scowled at Jennie. "Well, I don't care if you divorce me, toots, but just remember, you're still under contract to my studio!"

Tony couldn't believe what was happening. He hadn't said a word to Jennie about marriage—it had seemed beyond the realm of possibility—but my god, what a fantastic thing to look forward to! For a moment he was sorry he had been in such a rush to join the RAF. *What if he didn't come back?* Oh, but he would. He had to now. He'd come back a big hero and every newspaper in the country would have his picture on the front page, with Jennie on his arm, the two of them coming down the steps of the biggest goddamn church they could find to get married in.

*   *   *

Cal was really buzzed. He had lost count of how many bourbons he had consumed. He got into his sleek new silver Mercedes 500K—he had given the old Duesenberg to Vivien because she adored it—and, not feeling like going home, he headed northwest toward Los Angeles. His dashboard clock showed eleven-thirty and he made a bet with himself that at such a late hour, without much traffic, he could easily make it to his mother's Bel Air estate by one in the morning, *if* he could maintain his speed at ninety or more.

In his convertible, with the top down, he felt as though the combination of high speed and desert wind was going to blow his head off. But although the rushing air cleared his mind, he kept seesawing back and forth between despair and exhilaration.

Seeing his Aunt Ginger and Avery had made Cal seriously question his own life. There they were, his aunt past forty and Avery pushing sixty, and their vibrancy, their excitement with existence and their love for each other was so beautiful to watch that it left Cal breathless with envy. Here *he* was, not yet quite twenty, bored, restless, aimless, loveless, and sick of living. His marriage was a joke. And all little Todd did was make him feel guilty as hell. Cal was grateful beyond words to his mother and Jason for taking the little tyke off his—and Vivien's—very incompetent hands. At first he had resisted the idea of the two grandparents raising Todd. But now he could see that it was better for everyone concerned, especially for Todd.

As he roared along the dark highway bordering the orange groves surrounding San Bernardino, Cal realized that he either had to change his life or end it. There was no aspect of it he truly enjoyed. His work with Neil had lost its appeal—how much money did he need, for Chrissake? If he never made another dime, he would be stinking rich for the rest of his life, not even counting the inheritance from Frank Ricardo that he would get next year.

He could also see now, after watching Ginger and Avery together, that he had never been in love. Never. Not even with Jennie. With devastating clarity he realized that Jennie was a sex machine, an absolutely beautiful little creature who was charming and kind to everyone, but who was entirely without a heart or soul. She was an animated mannequin who, when she said she loved you, really meant she *liked* you. He just hoped to hell she wouldn't hurt poor innocent Tony. Not that she would do so intentionally. But Tony could always misunderstand and expect more from her than she could give.

Ah, but Tony would have to watch out for himself. Now Cal was more concerned about the need to change his own life. He didn't have an inkling as to where he should even begin. It was hopeless. Hopeless! As for suicide, he didn't have the guts to do it. At that moment, his tires screeching at ninety-five miles an hour, he swerved around a truck without taillights that he had seen only at the last minute. Grimly he told himself that if he kept driving this way, he no longer would have to worry about suicide or anything else.

When he reached his mother's Bel Air estate, it occurred to him that he hadn't eaten all day. He had been too busy drinking. Rather than wake up the servants, he went into the kitchen and, for the first time in his life, prepared a meal for himself. He found a can of tomato soup in the vast pantry, but he had no idea how to open the can, so he put it back. Fortunately, the refrigerator was full of food that didn't need a can opener. He took out a package of sliced, cooked ham, some lettuce, mayonnaise and mustard, and a loaf of white bread. With much dropping of utensils and dripping of mayonnaise and mustard, including a big gold blotch on his pleated shirtfront, he put together a thick, untidy sandwich. His developing headache told him to pass up the bar and have a Coke instead.

In the breakfast room, devouring his sandwich, he felt inordinately proud of actually having made it. In fact, he realized that this untidy sandwich was the first thing he ever had *created* in his entire life. It also was the first time he had ever done anything for himself. He was so spoiled, it was a wonder he didn't have a servant wipe his ass for him when he took a shit.

He lay down in his tuxedo on his mother's bearskin-covered bed, suddenly remembering that exactly a year ago today he had foolishly taken Vivien's virginity on this very bed, and then asked her to marry him. That surely was the dumbest thing he had ever done.

His thoughts wandered back to his Aunt Ginger and her Avery. He wondered what made certain people so capable of loving. Was it luck? Some sort of chemistry? Or was it an inborn talent? Whatever it was, he sure didn't have it.

I ought to ask Aunt Ginger to give me lessons in loving, he thought wryly. *Maybe she can give a few lessons to my mother too.*

He awoke at eleven the next morning, still in his party tux, still lying on his mother's bearskin-covered bed. A terrible sadness enveloped him, pressing on his chest and throat, as though he had swallowed a prickly barrel cactus. Then all at once it occurred to him that if he didn't have the guts to take a gun and shoot himself, he could let the crazy Japs do it for him. He went to his bedroom and showered, and put on his least flashy clothes. Leaving his own extravagant car in the driveway, he got into one of the Fords that his mother kept for the servants to use.

He drove directly to the Marine Crops recruiting office in Santa Monica and, without hesitation, enlisted as a buck private.

CHAPTER
10

(1943–1944)

Ginger was blithely pushing two-year-old Jiminy in a blue stroller along Palm Canyon Drive one bright, sunny September morning in 1943 when, staring at a low-cut red bathing suit in a store window, she turned the corner at the Plaza and crashed the stroller into a white one coming toward her. The strollers locked their front wheels and came to a jarring halt.

Ginger quickly looked down at the two babies, her own little Jiminy and the boy in the other stroller, to make sure they weren't hurt. Then she looked up apologetically at the other mother and found herself staring into Ella's frightened eyes.

Ordinarily, when the two sisters passed on the street or in a shop, they quickly averted their eyes and walked on. But now they were trapped, and Ginger's first impulse was to pick up Jiminy and run. Instead, she and Ella both bent down and tried to unlock the meshed wheels. They pushed and tugged, to no avail. The wheels were bent and refused to part.

They stood up at the same moment, and suddenly they burst out laughing because they were dressed in identical pleated dark blue blouses and belted white shorts.

"Did you get them at Magnin's?" Ella asked.

Ginger nodded. "We look like the Bobbsey Twins!" She felt an unexpected warmth flow through her when she impulsively reached out and touched Ella's arm. "Oh, Ella," she whispered, "Ella."

They hugged in the middle of the sidewalk with pedestrians detouring around them and giving them inquisitive looks. Their arms still around each other, they realized that the two babies were fighting. Todd, sturdy and blond, with his grandfather Jason's winsome gray eyes, was trying to grab a stuffed giraffe that Jiminy was holding. Jiminy refused to let go, and hit Todd's arm with her other hand, her dainty face turning red with anger. During all this, Jiminy and Todd were screaming at each other—in Spanish!

"Isn't that cute!" Ella said. "You must have a Spanish-speaking nursemaid too."

Ginger nodded, smiling. "She's your Clara's sister. It's such a painless way for the kids to be bilingual."

"Yeah, it's the one good thing I did for Cal. His Spanish is as good as his English."

"Remember how Polly made us suffer with French?" Ginger giggled.

"How can I ever forget?"

"So what are they to each other?" Ginger mused. "Your grandson and my daughter? Let's see. Cousins of some kind."

"Second cousins?" Ella guessed. "Or is it first cousins, once removed? I never can figure it out." She smiled at Jiminy, who at two was a miniature version of Ginger, with her mother's curly auburn hair and delicate features, but instead of Ginger's brown eyes, Jiminy had Avery's bright blue ones. "She's absolutely adorable," Ella said admiringly.

"So's your grandson."

"Listen, Ginger, don't go away. I'll be back in five minutes." Ella picked up Todd and disappeared around the corner.

Ginger looked after her, mystified. She pushed the damaged strollers into an unused doorway and leaned against the arcaded stucco building with Jiminy in her arms. She covered her daughter's head with little light kisses, thinking with a smile how delighted Avery would be that she and Ella were talking to each other. He had begged her time and again to stop hating her sister, not for Ella's sake, he had said, but for her own. And he was right, as usual. She felt a great sense of relief.

As Ginger waited, she watched the steady flow of traffic. Except for occasional outbursts, she had long ago stopped bemoaning the metamorphosis of Palm Springs from charming village to bustling city. It had lost the feeling it once had had of being isolated from the real world. The real world had long ago engulfed it. She either had to accept it or move away, and neither she nor Avery could bear the thought of leaving. After all, their privacy was safe up in their beloved pink mansion on its isolated mesa.

She smiled, realizing that she no longer owned the only pink mansion in Palm Springs. Pearl and Austin McManus had built one, not far from hers, and these days several luxurious pink houses dotted the fashionable Las Palmas area. Obviously, Ginger told herself, her grandfather wasn't the only one who thought pink was a good color for the desert.

The war had changed the city even more than the invasion of movie people and tourists had the previous two decades. Thousands of soldiers were being trained in tank warfare out on the desert east of Palm Springs. Instead of tourists in shorts strolling down Palm Canyon Drive, now skinny young men in khaki thronged the streets at night, looking for "action." They were lonely, and they were tired from their rigorous war exercises in the desert heat. They tried to find companionship and romance in a city whose recreation facilities, except for a few recently opened cheap bars and café's, were either too tame or too expensive for an enlisted man's wallet.

Fewer and fewer tourists came to Palm Springs these days. With rationing an unavoidable part of wartime life, ordinary people and movie stars alike had to make do with three gallons of gasoline a week, hardly enough for an outing to their favorite desert playground. Even Angelenos who owned vacation houses in Palm Springs had to hoard their gas for several weeks before they accumulated enough ration coupons for a trip to the desert.

Waiting for Ella to return, Ginger heard an airplane overhead. She glanced up at the clear blue sky and felt a familiar rumble of apprehension in her chest. Planes always reminded her of Tony, now a seasoned fighter pilot stationed in eastern England. Ginger wrote to him twice a week, hoping to mend the coolness he had felt toward her ever since she had divorced Jason. The constant threat of his being killed was far more painful for her than it seemed to be for him. Oh, the optimism of youth, she thought. But she worried enough for both of them.

As a fighter pilot, his job was to help protect the big B-17's and Mitchells that were sent from England across the channel to bomb Nazi-held targets. His letters were divided between lyrical descriptions of the thrill that flying gave him even in wartime, his sorrow when he helped destroy some of the beautiful places he had visited with Avery, his respect for his fellow Air Corps pilots and crews, his admiration for the brave British people, and his impatience for the war to end so that he could come home and marry Jennie.

Jennie had appeared in four more successful films since her divorce from Neil. Her provocative pinup photographs, along with those of Betty Grable and Rita Hayworth, were cherished by soldiers, sailors, and marines all over the world. With her studio's approval, she had told the press about her engagement to Tony. Her bosses wanted Jennie's image to be that of a wholesome young woman—who also happened to be very sexy—pining for her brave, patriotic sweetheart who daily risked his life serving his country. Now Tony was a celebrity too, the envy of millions of servicemen and civilians.

Ginger was out of work for the duration of the war. The Springs had been requisitioned by the Army for an officers' club, and Ginger had declined the Army's offer that she remain and manage the club. The few times she had visited The Springs, where she now felt like an interloper, she had been shocked by the banks of pinball machines lining the dining room and the blaring of canned music that uttly destroyed the serenity of her little gem. Fortunately, she had insisted that the Army put her fine antique furniture in storage. They had installed ugly light-wood "Danish modern" furnishings that had nothing whatsoever to do with Denmark.

Ginger hadn't realized just how much she enjoyed the challenge of running her beautiful little hotel. She missed her guests, especially the "old-timers" who had returned year after year and who had become her good friends, creative people whose stimulating conversations and imaginative ideas had greatly added to the richness of her life.

Above all, she missed Jean-Paul's cuisine. For years,

her talented chef had sent lunch and dinner over to the pink mansion on the days Ginger didn't feel like eating in The Springs' dining room. But when Hitler declared war on France, Jean-Paul and his Danielle were there for their customary summer vacation, and they had decided to stay "to fight the Huns," he wrote to Ginger. She had smiled at this. She couldn't see roly-poly Jean-Paul, a cigarette always dangling from the corner of his mouth, an expert with a saucepan and a novice with a gun, striking much terror into the hearts of the Nazis.

For the first time since she was sixteen, when she had gone to work in the Desert Inn kitchen, Ginger was forced into the role of "lady of leisure." She had welcomed it as an opportunity to spend more time with Jiminy and Avery. Ironically, Avery then had gone back to work. With the wartime shortage of medical personnel, the Army had requested his services as a civilian consultant at Torrey Army Hospital, which now occupied the El Mirador Hotel. Where once the greats of Hollywood had cavorted, wounded soldiers hobbled on crutches or whizzed around in wheelchairs. Sometimes Ginger saw blue-robed patients out on the hospital lawn playing baseball, despite the bandages on their heads or casts on their bodies. Usually a furious nurse or doctor would rush out and chase them back to bed.

Avery seldom had time anymore for leisurely rides on the desert with Ginger, or for the hours he enjoyed sketching out on the desert or painting in the studio he had built behind their house. But he and Ginger still rose early to greet the dawn at their favorite lookout spot high up Mt. San Jacinto.

Ginger's musings were interrupted when a grinning Ella came rushing around the corner with two new strollers, one blue and one white. Todd was strapped into the white one and Ginger lowered Jiminy into the blue one. "Thanks," Ginger said gratefully. "But I should pay for them. *I* was the one who came barging around the corner without looking."

"Oh, forget it." Ella couldn't stop smiling. "Ginger, I'm so pleased," she said shyly. "You don't know how long I've wanted to be friends." She hesitated. "Let's go somewhere and talk, okay?"

Ginger frowned. She wasn't sure she was ready for too

much intimacy with Ella. What would they do? Have chummy little dinners with Avery and Jason? It would be too uncomfortable for everyone. But when she looked over at the wistful yearning on Ella's still-exquisite face, she didn't have the heart to refuse. "Well . . . where can we go?"

"Let's go over to my place," Ella offered. "My car's right down the block."

Ginger held back. "What about Jason?"

"Oh, you know him, always off lecturing somewhere. He's in L.A. today."

Ella's car turned out to be a two-year-old Packard. "But . . . I thought you drove a Rolls . . . and a Bugatti," Ginger said.

"Yeah, well, I sold them. With rationing, they were gas guzzlers. I sold my big estate, too."

Ginger was mystified. "You're not broke, are you?"

"Oh, no, nothing like that. But now that Cal's off in the South Pacific with the Marines, and Vivien prefers living in New York, Jason and I talked them into letting us keep Todd permanently. Anyway, the point is . . . well, I don't want to attract kidnappers."

Ginger nodded. "I guess it's one of the penalties of being rich and famous."

"Yeah, I have to admit, even though I retired from films five years ago, my fans still remember me. I keep getting invited to make USO appearances."

"And do you?"

"Sure. I've been on four tours of Stateside Army camps so far. I won't go overseas, though. I'd have to be away from Todd too long."

Ella drove north along Indian Avenue, turned at the Las Palmas section, and parked in the driveway of a house with a high brick wall half-hidden by a thick hedge of pink oleander bushes. Though the house itself was larger than it looked from the outside, it was far less pretentious than Ella's former estate. A glass-walled living room filled with striking modern teak furniture overlooked an oval pool and a small but colorful garden with a row of royal palms around it.

"Well, I'm glad to see you're not living in total poverty." Ginger smiled.

"I really like being in a smaller house. With big estates, you're always at the mercy of hordes of servants. I mean, you practically have to shrivel up and die if they quit." Ella gestured toward the back of the house. "Here we manage with just a live-in nursemaid and a Japanese couple who do the cooking and gardening, and a woman who comes in every day to clean and do laundry. Life's much simpler now." Ella had been talking quickly, nervously, still afraid of her big sister.

But what are you afraid *of*? Ella asked herself as Ginger wandered around the living room, carrying Jiminy while looking at Ella's paintings. After all, Ella mused, what was the worst that could happen? That Ginger might be angry about Tonito all over again and walk out? That Ginger might slap her face, as she'd sometimes done when they were little?

"I'm impressed," Ginger was saying. "Two Picassos, a Degas, a Seurat, and a Mary Cassatt." She looked over at Ella. "Are they all originals?"

Ella's nod was a cross between pride and modesty. "I can't take credit, Ginger. I mean, sure, it was my money that paid for them, but to tell you the truth, one of my French boyfriends made me buy them in Paris. Honestly, I didn't know a Picasso from a Norman Rockwell magazine cover. I've since learned."

They watched Jiminy and Todd play together amicably on the carpet. Todd gave Jiminy a fuzzy black fur cat and Jiminy let him hold her giraffe. Soon Clara came in and led the two toddlers out onto the patio, where she had set up their lunch on a child-size table.

Ella went to the mirrored bar. "What'll you have?" she asked Ginger. "Champagne? To celebrate our . . . reunion?"

They drank a whole bottle of Mumm's and then Ella opened a second one when the cook brought them a lunch of chef's salad and spinach soufflé. And while Clara took the children off to Todd's room for a nap, the sisters talked nonstop for two more hours. They choked with laughter, recalling Polly's prim ways and their father's foppery. Ginger told Ella about family events that had happened when they lived in San Francisco, and stories about Grandpa John that Ella had been too young to remember. They gossiped about Neil's parade of mistresses and they shamelessly bragged about Jiminy's and

Todd's accomplishments. Ella described Cal's brushes with death on Guadalcanal and more recently on Tarawa. Ginger matched them with accounts of Tony's harrowing dogfights with German fighter pilots while flying over continental Europe. Finally they brought each other up-to-date on the major happenings in their lives during the twelve years they had been estranged.

Ella told Ginger about her screen roles, and which of her leading men she had had affairs with. "Did you know that I made twenty-three pictures—all but two of them hits—in less than twenty years?"

"I know. I saw every one of them. Several times."

Ella was stunned. "You did?"

"You became a very good actress, Ella. And . . . well, sure, I was furious with you over Tonito . . . but I was proud of you as an actress, too."

"You were? Honestly? Oh, Ginger, I'm so amazed! And so pleased!"

"What was it like," Ginger asked, "making love to all those gorgeous men?"

Ella shrugged. "It wasn't just my leading men. Looking back, I can't believe how promiscuous I was. I went to bed with everyone—directors, studio truck drivers, gaffers, messenger boys. I guess I was searching for reassurance or something . . ." Her voice trailed off. "I was lucky I never caught anything."

Ginger then described how she unexpectedly had fallen so madly in love with Avery, and how cruelly she had had to treat Jason. "I hope he's happy with you, Ella," she said, close to tears. "I'm still so fond of him."

Abruptly Ella said, "About Tonito . . ."

Ginger sat very still. "Yes?" she finally said in a strained voice.

"He didn't love me, Ginger. In fact, he *hated* me. But it was . . . well, a very powerful physical thing. Maybe after what happened to you with Avery, you can understand that better now." Ella looked at her sister questioningly.

Ginger slowly nodded.

"Oh, but I *was* rotten then," Ella confessed. "I was desperate for Tonito to love me, not because I loved him—I really didn't—but because I wanted to hurt you. I was so jealous of your happiness! If you only knew how Tonito suffered, how horribly guilty he felt. But, Ginger, he never stopped loving you!" Ella came over to sit next to Ginger, taking her hand. "I can attract hordes of men, Ginger. They always want to possess me. But not one of them has ever loved me. Not the way Tonito loved you, or the way Jason still loves you—and now I guess Avery too."

Ginger took a deep breath. "I'll never forgive Tonito. I can't, because I wasted too many years grieving over him. But I *will* forgive you." She smiled into Ella's eyes. "If you promise not to make a pass at Avery."

Ella beamed with relief. "But I've already made a pass at him!" she giggled.

Ginger jumped up indignantly. "When?"

"Oh, ages ago. In Paris. Long before he married you. I thought he was going to spank me right there in public."

"Whatever possessed you to go after Avery? Weren't there dozens of handsome Frenchmen panting after you?"

"Yes, but I saw Avery in a restaurant one day, and he suddenly looked very attractive to me. I was getting tired of French charm and I was feeling sort of homesick. But listen, Ginger, you have nothing to worry about. It's obvious even from a distance that Avery's crazy in love with you—and you with him. Nobody's ever going to try to get between you two."

Nobody can, Ginger thought smugly.

Ella sighed wistfully. "Ever since I can remember, my looks were the only thing that anyone ever valued in me. So I never tried to develop any good traits I might've possessed." She paused to catch her breath. "God, it's hard to talk like this. I'm not used to spilling my guts. Anyway, Ginger, do you think you can help me become the person I would have been if I hadn't had the bad luck to be born beautiful? Oh, I know that sounds terribly conceited, but I mean it—it turned out to be just plain bad luck. It hasn't brought me any happiness at all." She put her hand over her heart. "And honest, I swear: I'll never hurt you again. Never. So long as I live!"

"And you believe her?" Avery asked.

"She's changed. That baby's made a human being out of her. And Jason's had a good effect on her too."

"Well, I hope so." He hesitated. "D'you think she and Jason are in love?"

"In love with Todd. But not with each other."

"I'm glad you forgave her. Hatred is so corroding." He paused. "But what about Jason? How can you spend time with Ella if seeing Jason is awkward for you—for all of us?"

"Well, I can always see Ella alone."

"How did Jiminy like her little cousin?" Avery asked.

"They really hit it off—once our little darling decided to share her giraffe with him. Avery, it was so cute! When we left, she and Todd put their arms around each other and kissed. And now she keeps asking when she can see Tah-*dee* again. He calls her Yimimy."

Avery nodded and smiled, but he couldn't help feeling sad. His baby had taken her first tiny step out into the world . . .

. . . and away from him.

In late September Ginger received a telegram that read: "THE WAR DEPARTMENT REGRETS TO INFORM YOU THAT FIRST LIEUTENANT ANTONIO ALVAREZ IS MISSING IN ACTION IN OPERATIONS OVER EUROPE."

Like a mother bear whose cub has been taken from her, Ginger was inconsolable. She wept. She raged. She prowled around the house at night, afraid to sleep, because for the first time in years she had recurrent nightmares in which Tonito and Johnny fell screaming into the flooded creek while she scrabbled around in the mud, unable to get up.

Avery felt helpless. He couldn't bear to see her suffer and he knew of no way to overcome her fears. He held her when she screamed in her sleep and he tried to reassure her whenever she concluded with terrible certainty that Tony was dead. When all else failed, he reminded her that her premature grief over Tony was harming Jiminy, who was very much attuned to her mother's emotions.

"Well, what do you want me to do?" Ginger asked heatedly. "Make believe everything's hunky-dory? *I'm* not the actress in this family."

"I don't want you to act, Ginger. But there's a good chance that Tony's still alive. He's probably in a German prison camp. Or hiding out somewhere. I want you to adopt the sensible attitude that you will only worry when you have to, and not waste your energy worrying about what might be. Most of the things we worry about never happen anyway."

She hated it when Avery talked to her like a wise father giving advice to an unreasonable child. But, she realized, she *was* acting like an unreasonable child, wasn't she? Only she couldn't help it. She had already lost one son. Did she have to lose Tony too? "And just how do I go about adopting this sensible attitude you recommend?" Her voice was petulant. Caustic. Belligerent.

Avery held her close. "You know how," he said soothingly. "I don't have to tell you."

Ginger spent hours alone on the desert, riding aimlessly through the foothills and into the Indian canyons. She sat staring hypnotically at Tahquitz Falls. She took deep-deep shuddering breaths of the pungent dry air. She stared at the dazzling blue sky until her eyes ached. She let the sun warm her body and the breeze soothe her soul until she was able to stop grieving over Tony as though he were already dead. She felt more and more confident that he was safe. Somewhere.

Three weeks after the telegram arrived, Ginger received a letter from Tony's commander, telling her that her son had been shot down over Normandy, not far from the coast. The other pilots in his fighter detachment had sent the attacking Messerschmitt crashing into the English Channel in flames. They saw Tony's parachute open above a dense forest and they assumed he had survived, but whether he had been taken prisoner by the Germans or had been rescued by some friendly Frenchmen, they had no way of knowing yet. The Germans often were lax about sending prisoners' names to the Swiss Red Cross, he wrote, but the War Department would watch for Tony's name on the lists and would keep her informed if they heard anything further.

Weeks passed, and Tony's name failed to appear on the Red Cross lists of American prisoners of war held by the Germans. If Tony hadn't been captured, then he had to be hiding from the Germans somewhere in France.

Ginger *had* to believe that.

When she first received the telegram, Ginger had felt duty-bound to let Jennie know that Tony was missing in action. Ginger had great misgivings about Tony's engagement to the beautiful young film star. Not that she didn't like Jennie—it was almost impossible not to like her.

Jennie was adorable, gorgeous, sweet, kind—all the good words applied to her. Her divorce had been entirely Neil's fault. Neil cheerfully admitted it. Even the scandal-mongering movie columnists had only good things to say about Jennie. She was generous with her time, going all over the world with the USO to entertain the troops when she wasn't shooting a film. But Ginger admitted—only to Avery—that she would have preferred that Tony fall in love with a nice local girl who would give Ginger a half-dozen grandchildren.

"Well, you have no reason to believe that Jennie won't want children," Avery said. "And if she doesn't, you can always hope that someday Jiminy will make you a grandmother."

Ginger phoned Jennie's private number in Hollywood and told her the news. Ginger forced herself to sound even more optimistic than she felt. And Jennie seemed to accept it very well. "Oh, you know Tony," she said to Ginger, "he's so clever. I'm sure he's outwitted the Germans and is perfectly safe."

It was news to Ginger that Tony was either that clever or that capable of outwitting the Germans, though she didn't say so to Jennie.

Every newspaper and movie magazine in the country carried photos of Jennie looking charmingly worried, and pictures of Jennie and Tony embracing each other in happier days. Ginger secretly fretted over the photos—quite unreasonably, she knew. After all, Tony was *her* son, first and foremost, and she felt that Jennie was invading her territory by getting all the public sympathy for Tony's disappearance.

Ginger kept her feelings to herself, not even sharing them with Avery, knowing he would consider her attitude petty in the extreme.

One lovely morning in late December, Ginger was surprised to receive in her hotel mail a heavy letter in a soiled and crinkled envelope. She saw at once from its return address that it was from Pfc. Calvin Ricardo, USMC, Fleet Post Office, San Francisco, but she also noted from the postmark that strangely the envelope had been sent only the previous day, via the regular U.S. mail service, from San Diego. Ginger then sat in a shaded chaise by the pool and proceeded to read with great curiosity the first letter she had ever received from her nephew.

Fox Trot Beach,
Apia, Western Samoa
November 11, 1943

Dear Aunt Ginger:

Surprised to hear from me? I'm writing this to you because I have a story I have to tell—to someone, somewhere—about war and myself, and in all the world, I have no one to tell it to except you. We're on Rest and Recuperation on these beautiful islands, which haven't been touched by the war. I'm sitting here in my skivvies writing this letter with my back against a palm tree, on the kind of beach where any minute you expect Dotty Lamour in a grass skirt to bounce up out of the waves and Crosby to appear with a ukulele (is that how you spell it?).

But who needs Lamour? Western Samoa's a tropical paradise where the people are very friendly, especially the girls, who tell us that the greatest sin is to live without love. Even while I'm writing this, I have a sweet Samoan girl sitting beside me and she's playing with my toes and kissing my arms, where they're not bandaged. I was wounded, nothing much, a month ago in a battle on an island called Tarawa, but I'll be all better in a couple of weeks.

It's Tarawa I have to get out of my system. I must tell someone—you—what happened there and what happened to me, not the wounds, but what happened *inside*. It was sort of like seeing God, or, at least, myself, and for the first time to know where I've been and where I'm going. For the first time in my life, Auntie, I'm pouring my heart out, telling it as I feel it, so forgive the language, I don't want to stop to try to think of the nice words. There are no nice words in war.

This letter can't pass the censors, though there's nothing in it that'll give any comfort to the enemy, so when I finish it, I'm going to bring it to a guy in the field hospital down the road. His name's Rico, he's from East L.A. and his English is not so good. I speak Spanish to him so he feels like I'm a brother. Only now he's got the Goony-Bird Stare, which is what we call it when you've seen too much and your eyes get this empty glaze and, not saying a word, you just stare, like a Goony Bird lying dead on the sand. They're shipping Rico back to the States tomorrow, probably to the Navy Hospital in San Diego. All he does is just stare straight ahead, unseeing, but deep down I think he understands me, my voice, my Spanish. Anyway, I'll give him this letter. Then back in Dago, when they fix him up and let him out for a little fresh air, I hope to God he'll walk over to the souvenir shop in Balboa Park and buy some regular stamps and mail this letter to you from a civilian mailbox.

Let me tell you about Tarawa. It's a bunch of tiny atolls, two to three feet above sea level, little sand-and-palm-tree islands surrounded by a big blue lagoon and lots of coral reefs. On the biggest of these atolls, one that's maybe a mile or so in circumference, the Japanese had dug hundreds of palm-log bunkers and covered the bunkers with sand so all we could really see were the little slits through which they fired their machine guns. They thought they were invincible and were dug in for keeps, but we had to take Tarawa as the first stepping-stone on our island-hopping route to Japan, seven thousand miles further on.

As our landing began, our first wave hit long lines of barbed wire only a few feet from shore, and as our guys stopped to cut the wire or try to climb through it, the enemy machine guns opened fire, shredding that first wave to bits, so that only a few marines ever reached the beach alive. But there they were, pinned down and unable to move, while on the barbed wire behind them, the rest of our guys were dead or dying, hooked on the sharp barbs and hung out to rot in the tropical sun.

Our second wave then went in, but didn't do much better, though a few more got through to the beach. There they joined the first wave, so that now there were, maybe, a hundred marines ashore, all pinned down and sure to get wiped out unless reinforcements from the third wave could get in to them fast and help mount an attack in force.

I was in the third wave. But with the tide pulling out, our landing boats got hung up on the reef, and we all jumped out onto the coral and stood there up to our necks in the lagoon with our heavy weapons held high above our heads. Then the hidden machine guns in the bunkers began zeroing in on us, their fire getting closer and closer. Soon we were getting hit.

That's when I made history. If there'd been any officers around—but there weren't: by that time they were all dead—there'd have been the proper witnesses and I might've got the Medal of Honor. Hell, there weren't even any noncoms left, so all I'm going to get is the Purple Heart and a Silver Star. They always clean up the language in the medal citations so they can be printed in the hometown papers, like the *Desert Sun* in Palm Springs. But I'm spilling out my guts to you, and it's easier to tell it exactly like it was, with only the f-word cleaned up.

I turned to all the other guys up to their necks in the water, all paralyzed with fright and waiting to die, and I yelled, "All right, you effing bastards, all shitting in your pants, stay here and you're sure to die. Head for the effing beach and maybe some of us'll make it!" And you know how I got so gutsy? I wasn't afraid. *I really wanted to die.* The only reason I'd enlisted was that I wanted to kill myself. I didn't have the guts to blow my brains out or slit my wrists or even swallow a handful of pills, but I knew that in the Corps I'd have a good chance of dying and finally doing some good at the same time. Doing some good. Remember that, Auntie. That was always part of my thinking.

But nobody moved. So I headed for the beach all by myself. Then a second later, Rico joined me. Then another young gyrene, an effing little piece of white trash from Arkansas, who didn't give a shit about living either. Maybe that's what makes war heroes. Once the three of us started out, then the whole line joined us, all wading in toward the machine guns, each guy mumbling out loud the words remembered from his childhood, the old mumbo-jumbo that gave him comfort now: "Hail Mary, Mother of God!" "Our Father, who art in heaven!" "Hear, O Israel!" while the effing little Arkie beside me kept reciting all the counties of Arkansas, the dumb refrain he'd had to memorize in the third grade. I said nothing. The only counties of California I could remember were Riverside, San Berdoo, and L.A. and if there was a God to pray to, he sure as hell wasn't looking out for any of his children at Tarawa that day.

When we got to the bodies of the marines hooked on the barbed wire, shreds of shirts and pants and hunks of human flesh, all hung out on the barbed wire and stinking in the sun, I knew what to do. Don't stop. Don't pause to cut the wires or squeeze through. Use the bodies of your buddies, dead or alive, as stepping-stones, and keep on going. I went first, the others followed. Over the bodies of our own dead and dying.

So that's how we reinforcements landed. And kept going! With Rico and the effing Arkie beside me, I crawled up onto the blind side of one of the bunkers, and we dumped three hand grenades through the slit where the machine gun poked out. And all by ourselves, we three had knocked out the first machine-gun nest! Just the three of us, a Mexican, an Indian half-breed (me), and an effing piece of poor white trash. Then we crawled up on top of another bunker, a big one, dropped in more grenades, knocked it out too. By that time, the others guys on the beach got the word. Suddenly it was the Fourth of July and we kids were tossing firecrackers into empty tin cans. That's how it felt as we spent the rest of the afternoon knocking off, one by one, the poor bastards in the bunkers.

Then it was night, and the machine guns were still, and from here and there, all over the little island, while we were too dumbfounded to do anything, the Japanese rose up from one bunker after another, and they bowed, first to the east to their emperor, and then they bowed to us, their conquerors, and then each man put a hand grenade to his belly, and they all blew themselves up. Little bits of Jap flesh and blood hailed all over the atoll. We'd taken Tarawa.

I looked over at Rico and that's when I saw he was lying down on the sand, looking up at the stars with the Goony-Bird Stare. And I looked over at my effing little Arkie, and he, too, was sprawled in the sand and he was crying. Me, I was bleeding a little and vomiting. I must've puked for hours. Finally, drained, with pieces of dead marines and Japs all around us, we three lay there in the sand, side by side, grown men, marines, and we held hands. That's how we comforted each other and that's how we spent that night. Holding hands! Christ, if we'd done that in the barracks at Pendleton or on the streets of Dago, we'd have been drummed out of the Corps as flaming fairies. But that day and night, I learned brotherhood. On Tarawa!

And now I want to live.

You don't know how many hours we've spent in the Corps in bull sessions, especially during the long voyages across the Pacific in the ships and during invasions on the landing barges. In some ways, I knew my fellow enlisted men better than I knew myself—where they came from, what they hoped to get out of life, what they'd settle for and what they expected to get, which was always the shit end of the stick. I was the only one who was rich, and I never told them. They were all poor, none of them well-educated or favored in any way.

As we waded in, the machine guns knocking off one after another of us, I looked to right and left at what I then felt were my brothers. I loved them. I cried for them, cried all the way in. These were the poor bastards bleeding at my side and floating face-down in the water, who do all the killing and the dying in all the wars in all countries, who work with their hands in the effing factories and fields, who always draw life's shit details. Especially in the poor countries.

But I've got money and if I survive this hell, I'll have the time, and, I swore on Tarawa, I'll use it to help all those poor bastards, men, women, and especially children, and especially those like my father, with darker skins, to somehow get a better life, to fill their bellies and enrich their minds and lay down their effing arms. I've read no books on all this, Aunt Ginger. I've got no fixed ideas, know no sure path to Utopia, am not even sure who the real bastards are. But I know who my brothers are, and I will devote my life to helping them, wherever and whenever I can. And if I fail in that, well, I will have tried.

With love and respect,
Cal

P.S. One hour later:

Dear Ginger:

It's all spilling out of me and I can't stop writing. I went for a little swim, but hurried back up to my palm tree and my pen. I want to tell you more, more about you and me and those we know, some of who (whom?) we love, all of whom we're mixed up with for life.

Do you mind my not calling you "Aunt Ginger"? It seems kind of childish to me now, and I want to write as a friend and an adult, no more a kid. I've always liked you and wished you were my mother. I sure was jealous of Tony when we were kids because he had a real mother. My own mother's all fucked-up, as we say in the Corps. Back when I thought Frank Ricardo was my father, I really did love him, but he died a long time ago. As for my dear wife, Vivien's a very silly girl. I don't know why I married her except that I was drunk and lonesome, and it was Christmas. Now that Jason's my father-in-law, I could love him if he'd let me, but he's too disgusted with me and Vivien. He thinks we were irresponsible to bring a kid into the world that neither of us wanted. I don't know how he can say that, though, when he drools over Todd like he's the greatest thing since God invented people.

In the ten months since I enlisted, my mother's written me three letters so I know that you two made up. I'm awfully glad. Maybe you can teach her how to be human. She also wrote that Tony is missing in action. Ginger, I know Tony's still alive. I just know it. I guess you never told him that we're brothers. It makes me feel better, just knowing it. I hope someday you will tell him. Then maybe we can be true brothers to each other. I know now how I love Tony, but I think he sort of looks down on me as an empty-headed playboy. I don't blame him. That's all I've ever been.

Ginger, why didn't I get killed? Why did I survive when almost everybody else bought the farm? God's such a joker. He knew I wanted it so he didn't give it to me. Ginger, what is love? You're the only person I can think of who's terrific at loving. I mean, my mother told me that you and my father were madly in love, and I can remember when you married Jason how happy you both were, and from what I've seen of you and Avery, it's the love affair of the century.

Well, I guess I'm going to be around awhile. Maybe I'll lead a charmed life and live to be a hundred.

Please write to me.

Love,
Cal

Ginger did reply:

Dear Cal,

What dismayed me most about your letter was the fact that you ever feared life more than death. I hope you now will cherish life as the precious gift it is.

First, I want to tackle your questions about falling in love. Frankly, I don't know if the ability to love is inborn. For your sake, I hope it can be learned. I would say from my own experience that being good friends first is the best way to fall in love.

Love not only means giving, but even harder, sometimes, is being able to receive the intimacy that someone holds out to you. By receiving intimacy I mean being entirely open to whatever the person you love tells you—not only open, but *extremely attentive*! It isn't always easy. All this giving and receiving requires a certain amount of willingness to take chances. Women might be afraid that if they offer their love to you (and I'm not talking about sex), you'll slap it down. Lots of women have thrown themselves at you, but that isn't love. I hope you haven't been too spoiled by the wrong kind of women to recognize the right kind—the truly loving kind—when you meet one.

Your newfound sense of brotherhood is impressive. If you don't love people generally, it's difficult to love one particular person. It's important to feel that you're part of the human race, and now that you do, I think you are on your way to finding the kind of love you want, from a woman, from friends, maybe even from your mother.

I realize that you were never attached to Ella, or even to Frank, the way a child should be to his parents. That was their fault, not yours. But I don't think it's too late for you to start loving your mother, and you'll feel better about yourself if you do.

She's changed a lot, Cal. She no longer is so afraid to look her age, which has liberated her from the terrible energy-consuming need to always look youthful and beautiful. Her love for Todd has expanded her ability to feel affection for other people. In fact, she and I have become good friends. Once I stopped hating her for seducing Tonito—and I admit, that was very difficult for me—she and I began to communicate.

Also, it's not too late to start loving your son. It's fortunate for Todd that Ella is able to give him all the maternal love she never could give you. But don't resent him (or her) for that. She couldn't help it. You were born at the wrong time in her life. She was very young and insecure. Her career was just beginning, and I think she saw movie stardom as the only way of ever achieving any kind of self-esteem.

Her childhood wasn't the greatest. She herself was denied the kind of love parents should give. Our mother openly preferred me, and our father admired only her beauty. So be glad Ella loves Todd. He would be in bad shape were it not for Ella and Jason. I don't think Vivien is ever going to become very maternal, but I do believe you might have it in you, Cal, to become a loving father.

As for Tonito, you can be proud of him, Cal. Even though he hurt me, he also gave me much love and happiness. He was exceptionally strong and intelligent, and ever so charming and handsome. I can't tell you how difficult it was for him, a poor dirt farmer's son, to go all through school and graduate with honors from Harvard Law School, not because he wanted to make a lot of money, but to help his tribe. For too many years I let his one transgression blind me to all that was good about him. And since that transgression resulted in your life, I no longer hate him for it.

I have very good feelings about you, Cal. And I promise you, when Tony comes home, I will tell him that you two are brothers. He has always idolized his father and he will probably be very upset that Tonito wasn't faithful to me, but I think it's more important for him to know that you are his brother than for him to go on thinking that his father was a saint.

Cal, please write again. And again!

Love,
Ginger

CHAPTER
11

1943–1944

Tony held on tightly to Odette's thin veined hand. The Frenchwoman, Avery's friend and former neighbor in Paris, had shrunk from the plump, chic, sixtyish widow Tony had known in the thirties to a wasted wraith with wispy white hair. Tony and Odette were waiting—tense, miserable, furious—for the shots that would end the life of Odette's oldest friend.

Tony groaned when he heard a thin, tremulous voice in the distance singing, *"Allons, enfants de la patrie, le jour de gloire—"* Abruptly the words were cut off by a burst of gunfire. A blast of October wind noisily swept a carpet of crisp autumn leaves down the street and rattled the windows of Odette's house, as if in protest.

"Forgive me for coming here," Tony whispered to Odette with a strangled sob.

"Shhhh. Raimond was a very old man, *chéri*. A very sick man. He was not afraid to die." With tear-filled eyes Odette smiled reassuringly at Tony. She loved this boy, Avery's young friend. Now his stepson.

Tony looked down in frustration at his right leg, encased in a cast made by Raimond Forer, the elderly doctor who had just been murdered by the Germans for helping Tony. The execution had taken place in the town square, down the street from Odette's house, beyond Tony's line of vision through the window of the second-floor room where he was hiding.

Two days earlier, when Tony was shot down, he had landed in a forest a few kilometers from Odette's village.

His parachute had caught an unfortunate gust of wind that had slammed him against a tree and thrown him to the ground. Not only had his leg been broken below the knee, but he had suffered deep gashes on his arms and head as well.

He had known he was close to Odette's Normandy house, where he and Avery often had visited, because Odette's village of Fouzille was the reason Tony had been shot down in the first place. While flying back to his base in England after a bombing raid on the submarine pens at St. Nazaire, he had realized from his maps that their course would take them right over Fouzille and he had been watching for its white church, its distinctive pink stone city hall, and its tree-lined main square. His fighter detachment of P-51 Mustangs had been flying in a low-level sweep beneath the formations of twin-engine Mitchell B-25 bombers, protecting the bigger aircraft from German fighter planes that might suddenly swoop upon them and attack.

It had been his next-to-last mission. One more and he would have been sent back to the States as a flight instructor. It also was the easiest mission he had ever flown, with only a little flak around St. Nazaire and no German fighter planes around whatsoever, so Tony had been less alert and vigilant than usual. He had become so intent upon spotting Fouzille that he had drifted momentarily behind his squadron's tight defensive formation and hadn't even been aware of the lone Messerschmitt 109 zooming up behind him until a loud crack and heavy smoke and a stream of glycol flowing from his engine reminded him, with an agonizing jolt, of the ghastly consequences of his brief distraction.

Automatically he had jettisoned his cockpit hood, quickly inverted the plane, and pulled the ring on his safety harness. As he fell clear of the plane, he had slowly counted "one . . . two . . . three" and pulled the ripcord to open his parachute. His abandoned plane, he calculated, would probably lose altitude at a rate that would bring it down into the English Channel.

Drifting gently toward the forest's treetops, he had worried about being spotted by the Germans. He and his fellow pilots had been warned again and again at briefings that the Germans avidly watched for parachutes, that they were paranoid about Allied military men being dropped into France as spies. But there was nothing he could do about it now, except fervently pray that he hadn't been seen.

Once on the ground, in massive pain, he had tried to haul down his parachute, but it had become impaled on the tree's sharp branches. He had been forced to leave it there—he had no other choice—hoping that the Germans wouldn't find it and realize that he was in the area. He had inched along through the forest for an hour on his elbows and his undamaged knee. He saw no houses and he had no idea where he was, in relation to Odette's village.

He stopped crawling, trying to get his bearings and fighting the temptation to simply stay there and bleed to death. By the time dusk approached, he had lost all sense of direction. He was trembling from head to toe with pain and fatigue when he heard the squeak of wheels and childish voices coming toward him.

Dragging himself behind a tree, he saw three boys, about ten years old, pushing a rusty old wheelbarrow filled with the twigs and small pieces of wood they obviously had been collecting in the forest. They had fashioned guns from gnarled twigs and, listening to their shouts, Tony had to smile, despite his pain, because they were playing an exuberant game of Cowboys and Indians. He was thankful that his French was fluent enough for him to understand them.

The boy playing the Indian had fashioned a chief's bonnet by tying a ribbon around his forehead and sticking chicken feathers through the ribbon. A bent stick with a string connecting the two ends, and a straight twig with a pointed end were his bow and arrow. The two "cowboys" wore vests made from old shirts with the sleeves cut off. Battered fedoras doubled as cowboy hats.

Tony crawled out from behind the tree and called to them.

They stopped their game and stared at him as though he were a ghost.

"I'm an American flier," he told them in French, point-

ing up at the sky. "The Germans shot down my plane."
He paused and tried to smile reassuringly. "Can you help
me?"

One boy, the "Indian," took a few hesitant steps
toward Tony while the other two hung back. "Are
you a spy?" he asked. "The Germans will kill us if
we help you. They also will kill ten old men from our
village."

Tony had an inspiration. "*I'm* an American Indian,"
he said proudly.

The boy scoffed. "You don't look like an Indian. We
see them all the time in American movies."

"Let me show you." Painfully Tony shifted his position
on the ground so that he could take his wallet out of his
pocket. "See?" He held out the small photograph he had
made of Tonito's portrait in full movie-Indian regalia.
"This is my father."

Cautiously the boy reached out and snatched the picture from Tony. He brought it back to his two friends
and the three of them examined it with excited exclama-
tions that, yes, this man in the photo was a real Indian.
They compared Tonito's features with Tony's and concluded that Tony did indeed resemble the *peau rouge*—
the redskin. They returned the photograph to Tony and
stared at him with admiration.

"Where is Fouzille?" Tony asked.

They conferred. "I say it is two kilometers to the
north," the Indian replied, "and Jacques here says it is
three. We are from La Maroque, a half-kilometer in the
other direction."

Tony pointed at the wheelbarrow, then at his broken
leg. "Can you put me in that thing and wheel me to
Fouzille?"

The boys looked doubtful. "It is very dangerous," the
Indian said reluctantly.

Tony pointed at the sky. "It's getting dark. You can go
through the forest, away from the road . . ." He closed
his eyes in pain. He hated to endanger the boys, but this
was war, and he was desperate. Besides, bad as the
Germans were, he couldn't believe that they would actually execute children. "*Real* cowboys and Indians are
fearless," he told them.

They threw the wood they had gathered onto the ground. They helped him into the barrow, where he curled up in a tight ball. Then they covered him with the twigs as best they could.

"All right, act normal," he told them as they set off through the trees. "Keep singing while you go toward Fouzille."

With heavy French accents and a pronounced nasal twang, they began to sing, "I'm zee old cowhand . . . from zee Rio Grande . . ."

Luckily, Odette was home, alone. He almost didn't recognize her, she looked so emaciated and old. Her astonishment at seeing him would have been wonderful to behold, had he not been terrified and in so much pain. She had run down the street and brought back the elderly doctor, Raimond Forer. Short and slender, Raimond was a white-haired, florid-faced man with beautifully erect posture and tiny gnarled hands. Working quickly but with meticulous care, he had put a cast on Tony's leg and cleaned and bandaged his deep cuts. Then he had gone back home to fetch a pair of crutches and a bottle of pain medication.

"No one will suspect me of hiding you, *mon ami*," Odette had assured Tony that first day. "All along, I have forced myself to be civil to these horrible Germans who are occupying our village, because I wish for them to think, aha, this Madame Odette, we can trust her. I even invite the officers to tea every month. So you see, *mon ami*, this way they will never suspect me if someday I think of a way to harm them.

"I may be an old widow, Tony, but I have this great dream of putting a bomb into their headquarters and blowing up every one of them. *Malheureusement*, but where am I to get the bloody bomb? To tell you the truth, my dearest Tony, Raimond and I pray for the chance to kill them, but how? We have no guns, no weapons. What are we to do? *Mon Dieu*, strangle them with our bare hands?

"This village is full of frightened old people who cannot even trust each other. Raimond is the only other person here who I know positively is not a secret collaborator. He was my parents' dearest friend, and mine. Tony, you are a godsend to me because you see, *mon ami*, at least taking care of you makes me feel I am even a little useful to the Allied cause!"

But that had been two days ago. Now the dapper little doctor was dead and Tony knew it was all his fault. "How did the Germans find out that Dr. Raimond helped me?" he asked Odette.

"You see, Tony, this morning a German patrol found your parachute in the forest. *Quel dommage!* First they are searching the village of La Maroque, three kilometers from here. So! While the Germans still are in La Maroque, Raimond tells me, 'Odette, they will search us next and we must keep them from coming to your house. You must go to the German swine here in Fouzille and tell them that I am the guilty one who helped the American flier.' "

Tony frowned. "I don't understand, Odette. Are you saying that Raimond actually wanted you to go to the Germans and *inform* on him?"

"*Ah, oui*, exactly. I am very sad, of course, for Raimond is my friend, but I see no other way to save you. So, yes, I tell the Germans that our Dr. Raimond is a traitor, that he secretly treated the wounded American flier and helped him to escape."

Astounded, Tony raised himself up on his elbows. "Odette, how *could* you—"

"Shhhh, lie back." She gently pushed him down against the pillow. "It was Raimond's idea. He insisted. You see, Tony, if I am the informer, it takes all suspicion away from me, *n'est-ce pas*? It is really most clever, no? Otherwise the Boche might search my house, along with all the others in the village, and then they might find you, *mon pauvre ami*, even though this room is quite well-hidden."

"But to sacrifice Raimond's life?" Tony was outraged.

"Ah, Tony, the poor man was eighty-nine. He was not well, always coughing." She made a helpless gesture. "He has had a long and fruitful life. He is not afraid to die. So you see, Tony? This way he dies a hero to the cause of freedom and justice. This is very important to him as a patriotic Frenchman. We French are very low on pride these days." She caressed Tony's cheek. "*Mon ami*, be glad for him. He died very happy, as you heard, singing his beloved '*La Marseillaise.*' "

Tony closed his eyes. "Where do the Germans think I am, then?" he whispered hoarsely.

"Raimond also instructed me to tell the Boche that after he treated you, he secretly took you, hidden under some hay in his wagon, to Caen, only twelve kilometers from here. So, while the Germans still were making the search for you this morning in La Maroque, Raimond took his wagon full of hay to Caen and back. To make sure the Germans would see him leave the village and return, he drove slowly past our city hall, where two stupid Nazi *gendarmes* sit all day. Raimond told me to wait until he came back from Caen and then go and inform on him. So, Tony, I am hoping you will be safe here. The Germans did not search our village. Instead, the fools look for you now in Caen."

Tony exhaled with relief. "So I'm safe here now?"

"We still must be very, very careful, Tony. There are many in the village who are true collaborators with the Germans, and they would be only too happy to find you here and have the Germans shoot me in retaliation."

"Isn't there anyone here you can trust?" he asked.

"No, no one, now that Raimond is gone. I am afraid to tell another soul that you are here. I have known everyone in Fouzille all my life—I was born here. But even I do not know who is a secret collaborator and who is not. Nobody trusts anybody else." She shook her head sadly. "Sometimes fear and misfortune make people noble, Tony, but more often they show the very worst in us. I have heard that some villagers secretly help the Germans for extra rations, but nobody knows who they are. It is said they would inform on their own kin to get more food. I suspect some of the villagers even are in sympathy with the Nazis. But I must not judge too harshly. It is a hard life these days for all of us in France."

Tony gestured at his cast. "Who will remove it, if Raimond is dead?"

"I shall, *mon ami*. Raimond told me exactly how I must do it." She plumped up his pillows. "So, we must talk of happier things. Tell me all about Avery. Now he is a proud papa. I am so pleased when you tell me you have a little baby sister!"

"You don't mind, that he got married?"

"Oh, no, Tony. He and I, we are only good friends. We are not in love. Besides, I know all along that he loves your mother. Always, he was talking about her. He was saying, 'Oh, Ginger does this,' and 'Oh, Ginger does that.' Always, it was Ginger, Ginger, Ginger! And every time he speaks her name, his eyes grow big and show his great love for her."

Tony took Odette's withered hand and gratefully kissed it. "Let's talk later," he begged. "I'm so tired now."

After she left the room, Tony sank against the pillows and groaned in misery. He felt nauseous with guilt. It was his own fault that he had been shot down. He should have been more careful and stayed in formation. Now he was responsible not only for the loss of a valuable airplane, but much worse, for the death of the kind old doctor. He was also putting Odette herself in jeopardy. All because of his unforgivable moment of carelessness.

He looked out the window at the Normandy landscape. Odette had placed his narrow bed so that he could see out, obliquely, without anyone outside the house seeing him. His view included a corner of the church, a meadow with grazing cows, then the dense forest beyond. The treetops were swaying in a slight breeze; above them, small puffs of white clouds were like flak against the blue sky.

It amazed him how rural life went on, war or no war. The cows epitomized this more than anything else for Tony. They grazed, and produced milk, day after day, no matter what happened around them. He was sure that if a field of them were strafed and half of them were killed, the other half would just go on chewing their cuds. Then he found it worrisome that he considered this remarkable—what else could the poor dumb animals do, after all?—and he began to get very confused because he couldn't stop his mind from chewing on its own fearful, guilt-ridden cud.

His room was small and narrow and papered with a pattern of tiny pink roses from floor to ceiling. It was the dressing room and adjoining bathroom for the big master bedroom where Odette slept. Odette had told Tony that whenever she went downstairs now, she shoved a big armoire on wheels against the dressing-room door so that anyone searching her bedroom would not see that the door was even there. She herself was using another bathroom at the end of the hall.

She had warned Tony that when he went to the bathroom on his crutches he must be very quiet, and he must never, *never* flush the toilet unless she was up there with him, just in case some neighbor walking past her house saw her in the kitchen or in the salon through a downstairs window and then, knowing she lived alone, heard the toilet flush upstairs. The neighbor would surmise at once that she was hiding someone. And when he heard visitors arrive—after all, she had grown up in this village, and people dropped in all the time—he must stay in his bed and *not move* until he heard them leave.

Immobilized as he was, he quickly became attuned to every sound around him, not only inside the house but also in the village and in the sky. He exulted when he heard Allied bombers going over because the sooner the Germans were kicked out of France, the sooner he would be liberated from this life of imprisonment.

He was deeply grateful to Odette for all she was doing for him. His admiration for her, combined with his utter dependence upon her, made him love her almost as much as he loved his mother and Jason and Avery. He realized how insensitive he had been, taking the adults in his life for granted. He had been so wrapped up in his own activities—his studies, his flying, his pursuit of girls, his friends—that he seldom had thought much about Ginger and Jason and Avery, their needs, their concerns, their problems. He had blithely accepted their deep interest in him without much reciprocity, except when something unusual happened, such as when his mother left Jason for Avery. And even then, he had mainly been concerned about how it would affect his relationship with Jason.

Lying there day after day, he thought about his mother with a growing sense of shame. Instead of being glad that she was deriving so much joy from her marriage to Avery and from the birth of their baby, he had resented her, resented Avery, and unfairly taken Jason's side. Tony hid his head in the pillow, trembling with self-loathing. What had possessed him to treat her so despicably? She had always been so loving to him.

He remembered their early days together when they lived in the cabin his father had built, and how she had managed to play with him for hours, even though she worked very hard managing The Springs all by herself. She had set up a low desk for him in her office so that he could draw and paint and she could read to him while she was trying to run the hotel too. He had always come first. When the hotel's one maid had caught the flu and Ginger had had to make the beds and sweep the floors, she had taken Tony with her from room to room and together they had made a game of the work.

Always, whether poor or rich, she had given him her time and her loving attention, as well as all the material advantages a boy could want. Poor or rich, he had always had his own horse. Neat clothes. Books. By the time he was sixteen and she had money, she had bought him a blue Studebaker coupe. Oh, how he had complained, he was mortified to recall, because Cal had a Duesenberg and all he had was a "cheap" car. Ginger had smiled and said, "Count your blessings, darling, and then count Cal's, and see who's way ahead." She had meant, of course, his having her for a mother instead of Ella, whose neglect of Cal was a crime. She had meant his having Jason for a stepfather instead of all the creepy lovers Ella brought home. She had meant his warm home life and his attendance at his much-loved Palm Springs schools, instead of Cal's years of incarceration in a hated military academy.

In his head he wrote long letters of apology to his mother. If only there were some way he could actually send them to her! He was fully aware of how much she must be suffering, not knowing where he was or how he was. Probably she was in mourning, thinking he was dead.

Odette could see that he was deeply troubled. "What is it, *mon pauvre ami*?" she asked. "You look so unhappy."

He shook his head, unwilling to burden her with his problems. Odette had enough to worry her. "Tell me about your life," he urged, hoping to get his mind off his guilt toward his mother.

So Odette told him about her pleasant childhood in this house in the 1880's and 1890's, with loving parents and doting grandparents. Her happiest memories were of garden parties, picnics at the seashore, winter vacations skiing in Chamonix. There, the winter she was eighteen, she had met the wealthy young doctor Jules Cassin, had married him, and had gone to live in Paris, but always, always, they had spent their summers in Fouzille. Their only daughter, Mareille, had been killed in a train accident during a blizzard when she was fifteen, on her way home for Christmas vacation from her boarding school in Lausanne. A few years later, Dr. Cassin had died of a sudden heart attack, leaving Odette wealthy and lonely, but rich in happy memories.

"Why didn't you stay in Paris when the Germans came?" Tony asked one day. "Isn't it safer there? I mean, it's not like here, where everyone watches everyone else."

She shrugged. "Ah, *mon ami*, things were happening there that you do not wish to know about."

"What kind of things?"

She hesitated for several moments, and then spoke reluctantly. "Oh . . . swastikas everywhere. Collaborators everywhere. And I was so cold. All the time. There was no heat whatsoever. The Germans take everything for themselves and for those who help them. Often, I am thinking how foolish I was not to go with Avery to your wonderful hot desert when he was urging me to go home with him!

"Like the other Parisians, I was always hungry, too. The shops were full of bare shelves. And everyone so suspicious of everyone else! Paris had become a city of great distrust. And worst of all, Tony, there was the deportation of the Jews." She sighed deeply. "I had many Jewish friends . . . I could not bear it when they disappeared and there was nothing—*nothing!*—I could do to help them. They were gone before I realized it. So I came back here to my little village, where I can be an ostrich with my head in the ground and not have to see the great shame that has befallen France." She wiped her eyes.

They took turns speaking French and English, to improve their fluency in each other's language. To keep him from growing too bored, she searched through her library to find books in French that were easy enough for him to read. She taught him chess. She shared what rations she could find, but mostly they ate the local cheese and apples, and vegetables from her garden, which she had preserved the previous summer in glass jars. Food was scarce even here in the country, she explained to Tony, because the Germans took most of whatever food was produced.

By mid-December Tony had developed an overpowering desire to get out of this tiny room and out of this house. Odette had taken the cast off his leg the previous week. Now that he could walk without crutches, he doubly hated being cooped up in this damn cubbyhole.

When he first arrived, Odette had buried his bloody, torn uniform in her garden, saving only his wallet and boots. He never took off his identifying dog tags, not even to bathe. Now that he no longer had to stay in bed, Odette brought him clothes from her attic, pants and shirts and underwear that had belonged to her husband and which she had kept out of sentiment. Although Dr. Cassin had been Tony's height, he had been heavier and the clothes were loose on Tony. But as Odette pointed out, almost all the people in France, even the Germans these days, were emaciated and wore clothing that was too big for them. Truly, she said, he could pass as a Frenchman, if he had to, until he began to speak French with an American accent.

He spent hours brooding over the execution of Dr. Raimond. In November, ten more Fouzille citizens—two fifteen-year-old boys and eight old men—had been shot in the village square, in retaliation for someone's having thrown a grenade at a German truck on the outskirts of town, killing the driver.

Tony lived in terror that he might be discovered and that Odette and ten more innocent men would be executed too. He felt defenseless and demoralized. He became obsessed with the desire to shoot the Germans who had killed Dr. Raimond and the others. This craving to *kill, kill, kill* gripped him so fiercely that he often found himself crying silent tears of anguish that circumstances had made *him* so eager to kill other human beings.

As the months dragged on, he begged Odette to help him escape from France and return to England. "We aren't far from the channel," he fretted. "Why can't I get a small boat . . . even a rowboat, for Chrissakes . . ."

"Impossible, Tony. The fortifications between here and the coast are formidable. Day and night the Germans observe every inch of the shore. You would be discovered at once."

"Don't you know anyone who can help me get to Portugal?" he wheedled. "When two buddies of mine were shot down near La Rochelle last year, a guy in the French resistance took them over the border to Spain and then bribed some Basques to get them into Portugal. From there my friends flew back to England."

"Ah, my young friend, it is quite impossible. Am I suddenly a magician? I am an old woman without political connections. There are no *maquis* here, no resistance, none of de Gaulle's Free French underground fighters, at least none that I know of. No, Tony dear, you simply must be patient."

"Then let me walk at night in the forest. I'm going crazy, cooped up—"

"Tony, please. The Germans have patrols in the forest."

"Patrols? What *for*, in this godforsaken place?"

She was silent for a moment, regarding him with worried eyes. "Fouzille is not far from the sea, and the Germans are getting nervous, *mon ami*. They are bringing in many more of their soldiers. They think, soon the Allies will land near here. They think, what if American or British or Free French paratroopers come down and attack them? Ah, Tony, I understand how you feel. You are young, and strong, and restless. But you are safe here. If you are discovered, they will only send you to a camp for prisoners of war. But *me* they will shoot for harboring you, along with ten innocent villagers! So, *mon petit chou*, I beg you. Please! I very much wish to live, if only to see the Germans thrown out of France. Do not do anything foolish."

In early March, the Allied bombings of Normandy began in earnest. Tony was amazed at how much his ears could tell him. First he heard the heavy pounding of a railroad bridge that crossed the Orne River near Fouzille, and Odette afterward confirmed this, jubilantly telling him that the Germans now had to transfer their shipments by boat or truck from the trains on one side of the river, and then reload them onto other trains on the opposite bank.

A few weeks later, Tony surmised that all train traffic had ceased, for he no longer heard the rumble. Now, Odette informed him, the Germans had to ship everything by truck because the rail lines and their rolling stock had been so badly demolished by Allied bombers. Tony could hear the constant roar of truck convoys on the highway outside of the village, and often he was treated to the sound of American and British fighter planes strafing the trucks. Soon the highway became very quiet during the daylight hours, and he heard, instead, the convoys cautiously coming through only at night, to avoid being strafed.

"I think the invasion will be very soon," Odette whispered to him on the first day of June.

"Why are you whispering?" He whispered too, although with the window closed it was usually quite safe for them to speak normally.

"Because everyone here is very nervous, *mon ami*. We fear the Germans are planning to make much trouble at the last minute for us villagers. There is a rumor that the Boche will round us all up and shoot us before they leave. It is not beyond possibility. Also, we fear we will be shelled when the fighting starts, if the Allies land near here. Daily there are rumors, rumors, rumors! 'Paratroopers have landed in the forest,' someone whispers when we pass on the street. But it is what you call a false alarm. Then we hear bombs, not far away. 'Ah, they have landed! They have landed at last!' my neighbor says. But it is another false assumption. I am afraid when it actually happens, no one will pay any attention. It is like the little girl who cried 'Wolf!' Or was it a little boy?"

A few nights later, Tony suddenly awakened around midnight. When he looked out the window—it was a miserable drizzly night—he saw movement above the forest. He realized with a pounding heart that he was looking at a polka-dot sky, and the polka dots were . . . parachutes! He suppressed a shout, but quickly dressed in the gray pants and shirt that he had inherited from Odette's husband.

It was his intention to run into the forest to meet the Allied paratroops so that he could lead them back to Fouzille without delay. They could quickly capture it and liberate its people while most of the Germans slept. Oh, how he and Odette would celebrate! She had told him that she had a bottle of champagne and a tin of caviar hidden away for the day the Germans were thrown out of Fouzille.

Quietly he opened the window of his tiny room and climbed over the sill, letting his bare feet find the shingles of the sharply pitched porch roof, then sliding down into a lilac bush that broke his fall. He began running across the meadow toward the forest, taking delicious deep-deep breaths of the wonderfully fresh damp air, when a guttural voice rasped through the dark: *"Achtung! Halt!"* Tony kept running, propelled by sheer terror. He heard the thud of booted feet behind him, a dozen at least, and realized he had been seen coming out of Odette's house not by just one German soldier but by a whole fucking patrol!

When he reached the dark forest, he dared look back, and he saw that they had given up chasing him, no doubt figuring that he would be hard to find among the trees. But they were hammering on Odette's door, shouting for her to open it, and hollering in both German and French that she was a traitor for hiding an enemy of the Third Reich.

Tony heard a crash as he kept running, and he realized that they had knocked down Odette's door. Tears were streaming down his face, mixing with the light rain, and he bellowed in misery, but he kept running. The paratroopers were his only hope. He had to find them and get them to stop the Germans before they shot Odette.

But the Allied troops were farther into the forest than he had expected. He ran, slithering in the mud, bumping into tree trunks, sobbing now, shouting hoarsely for help. In the distance he heard Odette's terrified screams, and then shots rang out and her shrieks stopped abruptly.

The American paratroopers found him flat on his face. He had tripped over a gnarled root and had fallen, and when they helped him up, he babbled and stared at them with as much dazed confusion on his muddy, bleeding face as though they were men from Mars.

CHAPTER
12

1944

It was noon on a golden October day when Ginger steered her white Oldsmobile off Wilshire Boulevard and onto the long driveway of the Ambassador Hotel. She was tired after the trip from Palm Springs to Los Angeles, and she was disconsolate because at the last minute Avery had decided to stay home, feeling a sore throat coming on. It had become their little private joke to always reserve the bridal suite when they traveled. And even though Ginger was there to attend a three-day California Hotel Association seminar on "Looking ahead to a postwar travel boom," she had planned to put in only the most perfunctory appearances at the meetings and spend most of the time enjoying the city with Avery.

She would have canceled the trip altogether, but she had promised to conduct a special symposium on small, elegant hotels and she didn't want to disappoint the seminar chairman, who himself often had been a guest at The Springs. So she resigned herself to staying for just the one night, getting through her symposium in the morning, and then heading back home after lunch. She slid out of the driver's seat and handed the car keys to the doorman, feeling a little foolish about registering alone for the bridal suite.

She ordered a tuna salad and a bottle of beer from room service. Sitting alone eating in the suite's ornate living room, she turned on the radio and listened to the news. After a Chiquita Banana singing commercial she learned the dismaying news that the British toehold across

331

the Rhine had been wiped out by the Germans. The marines on Saipan were fighting against strong resistance. She snapped off the radio. At least Tony was safe at Letterman Army Hospital up near San Francisco. Safe in body, if not in spirit.

She took a long nap. In the late afternoon she decided to wander through the hotel's shopping arcade, hoping to find a present for Jiminy. While staring into the window of the toy store, she saw Jason on the other side of the glass. He was pointing out a handsome red fire truck to a salesman. She felt a sudden choking panic and she drew back, ready to run. But their eyes met and it was too late for her to retreat gracefully. He waved, a friendly gesture, and Ginger's fear of having to talk to him slowly began to fade. After all, four years had passed since their divorce, and Ella kept assuring Ginger that Jason's anger toward her had largely subsided.

He told Ginger that he was in town to give two lectures, one at USC, which he had presented that morning, and another the next morning at Occidental College.

"My symposium's tomorrow morning too," she said. "And then I'm going home. You need a ride?"

He shook his head. "I drove in too."

"Too bad. We could've driven in together and pooled gas coupons."

They were both well aware that they never would have arranged a trip together, even if they *had* known in advance that they both would be driving to L.A.

He grinned. "Do you still swear like a trouper when you drive?"

She nodded guiltily. "I can't help it. It offends my sense of justice when someone cuts in on me. Besides, I still resent the automobile."

"Me too. I was happier in the days when we went everywhere on foot or on a horse. At the worst, on a bicycle."

While he helped her choose an Indian doll and a coloring book for Jiminy, Ginger realized that Jason seemed totally at ease with her and she began to relax too. It was almost as if the last four years hadn't happened, and they were simply having fun shopping together, as they had done countless times during their marriage.

"What are you doing for dinner?" he asked.

"Well, the Hotel Association is having a dinner here at the hotel—"

"Chicken croquettes, mashed potatoes, and peas?"

"Probably."

"Speeches?"

"Undoubtedly."

"I have a much better idea, Ginger. Perino's is just down the street."

"Mmmmm. Isn't it a bit late to get a reservation?"

"I know the headwaiter," Jason said. "He's a great admirer of Ella's."

Ginger was increasingly surprised at how easy it was for them to be together. They took a long walk down Wilshire Boulevard to Westlake Park, they came back and had a drink at the hotel bar, they parted to dress for dinner, and it seemed perfectly natural for him to take her arm as they strolled over to the restaurant. Matching strides, they walked well together, always had. Jason was not as tall as Avery, with whom Ginger sometimes had to take a few extra-fast steps to keep up.

Jason noticed that most of the other restaurant patrons looked at them approvingly as they were led to their table. They had always been an attractive couple, enhancing their good looks with their healthy color and high spirits. Ginger was especially lovely this evening in a low-cut blue chiffon gown that gracefully swirled around her legs as she walked ahead of him in her usual forthright manner. He loved her in blue. Ah, well, he thought forlornly, he loved her in anything. Or even better, without anything.

They talked and laughed and enjoyed the dinner like good old friends, which in some ways they certainly were. They exchanged stories about Todd and Jiminy, about their present activities, about Tony's imminent medical discharge from the neuropsychiatric ward of Letterman Army Hospital in San Francisco, about Cal's phenomenal combat record, for which he had received a field commission and was now a first lieutenant. But though they talked about many subjects, neither Ginger nor Jason dared mention anything about their eight and a half years together as husband and wife.

"I went up to see Tony two weeks ago," Jason told Ginger. "He looks pretty good."

Ginger nodded. "Avery and I took the train up last week. Tony told me you've been coming up to see him every other week."

"Yeah. I hope you don't mind, Ginger, but . . . I'll always consider him my son." Jason hesitated. "He's not completely cured, you know," he added cautiously. "Far from it."

"I know." Ginger's lips trembled. "I don't think he'll ever get over feeling guilty about Odette's death."

"Well, maybe marrying Jennie will help. He's pretty excited about it." He paused. "Ella and I have been wondering—are we going to be invited to the wedding?"

Ginger stared at him in surprise. "Didn't Tony tell you? He wants you to be his best man."

Jason grinned, vastly pleased. "He does?" He looked carefully at Ginger. "Tell me . . . does Avery mind?"

"No, not at all. Avery thinks you've been an absolutely marvelous father to Tony."

"About Ella and me, Ginger—"

She held up a hand. "Please, Jason. You don't owe me any explanations."

"I know. But I still want to tell you. We both want to raise Todd, so the only practical way we can do it is by living together. But believe me, it's no great love affair. It's just . . . comfortable."

"I'm glad it's working out so well, Jason."

Yeah, he thought with a touch of bitterness, *it's easy for you to be magnanimous. You've got what you want.*

Returning to the hotel, Jason suddenly stopped walking and put his arms around her. His mouth took possession of hers, and she felt her earlier panic grab her again and then slowly abate as the memory of all their years of wonderfully playful lovemaking washed over her. He kept his arm around her waist when they continued up the long walkway to the hotel entrance, and she made no objection when he accompanied her in the elevator to her suite. They kissed again inside the living room, more fervently this time.

"Ginger," he implored, "let's make love."

She still adored this delightful man with whom she had been happy for such a long time. Just as she had felt, when she and Avery first became lovers, that part of her had always belonged to Avery, so she now felt that a part of her always would be Jason's. She decided to do as he asked, to help make up to him for all the misery she had caused him, and also because she herself wanted to share again, if only briefly, what they once had had.

"Well," she murmured, smiling up into his eyes, "if you're sure it won't reopen old wounds."

"No," he promised. "I won't let it."

"All right, then."

She let him undress her slowly, as he always had loved doing. He kissed each part of her as it became exposed. He lingered over her breasts, tracing with his fingertips the faint blue veins he remembered so well. He gently licked her delicate pink nipples while she shivered with little gasps of pleasure. She began to caress his still-youthful tanned body too, helping him unbutton and throw off his clothes.

Welcome back! his body silently rejoiced as they surged together. Their eight and a half years of throbbing unions were replayed in all their glory in this one bittersweet reunion. They called out softly to each other—*"A-a-ah, Jason,"*—*"O-o-oh Ginger"*—their voices groaning with passion and then suddenly with regret until they had to lock their trembling mouths together, desperately, to keep the threat of grief and tears from ruining their pleasure.

They were left spent and gasping for breath, as though spewed out of a churning cement mixer onto the sheets. *My God, it's all still there,* Jason thought, dazed, not knowing whether to exult or mourn. They both wanted to laugh and cry, and they clung to each other in gratitude and in consternation, she afraid of hurting him again, and he dreadfully aware that once more she was going to abandon him.

Ginger fell asleep, but Jason forced himself to stay awake. He didn't want to waste this precious night sleeping. Instead, he listened to her breathing and watched her serene face in the dim city night-light that filtered through the draperies. He held her close, his lips in her hair, and he tried to convince himself that he must stop loving her.

The euphoria he had felt before their lovemaking was gradually replaced by melancholy. His pain at losing her again was livid, but at least now it was without anger. He couldn't stay angry forever; it was against his gentle nature. He kept dozing, but each time he forced himself awake, wanting to be aware of every minute they spent together. It might be the last time in their lives they would be like this.

Ginger awoke refreshed, as she always did, just before dawn, only to find Jason already snugly inside of her. They shared a pleasant, quiet, unremarkable little orgasm, nothing like the previous night's cataclysm, and then, both of them in a subdued mood, they took a quick shower together and got dressed and had breakfast sent up. They found they weren't at all hungry and they didn't feel like talking. What could they say that wouldn't spoil what had occurred last night between them? They both knew, without any need for discussion, that it couldn't happen again.

Just before Jason left to change clothes in his own room and give his lecture at Occidental College, Ginger reached up and ran her hands through his unruly curls, then pulled his tired, troubled face down to hers and gently kissed his lips. She released him and stepped back. Fleetingly she wondered what his life would have been like if they had never met. Would he have been any happier now? "Are we friends?" she asked uncertainly, still terrified of hurting him.

He looked down at her, seriously considering her question. Finally he sighed deeply and shook his head. "You know that's not possible," he said sadly.

Avery had just put Jiminy down for a nap when he heard Ginger's car in the driveway. By the time he went out to greet her, she was standing beside the car's open trunk taking out packages. He knew that something unusual had happened to her as soon as she turned to him with a smile and a kiss—he was that attuned to every nuance of her facial expressions. He waited all afternoon and evening for her to tell him what it was. By the time they went to bed he was afraid that she wasn't going to tell him after all.

He was miffed—unreasonably so, he admitted to himself. She had every right to some privacy in her life. There was no reason in the world why she had to tell him every last thing that happened to her. But he was torn between curiosity and concern. She didn't seem upset, or even unhappy. Only . . . unusually thoughtful.

His sore throat had never materialized and he decided that the scratchiness in his throat had been caused by his having swallowed some sharp food without properly chewing it. So he kissed her with impunity, deeply, and she responded fervently, and they made love with all their usual heady rapture. He was relieved that, at any rate, whatever had befallen her wasn't interfering with their physical intimacy.

He kept telling himself to forget it, that it couldn't have been anything important. But perversely, his mind wouldn't let go of it, and he was becoming obsessed by it. If it hadn't been anything important, then why the hell didn't she just go ahead and tell him about it? Conversely, if it *had* been important, then certainly she *should* tell him, shouldn't she? Had someone at the convention made a serious pass at her? But he knew that would only have amused her and she would have reported it to him with a wry sort of conceit. Men often looked at her admiringly, but the security of her happy marriage gave her a "hands-off" aura.

In the morning, as they climbed up their trail, he kept peering at her face, searching for clues. Maybe her seminar had gone badly and she was ashamed to admit it. But he dismissed that possibility, knowing that her knowledge of the subject was too complete for her to have failed. Besides, she would have shared something like that with him right away.

They were standing side by side at their favorite lookout point when she turned to him and put her hands on his shoulders. "Relax!" she said firmly, a cross between a suggestion and an order.

He waited for more, but she turned away and squinted out at the view. "Did you ever see the Santa Rosas look so shockingly *pink*?" she asked.

"Never," he replied absently, realizing with reluctant resignation that she wasn't going to tell him anything after all.

Ella brought Todd over that afternoon to play with Jiminy. Todd was proudly carrying his new red fire truck. "Issa pwesent from Gwanpa," he told Jiminy.

"I got *two* pwesents from my mommy," Jiminy bragged, running to get her Indian doll and coloring book.

Ella laughed. "Jason was in L.A. for a couple of days. Lecturing, as usual. He says the toy store at the Ambassador is absolutely *stuffed* with goodies, the best he's seen since the war started."

Avery turned and stared at Ginger with flash bulbs going off in his piercing blue eyes.

"I know," Ginger said lightly. "I ran into Jason there. He helped me pick out Jiminy's presents."

Ella turned speculative eyes on Ginger. "Oh? He didn't mention seeing you."

Ginger shrugged. "Well, it was no big deal. We managed to be civil to each other for the few minutes it took to buy the toys."

The sisters gave their attention to the two three-year-olds, who were sharing their new possessions like little angels. Todd and Jiminy had been playing together almost daily for a year now, and were more like siblings than cousins. They fought and hit each other and made up and always hugged and kissed when they parted.

Ginger was aware of Avery's eyes still on her, full of questions and conjecture. Okay, now he knew that she had seen Jason. She realized that he was puzzled that she hadn't mentioned it to him. She also realized that he was wondering . . . well, she knew *exactly* what he was wondering . . . and it really was none of his business. Nevertheless, for some perverse reason, his jealousy pleased her.

But she had to be fair. Wouldn't she be jealous if he had been out of town without her and had run into an old flame? Wouldn't she be wondering if he had gone to bed with the woman for auld lang syne?

"Did you see Jason again?" he asked in a low voice as soon as Ella and Todd left. "*After* the toy shop?"

She gave him a reproachful look. "Avery!" she chided.

"Dammit, Ginger! It's not as though you're above committing adultery!"

She stared at him, shocked at his cruelty.

"I'm sorry!" Contritely he held her close, stroking the back of her head. "I don't know what's gotten into me. Plain old jealousy, I guess."

"Jealous of poor old Jason? Are you out of your *mind*?"

She raised up on tiptoes and kissed Avery lightly on the cheek. "It's all right, darling. I guess I'd be jealous too, if the situation were reversed."

He didn't mention it again. But every now and then he looked at her with great big question marks in his eyes.

Tony came home in November to something of a hero's welcome. Everyone, including his mother and Avery, treated him as though he were made of spun glass. Even three-year-old Jiminy was in awe of him. Only Jason seemed able to relax and treat him as he always had.

Tony found himself constantly cross with Ginger, despite all his vows back in Fouzille that if he got out of there alive, he would never hurt her again. He loved her and thought she was a beautiful, wonderful woman. He was proud of her, proud to be her son. Whenever he spoke sharply to her, and saw the pain in her eyes, he wanted to throw himself down on his knees and apologize. But he couldn't. Instead, he only made things worse by getting angrier and stomping out of the room.

He knew he was still sick. His psychiatrist at the Army hospital had been reluctant to discharge him, but Avery and Ginger had felt that Tony would be better off with a civilian doctor in a nonhospital setting. And Tony had agreed wholeheartedly, eager to get out of the military atmosphere.

He was happy to be back in the desert. He felt exhilarated when he was on his horse, roaming freely, or hiking up good old Mt. San Jacinto with his mother and Avery, or visiting Jason, which he did almost daily. But as soon as he was alone, he started to brood again. Nights, he was always back in Fouzille. Sometimes it was all right, when he dreamt that he and Odette were doing some pleasant chore together. But other nights he would be running through the forest, hearing Odette's screams.

Jennie was in the Pacific with the USO. She had visited him at Letterman before leaving, and they were planning a Christmas wedding in Palm Springs. They were going to be married in the gardens of Nellie's Desert Inn, as his own parents had been. For their honeymoon they were taking the *Super Chief* to New York, where Jennie had to make personal appearances for her latest film. Beyond that, they had made no plans. "We can talk about it on the train," was all Jennie would say.

"I'm sorry Cal won't be here," Tony said to Ginger one day two weeks before Christmas. They were riding together in Tahquitz Canyon.

"Let's rest awhile," Ginger suggested, dismounting and sitting on a rock facing the waterfall. When Tony joined her, she took his hand and looked into his eyes. Her mother's heart contracted with worry whenever she saw the sorrow in his eyes. He still had his hospital pallor, which made him look flat, washed-out, too thin, older than his twenty-three years. She hoped that what she was about to tell him would cheer him up. "I want to talk to you about Cal," she said.

"Is he okay?"

"Yes, last I heard. He writes to me quite often." She hesitated. "Tony, Cal is more than your cousin." She took a deep breath. "Frank Ricardo wasn't his father."

He watched her warily, waiting for her to continue.

The words seemed wrenched out of her. "As you know, Cal is two months younger than you are. What happened was that . . . Ella and your father . . ." She couldn't go on.

He swallowed painfully and stared at the waterfall as though it might save his life. *Don't let her say it,* he prayed. *Don't let it be true.*

"What I'm trying to say, Tony, is that Cal is your half-brother."

"I see." He cleared his throat. "So my father wasn't such a saint after all," he said harshly.

"Oh, Tony. Don't take it that way. Tonito really was a very good person. It was mostly Ella's fault. She was pretty irresistible then . . ." She let go of his hand. "Aren't you glad to have a brother? Cal loves the idea."

"He knows?"

"Oh, sure. Ella told him ages ago."

"He never let on."

"No. He didn't think it was his place to tell you." Ginger tried unsuccessfully to smile. "Tony. Please. Say it's all right."

"Sure," he said flatly. What could he say? People hopped from bed to bed, from partner to partner. His father, the saint, succumbing to Aunt Ella. His own mother, falling in love with Avery when she was happily married to Jason. And, Tony warned himself, he was goddamn stupid if he thought Jennie was always going to be faithful to him, if she hadn't already been screwing every male in Hollywood.

He turned over in his mind the concept of Cal being his brother. His *half*-brother. He had been perfectly content having Cal as a cousin. A brother was something else. A responsibility. You're supposed to love your brother. He didn't know if he *could* love Cal. He wasn't even sure he wanted to try.

He wondered if there was anyone in the world he could trust. Yes, there was Jason. Good old Jason. Jason never let him down. And there had been Odette. They had trusted each other with their lives. Sure. So he could get her killed.

He raised his stricken eyes to Ginger's face. Smug lady. Everything was *her* fault. She had never really loved him. Her eyes never ignited with maternal love when she looked at him, the way they did when she talked about her firstborn, Johnny, or when she hugged Jiminy. Oh, he hated her! He wished he could hurt her somehow.

He stood up and mounted his horse. There was a horrible ringing in his ears. He wanted to be flying. He realized that it was more than a year since he had been shot down. All that time without being at the controls of a plane. No wonder he felt sick all the time.

He felt better by the following week, when Jennie arrived looking more beautiful than ever. She traveled now with an entourage. Her parents. Her business manager. Her agent. Two secretaries. Her hairdresser. Her makeup artist. Her personal maid. Sometimes her lawyer. They were all staying at the Desert Inn because she didn't want to open her Italianate villa for just a few days. It was too difficult to get temporary servants in wartime.

"Darling, everybody, just *everybody* in Hollywood's coming to the wedding," she bubbled to Tony in her hotel suite the first night she was back. She kissed him. "Honey-bug, I can't wait till you see my wedding present for you."

He looked around her suite. "Where is it?"

She giggled. "It's not here, sweetie. I'll show you in the morning."

When they made love he felt awkward, like a machine that needed oiling. "Ooooh, you *are* rusty," she laughed softly. "So am I, darling. I was utterly faithful to you. Like a nun. But we'll have plenty of time to practice."

The next morning she drove him to the Palm Springs airport and stopped her red Cord convertible on the tarmac next to a blue-and-white Navion. "It's all yours," she sang out gaily.

He got out of the car and ran his hand along the sleek metal wings. *His!* He felt dizzy. Almost nauseous. Too much excitement. "I'll take you up later," he promised. "After lunch."

"Sure." She hugged him. "Darling, I'm sorry it's not brand-new. But it's completely reconditioned. There just aren't any new ones around, 'cause the aviation companies are only making military planes."

"I don't care, Jen. It's simply gorgeous. I can't wait to get my hands on the controls."

"And, Tony-love," she warned, "it's murder getting gas for private planes. I got an Army mechanic to steal enough to fill the tank. But after that . . ." She shrugged. "You might have to wait till the war's over."

Driving back to his house, she stopped the car under a row of tamarisk trees on Indian Avenue. "Confession time," she said, fixing her big blue eyes on him. "Honey, I did have one tiny little affair. With this English actor in my last picture. The studio absolutely *made* me do it, for publicity. Honestly, it didn't mean a thing."

"Then why are you telling me?" he asked, feeling like he was falling from the sky without a parachute.

"I think we should be totally honest with each other." She took his hand. "Darling, didn't you make love to any Frenchwomen while you were over there? Or any of those pretty British girls?"

He shook his head, drowning in misery.

"Well, you don't have to tell me if you don't want to," she said tartly.

"There's nothing to tell."

"I'll bet! The only reason I let the studio talk me into it was that I was so sure that *you* were screwing around too." She was miffed at him, at his refusal to "confess."

"Listen," he said, "there's something I want to tell *you*." He cleared his throat nervously. "As soon as we're married, I want you to quit making movies."

"Are you *crazy*?"

"I want a family, Jennie. Lots of kids. A big house. That's all I dreamed about, those terrible months when I was hiding from the Germans."

"No, Tony. Maybe in a few years, but not now. It's unfair of you to even ask." She turned on the motor and drove up the street so fast that the tires howled.

After lunch, Tony told Ginger and Avery that he was taking Jennie up in the Navion. "I'll buzz the house so you can see it. It's a beaut."

"Where are you going?" Ginger asked, hiding her fury at Jennie for buying him a plane when Ginger kept praying that he would give up flying.

"Nowhere. I just want to fly around for a while, for the fun of it."

Ginger kissed them both and watched them leave before she went upstairs to put Jiminy down for her nap. She decided she would rest too, as soon as Tony buzzed the house. She was unusually tired, and more than a little dispirited. Tony was far from well, and she had grave doubts about the wisdom of his getting married while he still needed psychiatric help. She couldn't stand the way he looked at her. So hostile. And at the same time so needy.

She looked down at little Jiminy as they mounted the stairs together. She prayed that this one would never give her any pain, although she knew there was bound to be some. Right now, at three, Jiminy was pure pleasure, even when she was being difficult and arguing with her parents. She was simply too adorable for Ginger and Avery to worry yet about her headstrong tendencies.

"I wanna see Tony's pwane," Jiminy said, stopping halfway up the stairs, hands on hips.

"Tomorrow," Ginger promised. "It's late for your nap now."

For once, Jiminy didn't argue. She yawned sleepily and lay down on her bed.

Ginger went out onto her bedroom balcony and scanned the sky for Tony's plane. She could see a white speck taking off from the airport, and while waiting for it to gain altitude, she waved at Avery, down in the garden, also waiting to see the plane.

They both looked up when they heard the drone of the approaching engine. Tony zoomed the blue-and-white plane over their rooftop—far too low for comfort! Ginger held her breath while Tony made a slow, lazy circle through the brilliantly blue early-afternoon sky and came back over the roof with a roar that made the whole house shake. Then he gained altitude, like a graceful swan, and flew east again, away from the house. Once more, he made a slow circle and came back toward them. Ginger thought he was going to buzz them a third time, but instead, he stayed high above the house, heading west toward the mountain. She waited for him to circle north again, but he kept flying straight toward San Jacinto. "Avery!" Ginger shrieked.

They watched in horror, both of them screaming, as the plane smashed into San Jacinto two thousand feet above them. They watched, still screaming, as the plane became a ball of flame. Then, like a slow-motion film, pieces of burning debris lazily cartwheeled down the steep side of the mountain, coming to rest on a ledge high above Palm Springs.

Ginger didn't hear Avery bound up the stairs. She hardly noticed when he led her off the balcony and back into the house. She didn't hear anything at all, except the roar inside her head that deafened her and finally turned the world black.

The press called it an accident. They blamed it on a malfunction of the plane's instrumentation. All over the country, people mourned for their beautiful Jennie and her hero sweetheart. Accompanied by poignant photographs of them taken in happier days, sob stories about Jennie and Tony were splashed over every newspaper and magazine in the country. Oh, the tragedy of it, the journalists and studio press agents wrote, that it should have happened to these two beautiful young people so soon before their wedding. Oh, how ironic that Tony, who had survived being shot down in combat and who had valiantly eluded the Germans for months, should die in an accident now. It was weeks before the press stopped running articles about the "accident."

Ginger and Avery knew better. But they kept their knowledge to themselves. It was much easier to make believe with the rest of the world that it *had* been an accident than to acknowledge that Tony had committed suicide and had taken poor, innocent Jennie with him.

Ginger and Avery worried about Jiminy's reaction to Tony's death. Ella had come right over, as soon as Avery phoned Jason with the news, and had taken Jiminy home with her. The next day, when Avery went to pick her up, he heard Jiminy explain to Todd that "God took my bwother Tony and his pwetty Jennie and they're angels in heaven now." Avery didn't know where Jiminy had gotten that idea—most likely from Todd's nursemaid, Clara, or maybe even from Ella. After all, what *did* you tell a three-year-old about death? Both Ginger and Avery were a little uncomfortable with this evasion of the truth, but they decided to let it go, afraid that further discussion would do Jiminy more harm than good.

Jason was as shaken as they were by Tony's death. At the funeral he came and sat next to Ginger, holding her right hand while Avery held her left. It seemed right for him to be there with them. Later, after they had buried Tony next to Tonito and Johnny, Jason came home with them and, taking turns with Avery, held Ginger in his arms while she cried uncontrollably. At one point, while an exhausted Ginger napped, Jason and Avery embraced each other and cried together in the frenzy of their own bereavement and the torture of watching the woman they both loved suffer such ferocious grief.

Their intimacy born of sorrow didn't last beyond the first few days of intense mourning. Then Jason withdrew to his former stance of having nothing to do with his ex-wife and her present husband. In time, life returned to some semblance of "normal." Ella continued to bring Todd to the pink mansion to play with Jiminy almost every day. When Ginger recovered from her bereavement enough to go out again, sometimes she and Avery would see Ella and Jason across the room at some social function. They would wave and nod, but never speak to each other when all four of them were present.

Ginger would have liked to be friends with Jason, but she knew that he was still too bitter about her abandonment of him. And she couldn't blame him. He had always been wonderful to her, had done everything in his power to make her happy, and she had destroyed it all. But she couldn't feel guilty. She belonged to Avery, body and soul, and if anything had been a mistake, it had been her marriage to Jason.

Christmas in the pink mansion was sad that year, as it was in much of the country. The American people were shocked by the unexpected German counterattack in Belgium, which the press called "The Battle of the Bulge." It had caught the public by surprise, at a time when everyone had been confident that the war soon would be over.

Ginger had bought her presents early, but she didn't have the heart to wrap them. She was too weepy to bother with a tree. Still, she didn't want to rob Jiminy of the holiday completely.

"Mommy is very sad because Tony isn't here anymore," Ginger told Jiminy.

"Is Daddy sad too?" Jiminy asked, knowing full well from his face that he was.

Ginger nodded. "So, sweetheart, you can go have Christmas with Todd and Aunt Ella and Uncle Jason at their house. Okay?"

"Okay."

Avery took Jiminy there Christmas morning, along with her presents for Todd. When Avery returned home he found Ginger sadly packing away the things she had bought for Tony and Jennie. She had Christmas gifts for both of them—expensive matching gold-and-diamond watches. A new camera was a belated birthday present for Tony. Their wedding present sat in a set of matching royal-blue velvet boxes: Ginger had commissioned a local Agua Caliente artist to make twenty-four six-piece cutlery place settings in sterling silver. The knives, forks, and spoons were fitted with ceramic handles, each of which was hand-painted in a different Cahuilla Indian design. There was also a matching set of fifteen serving pieces.

"What'll I do with them?" she asked Avery helplessly, waving at the silverware. "I can't bear the sight of them. But they're too beautiful to throw away. Or even give away."

He sighed. "You don't have to decide today, darling. Let me put them in the storage room for now."

She ran her hand over the velvet boxes and burst into fresh tears. She clung to Avery as he sat beside her trying to comfort her. Her grief was laced with guilt. She was sure that every suicide's mother felt responsible. *What did I do wrong?* had to be their theme song. She knew that being a parent seldom was easy. Her own parents' performance had been riddled with mistakes and she was sure that inadvertently she and Avery would make plenty of blunders with Jiminy.

She ran out of tears and tightened her hold on Avery. "Don't let go," she implored.

"I won't."

They sat that way, silently, rocking slightly in their joint misery. She knew the misery would pass, that life would be good again, would even be wonderful again—someday. She and Avery still had each other. They had Jiminy. They had more money than they ever could spend. Soon the Army would return her beautiful little hotel to her and she would have the pleasure of refurbishing it and making it better than ever.

Avery stroked her face and kissed her, trying wordlessly to remind her of the one unalterable truth in their lives: he loved her!

CHAPTER
13

The 1950's

One day in 1951, Ginger and Avery were invited by Ginger's friend and former sister-in-law Maria to watch the burning of the Tribal Big House. It was the round structure where, thirty years earlier, Ginger had sat through the Ceremony for the Dead for Tonito and Johnny. She still remembered vividly how Avery had comforted her during the long hours she had suffered in the smoke-filled room, watching the effigies of her husband and baby.

"We're burning it down because we've become too Americanized to use it properly anymore," Maria explained. "Too much intermarriage . . ." She shoved a playful elbow into Vittorio's ribs. "Will you tell me how I got Americanized by marrying an Italian?" Then she sighed. "So, now that Al Patencio's dead, there's no one left who knows enough about the old customs and ceremonies to take his place as tribal chief. From now on, our chief will be more of a political leader than a spiritual one."

And so Ginger and Avery stood beside Maria and Vittorio and watched the flames consume the old thatch-roofed building, thus ending an era that few people with even a drop of Agua Caliente Indian blood could relinquish without a sigh of regret.

Ginger walked away filled with sorrow. Tonito's hopes of legally dividing the reservation land among the tribal members still were unfulfilled. The two sons she and Tonito had created both were dead. Now Tonito's only links with the future were Cal and Todd, and Ginger wondered if Tonito ever would have a descendant truly worthy of him.

Ginger and Avery returned to Paris, with Jiminy, the summer before their sixteenth wedding anniversary. For Avery it was far more than a vacation visit to a city he loved; he constantly faced painful memories of having been there with Tony and Odette, and with friends who had disappeared during the war. Sometimes, walking down the familiar streets, he felt like a lover coming face-to-face with a charming mistress who had betrayed him.

He got goosebumps when he and Ginger and Jiminy were in a taxi on the Boulevard Raspail and the driver pointed out a hotel near the Bon Marché department store. "There," the man said matter-of-factly in French, "the Nazi S.S. tortured its victims." In his vivid imagination, Avery heard screams of agony echo along the carpeted corridors. It seemed impossible, unreal, as though the driver were talking about a horror film he once had seen. The day was too balmy, the sky too bright, the trees along the boulevard throwing too heart-stirring a dancing dappled shade for any cruelty ever to have taken place there. But it had. It had.

Avery reminded himself that this was a very old city, with centuries of history, and for all the years of tragedy there had been decades and decades of peaceful, vigorously creative life. Had the Revolution been any less revolting than the Nazi occupation? But, he half-excused the eighteenth century French murderers, at least they thought they had an idealistic justification for their bloody excesses.

Being wholly wrapped up in the present, nearly fifteen-year-old Jiminy did not share her father's ambivalence toward the city. She fell in love with the narrow cobbled streets of the Marais and St. Germain, the broad romantic vistas along the Seine, and she squealed with excitement whenever they came upon monuments she recognized from books and her father's paintings.

Besides taking his wife and daughter to all the usual tourist attractions, Avery had his own secret gems to show them, little private parks hidden behind big wooden gates, old bas-reliefs on the sides of buildings, tiny cafés where English had never been spoken, all places he had discovered when he lived there two decades earlier, and some even remembered from his student days at the turn of the century. He was able to tell Ginger and Jiminy the history of the city's most famous buildings, from the grand old palaces of the French kings to the art-deco edifices of the early twentieth century.

The three of them took a leisurely trip by automobile through the Loire Valley to visit the *châteaux*. They enjoyed one-day excursions to see the cathedrals at Rouen and Reims and Chartres, and the palaces at Fontaine-bleau and Versailles. Little by little, Avery was able to shake off his sense of sorrow over the past and live more fully in the beatitude of the present.

He derived enormous enjoyment from watching Jiminy's enthusiastic reaction to the landmarks he himself dearly loved. This child constantly delighted him with her vivacity and intelligence and loving nature. She was so much like Ginger—with a good dose of his own genes contributing to her capabilities, he thought proudly. He never failed to be thankful for the miracle of her existence.

But one day in late July, as they sat resting in the Tuileries Garden, Jiminy became restless. "Why couldn't Todd come with *us* instead of going to Italy with Uncle Cal?" she asked petulantly.

"Honey, Cal isn't your uncle, he's your cousin," Ginger corrected her. "Anyway, Todd couldn't very well refuse to spend the summer with his father, could he? So you'll just have to be patient until they meet us here at the end of August."

"I know, but that's a whole month from now," Jiminy complained. "Everything's more fun with Todd."

Avery and Ginger exchanged a worried look. They were concerned because Jiminy and Todd were inseparable. It had been cute when they were small. In grammar school the two children had cried when they were put in different classrooms. After Todd joined a Peewee Little League baseball team that didn't allow girls on it, Jiminy had thrown a tantrum. When Jiminy became a Brownie Girl Scout and Todd couldn't attend meetings with her, *he* had thrown a tantrum. But now Ginger and Avery were alarmed, and so were Ella and Jason, because Jiminy and Todd were together all the time. They wanted no other friends, only each other.

Jiminy had her mother's wavy auburn hair and her father's vivid blue eyes. Her oval face with its straight nose, flared nostrils, and smooth lips was almost as perfect as her Aunt Ella's. But unlike Ella, and very much like Ginger, Jiminy was an excellent student with many interests. She devoured literature, got A's in science, played a mean game of tennis, and was a jazz pianist of great verve if not talent.

Todd, on the other hand, was interested only in Jiminy—and golf. Sometimes he would be goaded by her into reluctantly reading a book that wasn't required for school. Often Jiminy did his homework for him so he wouldn't fall behind. Only on a golf course did he come wholly alive, winning one junior championship after another at the various desert country clubs. He was exceptionally handsome, with curly dark blond hair, Jason's warm gray eyes, and an enchanting, cheerful smile. Girls and even women were beginning to pay a lot of attention to him, but he cared only about his Jiminy.

Their early childhood habit of hugging and kissing each other had stopped when they entered first grade. They remained playmates and best friends, with the understanding that eventually they would get married.

Now, with Jiminy in Paris and Todd touring Italy, they were apart for the first time in their lives, and she missed him. Still, after her initial outburst, Jiminy didn't mention him again to her parents. She was baffled by their obvious discomfort over her love for her cousin. She knew they liked him. So why did they disapprove of her friendship with him? *Parents!* she inwardly groaned, and thereafter kept her longing for Todd to herself.

Every afternoon, while her parents took a nap, Jiminy roamed the streets of Paris. She was adept at using the Métro trains, enjoying the cool underground respite from the summer heat. She flitted around the city like a native. Now she appreciated the hours she had spent studying French at her father's insistence, because she could speak with the French boys and girls she met in cafés when she stopped for a *citron*, and she had no trouble asking for directions when she occasionally got lost.

One day, while she was waiting to cross Rue Montaigne, a limousine came slowly down the street and she was surprised to see the former French president, Charles de Gaulle, riding by only a few feet away from her. She grinned and waved to him. Although she was accustomed to meeting celebrities at her mother's hotel, this was the first time she had been so close to a head of state, even a former one, and she was thrilled when his long, austere face broke into a broad smile and he waved back at her.

"I know you don't like his politics," she told Avery afterward, "but, Daddy, don't you admire what he did during the war?"

"Being a great soldier doesn't necessarily make you a great statesman," Avery grumbled disapprovingly.

By early August, when Todd and Cal reached Rome after visiting Venice and Florence and the Italian Riviera, they were heartily sick of each other. Neither had anything to say to the other, never had, and every day was a strain. Cal had suggested the trip to Italy partly out of a deep-seated feeling of guilt toward his son, and partly so that Todd could spend some time with Vivien, who now lived in Rome. Although Vivien hadn't seen her son since he was four, Cal had contrived over the years to spend short holidays and Christmas vacations with Todd in Palm Springs. Then, a few slick, expensive presents had passed as a substitute for fatherly interest.

Thank God for Ella and Jason, Cal said to himself a dozen times a day. This summer was the first time since Todd's birth that Ella and Jason hadn't been tied down taking care of the boy. Ella had rented a Bar Harbor waterfront mansion for two months of socializing with New York friends who summered there. Even after nearly twenty years of retirement, the former movie star still was asked for autographs by an adoring public and she continued to be the darling of newspaper gossip columnists. Jason meanwhile had opted to spend most of the summer hiking the long John Muir trail with two fellow members of the Sierra Club.

Vivien had long since divorced Cal and had married Enrico di Lullo, an Italian film director. She had met him three years earlier at the Cannes Film Festival, which she and some of her "show-biz" New York friends attended that year, and where Enrico had won an honorable mention for his first feature. Vivien had married him and moved to Rome after a two-week courtship.

Todd was nervous when Cal dropped him off in front of Vivien's apartment building near the Piazza Venezia for a two-week visit. Cal was going to drive up to Milan to visit a countess he knew there. "Hey, Dad, c'mon up with me," Todd beseeched, looking up at the old ocher stones of the forbidding facade.

Cal grinned and revved the motor of his rented Ferrari. "You and your mom can get to know each other better without me, kid." He zoomed away toward the river.

Todd picked up his suitcase and took the creaking cagelike elevator to the top floor, the fourth. A plump dark-haired maid let him in, unabashedly staring at him and clucking approvingly.

"Todd!" His mother swooped upon him and kissed both cheeks, twice. "Let me *look* at you!" She turned him around and then kissed him again.

He looked at her carefully too. She was an earthy woman in her early thirties with tawny curly hair and a rather plain face that she skillfully jazzed up with cosmetics. She had a tremendous flair with clothes, and although he was accustomed to exotic Hollywood types—he saw them all the time at the Racquet Club and hanging around all the Palm Springs country clubs—his mother looked exceptionally glamorous to him in her tight black pants and clinging white silk shirt and big dangling gold earrings.

"Hey, kid, you sure got the shit end of the stick when it came to parents," Vivien chortled in a throaty voice. "There isn't a maternal bone in me. And God knows, Cal's no prize daddy."

"Don't worry, Mom. Gram and Grandpa take good care of me."

"You're lucky, ducky. We're all lucky for that. Otherwise you'd have been raised by servants, like Cal was."

She seemed to like him well enough, and he was surprised that he liked her too. He had thought from the way Ella and Jason always talked about Vivien that he would find her unsympathetic. Only her photographs and Jason's efforts to remind him of her existence had kept her from fading from Todd's mind altogether.

Vivien put an arm around his shoulders and showed him through her lavish *apartamento*, which was surrounded on all four sides by a broad marble terrace. From there she pointed out to him the glittering dome of St. Peter's, the Tiber River, the Campidoglio, Piazza Venezia, and miles of rooftops. It looked like a fairyland to him.

"Where's your husband?" he asked.

"Shooting a cheap western in Yugoslavia."

"Won't I get to meet him?"

"Maybe next time, kiddo. If he and I are still trying to talk to each other." She hooted. "He no speaka da English, I no speaka da Italian."

Some nights Vivien took Todd to luxurious restaurants to meet her eclectic friends, ranging from Italian millionaires to American beatniks. Other nights they enjoyed quiet meals together, just the two of them, at the colorful Trastevere *trattorias* across the river, where she made him try all kinds of food he had never tasted before, not even at his Aunt Ginger's hotel, where the French chef prepared some pretty fancy dishes.

"Are you rich?" he asked Vivien one day.

She laughed. "Yeah. Thanks to your father. He paid a fortune to get rid of me."

"How about your new husband?"

"Enrico? *Merda!*" She made a very Italian gesture, hitting the bottom of her chin with her fingertips. She leaned close. "Tell me, kid, how's my dad?"

"Grandpa Jason? He's okay."

"Did he ever get over, you know, being jilted by Ginger?"

Todd wrinkled his brow. "Aunt Ginger? What d'you mean?"

She drew back. "*Madonna mia*—they never told you? He used to be married to her. Before she threw him over for old Doc Avery."

Todd sat very quietly, in shock. "I didn't know," he said quietly. "I'm sort of engaged to their daughter. Jiminy."

"Ginger and Avery's daughter?" Vivien gave an explosive laugh. "Oh, my God! If that isn't ironic!" She peered at him. "Aren't you a little young to be engaged? What the hell are you now? Fourteen? Fifteen?"

"Almost fifteen." He turned red. "Well, sure, it's young. We'll wait till we're eighteen, anyway."

"Listen, don't rush things. I got married when I was sixteen, but really, kid, I don't recommend it. It's just a goddamn miracle that *cazzo* Cal didn't completely ruin my life!" She reconsidered. "Thank God he was rich."

Every afternoon, Vivien left the apartment at one o'clock and returned at four. She always looked radiantly splendid to Todd when she went out, wearing a different outfit every day, her hair and makeup flawless.

"Where're you going?" he asked her as she headed for the door the first day he stayed with her.

"Business, kid. Monkey business." She gave him a wink. "And it's none of *your* business. Just tell your daddy I'm a late bloomer." She pointed toward the kitchen. "Go tell Rosalba to fix lunch for you."

He found the maid vacuuming his room. "Lunch?" he said.

She gave him a blank look.

He looked up "lunch" in the small English-Italian dictionary Vivien had given him. "*Colazione*," he said, mispronouncing it.

Rasalba thought a moment, and then her face lit up. "*Ah, si. Un momento.*" He noticed that her spectacular breasts jiggled when she moved. Unexpectedly, as she brushed past him to leave the room, she stopped and put her arms around him. She was shorter than he was, but strong. Giggling, she pushed him back onto the bed. "*Bello mio,*" she crooned, getting on top of him. She kissed him with quick darts of her tongue seeking his.

Her hands were all over him while her mouth held his like a vibrating suction cup. Deftly she pulled up her frilly white apron and black uniform and pushed down his pants and Jockey shorts without letting go of his lips. When she finally stopped her marathon kiss it was to shove a nipple into his mouth.

He didn't know what to do with it. Tentatively he licked it.

"*No, no,*" she panted. She put the tip of her finger in her mouth and vigorously sucked it. "*Com' questo!*"

He got the idea and found that it stirred him in the

groin when her nipple grew large and hard in his mouth. She was still on top of him but she rolled them both over so that he was above her and could move more easily from one breast to the other.

She grabbed his penis and fondled it. *"Oooh, che gran cazzo!"* she crooned. *"Che rigidità! Che forma!"* Again, he didn't know what to do when she grasped his engorged penis and slid it inside of her. But she showed him. She had strong muscles that squeezed him and let go, again and again, with increasing frenzy, until they both stiffened and fell screaming in a heap of quivering flesh.

For the entire two weeks, as soon as Vivien shut the door behind her at one o'clock, Todd rushed to his room, where he never failed to find Rosalba waiting for him with a lascivious grin, naked on his bed. During that period she taught him almost everything about sex that he would ever want to know.

The day after Cal returned to Rome, he and Todd took the overnight train to Paris. Todd spent most of the night in their compartment with the window shade raised a few inches. He lay on his side in the lower berth and watched the dark countryside swish past the window. Shivering with longing for Rosalba, he was having a difficult time accepting the fact that he probably never would see her again.

He was struggling to figure out how his tumultuous encounter with Rosalba would affect his relationship with Jiminy. When he thought about the Italian maid, his entire body rocked with desire for her. When he thought about Jiminy, he felt no physical reaction at all. And yet he wanted to *be* with Jiminy, every minute. He didn't feel complete unless they were together. She was his buddy, his best friend, his playmate, his mentor. He *loved* Jiminy, and he wanted to spend his whole life with her. He couldn't wait to see her. Just a few more hours!

He decided that when he got to Paris he would kiss Jiminy and see what happened. He hadn't kissed her since they were little kids. But no matter how he tried, he simply couldn't imagine doing the things with her that he had done with Rosalba. Never!

Cal was counting the hours too. He was eager to see Ginger, who was his favorite person in the world. How often he wished that she had been his mother instead of Ella! But then, they probably wouldn't be such good friends, since one seldom can confide in one's parents. Ginger had saved his sanity during the war with her affectionate letters.

When he left the Marine Corps after the war, he had started to wander around the world. Travel became his salvation and his vocation. The time he had spent in Samoa after he was wounded on Tarawa had given him an interest in seeing countries that tourists seldom visit. He liked to tell people back home that he had gone to a *fia-fia* in a *lava-lava*, and when they looked puzzled he would grin and explain to them that a *fia-fia* was a native Samoan feast and a *lava-lava* was a colorful wraparound skirt that the men wore.

After the war he wandered through places like Penang and Burma, Nepal and Afghanistan. He knew more about yak dung than he did about Rembrandt and Monet. He discovered South and Central America, and particularly Mexico, places where his ability to speak Spanish—which was as much his native tongue as English—gave him instant rapport with the people. He acquired a reputation, especially back home in Palm Springs, of being a poignantly romantic figure—a rich, handsome war hero roaming the world and looking for the meaning of life.

What people back home didn't know was that he had become deeply involved with groups seeking independence from oppressive regimes. He was wary of being used by the far left, and he hated the far right. He tried to make contact with men and women who were sincere lovers of freedom and civil rights so that he could secretly give them his financial support. But often his inability to take himself or the world too seriously made him seem a dilettante to the very people he was trying to help.

Women ran after him more urgently than ever. He used them sexually if they appealed to him, always being perfectly frank with them. If they wanted a brief fling with him, great, but the only promise he would make was that he would make no promises. What always amazed him when an affair ended was the anger the woman almost invariably felt toward him. No matter how honest he had been with her, she thought that she could change him. He not only never had fallen in love, he didn't even want to fall in love. He was thirty-four years old and fervently dedicated to his precious freedom.

At dinner the first night they were all together at the Paris Ritz, Todd turned to Ginger. "Hey, Aunt Ginger, my mom told me you used to be married to Grandpa Jason."

Everyone at the table stared at him in shocked silence. Finally Ginger nodded. "Yes, Todd. I'm surprised nobody ever told you before now."

He blushed and looked down at his plate, aware that he had blundered. "I'm sorry. I guess I shouldn't have mentioned it."

She reached over and patted his hand. "It's all right. Really. It's not a big dark secret."

Later, Todd and Jiminy went for a walk around the Place Vendôme. "Did you know about your mom and my grandpa?" he asked her, disgruntled that he had never been told.

"Sure."

He stopped walking and scowled at her. "Then how come you never told me?"

"Stop looking at me like that. It never occurred to me that you didn't know. I don't see why it should bother you."

"Well, when you and I get married, suppose that after a while you decide you want to marry someone else, like your mom did?"

"So?" Impatiently she flicked her fingers against his arm. "What're you trying to say, Todd? What's your point?"

"I'm just trying to say . . . I'd be so sad I'd go crazy. So I can't help thinking that my grandfather must've felt the same way."

"Well, even if he did, there's nothing you can do about it, is there?"

"No, but if you love someone, you don't want them to be sad. Like . . . what if it was *your* father who'd gotten dumped? Wouldn't you feel awful for him?"

She put her hands on Todd's shoulders. "Sure. That's why you and I have to promise that we'll never fall in love with anyone else. Either of us. That way, we won't end up hurting each other."

"Yeah." He hesitated. "Should . . . should we seal it with a kiss?"

For a reply, she lifted her face toward his and closed her eyes. She felt his face come close, felt his breath on her cheek, and then slowly his lips touch hers. She thought: *This is our first grown-up kiss!* She liked it—it was really sweet.

He broke away from her abruptly. "What's the matter?" she asked. "Why'd you stop?"

"I don't know." How could he tell her that he had felt nothing—*nothing at all*—and it scared him?

"Well, I liked it. Didn't you?"

"Sure," he lied.

She put out her hand. "Let's hold hands."

He took her hand. They circled the square, then ventured out along the Rue de la Paix. They kept going until the street ended in front of the brightly lit Opéra. The outdoor cafés were full of people whose noisy chatter in polyglot languages gave the street a highly festive air. Crowds of people were coming down the Opéra's broad stone steps and going into nearby restaurants. The sidewalks were jammed with strollers.

"It looks like a painting, doesn't it?" she asked, squeezing his hand.

"Yeah. If it was, I'd buy it for you."

"If it *were*," she automatically corrected his grammar.

He grimaced; he hated when she did that. Walking past the Café de la Paix, he stared at a heavy dark woman—she reminded him of Rosalba—sitting at an outdoor table. He felt his penis stir against his tight Jockey shorts when the woman caught his eye and smiled up at him.

A few paces up the street, Jiminy stopped and put her hands on her hips. "I saw how you looked at that awful woman."

"What woman?"

"C'mon, Todd. It's really tacky to flirt with someone else when you're with me. Especially an old bag like that!"

"Honestly, Jiminy, I wasn't flirting. I can't help it if she smiled at me." He pulled her into a recessed doorway and kissed her again, vainly trying to feel aroused. Much as he loved Jiminy, he really wanted to be kissing that woman he had seen at the café.

He took her hand again and they returned to the hotel. He accompanied her to the door of the two-bedroom suite she shared with her parents, and he pecked her cheek in parting. Then, instead of going to his own room, he ran all the way back to the Café de la Paix. He had no idea what he would do or say, but he wanted to see that woman again.

When he arrived at the café, out of breath, the woman was gone.

The next morning Jiminy went into her parents' bedroom. She sat cross-legged at the foot of the bed while Ginger and Avery leaned against the antique rosewood headboard. At home, Ginger and Avery still got up before dawn to hike up Mt. San Jacinto, long before Jiminy was awake. But in Paris they did their walking after breakfast so that Jiminy could join them.

Jiminy felt suffused with love for her parents. They were so wise and kind and so beautiful to look at. Although she knew that her mother was fifty-six and her father was seventy-one, Jiminy found the numbers hard to believe because they both seemed so youthful to her. Most of the kids in her class had mothers and fathers in their late thirties, but Jiminy thought her own parents were much more youthful and good-looking than any of her friends' parents.

"What's up?" Avery asked his daughter. She looked a little peaked to him, with faint shadows under her eyes. "You didn't sleep well, did you?"

"Oh, Daddy! Stop being a doctor." She smiled at him. "You're right, though, I didn't sleep much."

"How come?"

She hesitated. "Well, last night . . ." She stopped, suddenly feeling very young and shy. "Last night, Todd kissed me."

Ginger and Avery exchanged a glance. They waited for her to go on.

"What I want to ask you," Jiminy said in a low voice, "is . . . well, what are you supposed to *feel*?"

"You're too young for serious kissing!" Ginger's voice was almost scolding.

"Yeah, but when I see you two kiss, you both look like you're going to faint with happiness." Jiminy glanced from one to the other. "How come I didn't feel that way?"

Avery felt his chest swell with love for his daughter. And with worry. She was everything a father could want in a child. She was so much like Ginger had been at her age—sweet yet spunky, bright, full of curiosity about life—and he could detect his own traits in her too, his tenacity, the strong desire to help people which had led to his becoming a doctor, his concern for the downtrodden despite having been born wealthy.

He cleared his throat. "Sweetheart, your mother is right. You're too young to waste time worrying about things like kissing. You're going through the most difficult period in a person's life, so why complicate it? You're no longer a child, and you're not yet an adult. You're feeling all kinds of new emotions. You have to make important decisions that will affect your entire future life, but you don't have enough experience yet to make the wisest choices. It's not easy, Jim-jim. Let me tell you, most of us suffered a lot in our teens."

"But, Dad, I'm not afraid of suffering a little," Jiminy said. "Isn't that how you learn? I mean, if everything's too easy—"

"Well, but you don't want to make it any harder on yourself than it has to be," Ginger interrupted. "As for kissing Todd . . ." She sighed. "It's not a good idea, honey-bun. Not now. Not yet."

Jiminy looked down at her hands. She gave an exaggerated sigh. "Oh, I know what you're going to say. That I'm too young for serious sex and I might get pregnant if we make love. I know all that. But I'm not talking about sex . . . only about kissing, for now."

"Well, believe me, Jim-jim, one thing leads very quickly to the other."

"But, Mom, now that we started kissing, it'll hurt Todd's feelings if I say I don't want to anymore. So how do you expect me to stop?"

"By not being alone together!" Ginger replied firmly, with angry glints in her eyes.

Jiminy was surprised that Todd didn't try to kiss her again the next day. She assumed that he might have talked to Cal and gotten the same advice that she had been given by her parents.

At dinner that night she realized that they would be leaving Paris in two days and that Todd had seen only the Eiffel Tower and the Champs Elysées, with lunch up in Montmartre, none of which had impressed him very much. "Mom and Dad have been with me every day since we arrived," she told Todd and Cal, "and I think they ought to have some time alone. So why don't I give you guys the Jiminy Rowland special tour of Paris tomorrow?"

"Sure." Cal looked at her with amusement. "If you don't expect too big a tip. What time do we start?"

"Tomorrow morning right after breakfast?"

"Okay. What's on the agenda?"

Jiminy thought a moment. "Well, I'll take you along the Seine, from here to the Ile St. Louis, with little side trips. It's loaded with history."

Cal smiled. "Is nine o'clock too early?"

"No, that's fine. Remember to wear comfortable shoes."

After dinner, Jiminy looked expectantly at Todd. "Want to take another walk? Like last night?"

He shook his head. "I'm awful tired." He yawned to prove it.

She shrugged. "Okay. See you both in the morning."

At nine o'clock the next morning, Jiminy went down to the lobby. The August day promised to be warm, so she wore a sleeveless pink dress with matching sandals and straw hat. She looked forward to showing *her* Paris to Todd, and of course to Cal too. She so wanted Todd to love this city as much as she did because she hoped that someday, when they were old enough to get married, they could come back here for their honeymoon.

The elevator doors opened and Cal emerged, without Todd. "He isn't feeling well," Cal explained. "Upset stomach."

"Is it all right to leave him?" Jiminy asked worriedly.

"Sure. He just needs a good rest." Cal gestured toward the lobby doors. "Shall we go?"

Jiminy felt all the excitement fizzle out of her, like air being let out of a balloon. She wasn't particularly fond of Cal—she hardly knew him, actually. She resented his neglect of his son and she couldn't understand why her mother liked this cousin of hers so much. He looked like a wastrel to Jiminy, albeit a very handsome one. But someday he would be her father-in-law as well as her cousin, so she felt she should make an effort to like him.

"Tell me," she asked as they walked briskly down the Rue de Castiglione toward the Tuileries, "do you know much about Paris?"

"Nope. I haven't been to Europe since before the war, when I did a student tour," he admitted. "I guess I know more about the eating habits of Borneo cannibals than of Paris gourmets."

She gave him a disapproving sidelong glance.

Cal was amused by her silent reproof. He admired this little cousin of his. She seemed intelligent and plucky, traits he cherished. He knew that she and Todd were inseparable, and he wondered how his son would be able to keep up with this bright, vivacious girl.

They walked east through the Tuileries Gardens to the Place du Carrousel, where she showed him that if he stood behind the Arc de Triomphe du Carrousel, he could see the much larger Arc de Triomphe, a mile away, framed by the smaller monument's center arch.

"Remarkable!" Cal said, trying hard to sound enthusiastic about the view. "Hey, look at that!" He laughed softly, nodding toward a couple inside the arch who were kissing passionately, oblivious of the world.

Jiminy dismissed them with a shrug. "They're weird, the French. They just love to kiss in public."

They crossed the Pont Royal to the Left Bank, where she kept pointing out important buildings. "That's the Invalides, where Napoleon is buried—want to go inside and see his tomb?"

When he shook his head, she led him back to the river, stopping to show him the French Academy, the Chamber

of Deputies, the Ecole des Beaux Arts—she rattled off
the names until he complained of thirst and they stopped
at a sidewalk café near the Petit Pont for a cool *citron*.

"You're the best guide I've ever had, Jim'ny." He
pronounced her name as though it rhymed with "chim-
ney," and she liked it. It had a nice lilt.

When Cal told her about some of his travels through
South America, Africa, Asia, and the South Pacific, she
listened to him attentively.

"Are you really interested," he asked wryly, "or are
you just being polite?"

His question surprised her. "Of course I'm interested.
I love hearing about out-of-the-way places. But I can't
help wondering . . . aren't you at all interested in seeing
Europe too?"

"No. Not really. Y'see, Jim'ny, I don't travel to look
at buildings or scenery." He paused thoughtfully. "It's
the people and *ideas* that I'm interested in. And basically, most Europeans are pretty much like Americans.
Same values. Same religions. After all, it's where most
Americans came from. But in countries like, say, India,
or Mexico, where I've spent a lot of time, away from the
tourist centers, they talk to me. Not just polite chitchat,
either. I learn about ways of living and thinking that are
completely different from what I'm used to."

"What's so wonderful about their being so different
from us?"

"Well, for one thing, it makes me question my own
values. Like, are the Eastern religions more spiritually
satisfying than our Christian traditions? It's hard to judge
your own ideas if you don't have something to compare
them with."

Jiminy looked at him thoughtfully. He was such an
enigma to her! She had always seen him as an utterly
self-centered man, and now he seemed . . . well, quite
admirable. She liked the way he looked, too. She never
had noticed before how compassionate his dark eyes
were, always looking as though they were smiling a little,
even when he was serious. Even though he had dark hair
and eyes, he resembled his beautiful mother, though his
features were more rugged, entirely masculine. And yet,
there were reminders—something about his smile—of the

pictures she had seen of her half-brother, Tony. "I never thought of it that way," she said. "Maybe I don't question things enough—you know, what I learn in school."

"I'll bet you're a good student." He smiled at her with such admiration that she felt herself blush.

"I love school," she admitted.

"How about Todd?"

She hesitated. "He does okay," she lied loyally.

"So what are you going to do with all your scholastic ability? Marry Todd and have a bunch of kids?"

"Yes, but I also want to be a doctor, like my father."

Cal shook his head in admiration. "You're something, Jim'ny Rowland."

"I *want* to be something," she said seriously. "Why waste your life?"

"Touché!"

She led him through the Huchette, where they peered into the dark little cafés that lined the narrow alley, and then into the church of St.-Julien-le-Pauvre. "He's called *'le Pauvre'*—poor St. Julien—because he murdered his parents by mistake, thinking they were burglars, and he never forgave himself," she explained. "At least that's what Daddy claims is the legend." Then they looked into Notre Dame, which Cal found "too big and too dark."

They crossed the river to the Right Bank and circled the Hôtel de Ville to examine the hundred and forty-six statues on its facade. "It's the city hall for the entire city of Paris," she informed him.

"Yeah," he said. "It's certainly impressive. If you like statues."

"Now I want you to see my favorite square in all the world. It's also the oldest one in Paris." She rushed him along the Rue de Rivoli past neighborhood shops and cafés, past a cluster of sidewalk food vendors, then into the Place des Vosges with its arcaded red-brick buildings surrounding a grassy park where couples were kissing on almost every bench. "Isn't it romantic? Henry IV built it in the early seventeenth century, but he was assassinated before it was finished. He was a pretty good king, as kings go. Victor Hugó lived over there. See?" She pointed at the southwest corner.

"My God, Jim'ny," Cal said, smiling, "you sound like an animated guidebook."

"Oh!" She flushed guiltily. "I didn't realize . . . I'm sorry—"

He grabbed her arm contritely. "Don't be sorry, honey. I meant it as a compliment."

She brightened. "Sometimes I get carried away when something interests me." Suddenly she realized that she and Cal were having a lot more fun alone together than if Todd had been with them. Todd would have been bored and full of complaints by now. She looked at her watch. "It's after one. Are you hungry?"

"Starved."

"There's a famous old seafood restaurant Daddy took me to near here, in the Place de la Bastille . . ."

"Sure. Let's go." He tucked her hand under his arm and they sauntered back toward the Rue de Rivoli. He noticed that when she took off her hat, the sun turned her auburn hair into a red-gold halo around her face. He thought she was the dearest child he had ever seen. He loved her enthusiasm and her forthright, self-possessed manner. He kept regretting that he didn't have a daughter like her so that he could have the thrill of guiding an intelligent young person into adulthood. He sighed, wondering if he would ever feel that way about Todd.

"I think you and Todd see too much of each other," he told her over a shared order of *belon* oysters. "And it's *much* too early for the two of you to be talking about getting married someday."

"I like you better when you act like a jolly friend and not like a strict parent," she said with a tinge of asperity.

He was unabashed. "I'm not trying to be a strict parent, Jim'ny, just a caring relative. I simply don't think Todd's right for you."

She was shocked at his disloyalty to his son.

"I mean it!" He leaned toward her, to make his point. "When people get married, it's better if they're fairly evenly matched. You're a very bright kid. I honestly don't think Todd can keep up with you."

"How can you talk that way about your own son?" she protested. "Don't you have *any* faith in him?"

"Of course. Todd has a lot of good traits. He's a magnificent golfer. He's kind and generous. He's got a lot of charm. But a great brain he isn't. And obviously you are." He touched her arm for emphasis. "Honey, I *know* what it's like to marry the wrong person." He smiled ruefully. "Don't forget. I'm an expert on the subject."

"Was Todd's mom that bad?"

"Not *bad*. It's just that we were completely wrong for each other."

"Then why did you get married?"

"Because I wasn't even eighteen yet and Vivien was barely sixteen and like most kids that age, we were sexually stirred and incredibly stupid."

"You make being a teenager sound like a terrible disease," she complained.

"It is, baby, it is. What you have to realize is that you don't have to be a villain to cause trouble. Todd isn't a *bad* person. Far from it. But he can make a sensitive girl like you very unhappy."

"You don't know him," Jiminy maintained. "He's just as sweet and dear as can be."

Cal sighed deeply. "I'm not saying he isn't. I'm just not sure . . ." He made a helpless gesture. "Ah, forget it. You're just kids anyhow."

Lunch took two hours. They followed the oysters with spicy steamed mussels *marinière* and baked lobster stuffed with shrimp. He gave her half a glass of wine from his bottle of *Pouilly-sur-Loire*. He told her about Fiji and Zanzibar; she gave him brief biographical sketches of van Gogh and Toulouse-Lautrec. He described being a boy in Palm Springs during the twenties, with a famous movie star for a mother; she told him about growing up there during the war, and she name-dropped some of the famous writers and artists she had met at her mother's hotel.

"Either you're precocious or I'm retarded," Cal said ruefully. "I feel like I'm talking to a contemporary, not a kid."

She bristled. "I'm fifteen! So don't call me a kid when I'm trying so hard to grow up!"

"Aw, Jim'ny, what's your hurry?"

The waiter interrupted with his dessert cart. He named each item and extolled its virtues. Cal and Jiminy both had trouble making a decision, and at one point Cal suggested ordering one of each and just tasting them, but Jiminy shook her head and chided him for being wasteful. He finally chose *framboises-chantilly* and she took the *tarte de pomme Leonardo da Vinci.*

"I wonder what Leonardo had to do with apple tarts," Jiminy said as she nibbled the last of it from her fork. "Sometimes I wish I'd lived in the Renaissance. It must've been exciting."

Cal shook his head. "With the life expectancy they had in those days, you'd have had a couple of kids by now, and I'd be dead." He held out a spoonful of his raspberries and whipped cream. "Want a taste?"

She licked his spoon clean. His mention of death reminded her of Tony. "My mother told me about you and Tony being half-brothers," she said, treading softly.

"Yes, and it just occurred to me, Jim'ny—he was *my* half-brother, *and* yours too!"

"That's right! I never thought of it that way either."

"Somehow, that makes us more than just cousins, doesn't it?"

She nodded. It was a bond, a strong bond, and she felt emboldened enough by it to touch the back of Cal's hand in shared commiseration. Then she bounced out of her chair. "Okay, lazybones, lunchtime is over," she announced briskly. "We have to explore the Ile St. Louis. Then on to the Boul' Mich and the Luxembourg Gardens and you absolutely have to see Montparnasse! We'll stop for another *citron* at La Coupole if you get tired."

He followed her out of the restaurant, grinning at her electrifying energy. *He* had never felt so alive in his life. He took her arm and they crossed the Pont Sully to the eastern end of the Ile St. Louis, shaped like the prow of a ship. They stopped in the little deserted park tucked into the island's narrow tip.

They leaned against the railing and watched the river branch around the island. "How can you be sure you're in love with Todd," he asked carefully, "when the two of you grew up like siblings?" He hesitated. "Can you really feel passion for someone who's like a brother to you?"

She gave him a hostile look. "I don't know what you mean."

"Well, when he kisses you, do you . . . do you feel . . . ?" He groped for words that wouldn't offend her. "Do you feel . . . excited?"

"Honestly, Cal, I think you're—"

"Like this." He drew her close before she could object and kissed her warm, vibrant lips.

She felt as though she had fallen off a cliff. Her body soared, plummeted, then was swiftly roaring down Niagara. Her agitated heartbeat drummed in her ears and she forgot to breathe. She had never felt anything so wonderful in her life. When he released her mouth, their bodies still tight against each other, she clung to his arms and hid her face against his chest, catching her breath.

"Well," he said, sounding breathless himself. *"Well!"* He put his hand under her chin and forced her to look up at him. "Tell me the truth," he said huskily, "is that how you feel when Todd kisses you?"

She blinked away a few sudden tears and took a deep breath. "Do you want the rest the tour?" she asked shakily, forcing herself to move away from him.

"Lead on, McDuff!" He took her hand and, their interlocked fingers throbbing, they walked quickly down the Rue St. Louis en l'Ile, afraid to look at each other.

Todd got out of bed as soon as his father left. He didn't have an upset stomach; he was suffering from a frantic case of unrequited lust. He tried masturbating, but it didn't help enough. He desperately wanted Rosalba, or someone like her—a plump, jolly, amorous woman. And, by God, he was going to find one!

He showered and dressed hastily and went out. He remembered that Jiminy had said they would walk along the river, so he went north, in the opposite direction, past the Opéra, past the big department stores, and into a residential neighborhood with food shops on the ground floors.

He was looking for Montmartre, where he and his father and Jiminy and her parents had gone for lunch the previous day. He had seen a lot of women up there who his father had said were prostitutes. For reassurance, he touched the wallet in the pocket of his light summer jacket—it was full of francs that his father had given him.

He asked several people how he could find Montmartre but nobody spoke English and they didn't understand his pronunciation of "Montmartre." Then, far above him on top of a hill, he caught sight of a dazzling white church with a distinctive high dome and a lot of cupolas, which he recalled having seen near the restaurant where they had all had lunch the previous day. He plodded uphill and finally found the square he remembered—the street sign said "Place de Tertre"—where several painters were displaying their work.

Todd saw a heavy blond woman sitting alone at a café, sipping coffee and smoking a thin brown cigar. He could see her generous breasts through the thin material of her low-cut green blouse. Despite the difference in coloring, she reminded him of Rosalba. When he sat down at her table and smiled at her, she smiled back and said something in French.

"No speak," he said.

She held up her fingers, all of them, made fists, then opened her fingers again. *"Vingt francs,"* she drawled with the cigar in her mouth.

He held up his own ten fingers twice. "Twenty? Twenty francs?"

She looked at his hands, then smiled and nodded.

He took out his wallet, counted out twenty francs, and handed her the money. She rose, dowsing her cigar in the dregs of her coffee, and led him along a narrow downhill street and up a stairway to a small room with blue walls and a sagging bed. He grabbed her at once and started to kiss her, but she pushed him away, slapping him playfully on the arm and wagging a chiding finger at him.

She began to undress slowly, methodically, folding each garment and putting it carefully on a chair. She gestured for him to do the same. When they both were naked, she pulled him over to a sink in the corner of the room and washed and dried his penis as matter-of-factly as if she were cleaning a cucumber. In his state of enforced patience, he noticed that she was shorter than Rosalba, fatter too, and a good deal older. He was surprised to see that her thin arched eyebrows were drawn on with a pencil. It didn't matter to him. She could be a purple-assed orangutan for all he cared. All he wanted was to shove his penis into her goddamn bloated body and find total bliss.

They all returned to Palm Springs shortly after Labor Day so that Jiminy and Todd could start school and Ginger could get her hotel ready for its October reopening. Ella and Jason already had returned from their separate summer vacations. Cal took a bungalow at the Desert Inn while trying to decide where in Mexico he wanted to spend the winter—San Miguel de Allende or Oaxaca?

Their first morning home, Ginger and Avery hiked up to their beloved lookout point. Arms around each other, they stood staring out at the valley below them. "I hate to sound like an old fogey," Avery said, "but I wish our little village had stayed the way it was the first time I brought you up here."

"So do I. Remember? It was my second morning in Palm Springs, and Nellie told me you knew more about the mountain trails than the Indians."

"Good old Nellie."

"Can you believe she's been dead for five years? I still miss her." Ginger rested her head against his arm. "Y'know, the town looks twice as big as it did when we left two months ago."

"I know. Just *look* at all those new roofs, all the way out to Rancho Mirage. And up on those hillsides . . . and look, over there to the south . . . was that big U-shaped hotel there before we left?"

"I can't remember." Ginger sighed. "Neil told me that he's building two new shopping centers and about a million apartments." She peered out at the view. "Avery, I can't believe it! I see two new golf courses!"

"Yeah. I read somewhere that we're now known as the 'Golf Capital of the World.' " He laughed hollowly. "Do you know what all this is doing to land values?"

"I can imagine," she said. "The prices must by skyrocketing. And you still own . . . what—almost three thousand acres?"

He nodded. "I might as well start selling some of them, Ginger. Hanging on to them won't stop development the way I thought it would."

"Well, do what Pearl McManus does. She won't sell

any of her land unless she gets the right to approve the building plans."

"I agree." Avery gestured out at the desert. "You know, with all our complaints about the way Palm Springs is growing, you have to admit, the sky's still the same as it always was, the mountains haven't changed, the air is still dry and fragrant. We can't help it if other people love the same things that made *us* love it here, can we?"

"No, darling. So let's not worry about it." She put her arms around him. "Remember the mornings when we'd forgo our hike and rush over to your old house and make love?"

He nodded dreamily. "Speaking of making love, Jimjim's going off somewhere with Todd this morning. We'll have the house all to ourselves."

Later that morning, Ginger started her preparations for The Springs' new season. After all these years, she still was excited about owning a hotel. She never tired of meeting new guests and greeting old ones. This October her old friend Gracie was coming for a whole month after four years in a hit Broadway musical. Hitchcock had booked a room for a week in November. Half the White House press corps had wired for reservations during President Eisenhower's next visit. And Ginger found more than two hundred requests for the Christmas holiday, when she had only forty rooms.

"It's such a happy business," she said enthusiastically to her assistant, Joyce, the granddaughter of Tonito's sister, Maria. "Everyone comes here to have *fun*—for their vacations, or honeymoons, or to celebrate birthdays and anniversaries. That's what makes the place always seem like a nonstop party."

"Talking about parties, Auntie Ginger . . ." Joyce grinned, showing Ginger a carton full of envelopes. "These all arrived while you were away. I put them in categories." She pointed. "This bunch is private parties. This pile is for benefits where they either want your hefty contribution or they want your presence as honorary chairman. Here's one asking you and Uncle Avery to be grand marshals of the Circus Parade next spring. Then all these are for—"

"Stop!" Ginger cried in mock agony. "Avery and I just want to spend our evenings quietly at home."

"Then you better move to Timbuktu," Joyce advised archly. "This town is getting more social every day. Anyway, I figured it all out for you. If you want, you and Uncle Avery can go in tux and formal one hundred and eight nights this coming season. There are seventy-six informal parties, forty-seven barbecues, and thirty-eight picnics and desert breakfasts—"

Ginger shook her head. "Joyce, do me a favor. Make a big bonfire . . . or better still, send them all over to Ella. She loves parties."

"If only it were that simple!" Joyce handed Ginger a neatly typed list. "Here. I put them all down, and I marked the ones you absolutely can't avoid—in red pencil!"

Ginger grimaced at all the red marks. "Okay, call the airlines and get us three seats to Timbuktu! Seriously, Joyce, did the painters show up?"

Joyce nodded. "They're in the dining room. You better check and see if there's enough pink in the beige."

Ginger had made many changes in The Springs over the past few years. Although her well-trained staff no longer needed her actual presence for the day-to-day operation of the place, she never stopped improving the physical plant and the service. She had had the old pool dug out and a larger one built in its place, along with two Jacuzzis and a sauna. Every year she had the entire hotel redecorated with fresh paint in soothing desert pastels, and the Mexican-style furniture was refinished or replaced whenever necessary.

Reluctantly she had installed television sets, hidden in cabinets, and telephones in all the guest rooms and bathrooms. Every "modernization" brought back memories of the hotel's simplicity in the early days, when the guests had come because they loved the desert ambience, and not to luxuriate in the sumptuous amenities they now expected.

After the war, Ginger had redecorated the dining room and lobby so that they looked like mini-museums of Indian, Mexican, and southwestern art, featuring her own collection of Agua Caliente baskets, some of which she had inherited from her former father-in-law, Juan Pedro. She had been buying Indian handicrafts from other tribes too, and she hadn't realized what a fine collection she had until she brought it all together. She had softly lit niches holding sculptures by Zuniga and Hauser. The rosy-beige walls were covered with desert photographs by Laura Gilpin and Ansel Adams, paintings by Carl Eytel, Jimmy Swinnerton, and Georgia O'Keeffe, and on the most prominent walls she had hung three dynamic desert canvases by her favorite artist in the whole world, Avery Rowland.

"Do you realize that The Springs is thirty-four years old?" Ginger asked Avery when he came to the hotel that first day to have lunch with her. Jean-Paul had promised them shrimp mornay, a platter of white asparagus that he had just brought back with him on the plane from France, and chocolate-covered profiteroles.

"Can you believe that you had the gumption to actually borrow the money to build a hotel and run it when you were only twenty-two?" He beamed at her with admiration. "No wonder Jiminy's so fearless. She doesn't think there's anything she can't do."

Later he asked, "What are we going to do about Jiminy? We can't very well forbid her to see Todd."

"No, we can't. Granted, he's limited, but really, he's so lovable, it's difficult to say anything against their being together."

Despite her parents' disapproval, Jiminy and Todd continued to spend every possible minute together. Whether bicycling to school, or going to school dances and dancing only with each other, or riding horseback after school, or doing their homework, they were inseparable.

Jiminy was surprised and a little hurt that Todd had never tried to kiss her again. She felt it was important for her to convince herself that he could kiss her as thrillingly as Cal had. "How come you stopped?" she asked him one afternoon as they rode their horses through Tahquitz Canyon.

He looked abashed. "Well, my Dad and Grandpa Jason both said we're still too young for that kind of stuff, so I promised them we wouldn't."

"That's what my parents said too."

"You mean you actually told them that I kissed you?"

"Sure." She stopped riding and gave him a curious look. "Don't you ever talk frankly about your feelings, you know, with Cal, or Aunt Ella and Uncle Jason?"

Embarrassed, he looked away. He could just imagine how his father and grandparents would react if he told them that every night he crawled into bed with Magda, their plump twenty-four-year-old cook. He couldn't help it. He was hopelessly addicted to the kind of lascivious sex that he couldn't imagine ever doing with Jiminy. "I'm happy, so what's there to talk about?" he asked huffily.

After weeks of indecision, Cal finally decided to spend the winter roaming all over Mexico instead of staying in one place. He refused to admit to himself that he had delayed making the decision because he didn't want to leave Jiminy.

Ever since Paris, they had avoided seeing each other alone. He knew that his kiss had frightened her, and he himself was puzzled by his own reaction to it. He had made love to so many women that he had long ago lost count. But his little cousin had touched him as no other woman ever had. He tried to make light of it, to treat it as a passing foolishness, to make fun of it to himself. Anything but take it seriously.

The day before he left Palm Springs, he had dinner at The Springs with Ginger and Avery and Jiminy. Afterward he asked Jiminy to walk him to his car, where he took her hand. "Now, honey, remember what I said about you and Todd spending too much time together. And, Jim'ny, if you're a good girl, I'll let you show me the rest of Paris someday." He smiled archly. "Especially that little park on the Ile St. Louis."

She looked at him coolly and withdrew her hand.

"Aren't you going to kiss me good-bye?" he asked mockingly, knowing she wouldn't, but desperately yearning with a shy schoolboy's hopeless longing that she might.

"Stop teasing me. You're going to be my father-in-law someday," she reminded him through trembling lips, fighting her own frantic desire to kiss him again. She fled back to the hotel's dining room.

After Cal left, she felt as though there were a huge hole in her life. She didn't have that many interesting people she could talk to besides her parents. Oh, she missed him, missed him! His very presence in the same room had excited her beyond belief, ever since Paris. But stubbornly she tried to deny his attraction for her. She loved Todd, not his father. She was going to marry Todd. They belonged to each other. Still, she wondered if she should follow Cal's advice—and her parents'—and try to make other friends. After all, she admitted to herself, Todd *was* limited when it came to carrying on an engrossing conversation.

In mid-November, Ella came over to the pink mansion and invited the three Rowlands to come to her place for Thanksgiving dinner.

Ginger looked at her in amazement. "You want me to come to your house? What about Jason?"

Ella grinned. "He says it's okay. He wants us all to be friends now."

"Well! What do you know!" Ginger hugged her sister. "It's taken him sixteen years to finally forgive me!"

CHAPTER
14

1961–1962

Everyone in the family was coming home to Palm Springs for Neil's annual Christmas Day party, which this year was doubling as an engagement party for Jiminy and Todd. Cal was flying in from Mexico, Jason from Morocco, Ella from Switzerland, and Jiminy and Todd were driving home from the University of Arizona, where Jiminy was a premed student and Todd was squeaking by in the physical-education department only through his prowess on the school's golf team.

Five days before Christmas, as they awaited Jiminy's and Todd's arrival, Avery's long-suppressed distress surfaced. "How can we stand by and watch her throw her life away?" he asked Ginger.

"I don't like it any more than you do, Avery." Ginger turned away from their bedroom window, where she had been watching for Jiminy's red Alfa Romeo convertible, a birthday gift from Neil.

"Ah, Ginger." Avery held her close and rested his head against hers. "I want so much for our little girl!"

"She's twenty now, darling." Ginger lovingly caressed his silver hair. "We can't tell her what to do anymore."

"No, but we can still advise her."

"My dearest, we've been advising her not to marry Todd since they were fifteen!"

"They were still kids then. I thought it would be years before we really had to worry. Now . . ." His voice trailed off for a moment. "I always hoped she'd find the kind of love that we have."

"She never will with Todd," Ginger sighed. "Oh, he's a nice-enough youngster. I'm actually very fond of him, but . . ."

"I'm fond of him too. As a nephew. But not as a son-in-law. Not as my Jiminy's *husband*."

Ginger hesitated. "You know, don't you . . . that she's in love with Cal? And Cal loves her."

"I've suspected as much. You can't help noticing how they look at each other."

"But she's so loyal to Todd! She'll never admit she loves Cal—not even to herself."

"Cal fascinates me," Avery said. "I like the way he's so open to new ideas. He's intelligent. And gentle. . . ."

"D'you think Jiminy would be happy with him?"

"Oh, they'd be wonderful for each other! But goddammit, she's determined to go ahead and marry that sweet idiot, Todd."

Ginger rose on tiptoe to kiss Avery's cheek. She wanted to cheer him. "You're sure a good-looking guy, Avery Rowland."

He smiled wryly at his reflection in the mirror above their dresser. "Damn right I am! Modest, too, in case you hadn't noticed." When Ginger returned to the window for another glance down their long driveway, he examined himself more closely in the mirror. He was seventy-six and it seemed to him that he looked no more than sixty. All right, sixty-five. He had never had a sick day since he had moved to the desert, except for a few colds when he lived in Paris. He climbed old Mt. San Jacinto almost as nimbly as he had in his youth. He continued to make love to Ginger with gusto, if somewhat less often than he had twenty years earlier.

But, to his chagrin, he still looked a lot older than Ginger, because at sixty-one *she* could pass for fifty! Maybe less. She took good care of herself. With facials and a little help from her hairdresser, she had very few wrinkles and no gray hair. Ah, he was proud of her, of everything about her. Above all he was proud because she loved him and made every day a joy for him.

Her lovely face and friendly smile and slim body still attracted men, even fairly young ones, much to Avery's annoyance. To his chagrin, he could see that she enjoyed having men admire her, even though she never encouraged them. When men flirted with her, he wanted to punch them out and shout that she was *his*, by God, that she belonged to *him*! Not that he ever did. Oh, he knew it was juvenile, a sign of wholly unwarranted insecurity on his part. He was possessive as hell, though he hid it well.

Still, he did sometimes worry that he would wake up one morning and find a ruined face in the mirror, with all the years caving in on him at once. He had to keep reminding himself that he was not immortal. Someday he was going to die. And when he did, Ginger would be inconsolable, just as he would be if she happened to die first, though that was unlikely. He remembered how Ginger had suffered—for years—when Tonito died in the flood, and she hadn't loved Tonito nearly as much as she loved him. The price of the kind of love Avery and Ginger shared was the devastating sorrow suffered by the survivor—and there was no way to prevent it.

"She's here!" Ginger cried from the window. She raced down the steps and out to the driveway, with Avery close behind her.

Jiminy hugged them both at once, then each one separately. How she loved them! And had missed them! And there was so much she wanted to tell them. But she had promised Todd she wouldn't, not until the Christmas engagement. How was she going to keep from blurting it all out?

"God, I'm happy to see you!" Ginger exulted, her arm tight around her daughter's narrow waist as they went into the house.

"Me too, Mom. And Dad! Honestly! You never change, either of you."

"We found the Fountain of Youth," Avery said dryly, following them into the living room. "It's called parenthood." *And making love a lot*, he added to himself.

"Where's Todd?" Ginger asked.

"I dropped him off at Aunt Ella's house," Jiminy said. "Todd said she's not due home till Christmas morning."

"I know." Ginger smiled fondly, thinking of her sister. "She called from Switzerland and said she doesn't want anyone to see her before Neil's party. She wants to surprise us all with her new face."

"*Her* Fountain of Youth is a Swiss surgeon's scalpel," Avery interposed.

"Uncle Jason's back from North Africa," Jiminy told them. "Looking very spiffy with his Sahara tan." She saw her father's jaw tighten. She kissed him again. "C'mon, Dad, you're not still jealous of him, are you?"

Avery smiled. He was troubled, not over Jason's return—he long ago had learned to live with his jealousy of Jason—but because Jiminy didn't look well to him. Oh, she was as pretty as ever—beautiful, he thought, with her long wavy auburn hair and blue eyes and delicate features. But his doctor's sixth sense told him that something was wrong. She seemed jittery, but of course it could be the long drive and the excitement of seeing them and—he suppressed a sigh—the hullabaloo of getting officially engaged.

"Cal's coming home tomorrow, from Guadalajara," Ginger said lightly, carefully watching Jiminy's face. "He'll be here tomorrow night for dinner."

"That's nice," her daughter said flatly, and Ginger noticed that Jiminy's cheeks flushed deeply at the mention of Cal's name.

"Of course I'll invite Todd and Jason too," Ginger went on.

"There's a pre-engagement stag party for Todd tomorrow night, so I know he can't come." Jiminy fiddled nervously with her wristwatch. Why had she let Todd talk her into secrecy? Oh, if only she could tell her parents what had happened! Maybe she would feel better about it herself.

By the next evening, Jiminy thought she would break apart into little brittle pieces, like a glass jigsaw puzzle. She always felt excited when she knew she was going to see Cal, and now, with everything that had happened, her nervousness made her flit around like a hummingbird. She changed her dress three times, and finally came halfway downstairs in a Christmassy red velvet sheath, then ran back up and put on a white chiffon, only to change again into gold satin pants and a clinging white silk shirt with a pleated sash that flattered her narrow waist and shapely breasts.

She found Cal alone in the living room, standing by the

fireplace. He hadn't seen her yet, so she watched him for a moment from across the room. He looked so youthful, more like Todd's older brother than his father. The flames' glow flickered over Cal's thoughtful face, highlighting the tinge of color across his high cheekbones, his legacy from his Indian father. His tan was accentuated by his embroidered white Mexican shirt. His dark hair was longer now than she remembered it, and like Todd's, one wayward lock fell over his forehead. He looked incredibly handsome to her. Exotic and . . . utterly wonderful.

She long ago had realized that they were in love with each other. Ever since their day together in Paris, Cal had timed his visits to Palm Springs to coincide with her vacations from school. Everyone else thought he was doing it to see his son, but Jiminy knew better because Cal hardly ever tried to spend any time with Todd, but he always made plans to be with her.

She wanted to rush into his arms and stay there forever, but instead she walked up to him and gave him a sedate peck on the cheek. Before she could move away from him, he grabbed her and embraced her tightly. Eagerly, shivering with desire, they kissed as though trying to absorb each other's very souls. Only when they heard voices approaching from the kitchen did they force themselves apart. Her heart was beating so noisily, and so fast, that she was sure it was reverberating throughout the house.

Silently noting the flush in Jiminy's cheeks, Ginger and Avery came into the living room with champagne and a tray of fluted glasses. They were followed by Jason carrying a platter of Iranian caviar, sour cream, and triangles of dark rye bread. Sitting in a semicircle around the oversize tile coffee table, watching the fire, they talked about the Russians having beaten the U.S. in sending a man into space, about President Kennedy's meeting with Khrushchev in Vienna, about Ernest Hemingway shooting himself to death in Idaho, about JFK telling Americans to exercise more and to build backyard bomb shelters in case of nuclear war.

Jason wanted to know what the point was in staying fit if we were all going to be bombed to death anyway, and Cal added with a chuckle that if everybody was out jogging when the bomb dropped, what good were their fancy shelters going to do them? Ginger chided that it was too serious a matter to laugh about, and Avery said that if they didn't laugh, they'd cry.

But they were in no mood for crying. How could you cry, Ginger asked, when your bellies were full of caviar and good French champagne and you were surrounded by people you loved? Their conversation kept bouncing from topic to topic, like a basketball being swiftly dribbled down the court, and most of what they discussed, like the Berlin Wall, was depressing, but their collective gaiety could not be suppressed.

Avery brought up the alarming rise in the use of drugs in America, Cal told them of the centuries-long addiction in the South American altiplano to coca and of the wild dreams some Mexican Indians induced by eating psychedelic mushrooms, and Jason described the North Africans' fondness for hashish.

"Just like LSD," said Jiminy, explaining the new chemical drugs to her seniors. "I've never tried it—I'm afraid of it—but some of my friends are into it."

"What's that new dance you kids are doing?" Avery asked her.

"You mean the twist?" Emboldened by the champagne, she stood up and gave them a demonstration.

"Call me old-fashioned," Avery laughed. "I like to hold my partner close when I dance."

The conversation moved on to the new international problem of airplane hijacking, and then they all expressed their sympathy for the Freedom Riders. Even though most of the subjects they discussed were, indeed, depressing, the talk remained lively and witty.

Jiminy suddenly realized, guiltily, how bored Todd would be if he were there. It was all her fault, she scolded herself. She should insist that he at least read *Time* or *Newsweek* once in a while, instead of practically memorizing *Sports Illustrated* every week.

Ginger led the way into the dining room for a Christmas Eve dinner of baked ham, sweet potatoes, Yorkshire pudding, vegetable and fruit platters, and mincemeat and pecan pies. She looked around the table with pleasure. Fine food, bright conversation, and such a lovely group of loving people. Her eyes went from face to face: Avery's silver hair and keen blue eyes, Jiminy's well-bred loveliness, Cal's dashing good looks, and dear old Jason's tousled graying hair and warm smile.

Jiminy was aware that Cal's eyes remained constantly upon her. She longed to be back in his arms. When she imagined kissing him again, she felt as though a miniature elevator were swiftly rising and falling between her groin and her throat, leaving a path of dizzying desire in its wake.

Cal couldn't take his eyes off her. He had never been in love before, had never experienced anything remotely like what he felt for Jiminy. He couldn't believe that another human being could be so perfect. Except for her obsession with Todd. She was so *foolish* to forgo the happiness he knew they could share, just because she felt responsible for Todd. God! How could a bright angel be so *estúpida*!

Cal realized that he had never wanted anything as much as he wanted to be with her, and to make love to her. At the very thought of it, his entire body prickled with desire. How incredibly sweet it would be. Sweet and sensual and voluptuous and rapturous and blissful, all at once. They were made for each other, meant for each other. They fit together mentally, physically, and spiritually as perfectly as the pages of a closed book.

Across the table, Jason was annoyed with Cal. *And* with Jiminy. Why did they keep looking at each other like star-crossed lovers? Intensely loyal to his beloved Todd, Jason wondered why the boy's own father was flirting with his son's fiancée. It was more than flirting. Cal and Jiminy looked like they were ready to dive under the big round dining-room table and rip each other's clothing off.

Jason glanced resentfully at Ginger. Like mother, like daughter? Was that it? Unable to be constant? Though Ginger certainly had been damn faithful to her precious Avery for twenty-one years! Except—ha!—for that one time at the Ambassador Hotel, Jason remembered gleefully, wondering if she had ever told Avery about it. Jason doubted that she had, because he didn't think Avery would have been so friendly toward him all these years if he had known. For a wild moment Jason wanted to tell Avery about it, just to smash that complacent look on the older man's face. But what would be the point? It would only make everyone unhappy, including himself after his brief moment of revenge.

Jason still felt uncomfortable in this house, which once had been his home. Every room had such happy memories for him. Even after all these years, he felt deprived that he couldn't walk up the stairs to the big comfortable master bedroom with its spectacular views from every window and get into bed with Ginger. He still felt abandoned by her, still wanted to be with her, still loved her, dammit! And always would.

After desert and coffee, when the others returned to the living room to sip brandy in front of the fire, Cal took Jiminy's hand and led her out to the front porch. It was a typical December desert night, cool, with a sky full of stars to gaze at, but neither of them was at all interested in stargazing that night. She was back in his arms at once. He kissed her, deeply, and all the imagined thrills that had plagued them both during dinner were increased tenfold by the reality of their embrace.

He held her tighter. "Oh, Jim'ny, I love you!"

She clung to him, wanting to tell him she loved him too, but she couldn't. Not now. Not ever, now.

"Jim'ny, I *know* you love me," he said urgently. "How can you marry Todd if you're in love with me?"

She shook her head, holding back tears. "Stop it," she pleaded. "I have to stay with Todd."

He wanted to tell her where her precious Todd was, but she would think he was making it up to get her to break the engagement. His son-of-a-bitch son! That story about a stag party was totally untrue. Todd was in the servants' quarters at Ella's house, engaged in a wild sexual marathon with Ella's latest hefty, raucous housekeeper. Before coming to Ginger's house, while trying to take a nap in the guest suite, Cal had heard their lewd snorts, gasps, groans, and giggles from clear over on the other side of the big mansion.

He kissed Jiminy again. "What do you mean, you *have* to stay with Todd?"

She leaned against him and hid her face on his shoulder. "Because I'm going to have his baby."

Cal gasped and was quiet while absorbing the shock. "I thought he didn't want to have sex with you," he finally mumbled. "Until you were married."

"I insisted. So we did it, several times last semester. I told him that I wouldn't ever marry him if . . . if . . . well, that I couldn't understand *why* he didn't want to. . . ."

"Didn't you *use* something? A diaphragm, a condom, an old *sock*, for Chrissake?"

She shook her head.

He grasped her shoulders, hard, angrily. "Was it good, Jim'ny?" He forced her to look into his stricken eyes. "Goddammit, did you enjoy it?"

She shook her head again.

"Then, my God, why did you keep on doing it? Why the hell did you stay with him?"

"Sex isn't everything." She felt so wretched, she didn't want to live. "He'd go to pieces if I left him."

"Sweetheart, that's his problem," Cal insisted. "Not yours."

"Ever since he was little, he's always depended on me. I love him like I'd love my Siamese twin. We can't be separated. Don't you understand? I can't abandon him!"

"Oh, you little fool! So you're sacrificing your life . . . *and* mine . . ."

"You can't understand what it's like, Cal. You've never loved anyone the way I love him. I mean, it's protective, the way you'd love a child. It's not like *being* in love, the way I love you."

"Then you *do* love me?"

"Oh, God, yes!" She hadn't meant to ever tell him, but she couldn't stop herself.

"Jim'ny, Jim'ny, it's not too late. I've waited five years for you to grow up so I could ask you to marry me."

"No," she whimpered. "Cal, don't—"

"But it's all I've lived for. Come away with me. Todd's child is my grandchild. I'd consider it my own."

She shook her head. "I can't, Cal. Not now."

"Why *not*?"

She tore herself out of his embrace and leaned forlornly against the porch railing. Then she spoke. "Because," she said slowly, painfully, reluctantly, "Todd and I got married yesterday, in Tucson."

Cal stared at her in utter disbelief.

"We're going to announce it at Neil's party," she added.

Cal walked down the steps and got into his car. His mother's car, a maroon Bentley. He drove back to Ella's house and strode directly to the housekeeper's room, where he found his son and the woman yowling their salacious pleasure as they writhed and thrashed and slammed against each other in their frenzied coupling. Todd's firm young buttocks, shiny with sweat, caught the gleam of the harsh ceiling light while he frantically lunged into his partner's body. As Cal hesitated in the doorway, Todd and the woman bellowed their climax like wounded lions and collapsed against each other, hoarsely gasping for breath.

Cal grabbed Todd's arm and hauled him out of bed. "How the *hell* can you whore around if you're in love with Jim'ny?"

Todd slipped on his pants and sheepishly followed his father out of the servants' quarters. "Hey, Dad, I'm sorry you saw . . . Listen, don't get the wrong impression—"

"What's the right impression, for Chrissakes?"

"Well, I mean, about Jiminy." Todd grabbed Cal's arm and made him stop and look at him. "I love her more than anything in this world. I'd never hurt her."

"Then what was that all about?" Cal nodded angrily toward the housekeeper's room.

"I can't help it. You know, every once in a while . . ." Todd gave a shamefaced grin. "I mean, with Jiminy it's . . . it's . . . sort of . . . well, not very exciting."

"Why not?"

"Because I can't do the things with Jiminy that I do with women like that. Jiminy's too . . . too ladylike."

"Bullshit! Sex is sex. There aren't any rules. You can do anything and everything it takes to make it enjoyable."

Todd shook his head. "I just can't do all that stuff with Jiminy."

"Then you had no business marrying her!" Cal started toward the guest suite.

Todd followed, astounded. "She told you we were married?"

"Obviously."

"Why'd she tell *you*? We were keeping it secret till Uncle Neil's party."

"Never mind why she told me." Cal stopped again and looked searchingly at his son. With all his faults, the kid was lovable. It was difficult to be angry with him. He had Jason's great gray heavily lashed eyes that were utterly candid and winsome and vulnerable. No wonder a sensitive, softhearted girl like Jiminy couldn't bear to hurt him.

Cal put his hands on Todd's shoulders. "Look, kid," he said kindly, "I understand what you're saying about that broad in there. You like a good rousing fuck and you don't get it with Jim'ny. But if Jim'ny ever found out, she'd be shattered."

"Nah." Todd shook his head. "Jiminy's not that crazy about sex."

"She might be, with someone else. Just like you are with someone else."

Todd looked frightened for a moment. "I'd die if she ever did."

"Todd, you're not making sense. It's all right if you screw around, but not if Jim'ny does."

"Yeah, Dad. It's that simple. I'm the jealous type, and she isn't."

"Don't count on it!" Cal sighed in frustration. He knew that the minute he left the house, Todd would return to his fat playmate. Well, he told himself as his anger returned, accompanied by a great gust of pain, Jiminy had made her choice. She'd just have to live with it.

But how was *he* going to live with it?

He returned to the guest suite and packed a duffel bag. He did everything mechanically, drained of all hope that life would ever be good again. He borrowed one of his mother's cars—he didn't want a flashy, expensive car so he chose a Chevy wagon she kept for the servants' use. He headed south, toward the Mexican border, toward the sound of mariachis playing the kind of music that matched his sorrowful mood.

Ella returned, more beautiful than ever. Although she

was almost sixty, she looked thirtyish. The Swiss surgeons had performed a miracle. Her facial skin was taut and smooth above a graceful, youthful neck. Her eyelids had been tightened, her hair had been thickened with transplants. Her breasts had been lifted, and her stomach, legs, and underarms trimmed. She looked brandnew and sculptured in a simple long gown of clinging gold velvet, dangling diamond earrings, and a giant diamond pendant against her chest.

Everyone clustered around her, full of compliments, which she received with aplomb and humor. After a year's absence, she was happy to be back, hugging her darling Todd and exchanging banter with Jason and Neil and Ginger and Avery. "But, Todd, where's your father?" she suddenly asked, looking around Neil's vast living room for Cal.

Todd flushed. "I don't know, Grandma. He packed and left in a hurry."

Only Ginger and Avery noticed the pallor on Jiminy's face during this conversation. "I have to talk to you," she told her parents softly, and led the way out onto the terrace.

Neil's newest mansion was more splendid than any estate he had ever owned, without the garish excesses of his previous homes. It was painted a warm gold, inside and out, all curves and arches, without a single rightangled surface. The lighting was soft, indirect, seductive, with the hiss of fountains and waterfalls creating a musical counterpoint of sibilance. Outside, swaying palm fronds clattered overhead, like a clapping claque. The estate was built on its own private knoll south of the city, nestled in a circle of thick white oleanders that from a distance made the sinuous amber-lit mansion look like a floating spaceship.

Jiminy sat between her parents on a curved marble bench beside a carp pond. She took their hands, squeezing them hard for courage. "I don't know how to tell you . . ." She hesitated, then blurted: "I'm g-going to have Todd's baby. So we got married in Tucson."

Ginger immediately thought of two words. *Abortion. Annulment.* But abort her grandchild? Misery enveloped her, momentarily paralyzing her vocal cords. She put a trembling arm around her daughter and looked past Jiminy's bowed head at Avery. She seldom had seen him look so woebegone.

Their silence was like a cruel slap to Jiminy. "Say something!" she begged.

"What do you want us to say?" Avery asked quietly. "That we're thrilled?"

"I want you to be happy for me!"

"Jim-jim, we're . . . totally surprised," Ginger said slowly. "First let us get used to the idea. Of course we'll try to be happy for you if . . . if it's what you really want."

What I really want, Jiminy thought in misery, *is to be with Cal forever and ever.* But it was too late. It had been too late ever since the days when she and Todd were toddlers and became so enmeshed in each other's lives. She could see now why her parents had always objected to her closeness to Todd, had begged her to make other friends too, to give herself—and Todd—space to make choices. Now she would never know what it was like to make love with Cal, to experience the exquisite thrills their fervent embraces had promised, to be ecstatically in love and revel in the daily joy of being together and sharing every aspect of life. The way her parents did.

Yet, she had done what she had to do. She was tied to Todd. Oh, sure, she knew that he was lazy and expected everything to be handed to him without any effort on his part. She knew that he was a poor student and had grave lapses of judgment. She knew that there was no sexual spark between them. But she appreciated his strengths. He was incredibly sweet and kind and fun to be with. They had common references, knew their family's dynamics. And they *knew* each other, although—being smarter and more perceptive—she knew him far better than he did her.

Deep down, she had to admit she was rationalizing. Marrying Todd had been a mistake, but one she couldn't have avoided. Maybe she was wrong to think he couldn't get along without her. But what if she had gone off with Cal, and Todd *had* fallen apart? Could she ever be happy, knowing she had caused his breakdown?

When she stood up, her eyes glittered with tears. She

looked down at the two people who were so dear to her, who had done so much for her, who had given her life itself. But now she needed more from them, and they were failing her. Their disappointment enclosed all three of them like a poisoned fog. And she had more unwelcome news to add to their dismay. "I'm quitting school," she told them in a faltering voice. "I guess I'll never be a doctor now."

Avery stood up in alarm. "But *why*? There's no reason you can't continue—"

"Yes, there is, Dad. Todd hates college. He wants to work for Uncle Neil, here in Palm Springs, and play golf on the PGA circuit. How can I expect him to go and live with me somewhere else while I go to medical school for years and years?" She turned and fled into the house.

Avery put a consoling arm around Ginger. It was cold outside, and turning dark. They shivered against each other, partly from the temperature, mostly from misery.

"Maybe it'll work out," Ginger said with forced brightness.

"Yes, Pollyana." He sighed so deeply that Ginger was afraid he would sprain his lungs—if that were possible.

"Don't take it so hard," she begged. "Darling, darling . . . what good will it do?"

"Let's go home," Avery growled.

"Avery, we can't. We can't abandon Jiminy." Ginger stood up. "Come on, darling, try to smile. For Jiminy's sake. Let's go in and toast the"—she almost gagged over the word—"the newlyweds."

Cal's footprints were all over the earth, but his heart was in Mexico. There, except for his native Coachella Valley, he felt most at home, and, when troubled, it was his place to find peace. And so on Christmas Eve he had fled to Mexicali, just south of the border.

He had spent the night in a nondescript motel and slept late. When he awoke on Christmas Day he went immediately to an old-fashioned cantina called La Paloma, where the ambience was dark and cool and imbued with the smell of stale beer. The patrons and barkeeps were good-humored and *simpático*, and as long as he tipped them a few dollars per hour, a band of eight smiling *mariachis* would play and sing for him the old, romantic Mexican ballads he loved so much, love songs in which three key phrases always seemed to recur: *Mi amor, mi corazón, mi vida*—my love, my heart, my life. Coincidentally, these same three words were painted on one of the dark wooden walls of La Paloma, while the other wall bore the time-worn Mexican toast: *"Salud, Amor, y Pesetas—y Tiempo para Gozarlas."* At this holiday time, Cal found the old drinking salute especially ironic, for he realized he had the health and the money and time to enjoy them, but he didn't have the *amor*. And without love, all else was worthless.

Whenever he was in Palm Springs, Cal would drive down to La Paloma once or twice. He would drink very little in the cantina, in the course of a few hours rarely having more than one or two bottles of Dos Equis beer or occasionally a lick of salt and a shot of tequila. He frequented the unprepossessing La Paloma—the Dove— for its old-fashioned name and quintessential feel of Old Mexico. Everyone there spoke only Spanish, since the bar's down-at-the heels decor repelled most gringo patronage.

Every time Cal entered La Paloma, the eight mariachis in their traditional sombreros, tight pants, and embroidered bolero jackets would salute him with wide mustachioed smiles and a collective, wholehearted *"Hola, amigo!"* With their guitars, fiddles, trumpet, and maracas, they always hurried to his table, where he greeted them all by their first names. After inquiring as to his health, the eight musicians would proceed to sing Cal's favorite ballads, the familiar bittersweet love songs his nursemaid Juanita had sung to him when he was a child. And thus, to the recurrent laments of *"Mi amor, mi corazón, mi vida,"* Cal was temporarily happy in a sad, sweet, Mexican way.

But the songs of the mariachis and the gentle ambience of La Paloma didn't work this time. Cal was too distraught by Jiminy's marriage and the dismal effect it would have on both her life and his. He needed solitude and a space where he could think of what he should do with his life. Since La Paloma and Mexicali during the celebration of the *Navidad* were hardly suitable for quiet contemplation, Cal decided to go deeper into the country, to the most remote place in Mexico, and there try to sort out the mess Jiminy was making of both their lives. With isolation and time, he hoped to gain enough strength and insight so that he could return to Palm Springs and cope with life without Jiminy.

He returned to his motel and at dawn the following day began driving to Barranca del Cobre—Mexico's Copper Canyon. Though less-well-known than Arizona's Grand Canyon, Barranca del Cobre was much larger, almost as deep, and far more isolated. Anxious to get there, Cal floored the Chevy down route 2, which slashed a straight path through the great Sonoran Desert to Los Mochis, his first night's objective, 630 miles south of Mexicali.

The paved federal highway was mostly straight, had two lanes, and traffic was light. But periodically he would be stymied by barely creeping trucks and even slower-moving horse-drawn wagons. Intermittently, too, he'd have to brake and swerve at the last moment to avoid potholes big enough to bite off a wheel. Cal was anxious to complete his 630-mile journey during daylight. After sundown, he knew, Mexican highways abounded with sudden Apparitions in the Night who wandered on the black pavement in total darkness: unwanted dogs and stray burros, wild horses and wayward cows, and, especially, staggering peons, *mucho borracho* on fermented agave juice. He had to beat the setting sun.

At a speed of eighty-five miles an hour, the Sonoran Desert, with its cacti, yuccas, and joshuas, looked to Cal much as he imagined the Coachella Valley must have looked before Palm Springs got saturated with swimming pools, irrigated golf courses, and the throng of go-getter developers like Uncle Neil. But rather than finding the Sonoran Desert drab or monotonous, Cal found it soothing. He had been born a desert rat and he had become a lover of Mexico and most things Mexican. But what was it, he asked himself as he sped furiously along the potholed highway, that he loved so about Mexico and the Mexicans?

He loved the innate sweetness of the people, he reminded himself, their gentleness, their courtesy, their desire to please, their slower pace, their love of music and dancing and partying, their ability to turn the drabbest and saddest commemorations into fiestas. They even celebrated their Day of the Dead with music and parades and family picnics in their gaudy cemeteries, where by candlelight they sat all night on the graves of their ancestors and ate their fiery foods and drank their hard liquors and laughed at the grim joke of death.

What was there about the Mexicans he didn't like and couldn't understand? Well, there were a helluva lot of exceptions, sure, but for so many of them, especially the very poor, who constituted the majority, their fucking patience, patience, patience! Their incredible submissiveness! Their passive, stoic, endless putting up with outrageous misrule, corruption, and deprivation. The few who were very, very rich had all the land, the wealth, the power, and the privileges, which they exercised with arrogance and no feeling of kinship to the very poor, while the poor, who comprised the vast majority, were never more than ten beans away from starvation. The *ricos* believed in the Trickle-Down Theory. As they got ever richer, they rationalized, their wealth trickled down to all the others. But in Mexico, Cal had observed, Trickle Down merely meant that the rich pissed on the poor.

Was this passivity, this stoic acceptance of injustice by the very poor, part of the Indian heritage? Cal wondered. Being half Indian himself, and knowing the history of the fierce defiance of oppression by hundreds of native tribes in both Americas, Cal immediately rejected this notion. He was not a Marxist or believer in any doctrine of economics or dogma of history. But in the pressure cooker that was Mexico, it was inconceivable to him that the Indians and *mestizos* would not eventually blow the lid off. It was overdue.

There had to be an explosion. This was also the almost unanimous belief of the gringos who lived in Mexico and knew it well. Cal had idled from time to time in all the American watering holes—Puerto Vallarta, Acapulco, Cuernavaca, Guadalajara, Chapala, Ajijic, San Miguel de Allende—and in all these retreats, the gringo *inmigrantes* had confided to him that the Day of Retribution had to come. The people were beyond desperation. Their lives were intolerable. Yet the Mexican population kept doubling every generation! Fifty-percent unemployment! Year after year of double-digit inflation! Five hundred years of governmental corruption! "Beautiful country," the Yankees who lived in Mexico agreed unanimously, "gentle people, wonderful way of life. But good God, get me out before the bloodbath comes! And it's coming! Inevitably! Any day now!" But they had been predicting bloodbath for years, and staying on for years, and still the smoldering volcano only smoldered.

To forget it all, including his own troubles, Cal turned on the car radio as he approached Hermosillo, hoping to hear some of his beloved Mexican music. But as he punched up station after station, all he heard was rock and roll, the U.S.A.'s top-forty hits, all heavily interlarded with commercials for Yankee colas and detergents. But at last, by dialing through the entire broadcast spectrum, he found a weak, crackling outlet that was playing the old ballads. *Mi amor, mi corazón, mi vida.* For a while Cal was content, until the static caused his teeth to hurt and he had to turn off the radio.

As he kept speeding on to Los Mochis, Cal recalled a scene that typified to him the crazy optimism of Mexico, a street scene he had witnessed one very rainy night, almost a hurricane, in the chic Zona Rosa section of Mexico City. He had stayed late at a club where the folk dancers and the mariachis were particularly good, and at three in the morning he had gone out to find a taxi that would take him to his hotel. But in the terrible downpour there were no vehicles or pedestrians to be seen. The gale whirling down from the mountains blasted the rain horizontally, and the street was dark and deserted. He took refuge in a doorway from which he would be able to see the lights of any approaching cab.

Then, hobbling down the sidewalk toward him, came two desperate hookers, both brunettes, wetter and colder than drowned alley cats, and just about as desirable. Optimistically they walked close to the curb so that potential customers cruising by in cars could easily assay and hire them, and they wore the universal uniform of that era's hustlers, miniskirts that barely covered their pubes, low-cut blouses that clung like wet T-shirts and revealed all but the hue of their nipples, and high spike heels that lent some shapeliness to legs that were a little too thick. But their clothes and skin were drenched, for the umbrellas they carried offered little protection against the sideswiping wind.

As they drew closer to Cal's doorway refuge, he saw that one of the women was quite young, maybe eighteen or nineteen, while her colleague looked twenty years older, though she might have aged prematurely from having spent so much time in bed. He saw, too, that the young hooker was limping severely and insisted on pulling the older woman along with her into the doorway adjoining Cal's, where they, too, took temporary refuge. They did not see that Cal was next door to them, within easy earshot.

"These fucking high heels are killing me!" the young one cried in Spanish. "We've been walking steadily in this fucking rain for six hours now without turning one fucking trick, and I'm soaked, I'm cold, I'm tired, I'm hungry, and I want to go home!"

"We've got to keep walking!" the older one insisted. "How can we make a peso if we aren't out there walking?"

"Oh, God, my aching feet!" the younger one lamented.

"Patience!" the older whore pleaded. "We need the money! We've got to keep going, keep walking, keep smiling, never, never give up! Who knows, even now, somewhere out in the storm, there's maybe a rich man with a hard-on. He'll come cruising by in his Rolls-Royce and want to make it with the both of us!"

And so the two hookers went back out into the storm and began limping patiently and hopefully down the street.

Cal was a rich man and he did have a Rolls-Royce—well, his mother's, back in Palm Springs—and although he didn't at that moment have a hard-on and was sure these two would never incite one, he did have *un corazón*. He rushed out after the two women and in English persuaded them to let him buy them their dinner at a very good all-night café on the next street. He spoke English because as a patriotic gringo who knew his country was not always in high regard in Mexico, he wanted America to get the credit for his generosity. He also didn't want the two women to suspect—if he spoke to them in Spanish—that he might have overheard and understood their revealing conversation.

They ate. *Dios mío!* How they ate! They ate soup, salad, six rolls, two huge steaks, rice, beans, two pots of coffee, and two orders, *each*, of flan with whipped cream. They dried out, surreptitiously pushed off their shoes under the table and rested their feet, put on fresh makeup, and even looked a little attractive, though obviously tired. They were also very proud. They insisted to Cal that in return for what he had given them, they must reciprocate with the only gift they had—themselves. Cal declined politely, and to protect their feelings, claimed that it was almost dawn and he was exhausted. They gave him a rain check then, writing down their names and phone numbers on a paper napkin, which they handed him. But they didn't believe his excuses and knew that later he would throw the phone numbers away.

As Cal seemed preoccupied in paying the bill, the older hooker crowed in Spanish to her young colleague, "See! What did I tell you! Patience always pays! If you keep walking, keep trying, never give up, a rich man will eventually come along and save your ass."

"*Es verdad,*" agreed the young whore, admiring Cal's good looks. "Too bad he's a fag."

The poor people of Mexico, Cal decided, were like the two whores in a hurricane, patiently waiting for a rich man with an erection. In the meantime, they kept walking, kept smiling, never gave up. But oh, God, they were wet and cold and hungry, and how their feet hurt!

It was just before sunset that Cal pulled into the hotel in Los Mochis. He showered and shaved and went down to the bar for a Dos Equis. Some mariachis were singing. *Mi amor, mi corazón, mi vida.*

Cal left his car in the hotel's locked parking lot in Los Mochis and departed for Copper Canyon on the morning train, the only way of reaching the interior of the canyon from the coast. He got off the train when it paused briefly at El Divisadero, a station close to the rim of the canyon, and he checked into a small hotel whose porch stood right on the steep canyon's edge.

El Divisadero was full of tourists. Eager American college kids with heavy backpacks plunged down the trail that zigzagged toward the canyon's floor. Older visitors were content to see the canyon from the fence along the rim. Train passengers going farther into the canyon debarked from their coaches long enough to buy snacks and plastic souvenirs from the hawkers alongside the tracks.

Cal found sitting on the cantilevered porch a dizzying experience. He had the feeling that this tiny speck of civilization clung to the side of the canyon as though fearful of sliding at any moment down into the very *barranca* whose existence had created it. Still, he felt peaceful, for the first time since he had hastily left Palm Springs. But not contented. That would take time, and more seclusion than El Divisadero afforded. He decided to find an isolated cabin where he could simply sulk until the pain of losing Jiminy receded enough for him to reface the world.

He knew that he couldn't expect to find anything very fancy. The area was primitive—some of the local Tarahumara Indians still lived in caves. But Cal was accustomed to making do with whatever housing presented itself. Countless times in Asia and Africa and South America he had slept without complaint in unheated shacks on stiff cots or even wrapped up in a blanket on the earth floor. *Semper fi*, he would tell himself, it was better than a foxhole. Oh, he wasn't so foolish as not to prefer a clean bed in comfortable surroundings. But he wasn't fussy. He took whatever came his way. Whether it was simply his revulsion for his mother's luxurious life-style or that his years in the Marine Corps had made a Spartan of him, or that, finally, he had learned to identify with those who made do with very little, Cal had no need for creature comforts or rich fare.

With the help of the hotel manager in El Divisadero, he found a cabin several miles up a rocky dirt road, too isolated to have electricity or a telephone. The one-room hideaway had a clean outhouse and a tin tub for a stand-up bath. Cal had to pump his water and carry it in an iron bucket to the house and then hang it on hooks over the rock fireplace when he wanted hot water. At least there was a reassuring woodpile outside the door. He had two kerosene lamps, a squeaking wooden rocking chair, and a comfortable bed with clean muslin sheets and a worn pile of blankets. When he sat in the peeling rattan chair on the front porch, he faced out across a small pond to the Sierra Madre Mountains, a bucolic view that filled his soul with peace. In Tibet and India he had learned how to sit quietly for long periods of time while meditating and practicing deep relaxation.

He arranged with the woman who owned the cabin to bring him three hot meals a day and to come and clean the place every other morning. She was a Tarahumara Indian, a tribe famous for its ability to run swiftly for long distances. Though she lived two miles away, she showed up at his cabin promptly with his meals still hot. He tried to explain to her that he, too, was part Indian, but she only shook her head and grinned, certain that this handsome gringo was teasing her.

He dedicated the next few weeks to calming his body and soul and trying to determine what to do with his life. But whenever he thought about Jiminy, his frustration and anger returned, so that he had to back off and teach himself to think about her without disrupting his serenity. Again and again she reared up in his imagination, lusciously if innocently seductive, making him sick with longing for her.

He stayed there for over a month. He had rented a horse from his landlady so that he could explore this remote land, and once a week he went into El Divisadero to use the hotel's phone. As had been his habit ever since embarking on his nomadic life, he telephoned Ginger to let her know he was alive. Thus did he learn, four weeks after Christmas, that Jiminy had had a spontaneous miscarriage.

His first impulse was to rush back to Palm Springs and make her annul the marriage. But before taking any precipitate action, he returned to the solitude of his cabin and meditated. He concluded, at last, that nothing he could say or do would make Jiminy waver from her stubborn loyalty to Todd.

He cried for her then, forlornly hoping that his tears would wash away his desire for her. In a month, he would be forty years old. It was time he realized that he couldn't have everything he wanted in life. He recalled his teens, when the money and good looks he had gotten from Ella had brought him, as they had for her, easy sex and every luxury, but these inherited advantages hadn't made him feel that life was worth living. He had always thought of those prewar days as his wasted years. And yet, he now realized, they had taught him to distinguish between life's real joys—love for others and understanding of self—and those one tried to buy.

He decided to stay in Mexico for a while, to return to Los Mochis and get the Chevy wagon and just roam around the country to all the places he hadn't yet visited. He got out his map of Mexico and circled the smaller routes, the ones less traveled by gringos.

He vowed to stay away from Palm Springs until the following Christmas, thus giving Jiminy and Todd a year to make their marriage work. Then, if he saw that Jiminy was unhappy, he would do everything in his power to convince her to divorce Todd and marry him.

CHAPTER
15

1962–1964

Ella was worried about Ginger. She seemed pale and withdrawn, and Ella wondered if her sister might be ill. They were having lunch at The Springs, but Ginger was only toying with her shrimp salad, pushing the food around with her fork but not eating any of it.

"Are you all right?" Ella asked.

Ginger nodded. "I guess." She raised sad eyes to her sister. "Just worried about Jiminy."

"Oh, but a miscarriage isn't serious, Ginger."

"I know." Ginger also knew that Ella had no inkling of how miserable Jiminy was, married to Todd, and there was no point in telling her. Ella would only get angry and hotly defend Todd.

Ginger gave Ella a speculative look. In the three months since returning from Switzerland with renewed youth and beauty, Ella had been behaving like a bitch in heat. Once again she was flitting from affair to affair, as fickle and flirtatious as she had been twenty years earlier, before Todd and Jason had given some stability to her life. Now Todd was married and living in his own mansion in Chino Canyon—a wedding present to Todd and Jiminy from their Uncle Neil—and Jason was off doing extensive research in the deserts of Jordan and Israel.

"What I really want," Ella confided, "is to fall madly in love." She gave Ginger a wry smile. "The way you have. Three times!"

"Any candidates?" Ginger asked, giving up all pretense of eating and putting down her fork.

Ella looked around the hotel dining room. "Look at all the handsome, distinguished-looking men staying here. They have to be *very* successful to afford your rates!"

"So? Do any of them appeal to you?"

"Not one."

"Then who does?"

"Avery." Ella grinned teasingly.

"D'you want to get stabbed with a fork?"

"Seriously, Ginger, remember Bert? Gracie's ex?"

"Ella, you can't be serious—"

"Yeah, I am. I was really crazy about him. He lasted longer than any other man I was with."

He's so boorish and vulgar, Ginger wanted to say, but didn't.

"Anyway, he's back in town, living in a miserable bachelor apartment. He's a salesman at one of those cut-rate furniture stores out in Cathedral City. And, Ginger, it's all my fault that he's down on his luck."

"*Your* fault? Ella, he was a rat! He ran out on Gracie and Amy—"

"Yes, all because of me. He gave up a good job, and his family, and then what did I do? I dumped him for some kid." Ella put a beseeching hand on her sister's arm. "Ginger, if he comes and lives with me again . . . will you and Avery accept him? You know, socially?"

I should be honest and say no, Ginger told herself. But she didn't have the right to tell her sister how to live . . . or how to love. "We'll accept anyone you want," Ginger said reluctantly, with a wan smile. "With the exception of General Franco, King Farouk, and Chairman Mao."

"Oh, goody! That's all that was stopping me!"

Ginger looked at her watch. "Damn! Where'd the time go? I've got a meeting in fifteen minutes."

"Yeah? What kind of meetings do you go to?"

"Today it's the City Planning Commission." Ginger grimaced. "Once more trying to save our dear little city from overzealous developers. These assholes want to put up an eight-story hotel right smack in the middle of town."

"So what?"

"*So what*?" Ginger repeated, outraged at her sister. "Do you want Palm Springs to look like Las Vegas, for Chrissakes?"

Ella really couldn't see what was wrong with that, but she was afraid to say so, knowing it would upset Ginger. "Don't you get sick of all that . . . crap? Going to meetings?"

"I get sick of having to fight the same battles over and over again."

"Well, have fun!" Ella jumped up from the table and threw Ginger a kiss as she ran toward the parking lot.

When Ginger came home from a stormy but successful meeting, she sat on Avery's lap and rested her head against his shoulder. "You claim that we have such good heredity," she began, "but what strain is there in my family that both my sister and my daughter have to screw up their lives by loving the wrong men?"

"At least there's still hope for Jiminy," Avery said archly. "After all, you didn't marry the *right* man until you were forty!"

Ella convinced herself that she was experiencing the love affair of her life. She knew that everyone, including her sister, found Bert loud and uncouth, but she got him to quit his job, and after she treated him to a new wardrobe and moved him into her mansion, he looked quite presentable.

He liked a "good time." Dancing at the Thunderbird Country Club, where Ella was a member, hobnobbing with the rich and famous at the posh Tennis Club, weekending in L.A. to eat at Chasen's and Scandia, flying up to "San Fran" or Tahoe on the spur of the moment, frequent trips for gambling and nightclubbing in "Vegas"—these were his favorite ways of spending his time and Ella's money. This frenetic activity gave their life together an aura of excitement, which Ella had sorely missed during the years she had devoted to being Todd's substitute mother and Jason's sometime lover.

"Hon," Bert said every morning when they woke up in her satin-sheeted bed, "you are the most beautiful thing in God's creation." And he proceeded to worship her body with his hands and lips and murmured endearments. He was an adept lover, with superb timing. He never entered her until she was thoroughly aroused, and then he did so just slowly enough to make her wildly excited. Her lust was a joy for him to see. It made him feel powerful and important, emotions his life had sorely lacked.

Day and night, he was attentive, anticipating all her needs—from a fresh martini to another lascivious bout on her bed. He felt that he more than earned his keep. He loved luxury—satin sheets, silk shirts, fine linen underwear, expensive food, premium single-malt Scotch, flying first class, staying in sumptuous hotel suites, and, above all, living on an estate with three acres of formal gardens, a tennis court, an oversize swimming pool, a million-dollar view, and seven servants, including one who took meticulous care of Bert's expensive wardrobe.

Much as Bert enjoyed the amenities of Ella's house, he loved going to Neil's estate every week for dinner. Now, *this* is the ultimate in luxury, Bert told himself the first time he was invited there. He lowered himself into a big easy chair in front of the fireplace after a dinner of creamed oysters in patty shells, châuteaubriand, potato soufflé, fresh asparagus with hollandaise, strawberries Romanoff, and a couple of bottles of some fancy wine that Neil boasted cost him two hundred bucks a bottle. Bert had strained his eyes to see the label, but the butler kept a napkin wound around it and Bert thought it would be gauche to ask.

"You shouldn't eat this way," Ella scolded her brother as he took his third helping of dessert. "For God's sake, Neil, you had your second heart attack less than a month ago. Are you crazy or something?"

"C'mon, Ella, lay off." Neil now weighed close to three hundred pounds. He was a blimp, a whale, a hippo, a sack of quivering flab, a bloated bag of blubber. He lit a cigar and gestured for the butler to pour cognacs all around. "Look, Ella," Neil said softly when the butler left the room, "if I do croak, there's a couple million stashed away in that safe I once showed you. Mostly hundred-dollar bills, easy to cash, no questions asked. I put it there when Jennie divorced me, before her lawyers could get their hands on it, and I left it there so you won't have to pay any inheritance tax on it." With sudden misgivings, Neil looked over at Bert. "Can I trust him?"

Ella shrugged. "He's got his faults, but robbing people isn't one of them. Besides, he'd never in a million years find your safe."

Bert laughed, embarrassed at Neil's lack of trust in him. "Don't worry, Neil, I won't squeal to the IRS either." But Bert sat there wondering how it would feel to be so filthy rich that you could just stash away a couple million bucks and not miss it.

Bert enjoyed three springtime months of this extravagant life with Ella, and a summer on a yacht docked in Cannes, but when he and Ella returned to Palm Springs in October, he became restless and insecure. Sometimes Ella snapped at him. She might look thirtyish, but the plastic surgery was only a surface cosmetic. She suffered the ailments of a sixty-year-old woman, with frequent headaches, tiredness, and digestive problems that kept her from going out to eat and drink as much as Bert would have liked. Often Ella went to bed early, leaving him with time on his hands.

On such nights, he returned to his old hangout in Cathedral City, a dark hole of a place called O'Hanlon's Bar, with cheap imitation Tiffany lamps, a couple of tired-looking fake plants, plywood-paneled walls that looked okay in the dim light, a sixty-foot-long black Formica bar full of nicks and scratches, and a line of saddle-shaped orange vinyl barstools that could cradle Bert's bulging ass without his flesh hanging over the sides.

He enjoyed showing off his expensive clothes and jewelry to his drinking buddies, ex-cons like Vic and Kelly and a collection of other shiftless men, bums and drifters who didn't have much to say and sat dejectedly watching whatever was on the TV set above the bar. The few women who frequented the joint were mostly washed-up hookers.

Bert took up again with Selma, the cocktail waitress there. He loved the irony of using Ella's money to buy this sexy twenty-four-year-old redhead gifts like a new gold wristwatch, a fake-fur coat, and half a dozen expensive dresses from Magnin's.

More and more often, he didn't feel like always being so goddamm attentive to Ella. It occurred to him that he could wake up one morning and be thrown out without warning. Or the bitch might die and he'd get nothing. Then what? Back to the furniture store and his shabby bachelor dump?

"Hon, let's get married," he suggested. He chose his time well: a romantic dinner *à deux* beside her pool, with a full moon and a couple of scented candles for illumination. Dinner had been preceded by a swim and a languorous coupling on a chaise next to the scented night-blooming jasmine.

She put down her fork. "Why?" she asked suspiciously.

"Why not?" He lightly stroked the back of her hand and smiled. He was still handsome, in a fleshy-faced way. His expensively styled hair was attractively streaked with gray. Poolside lounging had given him a ruddy, virile look. His body was heavy, but graceful. He felt he had a lot to offer her.

"I like our relationship the way it is." She picked up her fork and jabbed it into the lobster thermador on her plate.

"Ella," he said earnestly, "I'm afraid of losing you."

She smiled reassuringly at him. "Don't worry, sweetheart, you won't lose me. So long as you behave yourself."

"Meaning what?"

"Meaning you stay faithful and keep me happy. *In* bed and out of it."

Bitch! he thought, hiding his anger behind a smile. Suddenly he hated her. She had ruined his life twenty years ago, and he had never forgiven her. Too late he had realized how much he had loved Gracie and their daughter and their cute little house. He remembered how much pride he had had, how he used to insist that Gracie live on his income and not spend a dime of her own money. Then Ella had come along with that goddamm alluring body and gorgeous face of hers, and all her money, and he had been unable to resist her. Now look at him, reduced to being a goddamn gigolo.

Well, he was too old to change. Ella had corrupted him, and by God, he didn't want to take a chance on her dumping him, or suddenly kicking the bucket and leaving all her money to that nutty wandering son of hers. Nosiree! He'd have to think of a way to get his hands on some of her dough.

Meanwhile, he decided to break off with Selma. Just because he'd bought her some baubles and a few nice rags, she expected more and more expensive gifts. Now she was nagging him for diamond earrings and he was goddamned if he was going to be bothered with that kind of shit. She was just another piece of ass as far as he was concerned, and a damn ungrateful one at that!

Bert spent the next three weeks figuring out a plan. Late one morning, when he knew the place wouldn't be too crowded, he drove the white Eldorado that Ella had given him to Cathedral City—"Cat City," the locals called it—and parked in front of O'Hanlon's Bar. He was still seething with resentment against Ella. First off, she had promised him a gold Jag, and here he was driving a goddamn ordinary Cadillac. Hell, they were a dime a dozen in Palm Springs. Second, she wasn't being as generous with the bucks as she had been in the beginning of their affair. Finally, he had caught her giving the eye to a young hotshot tennis pro at the Racquet Club—Christ, the kid was younger than her grandson. If she took it into her head to try out the guy's youthful prick and stamina, he—Bert—would be out on his ass, for sure. It had happened once, it could happen again. Only this time he wasn't going to walk away empty-handed.

He heaved a sigh of relief when he spotted Vic and Kelly alone at the far end of the bar. The bartender was preoccupied at the front end, coming on strong to an aging blond with a raspy voice and a hooting laugh.

"Hey, Bill!" Bert hollered at the bartender, lighting a cigarette with a shaking hand while mounting the empty stool next to Kelly. "How about some service? Where the hell is Selma?"

The man looked up in annoyance and lumbered over. "Selma's been home sick, Bert, ever since you dumped her again."

Bert shrugged. "What'd she expect? It was hardly the love affair of the century."

"Yeah? Well, she claims you broke her heart."

"Her heart breaks easy. And often. Listen, Bill, mind your own business and bring me a double Scotch. Okay? Glenfiddich." He gestured at the beers Vic and Kelly were nursing. "Give 'em both a refill."

"Make mine Glenfiddich while you're pouring," Vic said quickly.

"Me too!" Kelly echoed, grinning. Kelly was young, maybe twenty-seven, with a pink-cheeked baby face and a lot of longish blond hair. He was a couple of years older than Vic, who had greasy black hair, a thin pale face, and mean green eyes. His elongated nostrils and buck teeth made him look like a nasty Bugs Bunny.

Bert drank slowly, screwing up his courage and waiting for the bartender to go back to his blond at the other end of the long bar. Finally Bert leaned conspiratorially close to Vic and Kelly. "You guys wanna make a buck?" he asked hoarsely.

"Shit," Kelly said, "for a buck I'd kiss Khrushchev's ass."

"Yeah, for two bucks I'd kiss his you-know-what," Vic added, smirking lasciviously. He took the pack of Marlboros from Bert's shirt pocket and helped himself, then offered one to Kelly.

"For Chrissakes, you guys're always broke!" Bert snorted. "What the hell do you do for a living? Steal church poor-boxes? Hold up little kids for their milk money on the way to school?"

"Don't give us no ideas." Kelly took a long drag on his cigarette and grinned at Bert while he slowly exhaled. "We ain't being kept by no rich dame, wise guy, that's for sure. So c'mon, out with it! What kind of bucks you talking about?"

"Believe me, *big* bucks."

"Is it foolproof?"

"Foolproof!" Bert glared at him. "Hell, I'll guarantee it. This plan *can't* fuck up!" He leaned even closer to them and spoke low and tensely. "You know this old gal I'm living with," Bert began, "you guys remember Ella Ricardo? The movie star from way back?"

Kelly and Vic shook their heads. "Never heard of her," Vic said.

"Guess she was before your time. Anyway, she's loaded. And her brother's got more money than Fort Knox."

Vic looked Bert up and down. "What's she see in a bum like you?"

Bert smirked. "I'm good in bed."

"Yeah, so am I, lotta good it does me," Vic whined. "So go on, tell us what you got in mind."

"Well, I want you guys to rent a cabin up off Seventy-four—you know, the mountain road to Idyllwild? I already checked the place out. You can't see it from the highway. Anyway, the old broad already pops plenty of pills for her headaches and bellyaches, so she won't notice if I slip half a dozen more barbs in her prune juice." Bert paused. "You guys got a gun?"

"Of course I got one!" Vic said indignantly. "But I don't want to use it."

"You won't have to," Bert assured him. "When she passes out, I'll call you. Then you stage a break-in at her place. I'll help you."

"How about the servants?"

"Hell, there's a couple acres of flowers and a high wall between their rooms and our master suite. So after you break in, you guys'll tie me up and then take her to the cabin and lock her up for a few days. I'll give you the money to buy a used station wagon."

"And where'll *you* be all this time?" Kelly asked suspiciously.

"I'll stay in her house and play Mr. Heartbroken. That way I can give 'em a false description of you guys and tell 'em you let slip you were taking her up north to Yucca Valley. That'll put 'em off the scent. I'll even go help look for her when they get up a search party."

"How much ransom you gonna ask for?" Kelly asked, blowing smoke in Bert's face.

"A nice cool million. I know her brother has that kind of cash stashed away in a safe in his house, and believe me, he'll never miss it. We'll split it fifty-fifty—half for me and a quarter-million for each of you."

Vic whistled, impressed. "Now you're talking!"

"Yeah, but I don't get it," Kelly said. "Why not just go rob the brother and save us the trouble of kidnapping the dame?"

"Because first, wise guy, I don't know where the hell his damn safe *is*. Second, his house is wired like Fort Knox. And third, nobody's going to squawk to the police if the dame is returned unharmed."

Vic pointed at his empty glass. "I'm dying of thirst."

"Me too," Kelly grinned.

"Hey, Bill!" Bert hollered. "Refills!" They waited while the bartender brought three more drinks and returned to his ladyfriend. "Okay," Bert continued, "once we get the dough, you guys keep the wagon and take off across the border to Baja and lie low for a while. But first you telephone the brother and tell him where to find the old broad, and that way everybody's happy and nobody gets hurt. What d'you think?"

Kelly shrugged. "Sounds too easy. What if the brother doesn't come across?"

"Worse comes to worst, we'll give it a week and then pull out. Only, be sure she never sees your faces. All we lose is a week's rent on the cabin, and I'll pop for that. And be awfully careful not to hurt the dame." Bert looked at them uncertainly. He wasn't sure . . . "You know what I mean? No funny business."

"Haw!" Vic put his arm intimately around Kelly's shoulder. "Don't worry. We got each other."

"Okay. If she's returned safe and sound, nobody'll bother looking for us that hard."

Vic exhaled his cigarette smoke slowly through his nose. "How do you collect the ransom without getting caught, Mr. Know-It-All?"

"Easy. I got it all figured out. She's got this sister and brother-in-law who climb a steep trail up the damn mountain. Every fucking morning at dawn. Can you believe it? We'll tell 'em to bring a backpack up there with the million in cash."

"Shit, Bert, how the hell are they gonna get all that dough up the mountain on foot?" Vic wanted to know.

"Yeah, what if it don't all fit in a backpack?" Kelly added.

"Well, first off, folding money isn't all that heavy. I figured it out—ten thousand one-hundred-dollar bills, hell, it sounds like a lot but it won't weigh more'n fifteen pounds, twenty at the most. And worse comes to worst, they can get two backpacks. Second, I'll be higher up, watching to make sure there's no cops around. You can see the whole town from up there. Third, after the sister and her husband leave, I'll pick up the backpack and come on down a different trail. I'll tell 'em we'll kill the old broad if they try any monkey business. But it's just a threat to scare them. Like I said, I don't want her hurt in any way. I just want the dough."

"I don't know." Kelly shook his head. "It just sounds too—"

"Come on, you guys, it's a breeze," Bert insisted. "You'll never get another chance like this!"

"Give us a couple days to think about it," Vic drawled. "C'mon back Friday."

"Same time?"

"Yeah, man. Same time, same station. We're always here."

Ella was terrified, and utterly humiliated. Whenever she had to use the toilet, she had to pound on the floor with the heel of her slipper and then wait until the dark-haired punk sauntered upstairs, unlocked her door, and took her downstairs to the bathroom. Worse, he would stand there next to the toilet, arms folded across his chest, a cigarette dangling from his grinning lips, watching her. He wore a red Halloween mask over his eyes and nose, but she would recognize those ugly lips and buck teeth anywhere.

The first time she had to use the toilet, she politely asked him to wait outside the bathroom, but he stood there leering at her. "Can't leave you alone in here, toots." He gestured at the small window.

"I promise," she said. "I won't try to escape."

"Listen, don't gimme a hard time, okay?" He laughed at her discomfiture. "C'mon! Shit or get off the pot!"

She had never felt so ashamed, and so degraded. To make matters worse, she had diarrhea. All they gave her to eat were candy bars and weak, lukewarm coffee. She hated sweets, had never liked them even as a child, and especially not all these years when she'd had to watch her weight. Now she was forced to eat them or starve, and they upset her stomach.

After a particularly bad attack of loose bowels, she tried to ignore the punk's presence as she wiped herself.

"God, your shit stinks!" He grimaced and took a book of matches from his pocket. After lighting three matches in a row, he threw the matchbook onto the back of the toilet. "Save 'em for next time, sweetheart."

The room where they kept her, on the second floor, was stifling during a late-October heat wave. The one window looked down on a leafy canyon that cut off any possible breeze. She couldn't see the road from the window, so she assumed that anyone driving on the highway, looking for her, couldn't see the cabin either. All that was visible to her was a dirt driveway going off into the trees. Now and then she heard the drone of a truck shifting gears, but it sounded pretty far away.

She assumed she was being held for ransom, because there was no other reason she would have been kidnapped. But she didn't trust these young creeps. What would prevent them from taking the ransom money, which she was sure Neil or Ginger would pay, and then simply killing her and abandoning her corpse there while they got away? Or they could even take off, leaving her still alive, but locked in the room. It could be weeks, even months, before she was found. She'd die either way.

She didn't want to die. Not yet. She was having too good a time with Bert, even though he seemed to be faltering lately, and not at all sympathetic about her aches and pains. She no longer thought it was such a great love affair, but they did know how to enjoy life together. She was willing to settle for that. Besides, if she died now, what a waste all that pain and boredom at the Swiss clinic would have been!

She had to escape. She looked carefully around the room. From the window there was a two-story drop onto a jumble of jagged rocks. Her captors hadn't even bothered to lock the window because they didn't see how she could possibly get out that way. Those young snots! It was obvious that they didn't even know who she was. She was miffed, and surprised, because her old movies had been showing on television for years.

One of her earliest silent movies had been a prison story in which she had played the innocent and beautiful heroine, falsely accused of murder and sentenced to life imprisonment in solitary confinement. But the enterprising hero had smuggled a file to her in a cake and she had sawed through the bars and escaped by tying her sheets together and letting herself out a window. At least here there were no bars.

She examined the two rough sheets on the bed—top and bottom—and the thin cotton bedspread. She was certain that if she knotted them all together, they would reach the rocks down below. She decided to do it that night, then feel her way up the dirt driveway to the road. She could hitch a ride and be back in Palm Springs before her captors even knew she was gone!

Avery carried the backpack up the mountain, breathing hard. The pack wasn't all that heavy, but he was unaccustomed to walking with any weight on his back. He and Ginger didn't dare stop and rest. Ella's life depended upon it.

They reached the point where two trails met next to a screen of creosote bushes—the spot where the muffled voice on the phone had told Neil to have them leave the money. Hastily Avery dropped the knapsack as though it contained a ticking bomb. Never in all the years they had been hiking up San Jacinto had they bolted back down the trail with such speed.

They had followed the telephoned orders explicitly. Neil had provided the money the night before, taking it out of the safe hidden somewhere in his house—even Ginger didn't know where. They didn't inform the police about what they were doing. It was too chancy. The caller had said that Ella would be killed *that morning*, without delay, if there were any sign of police interference.

Once back in their house, Ginger and Avery locked the door and closed the draperies. They both felt violated, exposed. They couldn't eat breakfast. They sat in the living room, tensely waiting—waiting to hear that Ella had been released.

"Do you think we should've called the police?" Ginger asked anxiously.

"Too dangerous," Avery said with some misgivings. "The man told Neil that Ella would be killed at once if we didn't follow his orders exactly."

"I know, but . . . Do you think someone was watching us?"

"Undoubtedly. Darling, stop fretting."

"Did you count the money?" she went on.

Avery sighed and shook his head. "Neil counted it four times." He came and sat next to her on the couch and put an arm around her. "Come on, sweetheart," he said soothingly, "I know how worried you are about Ella, but try to relax. All we can do now is wait."

During the previous night, knowing nothing about the ransom, Ella tied the bedclothes together, silently crying with frustration. She hadn't realized how difficult it was to make strong knots in bulky cloth. But somehow she twisted the sheets at the ends, and pulled the knots as tight as she could, and although they didn't look any too firm to her, she decided they would have to do.

Luckily the heavy wooden bunk bed was next to the window so that she was able to tie one end of her rope of sheets to the footboard and there was no danger of the bed sliding. She said a silent prayer and then climbed over the windowsill.

Outside the cabin, she gingerly lowered herself toward the rocks below, slowing her descent by "walking" down the outside cabin wall, pressing the bottoms of her bare feet against the siding while using her hands to hang on to the sheets, just as she had done in *The Lady Was Framed*. Her heart was banging with fright, but she concentrated on putting one foot down carefully after the other.

She still had ten feet to go when one of the knots she had made in the flimsy bedspread gave way. With a scream she couldn't stifle, she fell backward onto the rocks, hitting her head on a sharp boulder.

Just before she lapsed into unconsciousness, she realized that the breaking of her improvised rope of sheets wasn't in the script.

Vic and Kelly both awoke at once, hearing Ella's scream and the thud of her body. Grabbing a flashlight, they raced outside and found her draped over the boulders behind the house. The beam of light illuminated blood oozing onto the gray rock from her scalp and her back. It was the sight of all the blood that panicked them.

"Christ!" Vic gasped, "Is she dead?"

"I don't give a shit!" Kelly quavered. "Let's get the fuck outta here!"

"But the money—"

"Screw the money! Stick around and they'll nail us for murder. C'mon!" Kelly raced back toward the cabin.

Vic hesitated, then ran after him. "What the hell. We'll get the dough from Bert later."

Back in the house, they glanced quickly around the downstairs rooms they had occupied to make sure they were leaving behind no incriminating evidence. Then they snatched up their duffel bags and toiletries and threw them into the black Ford station wagon that Bert had provided.

They headed south toward the Mexican border and three hours later crossed over into Mexicali with no trouble at all.

Bert was jittery and drinking heavily. It was past noon and still no word from the boys. The plan had been for Kelly to drive down Highway 74 to Palm Desert every morning at ten and phone Ella's mansion from a pay phone. When the butler answered, Kelly would ask for Bert. If Bert didn't have the ransom yet, he would tell the butler to say he was too distraught to talk. And if Bert took the call, Kelly would say he was a friend from New York visiting Palm Springs for a few days, did Bert want to meet him for a drink? Bert would then reply that he wasn't feeling well and couldn't. That was the signal to Kelly that Bert had the money, and nobody would be suspicious if the police had a tap on Ella's phone, although Bert was pretty sure that Ella's family had not yet called the police.

Then Kelly and Vic were supposed to take Ella—blindfolded, gagged, and bound—in the black Ford station wagon, leave her on a picnic table at one of the National Forest campgrounds near Alpine Village, first finding one where nobody was around and then hightailing it down to Cat City. There they would pick up their share of the ransom from Bert in the men's room of O'Hanlon's Bar, call Neil from a pay phone and tell him where to find his sister, and then take off for Mexico.

Two days went by without the morning phone call from Kelly, and then a third day went by with no call. Unshaven, hung-over, with spasms of nausea churning his stomach, Bert didn't know what to do. But he didn't dare drive up to the cabin and get personally involved. He had the boys' share of the ransom in the back of his closet, all neatly packed in two flight bags and ready to give to them.

Meanwhile, Ginger, Avery, Neil, Jiminy, and Todd were frantic—they had been unable to get in touch with Cal, who was somewhere in Mexico. It had been three days since the ransom was paid, but there was no word from or about Ella. The entire family spent the days and nights at Neil's house, waiting to hear from her. Waiting. Waiting. Finally, on the third day, they phoned the police.

By coincidence, the police had just received a call from the man who owned the cabin up on the road to Idyllwild. He had gone to prepare the cabin for a new occupant, since the two previous tenants had rented it only for one week. When he got there, the upstairs bedroom door was locked. He unlocked it, but found no one in the room. Then he noticed the sheet tied to the foot of the bed and hanging out the open window. Puzzled, he looked out the window and saw Ella's body sprawled on the rocks below.

He rushed down to see if she were still alive, but she was dead, all right, cold and stiff. An autopsy later revealed that it wasn't the concussion that had killed her. She had slowly bled to death.

The police combed the cabin for clues. Whoever had kidnapped Ella had left only a few candy-bar wrappers in a wastebasket, but on the back of the toilet the detectives found a half-used book of matches. It was from O'Hanlon's Bar in Cathedral City.

"Any of your regulars no-show the last week or so, Bill?" the detective asked the bartender.

Bill was thoughtful. He wanted to stay on the good side of the cops. It never hurt. "Yeah. A couple of ex-cons—name of Vic and Kelly."

"Last names?"

"No idea."

"Where do they live?"

"Why you asking?"

"Curiosity."

"Hell, I don't know where they live."

Selma, the cocktail waitress, listened with a glint of revenge in her eyes. "They hang around with a shit-heel named Bert Elliott," she told the cops vindictively. "The bastard lives with some old has-been movie star . . ."

The detectives were out of there heading back to Palm Springs with their siren blasting before Selma could finish her sentence.

Earlier that day, Bert had packed part of his extensive wardrobe in two of Ella's biggest brocade suitcases and loaded them into the trunk of the white Eldorado. He put his share of the million dollars into a smaller case, then added the money he had hidden away in the closet for Vic and Kelly. This suitcase he kept safely and snugly on the floor of the passenger seat, where he could keep an eye on it. For a moment, while loading the Cadillac, still parked inside the four-car garage, he had been tempted to take Ella's silver Bentley, but he didn't want to drive a car that Ella's relatives might report as a stolen vehicle. At least Ella had had the decency to put the Eldorado in his name.

He decided to slip away without leaving a forwarding address. No reason Ella's family would want to get in touch with him, and after the way Vic and Kelly had botched things up, he wouldn't have given them their share of the money even if he had known where they were.

The past few hours had been hard on Bert. After Ginger had phoned to tell him Ella was dead, he had suffered wave after wave of guilt, alternating with bouts of jubilation that he would never again have to worry about money. Despite his grudges and resentments against Ella, he had loved her, in his way, certainly when he first met her twenty-two years earlier. But "love" was the wrong word, he decided. He had been smitten, not with love, but with lust. He couldn't help but regret that he would never again enjoy her silken, soft, clinging, ardent body.

Actually, he concluded, Ella had brought about her own death. She was selfish, lustful, willful, and impetuous. Years ago, she had selfishly snatched him away from Gracie, and then when a younger prick had smiled up at her, she had dumped him, wifeless, childless, penniless, and without a job. The subsequent twenty years had impoverished and embittered him and convinced him of the value of money, at any price. If she hadn't been so goddamn impatient, she wouldn't have jumped out of the window. Why couldn't she have waited just a few more hours? She would have been safely back in Palm Springs, and everybody would have been happy.

He was a little regretful that now he would have to leave Palm Springs forever. He liked the town. The dry, warm weather made him feel good. He had enjoyed being part of the ritzy bunch at the Tennis Club and the Thunderbird Country Club. He had felt like a real big shot being invited to the homes of all the famous movie stars Ella hung around with. But what the hell, he had a million bucks as consolation!

After his final four-course lunch at the table next to Ella's pool with its stunning view of Mt. San Jacinto and the Santa Rosas, Bert headed southeast toward the Mexican border. He decided he'd feel safer there because he had read about money laundering, just in case Ella's family had kept a record of the serial numbers of the ransom money. He was sure that in Mexico he could safely find a way to convert his stash of hundred-dollar bills into moola he'd feel safer cashing when he came back to the States. If he couldn't do it in Mexico, he'd go to the Cayman Islands or some other Caribbean refuge for hot bucks. Then he'd settle down for a few months in Mexico—maybe Cuernavaca—and rent a villa. He liked those dark-eyed brunette beauties down there. At least they wouldn't remind him of blue-eyed, blond Ella.

He sang all the way to the border, grinning whenever his eye caught the suitcase on the floor with its million gorgeous bucks inside. He thought that maybe he should've been a crooner, like Sinatra. He noticed that it was a beautiful day—the sky was blue-blue, the air was fresh, and he felt free, and so fucking rich! But as he approached the border, he had a stab of doubt. Did Customs ever examine cars headed into Mexico? Nah, he told himself, they only looked for stuff like dope and booze and wetbacks coming *into* the States. The Mexicans didn't give a good goddamn what you brought into their country, especially if you were white, well-dressed, and driving a Caddie.

He flashed a big smile at the U.S. Customs guard who held up his hand and came over to the car's window. "Driver's license," the man said tersely.

"Sure thing," Bert said genially. He was surprised, but he took out his wallet and handed the man his California license. Probably some new goddamn regulation. He'd never been asked for it on previous trips across the border.

The Customs officer studied Bert's license carefully, then pointed to an empty parking space alongside the Customs and Immigration building. "Pull over there," he said coldly.

"Hey," Bert protested, "whats a matter? I got a date in Mexicali."

The guard handed back the license and pointed again at the empty parking space. "Pull over!" he barked.

For one frantic moment Bert considered smashing through the barrier and speeding into Mexico—the motor still was running—but he decided to play it cool. By the time he pulled into the parking space and turned off the ignition, four policemen had surrounded the white Cadillac.

"What's in the bag on the floor?" one of the policemen asked, opening the door on the driver's side.

"Nothin', nothin'," Bert said, but his voice cracked and his hands were visibly shaking.

"Open it!"

Bert felt paralyzed. He couldn't move. "C'mon, guys," he pleaded with the whine of an innocent man being unjustly treated, "whatsa trouble?"

The policeman on the passenger side of the car opened the door and yanked the suitcase onto the seat. He ripped it open and grinned as he flashed the contents to the other three officers.

"How much is it?" the first policeman asked.

"A million dollars," Bert said weakly.

"I guess your little joyride's over, Mr. Elliott," the policeman said. "Get out of the car."

Bert complied. His legs were so weak he could barely stand. For a moment he was more mystified than frightened. His plan had been so goddamn foolproof! Why the hell had they pulled him over in the first place? "How'd you know . . . ?" he asked in confusion.

"Palm Springs police sent out an APB on you."

"What the hell's an APB?" Bert asked weakly.

"All-points bulletin. They also ˏsent out the license number of your Cad.

"Why?" he whispered, afraid he was going to faint.

"Why?" the cop repeated nastily. "Nothing much, buster. Just a slight charge of kidnapping. *And* murder."

Todd and Jiminy sold Ella's mansion because it was too big for them, and too pretentious for their taste. They were satisfied with their spacious house in Chino Canyon, where a number of movie stars had built secluded mansions. Then, in late November, Neil died of a massive stroke and left his entire fortune to Todd and Jiminy. The young couple couldn't resist moving into Neil's gold-walled villa on its private hill with sensational mountain and desert vistas in every direction. It was, after all, the most beautiful estate in Palm Springs.

As he always did, Cal came home for Christmas. When he had phoned Ginger from Mexico City to say he was coming back to Palm Springs, she had invited him to stay at her house. His anticipation of seeing Jiminy again made him look exceptionally animated and youthful. He didn't dare ask Ginger or Avery whether Jiminy and Todd were happy together, whether their marriage was working. God, he hoped not!

He felt vaguely disloyal to his son for wishing the marriage was a disaster, but knowing Todd, Cal couldn't see how it would work out any other way. Cal convinced himself that he wasn't only concerned about his own happiness, but much, much more about Jiminy's. He was certain he could make her happy. Blissful!

"I guess I'm actually sorry that there won't be any more of Neil's Christmas parties," Cal told Ginger shortly after he arrived, "even though I never particularly en-

joyed them. Unless . . . I don't suppose Jim'ny and Todd
will continue the tradition? Now that they're living in
Neil's house?"

"Well, I doubt it. Certainly not this year." She hesitated. "Jiminy and Todd aren't here, Cal." She was
mortified to see the shocked misery on his face. "They
flew to Switzerland for the holidays."

"She's not here?" he mumbled, dazed. All year, in the
self-imposed exile of wandering alone through Mexico,
he had waited impatiently for this moment, forcing himself to keep his vow to stay away from Jiminy until
Christmas. Not a day had passed without his wanting to
jump on a plane to come and see her, to hold her in his
arms again. And now she wasn't here. He couldn't believe it.

"I'm so sorry, Cal," Ginger said softly.

He turned desolate eyes on her. "Was it her idea?"

"I don't know," Ginger lied. Of course it had been
Jiminy's idea. Todd hadn't wanted to go, knowing that
even if there were any golf links over there, they'd be
under ten feet of snow. He was pretty damn sure, more-
over, that Swiss television wouldn't be carrying the bowl
games, certainly not the Orange or Cotton, probably not
even the Rose Bowl. But Jiminy had insisted on going.
She had been as terrified of seeing Cal as Cal was eager
to see her.

Cal went out onto the porch and sat on the railing. The
sun had dropped behind Mt. San Jacinto, leaving the
late-afternoon sky an electrifying turquoise. The rocky
slopes behind Ginger's house were in amber shadow, but
the Santa Rosas to the south and east were dipped in
coral. He remembered feeling a jolt of wonder, years
earlier, driving in his old Duesenberg to the Racquet
Club and having to stop, spellbound by San Jacinto.
Then he hadn't understood that mystical moment, but
now, at last, he did. He had traveled all over the world
looking for a spiritual home that he might have found
right here all along.

Ginger followed him outside. "Would you like to have
that old portrait of your father?" she asked.

"The one you used to have above the fireplace?"

She nodded. "It's been in Tony's old room all these

years. But you really should have it. That is, if you want it."

"I'd love to have it," he said, smiling fondly at her. She had always been so good to him, and so good for him. "I just realized something," he told her.

"Hmmmm?"

"I'm awfully tired of traveling, Ginger. And that's a pretty big painting of my old man. I'll need a permanent wall for it, won't I?"

"You mean, you're going to stay in Palm Springs?"

He nodded. "I'm going to find me a pretty little house with a view of old San Jacinto, and live there forever."

"I'm so glad, Cal. I miss you when you're away."

"Ah, Ginger, it hasn't been easy for me . . ." He peered out at the majestic rock pile of their beloved mountain behind the house and realized how much comfort he derived from the sight of it. Yes, he would have to find a house with a view like Ginger's. "Tell me . . . how are Todd and Jim'ny handling Neil's fortune? And my mother's estate too. What is it altogether, around seventy million?"

"Seventy-four. *After* taxes. It boggles the mind! Two twenty-one-year-old kids with that kind of money."

"You and Avery aren't exactly poor," he said dryly.

"We are compared to them."

"So's the whole world," he said ruefully. "Do you remember what it was like to be poor?"

"Once you've been there, Cal, you never forget. When I was twenty-one, all your father and I had was a little cabin—where my hotel is now. Tonito built it himself. We had a neat little outhouse—I actually made red curtains for it—and we had some of Nellie's cast-off furniture from the inn. Oh, but how we appreciated everything we had! It was so much fun! Little Johnny played with simple wooden toys that Tonito made for him, and Johnny cherished every one of them." Her eyes misted over as she recalled her toddler who had drowned. If he had lived, he'd now be forty-two! She couldn't picture her firstborn as an adult.

"So what do we do now, Auntie, when you and Avery and I all kick? Do we leave our estates to Todd and Jim'ny too? If not, who do we give them to?"

She sighed. "Cal, I wish I knew. I want mine to do some good. And you?"

"I've already given a lot away," he said.

"In Mexico?"

"Mostly. What's sad is that it's so hopeless. For every pauper you feed, a hundred more paupers are born every minute. What the peons need is their own land, and improved techniques to grow better corn and beans, but all our government gives is guns to the crooked bastards who rule them. We should be giving condoms, and the education to use them. Otherwise, with that birthrate, the whole goddamn region is gonna explode in the greatest bloodbath the world has ever seen!"

Cal looked so sad, Ginger decided to change the subject. "Tell me, Cal," she said cautiously, "does it bother you that your mother and your Uncle Neil left everything to Todd and Jiminy?"

He shook his head. "Nope. I'm having enough trouble getting rid of what I already have. Besides, the money that's left keeps generating more money. I could've gotten quite a bundle, you know, a few years ago when Congress finally divided up the tribal land. Anyone with even one-eighth Agua Caliente blood could apply for something like three hundred and thirty thousand dollars' worth of pretty choice Palm Springs real estate. And if they hold on to it, it'll be worth millions someday."

"So why didn't you apply? You're half Agua Caliente."

He hesitated. "It would've meant making my illegitimacy public, and embarrassing my mother. And everyone would've known that your first husband was unfaithful to you. I didn't want to do that to either of you."

"That was thoughtful of you, Cal," she said gratefully. "But have you ever thought of using Tonito's name? You know, Alvarez, instead of Frank Ricardo's name?"

"Sure I have. I'd be proud to. But, what I just said—about people knowing he'd been unfaithful to you . . ."

"I don't mind," she assured him. "It all happened such a long time ago. And now that Ella's gone . . . why don't you go ahead and do it legally? Maybe Todd would like it too."

Cal stood up abruptly. "When's Jiminy getting back?"

"Around the middle of January. Maybe sooner, if Todd gets too bored."

He hesitated. "Tell me, Ginger, are they . . . happy?"

She sighed. "You'll have to judge for yourself."

Neither said it, but both of them were thinking that Jiminy needn't have run all the way to Switzerland to avoid seeing Cal. When she returned to Palm Springs, she would have to deal with his constant presence there, and with the inescapable fact that he and she were madly, desperately in love with each other.

Jiminy was afraid to go home after she phoned her parents to wish them a happy new year and learned that Cal had bought a Spanish-style villa in Palm Springs. And that he planned to live there and stop traveling.

Todd shrugged when she told him the news about his father. "Maybe he finally wants to be pals with me."

Not with you, she thought. She longed for Cal all the time. She had reached the point where she knew that if he just touched her with his little finger, she would fall into his arms and never leave. And Todd was so jealous, it would kill him. She couldn't hurt Todd like that.

This past year, Todd had been away a lot, either running the company Uncle Neil had left them, which now had offices all over California, or else competing in golf tournaments around the country. When he was home, they had "played house" in their beautiful big estate, but no matter how much she tried to enjoy it, she always felt miserable. Unlike their schooldays, when they had only wanted to be with each other, they now had many friends, mainly because Todd was such a captivating fellow that he drew people to him. They were busy almost every night of the week, going to parties and dances and benefits, or entertaining at their place. Todd was restless when they had a quiet evening together, and they always ended up going out to eat and dance at the Racquet Club or at one of the country clubs where they were members. Todd loved being surrounded by people, lots of people. The only trouble was that the people were all like him: good-looking, charming, jocks—and Jiminy found them boring.

Jiminy had had lunch with her parents once a week, but a strain had developed between her and them, one they all made every effort to overcome, and when that failed, they all cheerily tried to make believe that everything was fine, just fine. Only it wasn't fine, because Jiminy knew they still were unhappy about her marrying Todd.

Todd hated Switzerland and was eager to get home. He had sacrificed all the holiday parties back in Palm Springs to come with Jiminy to Gstaad. He wasn't crazy about skiing, and he found the Palace Hotel too stiff and formal for his taste. Everything on television was in German or French. His sighs and fidgets were beginning to make Jiminy feel guilty.

"I guess you want to go home," she said, two days after New Year's.

"You bet!"

She wanted to say: You go and I'll stay here awhile. But it seemed a poor way to start the new year. "Okay," she said, "let's leave tomorrow."

There was only one way now that she could escape succumbing to Cal, and thus destroying Todd. While Todd was downstairs arranging for their departure, Jiminy wrapped her diaphragm in a wad of toilet paper and threw it in the wastebasket. Now all she had to do was get Todd to make love to her.

Jiminy saw Cal in the company of others, and managed to avoid seeing him alone. And by late January she was pregnant again. Protecting herself from Cal wasn't the only reason she wanted a baby. She hoped it would give some meaning to her life. She felt more and more alienated from the rounds of parties that filled her days and nights. There were always people in their house, boring people—houseguests Todd had invited, often forgetting to tell her.

"But, Jiminy," he would say when she complained, "it's not as if you have to cook for them or clean up after them. That's what we've got a houseful of servants for."

How could she tell him that she liked to be alone sometimes? Or that she would like to have a conversation on some subject other than golf or gossip? He would never understand. She began spending many of her afternoons at her parents' house and going to her old room for a few hours of privacy. But the awkwardness of her strained relationship with her parents bothered her—and them.

"Look here," she told Ginger and Avery one April day after lunch, "it's silly for us to be on less-than-perfect terms."

"It's worse than silly," Avery agreed, hugging her. "It's a crime."

Jiminy was flooded anew with love for them. "I know you feel badly that I married Todd. But it's done, and I'm pregnant again . . ." She touched her abdomen. "I'm three months along."

"Oh, Jim-jim!" It was Ginger's turn to hug her. "I'm happy for you. Really and truly."

They sat around a small table on the pink mansion's back porch and smiled at each other as if they had just met after having been separated for a long time. "While we're being honest with each other," Jiminy went on, "I guess you both know that I'm in love with Cal."

They nodded, speechless at her honesty.

Jiminy grasped each of their hands closest to her. "Mom, you know what it's like to be in love while you're married to someone else."

"It was different for your father and me," Ginger said. "We became lovers. We had that consolation."

"It's not as if I don't love Todd . . ." Jiminy said with a sigh.

"But your love for Todd isn't the kind you need for a happy marriage," Ginger said. "You knew that before you married him."

"I know. And I'd still marry Todd again if it came to that, even knowing in advance how unhappy it would make me. I feel so responsible for him! I can't abandon him. He'd die."

"Are you sure he'd die?" Avery asked.

"Oh Dad, of course I'm sure. Maybe he wouldn't literally, but he just can't function without me. And he's so jealous, there's no telling what he'd do if I left him." Jiminy stood up and took a deep breath. "The only thing is, I'm terrified of seeing Cal alone. I'm afraid I wouldn't be able to resist him."

"He understands," Ginger assured her.

"How do you know, Mom?"

"Because he told me so."

Jiminy was startled. "You and Cal *discuss* our . . . our . . . how we feel about each other?"

"Sure," Ginger smiled complacently. "I guess you could say I'm his confidante. Have been for years."

"I'll be damned."

"I'm very fond of him," Ginger went on. "He's a sensitive, caring man, and his love for you is beautiful to behold. If you love him half as much as I think you do, the two of you could have a wonderful life together. And darling, I so want you to be happy!"

"What else did he say about me?" Jiminy asked eagerly.

"He said he won't interfere in your life, Jim-jim, or try to push you into leaving Todd. He says you'll come to him when you're ready."

Jiminy gave birth to a boy one night in early October. Todd wanted to call the baby Antonio, after Cal's real father, and Jiminy readily agreed. "Imagine," she told Ginger the next morning at the hospital, "little Antonio is descended from you and all *three* of your husbands!"

"The fact hasn't escaped me," Ginger said dryly.

"But it's so amazing! Your first husband, Tonito, fathered Cal, who is Todd's father, so that makes Tonito the baby's great-grandfather. Then, since Jason's daughter, Vivien, is Todd's mother, she's the baby's grandmother, and that makes Jason little Antonio's great-grandfather too. Then, of course, you and Daddy are his grandparents on my side—"

"Darling, I know the statistics inside-out. And I assure you, it's *very* strange for me to hold this little creature who is part of all of us." Ginger smiled down at the infant in her arms. "It's too early to see who he's going to look like."

"All red like that," Jiminy said, "maybe he'll look like an Indian."

"Except that Indians aren't really red. Tonito's skin was like polished copper—like he had a good tan."

"Enough genealogy," Avery boomed, coming into the room. "I could hear you two all the way down the hall."

He took the baby from Ginger and sat down, holding his grandson in his lap. First he was all proud grandfather, goo-gooing and making silly faces. Then he turned all doctor and carefully examined the infant. "I'd say he's a fine specimen," he assured Jiminy and Ginger.

"Oh Daddy, I'm so relieved. After what happened with my first pregnancy . . ." Jiminy reached out her arms for her son.

"Has his . . . his *other* grandfather seen him yet?" Ginger asked cautiously.

"Cal? Oh, sure. He was with Todd in the waiting room all night while I was in labor. In fact, Cal talked Todd into legally changing his name to Alvarez. So all of us—Cal, Todd, me, the baby—we'll all be Alvarez from now on, instead of Ricardo. It really makes more sense."

"Why didn't you call *us* when you went to the hospital?" Ginger complained.

"Because there was no point worrying you and Dad until it was all over," Jiminy told her. "I think Cal's going to take after Aunt Ella. I mean, she was a terrible mother to Cal, but a wonderful grandmother to Todd. Then Cal was a terrible father to Todd, but he seems absolutely smitten with Antonio."

Only because you're Antonio's mother, Ginger could have said, but didn't.

Two weeks before Christmas, Jiminy unexpectedly brought little Antonio to her parents' house. They had created a complete nursery in one of their extra guest rooms so that the infant, now two months old, could stay with them whenever Jiminy was willing to let him out of her sight. Jiminy didn't tell them where she was going, but they had a pretty good idea from the determined, half-frightened, half-ecstatic look on her face.

Ginger was breathless with maternal concern for her daughter. Jiminy was going to the man she loved, and Ginger had to hold back all the advice she was desperate to give her. *Don't be frightened*, she wanted to say. *Don't hold back. Feel free, darling, free to savor every caress he gives you, free to touch his body, to explore, don't be shy, anything goes. Be happy, be happy, my darling. . . .* But she didn't say anything. These things had to be learned by oneself and from one's lover, not from one's mother.

Ginger saw that Jiminy had taken great care in preparing for her visit to Cal. Her hair was a mass of freshly shampooed waves. Her smooth skin glistened as though polished. The slight tremor of her lips betrayed her excitement. She was wearing a simple blue dress with snaps down the front and Ginger wondered with amusement whether her daughter had chosen that particular garment because it was so easy to pull open.

Ginger glanced at Avery, and she could tell that his thoughts paralleled hers. They both wanted so much for their girl! So much that Jiminy had denied herself when she married Todd instead of Cal.

As Jiminy drove away, down her parents' long steep driveway, every part of her tingled with anticipation. She trembled so much that she had trouble driving. God, she and Cal had waited so long for this moment! She was eager to see his face when she came to him.

She was liberated, free at last of Todd's hold on her. She didn't know who had been the bigger fool—Todd for thinking he was in love with her, or she for convincing herself that he needed her, that he would shrivel up and *die* without her. What a joke!

For weeks she had awakened in the middle of the night, an hour or two after giving the baby his middle-of-the-night feeding, only to find Todd gone from their bed. Too tired to investigate, each time she had fallen back to sleep. In the morning, when she asked him where he had been, he invariably told her that he'd had insomnia, that he hadn't been able to fall back to sleep after hearing her get up to feed Antonio.

The explanation seemed reasonable enough. Antonio's nursemaid had offered to give the baby a bottle for the night feeding so that Jiminy could sleep undisturbed, but Jiminy insisted on nursing Antonio. She couldn't believe how much she adored the tiny creature. Her love for him swept over her in great gusts that left her grinning with joy.

The previous night she had fallen back to sleep after feeding Antonio, and then had awakened with a start. Todd, as usual, was gone. Feeling restless, she had put on her robe and gone looking for him, wanting to suggest that they have some milk and cookies and then try to sleep. Todd wasn't in any of the rooms she looked into. She went to the kitchen, thinking he might be making a snack for himself, but he wasn't there either. She decided to sit out by the pool, but no sooner had she stretched out on a lounge chair than she heard loud grunts coming from one of their guest bungalows on the other side of the pool.

She knew they didn't have any guests staying with them at the moment. Or had Todd invited someone, and then forgotten to tell her? Or . . . could it be intruders? Barefoot, she went silently to the bungalow and looked into a window through the lace curtains.

Todd was having intercourse with one of their maids as he never had had it with her. Their grunts had turned into cries of erotic pleasure. Instead of the halfhearted thrusts he had always made into her body, he was ramming the woman with dizzying force and bellowing his ardor.

Watching them, she didn't feel at all like a betrayed wife, but more like a sister watching a younger brother make a goddamn fool of himself. It occurred to her that she had been married for two years, and had a baby, and yet she still felt like a virgin. Her tentative sexual fumblings with Todd had never given her an orgasm. The only reason she even knew what an orgasm felt like was that sometimes, in desperation, she gave herself one.

Dear God, she realized, *she was free!* Todd didn't need her. Not as a wife. Only as a caretaker, a leftover remnant of his childhood dependency upon her that he didn't want to relinquish. Well, he would just have to grow up now without her help, she thought, smiling about Todd's secret love life as she drove to Cal's house after leaving her parents.

Jiminy's heart began racing in anticipation. She would fly into Cal's arms, this time without having to tear herself away from him. She left her car in the middle of his driveway and rushed up to his door. It was locked, and when she rang the bell, there was no response. Shaken with disappointment, she looked through a window and was relieved to see Cal out behind the house, sitting in the shade of the ramada beside his pool. He was resting there quietly in a white wicker rocking chair, serenely gazing at the mountains.

She went around the house and stood before him. "Hi," she said softly.

"Hi." He gestured at a wrought-iron garden chair facing him.

She sat down. "I thought you'd be glad to see me."

"I am."

"Then why . . . ?"

"Why don't I sweep you into my arms?" He looked at her unsmilingly. "Because first I want to know exactly why you're here."

"*Why* I'm here?" She was dismayed. "Oh, Cal, don't you love me anymore?"

"More than ever." He waited. "Well, why *are* you here?"

"Because *you're* here."

He laughed. "That's a very good reason."

"And I'm free now. Free to love you."

"What happened?" he asked gently.

"I found Todd having sex with one of our maids."

"The big one you hired last month? Fat and blond?"

"Yes! How did you guess?"

"Because he's always liked to have sex with big fat women, Jim'ny. Ever since he was—I don't know—fifteen, sixteen."

"And all the time we've been married too?"

He nodded.

"Then why didn't you *tell* me?"

He shook his head at her stupidity. "You know you wouldn't have believed me. You've always been so goddamn pigheaded where Todd's concerned." He let himself look at her with the eyes of a lover, as he had been afraid to do ever since she had married his son. He didn't want to see her as his daughter-in-law, but as the woman he loved. She seemed more beautiful to him than ever— blooming with motherhood—but also with her newfound freedom to love him.

He stood up then, took her hands, pulled her up out of the chair, and held her close against him. He felt giddy, lighter than air, like a gaily colored balloon ready to soar. When he kissed her, she responded ardently, eagerly, and for the first time without any reservations whatsoever.

He took her to a long padded glider—where he often napped—and sat down with her. He just wanted to hold her for a while, to savor the *anticipation* of making love to her. They both had waited so long for this magic moment—seven years, since that first kiss on the Ile St. Louis. He felt new, freshly created, without a past, like Adam the first time he touched Eve.

Through the soft cloth of her dress, he let his hand lightly touch her breasts and slowly slide downward, stopping below her navel. He was in no hurry. They had all afternoon. And all night. *And the rest of their lives!*

Jiminy returned to her parents' house three hours later to get Antonio and bring him back to Cal's house. "I'm going to stay with Cal," she told her parents. "Forever and ever." Her eyes were lustrous with sensual satisfaction.

Impulsively she threw her arms around her mother, then her father. "I never used to understand exactly what it was, when I'd see you two look at each other, you know, like you shared some wonderful private secret." She giggled. "Now I understand. *Oh,* do I finally understand!"

Ginger hugged her. "I'm so glad, darling. So glad!"

Jiminy took a deep breath, still ragged with lingering bliss. "Oh, Mom, Dad . . . it's so wonderful!"

Avery put a proud arm around each of them. "My two beautiful girls!" He was thinking how much like Ginger his daughter was at this moment. After he made love to Ginger, she always had that same luminous, deeply sated look that he now saw in Jiminy's face, and he was grateful to Cal for loving his daughter, and for finally making her happy.

Two days later, Jason returned from his research trip to Jordan. Loaded down with Christmas gifts for the family, he took a taxi from the airport to Todd's and Jiminy's estate, since he hadn't told anyone when he was arriving. He walked into a scene of utter chaos.

Todd was screaming into the phone at Jiminy that he would kill her, kill Cal, fight her in court for the baby, shoot himself, and *by God* get even with her! Then Todd slammed down the phone and began to cry.

Jason held him in his arms and tried to comfort him, as he had done countless times when Todd was a youngster and Jason and Ella had been his substitute parents. At first Jason was furious with Jiminy for hurting his grandson. *Just like her mother*, he fumed to himself, *marrying one man and then falling in love with another*. . . .

But Jason had to be fair. He knew how loyal Jiminy had been to Todd, how she had taken care of him all during their years of growing up together. Jason had always admired Jiminy, had been exceedingly fond of her, especially when she grew into young womanhood and began to remind him so much of Ginger. "C'mon, Todd, tell me exactly what happened," he urged.

"She caught me having a little fun with one of the maids," Todd admitted. "So what? Everybody screws around."

Jason shook his head. "Not with a wife like Jiminy."

"Why not? She doesn't even like sex." Todd sat up straight and wiped his eyes.

"Then it was up to you to help her like it."

Todd gave Jason a troubled look. "I couldn't, Grandpa."

"Why not?"

Todd hesitated. "Well . . . she . . . I . . ." He sighed. "Y'see, I never . . . she was too . . ." He groaned. "How can I put it so you'll understand? Sex just wasn't much fun with her. I mean, for either of us."

"I see. So she left you for Cal? Is that what you were saying on the phone?"

"Yeah. My own *father* stole my wife!"

Jason remembered the way Cal and Jiminy had looked at each other every time he had seen them together the past few years. "Todd, I know what you're going through. I went through it myself, when Ginger left me for Avery. All I can say is, there's no point fighting it. When women fall in love like that . . ." He shook his head sadly. "She'll never come back to you. And maybe it's for the best."

Angrily Todd stood up and glared down at his grandfather. "Whose side are you on, anyway?"

"That's what I'm trying to tell you. There *are* no sides. You're acting like a spoiled brat, screaming threats at

Jiminy. You think that'll bring her back?" Jason looked at him shrewdly. "Are you sure you really want her back?"

"Of course I do! She's my wife! I love her!"

"Todd, let me tell you something. When a husband and wife don't enjoy sex with each other, it usually means that there's a fatal flaw in their relationship. Sure, you can have great sex without love, but when you really love someone, *making* love is an affirmation of that love."

"I don't care what you say," Todd barked with uncharacteristic anger. "I want her back! And dammit all, Grandpa, I want my baby back too!"

When Jason phoned Jiminy and asked if he could see his great-grandson, she assured him that he would be more than welcome. She kissed him cautiously when he arrived, not sure how he felt about her.

"Don't worry," he assured her. "I'm not blaming you." *Not the way I still blame your mother,* he thought. After all, he and Ginger *had* been in love. They *had* been happy together for more than eight years. She had had no right to go off and fall in love with Avery. It irked him that after twenty-three years it still hurt him so much.

He followed Jiminy into the makeshift nursery in Cal's guest room, where Antonio was just waking from his nap. As Jason stared down at the infant, a great sadness gripped him. This great-grandson of his would always be Jiminy's and Cal's, and Ginger's and Avery's. He himself would forever be the tolerated outsider. Oh, they all were friendly enough to him, but they were a closed corporation so far as he was concerned—the jilted husband whose presence made them feel guilty, no matter how pleasantly they acted toward him.

Jiminy picked up the baby and let Jason hold him. "We have to get this room properly fixed up for him," she said. She looked into his eyes. "Are you angry with me, Jason?"

He shook his head. *I'm used to you fickle Rowland women,* he wanted to say. But what good would it do? She and Cal were so obviously in love.

"You're staying for Christmas dinner with us, aren't you?" she asked.

He shook his head, having already decided it would be too awkward. "Todd and I are going to Rome next week to see Vivien," he said. "I thought it might cheer him up."

Ever since he had bought his house, Cal had loved to sit in his wicker rocking chair under the grapevine-shaded ramada beside his swimming pool and gaze at Mt. San Jacinto. The rocking chair was wide enough for him and Jiminy to sit tightly pressed against each other, with his arm around her, and with Antonio in his lap. The scene filled him with beatitude. He didn't know whether it was because his Indian blood felt some atavistic mystical bond with the mountain, which the Agua Calientes considered sacred, or whether it was simply the juxtaposition of water and palm trees and mountain and vivid blue sky. Whatever the reason, the inclusion of Jiminy and her baby in the scene filled Cal with a joy that he had never dreamed existed. Jiminy and Antonio had been with him only three days, but Cal couldn't imagine life without them now.

Never in his entire life had Cal expected to be so thrilled by an infant. He was endlessly fascinated by the miniature fingers, the minuscule nails, the brand-new skin, the toothless smile, the moist little lips, the alert dark eyes.

Cal enjoyed gently inserting a finger into the baby's grasp and feeling Antonio tighten his tiny fingers around Cal's with amazing strength. Most of all, Cal liked to watch his grandson greedily suck his nourishment from Jiminy's rosy nipples. To Cal, this seemed the epitome of human love and nobility. He could understand now why Renaissance artists loved to paint the Virgin and child, again and again trying to catch this symbol of the continuity of the human species.

Ever since he had fallen in love with Jiminy, Cal had assumed that when they finally made love, *he* would be the knowledgeable one leading the novice to the heights of passion. But he had been astounded by the intensity of her ardor. This was no submissive young maiden waiting to be shown what to do. She was like a wild thing in his arms, triumphantly aware of her youth and beauty and the glory of being in love.

Cal felt sorry for Todd. His sweet, ignorant son. To have possessed Jiminy and not been able to realize her potential for physical rapture seemed tragic, indeed, to Cal. To have had this dazzling creature in his bed and then to leave her for a loveless, mindless *fuck* also seemed the height of stupidity to Cal. Poor Todd, he thought again and again, full of pity for his son. To his sorrow, Cal never had loved Todd the way he loved this tiny, wiggling, gurgling, happy baby in his lap.

Guiltily Cal wondered whether, if he had made the effort to be a father to him, Todd might have been different, even though Jason had been an excellent substitute father. Still, Cal chided himself, he had cheated Todd *and* himself of a love, and a bond, that would have added much to both their lives all these years.

Todd telephoned Jiminy once or twice a day to berate her. Even from across the room Cal could hear Todd's howls of rage on the telephone. Jiminy listened to Todd quietly, knowing better than to try to placate him. She looked sad, but not guilty, Cal was thankful to see. She no longer was feeling *responsible* for Todd, as she had for so many years.

One afternoon before Todd and Jason left for Rome, while Jiminy and the baby napped, Cal walked over to the estate that Todd and Jiminy had inherited from Neil. The day was balmy, the air fragrant with the dry smell of desert plants. Cal felt fit, strong, and virile, bursting with a youthfulness that belied his forty-two years. He wished the whole world could share his happiness. The very last thing he wanted to do was confront his son's rage, but it had to be done.

He found Todd sulking in his den, a handsome teak-paneled room whose floor-to-ceiling windows alternated with book-filled shelves. Cal sat down beside his son on a soft green leather couch. After much hesitation, and feeling awkward, Cal took Todd's hand, which Todd angrily snatched away.

"Ah, c'mon," Cal coaxed, "it doesn't help to be angry."

Todd looked away.

Cal got up and went to the bar built into one wall. "How about a margarita?" he coaxed. "My specialty." When Todd didn't respond, Cal went ahead and made a pitcherful.

"It's like this, kid," Cal went on, putting the pitcher and two salted glasses on the coffee table in front of Todd and pouring each of them a drink. "Accept the fact that you and Jim'ny never should've gotten married. You were like brother and sister all your lives. You should've just been good friends, not husband and wife." Cal sat down again, next to Todd.

"I love her," Todd muttered, lifting his glass.

"Sure you love her. And she loves you. But you two never were *in* love."

"How would you know?" Todd sniffed. "You were always off somewhere on the other side of the world."

"Regardless," Cal continued patiently, "she *is* in love with me, and I with her. The sooner you accept that and get on with your life, the better off you'll be."

"So I'm supposed to sit back and let you steal my wife? And my son? Just because you tell me to?"

"I'm not stealing anyone, Todd. Believe me, I never tried to take Jim'ny away from you, once you were married. She came to me herself, as I knew she would someday. But for your information, she and I have been in love ever since that summer we all went to Paris. Remember the day she gave me a tour of the city and you were too sick to come with us?"

Todd nodded, guiltily remembering the prostitute in Montmartre. He downed the rest of his drink and refilled his glass.

"Well, that day," Cal went on, "Jim'ny and I both realized that we loved each other . . . but she was afraid to admit it for a long, long time. She felt committed to you. *Responsible* for you. As for Antonio, he's your son and always will be. And I sure hope you'll be a better father to him than I was to you. I'm sorry I failed you, Todd. I truly am."

Todd looked up in surprise at this admission from his father, and for a moment his anger subsided. Then he glowered again. "I want legal custody of Antonio."

"C'mon, Todd, don't be vindictive. You know the baby's better off with his mother while he's little." Cal refilled his glass. "But you can see him anytime you want. And when he's older, there's no reason why he can't stay with you part of the time. Even half the time. As long as it's all friendly." Cal's voice shook. "As long as you don't neglect him the way I neglected you."

Todd slumped back in his seat and stared disconsolately at the beamed ceiling. He felt a vast emptiness, as though he were a shell with his insides removed, like a scooped-out melon.

"Listen, Todd, look at the bright side. You're a very rich fellow. You've got this fantastic house. You're young and attractive. Without a wife, you won't have to sneak around to get some ass, either. You can screw a different woman every day. If that's what you want."

Todd remembered that his friend Al Steinberg called that kind of sex *"shtupping."* Such a comical word! He suppressed a smile, not wanting his father to think he wasn't suffering.

"But if you don't mind a bit of fatherly advice," Cal continued, "you'll take some of your money and get yourself a shrink and find out why you've got this crazy yen for fat slobs. Believe me, I've screwed all kinds of women in my time, but there's nothing like making love to a woman you really and truly love."

Todd scowled.

"I mean it. Get some professional help, Todd. I want you to be happy."

"Sure you do," Todd said snidely. "If you go around feeling guilty about me, it'll interfere with your own happiness, won't it?"

"That's not the main reason," Cal said quietly. "And you know it."

Todd shrugged. He didn't want to admit it, but his anger against Jiminy was fading. Maybe their marriage had been a mistake. His hatred for his father was fading too. All his life, he had wanted Cal to love him. His Grandma Ella and his Grandpa Jason had been wonderful parents, but Todd had always felt abandoned, not so much by Vivien as by Cal. Maybe it wasn't too late to at least be friends.

As though reading his mind, Cal smiled. "We've never had much to say to each other, have we? I can't talk about sports to you, and you can't talk about the Mexican peons to me."

"There *are* other subjects . . ." Todd said tentatively.

"So?" Cal said, standing up. "Are you going to be reasonable?"

Todd stood up and faced his father, reluctant to give up the role of the injured party. He wasn't ready to make any promises. And he certainly wasn't going to spill his guts to some dumb head doctor. "I'll think about it, Dad," he said.

"Ah, Todd!" Impulsively Cal threw his arms around his son in a Mexican *abrazo*. Todd stood there stiffly for a moment, resisting, and then slowly put his arms around his father and suppressed a sob.

As it turned out, Todd was no more interested in Antonio than Cal had been interested in Todd as a baby. Todd and Jiminy equally divided the fortune they had jointly inherited from Neil. They sold the lovely gold-walled estate that Neil had left them because Todd decided to move out to the El Dorado Country Club in Indian Wells, where he was building a mansion a few doors from President Eisenhower's place. Jiminy didn't want Neil's estate either. She preferred to live in Cal's pretty, much simpler house.

A year later, Jiminy's divorce from Todd was final. On their terrace facing Mt. San Jacinto, with only Ginger and Avery in attendance and Antonio standing between them, Cal and Jiminy were married.

CHAPTER
16

1966

One night in late August, Avery was jolted awake by breath-stopping pains in his chest and back. He immediately ruled out a heart attack; the symptoms were quite different. He tried to remember what he had had for dinner—or had he drunk too much wine? He was quite sure he was having an attack of acute pancreatitis and, if he were correct, he knew he should get to the hospital. The condition itself was not necessarily too serious unless he went into shock. Then it could be fatal without quick medical attention.

He was eighty-one years old and had been blessed with excellent health all his life. The first thing that occurred to him was that he wouldn't be able to watch the dawn from Mt. San Jacinto that morning. Except during violent rainstorms or when he had been away from Palm Springs, he had seldom missed hiking up his beloved mountain to watch the sunrise. *What if he could never do it again?*

He touched Ginger's arm and she awoke with a start. "Darling," he said softly, but there was no way he could avoid alarming her, "I don't feel well."

She sat up and turned on the bedside light. Then she leaned over and touched his face. "Oh, *Avery!*"

He could see the fear in her eyes. How many years had she been secretly dreading this day? "Call Sam. And an ambulance," he whispered, bracing himself against a fresh onslaught of pain.

*   *   *

After three days of tests, Sam Miller, Avery's doctor, reluctantly came into Avery's hospital room and stood beside the bed. It was a long moment before he could speak. "It's the worst news possible, Avery," Sam finally said, choking back his distress.

Avery blinked, shocked at the fear that gripped him. "Well? Go on!"

Sam cleared his throat. "The tests and X rays . . yes, it was acute pancreatitis, all right, but that's not the real problem. Avery, the tests showed you have . . . a primary cancer of the liver. Both lobes . . ." He gulped. "Inoperable." They stared at each other in agony. Sam didn't have to explain. They both knew what that meant.

Foolishly Avery had come to expect that he would live forever—well, at least to a hundred. Physically he now faced becoming a helpless invalid, with ever-increasing pain and a steady loss of weight and vigor, until he shrank into a shriveled parody of a human being. Mentally he would grow progressively confused and lose all dignity, until finally his brain's functions would cease altogether. He would be a helpless vegetable. And then he would die. He had watched several of his patients suffer that way, but he had never dreamed that one day it might happen to him.

And what of Ginger? What of *her* pain, watching him deteriorate day by day? Oh, if only he had simply died in his sleep, or fallen dead with a slam-bang heart attack! Not this! Not a slow, lingering, *loathsome* death!

With medication for his pain, Avery was able to come home from the hospital. His sudden loss of vigor was astonishing. He could walk around some with a cane, but since the stairs were too difficult for him, Ginger moved their clothes and toiletries down into the first-floor guest room and bath. The night after he returned from the hospital, she clung to him as though the sheer force of her embrace could cure him. Sam had tried to be honest with her, to warn her exactly what to expect, but she stubbornly refused to give up hope that Avery might recover.

Avery knew that sex was out of the question. *Old fool, you've had more than your share*, he tried to console himself. Still, he derived enormous comfort from the closeness of her body. He caressed her hair, loving its softness. She was still so beautiful. She never seemed to age. Or was it that he saw her through such thoroughly love-struck eyes?

"Ginger." He spoke softly—he tired so easily. "Darling, listen to me. You mustn't cling to false hopes. I'm not going to get better. I'll only get worse . . . and worse . . ." His voice trailed off.

"No! I can't live without hope."

"You must," he said wearily. "If you don't, you'll only make it harder for me."

She bit her lip and shook her head. Her eyes were drenched with tears.

"Please, Ginger," he begged, "you've got to accept the fact that I'm dying. You've got to help *me* accept it. . . ." He buried his face in her hair.

She trembled uncontrollably in his arms. What good was all their money now, what good was her *life* if he died? "Avery," she protested, "there must be *something* Sam can do! One of the new miracle drugs?"

"No."

She cried silently against his cheek. Her entire being rose up with fury. *This can't be happening!* She moved away from him and lay on her back, staring up at the dark ceiling. She thought of star-crossed lovers who jumped off cliffs together. "Then give me something, Avery. An overdose. I'll die with you."

He sighed. Why was she being so difficult? But what had he expected? That she would accept his death without protest? If the situation were reversed, wouldn't he feel the same way she did? But he couldn't let her even think of ending her life. She was only sixty-six. She was strong and healthy. She probably had years and years left, good productive years. Maybe in time she would even marry again. Why not? Someone like Jason, who still loved her . . . though the thought of her in Jason's arms made Avery's stomach lurch. He still was so jealous of Jason's years with Ginger. Anyway, she owed it to Jiminy to stay alive. And didn't she want to watch Antonio grow to manhood?

As always, Avery felt a warm glow when he thought of Jiminy's son. What a treasure! At three, he spoke beautifully, enunciating clearly in perfect sentences—no baby talk for him, except that he called Avery "Pa" instead of "Grandpa" and Ginger was his "Gamma." Antonio was fascinated by everything he saw and heard. Sometimes it bothered Avery that his grandson looked so much like Tonito. How strange heredity was! He really would have preferred that his grandson be in *his* image. Or Ginger's. Why should the boy look like that damn young fellow who had stolen Ginger from him in the first place?

Ah, but the boy was handsome. Sturdy and healthy, with expressive, laughing dark eyes. He had a way of bursting headlong into his grandparents' house with a mischievous grin and a shout of joy at seeing them. Whenever he sat on Avery's lap and put his adorable little arms around Avery's neck and kissed his cheek and said, "I love you, Pa," Avery thought his heart would melt with pride.

Before Avery became ill, Antonio had enjoyed "helping" Avery in the garden, using his own miniature trowel and rake. The two of them would get down on their hands and knees and pull weeds, stopping for frequent games of "horsie-back ride"—Avery was the loudly neighing horse and Antonio was the fearless rider, clutching the back of Avery's shirt and joyfully squealing, "Giddiyap, Pa!"

Avery's reverie ended abruptly when Ginger flung herself back into his arms. "Oh, *please* take me with you!" A great sob strangled her voice.

Ginger had nothing to console her. She had lost all desire to climb San Jacinto in the morning to watch the dawn. She knew how much Avery missed going up his mountain, and she was afraid that if she went up alone he would feel even more deprived. Besides, how could she bear ever again to stand on their favorite lookout without him?

She didn't even have Jiminy and Cal and Antonio to help her through these dreadful days. Cal had rented a house in Atlanta for a few months while giving moral and financial help to Martin Luther King.

"Shall I phone Jiminy?" Ginger asked Avery. "They'll want to come home—"

"No!" he barked vehemently. He made a violent gesture with both hands, as if to push them away. "I don't want them to see me like this! It's bad enough that you have to."

"But, Avery—"

His voice quavered. "I want Antonio to remember me the way I was. Not like this." Disgustedly his hand indicated his deteriorating body. Then his eyes softened. "I was three, just about the same age as Antonio, when my own grandfather died. To this day, I remember him so vividly! He was tall and robust. I look a lot like him . . . or I used to, anyway. That's how I want Antonio to always think of me."

A few days later, Avery realized he was going downhill daily. He had to take action while he was still lucid. He couldn't bear to face the indignity of the slow, painful disintegration of his body and mind. What was the point? Nor could he stand to think about the hardship that a long, drawn-out illness would impose upon Ginger. Sometimes it seemed to him that her suffering was more intense than his. She tried to smile and be cheerful around him, but he was aware of every tremor in her voice, every nuance of fake optimism in her manner. The skin beneath her eyes had darkened, and some mornings her eyelids bore the telltale redness of sleeplessness and tears.

Since the day he had met her, his foremost aim in life had been to make her happy. Now, to be causing her so much grief was beyond his endurance.

"Darling, I need some medicine," he told her, tearing the form off his prescription pad and handing it to her.

She looked at him suspiciously. "Shouldn't you check with Sam?"

"Why bother him? Anyway, I know more than he ever will."

"What's it for, Avery?" She looked down at his Latin squiggles. It always amazed her that a man who had such beautiful Palmer penmanship could write his prescriptions so illegibly.

"Oh, for God's sake, stop being so curious. It's just a mild painkiller."

"Pain." Her eyes filled with tears. "Is the pain awful, Avery?"

"No," he lied. "Not too bad."

"I'll drive down right away—"

"There's no rush." He smiled wanly at her, feeling guilty that his illness was keeping her so housebound. "Why don't you walk down later?" he suggested. "After lunch, when I take my nap. You haven't been getting nearly enough exercise."

She clasped his head against her chest. During all their years of happiness, especially the last two years with Jiminy blissfully married to Cal, and Antonio such a delight, Ginger had tended to forget how much she had suffered when Tonito and Johnny were swept away by the flood, and when Tony and Jennie had crashed into the mountain. Yet devastating as those events had been, she knew that the loss of Avery was going to be far worse.

But he was right: she did have to stay alive, much as she wanted to die with him. She couldn't impose upon Jiminy the double bereavement of losing both parents at once. Nor could she rob Antonio of her love. The family had shrunk so much that only she and Jiminy and Cal and occasionally Jason would be left to love the child, once Avery died. Todd was spending much of his time in New York now, developing construction projects on a national level. And except for a brief visit each Christmas, Jason always was so far away, studying the world's seemingly endless deserts. As for Vivien, she sent the boy a stuffed toy for Christmas and a beautifully embroidered Italian silk shirt for his birthday every year—a completely impractical garment for an active child living in the desert—but Vivien was no better a grandmother to Antonio than she had been a mother to Todd.

That afternoon, when Ginger walked down to the Village Pharmacy to get the prescription filled, she saw her beloved city with unusual clarity, with Avery's eyes, with the perspective of someone seeing the place he loves for the very last time. Palm Canyon Drive was gilded by afternoon sunlight filtering through the mile-long row of handsome Washingtonia palms that had been planted by the city. Ambling along the sidewalks and looking into shop windows were crowds of tourists in shorts and tank tops and even a few young women in the amazing new miniskirts—Ginger wondered what Avery would make of those! The shops sold everything from inexpensive souvenir T-shirts to designer clothes and jewelry costing thousands of dollars. With art galleries, antique shops, department stores, restaurants, ice-cream parlors, and the old Spanish-style Plaza Arcade standing side by side with sleek modern bank and office buildings, the street bore little resemblance to the pleasant little shopping area it had been even a few years earlier.

In the twenties and thirties, movie stars had roamed freely through the village. But no more. Oh, there still were plenty of them who had homes here—Frank Sinatra, Bob Hope, Dinah Shore, Mary Martin, Bill Holden . . . the list went on and on—but now they had to be as reclusive in Palm Springs as they were forced to be in Beverly Hills, with so many of their fans waiting to pounce upon them in both places. Ginger remembered walking here with Ella—in the days when Palm Canyon Drive had been plain old Main Street—and having the few tourists in town shyly ask Ella for her autograph. These days, someone as famous as Ella would be mobbed.

Ginger realized she was sighing a lot, partly for Avery, and partly for her beloved village, which had been swallowed up by this vibrant new city full of high fashion and honky-tonk. She felt bewildered by it all, as though she were desperately clinging to the past because the present suddenly had become so frightening to her.

She stopped and looked longingly into a bookstore window. She hadn't read anything—not even a newspaper—since Avery had fallen ill. She saw that there were new books by Walker Percy and John Barth and Barbara Tuchman, all favorites of hers. She smiled wanly at the display of *Human Sexual Response* by Masters and Johnson that everyone was talking about, especially the book's claim that some women enjoyed multiple orgasms. Well, she thought smugly, *she* certainly could have written that chapter!

Walking toward the pharmacy, she saw that the Plaza Theater was showing *Who's Afraid of Virginia Wolf?* and she felt a pang at not being able to see it. Ah, but so much was going on that she was missing. In the past, she and Avery had prided themselves on being *au courant*. They flew to New York at least once a year—last year they had enjoyed *The Odd Couple* and *Man of La Mancha* on Broadway and a Giacometti retrospective at MOMA, and this year they had seen *The Lion in Winter* and

Cabaret, and *Elektra* at the new Met. Now all she and Avery had the energy to do was sit in front of their television set, usually falling asleep from boredom before a program ended.

These days, when she heard the start of a newscast on the radio or television, she immediately snapped it off. She felt bombarded by all the misery going on in the world. She couldn't bear one more ounce of gloom in her life. It seemed to her that ever since the assassination of President Kennedy three years earlier, the world had been disintegrating at an alarming rate. Just last year almost three dozen people had died during riots in the black ghetto of Los Angeles. Crime and drugs were major problems now, not only in big cities, but sometimes even in small towns. Police brutality against demonstrators had become commonplace.

Ginger was proud that Cal and Jiminy had become ardent activists in the civil-rights movement, but it caused her a lot of worry too. When the police had clubbed and tear-gassed innocent freedom marchers in the South, Cal and Jiminy had been there. Fortunately, they had managed to avoid being hurt.

Even here, in the never-never-land that Palm Springs always had been, there were protests, she realized, as she stopped and watched a group of high-school students link arms and march down Indian Avenue shouting, *"Hey, hey, LBJ, how many kids did you kill today?"* Honking its horn and following along behind the students was a white van with red daisies painted all over it, bearing posters that said, "Make Love, Not War" and "Flower Power."

When she left the pharmacy, Ginger put Avery's bottle of pills in her purse and started back toward her pink mansion. Halfway home, she stopped and took the pills out of her purse. She examined the label, but it gave her no clue about the contents. She hesitated, wondering if she should find a pay phone and call Sam. She felt uneasy about the way Avery had written a prescription for himself. But she couldn't show so little faith in his judgment.

She found Avery sitting on the back porch, staring at San Jacinto. He hadn't heard her so she stopped and quietly watched him for a moment. He was withering before her eyes. His once-handsome face was gaunt, lined, pale. His beautiful silver hair—he'd always been so justifiably vain about it—had grown sparse. His blue shirt and gray pants were two sizes too big for him now. Most of all, though, it was the brooding sorrow in his face that broke her heart. What a terrible way for such a grand, happy life to end, she thought as her own sorrow gripped her throat.

She swallowed hard and forced herself to sound cheerful. "Here you are, darling." She handed him the bottle of pills.

"Thanks." He grasped her hand and kissed it.

When he went inside to take another nap, Ginger climbed the trail to their favorite lookout, even though she had vowed never to go there without Avery. But she needed the solace that the place gave her. She sat forlornly on the flat rock where they always had rested, where he first had told her he loved her.

Life stretched out ahead of her like a big, dark, empty, forbidding cavern. In contrast, death seemed enticingly desirable, an end to pain. She wanted to be buried in the same coffin with Avery so that throughout eternity they would be locked in a perpetual embrace.

Her cynical friends would scoff at such an idea, assuring her that after death there would be no perception of such a thing as a "perpetual embrace." But who could say what really happened after death? Even when their bodies disintegrated, might not their souls remain forever fused?

She thought she might be going insane. If she grieved so much before Avery's death, how would she cope *after* he died? Part of her wanted Jiminy to be there with her, so that they could comfort each other. And part of her was glad that her daughter was being spared this ordeal. It was going to be bad enough for Jiminy to lose the father she adored without having to watch him wither before her eyes. And how were they going to explain Avery's absence to Antonio?

As Ginger came back down the mountain, her anguish made her clumsy. She who always had nimbly sprinted up and down this trail now stumbled and slid and had to clutch a manzanita plant to keep from falling. She was annoyed with herself. For the first time in her life, she felt like an old lady. She wanted to throw herself down in the dirt and sob her heart out. But what good would it do? She knew that Avery hated to see signs of weeping in her eyes.

That night he asked her to put the pills she had bought, along with a tall glass of water, on the low table next to his side of the bed. "In case the pain gets worse during the night," he told her. Then he held her close for a long time. He stroked her face and her hair while he talked and talked, reminiscing about their happy years together. He sounded so strong, so much like his old, vital self, that Ginger felt a surge of hope.

"Oh, darling!" she said at one point, kissing his cheek. "If only I'd had the sense to tell you I loved you when I was sixteen!"

He wound a strand of her hair around his forefinger and let it corkscrew down. "Ginger," he said carefully, "I know you'll think I'm a very silly old man, but after all these years, you can tell me the truth. That night at the Ambassador Hotel, did you and Jason . . . ?"

She could tell from the sudden tension in his voice that he awaited her reply with great anxiety. "Oh, darling, of *course* nothing happened between us!" she lied kindly.

He exhaled with relief. "Well, I just thought I'd ask."

They reviewed every detail of their visits to Paris, with Tony in 1931 and with Jiminy in 1956. "Avery, can you believe our trip with Tony was thirty-five years ago? If only you had told me *then* that you loved me . . ."

"Silly girl, will you stop 'if only-ing' me?" he said fondly. "If things had happened any differently than they did, we wouldn't have Jiminy." He pulled her closer. "Those first three months when we ran off together . . . remember? Yosemite? Tahoe? Carmel? San Francisco? The Oregon coast? And then Reno! By God, I was happy! I finally was convinced that you really and truly loved me as much as I loved you."

"And, Avery," Ginger added, "remember those incredible mornings at your old house when we first became lovers?" She caught her breath at the memory.

"How could I ever forget? Ah . . . darling, how incredibly *lucky* we've been all these years. . . ."

Their breath mingled on his pillow. After a few minutes she realized that he was sleeping. For the first time in weeks, she felt a modicum of contentment. Their memories were so laced with love and passion! She moved back to her side of the bed and quickly fell asleep.

When she awoke in the morning, later than usual because they had stayed up half the night talking, the first thing she noticed was the open pill bottle lying on its side, empty. Then she looked at Avery, who seemed to be sleeping soundly. A shaft of sunlight across his head gave his silver hair a burnished glow. He looked almost youthful.

It took her a few moments to realize that he was dead.

CHAPTER
17

1966–1968

Ginger fell back onto her pillow. She felt faint, though still conscious. There was no point calling for medical help—Avery was dead, dead, dead. And since he had taken his own life, she felt it would be cruel of her to try to have him revived, even if she could.

She knew what an agonizing decision it must have been for him. He so loved life. But he loved *healthy* life, *robust* life, *active* life, not a life of rotting away as a helpless invalid.

She forced herself to sit up again, and after a few moments the dizziness passed. She felt calm, but removed from reality, as though she were a spectator of life, and not a participant. Leaning over him, she stared hungrily at his serene face, soon to be removed from her sight forever. His eyes were closed and his strong features looked almost healthy again. She touched his cool cheek and his forehead with her lips.

She could see through the window that they were both missing a lovely dawn, the kind they had watched thousands of times while standing together up on the side of the mountain, a gold-pink-violet-amber dawn that always had gladdened their souls and given them a feeling of tingling union, surpassed only by the unity they achieved in each other's arms.

She got out of bed and put on her hiking clothes—Levi's, boots, a red Pendleton shirt—and realized that this was the same kind of outfit Avery had been wearing the first night she met him, when she was twelve years old and had just arrived in Palm Springs. It was his favorite desert costume, and one which she had eagerly copied.

She hid the empty pill bottle, then phoned Sam and was relieved when he, and not his answering service, picked up the phone. "Sam, this is Ginger," she said. "Avery died during the night." She was having trouble breathing. "Listen, Cal and Jiminy are in Atlanta and God knows where Jason is. Sam . . ." Her voice broke.

"I'll be right over," he said.

He was at her door in minutes. They embraced silently, and wept a little together. She took him into Avery's study. "I found this on his desk," she said, showing him a paper covered with Avery's beautiful Palmer script. Avery wanted a simple graveside service. Sam read aloud, " 'My wife and daughter and grandson are aware of my boundless love for them, which I am certain will transcend my death and accompany them throughout their lives. I die with great affection for my other relatives and friends and with goodwill toward everyone else who deserves it.' "

Sam put the paper back on Avery's desk. "Can I fix you something, Ginger? Some breakfast? Coffee?"

She shook her head. "I'd like to be alone for a while." She hesitated. "Would you call Jiminy and Cal in Atlanta? Talk to Cal and let him tell Jiminy." She handed him a slip of paper with a telephone number on it. "I just . . . can't." She touched his arm with gratitude. "I'm going for a walk."

He went with her to the door, frowning with concern. He didn't want her to go off by herself like this, but he felt he had no right to stop her. Avery had been Sam's mentor and his dearest friend. All during Avery's illness, Sam had most feared this moment. He had expected a violent outpouring of grief from Ginger, not this tightly closed-up withdrawal. But he had learned long ago that the different ways people faced the loss of a loved one were varied indeed.

Ginger felt drained of all feeling as she climbed up the trail toward the lookout point. By the time she arrived there, the sun already was well above the Cottonwood Mountains guarding the eastern end of the valley. She sat on the flat rock where she had rested so often that she was surprised it didn't bear her imprint. She stayed there for three hours, thinking about Avery and remembering countless details of their life together. When the sun became too hot, she retreated behind the shade of a hardy stand of red-tipped ocotillo that had managed to put down roots and thrive between the thick slabs of rock on the steep mountainside.

She knew instinctively that she had to reabsorb her life *with* Avery before she could face her future without him. With a twinge, she remembered going through the same ritual when Tonito died. It was her way of trying to let go, to begin the process of accepting a world that existed without the man she loved.

She smiled and laughed and wept, according to which memory of Avery she was reliving. From time to time, when she thought of their lovemaking, great gusts of remembered rapture swept through her. Over the years their ardor had grown ever more intense, amazing them, delighting them, thrilling them, right up to the day before Avery had awakened in pain. "We're a couple of geriatric sex maniacs," Avery had liked to tease her, but she hadn't cared what he called it, she was just grateful that they had been blessed with such an extraordinary bonus to their love.

She recalled their shared laughter. Their carefree trips to places like Paris and New York and San Francisco and up and down the West Coast. Their joint appreciation of sunrises and sunsets and all of nature's bountiful gifts. Their love of books and plays and music and stimulating conversation with good friends. And above all, their joy in Jiminy and the breathtaking realization that in a frenzied moment of erotic transport the two of them had created the miracle of a new, precious human being.

She was grateful that Avery had lived long enough to enjoy his grandson and that Antonio now was old enough to remember his beloved "Pa." The greatest blessing she could wish for Antonio was that he inherit Avery's traits.

And then the rage came, unexpectedly swamping her with the force of a cloudburst. Rage that her life with Avery was over, finished, gone forever. Rage that people had to die. Rage that someday *she* would die. Rage at the unfairness of it all. She wept, not with grief, but with fury at the *out*rage of it all!

A sudden breeze startled her with its gentle, warm caress, as though Avery had floated past to remind her that all was not lost, that he would exist in her mind as long as she lived. She remembered his exceptional kindness to her when she was a child mourning her mother . . . during the years she was tormented by Polly . . . after her father and Polly left her homeless and penniless . . . and most of all when she lost Tonito and Johnny and then poor, sad Tony. For nearly fifty-five *years* she had basked in the comfort Avery had given her. In his arms she always had felt safe and protected . . . and utterly, totally loved.

Jiminy, Cal, and Antonio flew home that afternoon. Jiminy's grief was so shattering that she had to be sedated during the flight from Atlanta. While she slept in the reclining seat beside him, Cal held Antonio on his lap and tried to prepare him for the ordeal ahead.

"Why was Mommy crying?" Antonio asked, his forehead puckered with concern.

"Because Pa won't be there when we get home," Cal said cautiously.

"Why-y-y?" Antonio had a way of stretching the word out into three syllables. It was his favorite word.

"Because when people get old, or if they get very sick, they go to sleep and don't ever wake up again."

The boy frowned. He hated naps and tried to stay awake as late as possible at night. The idea of a perpetual sleep seemed very disagreeable. *"I'll* never do that," he declared.

"No, darling, you won't, not for a long, long time, anyway."

"E-ver!" Antonio insisted.

Cal sighed. "So when you get home, only Gramma will be there."

Antonio thought about this, twisting the top button on Cal's shirt. "Will she go to sleep and never wake up too, Papa Cal?"

"Oh, someday, but not for quite a while."

"Where is Pa sleeping? In his bed?"

"No . . ." Cal hesitated. "There's a special place . . ." He didn't want to talk about burying people in the ground. He hated the idea too much himself.

"I don't *want* Pa to sleep." Antonio shook his head for emphasis, making his dark hair fly around his head. "Let's wake him up when we get home. Okay?"

"We can't, darling."

"Well, but I want him to *play* with me."

"I know you do. But he has to sleep now." Cal gently pulled Antonio's head against his chest so the boy wouldn't see his sudden tears. "Try to rest," he whispered hoarsely, and was grateful that Antonio closed his eyes without his usual argument.

Cal often forgot that he was Antonio's grandfather, not his father. Cal and Jiminy and Antonio were a close-knit family unit, with Cal experiencing all the joys and problems of actual parenthood. He and Jiminy had tried to be fair to Todd by reserving the name "Daddy" for him, and even though Todd seldom came to see Antonio, Jiminy and Cal talked about him to the boy so that he would understand the relationship when his real father did visit. Jiminy had had a time sorting out who should be called what, ending up with Antonio calling Cal "Papa Cal," and Avery "Pa," and Jason "Grandpa Jason."

As the plane droned westward, Cal held the dozing child against his chest and looked over at Jiminy, who was frowning in her sleep. He could feel his heart sharply contract with love for her. She exuded affection, combined with no-nonsense efficiency, and she was a superb mother. Although Antonio, like the Rowlands, was gifted with a joyful disposition, on occasion he could be demanding and cranky. At such times Jiminy had a magical way of jollying the boy out of his petulance. When he was negative, she offered him choices that permitted him to retreat with honor. He didn't want to wash his hands before a meal? Well, then, Jiminy would say, he could choose between letting her clean them with a washcloth or washing them himself. Since he knew she was pretty rough with the washcloth, he usually went and washed his hands after all. When Antonio was overstimulated, Jiminy soothed him with music. Mother and son had learned the words to some of the songs from *Oklahoma!* and *The Music Man,* which they loved to perform for Cal and anyone else who would listen. Cal, on the other hand, sang to Antonio in Spanish, the sad, romantic Mexican folk and love songs that Juanita, his beloved nursemaid, had sung to him when he was a child, songs that the mariachis still sang.

Cal lowered the back of his seat and shifted the sleeping boy into the crook of his right arm. Gently he put his left hand over Jiminy's slim fingers resting on the seat beside him. If only he could protect the two them all their lives from sorrow and pain! But he knew that only if their plane crashed then and there could he achieve such an impossible wish.

Ginger didn't attend Avery's funeral. She came down with a high fever that completely immobilized her, a fever that Sam suspected was unconsciously self-induced so that she wouldn't have to watch Avery's coffin being lowered into the ground. Sam understood that she had to mourn Avery in her own way, very privately, and that she couldn't possibly endure public tears right now.

The funeral was held on a bright but cool November morning in the small Welwood Murray Cemetery nestled at the foot of the mountain that Avery loved so much. It was an old cemetery, full of the village's early settlers. Reading the headstones was a lesson in Palm Springs history. Oleanders and palm trees swayed in a light breeze—*just the kind of day Daddy loved,* Jiminy thought sadly as she and Cal stood beside the flower-draped casket.

Jiminy was surprised at how many people came into the cemetery from all directions to pay their last respects to her father. They were friends and former patients, old-timers and newcomers, Indians, Mexicans, movie stars, business people, industrialists, waiters, maids, carpenters, and auto mechanics, all those whose lives had touched his. Many of them were crying. Jiminy knew he had been well-loved. But by so many! Dozens of mourners crowded around the grave and hundreds more stood outside the low rock wall surrounding the graveyard.

As Avery had requested, there was no formal service. Instead, people spoke up spontaneously.

"He cured my husband and took no money for it."

"He kept my mother alive for years."

"He sent my daughter to medical school."

"That's nothing. He paid for all three of my sons to go to college."

"He gave me the courage to live when my two children died in a fire."

"His smile made me happy all day long, whenever he came into my shop."

"He a mighty good man, missy"—to Jiminy. "You-all be proud-a him, now."

Dr. Sam Miller spoke. "I'm sure Avery Rowland must've had a few faults. But I knew him as a friend and as his physician for twenty-four years, and I never saw the slightest sign of one little shortcoming. The man had a genius for living, and an innate nobility. He had the happiest disposition I ever saw. You may say that eighty-one years are enough for any man, but they weren't enough for him. I always expected him to live to a hundred at least. He remained youthful to the end. He found love relatively late in life, with his beautiful Ginger, and he was the most devoted husband and father and grandfather in all the world. He would be the first to laugh if he heard me call him 'Saint Avery,' but a saint he was, and one who wasn't afraid to get up on the dance floor and do whatever the current rage was, from Charleston to frug to lindy to jitterbug to twist, and he did the classiest damn tango you'd ever want to see. I loved this man. My mentor. My dearest friend. . . ."

Todd was there, but he stood behind the crowd outside the wall, afraid that his presence might disturb Jiminy and his father. He remembered Avery with much affection, first as his uncle and later as his father-in-law. Now, as Todd watched Jiminy's tears and the way his father tenderly comforted her, he felt a great wave of sympathy for both of them. He pushed his way through the crowd and joined them, startling Jiminy when he kissed her cheek.

She looked up, then threw her arms around him. Cal embraced them both. They stood that way a long time, comforting each other.

Jason didn't hear about Avery's death until two weeks later. He had been on a grueling field trip out on Chile's Atacama Desert and, bone-tired and dirty when he returned to his hotel in Antofagasta, found a telegram from Todd. He sat for a long time with the paper in his hand. His first impulse was to fly right home to comfort Ginger.

Then, on further consideration, he felt uneasy about seeing her while she still was in deep mourning for Avery.

The big question in his mind was: Would she want to see him? Was she taking Avery's death as hard as Jason suspected she would? He remembered how frantic her grief had been after Tony died. And before that, when he first met her, she had been grieving for that no-good Tonito for nearly ten years. Jason knew that her loss of Avery, the love of her life, must be the most traumatic of all. If he turned up now, Jason was afraid she might look straight through him and wonder where she had seen him before.

Of course, he was being unfair to her. When he had come home the previous Christmas, she couldn't have been more gracious to him, or more affectionate, even though she knew it bummed Avery out to see her being so friendly to her former husband. Ah, poor Avery, Jason thought sadly. Despite the fact that Avery had stolen Ginger from him, Jason still couldn't help but admire the old doctor's charm and integrity.

Jason got up and looked at himself in the hotel's small bathroom mirror. He had gotten better-looking with age. He was sixty-four, deeply tanned, with laugh lines around his eyes and mouth. His heavily lashed gray eyes were clear and youthful. He still had all his teeth—and all his marbles—and lots of graying hair. Most of his colleagues now sported beards, but Jason remembered how vehemently Ginger had hated hair on a man's face and he had resisted following the style. He felt wonderful, fit as a kid. Women found him more attractive now than they ever had when he was young. He was in the midst of a pleasant affair with Judy, his thirty-eight-year-old assistant.

Jason had been planning to go home for Christmas, but now he decided to wait a while and instead spend the holidays this year with Judy. They both were eager to see Lima and Machu Pichu. Much as he wanted to be with Todd and Antonio, Jason was afraid that right now his presence might only further sadden Ginger, stirring up her old feelings of guilt about having left him for Avery.

Maybe by next year she would be ready to look at him the way she used to: as her best friend. And maybe after that—someday—her beloved husband.

* * *

Exactly a year later, Jason finally returned to Palm Springs. Todd met his grandfather's plane in a silver Mercedes 500. "Like it?" Todd asked, waving at the car. "It's brand-new. Got seven miles on it."

Jason looked at the car appreciatively. "It's very impressive."

"Grandpa, wait till you see my new estate!" Todd bragged as he drove toward Indian Wells. "It's the *biggest* goddamn mansion in the entire Coachella Valley. And the most expensive."

"Still keeping score?" Jason half-teased. "Like when you played golf in school tournaments?"

"I still play a lot of golf. But really, Grandpa, I'm building the *biggest* hotel complex in Palm Springs, and two hundred luxury houses in Rancho Mirage alone. I tell you, good old Uncle Neil was small potatoes compared to what I'm doing."

"So you're getting richer and richer?"

"Yeah. Granted, Uncle Neil left me a lot of money—and his company—but I've done wonders on my own. Little old dumb me."

"What are you going to do with all your money?" Jason asked.

"Enjoy it. What else?"

"Well, usually people with big fortunes start to think about philanthropy of some kind," Jason said tentatively.

Todd laughed. "I'm too busy to think about it. Tell you what—I'll leave it all to Antonio and let him worry about it someday."

"How is he?" Jason asked.

"He's fine. I went to his fourth birthday party."

Jason shook his head. "But his birthday was two months ago. Haven't you seen him since?"

"Nope. I was in New York."

"You ought to be closer to him, Todd."

Todd thought about it. "Hell, Grandpa, the kid thinks Dad is his father. I feel more like Antonio's stepbrother than his father."

"God! What a screwed-up family!" Jason paused. "Do you ever see your Aunt Ginger?"

"Yeah, I've been up there a few times since Uncle Avery died. She calls me once in a while and invites me to lunch at her hotel."

"Um . . . uh . . . how *is* Ginger?"

"Okay, I guess. Why?"

"I mean, is she still . . . well, grieving over Avery?"

"I don't know. It's been over a year now." Todd smiled. "Ha! I see what you're driving at. Why don't you go over and ask her yourself?"

"Well, I don't know . . ."

"Tell me, Grandpa, d'you like this car?"

"Sure. How many cars do you own now?"

"This one isn't mine. I borrowed it."

"Oh?" Jason was surprised. He knew that Todd collected expensive cars the way other people collected restaurant matchbooks. "Whose is it?"

"Yours." Todd laughed at the look on his grandfather's face. "I was hoping it might induce you to stay here awhile."

Jason ran his hand over the dashboard. "My God, Todd, it's simply beautiful!"

"I'll be happy to buy you a house too, anywhere you want, if you'll just stay home from now on. Dammit, Grandpa, I miss you!"

"It's a powerful inducement," Jason conceded with a grin.

It was almost noon when Jason found Ginger in her office at The Springs. She was writing in a ledger and didn't see him when he walked in. She had reading glasses perched on her nose—on her they look cute, he thought—and he noticed that she was wearing a gold blouse, his favorite color on her. "Hey, boss-lady," he said softly, "wanna give me a job?" He stood near the door and smiled uncertainly at her.

"Jason!" She rose and came to him. She hesitated, then grasped both his hands and kissed his cheek. "How good to see you!" She stood back and looked him up and down. He was wearing a light blue sweater over a white shirt and darker blue pants. He looked so *youthful* to her. "I don't know what you're doing out on those deserts of yours, Jason, but it certainly agrees with you."

"You're looking well too," he said. Actually, he thought she was more beautiful than ever. A little too thin, maybe. Still, he had expected her to be gaunt and withdrawn, racked with grief. He gestured at her desk. "I see you still work here."

"Right now I'm working full-time while Joyce is on vacation. But I have to confess, she runs the place better than I ever did."

"And you never think of selling it?"

She shook her head. "It means too much to me. Y'know, at first I needed it mainly to make a living. Then I kept it because it was so much fun and I met so many interesting people. Now to sell it . . . it would be like putting a child up for adoption. Actually, I'll probably give the place to Joyce someday. She's earned it, and it's the last thing Jiminy and Cal need, with all their millions." She nodded toward the dining room. "Stay for lunch?"

He grinned. "Why d'you think I turned up at noon?"

They sat out by the pool at a table with a pink tablecloth beside a trellis laden with purple bougainvillea while they ate lobster in mornay sauce, asparagus soufflé, Caesar salad, and hot rolls. As a special treat—recalling how much he loved them—she had the chef make some flaming crepes suzette for Jason.

She encouraged him to tell her about his travels in South America and the new book he was planning to write. They talked about Antonio—her grandson and his great-grandson—and how adorable the boy was. "Can you believe he's four now?" she said in a voice full of love. "Last week I took him to play with Maria's great-granddaughter, and on the way home he scolded me for saying 'shit' when another driver cut in on me."

Jason laughed. "Still the same old Ginger. You look like the perfect lady, but you sure know how to cuss when you're driving." He couldn't get her to talk much about herself. She parried his direct questions with a smile or a shrug and changed the subject. He realized that beneath her charming, friendly manner, she was distracted, and it disconcerted him.

"I'm going to stay in Palm Springs," he blurted impulsively, not even aware he had made such a decision.

"Oh? Have you run out of deserts?"

He laughed. "Well, I've collected enough data to fill twenty books. Unless I stop traveling, they'll never get written. Besides, I want to spend more time with Antonio. And Todd."

"It'll be wonderful for Antonio to have another grandfather, Jason. He misses Avery terribly."

He looked at her, still hoping she would talk about her own feelings. Had she recovered from her grief? Remembering how passionate she was, he wondered if she missed having sex. Or—he paled at the thought—was there already someone new in her life? He wouldn't be able to stand it if he lost her again. Not that he even had her to lose.

Still, he suspected that if he simply took her in his arms and made love to her, they might be able to pick up where they had been before she left him for Avery. But what if he were wrong? What if she rejected him? How could he bear it? He decided to leave well enough alone. It was safer to live with hope than to take a chance on despair.

After Jason left, a highly agitated Ginger returned to her office. She had managed to get through lunch without letting Jason see how being with him had affected her. She felt silly, giddy, like a teenager with her first boyfriend. She wanted to giggle and behave like a complete idiot. But more than anything, she desperately wanted to go to bed with him. Oh, how she missed lovemaking! So why hadn't she told him how she felt? she asked herself. *God knows*, she thought, *his tongue was hanging out every time he looked at me!*

But of course it was impossible. Avery wouldn't have liked it. He had always been so jealous of Jason. She knew that she shouldn't live her life according to what a dead man would or would not have liked, but she still felt like Avery's wife, not his widow. Maybe in time she would be able to put some distance between herself and Avery's hold on her, but for now, she decided, the less she saw of Jason, the better.

But her desire for him wouldn't go away. It suffused her, followed her around like a demanding puppy, grabbed her at night and kept her awake, filled her with a chronic longing. She kept thinking of their night together at the Ambassador Hotel—my God, she thought, even after twenty-three years she remembered it in such vivid detail! She knew it could be like that again between them.

She felt guilty and wholly unfaithful to Avery. She called herself names. She reminded herself that sex with Jason would never reach the supreme heights that it had with Avery. But it still could be wonderful, she argued with herself. And why even compare? Anyway, the truth of it was that in all the years she had been happily married to Jason, she *never* had desired him as ardently as she did right now.

Jiminy and Cal kept throwing Ginger and Jason together, not as matchmakers—they really weren't even aware that there was any attraction left between the two—but because Ginger and Jason were both Antonio's grandparents and the boy himself wanted to see them at the same time.

"I realize it's awkward," Jiminy half-apologized to Ginger on the phone one day in early February, "but Antonio keeps insisting he wants his Gramma and his Grandpa to come for lunch *together*. He has this crazy idea that grandparents should come in pairs. Just like parents."

"Or like the animals in his Noah's Ark book," Ginger added.

"Well, do you mind, Mom?" Jiminy wanted to know. "I realize it might be awkward for you."

Ginger hesitated, but how could she deny the boy such a simple request? "I don't mind, Jim-jim. What time do you want me there?"

So they both came for lunch, she and Jason, and then later in the week for dinner too. Then, when Jiminy and Cal decided to fly up to San Francisco for a few days and asked Ginger if the boy could stay with her, Antonio piped up, "Okay, but Grandpa Jason has to come too."

"But Grandpa Jason lives in *his* house, darling," Ginger explained patiently, "and I live in *my* house, so this time you can stay with me, and next time your mommy and Papa Cal go away, you can stay with Grandpa Jason."

Antonio shook his head. "I want you *both*," he insisted. "Together."

They all chuckled and thought it was cute, but he started to cry because he hated to be laughed at, and finally Ginger said with great trepidation that all right, Grandpa

Jason could come and stay in her downstairs guest room for the three nights that Antonio would be visiting her.

"If having Antonio stay with you works out," Cal said, "we'd like to leave him with you for a couple of weeks next October."

"I'd love it," Ginger assured him. "Where are you planning to go?"

"Mexico."

"Again?"

Cal looked uneasily at Ginger, knowing that she worried about the way he and Jiminy ran around to civil-rights and student demonstrations. "This time it's mainly for fun," Cal said. "We want to see the Olympic Games."

"*Mainly?* No angry students?"

"Well, I might talk to a few of them while we're down there," Cal admitted. "See if they need any financial help."

"God, I wish we were all poor!" Ginger exclaimed. "I mean it. We're always worrying about how to give our money away. Now I've got all of Avery's money and land to contend with."

Cal laughed. "Would you believe, Auntie, I actually do feel poor? All I have left is a measly seven million, while my wife's inherited forty million from Uncle Neil."

"Stop joking, Cal," Ginger scolded. "I'm serious. Avery promised me he'd give away all his land before he died, land he bought for a few dollars an acre long before I even met him. But he didn't get around to giving it away, and now I'm stuck with it."

"Can you imagine what it's worth today?" Cal marveled.

"Anyone listening to this conversation would think you're all crazy," Jason broke in.

"We could just let it all pile up," Jiminy said. "It probably adds up to a couple hundred million at least. That way, if Todd doesn't have any more children, Antonio will inherit it all—and *he* can worry about it."

"What can I worry about?" Antonio piped up.

"Money, darling." Jiminy hugged him.

"Money!" Antonio dug into his pants pocket. "Oh, I got lots of money!" He held up a quarter and a dime. "See? Hey, Gramma, see? Grandpa Jason gave it to me!"

When Ginger was ready to leave, she kissed Jiminy and Cal and Antonio, and shook hands with Jason.

"Kiss 'im!" Antonio commanded. "Gramma, you din' kiss Grandpa Jason!"

Ginger wondered if a woman her age could possibly be blushing. She leaned over and pecked Jason's cheek.

"Kiss 'im *good*!" Antonio squealed.

Self-consciously, Ginger touched her lips to Jason's. She drew away quickly, shocked at how wonderful that brief contact had felt.

Ginger tried not to show how nervous she was when Jiminy and Cal left for San Francisco and Jason arrived at the pink mansion in his silver Mercedes. He carried his overnight bag into the house and looked around the entry hall and living room. "It hasn't changed a bit," he said.

"Put your bag in the downstairs guest room," Ginger said. "Antonio's at the stable, getting a riding lesson."

"How many horses do you keep now?"

"Four. As you know, I always have one for myself named Se-San, after my very first horse. I've lost count of how many Se-Sans I've had over the years. Todd gave Antonio a pony he named Pooh. Got his animals mixed up a bit, I'm afraid. Then I keep a stallion and a mare for Jiminy and Cal. They both like to ride, but they don't want to bother building their own stable."

"I don't have one either." Jason was renting a small furnished house down the street from Jiminy and Cal's place while looking for a suitable house to buy. "I'm boarding my horse over at Smoke Tree."

"Oh, Jason, my stable's half-empty. Feel free to keep your horse here."

"Well, thanks." He looked at her plaintively. "You know, Ginger, you're a lot more hospitable to my horse than you are to me."

She didn't know what to say. To quell her agitation, she started picking up the toys Antonio had left on the living room floor. She felt so foolish to always get so wrought up in Jason's presence. This was good old Jason, after all, but . . . he was so youthful and vivacious and bursting with vitality! He wasn't dead like Avery, dammit, he was incredibly, wonderfully sexy . . . and he was *alive*!

He saw what was on her face. He came over and took the toys out of her hands. He drew her to him, and when she didn't protest, didn't push him away, didn't slap his face or call him names, didn't do anything but stare up at him with frightened eyes and trembling lips, he kissed her. "Ah, Ginger, Ginger," was all he could say when their lips began to hurt from the fervor of their kiss. Their bodies remained melted against each other.

"How much longer is Antonio's lesson?" he asked huskily, still holding her close.

She held her wristwatch up over his shoulder. "Another hour." She took his hand and led him toward the stairs. She suddenly stopped and said, "You might as well bring up your bag," and then she added breathlessly, "Oh, Jason! Welcome home!"

CHAPTER
18

1968

"Jason and I are getting remarried," Ginger announced to Jiminy and Cal one windy March evening.

"It's about time," Jiminy giggled. "We wondered how long you two were going to live in sin."

"Ideally," Jason said, "we should do it on the same date as last time, December 15." He took Ginger's hand. "But we don't want to wait that long. So we picked April 15."

"Now we'll have two anniversaries a year to celebrate," Ginger added.

They were sitting around Jiminy's and Cal's cozy candlelit dining-room table, alongside a blazing fireplace. Their shadows, cast by the erratic flames, jerked up and down the walls like drunken puppets. Outside, a fierce desert wind threw a hail of sand and pebbles against the windows, while periodic gusts shook the house.

"Is this an earthquake?" Antonio asked in awe, raising his big black eyes to Ginger, who was sitting next to him. He had been frightened awake by a minor tremblor a few months earlier.

"No, darling," Ginger said, taking him on her lap. "It's just nature reminding us that we don't really own this land." She kissed his dark curls and let him go back to his food.

"Are you two going to spend your honeymoon like last time?" Cal asked Ginger and Jason. "You know, roaming through the Santa Rosas on your horses?"

Ginger looked wistfully at Jason. "What do you think? It's tempting!"

"Not unless you insist, darling," he replied dryly. "I've done enough camping on field trips to take all the fun out of it."

Jiminy was happy for them. She didn't want her mother to be alone for the rest of her life, and she knew that her mother and Jason had never really stopped caring about each other. Jiminy did feel a pang, though, at the idea of her mother with anyone but her father. Her throat tightened at the memory of her parents' extraordinary love. She wondered whether she could ever love anyone else if Cal died, but the very thought of losing him made her shudder. *Dear God, be kind and let us go together!* she silently prayed.

Antonio had been diligently eating during all this, but he never missed a word that was being said within a hundred feet of him. "What's 'getting married' mean, Gramma?" he asked Ginger.

"Why . . ." Ginger searched for words he would understand. "It's like, well, like your mommy and your Papa Cal. They love each other, so they got married, and he's her husband and she's his wife. And when Grandpa Jason and I get married, he'll be my husband and I'll be his wife."

"Oh!" Antonio thought about all this. "Then why don't *I* have a wife?" he asked in a tragic little voice.

They all wanted to laugh, but they held back, knowing he hated to be laughed at, that it sometimes made him cry. "Because you're only four years old, sweetheart," Ginger told him. "I promise you, someday you'll have a wife!"

One hot June day, Ginger put down her morning paper and remembered her girlhood, when people in Palm Springs knew very little about what was happening anywhere else. In those days nobody ever read a newspaper because there weren't any. There were no radios or movie houses, and television hadn't even been invented. Nor had electricity came to the village yet. The villagers could have been on Mars for all the impact the rest of the world made on them. The only news they heard was local gossip down at the post office in Carl Lykken's general store.

Now everyone knew everything that happened everywhere, whether they wanted to or not. Did she *really* have to know that a bus overturned on a dirt road in India, killing eighty-seven people whose mangled corpses were shown on the late TV news she had watched the previous night? Did she *really* have to see the grisly photographs that were splashed all over the front page of her morning newspaper, showing a young mother and father and their five small children on a farm in Kansas who had been senselessly shot by a madman exercising his so-called constitutional right to bear arms? There seemed to be no escape from the world's agonies and insanities.

She knew she could cancel her subscription to the newspaper and pull the plugs on her TV's and radios. But she was hooked on the news, with a morbid curiosity. As the movie and television moguls knew only too well, Ginger reminded herself, we all are fascinated by the appalling, the horrifying, the monstrous, the evil.

She couldn't believe what a terrifying year 1968 was turning out to be. The assassination of Martin Luther King. The riots and burning of inner cities all over the country. The endless war in Vietnam. Student rebels rampaging all over the world, occupying campus buildings and screaming for peace and justice, and the riot police attacking the youngsters with a savage cruelty that shocked the civilized world. And now the killing of Robert Kennedy in Los Angeles by some rotten little man with a goddamn gun. And the year wasn't even half over yet!

She needed cheering up. She went into Jason's study and found him sitting at his desk wearing only shorts and a tank top, busily typing his notes on his new electric typewriter. "Like to play hooky?" she coaxed, sitting on his lap and cutting him off from his work.

He kissed her at length, then came up for air. "Why don't you go buy yourself another hotel to play with, lady, and let a poor guy work?"

"I didn't marry you for your brains, sir, but for your body." She slipped a hand under his shorts and found what she was looking for.

"*Uuuuuh . . .*" He inhaled sharply. He kissed her again while groping under her silk robe, only to happily discover that she was wearing nothing beneath it. He checked her breasts, slowly slid his hand down her torso, and paused between her legs—all deliciously bare and quivering at his touch. Every time he saw her naked, he was astonished at the beauty of her body. It seemed no different from the way it had been when he first met her thirty-seven years ago, when she was thirty-one. A little softer, perhaps, but still smooth and unblemished.

She was pulling up his shirt now and pushing down his shorts, and they practically leapt across the few feet separating his desk from his soft leather couch in their eagerness to get at each other.

This day, as sometimes happened, when she was close to orgasm her mind slipped gears and started to slide toward the memory of making love with Avery, so that she had to pause and quickly jerk her thoughts back, afraid she might burst into tears in the middle of her really marvelous sex with Jason. He seemed to sense what had happened, because he hesitated a moment. Then they continued.

Afterward they relaxed over coffee in the cheerful blue-and-white kitchen, both of them a little subdued as their bodies slowly recovered from the tumult of their climaxes. "Do you think you'll ever get over him?" Jason asked quietly.

She resented the question. "You don't get *over* people," she said coldly.

"Don't I know it. I never got over *you*, worse luck!"

"Jason!" She sighed. "Why are you making trouble, where none exists?"

"Because, dammit, I don't like you to think about *him* when you're making love with *me*!" he shouted.

She wondered why he was being so obnoxious. Everything between them had been so great since their remarriage two months earlier. She put a conciliatory hand on his. "Darling, I love you. Avery's dead and you're alive. Isn't that enough?"

"No," he muttered sullenly. "And another thing. I don't like the way you still run up that mountain every morning. I think you go up there to commune with his spirit or something."

She slowly shook her head at him, amazed at his unreasonable jealousy of a dead man. "If you're so worried, why don't you come with me?" she demanded.

"Because I'm afraid Avery's ghost will push me off the goddamn ledge," he grumbled.

"Tell me the truth," she said. "Have you ever really forgiven me for leaving you?"

He thought about it. "Probably not."

"I don't blame you, Jason. But we're so happy now. Can't you put it all behind you? Can't you accept the fact that . . . that you got caught in the middle between Avery and me, that our timing was all wrong, but now he's gone . . . and I love *you* very, very, very much?"

"I guess what I really want is to hear you say—" He stopped abruptly. "Ah, forget it."

"I know. You want me to say that I love you more than I loved Avery."

"Give the lady sixty-four thousand dollars. That's *exactly* what I want to hear."

She knew it would be easy to lie and put his mind—and his jealousy of Avery—to rest. But she couldn't lie where Avery was concerned. "Ah, darling . . . I've loved you both in such different ways," she said softly. "Avery was everything to me—husband, lover, father, mother, sister, brother, friend, healer, protector. He made up for all the losses in my life from the time I was a child. But you . . . you and I came to each other without any psychological strings attached—as two *very* consenting, independent adults. So how can I say I love this one more or that one less? Both loves are so different!"

He stared at her in admiration for a moment, then smiled sheepishly. "Darling, that was beautiful. Look, I'm sorry I was such a fool. I promise, it won't happen again."

Jiminy was positively bubbling on the telephone. "Mom! I've got such good news! But I want to tell you in person."

"Why can't you tell me now?"

"I want to see your face when I tell you. So come right over. I've got lunch all ready and I'll expect you and Jason in ten minutes flat."

"Ten minutes! Jim-jim, I'm . . . uh . . . not dressed yet."

"Not dressed!" Jiminy screeched. "It's eleven-thirty!"

"Sweetie, at my age I can afford to be lazy now and then." *And spend the morning in bed with my adorable husband.* "How's noon? I'll take a quick shower and throw on a sundress and we'll walk on over. Can your news wait that long?"

"It's a deal!"

They arrived promptly at noon and Jiminy, flushed with excitement, led them out to the shady ramada facing Mt. San Jacinto. Antonio was sitting on Cal's lap on a chaise next to the pool.

Ginger loved this little family. They were young, beautiful, healthy, happy, fun-loving, and generous. Their only problem was having too much of a social conscience, so that their vast inherited wealth had become a grave responsibility, a heavy burden.

Antonio jumped up and rushed over to kiss his grandparents. After Cal greeted them, he took a bottle of Dom Perignon from a bucket of ice and popped it open. By the time they all were seated with fluted goblets in their hands—Cal gave apple juice to Antonio in a two-hundred-dollar Baccarat crystal glass like everyone else's—Jiminy was ready to burst with the news she had been holding back.

"Well, darlings," she addressed Ginger and Jason, "Cal and I are deliriously happy. We're going to have a baby. In early February."

"Oh, Jim-jim! How wonderful!" Ginger embraced her daughter, then Cal. Another grandchild to love, she silently exulted. Another link with the future, the true form of immortality.

"That's just the beginning of our news," Jiminy laughed. "As you all know, ever since I was little, I wanted to be a doctor, like my father. But a pediatrician. So a year from September, when the baby is seven months old, we'll move to Tucson and I'll finish up my bachelor's degree there. Then I'll go to medical school."

"Are you still planning to go to Mexico in October?" Ginger inquired with maternal concern.

"Oh, sure. I'll only be in the fifth month. And I'm really excited about seeing the Olympics." Jiminy paused. "It's okay, isn't it, for Antonio to stay with you those two weeks?"

"We can't wait to have him all to ourselves!" Ginger assured her. Then she frowned. "Oh, darling, I'll miss you when you move to Arizona!"

"Shit, Ginger," Cal mockingly scolded, "Tucson's not the end of the world. It's maybe a four-hour drive from here."

"Cal, watch your language," Jiminy warned, nodding toward Antonio.

"And what'll *you* do," Jason asked Cal, "while Jiminy's in school?"

"Me? Oh, just about what I do here. Sit and contemplate my navel." Cal grinned. "And try to decide what to do with all our money."

Jiminy gave Cal a proud smile, then turned to Jason. "Well, you know, don't you, that Cal's already given a lot of financial help to the civil-rights movement in the South? And that he is *muy simpático* with student activists here and abroad?"

Jason frowned. "Frankly, from what I've read, some of those student hotheads are just a bunch of bored kids looking for a little excitement."

"Yeah, some are. Actually, you'll find all kinds of factions among them—commies, fascists, socialists, Che-Guevaristas, anarchists, Maoists, religious freaks."

"But a lot of them are sincere idealists," Jiminy pointed out to Jason, "fighting some pretty severe repression."

"A French student once told me," Cal said, "that they weren't going to let anyone meddle with their liberties, not even de Gaulle."

"What about all those riots in Paris, back in May?" Jason said. "What the hell did they accomplish, anyway?"

"Well, what started out as a protest against university policy ended up as a demonstration against the entire de Gaulle regime. Those entrenched, ossified governments tend to overreact. What these kids hate is the rigidity of an old-fashioned French educational system that allows no room for individuality or change. And they're outraged by what modern industrialization has brought about—you know, the pollution, the materialism, the corruption, the greed—"

"I think it's important to remember," Jiminy interrupted, "that four out of five Parisians were in sympathy with the students. They marched with them and supported their stand against the government. And *I* think that's pretty damn amazing."

"It is." Jason pondered a moment. "Don't think I'm

antagonistic to these kids. But I get the feeling that half the time they themselves don't know what they're doing . . . or what they're trying to accomplish. I guess my orderly scientific mind is offended by such disorganization. So tell me, Cal, what exactly is your role in all this?"

"Mostly, I stand on the sidelines and watch," Cal said. "It's my favorite spectator sport."

"Cal's being too modest," Jiminy said. "If he thinks the kids' grievances are legitimate, that their cause is just, he helps them out financially."

"I've found that what most of these kids want is freedom," Cal said, "some breathing space, more openness and honesty in society, a feeling of having some *control* over what happens to them. So, I've got a lot of money to spare. Why not do some good with it? Not big crazy things, not fomenting revolutions or buying guns. That's not my bag. But if these idealistic young people need a few bucks or francs or pesos to help print up pamphlets or rent a P.A. system, or pay their medical bills when the cops bust open their skulls, well, they know they can count on me to help."

"Are you saying," Ginger wanted to know, "that this trip to Mexico isn't just to see the Games?"

Jiminy detected the worry in her mother's voice. She reached over and hugged her. "Don't be such a worrywort, Mom. Yeah, we're going down a few days before the Games begin to meet with some of the student leaders there, but all we'll do is have lunch with them and talk."

"And what faction do *they* belong to?" Ginger asked.

"They come in all flavors too," Cal replied. "A really sweet kid named Kiki—short for Enrique—told me that he and his friends want to be the 'conscience of Mexico.' They feel alienated because a few rich bastards control the government and use it to get richer and richer—like Marcos is doing in the Philippines. It's the same all over Latin America. They've got a situation where profits keep rising for the rich bastards running things, and the workers' real wages keep dropping. I mean, kids everywhere—and especially in poor countries—are totally pissed off with the crookedness and greed they see all around them."

Jason sighed. "Aren't you afraid these Mexican student riots might lead to a full-blown revolution?"

"That's not bloody likely," Cal replied. "For Chrissakes, the kids are trying to avoid violence. But the police keep hounding them right on their campuses, chasing after them and beating them up, and then arresting them in droves. The cops are so goddamn vicious, it only makes the kids angrier."

"Cal, I agree that it's an ugly situation down there. But why do you have to get *personally* involved? It's not your country."

"Well, Mexico's always had a very special place in my heart—I consider it my second home. And when I help these kids, it's for practical reasons. Selfish reasons, actually. Because I think that repression in other countries threatens our own democracy. I'm for freedom everywhere, Jason, and I sure as hell can't imagine living under any system that isn't completely free. Anyway, these kids are all trying to tell us something, and we damn well better listen to them."

Jason turned to Jiminy. "Do you feel the same way?"

"Well, sure, I agree with all that Cal is saying," she said. "But as for investing my money, I'd rather put it into some kind of medical foundation, maybe setting up hospitals in slums and rural areas that don't have them. I think it's criminal that in this rich country of ours we still have people who aren't getting the medical attention they need."

Antonio listened to all the grown-up talk with his usual rapt attention. Mommy and Papa Cal had explained all this to him already—about a new baby coming, and next year moving to a new city and Mommy going to school to become a doctor. He got off the chaise where he was sitting with Cal and went over to Ginger. He leaned against her knees while she gave him her full, loving attention. "Gramma," he asked, "will you move to Tucson with us?"

"No, darling, but Grandpa Jason and I will come and see you often. And you'll come here and see us too."

Antonio hesitated before asking the next question. He looked around at everyone first, sensing that they might not like what he was going to say. He leaned closer to

Ginger and spoke in a loud whisper. "Gramma, can we wake up Pa now so he can come 'n visit me too?"

Ginger blinked to hide her shock. "No," she whispered back. "Pa doesn't want us to wake him up."

Antonio raised his voice. "Well, shit, Gramma, why the hell not? Isn't Pa goddamn tired of *sleeping* by now? Chrissakes, I'd be!"

Jiminy rolled her eyes reprovingly at Cal over Antonio's language and scooped the boy up in her arms. "Now, sweetie, I explained it all to you. We can't wake Pa up, but all the rest of us here love you. So whenever you start missing Pa, just tell one of us and we'll give you a great big hug and kiss for him."

Ginger suppressed a sigh of worry over her daughter's forthcoming trip to Mexico City. She hated the way Jiminy and Cal went gallivanting around to dangerous places so that Cal could "observe" civil-rights marches and student riots. At an anti-Vietnam demonstration earlier that year in San Francisco, a policeman's baton had just missed Jiminy's head and had grazed her shoulder.

Still, what could Ginger do? She felt she had no right to tell an adult daughter and son-in-law how to live their lives. Not that some mothers would let that stop them, but it wasn't Ginger's style to interfere. Besides, she knew that Jiminy would simply smile and kiss her and go ahead and do whatever she wanted. After all, Ginger and Avery always had been proud that they'd brought up their daughter to think for herself.

Jason viewed Cal and Jiminy quite differently from the way Ginger did. Jason's allegiance was to Todd, and he felt that Todd was the one who had been wronged. Of course, Jason had to admit that Jiminy *had* caught Todd red-handed—or should he say red-pricked?—having sex with their maid. But was that a good enough reason to bust up a marriage and rob Todd of his son? And then run off with Todd's *father*, of all people?

In the past, Jason hadn't mentioned his feelings on the matter to Ginger because he knew she would vigorously defend Jiminy and it would only cause hard feelings between them. But still, as they walked home along Palm Canyon Drive, he couldn't resist saying, "I *do* wish Jiminy and Cal would let Todd see Antonio more often."

Ginger stopped walking and turned to him in astonish-

ment. "*Let* him! My God, Jiminy and Cal keep *begging*
Todd to come and visit the boy, and Todd's usually too
busy. I think he deliberately keeps from having too much
contact with Antonio to prove to the world what a bum
deal he got. And it just isn't true! He was unfaithful to
Jiminy from the day they married, and all that time she
was as loyal and devoted to him as a wife can be."

"Well, of course *you'd* stick up for her, no matter *what*
she did!"

"Jason Sisley, I don't know what's gotten into you
today, but you're as cranky as a sick baby!" She put her
hands on his shoulders. "Now, you just better give me a
great big passionate kiss right here in the middle of the
street, or—"

She didn't get to finish the sentence because Jason did
exactly what she had told him to do—to the applause of
the tourists on crowded Palm Canyon Drive, many of
whom snapped photographs of the kissing couple.

The next day, the *Desert Sun* came out with a front-
page picture of their torrid kiss and the smiling tourists
watching them. The caption read: "Palm Springs pioneer
Ginger McKinntock-Alvarez-Sisley-Rowland-Sisley and
husband Jason demonstrate local mores to applauding
visitors."

A few days before he left for Mexico, Cal got a phone
call from Todd, inviting him to lunch at the El Dorado
Country Club in Indian Wells.

"Why not at your house?" Cal asked. "I've never seen
it."

"I'm having new tile put in the kitchen, so I gave my
cook the week off. I'll give you the grand tour when you
get back from Mexico."

They met in the club's bar, where Cal could tell from
Todd's eyes that he already had had a good head start.
"A Dos Equis," Cal told the waiter.

Todd gestured expansively. "Hell, have champagne,
Dad. The tab's on me."

"I feel like a beer," Cal insisted tartly, while Todd
ordered another dry martini.

"Your table's ready, Mr. Alvarez," the waiter told
Todd, carrying their drinks into the high-ceilinged glass-
walled dining room.

Cal paused at the entrance, enchanted by the sweeping view of the undulating fairway dotted by royal palms and embraced by one of the most stunning mountain panoramas Cal had ever seen. The sky was cobalt, the grass emerald, the mountains faintly lavender. *Heaven must look like this*, he decided. "Wow! Spectacular!" Cal burst out. "Is the view from your house this fantastic?"

Todd gazed out the windows as if seeing the vista for the first time. "Yeah, I guess so." He gave his father a curious look. A boring thing like a view was just the kind of thing Jiminy went gaga over too. No wonder the two of them fell in love, he thought wryly, they're *both* nuts!

Once they were seated at a corner window table, Cal nodded out at the golf course. "How's your game these days?"

"Better than ever. Wanna play sometime?"

"Against you?" Cal shook his head. "I'm not in your class."

"We could play in the Bob Hope Classic next winter. You and me and a couple of other guys for a foursome the first day. Maybe I can arrange for you to play with Hope himself the second day. How about it, Dad?"

Cal shook his head. "I'm not impressed. I grew up with movie stars, kid."

"Aw, come on, Dad. You've never even seen me play."

Cal reconsidered. It was the kind of thing he should have been doing with Todd all his son's life. Maybe it wasn't too late to start. "Sure," he said, "count me in."

Todd grinned with pleasure. "All *right!* We'll wow 'em, Dad!"

The maître d' was waiting for their order. Cal wanted beef Wellington and Todd chose a filet mignon, and from the sommelier he ordered an eighty-dollar bottle of Aloxe-Corton. "And uncork a second one," he told the man.

"Two bottles?" Cal objected. "I can't drink that much."

"I can."

"Well! What's on your mind?" Cal asked. It was the first time Todd had ever invited him anywhere. Not that he could blame his son, given their history.

"It's about my mother," Todd said. "I went to see her this summer."

"Vivien's okay, isn't she?"

"Yeah, sort of. But it cost her a bundle to get rid of that Italian director she was married to, so when I saw her she was running out of the money you gave her when you got divorced. She had to move out of her penthouse into a little one-bedroom apartment near the Piazza di Spagna."

"So? Can't you afford to give her a few bucks? With all your millions?"

"Yeah, I did. I bought her a nice little palazzo over-looking the river and I put a few hundred thou in the Rome branch of the Bank of America for her. But she's living with this crazy Yugoslav, a charming guy who claims he's a fucking Serbian prince. Can you believe it? He's trying to raise an army to overthrow Tito, for Chrissakes. Mostly, he drinks Mom's booze and talks about bombing the Yugoslav embassy."

"Sounds delightful. What's the problem?"

Todd shrugged. "I don't mind supporting Mom. But what the hell, I'm not about to finance this idiot's damn revolution."

When the waiter brought their salads, Todd told him to bring another martini before serving the wine. Todd looked at Cal defiantly, as though expecting him to object. Swallowing his concern, Cal didn't say anything.

"Anyway, Dad, what d'you think I should do about this Serbian nut? If he's a prince, then I'm the King of Naples. He keeps talking about how loyal his serfs will be. Can you imagine? *Serfs?*"

Cal pondered. "I wouldn't worry, Todd. Sounds to me like the guy's just shooting off his mouth. If you find that Viv goes through the money too fast, then you better do something about it." Cal ate some salad. "What's Viv like these days?"

"Plump. Fun. She's got gorgeous clothes. She knows how to enjoy life."

"Good for her." Cal paused. "You know I'm . . . we're going to Mexico for the Games, don't you?"

Todd nodded. "Aunt Ginger told me. Since when do you like sports?"

Cal shrugged. "Well, I understand it's quite a spectacle, and it's something I've never done. Jiminy's all jazzed about going." Cal gave his son a quizzical look. "What would happen, Todd, you know, if our plane crashed or something? Would you take Antonio?"

"Me?" Todd looked frightened. "Hell, what would I do with a kid?"

"Well, what do you suggest?"

"What's wrong with Aunt Ginger and Grandpa Jason raising him if you and Jiminy kick?"

"They're taking care of him while we're gone, but they're getting old, Todd. Ginger's almost seventy and Jason isn't far behind. It's too much to expect them to raise a little kid at their age."

Todd was thoughtful. "I suppose I could ship him off to Mom in Rome."

"Oh, sure. Have her boyfriend teach him how to throw Molotov cocktails at the Yugoslav embassy!"

"Well, what do *you* suggest, Dad?"

Cal laughed wryly. "Ah, forget it, Todd. Let's not worry about things that probably won't happen." He finished his salad and leaned back. "I've been hearing some strange rumors about you, kid."

"Yeah? Like what?"

"That' you're a fag. A queer. You know, a homosexual."

"Meeee?" Todd was astounded.

"Well, people say you're never seen in public with a woman. So they assume—"

"Are you kidding? Women are crawling out of the woodwork after me."

"I'm sure. You're tall, blond, and handsome, and a twenty-seven-year-old multimillionaire. So how come you never go out with any of them?"

Todd smirked and leaned confidentially toward his father. "I'll tell you why. I've got several very loving ladies strung out from one end of this goddamn valley to the other, in *casas chicas* that I bought for them. No matter where I am—Palm Springs, Cathedral City, Rancho Mirage, Palm Desert, Indian Wells, Indio, or anywhere in between—I'm never far from a good, rousing piece of ass." He chortled. "I've even got one up in Desert Hot Springs."

"Just like Father Serra stringing out his missions so he'd never be more than a day's ride from one to the next."

"Father who?"

"For Chrissakes, Todd, every grammar-school kid in California knows about Father Serra . . ." Cal gave up. "Tell me," he asked snidely, "are all your ladyfriends fat and . . . well, uncouth?"

"Yeah, they sure are. Just the way I like them. That's why I don't take them out in public. They're too vulgar." Todd gave his Father a defiant look. "But let me tell you, they're all great in bed."

Cal sighed. "I guess you never took my advice and saw a shrink."

"Hell, no. Listen, Dad, I *like* the way I am, dammit! I've got a hundred million bucks, I've got a fabulous estate, I win almost every golf tournament I enter, I sponsor college golf teams all over the country, I enjoy everything I'm doing . . . so why change?"

"If you're so goddamn happy," Cal snapped, "then why the hell do you drink so much?"

Todd carefully swirled the wine in his glass and then drank it slowly and deliberately. "Well, Dad—" he grinned as he refilled his glass—"I knew you'd get around to my drinking eventually."

Five-year-old Antonio loved staying at his Gramma's big pink house. It was full of nooks and crannies and window seats filled with treasures, things like his mommy's old toys and some that had been her big brother's too. All Antonio knew about his mommy's big brother was that his name had been Antonio too, except that everyone had called him Tony, and he used to fly airplanes and he was sleeping forever, just like Pa. The dumbbells!

Antonio loved his Gramma, and his Grandpa Jason too. This grandfather didn't get down on the ground and play horsie, like Pa used to do, but he had lots of strange pictures and specimens that he showed to Antonio—flowers and animals from different places, and rocks that looked like plain old rocks but were actually full of things Grandpa Jason called minerals and had streaks of wonderful colors, some of them.

Mornings, if he woke up early enough, Gramma took Antonio hiking up the mountain with her when it was just beginning to get light, before the sun came up. They would sit on some flat rocks, way high up, and watch the sun peek over the pale blue mountains across the valley, and soon the sun looked just like it was sitting right on top of the mountains! That always made him laugh. But the sun stayed there only a minute. It kept moving higher and higher in the sky, making all the mountains glow in different colors, mostly pink and purple and bright sparkling gold. Gramma explained to him about the earth revolving so you had day and night, and why some nights you saw the moon and some nights you didn't. He understood most of it, especially later at her house when she used a big ball from the swimming pool for the sun and a softball for the earth and a golf ball for the moon and showed him how it all worked.

Some mornings, when they were watching the sun rise, she told him stories about Pa, and how much he always had loved this mountain. Antonio noticed that whenever Gramma talked about Pa, a special shine came into her eyes and her cheeks grew pink and her voice was just a little shaky. She told him what it was like living there in her pink house when she was twelve years old. He knew how big twelve was because his great-Aunt Maria had a great-granddaughter named Anita who was twelve.

Gramma told him many, many stories about the Indians who used to live here on this land. He already knew that one of his great-grandfathers had been an Indian, the one who was his Papa Cal's father and whose portrait was in the living room of their house.

Antonio found all of it fascinating. Of course, he missed his mommy and Papa Cal, off in Mexico for a vacation, but Gramma and Grandpa Jason kept him so busy that at first he didn't have much time to think about it. But after he had been in the big pink house a few days, he began nagging Gramma, asking when his parents were coming home. He wanted his mommy, he whimpered. And Papa Cal too.

Gramma hugged him and told him about the beautiful old city called Mexico City that Jiminy and Cal were visiting. She told him that when he was older they would take him there too. Gramma said everyone in Mexico City spoke the same language as his nursemaid, Pepita, who had come with him to the pink house. Pepita had been speaking only Spanish to Antonio ever since he was born, and he knew it as well as he knew English, just the way his mommy and Papa Cal had learned Spanish from *their* nursemaids when they were little.

One day when he was walking with Gramma and Grandpa Jason on Palm Canyon Drive, on their way to get ice-cream sodas, the man he called Daddy came toward them. Daddy stopped and kissed Gramma and Grandpa Jason. Then he picked up Antonio and hugged him.

Jason looked hard at the man. "Well, Todd, how long since you've seen him?"

Todd shrugged. "Three, four months. I spent the summer in Europe." He kissed Antonio's cheek. "Pretty neat kid," he said.

"C'mon, Todd, join us for an ice-cream soda," Grandpa Jason urged.

"Okay, Grandpa," the man said.

All the time they were sipping their sodas, Todd kept looking at Antonio and half-smiling. When he said good-bye, he picked Antonio up once more and kissed him on both cheeks.

Afterward, walking home, Antonio suddenly stopped with an exclamation. "Hey, Grandpa Jason! Why does Daddy call you Grandpa too?"

"Well, because he's my grandson."

"But *I'm* your grandson!" Antonio objected.

"Yes, slugger, you are," Grandpa Jason said gently. "And so is he."

Antonio gave up. It was all just too confusing to have a daddy *and* a papa. He ran ahead of his grandparents, hopping and skipping, and put the whole thing out of his mind.

It wasn't as easy for Todd to put Antonio out of *his* mind. The kid was cute as hell. He remembered the night Antonio was born, when Todd and Cal had sat together in the waiting room, not saying much because they never had much to say to each other. Todd remembered being frightened that Jiminy might be in danger, but he couldn't remember being terribly excited about having a son.

All at once he understood how his own father had felt about him when he was a child. "You ought to thank God for my mother and Jason," Cal often had said to Todd over the years. "Without them, you'd have been up shit creek with a mother like Viv and a father like me." Well, now here he was, thinking that little Antonio ought to thank God that Cal loved him like a father.

Some of Todd's resentment of Cal drained away from him, along with the sense of guilt he had developed over his own neglect of Antonio. As Grandpa Jason often said, they were simply a strange family. So what was the point in wasting one's life feeling either resentful *or* guilty? In his will Todd had made Antonio his sole heir, so someday the kid would be loaded. That ought to take the curse off any neglect Antonio had suffered, Todd assured himself.

"Mi amor. Mi corazón. Mi vida!"

The eight mariachis began serenading Jiminy with songs of "my love, my heart, my life" as soon as she and Cal stepped onto the tarmac of Mexico City's International Airport. In their traditional sombreros, bolero jackets, and embroidered pants, backed up by their guitars and fiddles, their trumpet and maracas, the eight mellow-voiced musicians sent wave after wave of love songs washing over Jiminy, their ballads caressing her wherever she and Cal went that night. Through Customs, through baggage claim, throughout the terminal, festooned with Olympic flags and bunting, they continued to serenade her. Then at the curb where a stretch limousine was waiting to take them into the city, the eight mariachis piled in back while Jiminy and Cal sat up front next to the driver. The musicians never stopped singing.

Thrilled and delighted, Jiminy kissed Cal, and all the way into the city she held his hand. "How in the world did you arrange all this?" she asked.

"Easily," said Cal. "I asked two young friends here to go down to the Zócalo where the musicians hang out and make a deal with eight of them. They'll sing wherever we go. As long as I pay."

"Very much?"

"Only a few dollars per man. Incidentally, they're joining us for lunch tomorrow."

"The eight mariachis?"

"No, my young friends. Francisco and Kiki. Two of the student leaders here."

During the long ride into the city, Cal soon became depressed. Seated by the right-front window and aided by the headlights of the limousine, he let his mind's eye film a traveling shot of the lives of the desperately poor, with glimpse after glimpse into their flimsy, overstuffed warrens with tin-can roofs and cardboard walls, some lit by a bare bulb, others by a stub of candle. But Jiminy, who was seated between Cal and the driver, her head resting on Cal's shoulder, looked upward through the windshield. She saw only the rosy sky-glow of effusive neon and the Olympic banners that hung over the pot-holed streets. Wave after wave of happiness flowed over her. She kissed Cal, who *was* her love and heart and life—just as the musicians sang in Spanish.

"Thanks for the mariachis," she said. "It was a lovely idea."

"My dream of heaven," he said, gazing at her and snapping out of his gloom, "is you and me, *mi corazón*, riding horseback together through eternity. And eight mariachis will be riding alongside, serenading us with Mexican love songs."

"Oh, Cal," she said, drifting back down earth, "it's never been so good!"

"It must be the altitude."

"No," she said, "it's the lover."

They were in bed, an hour before lunch. Cal put his palm on Jiminy's bare belly. "What do you think *she* thought of all that?" he asked. They were both convinced it was a girl—Alicia Alvarez, they called her.

"I hope she paid strict attention," said Jiminy, putting her hand on top of his. "I want her to be good at it too."

"Like mother, like daughter?"

"Like grandmother, like mother, like daughter," Jiminy laughed.

"What do you know about your mother's sex life?" he asked, kissing the tip of Jiminy's nose.

"Her face never holds anything back. I can always tell when she's been laid." She laughed again. "Which is pretty damn often!"

"I need another shower." He rose from the bed and padded off to the bathroom.

Jiminy hugged herself with contentment. How she loved him! Despite the difference in their ages—she was twenty-seven and Cal was forty-six—they were soul mates, cut from the same healthy stock, and she wasn't the least bit worried about having a child with him, even though they were first cousins. She didn't know what she would do if Cal died first and left her stranded, the way her father had left her mother. Ginger was lucky to have had Jason waiting in the wings and still in love with her after all those years. All Jiminy had was Todd, and she'd enter a convent before she'd go back to him. If he'd even have her. Yet she still cared about her childhood companion and hoped Todd was happy.

She studied the sturdy dark beams spaced evenly across the high ceiling of their old-fashioned hotel room. The beams were four hundred years old—the building had been erected as a convent in the sixteenth century. Trying to imagine all that had transpired in this room, over so many centuries, put her own life into perspective for her. *Time,* the beams warned her, *is all you have. Don't waste it!*

They were staying in a suite at the Hotel de Cortez, facing the Parque Alameda. The Alameda was no longer the most fashionable part of the capital. Most North Americans preferred the newer hotels in the Zona Rosa or the high-rises farther out on el Paseo de la Reforma. In the early forties, the old convent building had been restored and made into a deluxe hotel, complete with heavy colonial furniture, modern black-tile bathrooms, and a romantic courtyard where the guests could take their meals leisurely amidst flowering trees and a flowing fountain. Cal stayed there whenever he visited Mexico City because, he said, "it isn't plastic." It had been recommended to him by Orson Welles many years earlier when Welles was a guest at Ginger's hotel.

Lying in bed, Jiminy could look out through the tall French windows, past their tiny wrought-iron balconies, and see the plaza below. In preparation for the Olympic Games that were to start in a few days, the city was adorned with the colorful pennants of all the participating nations, flag after flag fluttering on tall poles as far as she could see up the broad Paseo and around the Alameda. She watched an overcrowded bus, trailing foul black smoke, chug noisily through the plaza. People jammed every inch of space inside the bus; others hung on to every possible hand- or toehold on the outside.

The streets, the sidewalks, the vehicles, all were supersaturated with people, people, people everywhere. But at that moment, she refused to dwell on overpopulation-and-poverty, the Siamese-twin monstrosity of Mexico. She wanted to savor her present interlude of happiness without having to concern herself with anything else. This was uncharacteristic of her. Cal always called her a "bleeding heart," and he loved her even more for it.

She knew she worried too much about problems she could do nothing about. She couldn't help it. If she were a few years younger and not a mother and wife, she might have been a "flower child," tramping aimlessly through Europe with a pack on her back, or living in a commune in San Francisco's Haight-Ashbury district and trying to remake the world by eating tofu and smoking pot and dropping acid. . . .

Cal came out of the shower dripping all over the carpet and bounded back into bed with her. "Here's your chance," he offered playfully, getting her all wet when he took her into his arms, "to make it with an absolutely clean man!"

"Oh, Cal . . ." she whispered as his lips and tongue found all the places on her firm young body that made her ripple with pleasure.

He loved to watch her when she was aroused. Her eyelids flickered, her mouth twitched, her belly became engorged. She heaved and thrashed with complete abandon. When they first made love, she had worried because she was slow in climaxing. Her only sexual experiences had been with Todd, who had neither the forbearance nor the finesse for protracted lovemaking. But Cal assured Jiminy that the act of love was not a race against a clock. He relished every minute of it. The longer it took her, he insisted, the longer it prolonged his own delight. And when she finally did climax, every part of her was convulsed with pleasure.

To Cal, she was an endlessly enchanting combination of innocence and sensuality. In all his profligate years with so many women and so little love, he never had met anyone who came even close to kindling his love and warming his heart as she did. For the rest of his life, he knew, he would never want to make love to anyone else.

At last he got up reluctantly and began to dress. "Enough, you wanton woman. It's time for lunch! We're supposed to meet Francisco and Kiki in the patio in twenty minutes."

The foursome had a leisurely Mexican lunch in the hotel's flower-filled patio, at a table close to the nuns' still-flowing fountain. Though Cal and Jiminy were fluent in Spanish, Francisco and Kiki, who were both nineteen and long-haired, asked if they could practice their English, in which they were already proficient. The son of the owner of a small hotel in Cuernavaca, Francisco had been speaking English with the hotel's guests since he was a child. The son of a distinguished petroleum engineer, Kiki had learned English from a succession of American *au pair* girls who had lived with his family in the elite Lomas de Chapultepec section of Mexico City.

"Are you staying on for the Olympic Games?" Kiki asked Jiminy as the waiter brought them all fresh papayas for their first course.

"Of course. That's the main reason we're here," she replied.

"What about your . . . ?" Kiki didn't quite know how to refer discreetly to Jiminy's pregnancy. He simply pointed at her belly.

"The baby's not due until February," she replied.

"You'll come to our rally this afternoon, won't you?" Francisco asked. "Five o'clock at the Plaza of the Three Cultures?"

Cal glanced with concern at Jiminy's abomen. "I don't think so."

"Don't worry," Kiki assured him, "it'll be peaceful. The government's had a change of heart toward us."

"You believe that?" Cal's tone revealed his doubt. "I hear your president's scared shitless that you students will deliberately screw up the Olympics. If that happens, the government's hundred and fifty million dollars tied up in the Games goes right down the toilet. And it's not just the money. The president feels Mexico's national honor is at stake."

"Well," Francisco said proudly, "we're the first Spanish-speaking country to host the Olympics. But they've got nothing to fear from us. If the government will negotiate with us—and like Kiki says, they're suddenly getting reasonable—we've promised to help beautify the city and act as guides for the Olympic visitors."

Cal waited until the waiter served their second course of ice-cold *seviche.* Then he asked, "Could you use a few bucks? Like for rental of a good P.A. system? Forgive me, but I can never understand what the hell they're saying over your Mexican squawk boxes."

"Thank you, no," said Kiki. "It would destroy us if it ever got out that our movement's getting help from foreigners, especially from . . ." He glanced at Cal and Jiminy warily, not quite sure what word to use.

"Gringos?" Cal grinned.

Kiki nodded. "We just can't afford to take outside help."

"Did you know," said Cal, "that in Paris last week a thousand students marched down the Boul' Mich' to proclaim their solidarity with the students of Mexico?"

"I read about it," Kiki said with a grin.

"To this afternoon!" Francisco raised his glass of wine in a toast. "To the celebration!"

"Celebrating what?" Jiminy asked. "I haven't been paying much attention. *Que pasa,* anyway?"

They were quiet as the waiter arrived with their entrées of *aguacate relleno con camarones,* fist-sized Mazaltlán shrimp in two huge halves of avocado, all doused in *salsa.* When the waiter left, Francisco explained to Jiminy that a few weeks previously, in reaction to several incidents of police brutality, students at the National University had gone on "strike." In retaliation, the government had sent troops to occupy three university campuses in Mexico City, breaking the long Mexican tradition of freedom of speech for students and faculty.

But surprisingly, Kiki continued, in response to nationwide outrage at the government's action, and even stronger student demonstrations, the government suddenly had backed off. President Díaz Ordaz had withdrawn the Army from two of the three occupied campuses. "We're winning," concluded Kiki. "The government's seen the light. And this afternoon, we celebrate our victory!"

Cal suddenly felt chilled by a premonition of trouble. These Mexican students, he saw, were younger and more enthusiastic than their French counterparts, and much more naive about the reasonableness of their government. For many years, one party, the Partido Revolucionario Institucional, or PRI, had dictated every aspect of Mexican life, rigging elections, dominating the government, industry, labor, agriculture, and the press, amid accusations of widespread corruption. The Mexicans joked that their lives had been PRI-ordained and PRI-fabricated. During all this, each university campus had remained an oasis of freedom, until now. Cal was not convinced that this all-powerful government was going to make concessions to a handful of wild-eyed, long-haired, unarmed students.

"Victory or no victory, I don't think we better go," Cal said to Jiminy.

"Mexicans honor pregnant women," said Jiminy. "God knows they have enough of them."

Cal shook his head. "I think we better skip it."

"*Jesucristo,* Cal!" Francisco burst out. "It's just a little victory rally."

"We'll meet peacefully," Kiki added with equal enthusiasm, "hear some speeches, and go home. What's there to be afraid of?"

To be Mexican, Cal concluded, you must first be an optimist. And second, be blind.

"In all these student demonstrations," Jiminy asked, "throughout the world, how many people have been killed?"

"Not many really," Kiki replied. "In Paris last May, with thousands of students fighting the police, only one person was killed. A policeman. He was run over by a truck."

Jiminy turned to Cal. "Oh, let's go, darling. It should be fun to watch."

Cal did want to go. He wondered if he were being too much the pessimist. Besides, he couldn't hold out against the combined entreaties of the three others at the table. Their youthful enthusiasm was contagious. "Why not?" he conceded to Jiminy. "It can't be any worse than Tarawa. And I survived that!"

The Plaza of the Three Cultures comprised an Aztec ruin, a Spanish-colonial sixteenth-century church, and a score of modern high-rise apartment buildings, all surrounding a great airy square. By five o'clock, six thousand people filled the plaza. The vast majority were students in their late teens or early twenties. With them were some older relatives and friends, and from a housing project in the neighborhood there came many women and children who were curious and had nothing better to do. In addition, a few foreign journalists came, including a famous female writer from Italy.

Standing in the center of the plaza were two visitors from Palm Springs, California—Cal, in white slacks and blue sport shirt, taller than most men in the crowd, and Jiminy, lovely in a white silk dress with a white orchid clipped in her long auburn hair. At first, Cal and Jiminy caught the festive air of the thousands of happy, excited students all around them, but as the crowd kept growing larger, Jiminy became apprehensive.

"I don't know, Cal," she said, surreptitiously touching her belly and frowning. "I'm getting a little nervous. I need more space. I guess Alicia and I don't like crowds."

"C'mon, *mi corazón*," Cal said, seeing that all exits from the plaza were now so packed with humanity that it would be almost impossible to leave. "They honor pregnancy here, huh?" he said to Jiminy. "Let's find out." He put his right arm protectively around her shoulder, and with his left hand, he kept pointing to her swollen belly while shouting, *"Compañeros, está preñada!"* His words were a blowtorch cutting through wax. Every obstacle in their path instantly melted away, with smiles and appreciative nods at Jiminy's bulging abdomen and many a hearty *"Felicitacíon!"* for the expectant father. Within a few minutes they attained the sanctuary of an apartment building whose recessed doorway offered protection from the press of the crowd. With ample breathing room, Jiminy was glad she had come to the demonstration.

Cal's and Jiminy's new position on the perimeter also offered a superb vantage point for surveying the entire panorama. From a rostrum on the third-floor balcony of the apartment building across the plaza, the first speaker had already begun. The crowd was attentive and good-natured, clapping and laughing, whistling and stomping their feet whenever the speaker's remarks especially their feet whenever the speaker's remarks especially pleased them. But it was the quality of the public-address system that pleased Cal, who also noted that the happy, cheering crowd not only filled the center of the plaza but also had joined with the tenants of the buildings to jam all the lower balconies of the surrounding high-rises. On these balconies, too, Olympic flags and banners flapped in the breeze and caught the last rays of the afternoon sun.

All the speakers preached peace. Kiki, who was the third student to speak at the rally, began with, "We are fighting against police repression. We are fighting for the rights of the peasants. We are becoming the conscience of Mexico. But when this meeting ends, we will all go home. Without violence. Peacefully."

During Francisco's turn on the rostrum, he acknowledged that the student committee had planned to call for a hunger strike and then march on the one university campus still occupied by the Army. "But, *compañeros,*" he explained, "we are going to have a change of program. We will not go to that school. Nobody will go to that school because the Army is waiting there for us. Instead, we shall turn this meeting into a celebration. And when it's over, everybody will go home. Straight home."

Next, a seventeen-year-old-girl, with a sweet child's voice, said from the rostrum, "I want to ask you all to remain peaceful." Then, as the crowd applauded her plea, a helicopter suddenly appeared, descended swiftly over the plaza, and dropped two green flares into the midst of the crowd.

Cal had seen flares before, at Tarawa, and at Iwo and Okinawa. Flares, he knew, were the signals pathfinder aircraft used to tell an approaching armada behind them where to attack. And this helicopter, he suspected, was more than a pathfinder. From the news films he'd seen on television, he recognized that this huge chopper, hovering over the Plaza of the Three Cultures, was also a gunship. Incredible! They wouldn't dare! *God! God! God! Grab Jiminy and get the hell out! Now! But how? Where? Which way?*

There was no place to run. Armored troop carriers were roaring into the plaza, blocking every way out. At least a thousand foot soldiers and riot police also double-timed into the square. An Army mortar, with a "whoomp," dumped a white phosphorus flare into the midst of the crowd. On the third-floor rostrum, standing under a huge Olympic banner, Kiki seized the microphone. *"Compañeros,"* he cried, "don't run! Don't be frightened! It's a provocation! They want to scare us! Don't run! Don't—" Three bursts of fifty-caliber machine-gun fire from the helicopter gunship shredded the Olympic banner above Kiki's head and riddled his body straight down the middle.

There was a word the Nazi SS men muttered jubilantly when they fired again and again into the mass of defenseless Jews in the squares of Warsaw's ghetto, and the SS used the same word when they murdered the swarm of unarmed American prisoners who had surrendered in the snowfields of Malmédy. The German shout was *"Rabatz! Rabatz! Rabatz!"* It meant "the joy of killing." The Mexican government's police and soldiers had never heard of *rabatz,* and Cal knew of no Spanish word that was its equivalent. But on that October 2, 1968, in the Plaza of the Three Cultures, they knew the Joy of Killing.

Simultaneous with the murder of Kiki, the soldiers in the armored cars, submachine guns in hand, leapt off their vehicles and began firing into the crowd, at the thousands of people massed in the plaza. The foot soldiers and riot police joined in the assault, moving in on the unarmed and incredulous multitude, shooting at such close range that their weapons left powder burns on their victims.

Then, from on high, from the roofs of the buildings where they had been hiding, other soldiers with submachine guns and automatic pistols helped turn the plaza into a three-dimensional shooting gallery. All the while, the machine guns of the helicopter gunship kept firing. Twirling round and round above the plaza, the gunners aboard the huge chopper raked all the building ledges where agile students had taken refuge, and onto the lower balconies of the apartment houses, they fired burst after burst on anyone who moved. They hit the Italian journalist Oriana Fallaci twice in her leg and once in her back. They killed the two male journalists who had been standing alongside her.

Cal tightened his hold on Jiminy and propelled her

toward the double glass doors of the apartment building directly behind them. But just as they reached the entrance, the male porter, inside, locked the doors. Cal and Jiminy screamed, they gestured, they begged the porter to let them in, but he shook his head, his eyes bulging with terror, and ran deep into the recesses of the building. Frantically Cal pulled on the doors, pushed on the doors, pounded his fists on the doors, hurled his entire body at the goddamn doors. They wouldn't budge. Then he heard the steady pit, pat, pat of a stream of bullets coming relentlessly his way, a spitting out of lethal spray like a rainbird lawn sprinkler. He again seized Jiminy and they ran away from the deadly shower and from the invincible glass doors. They headed out into the crowd, intending to turn in the direction of the next building and the next set of doors.

But as they ran toward the crowd, masses of terrified people were running toward them, and bullets began hitting all around them. A ten-year-old boy, crying, "Mama, Mana," ran directly into Jiminy. Then a random rifle round drilled the boy in the heart. He died in Jiminy's arms. She stood there paralyzed, clinging to the dead child, his blood dyeing the front of her white dress red. Another hail of bullets spattered all around them. "For God's sake, drop him!" screamed Cal. "He's dead! Let's go!" He snatched the boy out of Jiminy's grasp and threw him to the ground. "Hit the dirt, for Chrissakes! Crawl!" he yelled at Jiminy, and he hurled her facedown onto the pavement. *Oh, God!* he silently groaned in agony, *right on her belly!* He threw himself on top of her to shield her. Then frantically the two of them began crawling toward the next apartment building and its set of double glass doors. Jiminy was crying and Cal was cursing, but they both moved swiftly, slithering across the ground like terrified snakes fleeing a forest fire.

In the center of the plaza, most of the crowd was still so paralyzed by what was happening that they did nothing but scream, their screams almost as loud as the gunfire. But suddenly there was a moment of horrified silence. Then panic. The group of women and children from the neighboring housing project thought they saw an opening at one end of the plaza. Followed by masses of students, they broke for it. In their terror, they stampeded, losing their heads and their humanity, bumping into each other, knocking each other down, scrambling, sobbing, cursing, crushing the bodies of those who had fallen underfoot. A five-year-old boy and his three-year-old sister, swept away from their mother, stood hand in hand and cried, "Mama, mama!" Other mothers trampled them to death.

By the time those stampeding had reached their hoped-for way out, the police and the military had closed the gap. Now the women and children had to run a gauntlet of cops and soldiers who slugged them with clubs, beat them with rifle butts, bayoneted them. A bayonet blade jabbed into a sixty-year-old woman's back. She died. Another bayonet thrust went deep into the head of a thirteen-year-old-boy. He died. The Joy of Killing extended to women and children too.

Now it was getting dark. Now there were more screams of pain than of terror. Now there was no one standing in the plaza. They had all fallen dead or wounded or were crawling hysterically toward some other side of the square where they desperately, and vainly, would seek sanctuary. The firing continued, but now the soldiers used tracer bullets, their rounds redlining the darkness, and when they ricocheted off the buildings, zinging and zig-zagging like drunken fireflies.

Cal and Jiminy approached the next apartment building. Still crawling painfully on their bellies, still crying, still cursing, they saw that a young man and a young woman were already standing outside the entrance, their backs to the plaza, pounding their fists and bodies furiously against the thick double doors of glass. The doors would not budge. The glass would not shatter. Then a spray of tracer fire, deadly little darts of red light, sprinkled the young man and woman and they fell dead at the foot of the glass doors.

"We got no other choice!" Cal yelled over to Jiminy. The two of them rose, ran to the doors, and spreading their feet wide so that they would not be standing on the corpses of their predecessors, began smashing their bodies and their fists again and again against the unyielding glass. Cal was still cursing, Jiminy still crying, and the glass still unyielding. But thankfully the guns seemed to be silent for the moment.

Behind Cal and Jiminy, a group of six students, boys

and girls all in their teens, came crawling up to the building's entrance. They rose and joined Cal and Jiminy in the assault on the glass doors. Now there were eight desperate, terrified, agonized people pounding repeatedly on the glass, which finally began to give way when the doors started to come off their hinges. At that moment a red tracer spray of fifty-caliber machine-gun fire shattered the glass doors into thousands of tiny shards, even as it cut down the entire group struggling in front of the doors. A few minutes later, all firing ceased. The Joy of Killing was over.

In remembrance of the night almost five centuries earlier when Cortez and his Conquistadors were decimated by the Aztecs, a night known in Mexican history as La Noche Triste, or Night of Sadness, the Mexican press, in referring to the massacre in the Plaza of the Three Cultures, called the night of October 2, 1968, another Noche Triste.

The official body count reported twenty-nine dead, eighty wounded, and three hundred and sixty-three students jailed. Unofficial accounts, made by foreign journalists who were there and who survived, estimated more than three hundred dead, maybe five to six hundred wounded, and sixteen hundred people arrested. A week later, the Olympic Games commenced peacefully, except for one young Italian track star who protested that he didn't want to "run on the blood of other people."

Cal and Jiminy were among those who died in the plaza that evening, surrounded by six of the young people they had believed to be the hope of the future. All eight lay together, facedown in the shards of glass, in an ever-widening pool of commingled Mexican and gringo blood.

Cal was still holding Jiminy in his arms. Each was shot through the heart. They died—along with baby Alicia—in the Mexico that Cal so loved.

Mi amor, mi corazón, mi vida.

CHAPTER
19

1976–1977

Antonio had his first date in October 1976, not long after
his thirteenth birthday. Her name was Rosemary Ryan
and she was half a year older than he was, which had
appeared a great tragedy to him when he first met her,
since the age difference had made her seem utterly unat-
tainable. But she was the one who made the effort to
seek him out and suggest the date.

She was new at school that semester, a pretty, vivacious, blue-eyed brunette who achieved instant celebrity.
All the girls wanted to be "best friends" with her, and
she made the eighth-grade boys suddenly realize that it
was time to stop ignoring girls. Like Antonio, she was a
straight-A student, often sharing top honors with him in
the classes they shared.

When she suggested they go out together, Antonio
couldn't believe she had chosen *him*. Sure, he was okay-
looking, but on the quiet, studious side, and not nearly as
popular as some of the other boys in his class. She invited
him to go bike riding on Saturday morning and then have
a picnic—he suggested Tahquitz Canyon. "I'll bring the
food," she said, "only I don't know how much you eat.
D'you scarf up everything in sight, or what?"

"Well, yeah, I eat a lot. Like, maybe three sandwiches?"

"Sure. That's cool."

Antonio had a new ten-speed bicycle, a blue beauty
that he had bought with money he earned doing chores
around the house. Cleaning the pool. Pulling weeds.
Sweeping the long brick driveway. It had taken him five

months to save the money. Oh, he knew his family was wealthy. But Gramma and Grandpa Jason had explained to him a long time ago that the money he was going to inherit from Jiminy and Cal was a sacred trust that he couldn't touch until he was twenty-five, and even then the money was to be used for the good of humanity—as his mother and Papa Cal had intended—and not just to satisfy his own whims. Until then, his grandparents would provide the necessities, they told him, but any luxuries he wanted must be earned, or else he would never appreciate anything he had.

Compared to his old three-speed, this new bike was a joy! He soared on it. His grandparents were right: he did value it more for having earned it himself than he would have if they had simply given it to him. And his sense of achievement made him feel very mature indeed.

At thirteen, Antonio was tall for his age, and thin despite his enormous appetite. His resemblance to his great-grandfather Tonito became more striking as Antonio grew older. The boy had the same dark hair, black eyes, sculptured cheekbones, and brilliant smile that had so captivated Ginger when she first met Tonito. "You have your Great-Grandfather Tonito's features, and your Grandfather Avery's tenderness," Ginger told him, "and your Great-Grandpa Jason's charm, and your Great-Grandmother Ella's exquisite beauty, and your mother Jiminy's brains and sensitivity, and your Papa Cal's generosity, and your father Todd's playful nature."

"What did I get from *you?*" Antonio wanted to know, half-seriously.

She thought for a moment. "Well, darling, I hope my capacity for happiness!"

Saturday morning, Antonio dressed carefully for his date with Rosemary, choosing white shorts and a light blue tank top that he thought made him look manly. As usual, he slid down the banister and almost collided with Ginger in the entry hall.

"Don't you ever walk down those stairs?" she asked with mock annoyance.

"Not if I can help it!"

"I remember when you were too small to slide down on your behind. You'd do it feetfirst on your stomach, and I used to worry that—" She stopped and grinned.

"It's still there," he laughed, kissing her cheek and rushing out the door.

As he coasted down the pink mansion's driveway on his new bike, he saw that a border of yellow chrysanthemums was in full bloom. He stopped and picked a dozen of them.

Rosemary was outside her house, waiting for him. She was wearing short-short white shorts and a red scoop-necked sleeveless top. Almost as tall as he was, she was deeply tanned and precociously shapely for her age. Her blue eyes were enormous, her thick blue-black hair fell straight and shiny to her waist, and her pink lips were so smooth that Antonio couldn't stop staring at them. She lived east of Indian Avenue in a pleasant housing development on a palm-lined street.

Antonio forced his eyes away from her lips. He looked around for something to divert him, and her beige stucco house caught his eye. "My Great-Uncle Neil built all these houses," he said, not knowing what else to say.

"I know." She smiled.

He was surprised. "Yeah? How did you know?"

She blushed, embarrassed. Too late, she realized that she wasn't supposed to let on that she knew his family was wealthy. "Oh, I . . . um . . . I heard my parents talking . . ." Quickly she pointed at the brown bag in the wire basket attached to her bicycle's handlebars. "I brought lots of goodies." She glanced at the yellow flowers in his hand. "Are those for *me?*" she trilled.

He looked down at the bouquet. "Oh, well . . . no." It was his turn to be abashed. "Actually, I hope it won't bum you out if we stop a minute and put them on my parents' graves. I do it every Saturday."

Rosemary had heard about the tragic death of his mother and stepfather. She also knew that his stepfather actually had been her grandfather. As soon as her mother had heard Rosemary mention Antonio's name, when she and Antonio had tied in a spelling contest, her mother had begun her campaign to have Rosemary make friends with him. "He's loaded," Mrs. Ryan had said. "From one of the richest families here."

"So what, Mom?" Rosemary had shrugged. "Everybody here is rich. Except us."

"Not everybody is as *stinking* rich as he is," her mother

had drawled. "Don't be a fool . . ." She looked at her husband and the unspoken words "like I was" hung in the air. "Believe me, it's just as easy to love a rich man as a poor one."

"Knock it off, Flo," Rosemary's father had bristled. "For God's sake, they're just kids."

"It's never too early to start feathering your nest," Flo had insisted. "Anyway, what's wrong with them going steady? All the kids do."

When Antonio and Rosemary reached the little historic cemetery at the foot of Mt. San Jacinto, they leaned their bikes against the trunks of adjoining palm trees and he led the way to the graves. He laid down the flowers lovingly, half on his mother's grave and half on Papa Cal's. Then he had second thoughts and took two off each grave and put four on Pa's grave too.

He was shaken by the desire to cry. But cry in front of Rosemary? That would be totally uncool. He realized that he should have come here first by himself. They sat down on a stone bench while he tried to compose himself.

She took his hand. "Trust me, Antonio. You can tell me about them," she urged softly.

He didn't know where to start. Anything he said might bring on a burst of tears.

"Come on, get real." Her voice was kind and understanding. "It's like totally okay to cry if you feel like it."

He basked in her sympathy. "I was five when it happened. They were at this student rally in Mexico City, and they got shot by the fuzz. I mean, a whole bunch of people were killed." Silent tears were sliding down his cheeks but he was unaware of them. "I was staying with my grandparents, and when the phone rang, my grandmother answered, you know, cheerfully, like she always does, and then she just keeled over. She had only fainted, but boy, I was scared, to the max. My grandfather ran over and picked her up and listened on the phone a minute, and when he put it down he burst into the most awful tears I ever heard. I mean, it was totally a scary scene. And all the time he was putting her on the couch and calling our family doctor—you know Sam Miller?— anyway, I just stood there like . . . flipping out. They didn't have to tell me. I knew something really bad had happened to my parents."

"Oh, you poor thing!" she murmured, wondering how she would react if her parents died.

"My grandmother stayed in bed a long time. My grandfather took care of me, and explained how I'd never see my parents again. When Gramma finally got up, boy, was she ever thin and sickly. You'd hardly recognize her. She'd just cry and cry and Grandpa would put his arms around her. But after a while she started to eat more and look like her old self, and even laugh once in a while. I mean, that was eight years ago, and she's totally okay now. Anyway, I've lived with them ever since it happened."

Rosemary squeezed his hand. "You're an awesome dude," she whispered. "Like, most kids would've really freaked out." She leaned over and kissed his cheek.

Antonio wiped his tears with the back of his hand. He stood abruptly. "Hey, it's dumb of me to dump on you like this."

"No, Antonio, really, it's cool. It makes me feel connected to you."

"Well, thanks." Her sympathy embarrassed him a little. "Come on. Let's go eat."

They locked their bicycles around the trunk of a palm tree near the entrance to Tahquitz Canyon and walked in on the trail as far as the waterfall. Antonio loved this spot. "Hey, isn't this place something else?" He spoke in hushed admiration as they settled on a big rock.

Rosemary was opening the bag of food. She looked up and took in the view. "Mmmm," she agreed without much enthusiasm. She handed him three ham-and-swiss-cheese sandwiches on rye, thick with lettuce and tomato and mayonnaise, all neatly wrapped in foil, and she opened one for herself. Then she took two cans of beer from the bag and gave him one.

He looked down at it like it might bite. But he didn't want her to think he was a nerd or something. He popped it open and took a swig. It was so bitter, it was all he could do to keep from spewing it out. The second mouthful was better, and by the tenth, he sort of liked it.

"What about your family?" he asked, chewing.

"Oh!" Offhand, she couldn't think of a good lie to tell him about her father's occupation. Besides, what was the point? In a town like this, everybody knew what everyone else did. "My Dad's a . . . a bartender," she admitted reluctantly, "at the Spa Hotel. My mom was a cocktail waitress before she got married, but my Dad's real lame. He won't let her work anymore."

"Any brothers or sisters?" he asked as she handed him a foil package with three thick brownies in it.

She hesitated. "Well, I have this older sister Marie in Seattle. She's nineteen."

"At the university there?"

"Uh . . . no. She's . . . um . . . married." She lied outright this time. Who was going to check out what Marie was doing, that far away? The truth was that Marie had run off with some married geek who had left his wife and a couple of kids. Rosemary's mother was all broken up about her older daughter, and now was putting pressure on Rosemary to marry young before she got into trouble.

Rosemary brought out two more cans of beer when they finished eating. They drank them while watching the waterfall, which was low this time of year. "Do you have any relatives besides your grandparents?" she asked.

Antonio's head was pleasantly buzzing from the beer. "I've got a grandmother in Rome. My father—my *real* father—lives in Indian Wells."

She nodded, as if this were news to her. Actually, her parents knew all about Todd, the "multi-multi" they called him, meaning multimillionaire. She threw the four empty beer cans and the crumpled foil into the creek at her feet.

"Hey!" Antonio leapt up and retrieved them before they floated away. He carefully put them into the empty paper bag. "This is hallowed Indian land," he said. "Besides, it's really gross to litter!"

She was miffed at his scolding tone. "Indian land!" she scoffed. "So what?"

"I'm part Indian," he said proudly.

"Oh." She gave him a doubtful look. "You don't look it."

"Yes I do. I take after my Indian great-grandfather."

She wondered what her parents would make of that. The way they talked, they didn't seem to think that Indians were any better than . . . well, they called them "red niggers." She remembered her father saying, "Hell, they walk around this town like they own the place."

And her mother had laughed rather nastily and said, "But, Herb, worse luck, they actually *do!*"

Now Rosemary wondered if her mother would still want her to go steady with Antonio. But if only his great-grandfather had been an Indian . . . well, Antonio probably was mostly white by now. Besides, there was all that money.

Rosemary had a healthy respect for money. Every time she wanted something—for example, back in Chicago where they came from, she would have *killed* for a beige cashmere coat like her best friend Audrey had. But all her parents ever could say when she wanted something was, "No, we can't afford it." She wanted more than anything to have enough money so that she never would hear those words again.

She was an avid reader of the *Desert Sun*'s society columns and the slick, beautifully illustrated *Palm Springs Life* that came out every month and cost a chunk of her allowance. She dreamed of dressing up in all the exquisite clothes advertised in the magazine and going to parties at the Sinatras' compound—that Barbara was so gorgeous!—and at the Annenbergs' estate with all the beautiful people who got invited there. Rosemary was vaguely aware of what a burden of envy she was creating for herself, drop by drop, every time she read about the lives of the superwealthy and superfamous. She didn't think she'd ever be famous because she had no talents, but there was no reason she couldn't be rich, if she married someone like Antonio. And it wasn't as if she didn't like him. She thought he was sweet, if a little dorky.

She lay down on the rock to take a sunbath. Antonio sat beside her awkwardly, not knowing whether to lie down too, or what. She solved the dilemma for him by taking his arm and pulling him down next to her. She rolled over on her side and leaned over him, grazing his chest with her small firm breasts in their light blouse. Instinctively he turned toward her. Their lips suddenly were pressed together and her darling little tongue was inside his mouth, fluttering against his tongue.

She pushed herself against him while they held the kiss, and all at once he felt a rapturous rush in his groin and a sensation of sticky wetness in his pants. Shocked, he abruptly broke off the kiss and rolled away from her. He was too ashamed to let her see what had happened. He grabbed the bag full of trash and held it in front of him. "L-let's go g-get an ice cream," he stammered.

He rode in front of her all the way back to town. She locked her bike around a light pole on Palm Canyon Drive, in front of the ice-cream parlor. Agitated, afraid the whole world was staring at the wet spot on his shorts, he rushed inside ahead of her and sat down at a table where he could hide his shame. He asked the waitress to bring a glass of water with the hot-fudge sundae he ordered, and when it came he accidentally-on-purpose spilled some water in his lap. "Oh," he cried in mock alarm, "I got myself all wet." He dabbed at his shorts with a paper napkin.

Rosemary, whose sister, Marie, had given her a liberal education in the sexual habits of boys, knew all about ejaculations. She was still a virgin, but she had been making out with high-school kids and even college boys since she was eleven, and this wasn't the first time she had made a boy come in his pants. She smiled at Antonio, delighted that he was so crazy about her. She hoped that from now on he would have wet dreams about her every night! It made her feel powerful to know she could do that to him.

When they went back outside, only Rosemary's red bicycle was there. His beautiful brand-new blue ten-speed was gone. "Wow, didn't you lock it?" she asked, horrified.

He thought back. In his insane hurry to get inside the parlor and hide his wet shorts, he must have forgotten to lock it. "I guess not," he said ruefully. All that work he had done to buy it! Now he'd have to go back to his grungy old three-speed.

Trudging uphill toward the pink mansion, he was in a strange mood of contradictions—elated one minute over the kiss, ashamed and yet excited by his spontaneous ejaculation, worried that Rosemary would think he was a nerd, and dejected over the loss of his new bike. He looked down at his shorts—at least the arid desert air had dried the wet spot. The material was still a little stiff, but it wasn't noticeable.

When he reached the top of the steep driveway, he saw Todd's Rolls-Royce parked in front of the house. Antonio found his grandparents and Todd in the living room having drinks and nibbling cashews. Dutifully Antonio kissed his father and sat down next to him.

"I brought you a present," Todd said. "Sorry it's late. I was out of town on your birthday." He looked at Antonio critically. "What are you now? Eleven? Twelve?"

"Thirteen."

"Well, the years sure fly." Todd stood up. "Come on, I'll show it to you."

Antonio followed his father into the next room, noticing that Todd was spiffily dressed for golf. "Do you have a tournament today?" Antonio asked politely.

"Yeah." Todd looked at his watch. "Over at Bermuda Dunes. Do you ever play?"

"Well, tennis is my game, Dad."

"Anytime you're intersted in taking up golf . . ." Todd checked himself. He was about to offer to teach the boy, but he didn't have that kind of time. "I . . . uh . . . I'll be glad to pay for lessons."

"Thanks." Antonio stopped short at the dining-room entrance. Propped up against the wall was a blue bicycle, the exact twin to the one he had bought with his own money—and then lost.

"Well, like it?" Todd asked, taking his son's surprised look as speechless delight.

"Yeah, yeah, it's . . . uh . . . it's a real beauty. Fantastic." Antonio tried to hide his astonishment at the coincidence. "Uh . . . thanks, Dad." He hugged Todd awkwardly.

As soon as Todd's Rolls sped down the driveway, Ginger said, "But, Antonio, you already have one exactly like it!"

"No more." He told them about the theft. "It's, like, really awesome that he bought me the exact same one!" Antonio laughed. "Y'know, sometimes my dad isn't such a bad dude after all!"

Todd surprised them all by offering to take Antonio to Rome to spend Thanksgiving with Vivien. "Hell, it's the least I can do for the kid," he told Jason. "If he skips the three days of school at the beginning of the week, we'll have eight days there."

"We'll miss him," Jason said. "But I think it's great that you want to do it, Todd. The boy needs your love."

The morning after Antonio's departure—it was the Saturday before Thanksgiving—Ginger faced Jason at breakfast. "So, darling, it's just you and me. Think you can stand it?"

Jason seemed distracted. He looked at her strangely for a moment, then said, "Hmmm? What?"

"Oh, nothing. Listen, I'm going to have to work all weekend. Ever since Joyce went on maternity leave last month, I've had to do everything myself. Our *sous-chef* decided to go back to France yesterday without giving me any notice, and we're short two maids . . . so, Jason, would you mind coming over to The Springs later for a quick dinner with me? There's going to be a private banquet tonight and I'd better be there—"

"I can't." Jason looked uncomfortable, then blurted, "I'm going to San Francisco this morning."

"San Francisco!" she repeated, dazed. "How come you didn't tell me?"

"I . . . uh . . . just decided."

"Oh. How long will you be gone?"

"I don't know."

She put down her fork and stared at him. It seemed to her that at seventy-four he was better-looking than ever. His boyish cuteness had evolved into a captivating self-confident maturity. He had a mass of graying sandy hair, unruly as ever, and his features had developed a harmony with each other that they had lacked when he was younger. "Jason," she said nervously, "what are you trying to tell me?"

He looked down at his plate, gathering his courage. He took a deep breath. "I'm leaving you, Ginger."

"You mean . . . for Thanksgiving?"

"No. For good."

She put a hand over her mouth to keep her lips from trembling. It occurred to her that he had been rather distracted lately, but she had been so busy at the hotel that she hadn't paid much attention to him. "Why?" she whispered.

"Because you don't take me seriously. You never have. I'm just a . . . a sex object to you. Someone to play with."

She shook her head, blinking away tears. "Nothing could be farther from the truth."

"The only truth that matters to me is my own perception of it. Anyway, I've met someone who appreciates me. *Really* appreciates me."

He's never forgiven me for running off with Avery, Ginger thought forlornly. *He's doing this to get even.* Now she was getting a taste of what it was like to be abandoned for someone else. "Who is she?" she asked dully.

"Millie Simpson."

"Ah, Millie." She should have known. Millie Simpson was a graduate student from San Francisco, divorced, in her mid-thirties, an attractive blond who had come to Jason a few months earlier asking for advice about her master's thesis on desert flora. She was bright and efficient and Jason had promptly hired her to organize the mountain of research material he had gathered in his years of travel. She had taken an apartment on Indian Avenue and spent her days in the pink mansion working on the desk in the guest room adjacent to Jason's study. She had seemed like a godsend to Jason, after all the trouble he'd had the past few years finding a good assistant.

Now Ginger could see it all. The long hours together, Ginger conveniently away at the hotel all day, the adoring, attractive younger woman flattering his ego. Ginger remembered hearing Millie gush, "Oh, Dr. Sisley, there's no one in the whole *world* who knows as much about the deserts as you do!" At the time, Ginger had turned away to hide a smile, thinking that surely Jason was smart enough to spot an outrageous flatterer.

It all added up. Millie's youthful good looks, her flattery, her avid attention to everything Jason said, combined with his deep-rooted resentment against Ginger for having left him for Avery, had made the young woman irresistible to him. No doubt Ginger had unwittingly aided and abetted the "romance" by sending over luscious lunches for the two of them from The Springs' kitchen. She could imagine the idyllic meals Jason and Millie had shared out on the terrace with its incredible view. *And* with the French wine Ginger always had thoughtfully sent over with the meals! And afterward, the guest room's king-size bed was so conveniently close by . . .

Ginger pushed her plate away. "I don't suppose I can

convince you," she said in a trembly voice. "that I love you very much."

"Not the way Millie does. She positively *worships* me, Ginger . . . and I love it!"

Ginger knew she was beaten. No, she didn't worship Jason, but she did love him, with all her heart and body and soul. She got up from the table and went out to the back porch. She told herself that if she could learn to live without Avery, she certainly could learn to live without Jason. But there had been too many losses in her life. How could she bear another one?

She felt a fit of weeping coming on and she didn't want Jason to see her lose control. She suddenly felt old, old, even though her mirror kept assuring her that she didn't look seventy-six. For years she had been grateful that she didn't show her age, that in fact she had an ageless sort of beauty. But how could she compete with a woman who was less than half her age?

She was a firm believer that being old was a matter of attitude, that the years added to one's wisdom, if you were lucky enough to have good health. No, her age wasn't the reason Jason was leaving her for Millie. It was this "worship" business Jason had fallen for. Maybe he was feeling *his* age. Maybe having a woman in her thirties idolize him made him feel younger. But people shouldn't deify each other, Ginger thought angrily. With all her overwhelming love for Avery, no, no, she never had *worshiped* him.

She went partway up the trail behind her house. Sitting on a rock, she let the tears come in great gasping waves. She realized how very much she *did* love Jason. She was sure she had always shown him that she loved him. It was true, she had been busier than usual at the hotel, with Joyce away and with a massive redecorating project she was trying to finish before the high season began in January. Besides, she needed Jason more than ever now, to help raise Antonio during the difficult years of adolescence. How was she going to do it alone?

Oh, she supposed she could always find another man if she had to. Every time she had lunch alone in The Springs' dining room, most of the unattached male guests over sixty gave her the eye. A geriatric belle, that's what she was, she thought mirthlessly. But she didn't *want* anyone else. She only wanted Jason. They were so good together!

Now she knew how he had felt when she left him for Avery. God, she had been cruel! But she had loved Avery so desperately that she hadn't been able to help herself. She very much doubted if Jason loved Millie that same overpowering way.

Ah, she just couldn't believe that Jason didn't love her anymore. His love for her had ruled his life from the day they met. Those entire twenty-six years she had been married to Avery, Jason had mooned around, still loving her. Why would he stop now, after they had been so happy together for the last eight and a half years?

When Ginger ran out of tears and returned to the house, Jason was packing his papers in his study. She went upstairs to her bathroom and bathed her eyes and put on fresh makeup. She examined herself critically in the mirror. She had lines across her forehead and around her eyes and mouth. Her skin was getting a little puffy, especially under the eyes, despite frequent facials. Only her hair still was glorious: the auburn waves framing her face had few gray strands, and those were skillfully blended with the gold streaks that her hairdresser wove into her hair. Ginger ate carefully and still hiked up the mountain every morning and was almost as slim as she had been at twenty. *And dammit, she wasn't ever going to act like an old lady!* she vowed to herself. Not that she was going to run right out and buy herself a string bikini either.

Yes, she looked good *for her age*—but maybe that wasn't good enough. Jason's defection badly shook her self-confidence. Get a face lift, she told herself. Why not? By God, if Jason wanted a younger face, then she would buy herself a younger face. Why give up without a fight?

Jason came up to their bedroom and packed some of his clothes while she sat quietly at her dressing table and watched him. After he finished, he looked at her for a moment, and then he went out without saying good-bye. She heard his car start and go down the driveway.

She remembered that when she left Jason to go away with Avery thirty-six years earlier, *she* hadn't said good-bye either.

* * *

Antonio was having a wonderful time in Rome. His Grandmother Vivien told him at once that he was not to call her "Grandma" or any variation thereof. "Just call me Vivien," she said. She was a lot of fun to be with. Except for warning him not to call her Grandma, she never said "you have to do this" or "don't do that" the way Ginger often did. Vivien just let him be himself.

Vivien had gotten fat and went around in wildly colorful clothes that floated around her big body. She wore a lot of clinking jewelry and liked to drape filmy scarves around her neck and sometimes over her long silver-gold hair. She smoked a lot and cussed a lot and had a deep throaty laugh that Antonio thought was neat. But he just couldn't see her ever having been married to Papa Cal, not even briefly.

Vivien hired a guide to show Antonio the ruins and museums—"no point both of us being bored," she said. Actually, nothing he saw bored him. He was overwhelmed by the sheer magnitude of the city's multilayered past. If he had been forced to choose which period he liked best—the Roman Empire, the early Christian period, the Renaissance, the Garibaldi revolution—he would have had a difficult time deciding. He liked studying history in school, but he was thrilled to *see* where momentous events had taken place. *I'm actually breathing the same air as Caesar!* he told himself after visiting the ancient Senate in the Forum. It was awesome.

Vivien took Antonio and Todd to parties, parties, parties, in modern penthouses and ancient palazzos, in elegant restaurants and noisy trattorias. When Vivien told Antonio, "My life's like *La Dolce Vita,* except that it's happier," he didn't know what she was talking about, but he got the drift.

She took him across the Tiber to an old area called Trastevere to visit one of her artist friends. Antonio was fascinated by the ateliers that were hundreds of years old—"Just think, kid," one bearded American sculptor said, gesturing at the stone walls surrounding them, "artists have been working here in this very building since the seventh century!"

Vivien took Antonio to the outdoor produce market next to Ponte Milvio. "That's where Constantine saw a cross in the sky and brought Christianity to the Roman

Empire," she told him. Antonio stared at the sky over the bridge until his eyes began to hurt, but he didn't see one little cross.

She took him for a boat ride in a driving rain on the little lake in the Borghese Park, and out to the Villa d'Este at Tivoli to see more fountains of different variety in one hour than he had expected to see in his entire lifetime. She took him shopping for presents on Via Condotti—a pink silk scarf for Ginger and a blue silk tie for Jason. Later, Antonio went back by himself and bought a gold scarf for Rosemary.

Vivien and Todd let Antonio wander around Rome on his own. He loved the narrow old streets and ocher buildings and the hills giving onto broad vistas of winding river and treetops and glittering church domes. It was as different from his beloved desert as a place could be, and yet he felt the same pull of the past that he always felt in Palm Springs.

After visiting the museum in the Villa Giulia, he fell in love with the ancient Etruscans. He was amazed that people who had lived so long ago could have been so fun-loving and humorous, at least as depicted in the art they left behind. A one-day bus trip to Pompeii and Herculaneum sent him on a high that lasted for days—he couldn't believe how closely he identified with those places, as though he had lived there in some previous life.

They were invited for Thanksgiving dinner at the home of some American friends of Vivien's named Gilbert who lived in the penthouse of a high-rise in Vigna Clara, a modern section popular with American residents. The dinner was supposed to start at six o'clock, but by eight o'clock the turkey was only half-cooked, even though it had been in the oven since nine that morning.

"Kee-rist! Every damn American in the building is cooking a turkey today," Annie Gilbert wailed from the kitchen. "Whenever someone else turns on their stove, it robs *my* oven of a little more gas." The twelve guests sat around drinking champagne until ten o'clock at night, and then gave up and went to a local trattoria for dinner. The next morning Annie phoned Vivien and told her that the damn turkey finally had turned a beautiful golden brown at three o'clock in the morning.

Antonio felt like a different person in Rome. When he

went to parties, he was treated with a deference he never before had experienced. He gradually realized he was respected because he was from such a wealthy family, and that his grandparents had protected him from letting money make a difference in his life. It did seem strange to him that being rich should automatically make people admire you—or at least *act* as though they did. Even though it didn't make sense to him, he *liked* it!

He enjoyed spending time with his father, too. Todd was a lot like Vivien—relaxed and easygoing. Antonio was sure he could stand on his head in the middle of the Trevi Fountain and it wouldn't bother Todd one bit. Todd simply accepted Antonio the way he was and didn't try to teach him anything or change him in any way. It occurred to Antonio that it might be fun to live with Todd instead of his grandparents. Much as he loved them, he had to admit that Ginger and Jason were old-fashioned and strict, compared to Todd.

His first night in Rome, Antonio dreamed he was kissing Rosemary and he was startled awake to find his pajamas and sheet soaked with semen. He washed his pajama bottom and hung it to dry over the bathtub, then rinsed off the sheet with a washcloth and dried it with his hair dryer. It was hardly noticeable. The next night, *before* going to sleep, he masturbated into a wad of Kleenex while thinking about kissing Rosemary, and then imagining that he was entering her. By doing that, he didn't dream about her and it saved him a lot of middle-of-the-night laundering.

Antonio got drunk at a couple of the parties they attended. Nobody seemed to mind. He liked the buzz it gave him, the floaty-giggly sensation, although he didn't like being hung-over the next day. One night when he was intoxicated, he met a big-bosomed German friend of Vivien's named Greta. Before they went to the party, he heard Vivien say that Greta was a "nympho," but he didn't know what it meant.

Late in the evening, Greta and Todd went into a bedroom, giggling, and when they came out, Greta pulled Antonio down on a couch right in front of everybody else and gave him a long, deep kiss that made Rosemary's seem tame. Greta unzipped his fly and reached for his penis, but while she was fondling him, Vivien came and pulled Antonio away from her. "He's just a baby!" Vivien hissed. Antonio passed out after that, and in the morning he was too confused to know whether it really had happened or whether he had dreamed it. Either way, he was too shy to ask Vivien about it. The next night, though, while masturbating, he imagined "doing it" with Greta instead of Rosemary.

All in all, he enjoyed the trip to Rome immensely. He returned to Palm Springs feeling years and years more mature. It didn't even bother him too much that while he was gone, Rosemary had started going steady with a seventeen-year-old high-school senior named Derek whose father owned shopping centers all over the country.

In early December, Ginger received a short letter from Jason—the return address was an apartment hotel in San Francisco's Nob Hill area—suggesting that she start divorce proceedings. She tore up the letter and threw it in the fire. She was damned if she'd let him go that easily!

She invited Todd to lunch at The Springs after he returned from Rome. As soon as the waiter brought their salads and a bottle of Vouvray, Ginger got right to the point. "Todd, with Jason gone, Antonio needs an older man in his life," she said. "Can't you spend more time with him?"

"Come on, Aunt Ginger, be realistic. I'd be a bad influence . . . and do more harm than good." He gestured airily with his fork. "I've got screwed values. I know it and you know it. So why expose the poor kid to me?"

"He's such a good kid, Todd."

"I know. But I'm not sure he even likes me. Maybe I'll uphold the family tradition of being a lousy father but a wonderful grandfather." He pondered a moment, darkly, his voice turning bitter. "Or maybe the tradition really is for me to steal my son's wife someday."

"Ah, c'mon, Todd, you and Jiminy never were happy together. All I'm asking is that you see Antonio on a regular basis. Even just once a month. Let him know you're there if he needs you. Take him to a golf tournament with you . . . better still, teach him how to play golf."

"Well . . . I'll think about it. The visit to Rome *was* fun for both of us. He was really taken with Vivien."

"What exactly is it about Vivien that you and Antonio like so much?" Ginger wanted to know. "I haven't seen her in years."

Todd thought a moment. "She's just . . . herself. No airs. No pretensions. She loves a good time—you know, fancy restaurants, dancing, lots of rich and interesting people around, party weekends on yachts. Even if you don't like those things yourself, it's great to be around someone who's having so much fun and who's so easy-going and happy all the time."

"Well, I'm glad Antonio likes her. He has so few relatives . . ."

"Have you heard from Jason?" Todd asked.

"No." She suddenly felt overwhelmed with grief. "Excuse me a minute, Todd . . ." She fled to her office and locked the door, determined not to cry. There had been too many tears in her life. She stood at the big picture window and surveyed her hotel, her creation. A stir of pride mingled with her sorrow. The Springs was beautiful. Perfect. And she had been working hard to make it that way. It didn't have one weed in its grounds, or one spot of chipped paint on its walls. The guests were pampered, superbly fed, given a respite from whatever it was in their daily lives that made them need an escape. But where could *she* go to escape?

When she rejoined Todd in the dining room she noticed that he had ordered a second bottle of Vouvray while she was gone and had already consumed most of it. She felt a momentary twinge of worry, since she had had only a half-glass of the first bottle. Was he becoming an alcoholic? But she had more pressing worries. "Well," she said heatedly, "with Jason gone and with you so basically uninterested, I guess I'll simply have to be everything to Antonio myself. Mother, father, grandmother, grandfather—"

"Ah, c'mon, Aunt Ginger, don't get angry. Listen, I'll really try to spend more time with the kid. But I'm warning you—don't blame me if I'm a bad influence."

"Can I count on your seeing him, say, once a week?"

"Well, maybe every other week." Todd looked uncomfortable. "It's not that I don't like him—actually, I do, a lot—but I'm just not cut out to be much of a father."

"What would you do if Jason and I both died? Put Antonio in an orphanage, for Chrissakes?"

Todd shrugged. "I'd ship him off to Vivien in Rome."

"Oh, Todd! She may be fun, but she's totally irresponsible! That's no life for a kid."

"Well, let's not worry about it till we have to." He emptied the bottle into his glass. "Y'know, I've already given a couple million bucks to Vivien and Grandpa Jason. But I want you to know that I'm leaving everything I own to Antonio." Todd beamed proudly, as though that made up for everything. "I'm worth a hundred and thirty-four million, and I expect it to grow a lot more before I croak."

The figures meant nothing to her. If anything, she thought, that much money was nothing but a pain in the ass. She still had almost all of Avery's money and land to get rid of, and when Antonio was twenty-five he was going to inherit nearly fifty million from Jiminy's and Cal's estates. It was frightening!

"Well, meanwhile, do me a favor and don't give him any money, Todd," Ginger pleaded. "I give him an ample allowance, and he has to work for extras. I'm trying to raise him to appreciate what he has, so when you throw a lot of money at him, it just makes him lazy."

"Ah, don't be so hard on the kid, Aunt Ginger."

After Todd left, she returned to her office and went once more to her window. Life seemed very joyless to her as she stood there suppressing her tears. She was so tired and angry and frustrated that she thought her head would burst. Quickly she went outside, and even though she was wearing a mauve silk suit and high heels, she went up the steep trail to her lookout ledge. She was breathing hard, not from the climb but from combined rage and sorrow. She sat on her rock and forced herself to take deep-deep breaths to slow her racing heart.

She put a hand up to block the city from her vision so that she saw only the farthest reaches of the valley, the empty spaces and mountains that still looked the way the desert ought to look—*real* desert without a sea of red-tile roofs and emerald-green golf courses and deep-blue swimming pools. She was afraid that the whole damn valley would be built upon and grassed over in another ten or twenty years. Then there would be no desert left whatsoever.

She remembered the days when riding her horse on the empty desert floor had given her the gift of unbroken solitude. It had been a harsh land in those early days, fierce and defiant and savage with its hot skies and relentless winds, but majestic and satisfying to those willing to accept its haunting, mysterious beauty.

She realized that Tonito had made her see the desert, that Avery had made her love it, and that Jason had made her understand it. Ah, if only Avery could rise up from his grave—loving and wise and strong, the way he had been before his illness—and hold her in his arms. And since that was impossible . . . dammit, she wanted Jason back!

She stayed there until the sunset turned the air pink and the mountains purple. Her pulse was normal now, and her depression had been carried away by the brisk dry wind that ruffled her hair and billowed her skirt. She would manage! She vowed to give Antonio all the love and guidance he needed to bring him to healthy adulthood. Without Jason. Without much help from Todd. Just by herself. She had raised a child alone before, under far more difficult circumstances, and, by God, she'd do it again!

In February, Ginger began thinking that maybe she ought to have an affair. She knew that the moodiness and crankiness she had felt lately weren't at all characteristic of her. She wondered if her problem might not be that she was just plain horny.

She looked wonderful. Her face lift in early January had been a smashing success—every time she looked into a mirror she had to grin with secret glee. It wasn't so much that she wanted to look young; she just didn't want to look old, because then she would *feel* old. Her face and neck were smooth, her eyes were big again—she hadn't realized how much the loose skin around them had encroached on their size. It was years since she had looked this youthful. It could be that a little casual sex would raise her spirits.

A guest at the hotel named Henry Hooper, a tall, tanned, silver-haired man, seemed like a possible candidate to her. Ginger felt a heart-stopping jolt whenever she saw silver-haired men who at first glance reminded her of Avery, although a closer inspection usually proved disappointing. Few of them had Avery's noble features or compassionate eyes. Henry was an insurance-company executive from Connecticut who for many years had been coming to The Springs in February with his wife. Now his wife was dead and he was trying to recover from his bereavement.

Ginger invited him to have lunch with her at The Springs. Then he asked if they could have dinner together the following night at Melvyn's. The next morning they lined up on the sidewalk with all the tourists to have breakfast at Palm Spring's old standby, Louise's Pantry.

They spent a good deal of time together after that. She took him for a picnic and a walk in Palm Canyon. They took the aerial tramway to the top of Mt. San Jacinto to see the snow and pine trees and the view clear into Arizona. She showed him parts of the desert floor that still were wild, although she was dismayed that he immediately envisioned more golf courses and luxury hotels and shopping centers on the sites, while she, as always, thought in terms of protecting the barren land from further development.

She could tell that he wanted to have sex with her from the way he touched her hand and held her arm. It amused her that they were both so reticent, worse than teenagers with braces on their teeth nervously embarking on their first kiss. She thought it might be interesting to go to bed with him, but then again, she really wasn't all that intrigued. Not that she was a prude. Nor did she object on moral grounds. It was just that she had never had sex with someone she didn't love. When he finally summoned up the courage to invite her to his suite, she lost her nerve and gently declined on the grounds that she still was married.

Then he proposed to her and asked her to get a divorce. He offered to retire, to move to Palm Springs, to take her on a trip around the world, to buy her the most expensive mansion in town. As an added inducement, he boasted that he had accumulated an estate of twelve million dollars, that he had no children, that he'd leave it all to her. She didn't tell him that her own net worth was twice that amount, that she didn't need his money, and that if she wanted the "most expensive estate in town" she could jolly well buy it herself. She said she was flattered at his proposal and was sorry if her friendly behavior had misled him, but she had no intention of getting a divorce because she hoped her husband would return before long.

"If he doesn't, he's the biggest goddamn fool who ever lived," Henry said, bitterly disappointed.

He stayed two weeks longer than he had intended, trying to get her to change her mind about marrying him. She felt guilty because she had trifled with him and had only succeeded in adding to his unhappiness. Finally, to assuage her guilt, she relented and went to bed with him. He was an adept lover, but she was gripped by a terrible sadness and felt nothing, nothing at all.

It was a strange new experience for her. At seventy-seven years of age, she'd had her first copulation without orgasm. But there he was, his brow slick with sweat, his mouth slack as he panted for breath, and his eyes fastened upon her, pathetically asking the question that was so important to his ego: Was it good for you?

"Oh, that was lovely," she lied, giving him a priceless going-away gift.

The whole experience only made her miss Jason more.

Antonio knew that adults tended to be screwed up, but he never thought his grandparents could be *this* bad. What on earth was his Grandpa Jason thinking of, running off like that? Was he in his second childhood?

Antonio was familiar with his grandparents' whole story, how Gramma had been married to Grandpa Jason, then she had left him for Pa—his Grandpa Avery—and then she had remarried Grandpa Jason a year or so after Pa died.

Antonio could hardly stand reading the short letters that Grandpa Jason sent him every week. They didn't say much anyway, just that he loved Antonio and missed him. Antonio felt that his great-grandfather had deserted him too. They always had been such pals, and had had such good times together. He recalled their yearly camping trips to Death Valley, which was one of Grandpa Jason's favorite deserts. He had taught Antonio about all the plants and animals that lived there, down to the tiny pupfish that were almost extinct. Antonio and his grandparents had spent one Easter vacation in a rubber raft with a Sierra Club group, going through Grand Canyon down three hundred miles of the Colorado River's swirling rapids. They had taken him to Yosemite and Yellowstone, to Alaska and Hawaii, to New York and San Francisco, and everywhere they had gone, they had been a real family. A team. *They belonged together!*

Antonio had mixed feelings for this Millie woman that Grandpa Jason had gone away with. Antonio had seen her every afternoon when he came home from school during the time she had been working in the pink mansion's guest room. She'd always come out and given him a big smile when he arrived, and then she and Grandpa Jason sat and had cookies and milk with Antonio in the kitchen. She'd look at him with her big smiling blue eyes and tell him that he rode his bike like a champion racer. Or that he ought to •take acting lessons because he was handsome enough to be a movie star. Or that he looked even better on a horse than John Wayne.

She always wore tight jeans and low-cut T-shirts, so that when she sat leaning forward at the kitchen table, Antonio could see her breasts cradled in her pink bra. Now that he thought of it, he remembered Grandpa Jason sneaking looks at her boobs too. Oh, she was pretty luscious, all right. Antonio could partly understand why his Grandpa Jason wanted to be with her. But still, Antonio thought that his grandmother was much more beautiful than Millie, not just in looks, but in *every* way.

When Antonio sensed the great sadness his grandmother was suffering, it broke his heart. How he wished he could make her feel better! He tried to be helpful to her. He worked hard at school so that he could cheer her with an all-A's report card. Many afternoons, after school, he asked her to go horseback riding with him, even though he would have preferred going skateboarding with his friend Diego.

Whenever Ginger was home, Antonio gave up listening to his records of the Rolling Stones and Elton John and Stevie Wonder. His father had given him twenty-five hundred dollars' worth of electronic and stereophonic-sound equipment for Christmas, and for weeks the house had reverberated with rock and roll, until Antonio realized that it bothered his grandmother. They discussed it, and knowing how much the music meant to him, Ginger moved him to a room in the most remote part of the house and had her carpenter from The Springs soundproof it.

One Saturday morning, when he couldn't stand his grandmother's unhappiness any longer, Antonio told her he was going for an all-day hike with Diego. Instead, with money he had secretly gotten from Todd, Antonio flew to San Francisco and took a taxi to the address on Grandpa Jason's letters. It was a grand old four-story apartment building on Nob Hill with tall bay windows and a view of the Golden Gate Bridge.

The return address had said "third floor," so Antonio went through the round marble foyer and took a mirrored elevator up three flights. He rang the bell of the apartment that had a card on the door with "Jason Sisley—Millicent Simpson" on it. His grandfather opened the door and just stared at Antonio with such astonishment that Antonio couldn't help smiling, although he had intended to be very unfriendly. Grandpa Jason hugged him, hard, and Antonio found himself hugging him back and fighting tears.

This time when Millie came at him with a big smile, he really hated her and dodged her kiss. She pouted and threw her hands up in mock distress. "Oooh, big handsome Antonio is mad at poor little old Millie?" she cooed.

When his grandfather hugged him again and said, "God, I've *missed* you," Antonio's anger returned.

"If you miss me so damn much," Antonio said coldly, "why the hell don't you come home?"

Jason looked at Millie, then back at Antonio. "Let's take a walk," Jason suggested to his great-grandson.

Once outside the apartment building, Antonio turned on his grandfather. "Why are you making Gramma so unhappy?"

Jason gestured helplessly. "Ah, she doesn't care about me."

"But she does! She does!" Antonio insisted. "She's miserable without you! You should see . . ." He grabbed his grandfather's arm. "Grandpa, *please* come home!"

"I'm sorry, Antonio, I can't. Someday you'll understand . . ."

"Oh, *damn* you!" Antonio shouted. He raced down the street. He could hear his grandfather running and calling after him, but Antonio could run faster and he left Jason far behind. He ran all the way to the street with cable cars and he jumped on one heading down toward the bay. He wandered around Fisherman's Wharf, stopping to buy a shrimp cocktail from a vendor and eating it while he walked. He went to Ghirardelli Square and looked aimlessly into shop windows. He counted his money—he needed enough for a taxi back to the airport—and then he treated himself to some Ghirardelli chocolates.

He felt drained of emotion. It seemed to him that love only caused unhappiness. He just couldn't believe that his own beloved Grandpa Jason was behaving so badly and giving his beautiful Gramma so much distress. And yet, he reminded himself, hadn't she done the same to Grandpa Jason when she left him for Pa? Ah, grown-ups! Try to figure them out!

Sitting on a bench and looking out at the weekend sailors crisscrossing their small boats over the sparkling blue bay, he thought first about Rosemary, and then about Greta, and for a little while his heart beat faster. But then he felt deflated. Rosemary was fickle, and Greta threw herself at every man she met. It was all too much for him.

He hailed a taxi and returned to the airport. He got home in time to have dinner with his grandmother. He didn't tell her where he had been.

Late the following Wednesday afternoon, Ginger was at The Springs doing some paperwork at her desk when she heard the office door squeak open. Reminding herself to get her handyman to spray some WD-40 on it, she looked up in annoyance to see who was interrupting her. Jason was standing there, staring at her and looking frightened.

She took off her reading glasses and stared back at him. She was dimly aware of the hotel's sounds around her—a diver splashing into the pool, the tinkle of glassware in the bar, a burst of laughter on the terrace—but she was almost deafened by the ringing in her ears and the echo in her head of her suddenly pounding heart. She found her voice. "Save your breath, Jason. I refuse to give you a divorce!"

"Why?" he asked softly. He was actually smiling.

Oh, the nerve of him, she thought angrily, to come in here looking so happy! She shook her head, unable to speak through a throat paralyzed by held-back sobs. She wanted to get up and run away from him, but she couldn't move.

He closed her office door, then came around to her side of the desk and sat on the edge of it, close to her. He felt a surge of love for her that made him tingle all over. How could he ever have left her? She was more beautiful than he remembered, and he wondered, with a stab of terror, whether she might be in love with someone else by now. "I forgave you once and took you back," he said. "Can't you do the same?"

She was dumbfounded. "I don't understand."

"I made a mistake. I was stupid. Out of my mind. *Mea culpa.* Ginger, I've been so miserable!"

"Why?" she whispered.

"Why?" he almost shouted. "Because I made a total and complete ass of myself! I left the most wonderful woman in the world for a very shallow, self-centered girl who flattered me into believing I loved her. She was *suffocating* me with flattery. What else can I say?" He knelt in front of her and grabbed both her hands. "Ginger, Ginger, say you still love me!"

She pulled one hand out of his grasp and ran it affectionately through his unruly graying hair. Sliding out of her chair so that they both were on their knees with their bodies pressed together, she put her cheek against his. "I never stopped loving you," she said into his ear.

He gave a sob of relief. "I've missed you so!" He tightened his hold on her. "Whenever I . . . I had sex with her, I would end up wishing it was you in my arms."

Ginger stiffened at the thought of his having sex with Millie.

"Ginger, let's go home . . ."

"No. Antonio's there with his friends. I want you all to myself for a while."

They helped each other up and went out to a far corner of the terrace where nobody would bother them.

Holding hands, they sat side by side on a blue-and-white-striped glider overlooking the city.

"I'm sorry," she began, "if you ever felt that I didn't love you, or that I didn't show it enough. Maybe I'm afraid to love anyone too much anymore, Jason. I've lost two husbands and all three of my children. Grief is the one experience in life that never improves with practice."

He squeezed her hand.

"I learned a long time ago," she went on, "that dwelling on grief only makes it worse. But it's there all the same. Even when I'm happy, it's just waiting to suddenly rear up and slap me in the face. Usually when I least expect it." She gestured toward a row of giant pink oleanders downhill from them. "Time after time, I look at those wonderful bushes with great pleasure, until I suddenly remember the day I planted them, with three-year-old Tony helping me. Everything around me reminds me of my losses." She stopped and took a shaky breath. "Losing you was the last straw!"

He held her close. "Ah, Ginger, I was out of my mind to leave you. But . . . I don't know, I just didn't think you cared about me anymore." He kissed her eyes and her forehead and let his lips linger on hers. "The truth is," he went on, "I think you're constantly comparing me with Avery . . . that he's always on your mind . . ."

"I do think about him a lot," she confessed. "I can't help it. But, darling, I'm enough of a realist to live in the present, not the past. If you could only get it into your head that *you're* my whole life now!"

They sat quietly, lulled by the gentle motion of the glider. They watched high white puffy clouds sail through a cobalt sky, sending polka-dot shadows leapfrogging along the ground below. A fresh brisk breeze mingled the sweet smell of orange blossoms with the pungency of mesquite.

Jason tightened his arm around her. "My God, you look terrific," he said.

"I had a face lift."

"No kidding! You look so young!" He touched her smooth face. "Maybe I should have one too."

"Oh, you look wonderful as you are!"

"Ginger, Ginger, I was so afraid you'd found someone else while I was gone."

"I did have a very flattering proposal. From one of my guests."

Jason inhaled sharply. "And?"

"I told him I was still in love with my husband. But, darling, I was so afraid you'd never come back." She gazed up into his face. "Tell me, what changed your mind?"

"Antonio. He was madder than hell at me when he came up to see me last Saturday."

"Antonio came to see you?" She was stunned.

"You didn't know? Anyway, he convinced me that you still loved me."

She rested her head on his shoulder while a delicious wave of anticipation slid through her torso. "Remember the first time we made love?" she asked softly. "In front of the campfire?"

"How could I forget?"

"It's crazy, Jason, it was . . . what . . . ? More than forty-five years ago! And I still feel as young . . . as full of desire. . . ." She sat up and faced him, her eyes gleaming with love. "Darling, with Antonio home, we can't go there . . . but bungalow twelve is empty. A couple from Calgary got snowed in and won't arrive till tomorrow."

Still holding hands, they walked beneath a curving row of towering royal palms toward a cluster of hotel bungalows half-hidden by purple bougainvillea. The afternoon sun had turned the rock pile of a mountain behind them into a wall of blazing copper chunks. Beds of pink petunias vied with clumps of crimson carnations for their attention, but Ginger and Jason saw none of it.

They saw only each other.

CHAPTER
20

1979–1980

The Christmas that Antonio was sixteen, he awoke to find a powder-blue Porsche, with a big red-and-green ribbon around it, sitting in the driveway in front of the pink mansion on Christmas morning. It was, of course, a present from his father. On the driver's seat he found a box containing an American Express card, a Visa card, three oil-company credit cards, five one-hundred-dollar bills, and a gross of condoms. One of Todd's business cards carried a simple scrawled message: "Have fun!"

Antonio put the money and credit cards in his pocket. He was embarrassed by the condoms. Twelve dozen! He couldn't imagine having that much sex in a decade! Especially since he had never had it once. He hid the box under the driver's seat before his grandparents caught sight of it. He could see from his grandmother's face that she wasn't any too happy about the car, anyway.

The Porsche was a sensation wherever he went. During the rest of Christmas vacation he drove it all over town, showing it off to his friends. He whizzed into L.A. for a day, he zoomed up the Palms to Pines Highway to Idyllwild, he cruised again and again down Palm Canyon Drive, basking in the admiring glances he got from girls and the envious looks from boys. He felt infinite joy when he stopped for a red light and Rosemary, crossing in front of him with some college geek, waved at him with a big, impressed smile.

While he was eating breakfast the following Saturday morning, the phone rang. It was Rosemary, suggesting they have lunch together. He accepted gleefully. He had never stopped liking her, but she had gone from one boyfriend to another during the last three years—all of them high-school seniors or college students—and Antonio had given up all hope of ever going out with her again. He had to laugh inwardly when he thought of all the semen she unwittingly had been responsible for pumping out of him.

Getting ready to see her, he was as nervous as a nineteenth-century bridegroom. He took a long shower and brushed his teeth for two full minutes and found a little facial fuzz to shave. He liberally applied deodorant, after-shave lotion, and talcum powder in the appropriate places and then put on new Levi's and the snappy red-and-white University of Rome T-shirt his Grandmother Vivien had sent him for Christmas. He wore the hand-tooled leather boots Ginger and Jason had given him for Christmas. He couldn't help feeling that a hundred-and-fifty-dollar pair of boots was a pretty paltry present, compared to the Porsche.

Later that morning, when he picked up Rosemary, she looked incredibly sexy to him in high-heeled copper-colored boots, a blue scoop-neck T-shirt the color of her eyes, and the tightest jeans Antonio had ever seen. "I have to lie down on the floor and wiggle into them," she confessed with a giggle. Her long black hair gleamed in the sunlight and smelled sweetly of shampoo.

She walked clear around the Porsche three times, admiring it. "Wow!" was all she could say. *"Wow!"*

"Where we going for lunch?" he asked when he finally got her inside the car. He noticed that she was carrying a Kentucky Fried bag.

She smiled mysteriously. "Drive out One-eleven and I'll tell you where to turn."

He was suffused with the thrill of driving the powerful car. He had learned to drive on a dumb Ford at driving school, and had practiced on his grandmother's Dodge station wagon. He never had been able to convince her that she ought to buy a real luxury car, even though Jason drove a Mercedes because Todd bought him a new one every year. "So," Antonio said to make conversation, "whatcha been up to?"

She giggled. "Sex, drugs, and rock and roll."

"Ah, that's what everyone says."

"Well, the drugs part isn't true," she admitted. "Just a little pot at parties once in a while. How about you?"

His head was still buzzing from the "sex" part. Was she hinting that she wanted to have sex with him? He felt like a nerd with her, young and inexperienced, after all the older guys she had dated.

Antonio's sexual knowledge was all theoretical, partly from books his grandparents had given him and partly from a talk with Todd, who made it all sound pretty fantastic. "Remember the three C's," his father had said with a grin, "be carefree, be carnal as hell, and always use a condom. And for God's sake, don't fall in love!"

Rosemary told him to turn south at Sunrise and then go right and left and finally into the driveway of a pleasant ranch house.

"Who lives here?" he asked, mystified.

"Remember my girlfriend Becky?"

"Yeah. You mean, we're having lunch with her?"

Rosemary shook her head. "She's in L.A. with her folks. She gave me the key."

He got the picture, and began to feel nervous as he followed her into the living room.

"Wait here," she said, waving toward the couch. She went down a hallway and disappeared from his view. When she came back, she was wearing a gauzy beige negligee. She brought in a tray from the kitchen with the Colonel's chicken, which she had reheated in the microwave oven, and two tall cans of beer. Neither of them ate very much, and they drank the beer fast.

Then she came over and sat on his lap, facing him with her knees drawn up on either side of him, letting the flimsy robe fall open so that her bare breasts and vulva were pressed against his still-clothed body. She gave him a long, deep, beer-tasting kiss. "I'm on the pill, so you don't have to worry," she told him while she undressed him, kissing his neck and chest as she removed his shirt, caressing his abdomen and buttocks when she took off his shorts and underwear, and after a moment's hesitation she gently stroked his engorged genitals.

Timidly he let his mouth touch one of her nipples. He was amazed at her reaction. She jumped involuntarily and moaned. He loved her breasts. They were full and firm and upright, with soft little pink nipples that quivered and grew big and hard when he licked them.

He remembered Todd's "three C's"—to be carefree and carnal as hell, and he didn't have to worry about a condom now, with her on the pill. He became more adventuresome and explored between her legs with his fingers while his lips and tongue continued to titillate her breasts.

"Okay, do it!" she whispered breathlessly, lying down on the couch. *"Hurry!"*

At four, when they finally left Becky's house and got back into the Porsche, Antonio's entire body was in a delicious uproar. He felt absolutely drowned in the sweet, pulsating, maddening, cataclysmic sensations his genitals— his entire body—had experienced.

After that, they were frantic to make love every day. They were reckless, enjoying the danger of coupling under the thick tangled weeds of vacant lots, or in ditches alongside busy highways, or standing up in a broom closet at school, and once even on the filthy floor of a gas-station rest room when they were desperate and couldn't think of any other place. They couldn't go to Rosemary's house because her mom was almost always home, and Antonio couldn't bring her to his house because he couldn't quite see his Gramma and Grandpa Jason being that permissive. Sometimes they borrowed a friend's house when the kid's parents were out of town, but they never could count on that. Antonio finally phoned his father and told him his problem. He had a feeling Todd would be sympathetic, since he had given him all that good advice about sex.

Todd was delighted that he finally could do something for his son, beyond buying him expensive presents and taking him to Rome. He told Antonio to come on over and they'd talk about it.

"Listen, kid," Todd said expansively as he and Antonio sat beside the pool drinking beer, "there's this great little house I own—it's even got a water bed. It's nice and secluded, down south of town where you and your girlfriend probably don't know anyone."

Todd didn't tell his son that it was a house he had used for his own assignations—he had expanded his sexual interests to include restless young matrons who didn't want to be seen coming to his home through the guarded El Dorado gate. Todd was having problems sexually, but lately he wasn't doing much better with the horny matrons than he was with the fat cows.

"Better still," Todd said, putting his arm around his son and feeling fatherly for the first time since Antonio's birth, "why don't you just come and live with me? Ginger and Grandpa Jason have had you long enough."

Antonio drew back. "Oh, I couldn't do that to them!"

Todd shrugged. "Well, think about it, kid. You're old enough where we could have some damn good times together. You could live in that guesthouse"—he gestured toward a fairy-tale white stucco building full of arches and cupolas on the other side of the pool—"and you'd have all the freedom you want."

"Yeah, well, thanks, Dad. But I better stay with Gramma and Grandpa Jason. At least for now."

"Suit yourself. Let me know if you change your mind."

Antonio went around grinning in a euphoric daze. He could think of nothing but Rosemary and their convulsive orgasms. At first, he was careful to keep up his schoolwork. He played tennis every day, he always came home in time for dinner with his grandparents, and he continued to do his chores around the house. His grades slipped slightly, but not enough to alarm Ginger and Jason. They were aware that he seemed singularly happy, if somewhat abstracted, but neither of them even began to guess the source of his happiness. At sixteen he still seemed such a child to them.

They were annoyed at Todd for having bought Antonio the Porsche and also giving the boy an allowance of a hundred dollars a week, plus the credit cards. But when they invited Todd to lunch to discuss it, he reminded them with a touch of asperity that he was, after all, Antonio's father and that they never had legally adopted the boy.

"He's beginning to get interesting," Todd said, gulping his sixth glass of Puligny-Montrachet. "Maybe I'll take him back altogether."

"Take him *back!*" Ginger was aghast. "You never had him in the first place! Or even wanted him!" But she and Jason immediately backed off. Because they never had seen any reason to legally adopt Antonio, they both were genuinely frightened by Todd's threat of taking the boy away from them.

They did talk to Antonio about money, how he should learn to use it sensibly and responsibly. They said that although he wasn't accountable to them for what he did with his allowance, they trusted him not to be foolish. They warned him that his unearned money and his unearned car would win him a lot of unearned admiration, but it was admiration not worth having. Antonio nodded and smiled and apparently accepted the wisdom of every word they spoke.

But he loved the delicious secret he shared with Rosemary—the wild sex, the hidden house, even the lies he told his grandparents to cover the hours he began to spend away from home.

He treated his friends to food and drinks and movies when they went out together. Most of his and Rosemary's friends were themselves from wealthy families, but none of them had as much money to spend or the unlimited use of credit cards that Antonio had. He enjoyed being the richest one among them, and the most generous. He liked having everyone beholden to him. It gave him a new kind of respect and a sense of power. He began to feel it was his due.

He still loved his grandparents more than anyone else in the world, except Rosemary. But they were "out of it." He couldn't share his life with them anymore. He looked forward to the day when he graduated from high school and could move out of the pink mansion into his own place.

He loved his Porsche almost as much as he loved Rosemary. He washed and polished it himself. He no longer touched his skateboard or his bicycle, and he never walked anywhere. He didn't go near his horse. He jumped into the car even if he had to go only two blocks.

He and Rosemary began to invite their friends to their hideaway, swearing them all to secrecy. Some of the kids brought wine and pot, while the more daring ones brought vodka and dropped acid and snorted coke. At first, Antonio and Rosemary shied away from the alcohol and drugs, being high on love and satisfied with soft drinks. But their friends called them "chicken." They laughed at the two "babies." They assured Antonio and Rosemary that alcohol and especially drugs would make their sex "totally awesome."

"It already *is*," Antonio laughed smugly, hugging Rosemary possessively. Still, everybody was doing drugs and booze. And challenging him. And, by God, he wasn't a baby anymore. Above all, he wondered if it really were possible that sex could be even better. He reached for the joint being passed around and took a hit. Then he passed it to Rosemary.

A week later, he started doing cocaine. Rosemary tried it a couple of times, but she didn't like it.

Ginger was uneasily aware that something wasn't right. There was an evasiveness in Antonio's eyes that worried her. He was getting thin and pale. He hardly ever came home for dinner anymore. "I like to grab a bite with my friends," he explained glibly, "and then we study together."

One Saturday morning, before he rushed off in his Porsche, she stopped him at the front door. "Darling, is anything wrong?"

He rudely brushed her hand off his sleeve. "Why're you always nagging me?"

"Nagging you!" Ginger was astonished. "But I never—"

"You should hear yourself," he growled, going out and slamming the door behind him.

"I can't believe what just happened," Ginger told Jason when he came downstairs for breakfast. "I tell you, there's something strange going on."

"I know," Jason said, worried. "He's been crabby as hell lately. Bites my head off when I try to talk to him."

"He's always been such a good kid," Ginger said.

"Now he's like Dr. Jekyll and Mr. Hyde."

His grades were going downhill, and finally, in late January, the school counselor asked Ginger and Jason to come in and talk to her.

"He's getting passing grades this semester, because his work before Christmas vacation was good enough to carry him through. But all this month, he hasn't even tried. He's distracted in class," the young woman said earnestly, "when he even bothers to come to class."

"You mean . . . ?" Ginger faltered. "You mean, he's been absent a lot?"

"Two or three times a week. We thought you knew."

The woman opened her desk drawer and took out a pile of notes. "Didn't you write these?"

Ginger and Jason reached for the notes. They both stared in astonishment at their forged signatures, giving their "ill health" as the excuse for Antonio's absences. "We didn't write them," Jason said, dazed.

"Frankly, we're worried," the counselor said. "He's always been one of our very best students."

"We've noticed a change too,' Ginger admitted. "But he won't talk to us."

Jason cleared his throat. "Isn't it unrealistic to expect perfection at his age? At sixteen, there's so much else on a kid's mind besides schoolwork."

"Granted," the young woman agreed pleasantly. "But we're not talking about perfection. We feel there's a serious problem here. We'll talk to Antonio about his academic situation. But it's up to you to find out what's happening to him outside of school."

Driving home, Ginger angrily slapped the steering wheel with her hand. "It's that damn Porsche, Jason! I swear, it's changed Antonio's personality overnight!"

"It's worse, Ginger," Jason said quietly. "It's drugs."

She stared at him in such shock that she almost drove into the car in front of her. She braked hard. "Drugs!" She was aghast. "You're crazy!"

"You read the newspapers and watch TV, Ginger. It's in the news all the time, the way kids use drugs these days. . . ."

"Only in the ghettos."

"No, darling, in places like Beverly Hills and, goddammit, here in Palm Springs too! It's everywhere. An epidemic! Even grammar-school kids are on drugs. Where've you been the last few years, Pollyanna?"

"I guess I've been hiding my head in the sand like an ostrich," she admitted.

"Well, for God's sake, Antonio's showing all the signs they talk about on those TV shows on drugs. A drastic drop in grades. Bad temper. A complete change of personality—"

"No! I don't believe it! He's always been such a good kid."

"Ginger, you don't *want* to believe it. Sure, he's always been a good kid. But he's at an age when kids are easily swayed by their friends. You can't expect him to escape the peer pressure unless you lock him up in the attic."

Later, when Antonio phoned to say he wasn't coming home for dinner, Ginger said, "Oh, darling, your school counselor had us come in today, and we really ought to discuss it."

He groaned into the receiver. "Oh, that woman's such a pain in the ass! Okay. I'll be home in an hour."

When he walked in two hours later, Ginger took a good look at him. He had always been tall for his age, but now she realized that he was as tall as Avery had been, although very thin. His arms and legs were covered with fine dark hair: they were the arms and legs of a man, not a boy. She wondered why she had failed to notice how grown-up he looked. Of course, she had been observing him with eyes accustomed to seeing a child. The day-to-day changes in a young person were imperceptible. She remembered feeling this way when Tony and Jiminy were teenagers.

At dinner, Ginger realized that Antonio, always the voracious eater, had no appetite. She told him about their meeting with the counselor. "Darling," she added, "I know what it's like to be your age. Believe it or not, I can remember when I was sixteen. Honestly, Antonio, we don't expect you to be perfect. Nobody is. But your grandfather and I do expect you to be honest with us. If you're doing things you don't want us to know about, because you think it'll shock us or something, well . . . I just want you to know, I'd rather be shocked than be shut out of your life." She smiled lovingly at him.

Jason cleared his throat. "I know you think we're a couple of old fogies, but we're as young at heart as you are. So don't let our age fool you into feeling . . . you know . . . too far removed from us." He reached into his jacket pocket and took out the notes Miss Butler had given them. "However, I do think you owe us an explanation for these."

Antonio took the papers and turned red when he saw what they were. He threw them down angrily, and they fell into the platter of grilled chicken. "Ah, shit!" he snorted. "The bitch had to go and squeal on me." He looked at his grandparents defiantly. "Okay, so I signed your names. So what?"

"So *what?*" Jason echoed, furious with the boy. "I won't stand for it, that's what! We want to know what's going on!"

Antonio's mind was racing. Were they really dumb enough to expect that he'd tell them the truth? He could just see himself saying that he fucked Rosemary and used coke and didn't give a good goddamn about school. Sure, they'd be kind and understanding and end up piously telling him he shouldn't do those things, especially the drugs. Hell, he no longer needed their advice. Yeah, he still loved them, but they sure were "out of it."

He realized that he'd be better off living with Todd, who wouldn't give a shit what he did. "The truth of the matter is . . ." He hesitated, not really wanting to hurt his grandparents, but seeing no way to avoid it, "I'm going to go live with my father. He's been pretty nice to me lately, and he invited me . . . he thinks I ought to . . . that I *owe* it to him . . . you know, to spend some time with him." Antonio stared at his hands, avoiding his grandparents' stricken eyes.

Ginger gave Jason a frantic look while she fought for breath. Jason was staring at Antonio as though the boy had turned into a rattlesnake in front of his eyes.

"I forbid it!" Jason shouted. He came around the table and grabbed Antonio by the front of his shirt.

"Wait!" Ginger rose, pleading with both of them. "Let's talk without getting angry—"

Antonio stood up and roughly pushed his great-grandfather away. "There's nothing to talk about!" he snapped.

As Antonio rushed from the house, Ginger fell back into her chair with a forlorn cry. Jason embraced her, trying to console her, trying to console himself. "I was a rotten father to Vivien," he mourned, "and I guess a rotten grandfather to Todd, and now a rotten great-grandfather to Antonio. I failed with all of them."

Ginger captured his hand and kissed it. "Don't say that!" she reprimanded. "You were wonderful to them."

"Then why did they all turn out so badly?"

She stood up and held him close, wanting to console him, but not knowing how. She began to cry against his chest, jerky little sobs. She felt she had failed Jiminy. If Jiminy and Cal had lived, surely Antonio wouldn't be like this.

She forced herself to smile up at Jason through numb lips. "Look at it this way. We're living in the midst of a terrible epidemic, and somebody we love has caught the disease. Now it's up to us to help him recover."

"How do we do that?" Jason asked forlornly.

They stared at each other and realized with burgeoning horror that neither of them knew the answer.

On February 13, Ginger quietly celebrated her eightieth birthday with Jason. Jacques-Claude, Jean-Paul's grandson, who now was head chef at The Springs, personally brought over the meal he had prepared for her and he served it to her himself. It included all her favorites: fresh oysters on the half-shell, shrimp mornay, pheasant soup, lobster thermidor, butter-lettuce salad with warm *chèvre*, raspberries and whipped cream, and a chocolate cake. She and Jason didn't have much appetite, but they tasted a little of everything to please Jacques-Claude.

Eighty. Ginger just couldn't believe it. It's only a number, she told herself rather desperately. Don't pay any attention to it. But she couldn't help feeling some panic. She remembered Avery's eightieth birthday, and how he had shrugged it off. But she had been only sixty-five then, and she had made him feel as youthful as she was.

Her heart ached for all the people who should have been at the table and weren't. First and foremost, Antonio. She had phoned to invite him but he said he had a cold and couldn't come. And happy as she was with Jason, oh, God, how she missed Avery! And Jiminy and Cal—and their unborn baby, who would have been eleven years old now. And Tony. And little Johnny, who would have been almost sixty. And Ella. And even Tonito. *The more candles on your birthday cake, the more ghosts you have sitting at your table.*

She raised her glass bravely to Jason, refusing to let her sorrow ruin such an important occasion. "To the future!"

A few days later, Antonio realized that he had left his grandparents in a state of acute alarm and he loved them too much to hurt them that way. He phoned them and apologized for his bizarre behavior. "Can I come over for dinner tomorrow night?" he asked.

"Oh, darling," Ginger said, her voice lilting with relief, "of course, of course! Anytime you want. This will always be your home."

The next day he stayed off the stuff, dressed carefully, and returned to the pink mansion to have dinner with Ginger and Jason.

"I'm sorry I caused you any trouble," he said as soon as he kissed them. "I was, you know, trying some of the drugs. It's like, all the kids do a little experimenting. But honestly, I didn't like it at all. I'm clean now."

Ginger looked at him carefully. "But you're getting so thin!"

"Yeah, I caught this stomach virus a few days ago and it sort of knocked me out." He was amazed at how easy it was to lie, once you got started.

"How's school?" Jason asked.

"Oh, fine, fine," Antonio lied. They didn't know he hadn't returned to school when the new semester started.

"Well, do you think . . . do you want to move back here?" Ginger asked, full of hope.

"I don't know, Gramma. I sort of think, you know, like I owe it to my dad to stay with him awhile. He's pretty lonely." He gave her his most ingratiating smile. "I love you guys, you know that. And I promise, I'll come over and see you every week. But . . . Todd *is* my father. . . ."

After he left, Ginger and Jason turned to each other with enormous relief. "Oh, darling," Ginger said, "he seems just fine, doesn't he?"

"He does," Jason happily agreed. "Now, look, boss-lady," he went on, "we've both been working much too hard and we've been under a terrific strain with Antonio. So, what say we take ourselves a little vacation?"

"Where?"

He thought a moment. "I've never been to Australia or New Zealand. It's going to be fall there soon, so the weather should be nice."

"I think it's a wonderful idea!" She beamed at him. "Now that Antonio's okay again and seems happy with Todd . . . I never realized how tied down we've been all these years. I mean, we've never taken a vacation without him. You know, just the two of us? A second honeymoon!"

He nodded. "It's about time!"

Antonio loved the guesthouse that now was his home. It was far more luxurious then the pink mansion. Oh, his Gramma's house was beautiful, in a plain sort of old-fashioned way, and he always had been entranced by the fact that his great-great-grandfather had built it nearly a century earlier. The rooms were big, the walls thick, and it had a feeling of serenity and solidity. But Todd's guest-house was modern, full of floor-to-ceiling windows and mirrored walls and marble floors. The thick, luxurious carpeting was hand-loomed from an original design. The paintings on the walls had cost a fortune. Doors and windows and draperies opened and closed at the touch of a button. The furniture screamed "money."

Antonio had a formal living room, a full kitchen, and a bedroom with a king-size water bed. The bathroom was all pink marble. The big sunken tub had eight Jacuzzi jets embedded in its marble sides. He and Rosemary turned on all the jets so that the water seethed and roiled. They cavorted in it, splashing like children one minute and throbbing with sexual delight the next. They could order anything they wanted from Todd's kitchen by picking up the phone—just like hotel room service, only better, because Todd's chef was one of the best around.

Todd encouraged them to use his tennis court and pool. Often he joined them, cannonballing off the diving board and playing Marco Polo with them just like one of the kids. He horsed around with Antonio and whistled at Rosemary when she appeared in the new string bikinis that Antonio bought for her.

Antonio and Rosemary fascinated Todd. Their aura of carnality dazzled his jaded soul. He liked to stand hidden in the foliage outside their windows at night—they were careless about drawing the draperies—and watch them frolic on the king-size water bed. The intensity of their climaxes was palpable in their frenzied movements and uninhibited cries. He was jealous because he no longer enjoyed sex.

Antonio wanted Rosemary to move in with him. He hated the way she always had to be home by ten on school nights and by midnight on weekends. But she didn't quite yet dare defy her parents. "When I'm eighteen," she promised.

"Well, screw you, sister. In case you hadn't noticed, plenty of girls around here would love to move in with me." He stormed out of the guesthouse and she heard his car's tires screech down the street.

She was worried about Antonio. In fact, she was so alarmed that she even phoned his grandparents, but the housekeeper said they had gone to Australia for a few weeks. Antonio never came to school anymore. He was on coke every day now, which frightened her. She hated watching him getting all the paraphernalia ready, the mirror, the vial of powder, the razor to push the stuff into a neat line, and finally sniffing it up into his nose through a short straw or a rolled-up dollar bill if he ran out of straws. She wanted to scream every time he did it. He'd have a period of high, when he bragged about all the things he was going to do, really impossible things like going back to school and making up for the weeks he had lost—it was too late, he'd never be able to catch up now even if he went off the stuff cold. But when the high wore off, he'd be unreasonably nasty and cold to her. Either he'd want sex—it was becoming angry, hurtful sex—or else he would pick a fight with her and stomp out, slamming the door.

Rosemary came over every day after school, hoping to make up with him, but Antonio never was there. She had a key, and she'd go in and wait for him by the pool. They hadn't had sex for a whole week and she felt like a taut string on a guitar. She was lonesome for him, and hurt at his neglect of her. Most of all, she was terrified that he had found another girlfriend.

Late one afternoon, when Rosemary was stretched out on a chaise beside Todd's pool, forlornly hoping that Antonio would come home, Todd came out of the main house in his bathing suit and smiled archly when he saw her. "Well . . ." he drawled. "Aren't we looking pretty today!"

For some time now she had been aware of his admiring glances at her bikini-clad body. She liked him. He didn't seem so old to her; he wasn't even forty yet and he looked much younger. She thought he was quite a hunk, though not nearly as good-looking as his son. But he had a breezy assurance that Rosemary found intriguing. Even sexy. Only, now she was a little frightened. She wasn't sure she wanted to be alone with him.

He came over and joined her on the chaise so that they were close against each other. "Where's your lover-boy?" he asked archly.

"I guess he needs his space," she replied sadly.

Todd's kiss and his hands were swift, demanding, supremely self-assured. At the back of his head was an ironic laugh that he was doing to his son exactly what his own father had done to him—stealing his girl. Unreasonably, he felt that by seducing Rosemary he was finally getting even with Cal. He realized that she felt wonderful —so small and light and clinging. He sank against the little darling and drowned himself in her nubile body.

They spent the next few hours lost in a tempest of intoxicating couplings, on the chaise beside the pool, in his bed, on the thick fur rug in front of his den fireplace. She couldn't believe how much fun he was. And he was vastly relieved that he finally was aroused again.

They laughed and played and chased each other naked through the house—the discreet servants never left their quarters if their employer was entertaining a woman. When Todd and Rosemary felt hunger for food instead of each other, they wrapped themselves in silk bathrobes and rang the kitchen, once for hamburgers and fries and root beer—her idea—and another time for cold lobster and French champagne—his idea. She had some marijuana in her purse, and he had some very fine cognac. They smoked and drank and giggled and screwed, and when it grew late she phoned her parents and said she was spending the night with her girlfriend Becky.

When Antonio returned to the guesthouse at midnight, he was surprised—and relieved—to see Rosemary's Toyota parked at the curb. She always rushed home at ten because she didn't want her parents to worry about her. Antonio desperately wanted to see her, to make love to her. He had spent the past week having sex with a different girl every night, and in each case, his orgasm had been about as exciting as a belch. He wanted to make love to Rosemary. He was sure it would be better with her. But he was mystified when he couldn't find her anywhere in the guesthouse.

With a stab of fear, he dashed out to the pool—what if she had drowned?—and he groaned with relief when he found the lighted pool empty. Then he went into t. main house and tiptoed through the rooms. In the master suite, by the night-light's soft illumination, he finally found her. She was fast asleep in his father's arms, and from the way they were entwined, it didn't take much imagination to figure out what they had been doing.

Antonio felt sore all over. His internal organs seemed out of whack. He had recurrent nosebleeds from the dryness of his nasal passages, caused by sniffing cocaine. His genitals felt dead. He decided that the pleasures he and Rosemary had shared weren't worth the agony he now was suffering.

At first, he stayed in the guesthouse with the draperies drawn—he lost count of how many days. He refused to talk to Todd or to Rosemary. Whenever he heard the two of them out by the pool, he threw himself on the water bed, shaking with self-pity. He only went out to replenish his coke supply and stop for a hamburger or a pizza. Some days he forgot to eat altogether.

He invited one girl after another to come over for a sexual romp, each time hoping to enjoy it again. And each time it ended up being a bummer. He would snort a line to get into the mood, but his whole body, not only his penis, went limp when the moment came to get it on with his partner. He would snort another line to get over his disappointment.

Todd was alarmed, but when he went over to the guesthouse and tried to talk to his son about the drugs, Antonio laughed in his face. "Hey, man, you've got a worse problem with booze. So why should I listen to *you?*"

"I'm sorry about Rosemary," Todd said sincerely. "But she knew you were going out with other girls—"

"Ah, who gives a flying fuck?" Antonio stormed into the bathroom and locked the door and didn't come out until he heard Todd leave.

Todd cut off Antonio's allowance, only to find that Antonio had taken six paintings from the guesthouse walls, had found the receipts for them in Todd's files, and had driven into Beverly Hills, where he sold them to a dealer for a fraction of their value.

Todd was thoroughly shaken. He got Ginger's and

Jason's itinerary from Ginger's secretary at The Springs, but when he tried to phone them in New Zealand, they were off on a trek in the Milford Sound and couldn't be reached. The friends he talked to at the El Dorado only laughed at him and said that "kids will be kids."

And finally, that was exactly what Todd told himself. After all, he'd done some crazy things when he was sixteen. And was *still* doing them!

Antonio found it easy to buy all the drugs he wanted. He had connections all over town. He went with his friends who were users to parties where dining-room tables offered marijuana and coke and hash and an assortment of uppers and downers, along with dips and chips and brownies. Once in a while, in a drugged haze, he tried to have sex with one or another of the girls—it never mattered to him which one—but it was always unsuccessful. Mostly he liked to sit off in a corner by himself and listen to Rolling Stones albums.

He convinced himself that he wasn't really addicted. It was just a habit he enjoyed, like smoking cigarettes or eating fudge. He was sure he could quit anytime he wanted. Hell, everybody knew coke wasn't addicting.

Sometimes his old friends didn't recognize him. He dressed carelessly in clothes he had slept in for days. He forgot to shower. He never tucked in his shirt. He was so thin that his clothes drooped on him like they would from a hanger. He didn't comb his hair. Some days he was strung-out—irritable, touchy, withdrawn. Other days he was wired, really high, feeling himself capable of walking on the ceiling if he wanted to, or running straight up the steepest trail on Mt. San Jacinto. Not that he ever did any of these things.

Then he started feeling sick. Really sick. Vomiting. Nausea. Worse nosebleeds. Aching all over. He couldn't get out of bed except to go to the john or to get himself a line of coke. By the third day he was thoroughly frightened. He wanted someone to help him, but he didn't know where to turn. Todd had gone to New York for a few days, and Rosemary didn't come around when Todd was gone. Antonio's grandparents still were on the other side of the world. He was too ashamed to call Dr. Sam.

He stopped taking cocaine and got Todd's chef to fix

him some bland meals. Rice. Chicken soup. Toast. His stomach improved, but he felt rotten without the crutch that cocaine had become. He sat out in the sun and swam a little. After a few more days he felt better.

He knew his grandparents were coming home on Good Friday and he was eager to see them. He was proud of the fact that he had been able to quit drugs on his own. His body had filled out a little in just these few days of being "clean" and eating sensibly.

On Good Friday he decided to surprise Ginger and Jason by showing up unannounced to welcome them home. He showered and dressed carefully that evening and drove into Palm Springs. On his way to the pink mansion, while stuck in a traffic jam on Palm Canyon Drive—a tie-up created by the thousands of high-school and college kids crowding into town for their Easter vacation—two girls approached his Porsche. The brunette was wearing a green bikini and the redhead was in shorts and a skimpy bra top. He smiled at them, out of habit, when he saw how they were admiring his car.

They took that as an invitation and squeezed into the passenger seat. They introduced themselves as Sheila and Sandy from San Diego. "We're having a party," Sheila said. "Wanna come?"

She was cute—they both were—and he could tell from the way they looked at him that they would be happy to put out. He hadn't had any sex for weeks—first having been too sick and then having concentrated on getting better. He felt fit and ready to tackle new opportunities. "Sure." He grinned. His grandparents could wait.

Antonio was jazzed by the sight of swarms of young people in a festive mood. The weather was hot and most of the girls were skimpily dressed. The boys paraded around in shorts and tank tops. Wildly clashing hard rock reverberated from car radios and ghetto blasters set to different stations.

The shops and restaurants were seething masses of youthful humanity, most of the kids looking, looking, looking for something—someone to love, someone to bang, excitement, kicks, a hit, a joint, a score, any goddamn thing to make them feel they were having a wonderful time and to cover up their anxieties. He knew the feeling only too well: the pervasive restlessness, the numbing sense of inadequacy, the panic that somehow you were missing out.

"Where's the party?" he asked the girls.

"At our hotel. On Indian Avenue. Hang a left here."

In Palm Springs there was a restriction against using the word "motel," so every place that rented rooms, be it ever so humble, was a "hotel" or a "manor" or an "inn" or a "resort" or a "villa." When they arrived at Sheila's and Sandy's modest hotel, Antonio couldn't find anywhere to park. The place was a zoo!

"You can double-park," Sandy said. "Everyone else is." She pointed at all the cars left carelessly on the street.

"Why not?" Hell, he figured, the police probably had their hands full on a night like this. They weren't going to bother with how anybody parked.

The hotel was crawling with bombed-out kids. The pool was so full of bouncing heads he could hardly see the water, much of which had surged out over the concrete decking anyway. The noise was incredible. Shouts, laughter, Donna Summer's "Bad Girls" vying with the Doobie Brothers' "Minute by Minute," and floating over the entire scene was the pervasive smell of marijuana. Couples were coupling right out on the pool's chaises and on the lawn and standing up against the sides of the pool. It was wild! And it turned him on.

Antonio and the two girls were jostled from room to room of the L-shaped building, sampling whatever was offered. The white powder of crazy-making PCP mixed into marijuana cigarettes. Cocaine. Vodka. Rum. They finally reached the girls' room.

"Hey, honey, you wanna ball us?" Sandy whispered in his ear. The three of them had their clothes off in ten seconds flat. He was high. *High!* He didn't know if it was the PCP or if someone had mixed some speed in the coke. The girls pulled him down on the bed and took turns getting on top of him and kissing him.

He could hear the music from down at the pool, its frantic beat in sync with his heartbeat. Wild! Wild! He had never made it with two chicks at once. They were a good team, taking turns at making him come. All he had to do was lie there. One would start to suck him off and then the other would get on top of him. Like a galloping rodeo rider, she'd lunge herself to a shouting orgasm. They they'd trade off. They were adorable with their sleek slender bodies and pert bouncing tits looming up in front of him. They looked almost surreal in the flickering pink light of the hotel sign coming in through the windows. He fell asleep for a few minutes and when he woke up the two girls were giggling and fooling around with each other.

He pulled his pants back on and left the room. A little later he realized he wasn't wearing his shirt or shoes. Then he was in Ruth Hardy Park with five guys he'd never seen before. They lay down on the grass and shared a couple of joints. "Look," he screamed, "I see four moons!"

"I see six," the boy next to him said.

"Nah, there's only four," Antonio insisted.

The other boy pounced on Antonio. They rolled in the grass, punching and kicking each other. Then Antonio was all alone. His face felt wet and when he put his hand up to his cheek his fingers looked bloody. He thought it was another nosebleed, but this was higher up, a cut near his eye. It made him furious.

He went back to Indian Avenue and found the hotel. He went up to the first kid he saw and punched him out. The guy pushed him into the pool. Antonio's anger grew to murderous proportions. He hoisted himself back onto the deck, picked up a lawn chair, and smashed a window. Then another. It was contagious: all around him young men were following his lead. His anger dissipated because he thought it was hilarious. He couldn't stop laughing.

He heard police sirens and ran out to where he had left his car. Four guys were smashing the windows of his Porsche with golf clubs. "Hey," he screamed, "whatcha doin'?" They had broken all the windows and the headlights and were making dents in the hood and doors.

"Asshole! Zis your car?"

He nodded, swaying a little.

"Well, fuck you, ya bastard! How d'ya expect me to get my fuckin' car out?" The speaker pointed at the red Buick convertible next to the curb.

"Fuck your car," Antonio said calmly. He unzipped his fly and pissed all over the Buick. His four antagonists threw down their golf clubs and pissed on the Porsche. They all burst out laughing.

Oh, God, it was funny! Antonio leaned against the trunk of his car and got hoarse, screaming with laughter. He just couldn't stop. Then he got angry with himself. He picked up a mashie and started attacking his Porsche. He couldn't think too straight, but in a haze, like the disintegrating letters written by a skywriter on a windy day, he got the message that the goddamn Porsche was the cause of all his troubles.

The owner of the Buick and his friends disappeared when a fuzz came toward them. The cop asked Antonio what the hell he was doing, and Antonio explained that it was his own stupid car he was trashing, so not to worry. But when he reached into his shirt pocket for his wallet to get his I.D., he realized that not only was his shirt gone, but his wallet too, so there was no way he could prove it was his car. He thought that was absolutely hilarious. He kept laughing, even when he was arrested, and all the time he was being booked at the police station out near the airport. It was just so goddamn *funny!*

Jason sleepily answered his bedside telephone at two in the morning. He shot straight out of bed when he heard the word "jail." He hung up the phone and looked with fright at Ginger, who also had been jolted awake. "Antonio's in jail," Jason told her.

They stared at each other. "Jail!" she breathed. "Why?"

"The policeman just said to come on down and get him in a couple of hours."

"Why the hell didn't you ask *why* Antonio's in jail?"

"Don't get angry with me, Ginger. The guy hung up on me before I could ask him anything."

"I'm not waiting two hours," she snapped.

She threw off the covers and started to dress, but she was so agitated and so jet-lagged that she put her bra on over her nightgown. She looked down in confusion, and had to start all over again. She rinsed her face in cold water, again and again, to wake up.

Staring into the bathroom mirror, she applied a little eyebrow pencil, a touch of lipstick. Vanity, she thought bitterly, never stops. Men only had to look clean, goddammit; women always had to be beautiful. Or at least pretty. Or anyway presentable.

The police station was pandemonium—demoralized parents milling around, mothers sobbing, fathers shouting their anger and impatience at being made to wait. Two hours. Three. "Sorry, folks," the desk sergeant roared. "We're three hours behind. Got a lot of business tonight."

All the policemen knew Ginger. Ginger McKinntock Alvarez Rowland Sisley was a pioneer, an old-timer, owner of a prestigious hotel, benefactor to countless charities, member of numerous civic committees—she'd even been the guest of honor at last year's Policemen's Ball. The sergeant treated her and Jason with deference, even found a place for them to sit on a bench against the wall, behind his desk, while everyone else had to stand.

Ginger sat on the hard wood, unsteadily swaying with sleepiness and agitation. Jason sat next to her with a pain in his heart. The police captain came over after the first hour and personally apologized to Ginger and Jason. "Sorry, Mrs. Sisley . . . Dr. Sisley—don't know why, Good Friday's the worst night of the year around here."

"Is he all right?" Ginger asked, trying to control the tremor in her voice.

"Yeah, just awfully whacked-out. Looks like he was in a fight." He gave her a sympathetic smile. Damn, he thought, she didn't deserve this.

"Where is he?" Jason asked.

The captain jerked his thumb back toward the rear of the building. "In a cell with a couple of other kids. You can take him home the minute we finish booking him and get him photographed and fingerprinted." He hurried back toward his office.

Ginger was horrified. "You mean . . . he'll have a record?" she called after him, but he had already disappeared through a door.

Finally Antonio walked out. He was totally crushed, crestfallen, miserable, sick, weak, and very ashamed of himself.

Jason roughly took Antonio's arm. Looking at the boy's inane face, he wondered why people had children. He started to berate Antonio, but the station was too crowded and noisy for the boy to hear him. Jason noticed that Ginger had fallen asleep with her head against the wall behind the bench. He let go of Antonio and tenderly gathered Ginger into his arms. He loved her so—always had, from the minute he had walked into her office so many years ago and told her she needed him. Always, he had needed her more.

Outside the police station, all over the sidewalk and on the lawn, there stood knots of parents and children, a mother and father with their teenage son or daughter, a single parent with his or her adolescent, all engaged in intense scenes of bitter recrimination. It was almost dawn and everyone was tired and irate.

For the first time since Antonio had been born, Ginger wanted to hit him. Hard!

Antonio flinched. "You really want to hit me, don't you?"

"You're damn right!"

"You never have. Neither you nor Grandpa Jason."

"We don't believe in hitting."

"Maybe you should have," Antonio muttered. He stared at her through swollen, blackened eyes, challenging her to hit him.

With all her strength, she slapped him across his right cheek.

He smiled, though there were tears in his eyes. "Last year I saw one of Great-Grandmother Ella's old movies on TV. She had a line where she said, 'Thanks, I needed that!' "

"So did I," Ginger said softly, with tears in her own eyes. Then she threw her arms around him.

"I feel awful," Antonio sobbed against her cheek. "I'm so ashamed!"

"I'll bet you are," Jason said bitterly.

"I know you won't believe me, but I swear, I'll never do anything like this again. Never! *Ever!*"

Jason, who had managed to talk to one of the arresting officers for a moment, explained that Antonio would have a hearing in a couple of weeks in front of the juvenile commissioner. He would probably get off with a fine and six months' probation, during which time he would have to attend a drug rehabilitation clinic at the hospital. If that didn't work, he would have to be hospitalized. "Do you want to go see Dr. Sam?" Jason asked, pointing at the cuts and bruises on Jason's face.

"No," Antonio said, "I'd just like to go home. With you. If you'll have me." His lips trembled. "I love you both so much! I promise, for the rest of my life I'll do everything I can to make you proud of me."

In August, Antonio borrowed Ginger's Dodge and drove to his father's estate in Indian Wells. His battered Porsche was parked in the garage at the pink mansion. When he earned enough money working weekends as a busboy at The Springs, he'd get it repaired. Until then he was getting around on his feet, his bicycle, his horse, or his grandmother's car if he had some distance to go.

"I hear you and Rosemary broke up," Antonio said when they settled down in chaises next to the pool.

Todd got up and poured himself a drink at the outdoor bar. "Want one?" he asked.

Antonio shook his head. "I'm not supposed to." He hesitated. "Dad, you drink too much. There's this program at the hospital—"

"Nah, forget it. It's nothing I can't handle." Todd sat down and put a hand on his son's shoulder. "Listen, I'm really sorry I took Rosemary away from you."

Antonio looked squarely into his father's contrite gray eyes. "I guess she was, like, totally bad news for both of us."

"She's really a good kid," Todd said thoughtfully. "Smart, too. It's too bad she's so fucked up."

"So what happened, Dad?"

"Well, it was my fault, mostly." Todd sighed with regret. "I can't stay with one woman too long. I get restless . . . and then she began nagging me about my drinking. Ah, I don't know . . . she's got such screwed priorities, it pissed me off! Money and sex. Sex and money. That's all she thinks about. I tried to make her see that she'd end up unhappy, like me, if she didn't make something of herself that she could be proud of, and not waste the God-given brains she'd been born with."

"Did she buy it?"

Todd shook his head. "She took up with Bob Warren— they met at the club. She's still going to school—I'll say that for her. She's living with him now, up the road from here. Jeez, he's a good ten years older'n I am." He paused. "So how are you doing, kid? After that fiasco . . ."

"I'm fine. Gramma and Grandpa Jason got me a couple of tutors so I could catch up with my class when school starts next month."

"And the hospital program?"

"It's been wonderful. I'll never touch anything again. No drugs. No booze. Nothing."

"Not even a little fancy white wine with dinner?" Todd laughed.

"Well, maybe. Someday, when I can handle it." He gave his father a shy smile. "That was the whole trouble, you know, with Rosemary. It was just too intense for me. I was too young. I don't think I'll be ready to love anyone for a long, long time," Antonio added thoughtfully. "I don't know. . . . I feel all screwed up about sex right now."

"Yeah, like I've been all my life." Todd smiled sadly. "To tell the truth, I'm not capable of loving anyone. Never was. And, kid, I don't wish that on my worst enemy. I certainly don't want *you* to be like that."

"I've been talking a lot to Gramma and Grandpa Jason about love. I mean, they think you have to start with friendship, and then when you fall in love, well, love-making should be an *expression* of your love."

"They're probably right," Todd sighed.

"Dad . . ." Antonio touched his father's arm. "Let's take a vacation together. For a few days."

Todd was delighted. "Sure. Where do you want to go?"

Antonio hesitated. "Mexico City."

Todd flinched. "Why on earth . . . ?"

"Because I want to see where it happened, Dad."

Todd turned away, suddenly overwhelmed with sorrow for Cal, who, after all, had been his father, and for Jiminy, his beloved childhood companion—who *never* should have been his wife. He had been too angry with them to let himself mourn for them when they died, but now his resentments were buried by his long-delayed grief.

Antonio saw the deep sorrow and regret on Todd's face, and suddenly he felt a sharp pity for this man who had fathered him. He wished he could help him. Todd had everything—money, good looks, an engaging personality—and yet he had nothing. Nothing at all! *No,* Antonio told himself fervently, *I don't want to be anything like him. No way!*

Todd reserved two suites at the Hotel El Presidente Chapultepec and spent most of his time at the bar for the three days that he and Antonio were in Mexico City. Antonio raced around the city on his own. Jason had insisted that he visit the National Museum of Anthropology and the Palace of Fine Arts. The latter fascinated Antonio less for its contents than for the fact that it was slowly sinking into the soft soil beneath it and had to be bolstered with tons of concrete. He felt a little foolish, but he couldn't resist standing outside the building and waiting to see if it would settle another inch while he watched. Of course, it didn't.

He walked through the Zona Rosa and window-shopped. He went to the Zócalo and glanced into the old cathedral. He stopped and listened to a group of mariachis singing about *amor*. He climbed Aztec pyramids and went into Spanish colonial palaces and took a bus out to some floating gardens. He ended up at the Hotel de Cortez, where his mother and Papa Cal had stayed during that visit when they died. Antonio stood in the romantic courtyard, wondering which doorway led to the suite they had occupied.

The next day, Antonio lured Todd out of the hotel bar long enough to take a taxi to the Plaza of the Three Cultures. "Hey," Antonio said in total awe, "did you see what he did?" He pointed at their driver, who had just taken a squealing right turn from the farthermost left-hand lane across four lanes of heavy traffic on the broad Paseo de la Reforma.

As they approached the plaza where his mother and Papa Cal had died, Antonio was overwhelmed with a sadness that prickled his skin. They got out of the taxi and walked slowly to the center of the plaza. It was a peaceful day, with people ambling across the square under the hot August sun.

Antonio and Todd gazed at the pyramid bases built in pre-Columbian times, then at the colonial-era Church of Tlatelolco, and finally they stared over at the modern high-rise buildings.

Fighting tears, Antonio grasped his father's hand for

comfort. With his other hand he pointed at the modern apartment houses. "They were shot over there, Dad, in front of one of those buildings."

"How do you know?"

"The American embassy interviewed witnesses after it happened. They sent a report to Gramma and she let me read it before we came down here."

"You want to walk over there?"

Antonio shuddered. What if he stepped on the very spot where they had died? *What if their bloodstains were still there?* "No. I only wanted to see the plaza. I'm trying to imagine it, you know, with thousands of frightened people trying to escape and the police firing on everyone. . . ."

The memory of his happy hours with his mother and Papa Cal washed over Antonio as he stood there. He remembered the summer he was four-going-on-five and they had spent such joyous hours out on their terrace, sitting under the shady ramada and looking out at Mt. San Jacinto, or jumping into the clear blue pool, all three of them skinny-dipping. He began to sob and he made no effort to stop his tears.

Todd embraced him, letting him cry. For a moment Todd felt like a father, a *real* father. Then he cried too, when he realized that no matter what he did for the boy, or how much he gave him, Antonio would never love him the way he had loved Jiminy and Cal. Todd finally understood that he had forfeited his son's love by not caring enough about Antonio from the day the boy was born.

CHAPTER
21

1987

Ginger took a critical look at herself in her dressing-table mirror. Her hair was more silver than auburn now, but the face lift she'd had ten years earlier had held up well. She really looked . . . oh, not so much pretty any more as handsome. So it had to be some kind of awful joke for her to be eighty-seven. She didn't look it. She didn't feel it. And she hoped to hell she didn't act it! She still hiked up San Jacinto every morning to greet the sunrise and commune with Avery. When people called her "spry" she bristled; that was a word for old people, and she was just doing what she always had done.

I'm a greedy old lady who wants to live forever, she silently told her reflection.

There had been times she hadn't wanted to live: when Tonito and little Johnny were swept away by the flood, when Tony flew his plane into the side of the mountain, when Jiminy and Cal were senselessly shot by the Mexican police, when Jason had a massive coronary and died in her arms the previous year. And the worst, the very worst, when Avery closed his bright blue eyes and floated away from her, a loss from which she still hadn't completely recovered, even after twenty years. But every time she had been paralyzed by grief, wanting nothing more than to lie down and never get up, there had been a young life for her to guide, and her own zest for life waiting to be reborn.

And now there was young Antonio. What a strange twist of fate that he so resembled his great-grandfather,

Tonito, and that Antonio's link with Tonito had come through Ella, and not through Ginger. Dark-skinned, with the high cheekbones of his Indian heritage, Antonio was tall, lean, spirited, stubborn, and fearless. He was becoming more and more like Avery, not in looks, but in his compassionate nature and his inborn nobility.

Also like Avery, Antonio had decided to become a doctor. Now in his second year at UCLA Medical School, he was an avid, dedicated student. He was not only following in Avery's footsteps but also making up for his mother's never-realized dream of becoming a doctor, and he hoped someday to carry out Jiminy's vision of using her fortune to build rural and inner-city hospitals and clinics. Now, Ginger thought, if only he would fall in love, the way she and Avery had loved each other. The way she and Jason had. The way Jiminy and Cal had.

Ginger sighed. She ought to be getting dressed for her testimonial dinner instead of mooning over the past and worrying about Antonio's future. What's done is done, and what will be, will be. If that hadn't been her philosophy all these years—face lift or no face lift, she'd certainly have a lot more wrinkles staring back at her in the mirror today!

She was distracted by the rows of photographs on the wall next to her dressing table. She had carefully arranged them chronologically, starting with stiffly posed pictures of her two sets of grandparents and ending with a newspaper photo of her and young Antonio taken only a few months earlier at an Indian powwow in San Andreas Canyon.

They all were there: gorgeous photogenic Ella as a baby, as a little girl, as a teenager, as a sultry movie star, as a grandmother, after her Swiss face lift. There was Neil, thin and sickly as a child, fat and dissipated before the age of thirty. Polly and George at their wedding. Tonito and herself at their wedding. Avery and herself at their wedding. Jason and herself at *both* their weddings. Then Tony from infant to dashing airman in uniform. And Jiminy. Oh, Jiminy! At every age, so bright and beautiful. *Don't cry*, Ginger begged herself, *oh, don't! You've cried enough.*

And there were more. Jiminy's marriage to Todd and Jiminy's marriage to Cal. A half-dozen of Jiminy and Cal with Antonio from infancy to his fifth birthday. A few of Todd and Antonio and Vivien taken in Rome. Poor Todd had refused to stop drinking—had insisted to the end that he wasn't an alcoholic—and had died the previous year of liver failure. And all the photos of Avery, invariably looking robust and handsome. She hadn't taken any pictures of him after he fell ill.

What struck Ginger now was how many snapshots she had of herself! They were like a fashion show, portraying nearly a century of women's styles. God, she'd worn them all. Long skirts, short skirts, wide pants, narrow pants, hot pants, bell-bottoms, miniskirts, even mini-minis. Long hair, bobbed hair, slick hair, wild hair, pageboys, flips, ponytails, ringlets, chignons. No, she had never been as beautiful as Ella, but she hadn't been exactly plain, either.

She touched a portrait of Jason, smiling straight into the camera, taken on his eightieth birthday and catching all his humor and charm. She gave a small laugh, remembering how he had come to her one day in 1985, his eyes bright with mirth and a piece of paper covered with calculations in his hand, and announced triumphantly that, including their eight-and-a-half-year marriage in the thirties, they had now been married *one day longer* than she and Avery had been married.

Just before Jason died with his head in her lap—while waiting for the paramedics, she had staggered with him in her arms to the couch in his study after he collapsed at his desk—he had looked up at her and asked, with desperation in his faltering voice, "Ginger, tell me . . . do you still . . . love Avery . . . more?"

"No, dearest," she had lied, "of *course* I love you more now. I have for years."

Reluctantly walking away from the wall of photographs, she went to her closet and took out the gown which had cost her more than a gown ought to cost. But she had figured, what the hell, how often am I going to have an eighty-seventh birthday and have a banquet in my honor?

At that moment she recognized Antonio's forthright knock, and when she opened her bedroom door the young man bounded into the room with a grin. Antonio never walked; he always seemed to be leaping, or loping, or bouncing with energy. "You're not dressed!" he scolded affectionately.

He was spectacular in his tux, though she liked him better slouched on his horse and wearing jeans and a T-shirt. "You look like a headwaiter," she teased, kissing his cheek.

Of course, it was a huge joke. He was one of the richest young men in the world. Not only would he inherit Ella's and Cal's and Todd's and Neil's and Jiminy's millions when he was twenty-five, but someday her fortune would be his too, unless she hurried and gave more of it away.

She never had allowed their money to be a major factor in Antonio's life. Except for those horrible months when he was sixteen and had moved into Todd's guesthouse, they had lived quite simply here in the pink mansion built by her grandfather nearly a hundred years earlier. It was a fine house in its plain, old-fashioned way, but it was nothing like the outrageously sumptuous estates that existed all over the Coachella Valley, and it wasn't a tenth as lavish as Todd's El Dorado estate, which, as Antonio's financial executor—and with his fervent consent—she had sold shortly after Todd died. "I never want to see that place again!" Antonio had muttered.

"Come on, Gramma," he urged now. "It's late. I drove all the way from L.A. like Papa Cal used to, just to get here on time."

"Can you stay overnight?"

He shook his head. "I have an eight A.M. class that I should be studying for right now." He gave her a mock-scolding look. "So c'mon, get dressed. You can't be late to your own testimonial dinner."

"Why not?"

He looked down at the dress spread out on her bed: pale layers of wispy blue chiffon with hand-sewn pearls in a swirled design.

Frowning, Ginger picked up the dress. "Ugh. It's just not me."

"Then wear something else."

"I'll go like this." She gestured at the jeans and red Pendleton shirt she was wearing. "They can take me as I am. Why should I get all gussied up for the very people who ruined my sweet little village?"

"Gramma, stop wasting time!" Antonio went to the door. "Hurry. I'll wait downstairs." He left her room and slid down the polished banister. Not once since he was tall enough to reach the banister had he ever walked down those steps. If he could only figure out how to do it, he'd slide *up* the banister too!

He watched her come down wearing her new blue dress after all. She carried a white velvet cape over her arm. With her auburn-and-silver-streaked hair and serene smooth face, she looked better to him than many women half her age. He wished he could have known her when she was young. What a team they would have made! How was he ever going to fall in love, when every girl he met seemed so tame and shallow compared to his grandmother?

"You look fabulous," he told her when she joined him at the door. He took her arm with exaggerated gallantry and led her out to the white limousine sent by the dinner chairman. Ginger refused to keep one of her own and still drove a Dodge station wagon.

"Wait!" Ginger commanded.

"What now, Gramma?"

"Let's get our horses and go riding!"

"Like this?" Antonio gestured at their formal clothes. Then he laughed. "'Sure! Why not?"

They went to the corral, where she carelessly threw her expensive cape on the fence and they mounted their horses. In the cool, clean February air, the moonlight glistened on the mountain, plating the rocks a bright burnished silver against their deep gray shadows. The air was redolent with sage and mesquite and wild plum.

They rode up Ginger's favorite trail, neither of them mentioning the testimonial dinner. Ginger smiled to herself, feeling wicked. It was the first time in her life she had been so blatantly truant, and it was kind of liberating. The city officials would blame her absence on her advanced age and forgive her.

She smiled over at Antonio as he slouched in his finery. Why did he always lounge that way on a horse? He who had such splendid posture when he stood on his own two feet. Tonito had ridden that way too, as though the lower part of his spine and the animal's were bonded to each other.

Antonio loved this trail almost as much as his grandmother did. Of course, he knew she had her memories of sharing it for so many years with her beloved Avery. But Antonio saw it as a place where his forebear's feet had walked, and whenever he climbed it, whether on foot or on his horse, he felt close to those who had walked here before him. Being on Mt. San Jacinto always gave him goosebumps. Was it because the mountain was sacred to the Agua Caliente tribe? Or was it simply his love of the desert? Its serenity made him feel as though his soul were taking a cleansing shower and his mind were being wiped clean of annoying trivialities.

They reached a plateau and stopped to gaze at the city whose lights extended far out into the desert, as far as they could see. "The first time I ever came up here," Ginger told Antonio, "was with your Grandfather Avery. We walked up here every morning to greet the dawn. In the early days, you could see endless sand dunes, and every mountain for miles and miles around. A few houses and shops were down there in the village, and your Indian great-great-grandfather had a dirt farm over that way" —she gestured toward Palm Canyon. "And was it quiet! You can't imagine such silence. It almost hurt your ears."

"Yes, Gramma. You've already told me . . . a thousand times."

"Indulge an old lady, smart-ass."

"Oh, look!" Antonio chortled, indicating the row of limousines lining up at the entrance to the elegant new hotel where the banquet in her honor was being held.

They both laughed.

Abruptly Antonio was serious. "I'm glad I'm part Indian. Even a little part."

"Why? What difference does it make?"

"Because I belong here. On sacred tribal land. Not down there, with all those interlopers."

"But I'm one of your interlopers, my darling. Don't I belong here?"

"Of course you do, Gramma, but not the same way *I* do. I can't explain it. I feel tied to this land. It's in my blood." He hesitated. "I didn't have a chance to tell you, some of the tribe's young people are trying to keep alive the old legends and ceremonial dances. I went to one of their meetings with some of my Indian cousins when I was home for Christmas. Did you know there's a twelve-hour song about the history of creation?"

"Yes, I heard part of it once with Tonito. Years ago."

"I'm beginning to feel the way you do about the desert," he confessed. "I mean, I look at it now, and it's like a noble animal—say, a lion or a tiger—that's been put in a cage and tamed until it's lost all its character. But even so . . . it's still beautiful. I miss this place terribly when I'm away from it."

"Yes," she murmured, stirred by the love they shared for this land. True, she no longer legally possessed much of the desert, except for her house and her hotel. She had sold or given away most of the land Avery had left her. But she still owned the *entire* desert, the same way she owned this entire mountain, and the entire sky, and the air she breathed.

The full moon cast dark shadows in an eerie imitation of daylight. As always, the stars looked unreal to her, their brilliance outshining their puny electric imitations on the ground. She took her grandson's hand and held it so tightly she could feel his blood coursing through his fingers.

How wonderful, it seemed to her, that he had inherited the best traits of all of them: courage from his Great-Grandfather Tonito . . beauty from his Great-Grandmother Ella . . . curiosity from his Great-Grandfather Jason . . . humanity from his Grandfather Cal . . . tenderness from his Grandfather Avery—*Oh, my darling Avery, my beloved, if only you could see him, you'd be so proud!*—playfulness from his father, Todd . . . integrity from his mother, Jiminy—*Ah, Jiminy . . . your beautiful baby now is such a splendid young man!*—but most of all, from Ginger herself he had inherited his joy in living, and his strong affinity for this vast, brooding, garish, weird, wonderful land.

She made a fervent birthday wish that she would still be around to see what he did with all these inherited traits, combined with his vast inherited fortune.

She let go of his hand and turned her horse around before starting back down the trail. "Come on, my darling," she called out gaily, "we've had our fun. Now it's time to go join the interlopers!"

Buy them at your local

bookstore or use coupon

on next page for ordering.